SAM TATE

Heroes of Janaan: the Power of Belief

To: Alex Bak
From: Sam Tate

Copyright © 2024 by Sam Tate

All rights reserved. No part of this publication may be reproduced, stored or transmitted in any form or by any means, electronic, mechanical, photocopying, recording, scanning, or otherwise without written permission from the publisher. It is illegal to copy this book, post it to a website, or distribute it by any other means without permission.

This novel is entirely a work of fiction. The names, characters and incidents portrayed in it are the work of the author's imagination. Any resemblance to actual persons, living or dead, events or localities is entirely coincidental.

Sam Tate asserts the moral right to be identified as the author of this work.

Sam Tate has no responsibility for the persistence or accuracy of URLs for external or third-party Internet Websites referred to in this publication and does not guarantee that any content on such Websites is, or will remain, accurate or appropriate.

Designations used by companies to distinguish their products are often claimed as trademarks. All brand names and product names used in this book and on its cover are trade names, service marks, trademarks and registered trademarks of their respective owners. The publishers and the book are not associated with any product or vendor mentioned in this book. None of the companies referenced within the book have endorsed the book.

First edition

ISBN: 9798341069978

Cover art by George Patsouras

This book was professionally typeset on Reedsy.
Find out more at reedsy.com

Contents

Cast of Characters		vii
Cartography		ix
1	In the Depths of Irkalla	1
2	Delusions of Adequacy	8
3	The Princess and the Infinite Falling Object	21
4	A New Recruit	39
5	The Joys of Job Applications	45
6	The Dragon Archive	51
7	Desert Storm	58
8	Necrocracy	67
9	Buying Money	72
10	Welcome to Dihorma	79
11	Fire and Darkness	86
12	How to Save a Life	95
13	A Brief Examination	108
14	Messaging the Divine	115
15	Pryomania	123
16	Lopsided Law	132
17	Resignation of a God	146
18	The Waters of Harlak	150
19	Strong Words	159
20	A Desperate Enchantment	163
21	A New Idea	171
22	Grave Preparations	176
23	A Reclusive Alchemist	181
24	A Gassy Experiment	191

25	Ogre Country	201
26	Cause of Death	214
27	The Perfect Citizen	221
28	Warded Glass	227
29	What Really Matters	235
30	The Time to Fight	247
31	Zombie Ogre Soup	256
32	Gaslighting: A Primer	265
33	Ephorah's Homecoming	272
34	How to Redeem a Bomber	278
35	Market Crash	284
36	Blowing Hot Gas	300
37	Settlers of Canasta	309
38	The Brown Wedding	318
39	Family Feud	327
40	The Institute's Salvation	335
41	A Simple Trip to get Wine	343
42	The Origin of Elementals	350
43	Weakness	357
44	The Eternal Boiler	369
45	Ancient Tyrant	374
46	The Research Facility	378
47	Courage of a Hundred Men	389
48	Mereshank's Palace	405
49	It Came From a Lab Down Under	413
50	Basic Training	424
51	The Demon in the Tunnels	434
52	The Good Enough Escape	447
53	The Root of the Problem	454
54	The Underground Market	469
55	Crossing the Nile	480
56	The Source of Authority	494
57	Raiding a Lich's Laboratory	502

58	Stranded by the Tainted Desert	510
59	Posters	519
60	Desert Survivalist	528
61	Power Lunch	538
62	Homecoming	548
63	The Translator	559
64	Business in Kemet	565
65	Origin of a King	575
66	The Inn at the End of the Road	580
67	Nightmares	592
68	The Ruins of Sekhet's Lab	596
69	Escape From Azzitha	604
70	Setting the Trap	629
71	Sibling Reunion	631
72	How to Design a Spirit	638
73	Unforeseeable Consequences	646
74	A Guilty Conscience or Two	651
75	Fiery Introductions	660
76	The Game of the Pharaohs	668
77	Memories of Eternity	675
78	Is This Thing On?	682
79	Secret Wrestling	689
80	Final Preparations	695
81	Alchemical Healing	701
82	Dispatch of the Gods	707
83	Lessons Recapped	714
84	Unmasked	717
85	Son of a Fish	720
86	Fireworks	724
87	One Bad Idea After Another	729
88	Street Fighter of the Dead	733
89	Divine Food Fight	740
90	Face the Music	745

91	No Witnesses	752
92	Cooking with Gas	758
93	New Solutions, New Problems	763
94	One Step Closer	768
95	An Incorporeal Warning	772
96	No Going Back	775
Glossary		780

Cast of Characters

Rostam (ros'tam) Tar'ik (tärik)
  Amri (am'rē) Sadi (sâd'ē)
  Namid (na'mēd) Sadi (sâd'ē)
  Ephorah (ē'fô'rä) el-Sabet (sa'bet)
  Cyrus (sI'rus) Levitch (le'vich)

The Tarik Family:
  Arslan (är'slan) Tarik – Rostam's father
  Mirasol (mi'ra'sol) Tarik – Rostam's mother

The Sadi Family:
  Kasto (cas'tô) Sadi – Amri and Namid's father
  Lapis (la'pis) Sadi – Amri and Namid's mother
  Panya (pan'ya) Seluk (se'lük) – Amri and Namid's aunt, Kasto's sister
  Mido (mē'dō) Seluk

The el-Sabet Family:
  Shaheer (sha'hēr) el-Sabet – Ephorah's father
  Haama (ha'ma) el-Sabet – Ephorah's mother
  Aziz (az'ēz) – Ephorah's younger brother

The Levitch Family:
  Chorev (chô'rev) Levitch – Cyrus's father
  Ilana (il'an'a) Levitch – Cyrus's mother
  Eina (ē'na) – Cyrus's oldest sister

Tomb Lords:
    Amenhotep (a'men'hō'tep)
    Djedefre (Jed'e'frā)
    Mereshank (mer'e'shānk)
    Amasis (a'mā'sis)
    Khufu (kü'fü)
    Arkeon (är'kē'än)
    Sekhet (sek'het)
    Pausiris (pä'sI'ris)

Other:
    Daurgo (där'gō)
    Aquila (a'kwē'la)

Esfan Dyer

Cartography

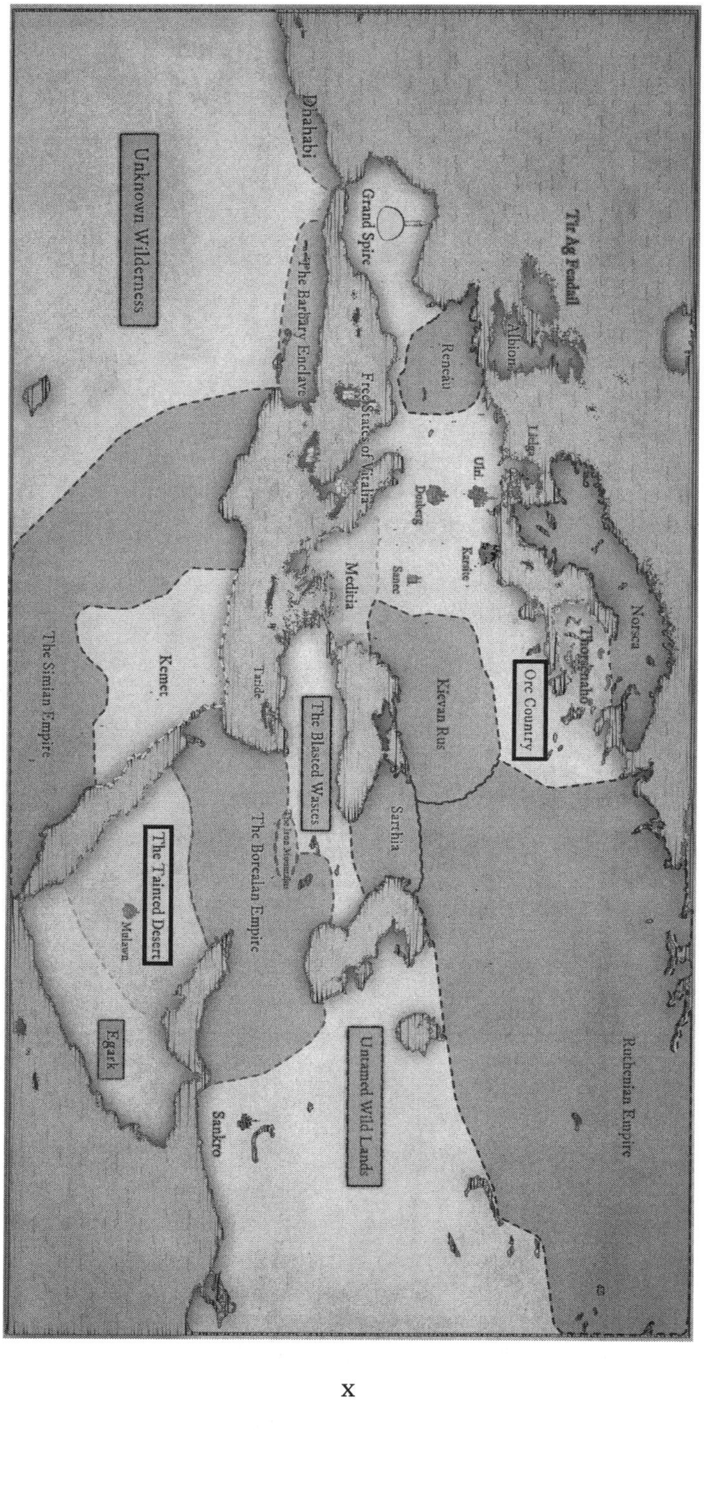
Unknown Wilderness
Dhahabi
Grand Spire
The Barbary Enclave
Free States of Vitalia
Albion
Norsca
Orc Country
Kievan Rus
Kemet
The Blasted Wastes
The Simian Empire
The Tainted Desert
The Borealan Empire
Untamed Wild Lands
Sankro
Ruthenian Empire

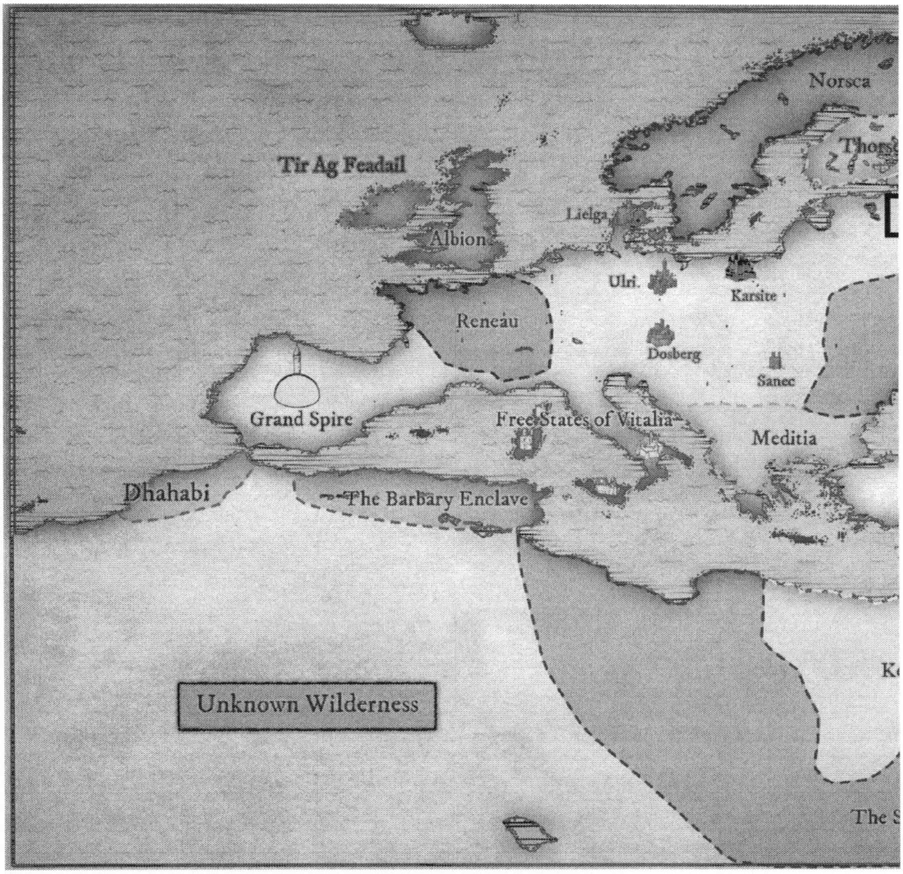
Norsca
Tir Ag Feadail
Lielga
Albion
Ulri
Karsite
Reneau
Dosberg
Sanec
Grand Spire
Free States of Vitalia
Meditia
Dhahabi
The Barbary Enclave
Unknown Wilderness

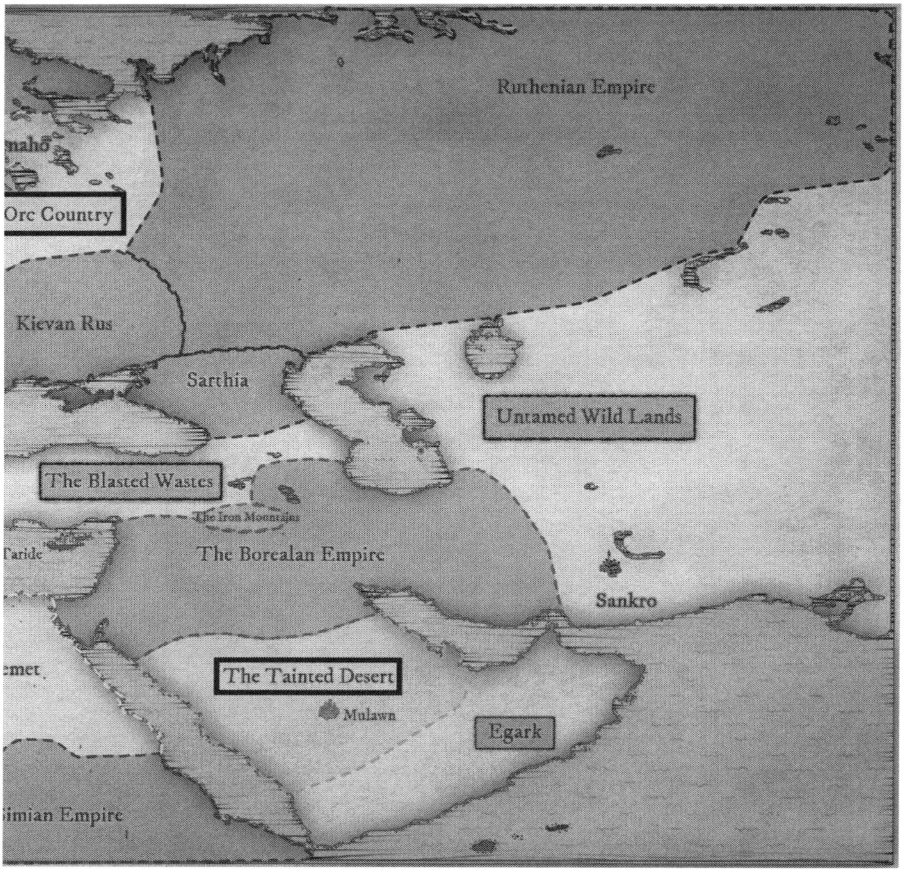
Ruthenian Empire
Orc Country
Kievan Rus
Sarthia
Untamed Wild Lands
The Blasted Wastes
The Iron Mountains
Taride
The Borealan Empire
Sankro
The Tainted Desert
Mulawn
Egark
Simian Empire

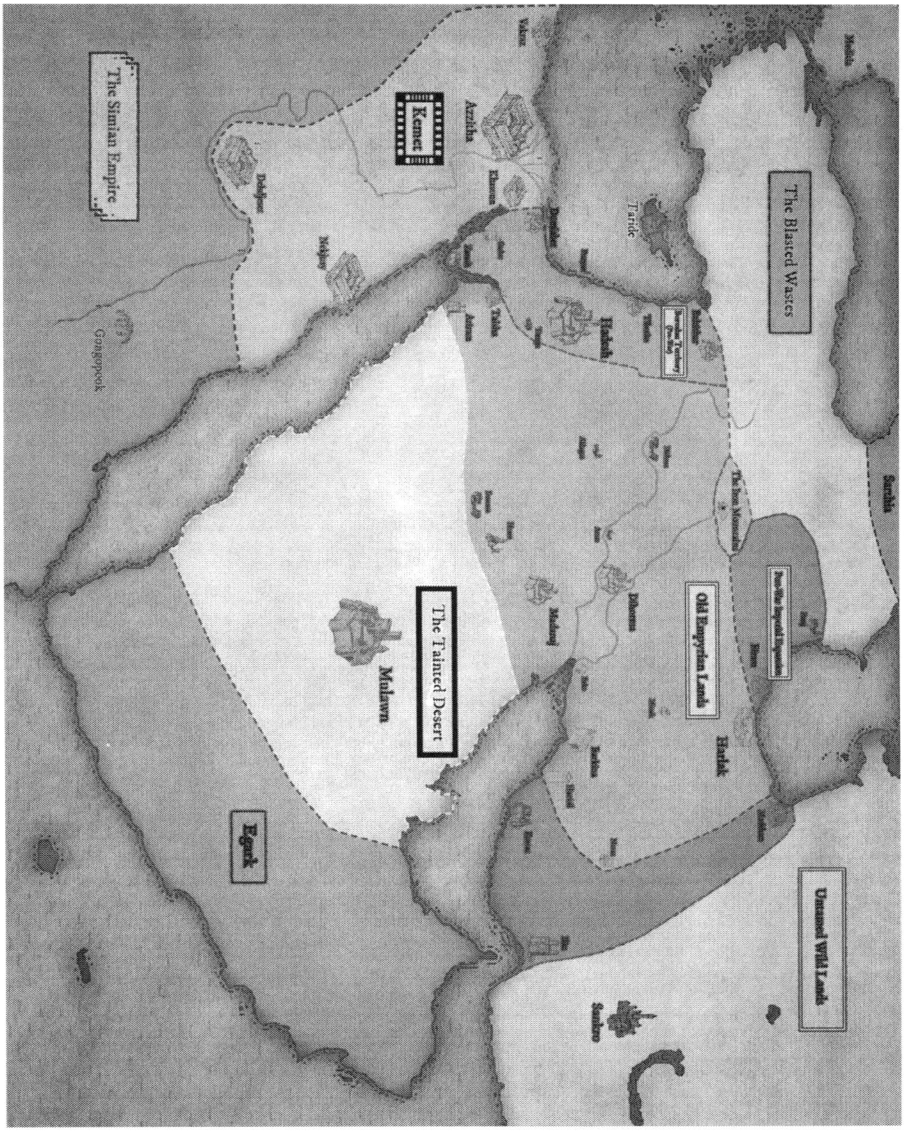
The Simian Empire
Kemet
The Blasted Wastes
The Tainted Desert
Mulawn
Old Empyrian Lands
Untamed Wild Lands
Gongopook

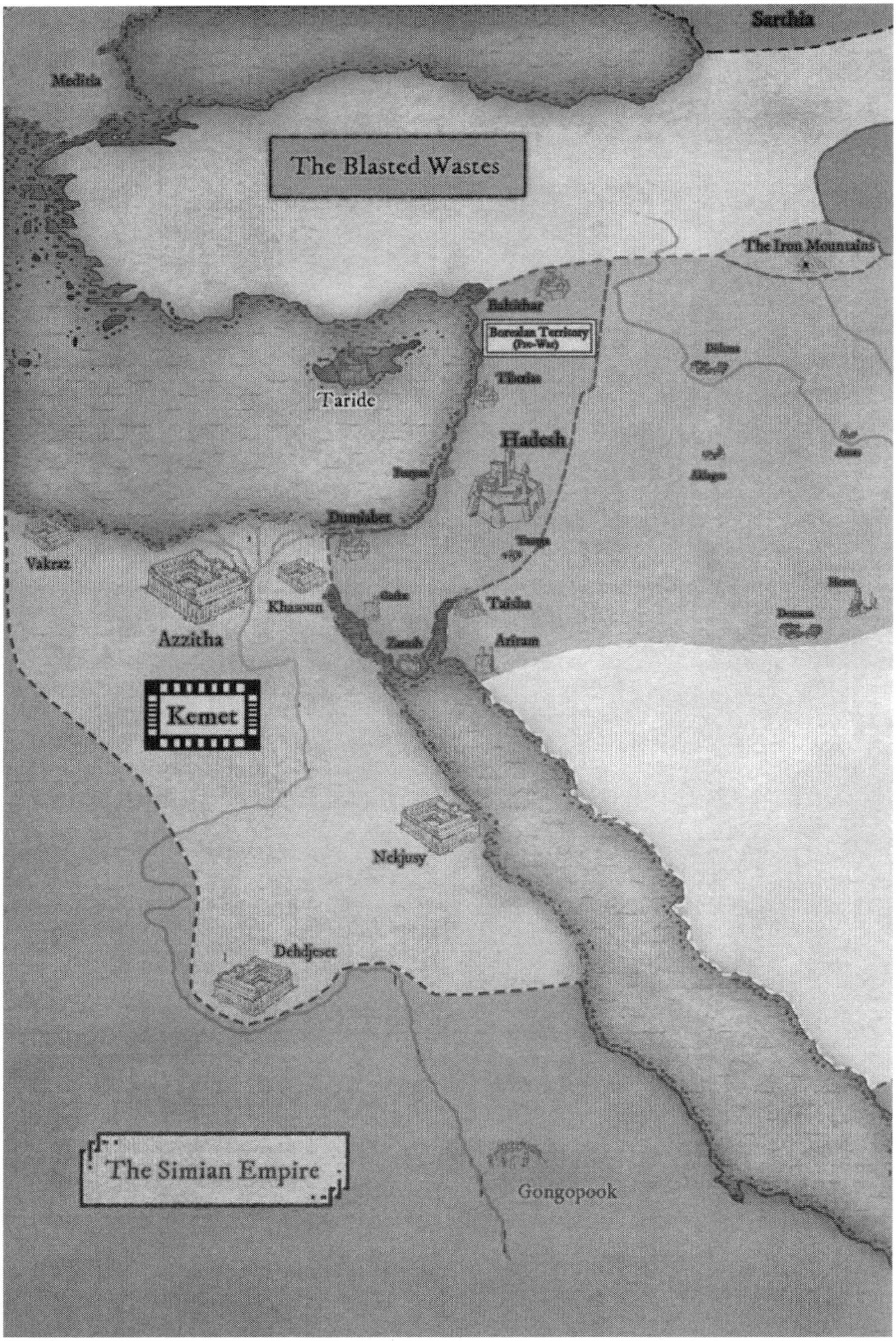
Sarthia
Meditia
The Blasted Wastes
The Iron Mountains
Borealan Territory
(Pre-War)
Taride
Hadesh
Vakraz
Khasoun
Azzitha
Taisha
Afiram
Kemet
Nekjusy
Dehdjeset
The Simian Empire
Gongopook

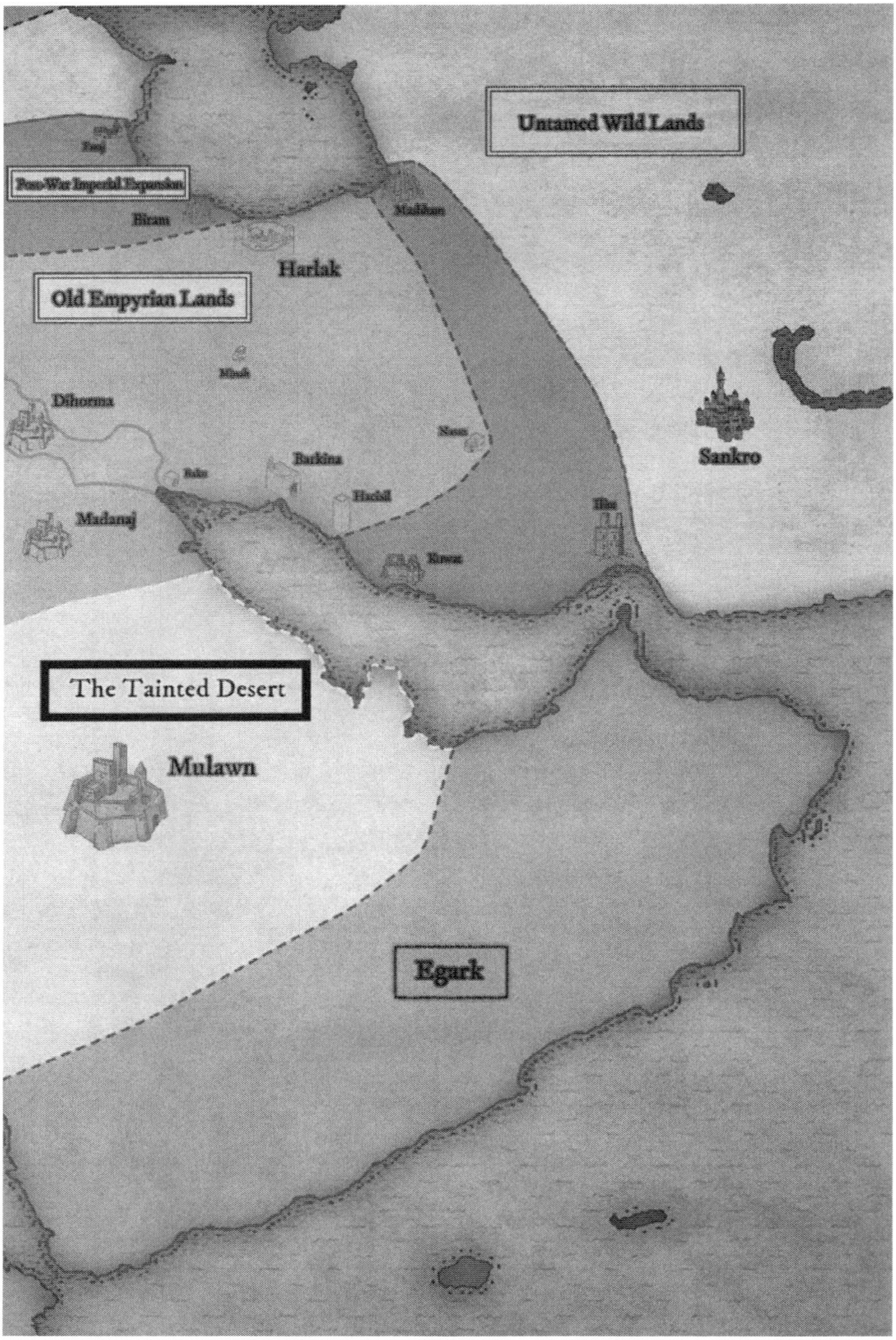
Untamed Wild Lands
Post-War Imperial Expansion
Harlak
Old Empyrian Lands
Dihorma
Barkina
Madanaj
Sankro
The Tainted Desert
Mulawn
Egark

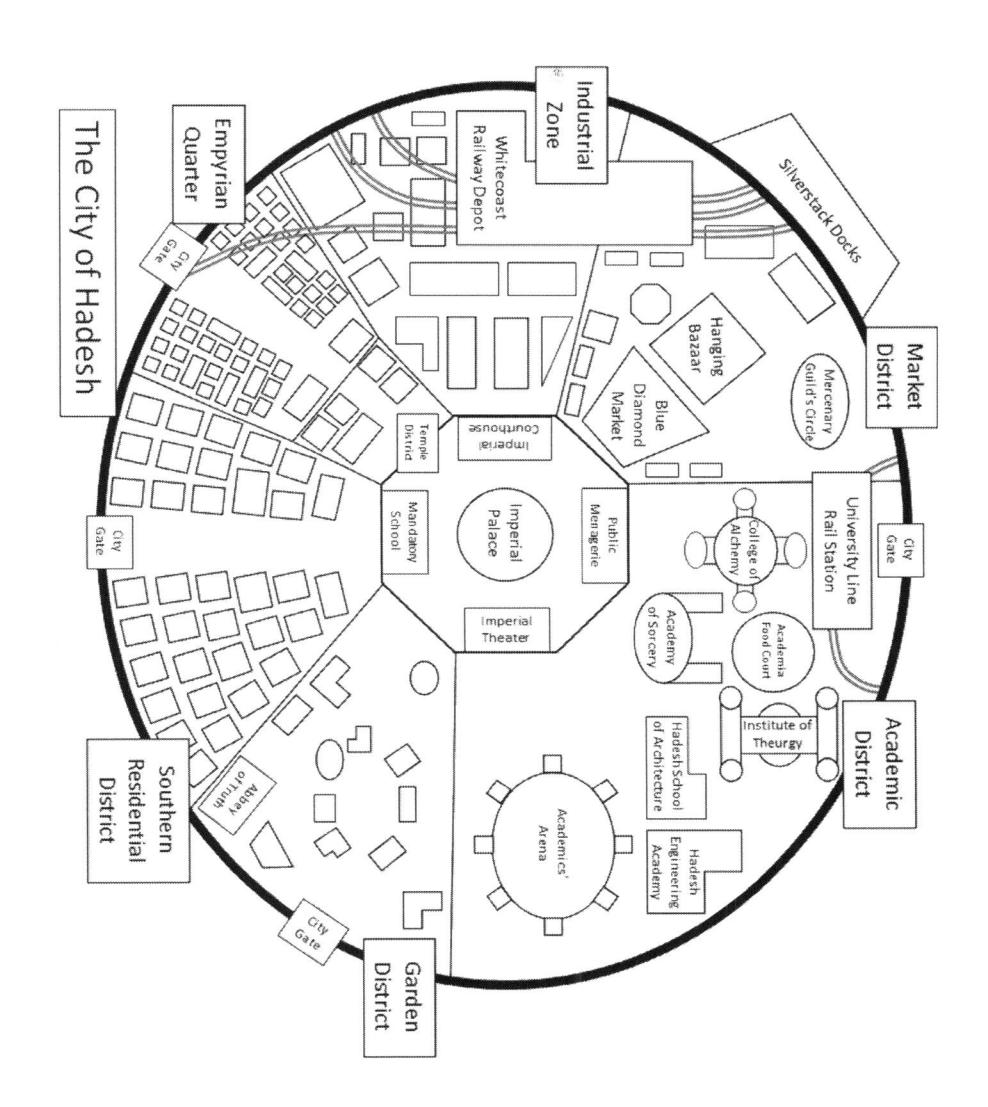

Nations Outside of Janaan:

Albion – Take a wild guess where this country is. The Greymarch cannot sail ships even after infecting sailors, making the nation's natural borders secure from attacks. They worship the old Celtic gods, and have attempted to push outside their island borders in the past, but their military has little experience in fighting the Greymarch and they quickly retreat to the sea. What Albion lacks in land military, they make up for in having one of the strongest navies in the known world.

Téir Ag Feadaíl – An island nation to the northeast of Albion. Its people worship the old Celtic gods, and are relatively safe from the Greymarch. However, they face regular invasions from the Tuatha de Danann, a supernatural race that emerges from the Spirit Plane and tries to claim the island for themselves.

Reneáu – A nation that has slowly, but surely, managed to assemble from several city states and built walls to protect themselves from the Greymarch. These defenses aren't perfect, but between the walls around the nation and the cities themselves, the populace is able to stay relatively safe. They primarily worship the Roman gods, but some cults worship the Lusitanian pantheon.

Grand Spire – A city state that grew out of an Ark, whose population more or less never left. Instead, they just kept building up and up using materials from the Ark and salvaged resources gathered from ruined cities of the ancients, which were reclaimed in part using recycling equipment unique to the Ark their ancestors emerged from. Though the people of Grand Spire have established outposts outside of the spire, these are mostly for the purpose of building trade routes along the coast. Grand Spire's religion is heavily divided; some worship the Roman gods, a small sect worships the Celtic gods, but the crown officially follows the Lusitanian pantheon, even though they are not always the majority religion.

The Free States of Vitalia – A group of cities states, three of which are located on islands, who have managed to avoid the Greymarch and similar monsters. However, slaver raids from the south have forced most of these city states into keeping their populations inside walled towns, fortifying their shores when and where they can. Although not officially a unified nation, the city states have a military alliance, most of which is dedicated to fighting off slavers. They primarily worship the Roman pantheon.

Meditia — A nation that relies heavily on natural borders to protect itself from invaders. The sea, the Blasted Wastes, and the Kievan Rus protect most of the nation from the Greymarch, while its people have focused heavily on using earth elementals to guard its cities from invasions. Although they occasionally struggle with attacks from slavers of the barbary Enclave, Meditia's shores are mostly safe, making the country a major trading hub between nations. They primarily worship the Roman pantheon, but it is not unheard of for people to follow the Egyptian or Lusitanian gods.

Lielga, Ulri, Karsite, Dosberg, and Sanec — a group of city states that have established walled cities, but live in a region of the continent that is a hotspot for the Greymarch to congregate, so building a larger nation has been proven difficult if not impossible. They each have a unique culture, with Lielga claiming to be originally a colony of Norsca that ended up declaring independence due to Norsca being unable to support their military defenses from various monsters. Sanec seems to exclusively worship the Roman pantheon, while the others follow the Norse gods.

Norsca — A nation almost entirely surrounded by the sea, this country is sheltered from Greymarch attacks. They predominantly worship the Norse gods, which has brought about conflicts over the years regarding the Norse beliefs about the afterlife. Since only warriors who die with honor go to Valhalla, there have been clusters of the population pushing for the nation to adopt a more militaristic policy. The general belief, however, is that "die with honor" does not mean "go to war with innocent neighbors just for the hell of it." However, the worst afterlife available in the Norse mythology is Hel's world, and Niflheim, though not as glamourous as Valhalla, is not a bad place to end up depending on the life you lived. As a compromise, Norsca allows people interested in Valhalla to join incursions into Orc Country, along with allies from Thorsenaho, where they can seek a glorious death against the orcs.

Thorsenaho – Literally "Thor's Grove." Another nation that takes advantage of the seas and lakes to protect itself from the Greymarch. Short walls built along each isthmus where an invasion might occur keep the country safe, although it isn't just the Greymarch this nation needs to fear. Orcs, supernatural beings brought into existence by humanity's fears of invading savages, regularly try to breach the nation's borders, along with the Kievan Rus and the Ruthenian Empire, where the spirits of those nations do not recognize the supernatural race as invaders. Orcs are an all male race, who can reproduce either by abducting human women or by simply being born out of humanity's nightmares, so no permanent extermination of their kind appears to be possible. Orcs are immune to the Greymarch infection, and the two groups are reported to ignore each other.

Kievan Rus – A nation that, like its neighbor, sits upon a colossal titan-class earth elemental that governs not only the land but to a lesser extent, the weather of the nation. The land itself rejects the taint and pushes it away, and whenever the Greymarch tries to invade the nation, landslides, frigid weather, and even the trees themselves are rumored to destroy the dreaded horde.

Ruthenian Empire – Like the Kievan Rus, the Ruthenian Empire rests on a land that is itself a titan-class earth elemental that protects them from the Greymarch. It is believed by some that the two earth elementals were once one, but they split at some point. Because of this belief, the empire has tried many times to invade the Kievan Rus, on the belief that they can reunite the two spirits. However, both elementals have been known to lash out against invading human armies, and since neither elemental has any power outside of their respective nations' borders, the two countries have been locked in a stalemate for centuries.

Sarthia – A nation known to worship the Altaic gods, this country benefits from having its northern borders surrounded by the Kievan Rus and the Ruthenian Empire, both of which have powerful defensive spirits that won't allow Greymarch incursions, but neither spirit can assist their nations' respective armies for invading their neighbor to the south. With the mostly uninhabitable Blasted Wastes covering Sarthia's only other land border, the country is easily able to defend themselves, although they have no ability to expand.

Sankro — A city that more or less appeared near the eastern border of the Borealan Empire, not too much is known about this independent state. It is rumored that the city is capable of relocating itself, and originally came from further out east, but if this is the case, the city guards any secrets about how this works very closely. Sankro is the only known settlement in the Untamed Wild Lands east of the Borealan Empire, and pockets of tainted regions have been reported by scouts in the area.

Mulawn — a city state that exists in a curious valley sheltered from the storms and poison of the Tainted Desert. The people living there are known to have odd features, including unusual hair and colors, oddly shaped ears, and a surprisingly large number of people with six fingers. Due to the fact that the taint tends to be more of a problem on the ground than in the sky, if an airship can avoid the taint storms that ravage the desert, trade with this city state is still possible.

The Barbary Enclave — A cluster of settlements that have formed along the north coast of the southern continent. These people are feared slavers known to raid the various civilizations across the sea, known to pose as merchant vessels when possible. Not much is known about their culture, apart from the fact that they seem to believe they have an actual right to enslave anyone who isn't the same race as themselves. Curiously, the barbary pirates recognize the people of Dhahabi as being part of that race, which is why they never attack Dhahabi and prefer to sell their captives there. Other known customers for the slave trade include the chimpanzees of the Simian Empire, who are more interested in the souls of the captives than actual labor, and the Tomb Lords of Kemet, although reports that this doesn't account for all of their slaves suggest that they have contact with another buyer, possibly to the distant south.

Dhahabi – A nation small nation on the coast of the Unknown Wilderness, this country is rich in mineral wealth, including gypsum, copper and iron ore, and natural diamonds. Before alchemists discovered ways of fabricating diamonds, Dhahabi was the only known exporter of the gems, making their economy boom due to the use of diamonds in a wide variety of thaumaturgical inventions. Their wealth has dropped somewhat after alchemical diamonds were invented, but other exports, particularly copper, have maintained the country's reputation as a golden nation. To the point that countries who admonish their open practice of slavery and general disdain for other races still trade with them.

1

In the Depths of Irkalla

DAURGO

There was little light in this craggy underworld. Daurgo had seen a number of afterlives, but this one seemed to be steeped in supernatural darkness. Some of the shadows seemed to move on their own, watching the dracolich out of curiosity. Whatever they were, they were not used to seeing something like him in their stalactite-filled halls.

"Yeesh, this place is a dump." Daurgo lazily smacked two guardians out of his path with his tail. "At least the Asphodel Fields were organized. This place looks like it hasn't been swept since the dawn of time. How much effort does it take to clear out stalagmites every few thousand years?"

As Daurgo stormed his way through the sixth infernal gate, a dozen lamassu tried to tackle him. Each monster had a human head, the body of a lion, and wings of an eagle. Leonine claws scraped harmlessly against the lich's armor of steel and brass. Some of the guardians tried to fly onto his back to look for a weak point. Daurgo flicked a switch on his armor and activated the tesla coils on his back. Lightning arced through each of the lamassu and left them twitching in pain at Daurgo's feet.

"Good grief. Valhalla's guardians could put up an actual fight," Daurgo muttered. "Pathetic."

A gallu stepped in the dragon's path. "You are supposed to sacrifice something at each gate!"

Daurgo snapped up the underworld guardian in his jaws, chewed him for a bit, and spat out the monster as a mangled wad against a cavern wall, then strolled through the seventh infernal gate unimpeded.

As soon as the lich passed through the last of the seven gates, the ground began to shake. Daurgo could see Ereshkigal's palace only a short distance away, but between him and the queen's doors, a massive black serpentine dragon erupted from the ground. It looked like a giant snake with a head ten meters tall like a scaley lion with four bull's horns and a pair of red eyes that locked onto the much smaller dragon trespassing in Irkalla.

"Hmm, you must be Kur[1]," Daurgo mused. "This should be interesting."

Kur lunged at Daurgo and engulfed the armored lich in his jaws, swallowing him whole in less than a second.

"Pfft," Daurgo extended the blades on his armored tail and stabbed Kur in the throat from the inside. "Eat me alive? Tactless and trite."

Daurgo released the full blast of his tesla coils. All of the electricity traveled down his grounded tail and flowed into Kur. The serpent roared and thrashed, with Daurgo chuckling inside as he held on for the ride. Eventually, Kur collapsed on the ground.

The dracolich was about to congratulate himself on his victory when he felt a burning sensation in his tail. Withdrawing it from Kur's throat, Daurgo saw that the blades had melted and blackened bone peeked through holes in the armor. From the wound he'd made in the underworld dragon's throat, magma flowed like lava from a fissure and closed up the hole like a scab.

"He has lava for veins?" Daurgo grabbed a bomb from his armor and planted it in Kur's esophagus. "Must be some kind of primordial. But that means—"

Daurgo braced himself as Kur shifted and roared back to life. The dracolich teleported outside of Kur's throat as the bomb he'd planted went off.

The blast blew Kur's neck to bits, sending pyroclastic rocks everywhere. More and more, Kur seemed less like an organic being and more like a living mountain shaped like a snake. Immediately Kur's head started to grow back

---

[1] Kur was a Sumerian dragon of Irkalla, the Mesopotamian underworld. In some myths, Kur *is* the underworld, *and* the dragon.

from the magma that flowed from his neck. Daurgo wracked his brain for everything he knew about this underworld dragon.

"Okay, he kidnapped Ereshkigal when she was a baby and took her to the underworld, Irkalla is his home, he was killed by Enki, none of him came with me when I teleported— wait a minute, killed by Enki, lives in the land of the dead..."

Kur regenerated his head and scanned the area for the dracolich. Spotting him on the ceiling of the cavern, the ancient serpent lunged with his jaws again. Daurgo teleported away, letting Kur get a mouthful of stalactites instead. The lich reappeared behind Kur and willed thermal energy to leave the underworld monster's body.

Frost appeared on Kur's skin and ice slowly cracked its way through his form. The black dragon became frozen solid just in time for Daurgo to drop another bomb right below his head.

This time, Kur's entire body shattered into glassy pieces that clinked against the stone crags of the cavern. Daurgo landed and watched the shards for movement.

As expected, the shards liquified and started drawing together, forming the underworld dragon anew.

"Figures." Daurgo growled. "What are you really? You're no death god, that's for sure; you don't even speak!"

As if in answer, the pieces slowly morphed into Kur, who angrily glared at the dracolich. It opened its mouth and flooded the cavern with its breath; some noxious, poisonous gas the likes of which one would find in the deepest volcanoes.

Foul as it was, this gas had no effect on the annoyed lich, apart from offending his sense of smell. "You call yourself a dragon? I've met human hunters with better predatory senses than you!"

Kur let out an angry hiss and headbutted Daurgo, ramming him into the wall of the cavern. Slowly, Kur slid the lich down from the wall and into the ground. Daurgo struggled, but in addition to Kur's sheer size and mass, there was a supernatural weight that forced him further into the dirt. Finally getting serious, Daurgo teleported out from under Kur and reappeared right underneath the ceiling.

The underworld dragon smashed his head on the ground, visibly confused as to where the dracolich went.

"That's not right," Daurgo thought to himself. "How come he didn't teleport with me? He couldn't get any closer. Unless…"

Kur looked up and spotted the lich. Lunging again, this time the primordial serpent grabbed Daurgo with his jaws and pulled him down to the ground. The ancient dragon coiled itself around the dracolich and tried to squeeze him like a python.

"Okay," Daurgo struggled. "Time to test this."

Twisting his claw, the lich made time slow to a stop. Kur became a black statue. The anger was still visible in his eyes, but he was completely frozen.

"Just as I thought." Daurgo examined his opponent. "You're not a real creature at all. An animal could still move, albeit slowly, and a man, god, or other sapient wouldn't be restrained, but your completely stuck. Which means…" Daurgo peered into the other dragon's eyes more closely. A kind of nothing, not just empty pupils, but the void itself was hidden in Kur's eyes. Death, not just the underworld, or a god ferrying souls to the afterlife, but the literal concept of death itself lurked beneath the dragon's gaze. Kur wasn't simply a dragon of the underworld; in a way, he *was* the underworld. A dragon that once stole a newborn baby princess away and whisked her off to a dark void from which she could never return.

"I get it now." Daurgo leaned closer to his captor's neck and whispered into Kur's ear. "*Morto, Tiran, Exume, Eiros.*" A wave of unholy energy washed over Kur as Daurgo's necromancy took hold. "*Recor, Oblivio, Perditio.*"

Kur's body started to disintegrate. Necromancy beats death like scissors cut paper. Like ash flaking off of a dead wooden log burning on a fire, death gave way to the stagnation that comes from the end of all life. As Daurgo allowed time to return to normal, he found himself alone in the cavern next to a massive pile of dust.

"You stood no chance against one who has already conquered death." The lich turned towards Ereshkigal's palace. "Now, then."

Smashing down the massive brass doors, Daurgo stomped into the palace and spread his forearms wide. "Sal-you-tations!"

A confused queen of the underworld sat on a basalt throne at the end of a massive main hall held up by pillars of bones and lit by many tallow candles that smelled to Daurgo like they were made from human fat. The goddess was as shapely and beautiful to humans as any mortal princess, and wore fine golden jewelry on her ears and around her waist, but quickly covered the rest of her undressed body at the sight of the armored dracolich.

Daurgo glanced at the souls of humans who had been brought before the queen for judgment. He hadn't been paying attention until now, but it seemed all mortal souls whether they were rich or poor, highborn or peasants, were brought naked and helpless before the queen of the dead. Apparently, Ereshkigal was normally the best-dressed person in her kingdom, even if she was mostly nude.

"Not my species, not my problem." The lich stomped towards the queen. "I take it you weren't expecting company?"

Ereshkigal stood from her throne. "Stop him!"

A score of gallu stormed into the throne room and tried to attack Daurgo with claws, fangs, and weapons. Bored, Daurgo triggered his tesla coils once again.

"How many times are your minions going to try that?" Daurgo asked. "I mean, really? It didn't work the first few times. Why would it work now?"

Ereshkigal covered herself with her left hand and conjured a ball of purple energy in her right. She hurled it at the lich, frying most of the equipment on his armor.

Daurgo sighed. "I just had this repaired. Oh well." Daurgo willed the ground to become hard and cold as ice; frost creaked across the floor. The queen of the dead and all the souls in her palace shivered as the normally warm, somewhat volcanic underworld became a frozen wasteland.

"Feeling a bit exposed?" The dracolich mused as he lumbered towards the goddess. "Why don't you make this easy and tell me how to bring back the dead?"

"I-is that what th-this is about?" Ereshkigal's teeth chattered, but she held her ground. "What you seek is im-mpossib-ble. N-no one escapes death!"

"Oh, but I've come all this way, and I even brought you a present." Daurgo impaled Ereshkigal with his tail and strapped a device from his armor to her chest. "It looks good on you! And don't worry about your little light show from earlier, this one is all clockwork."

The device was a contraption of metal gears and springs that covered Ereshkigal's torso and locked around her back. In the center of the machine were several large brass keys that Daurgo turned with his claw. As he did, a sharp blade shaped like a screw extended from the device and plunged into Ereshkigal's chest.

The goddess screamed as a metal corkscrew burrowed its way through her rib cage. "My heart!" She cried.

"That's where that one goes." Daurgo chuckled. "Are you ready to talk? Or do you want to try another one?"

Ereshkigal spat at the dracolich in response. Daurgo shrugged and turned another key. This one wound up a small hammer mechanism that punched a hole straight through Ereshkigal's torso below the screw.

"My liver!" Ereshkigal groaned.

"You know, when I'm dealing with mortal humans, I have to be really gentle. They break so easily. They're like eggshells." Daurgo tapped a third key with his claws. "But an immortal goddess? I can do all sorts of things to you and you'll still be able to tell me what I want to know. Tell me, death goddess. Do you like to play rough?"

Daurgo turned the third key, and a pressure plate crushed Ereshkigal's chest and squeezed the air out of her lungs. She tried to scream, but there was nothing left. Eventually, Daurgo turned the keys back, withdrawing all three torture mechanisms, and allowed Ereshkigal to regenerate.

"Are you ready to talk now?" Daurgo whispered into her ear. "If not, I have so many other things I want to try. Have you ever heard of tetherball? It's a game we can play where I tie your feet to one of those bone columns, and then I score points by seeing how long I can keep you spinning from clockwise to counterclockwise using just my tail. Want to try it?"

"You can't bring back the dead by force, fool!" Ereshkigal caught her breath. "Everything comes at a price! Even the gods are bound by that law!"

"Wait a minute..." Daurgo paused. "I remember something about that. Your sister who-must-not-be-named couldn't come back after you murdered her in a petty sibling-grudge-fest until she sacrificed her lover in her place. A soul for a soul. But would it work with another species? With a different afterlife?"

"I...why would I know that?" Ereshkigal grimaced. "That's your problem! Now get this thing off of me!"

Daurgo tossed the goddess over his shoulder, not bothering to check where she landed. "I'll need to learn how to collect and store souls. But what kinds? Do I need the souls of other dragons? Would a different species work? Another type of dragon? The slaves of the east, maybe? But how many? Does the age create a problem?"

The dracolich walked out of the underworld palace, continuing to ask questions to no one in particular. "I might even have to consult the Weavers, one more time."

2

Delusions of Adequacy

ROSTAM

"Is everything ready?" Captain Nadia checked on her crew.

"We've got fuel, provisions, and our passenger's luggage loaded," Simon Leverson, one of the new crewmates, reported. "We've got enough silver in capital to fill the hold with cargo."

Capital. Money the ship had on hand to buy cargo, which in this case meant lumber and quarried stone from Meditia, ready for any construction company looking to make repairs after the events of the Grand Wizard Tournament. All they needed was an eager merchant ship to deliver the supplies.

"And the passenger herself?" Nadia asked.

"She's been...a bit difficult." Simon grumbled. "But we got her to come aboard."

Nadia raised an eyebrow. "Difficult how?"

"Are you sure this is safe?"

Irene Rothstein stood at the end of the gangplank and tested it with her shoe. The airship swayed slightly in the wind, and she retracted her foot.

"Everything else is loaded, Miss." Simon waved for Irene to come aboard. "But we have to shove off soon."

Gingerly, Irene stepped onto the plank and flinched when it shifted under her weight. Simon must have had enough, because he grabbed her by the armpits and picked her up.

"We've got to get moving," he grumbled as he set the theurgist on the deck and pulled up the gangplank.

Irene got her bearings on the ship, and dusted herself off. The terrified look on her face made it clear that she was not accustomed to being picked up like a sack of potatoes.

From the high vantage point of Silverstack Docks, Rostam could get a good view of the damaged buildings throughout the city. Even though the damage the dracolich caused had started in the Academics' Arena, the Academic District had avoided the worst of it. Rumor was, the Institute of Theurgy had puppets summoned to deal with the undead that reached their school, and the faculty of the Academy of Sorcery left their campus to directly engage the zombies and drove the hordes from their university.

Noble as their efforts were, the sorcerers were not able to protect the Garden, Imperial, and Southern Residential districts from the dead. The Empyrian Quarter should have fared better, due to the nearby Temple District, but it wasn't just the undead to worry about. As soon as the initial fear of zombies and skeletons wore off, looters started raiding shops and homes, sometimes starting fires in the process. And for whatever reason, the Empyrian Quarter had been hit the hardest by looting, possibly because there were fewer zombies to worry about. Of course, rumor had it that most of the looters had been Empyrians themselves.

"Captain," Rostam looked over at Nadia. "What we're doing, buying up supplies to repair homes and businesses, does it seem...weird to you? We're effectively making a profit off of other people's losses."

Nadia thought for a moment. "Let me ask you this. If we don't go to Meditia and bring back supplies, what will construction companies use to rebuild the houses? How will people who lost their businesses make a living again if they can't fix their shops? If ships like ours don't bring the goods, will they just have to make do with damaged buildings?"

"But will we get into trouble?" Rostam asked. "I don't think what we're doing is wrong, but aren't there laws against racketeering? Profiteering off of destruction, or something like that?"

Nadia shook her head. "Only if you caused the destruction. Deliberately blowing up someone's house and then charging the owner to rebuild it would be illegal. Are we ready to shove off?"

"Our passenger is aboard!" Leverson hollered.

"All hands are on deck!" Joseph, the other new deckhand called.

"Tarchus?" Nadia called up to the crow's nest. "How are the skies?"

The spymaster looked down to his captain. "Couldn' be clea'er."

"Then take your posts!" Nadia ordered. "We're casting off."

Leverson released the docking clamps securing the ship to Silverstack Docks, and *The Endurance* was airborne. Rostam adjusted the ballast pipes, which let salt water flow through the ship to keep it balanced as it turned away from port and sailed off into the sky.

Once the ship was flying in the open sky and headed for Meditia, Rostam locked the ballast fluid and stepped away from the controls. He looked over the luggage they had stored in the ship's cargo hold just below deck. Irene had brought multiple instrument cases that Rostam couldn't identify. One of them looked like a cello, while another might have been a drum.

Rostam looked over at Irene, who was standing on the edge of the ship with her hands behind her back while she stared out at the scenery. She wore a brown trench coat that was too big for her, and a purple sports cap with a pair of cat ears on top. Rostam somewhat remembered Irene from the combat arena in the Grand Wizard Tournament. She'd worn her straight dark brown hair in twin-tails then, but now she had it down.

"I see you changed your hairstyle," Rostam commented.

"Hm?" Irene turned to face him. "Yeah, the twin-tails were pretty immature. I'm going to Meditia to try and sell some of the artifacts I've made. I'm trying to start my own business and establish my brand name, and that means I need to dress and act more mature."

Rostam glanced at the cat-eared hat she was wearing and wondered how that qualified as mature. Not wanting to push the issue, he tried another approach. "So, you work a lot with music, right?"

"Oh, yeah." Irene went over to a small case in her luggage and took out a tiny string instrument. "I've been working a lot with this ukulele lately. I like them because they're small, portable, easy to carry around for everyday things. My cello is too heavy to bring with me in most places."

"Okay." Rostam nodded. "I saw you in the combat arena, and you had a lot of enchanted instruments. What does this one do?"

Irene looked down at her ukulele. "This one? Nothing yet. I'm still trying to decide what to do with it. The thing is, music is inherently magical, and responds well to enchanted instruments. There's a lot of possibilities with a small instrument like this, but it doesn't have any enchantments yet."

"So, you couldn't use that to show me any of your magic?" Rostam asked.

"Hmm." Irene tapped the body of the ukulele. "I know a note that can make you poop your pants. Want to hear it?"

"Um... I think I'll pass." Rostam backed away from Irene and went over to talk to Nadia, who was looking over a clipboard.

"So, tell me why we're going all the way to Meditia to get building materials for Hadesh." Rostam propped himself next to the new captain. "Why go all the way to another nation, and how will it make us a profit?"

Nadia looked up from her clipboard. "What did Captain Zaahid teach you about supply chains?"

Captain Zaahid. The man who'd led the crew of *the Dutchess Authority*. He'd hired Nadia, Rostam, and Tarchus, and when his ship was destroyed by pirates, he chose to die with it. The captain went down with his ship.

"He told me about supply and demand, the Tragedy of the Commons, and how we ship captains can watch events that will cause changes in prices, such as a lot of property damage bringing in new demands for materials," Rostam answered. "But, wouldn't it make more sense to go somewhere closer? Baltithar and Zarash usually have stone and cement available. Why are we getting things from outside the Empire?"

"Okay," Nadia took a page from her clipboard and started drawing a picture. "Think of it like this. Baltithar and Zarash have some stone and cement mixed and ready for sale each year. However, the stone and cement they have stored is usually set aside for construction companies who buy from them every year. A certain percentage of their stock is set aside each season to supply their routine buyers, and it's incredibly bad for a supplier to sell stock to a small merchant like us and betray loyal customers, who now have to look elsewhere for materials and potentially find new trading partners. Think if we bought fifty bags of cement from a supplier that normally sells to a nearby construction company. The construction company will then have to buy from a different supplier, and they may decide they like the new supplier better, or may feel spurned by their previous trading partner and just make the new supplier permanent. Remember, we're only buying cement and stone because there's an emergency demand for the materials; we won't be around again next year to buy more cement."

"So it's a customer loyalty thing?" Rostam asked.

"Partly," she nodded. "Anyone who sells their stock to us and doesn't reserve enough for their normal buyers could end up hurting themselves badly in the future, and to cover their chances, any company that does sell to us will probably do so at a much higher price. Some companies even buy something called an 'option contract,' which is where you pay a supplier to keep some stock in reserve so that the company has the option to buy it later depending on the market."

"Why pay a supplier for the option to buy reserve stock instead of just buying the stock?" Rostam asked.

"Risk management." Nadia replied. "And storage costs. You can't just leave bags of cement out in the wind and rain for months, and every company has a limited amount of storage space for things like this. But on top of that, things can happen that change whether people want to hire construction companies, and on a bad year, the company might not need more material. If something should happen to reduce the number of houses or roads that people want to build on a given year, a construction company might find themselves with excess material and nothing to do with it."

"Okay," Rostam ran all of this through his head. "I think I understand. So how does all of this come back around to buying foreign goods?"

"We're going to one of the largest suppliers in a nearby country, who are further away, but they deliberately produce stock and keep it in storage for when demand is high, such as now." Nadia explained. "They have the warehouses to store so much excess stock that they can afford to sell low to a merchant ship like ours, and because they're based outside the Empire, it's possible that they haven't had many merchants come looking for supplies yet. Once they do, you can bet they're going to raise their prices."

"An' when we get to Meditia–" Tarchus's hand clamped onto Rostam's shoulder. "Be on tha' lookou' for any strange women. Don' trust any girl unless you ca'n see her legs."

"Uh…okay…" Rostam looked to Nadia to clue him in.

"No, he's right." Nadia crossed her arms. Where headed for one of the larger cities, and arachne like to slip in various places and lure men to their deaths. You'd be amazed at how creative they can be in hiding the fact that they're spiders from the waist down. And whatever you do, don't trust anyone handing out spider-girl comic books."

"Um…right. That's a little weird, but sounds pretty straightforward." Rostam nodded. "Anything else I should worry about?"

"Hey, there's another ship approaching." Irene pointed to the starboard side.

Rostam looked where she was pointing, but he couldn't see a ship. Squinting, a tiny speck was visible against the horizon getting closer and larger. He looked over at Irene again, wondering how she'd seen something so far away before Tarchus did. As he did, he could have sworn the cat ears on Irene's hat wiggled.

Tarchus looked through his spyglass at the speck. "I'll be. Tha's a ship, al'righ'. Na' sure wha' kind, though."

"If we don't know who, or what they want, we have to assume they're pirates." Nadia turned to Rostam. "Tell that fireball to give us some speed."

Rostam went to the lower deck of the ship and headed for the boiler room. A large, hot steam boiler with pipes flowing in, out, and around it sat in the middle of the room, heat coming off of the boiler filled the chamber. A steel door with a large handle and a latch covered the main portion of the boiler. A large stack of coal sat in a corner of the room, along with a thermal mitt hanging on a hook along one wall. Rostam put the mitt on his right hand and grabbed the latch on the boiler door, opening it to reveal the spirit inside.

"Hello, Cindrocles." Rostam told the elemental. "We need to pick up speed."

The fireball opened a pair of…well, you could call them eyes, though they looked like embers flickering in the flames. "Are we being chased?" He asked in a groggy voice. He must have been in a restful mood up until now.

"Not yet, but there's another ship out in the sky, and we're not sure who they are or what they want." Rostam grabbed a piece of coal and tossed it to the fire elemental. "Can you give us more speed?"

"No problem." Cindrocles gobbled up the coal and started glowing brighter.

Rostam stood back and closed the boiler while the heat started to rise. He felt the ship lurch as they went faster. Quickly, he went back up to the main deck and took his post at the ballast controls. "Ready for evasive maneuvers, captain!"

"Let's hope we don't need them." Nadia gripped the steering wheel. "Tarchus, how are we doing?"

"Righ' now, we're all righ'." The spymaster peered through his telescope at the ship. "They migh' be smaller 'an us, bu' I don' think they've spot'ed us yet. We shoul' be— wai' a mi'ute!"

Rostam looked over his shoulder at the speck on the starboard side. He couldn't get a good view of it, but the speck seemed to be getting larger. He could now make out the outline of a small airship moving faster and closing the distance between them and *the Endurance*.

"There's no friendly reason why they'd be on a course to catch us." Nadia gritted her teeth. "Rostam, time for those evasive maneuvers!"

Disengaging the ballast lock, Rostam grabbed a crank wheel and turned it as quickly as he could. As Nadia turned the ship's wheel to steer the ship left, fluid from the pipes flowed to the starboard side and kept the airship level. Were it not for the ballast fluid, the ship would capsize in the sky making such tight turns.

"They're gainin'!" Tarchus called. "They're small, fas', an' eager!"

Nadia turned to the new deckhands. "Joseph, Simon – each of you grab a rifle and discourage them from following us!"

The two grabbed rifles from below deck and tried to get a vantage point from the masts. Rostam heard two loud gunshots that pierced the air.

Tarchus kept his spyglass trained on the other ship. "No good. They're still a comin'!"

"What kind of firepower are they carrying?" Nadia asked.

"No ship guns." Tarchus answered. "They're smaller 'an us, cannae han'le the recoil."

"Then prepare to be boarded." Nadia drew her own pistol. "They won't take us without a fight."

"Irene, have you got anything?" Rostam asked the wizard.

"Um, I...uh, didn't prepare for a fight today." She scrambled around, looking for options. "Most of my stuff isn't meant to work so far from the ground, and all of the elementals I can summon don't like ships."

As she looked for something to help fend off pirates, Rostam heard the sound of a hook piercing the hull of their ship and pulling them closer to the sloop. The pirates would be on their deck in seconds.

Rostam grabbed a pistol and an axe, ready to fight, but as the sloop pulled itself side-by-side with *the Endurance*, he saw a dozen men with guns. *The Endurance* had no chance.

"Greetings and salutatorians!" A strange-looking man wearing a captain's hat and wielding a pistol stepped forward to address the crew of *The Endurance*. "We'll be taking your cargo, valuables, and other assets. Lower your weapons."

Nadia sighed and ordered for Joseph, Simon, and Rostam to drop their weapons. The four of them weren't going to fight off that many pirates in a gun match. The crew and Irene put their hands up in surrender.

"Excellent," the pirate captain said. "Now, Kaseem, subjugate them!"

"Subju– what?" One of the pirates, who must have been Kaseem, turned to their captain in confusion.

"Oh, you idiot, take their weapons!" The captain hollered.

"Alright, but that's not what 'subjugate' means," Kaseem grumbled. He grabbed the side railing of *the Endurance* and climbed aboard. He then scooped up the weapons that Nadia and the crew had set down.

"Akbar, Jallal!" The captain called. "Commerce perforating their stores!"

Two of the pirates gave each other a look. "Boss, do you want us to pick you up a thesaurus next time we're in town?"

"Oh, just do it, okay!" The pirate captain clearly didn't take kindly to backtalk.

The two pirates climbed over to *the Endurance* and headed to the lower decks.

"Um, who are you?" Irene asked. "I get that your pirates, but who specifically?"

"Well, I'm so glad you asked, little lady." The pirate captain smiled and bowed, taking his hat off to reveal his balding head. "I am Captain Amed, and we are–" A look of utter shock filled his face. His eyes grew so wide Rostam had to look over his shoulder and follow the pirate's gaze to make sure he hadn't spotted some monster in the skies behind them.

"By the gods," Captain Amed stammered. "Did we actually forget to think of a pirate gang name?"

The three remaining pirates on his ship glanced at each other.

"I think we did." One said.

"We're the…sky…pirates." Another offered.

"That's literally every pirate gang that has an airship." The third replied.

"The…what rhymes with sky?" The second pirate asked.

"…Hm…pie?" The first suggested. "The pie…in the sky, pirates."

Captain Amed smacked the handle of his pistol against the back of the first pirate's head. "That is quite possibly the dumbest pirate gang name I have ever heard."

"Hey, there's not much for cargo on this boat." One of the pirates called from below deck. "It's mostly luggage, and a bunch of instruments no one aboard knows how to play."

"How much do you think we could profiteer from selling these musical instruments?" Captain Amed asked.

"You can't take my babies!" Irene protested.

"Sorry, young lass." The captain chuckled. "But loot is loot."

An infuriated look filled Irene's face. Rostam didn't think much about it. There wasn't a lot Irene could do in this situation.

"Don't you think you could come up with a better pirate gang name than that?" Irene did her best to mask her anger. "I feel like a captain with such an…advanced vocabulary as you should be able to think of something."

Captain Amed stroked his chin. "Well…"

"Oh no," the remaining pirates with guns aimed at the crew of *the Endurance* grimaced like they were preparing for a storm. "She encouraged him. We're doomed!"

"Let me pontificate for a moment. We should have a name that encapsulates our ferocity. Something bold, brazen, like...feisty? The feisty pirates?"

"Captain," one pirate scowled. "That's terrible. Why not 'bloody?'"

"Don't be gross, Amir," the captain stroked his chin while the other pirates groaned. "It's still missing something, though."

"Why did that girl have to enable him?" One pirate rubbed his eyes with his thumb and index finger.

"Wait," one pirate looked back at the crew of *the Endurance*, as if noticing something wrong. "Where'd that girl go?"

Rostam quickly looked around for where Irene could be. He spotted her near one of her instrument cases. It was the unenchanted ukulele.

Realizing what she was doing, Rostam had just enough time to cover his ears. He pressed as hard as he could against the sides of his head, desperately trying to make certain the sound didn't get through.

With his ears covered and no sound, Rostam could see as everyone, the pirates, Nadia, and the rest of the crew clutched their stomachs and their rear ends. Captain Amed was so surprised he lost his balance and fell over, crashing into another pirate.

"What in the Abyss was that noise?" One pirate asked.

"Hell!" Another cried. "Hell is that noise!"

Rostam tackled Kaseem and knocked him on his back. As Kaseem tried to get to his feet, Rostam kicked his head into the side railing. Before the pirate could recover, Rostam grabbed two of the pistols and fired one into Kaseem's right hip. While the pirate rolled over in pain, Rostam pointed the other at the pirate captain.

Captain Amed held up his hands. "Now, wait just one nanosecond!"

Keeping the pistol aimed at Amed, Rostam knelt down and kicked another gun over to Captain Nadia. Visibly uncomfortable and needing a change of pants, Nadia grabbed the pistol and pointed it at the pirates.

Akbar and Jallal, the pirates sent to raid *the Endurance*, returned from below deck with several musical instrument cases. One carried a cello case, while the other carried two violins. Rostam notices that the instrument cases all had what looked like steel framing that had been ornamentally designed to look like spider legs.

The two looked at everyone's soiled trousers and the guns held by Nadia and Rostam.

"Okay, I don't think I want to know what happened up here." On pirate put down the violin cases. "Are we fighting, or something else?"

As if in answer, Irene clapped her hands twice. The violin and cello cases twitched. What Rostam had thought was an ornamental frame came to life as the violin cases stood up like large spiders. The pirate still holding the cello case froze in horror as he realized what he was holding had more limbs than he did.

The instrument cases attacked Akbar and Jallal. They weren't particularly dangerous; Rostam realized that they had no mouths, mandibles, or any of the things that make spiders a threat, but the pirates didn't seem to notice. They scrambled back to their pirate ship while the instrument cases stood at the edge of *the Endurance* menacingly. They might not have been actual fighters, but they were very creepy.

Rostam grabbed Kaseem and shoved him towards the edge of the ship. Although he was limping, Kaseem managed to crawl back to the pirate's vessel.

"I think," Nadia wheezed, still recovering from Irene's note. "We've had just about enough of this. Take your ship and get lost before we put any more holes in your crew."

Captain Amed nodded frantically. "You don't have anything worth constipating, anyway. We're going, men!"

The pirates unhooked their ship from *the Endurance* and pulled away.

Nadia sighed and lowered her pistol. "Everyone, go change your pants. I have to go check how far off course we've drifted. Even while boarded, we were still moving."

Rostam walked up to Irene. "Thanks for the assistance there. You all right?"

She nodded, and took two small wooden objects out of her ears. "I had my earplugs in, so I wasn't affected."

"What's with the spiders?" Rostam gestured to the instrument cases. "You used spider elementals in the combat arena, too. Do you like spiders?"

"Sort of." Irene sat down next to one of her violin cases and stroked its back like it was a pet. "Elemental spirits with spiderlike features work well with string instruments. Spiders use their webbing to communicate and even attract mates by plucking the strands. They're also very receptive to vibrations. And I also like how spiders can setup their webs in secluded spots and don't like being watched. I can definitely relate to that."

"You're not good with people?" Rostam asked.

Irene lowered her head. "I'm not even good with humanus elementals. I work a lot with bestia spirits, but I can't make more powerful artifacts because I can never convince the higher level spirits to submit. My friend Ariella from school showed me how to enchant parts of a more complicated device with lesser spirits. That was how I made the organ I used in the first round; each piece had a minor enchantment. Same with the instruments I'm trying to sell."

Rostam looked at the cello and violin cases. "What do they do?"

"They're mining equipment." Irene replied.

After a three-day flight, *the Endurance* pulled up to Gangryros, one of the larger cities in Meditia. The port for airships overlooked the sea. Carved into the hillsides were large, stone docks for ships to land and lock into while loading cargo. Being one of the smaller ships, *the Endurance* pulled into a narrow dock on the western side of the port.

The city of Gangryros was mostly shorter houses spread out along grasslands. There were few apartment buildings where multiple families would live. Rostam had never seen so many homes spread out across such a large area; Hadesh was one of the largest cities in the Borealan Empire, and the wall that enclosed the city limited their growth.

"What keeps this city safe from the Greymarch?" Rostam asked Nadia.

The Greymarch. An army of infected people attacking anyone they could to spread their disease. They were poorly understood, and feared by many.

"Elementals along the land," Nadia pointed to the east. "And the sea makes a nice natural barrier. Greymarchers don't swim."

"Elementals?" Rostam scanned the edge of the landscape. "I don't see any elementals. Only some rocks."

"Yeah, but if the Greymarch were to attack, those rocks would stand up and pound them into sludge. The Greymarch can't turn spirits into new marchers." Nadia said.

As *the Endurance* locked into the docks, a port official came up to their ship.

"I'll need to know your captain's name, the contents of your vessel, origin, and purpose for visiting." The official held up a clipboard.

Nadia went up to the official and filled out his questions. After a few moments, she shook hands with the man and he cleared their ship for unloading.

"Alright, Miss Rothstein." Nadia turned to Irene. "We've delivered you to Gangryros."

"Thank you," Irene curtsied. Then she stood up and clapped her hands.

Irene's luggage stood up at her command. In addition to her music cases, a large trunk that Joseph and Simon brought up from below deck got up on four paws like a large cat. The enchantress walked off the ship's gangplank with her ukulele in hand, and three spidery music cases and a lion-trunk following her like a group of ducklings.

"Good luck to you!" Rostam called.

Irene waved goodbye and set off.

"I was gonna ask why a girl tha' small was travelin' alone," Tarchus commented. "Bu' it doesn' look like tha' girl is ever alone."

3

The Princess and the Infinite Falling Object

AMRI

Swimming around in the aquarium was a creature with a bioluminescent bulb like an angler fish, tentacles of an octopus, lobster claws, and colorful stripes. All of these things seemed to be attached to a tuna.

"Okay," Namid examined the chimera in the tank. "Who smoked one?"

"That is a chimeric experiment regarding DNA combinations." Doctor Julio Castejón explained. "Alchemists use some of our aquatic animals to detect various properties that can be transferred to chimeras."

"So, what does your aquarium do with telepathic sorcery?" Amri looked around the facility. He and his sister were visiting Grand Spire's Aquatic Research Facility as part of their off-season studies. Amri had suggested studying abroad for the season to Namid after one of her fights in the combat arena resulted in her opponent becoming critically injured. They had been invited to visit the aquarium regarding studies in sorcery, and the aquarium had advertised telepathic sorcery experiments.

"We have been studying the ways that animals react to various types of telepathy." The doctor directed Amri and Namid to a large tank containing dolphins. A massive glass wall allowed them to see inside of the tank. "Some animals, such as dolphins, show enough intelligence for us to communicate with them using telepathy. My student Carmen, will demonstrate for you."

A pale girl about Namid's age with straight black hair and wearing a one-piece bathing suit climbed into the dolphin tank and sat on a shelf near the glass wall. A speaking tube traveling through the wall allowed her to talk with an outlet where Namid and Amri were standing. The girl dipped her legs into the water and waved to her audience as the first dolphin swam up to her.

The girl, who must have been Carmen, placed her hand on the dolphin's head. Amri had heard that the most basic and important technique of a telepathic sorcerer involved turning one's fingertips into a receptor for another creature's nerves. Thoughts could travel through the sorcerer's fingertips, allowing them to hear what their target was thinking.

"This is Blue," Carmen happily announced. "He is a four-year-old Atlantic bottlenose, and he would like the girl to climb into his tank and…" Carmen's eyes widened. "Um, I'm not going to repeat that."

Carmen shooed the dolphin away. It snipped at her before swimming off.

Namid turned to Doctor Castejón. "Do I want to know what that dolphin was thinking?"

The doctor frowned. "Probably not."

A second dolphin swam up to Carmen. Once again, she placed her hand on the dolphin's head.

"Okay, this one is Ray. He's usually more polite. I just told him your names are Amri and Namid, and he says he's pleased to meet you."

Amri and Namid nodded and waved to the dolphin, who made a happy expression and joyful noises.

"Ray says he'd like to know you both better," Carmen continued. "He says that he'd very much like for both of you to—oh gods!"

Carmen recoiled away from Ray and pulled her feet out of the water. Ray looked up at her for a moment, and after a while swam away.

"Carmen is new to the aquarium," the doctor said. "She's only been working with the dolphins for a week. It is possible she's getting some of her readings wrong."

"Do you have anybody who's been working here longer?" Amri asked.

"Sadly, no." The doctor shook his head. "I always try to get students from Grand Spire's Thaumaturgy University to give them opportunities to learn what they want to do with their careers, and the university likes to advertise working with dolphins to young women, in an effort to get more females interested in Thaumaturgy. Unfortunately, all of the girls that have worked with the dolphins usually quit after a week."

Thaumaturgy. That was what the people of Grand Spire, and many of the other northern countries called "sorcery." Apparently, up here, "sorcery" was another thing entirely, and had less to do with actual magic and more to do with hallucinogenic mushrooms. They also called Theurgy "conjuration." And for some reason, "alchemy" was still called "alchemy" here. Strange.

A new dolphin came up to Carmen, and once more, she placed her hand on the dolphin's head. "Oh, a female dolphin! This should be better." Carmen let the dolphin think and send thoughts up her arm. "Her name is Gracie. She wants to know what the boy's name is."

Amri looked at the speaking tube, which seemed to be a one-way device. "How do I tell her my name?"

"Hold on," Carmen continued. "I told her your name is Amri. She says she wants Amri to swim with her and—Aaahhhh!"

Carmen took her hand off of Gracie and climbed out of the dolphin tank. "They're all awful! Every last one of them is a pervert! I quit! Find someone else to talk to your stupid pervy animals!"

"I think we've solved the mystery of the disappearing female interns," Namid muttered. "What else have you got to show us today?"

"Well," Doctor Castejón looked flustered. "We have a new experiment that will allow a person to see and experience life as an animal. One of my other assistants, Miss Luna, can use telepathy to allow a person to plug into the mind of an animal, feel, see, and explore the world through the animal's senses."

"What's the point of that?" Amri asked.

"Well, seeing the world through the eyes of an animal could help us better understand—"

Namid tackled Doctor Castejón with all fifty kilos of her tiny body. "IWANT-TOBEA SNAPPING TURTLE!" She grabbed the doctor by the collar of his shirt and tried to shake him. "Make me a snapping turtle!"

"Okay, okay!" The doctor pried Namid's hands off of his shirt. "Yeesh. I'll ask Miss Luna to set everything up."

Within the hour, Miss Luna, a young woman in her mid-twenties, had a snapping turtle from the aquarium that was docile enough to run the experiment. With Namid seated on a stool next to Miss Luna, the telepath placed her left hand on the turtle's head and right hand on Namid's.

"This turtle's name is Pandora," Doctor Castejón explained. "She's lived with us for forty years now, and her entire species as we understand it only lives in captivity. As you can see, Pandora is very comfortable with people."

"Beginning the neural connection," Miss Luna said. "She should be seeing through Pandora's eyes...now."

As she began her spell, currents of energy flowed between Namid and the turtle. Namid's hair stood on end as electricity passed through her scalp. The turtle's eyes widened, as if possessed by a new spirit. Namid's eyes closed and her body slumped, but a comfortable smile spread across her face. Pandora withdrew her legs into her shell and mimicked Namid's own smile.

"Is she...controlling the turtle?" Amri asked.

"She shouldn't be." Miss Luna struggled to maintain the spell.

"Highly unlikely." Doctor Castejón placed a tray with a paper bag of food mix in front of the turtle. "Taking control over another creature's body when she's not even the one controlling the spell would require an extreme force of will, especially to overpower a turtle like Pandora."

Pandora stretched out her neck and took a bite of lettuce. As she ate, Namid mimicked chewing with her own mouth. Pandora looked around with her head stretched out, stopping to examine the food bag's ingredient list while chewing the food.

"Can Pandora read?" Amri asked.

"No..." Doctor Castejón raised an eyebrow. "She shouldn't be doing that."

The doctor reached for the bag to pull it away. The turtle responded by trying to bite off the doctor's fingers. He had just enough time to withdraw his hand in shock as Namid's mouth made a similar biting motion. Amri thought for certain that the turtle was cackling as it pulled its limbs and neck into its shell, leaving only enough of her head outside for Miss Luna to maintain the connection. Namid pulled her own head into her shoulders. Both Namid and the turtle looked incredibly cozy.

"I think I'm at my limit." Miss Luna winced. "I'm severing the connection... now."

Namid's body started moving again. She blinked her eyes and smacked her lips, wiggling her tongue around like she was getting used to the feel of her own mouth again.

"Did you enjoy yourself?" Amri asked.

"Yes," Namid stretched out her arms. "But now I'm hungry. I could really go for some shrimp with lettuce."

"Good grief, are these the foreign exchange students?" A voice with an heir of royalty to it came from behind Amri. He turned to see a girl his own age with ivory skin, brown hair in flowing curls that almost glowed, wearing an expensive-looking yellow dress with red trim. Following her were two armed soldiers carrying short swords and pistols. The girl walked up to Amri and looked down on him, standing a good ten centimeters taller. "Gods, your short. And what's with the girl and the turtle? Is she trying to grow a shell so she can hide her hair?"

"What's wrong with my hair?" Namid felt her head and realized how frizzy it was from the telepathic connection. "Oh no." She looked around for a mirror and found a reflective piece of metal on one wall. "Aw, crud." She pulled her neck into her shoulders and lowered her head. "Damnit, I don't have a shell!"

"Um, your highness," Doctor Castejón approached the new girl. "These are foreign students from the Borealan Empire. They're here to study thaumaturgy with the university."

"Oh, so that's their ordeal?" She looked over Amri and Namid dismissively. "Well, that's that, then. I have my own studies, which I don't need to remind you are more important than anything else you have going on here. Carry on."

The fancifully dressed girl turned and walked away, with her entourage following closely behind.

"Who's the rude rich girl?" Namid asked.

"That was Princess Elvia Valiente, heir to the throne of Grand Spire." Doctor Castejón rubbed his temples. "Gods help us all."

Amri looked at Namid's still-frizzy hair. "Is there a reason she's so hostile? She walks up to a couple of strangers and immediately insults them."

"I will not speak ill of my future queen," Doctor Castejón regained his composure. "However, she *is* the future queen. That should tell you all you need to know. Her royal education requires a basic schooling in virtually all subjects, including thaumaturgy and animal biology, so she comes here once a week for her studies."

"Perhaps we should move on to something else," Amri said. "We're only here to expand our thaumaturgy studies, and there's so much here you can show us that won't interfere with the princess. Is there anything else you can show us today as part of the program?"

"I think that would be best." Doctor Castejón took out a sheet of paper detailing the foreign exchange program. "I believe the thaumaturgical development center would be perfect for you to visit next."

Amri and Namid gathered their bookbags and stepped out of Grand Spire's Aquatic Research Facility and onto the streets of the spire itself.

Three days after their arrival, Amri was starting to get used to the layout of the city. A massive spire standing at over six hundred meters tall, the entire city had been built up rather than out. Concrete reinforced with steel formed the center of the spire and all of its branches, with thirty pillars of the same materials surrounding the city and supporting its weight. Encircling the spire were everything from schools, research buildings, residential housing, shopping centers and restaurants. Massive pipes traveling along the pillars pumped water up and allowed foul water down back to the ground, while elevators along the center served as the primary means of traveling up and down the spire. In addition, there was a massive staircase and sloped road that spiraled around the center of the spire to allow people to walk and haul goods on carts up and down the levels of the city.

Amri had never seen them, but he had heard that the spire extended into the ground itself, where food was grown through hydroponics that extended from the ark where the people of Grand Spire were said to have originated. An advanced facility designed to preserve humanity through the Calamity supposedly lay at the heart of the spire's foundation, and was the source of the original technology that made the vertical city possible.

"So...thaumaturgy?" Amri took out a map of the city they'd been given when they'd arrived. "Where is that?"

"Three levels below us," Namid pointed to a spot on the map. "It's weird that they call it that here. Elevator, or stairs?"

"Let's take the stairs." Amri folded up the map. "The elevators are always so busy, and three levels isn't that far."

The central road of Grand Spire stretched out before them, curling around the base of the center. Towards the middle, Amri could see elevators, each looking like a birdcage, sliding up and down the main column. They were supposedly powered entirely by steam, without any magical assistance, but Amri didn't know how they worked. How one could efficiently drive a metal box like that up and down such a massive city was beyond him.

Walking along the gentle slope of the spire's main road, Amri took in the sights of the city's people riding the trolleys, elevators, and wagons. It was strange to see a vertical city like this operate so much like Hadesh back home. Supposedly, Grand Spire was built in an effort to continue expanding without exposing its populace to the Greymarch, and a field of landmines stood between the spire and any potential invaders on all sides. Only a handful of roads lead away from the base of the spire, and they were not easy to spot unless you knew they were there.

As they walked along the helical road, Amri noticed a runner jogging up the curved walkway. Running up and down the spire seemed to be a popular form of exercise. It must have been difficult, but sorcerers needed to keep up their health in order to handle magic flowing through their bodies. Perhaps he'd have to try jogging up to the top of the spire once or twice before he and his sister finished their abroad studies.

After walking three levels down, the sorcery, no, *thaumaturgy* students approached a large building on a terrace extending from the main pillar and supported by the surrounding columns. A large set of double doors welcomed visitors inside.

"Greetings!" A cheerful receptionist smiled inside. "What can our illustrious institute do for you today?"

"We're here as part of a foreign exchange program." Amri handed the receptionist their papers. "We're from the Borealan Empire."

"Oh." The receptionist looked over the paperwork. "Let me get someone for you."

She rang a bell, and before long a clean-shaven man in his forties came from a back room to meet them.

"Hello. I am Professor Santiago Cantero." He gestured for the students to follow him. "Please, come with me."

Following behind the professor through a hallway, Amri got a good view through a glass window that lined the wall to his right of some of the strange experiments on which the facility was working.

"Thaumcraft is the art of using wards and other magical etching to create and develop magical apparatuses," the professor explained. "On your right, you'll see the kinetic reduction project, where we're currently trying to create a device that can reduce the rate at which potential energy is converted into kinetic energy for a falling object."

"And by falling object, you mean a person?" Namid pointed through the window to a man jumping from at least ten meters while wearing a belt. Wards etched into the belt glowed as he jumped, and a golden energy field enveloped the man like a ball, making a lot of noise and light, but he fell slowly and landed on his feet unharmed.

"Precisely," the professor pointed to the man's belt. "Wards resist change, and different wards can resist different kinds of changes. They can also allow changes in energy to occur in ways they naturally wouldn't. When an object normally falls, all of the potential energy the object possesses at its maximum height is converted into heat, sound, and kinetic energy, mostly the latter. The belt that the man wears increases the amount of energy that becomes sound, and even turns some of it into light, all to reduce the kinetic energy; that is, the speed at which the man wearing the belt falls. Very useful if you fall out of an airship."

Amri thought about everything the professor said. "Increased sound, and added some light, but what about heat? Does the belt change how much energy becomes heat?"

Professor Cantero grimaced. "The first experiments did. The test dummies were too burnt for us to try those on a human test pilot. But never mind that.

I'm going to show you the portal we've been working on."

Intrigued, Amri and Namid followed the professor down the hallway passed a number of strange experiments, including staves etched with ward lines, metal balls magnetized with wards, and clothes with wards woven into them to keep cold or hot weather out.

Eventually, they came to a large room in which a massive contraption was setup surrounded by railings. Five large, round, brass tanks lined one wall with pipes flowing in and out of them. In the center of the room were two large rings made of bronze, each two meters in diameter. One ring was located on the middle of the ceiling, and the other was on the floor, right above a strange green surface that looked like burlap. Catwalks to and from the bottom runegate formed an X-pattern with a circle in the center for the ring.

Amri could tell that the rings themselves were a pair of runegates, portals to and from the Spirit Plane, the realm of magic. Some called it the Duat, or the Aether, or simply the plane of magic, but it was from this dimension that all magic flowed into the material world, making wizardry possible. Runegates were portals to and from this eldritch location, where the rules of Euclidian geometry did not apply.

"These portals have been setup in an effort to hopefully create an infinite loop, or a perpetual motion machine," Professor Cantero explained. "Maintaining them is difficult; runegates use a lot of magical energy. Have your studies explained how magical energy follows diffusion?"

"Not really." Amri shook his head.

"So, diffusion is the process by which substances will try to reach equilibrium." The professor demonstrated by bringing out a large glass rectangular tank filled with water. He placed a transparent piece of material in the tank so that it divided the water in half. "This is a semipermeable membrane," he explained. "Water can pass through, solid mater cannot. The water will naturally try to even itself out until both halves of the tank have the same amount of water. Magic follows the same rules; magical energy will try to even itself out throughout the material plane until it reaches equilibrium, barring the occasional warpstorm in the Aether. But watch what happens to the water when I do this."

The professor took a salt shaker and sprinkled some salt into one side of the tank. Some of the water from the unsalted side drained into the salty side, until the salty side held significantly more water than the other.

"Add some salt, or other solute, and the water will try to balance out the solids," the professor continued. "Since the salt can't flow through the membrane, the water will shift until one side has more water than it normally would. Magic can be tricked into doing the same thing."

Gesturing over to the five brass tanks, Professor Cantero opened one and showed Amri the contents. Inside, there was a large, blue crystal packed with ice cubes and cold water.

"Certain types of crystals can attract magical energy when cooled." The professor took a pair of tongs and held one up for Amri to see, though Amri kept his distance. "The cooling isn't easy, especially once we fire up the runegates and the magic starts producing heat, but we can keep two gates open right next to each other for eight hours, when normally we'd only be able to sustain them for a little more than a few minutes."

Returning the crystal and closing the tank, Professor Cantero gestured for several lab assistants to turn on the runegates. As the gates flickered to life, Amri looked up into one and saw a strange world that looked like an open night sky with floating rocks and a sea flowing vertically upwards in the distance. Directly above the portal, Amri could see the other end of the lower gate, getting a good look at Namid looking down at him.

"This is too weird." Namid blinked. "What's the point of this?"

"We believe that if we can harness the energy of an infinitely falling object, we could generate an infinite supply of energy." The professor beamed. "We're still working on that, though."

"Infinitely falling object?" Namid asked. "How is that supposed to work?"

She leaned closer so she could get a good view of both the upper and lower portals.

"Sis, you shouldn't stand so close." Amri reached out to grab his sister, but as he did she stumbled and fell into the lower portal.

"Namid!" Amri called as his sister fell into the void. He could hear her scream get further and further away, before getting closer and closer. He had just enough time to step back from the runegates to avoid her crashing into him as she fell through the upper portal and back into the lower portal.

Amri blinked as his sister fell from the ceiling portal into the floor and back through the ceiling again. "How do we stop this?"

"Turn off the bottom gate!" Professor Cantero ordered.

A lab assistant shut off the gate on the floor, revealing the green surface below. From the catwalk railing, Amri watched as Namid fell through the ceiling portal and slammed into the material, which turned out to be a large trampoline. It launched her back through the ceiling portal, only for her to fall once again onto the trampoline.

As she continued to bounce in and out of dimensions through the portal, Amri looked around at the catwalks and trampoline in confusion.

Professor Cantero gave him a knowing expression. "This has happened before."

Eventually, Namid's bouncing came to a halt, and the runegate along the ceiling was shut off. She lay sprawled out on the trampoline with a dazed look on her face.

"Namid?" Amri held up three fingers. "How many fingers do you see?"

"I want to go again." She grinned.

"These two again?" A familiar haughty voice came from behind Amri. He turned to see Princess Elvia, followed by her train.

"Why are these two draining all of the magic from the area with this project?" She asked.

"Your highness," Professor Cantero stammered. "We were demonstrating our research to these foreign exchange students. It is part of our–"

"You are wasting the magic that I need for my studies," the princess remarked. "I am in the middle of my own lessons, along with other wizards in the building, and your demonstration to these foreigners is draining more magic from this area than everything else going on combined."

"Are you following us?" Namid asked. "Don't you have anything better to do?"

"Excuse me?" The princess roared. "Who do you think you are? You are a guest in *my* country distracting me from *my* studies that relate to how I run *my* kingdom. Who gave you permission to speak to me?"

"Your highness, they are foreigners!" Professor Cantero pleaded. "Please excuse their rudeness, for diplomacy's sake!"

"Quit your groveling," the princess scoffed. "You look pathetic!" She turned to Namid and her brother. "Don't let these two in my sight again, and keep them away from important projects like this!"

"Um..." The professor turned to look at the two students. "Of course. I'll...I'll make sure of it."

Before either of them could protest, armed guards escorted Amri and Namid to the Grand Spire's Thaumaturgy University.

A concierge directed the two to their room at the university. "I regret to inform you that you have been restricted to campus grounds for the rest of your stay with us." He bowed to them before leaving. "My sincerest apologies."

The concierge left and gently closed the door behind him, leaving Amri alone in the room with his sister. Once it was quiet, Namid dug through her bookbag and took out a notebook and a pen.

"Okay, here's the plan." She scribbled something in her notebook. "We ask one of the girls here on campus to recommend Princess Crabby-Pants to the aquarium for the Flirting with Dolphins project. Once the dolphins get frisky and the princess gets salty, she'll want to return home in a huff." Namid showed a drawing of a soggy stick-figure version of Princess Elvia. "I'll be waiting for her disguised as a party clown to cheer her up." She scribbled a picture of a grinning clown with the words 'clever disguise' and an arrow pointing at the clown. "She'll never know it's me. When I squirt her with a flower on my costume, the water will be laced with sugar. Then, I'll let a jar of killer bees loose, who will smell the sugar and swarm her." Namid followed her last drawing with a picture of the princess surrounded by dots, who must have been bees.

"Once they start to sting her, and she's stumbling around all confused and hurt, I'll switch to a beekeeper's outfit, douse her with barbeque sauce, and shove her off the platform level we're on so that she falls to her death on the spire floor below."

"What's with the barbeque sauce?" Amri asked.

Namid frowned. "Please, hold all questions until the end. Now, the barbeque sauce will attract rats, cats, heck, maybe even some pigeons, too. All are welcome. They start chewing on the corpse before anyone can grab the body and when they find the half-eaten princess, she'll be too stung and chewed up to bury in a conventional grave. Instead, they'll cremate her and put her ashes in a nice, convenient, easy-to-steal urn. While they prepare the cremation, you'll need to figure out where they plan to store her ashes and then dig a hole in the campus gardens while I take flamenco dancing lessons."

Amri squinted at Namid's latest drawing of herself attending the university's flamenco dancing class. "This plan is getting weird."

"Hold all comments as well," Namid continued. "Now, once the princess is literally dust, we'll need to dump her ashes into the hole you've dug and then cover it up as a proper grave so I can dance on it." She showed her last drawing, a crude stick figure of herself dancing on a pile of dirt. "Okay, now. Are there any questions?"

Amri looked at the series of drawings his sister had made and let the contents of her scheme sink in. "I have a few. For starters, why are you plotting to murder the crown princess in the first place?"

"Uh, because she got us banned from exploring the city and studying cool stuff?" Namid looked at Amri like she couldn't believe he needed to ask. "Because she's trash? Because she's a whole bunch of other words I can't say?"

"Namid, we've got less than two more weeks here before we're headed back home anyway. There's a lot of reasons not to murder someone, like the fact that assassinating the crown princess will probably get us both executed, but the fact that they'll already be out of our hair in a short amount of time should be enough by itself to just be patient."

"She ruined our chance to study." Namid sat on her bed and crossed her arms. "I was actually enjoying this. I got to fall through an infinite loophole!"

"We still have access to the university library," Amri offered. "There could be all sorts of interesting–"

"BORING!" Namid flopped back onto her bed. "I didn't come here to look through old books. I can do that at home."

Amri rubbed his forehead. "Look, I'm going to check the library and see if there's anything worth our while. Who knows, I might find a new bedtime story for you."

Namid rolled her eyes and groaned.

"Don't commit regicide while I'm gone." Amri closed the door to their room and headed for the university library.

The dorm they'd been provided for their stay at the university was on the opposite end of the campus from the library. Since most of their studies had taken place throughout the Grand Spire, away from the library, neither of them had noticed. But now, Amri had a chance to take a good look at the university's campus as he walked.

The campus fit into the northeast quadrant of the spire's seventeenth level. Each level of the spire was fifteen meters tall, and the seventeenth level had a radius of three hundred meters, with each level's radius ten meters less than the one below. This meant that the campus had plenty of room to build offices, classrooms, laboratories, dormitories, and research facilities, all connected by catwalks.

As Amri climbed a third flight of stairs to reach a catwalk that led to the library, he realized he hadn't seen a single overweight person in Grand Spire. "It's the stairs," he wheezed. "So many stairs – they must get a lot of cardio."

When they'd arrived at the spire, Amri had heard that it wasn't simply a city-state. They were an entire nation contained in a single city that had built itself upwards instead of out, so as to make it easier to defend themselves from the Greymarch. Memories of his old home, Aklagos, that had been overrun by Greymarchers flooded back to him. Him, Namid, Rostam, and Ephorah meeting on the evacuation ships. Moving to Hadesh with Namid and living with their aunt and uncle. His parents were never found. But the worst memory was the sight of a kid who'd fallen from the evacuation ships. He'd watched a Greymarcher grab him, vomit whatever grey crud spreads their curse, and turn him into a new marcher.

Amri reached the library and wondered if they might have any information about the Greymarch inside.

Two large, bronze doors filled with rivets greeted him. The doors were heavy, and as Amri tried to open them, he was further reminded how out of shape he must have been compared to the natives of the spire.

Inside the library, Amri was greeted by a huge skull of a dragon resting on a pedestal in the middle of a large, marble floor. The skull was massive, at least three meters tall, and reminded Amri of the dracolich that had attacked Hadesh during the Grand Wizard Tournament.

"Can I help you with something?"

Amri looked to his right to find a librarian a head taller than himself. He had gold-rimmed glasses, wiry gray hair, and wore a white button-down shirt with brown pants.

"Is there something specific you're looking for?" The librarian asked.

"Um," Amri looked around at the library, which was so massive he had no idea where to start. "Possibly. Do you have anything on...well..." Amri had to be careful. This was a touchy subject back home. No one mentioned the Greymarch in polite society and expected a welcome response.

Amri whispered into the librarian's ear. "I'm looking for information about the Greymarch."

The librarian blinked. "I'm sorry, but I'm afraid we don't have much on that subject." He gestured to a diagram of Grand Spire on a wall, which showed how the city was built. "We've been safe from the Greymarch for as long as anyone can remember, and we simply haven't collected much information about them. All we really know is that they don't follow the normal rules regarding necromancy."

"Normal rules for necromancy?" Amri cocked his head. "What are those?"

The librarian paused. "Why would you be asking about that? I can see you're not from around here, but necromancy is a touchy subject, especially the further north you go."

"Why is that?" Amri asked.

"The Great Fimbulwinter War," the librarian replied. "A half dozen necromancers raised an army that nearly took over the entire continent, like the armies of the dead that the Norse believe will come from Hel after three winters without an intervening summer. Armies from Norsca, Albion, the city-states, even Saarthia and Grand Spire got involved. You might not have heard about it in the south, as it never reached that far, and there wasn't much trade or news traveling back then. This was three hundred years ago; the Borealan Empire didn't exist yet."

Amri nodded. "So, what happened? Why was it called the Fimbulwinter War?"

"The undead marched in cold weather, and attacked the living in their homes during the winter." The librarian directed Amri to a section of the library where he pulled a large book from a shelf and set it on a big table. The book detailed maps of the city-states in the northwest, just south of Norsca. "The war started here, in between the city-states of Ulri, Karsite, and Dosburg. A group of necromancers found some sort of mass grave, at an Ancient ruin known as Auschwitz. From there, they raised an army of undead who were far more powerful than your typical zombies or skeletons."

"Why were they so powerful?" Amri asked.

The librarian paused. "That is a question we are...leery about answering. I can tell that your interests are purely scholarly, but it's essential to understand how sensitive a subject this is to people around here. The undead nearly enslaved the entire continent."

"I'm sorry." Amri bowed his head. "I meant no offense. It's just...my family originally fled from Kemet, which is still ruled by the Tomb Lords, and I know very little about the dark powers used to enslave the people who are still trapped there."

"Oh!" The librarian's eyes widened. "Of course. Well, then it should be okay." He took an iron key from his pocket and guided Amri to a room at the back of the library. A locked iron door blocked the entrance, but the librarian opened it with his key. "This is our restricted section on necromancy. It's a grim subject, but 'know thy enemy,' you know?"

Leading Amri inside, the librarian took out a leather-bound tome and placed it on a large, wooden table that could use some dusting. "This is everything we know about the dark art of necromancy." The librarian cleared some dust away and flipped the book to a particular page. "The black arts rely on using the grief of the dead to raise them from their graves. The more horribly a person suffered in life, the stronger they are as a corpse. We do not know what the Ancients used Auschwitz for, but the bodies buried there had been so badly tortured in life that a half dozen necromancers turned them into nigh-unstoppable abominations."

He showed Amri a drawing of a humanoid creature that looked like an old corpse, with empty pale eyes, and pale, papery skin. It had no nose; its head was mostly a skull, and its body had been filled with bullet holes, arrows, and even a sword lodged in its stomach. From the way it was drawn, none of the weapons seemed to slow it down, and a look of burning hatred filled its eyes. On the monster's left wrist was a tattoo of a number Amri couldn't make out, and its hands looked like they were strong enough to rip a man in two despite centuries of age.

Amri recoiled from the page, as if the creature would jump out of the picture and attack him. "How many of these things were there?"

"Thousands, tens of thousands." The librarian shrugged. "But that was just the physical monsters. The wraiths were even worse." The librarian flipped a page and showed some kind of horrid ghost with a furious, tortured expression. "Normal weapons didn't hurt these things at all, because they were purely spectral. Some say there were millions of these, though I have my doubts. You see, necromancy has its limits. How many undead a necromancer can control at once is finite. It differs from person to person, but if a necromancer tries to animate too many corpses at once, he can run into trouble. A zombie doesn't go back to being a lifeless cadaver when the necromancer is killed, or stops animating it. They'll keep shambling around, attacking the living, with no one to control or direct them. If a necromancer calls up too many of these things at once, they'll become too much for him to control, and turn on him. Many a necromancer has been torn to shreds by calling something up that they couldn't put down."

"Wait," realization hit Amri like a spark of lightning. "That's why the Tomb Lords need living slaves!"

"Yes," the librarian nodded. "A necromancer cannot live entirely on the backs of his animated puppets. And the stronger the undead, the more likely they are to break free of his control. A person who died peacefully can be animated fairly easily to do menial work, but it won't take much more than bullet to the head or chest to put them down. The monsters raised from Auschwitz, on the other hand, were almost unkillable. It took a direct hit from a cannonball to put down a single one of these wights, and only magic had any effect on the wraiths. Wizards from around the continent tried everything they could to destroy the undead army."

"Was there anything that worked?" Amri asked.

"Not much," the librarian shook his head. "Some pyromancers had limited success with fire, but human bodies aren't very combustible. Burning bodies can keep them from getting back up, but it's not easy. Ice magic could hold them in place while gun fire tore them apart, but a lot of weapons were useless. However…" the librarian turned to another page. "Apart from brute force, one thing was fairly effective. A religious order, known for worshipping Truth itself, organized other temples of other gods to focus on countering the grief that gave the undead their power." He showed Amri a picture of a priest surrounded by men with shields and spears to keep the undead at bay. The priest was clearly delivering some form of prayer. loud enough for the wraiths to hear. "These priests would give the undead their final rights, and also try to calm the restless spirits within, in an effort to ease the pain they suffered and lay them back to rest. It worked, and the Great Fimbulwinter War came to an end."

"Wait," Amri cocked an eyebrow. "So a bunch of priests just prayed in front of the undead and they fell apart?"

"No, it wasn't just prayer, or a sermon." The librarian explained. "The priests had to convince the tortured souls to let go of their anger, their pain, their suffering. That's what ended the war."

Amri examined the picture of the priest surrounded by soldiers again. "Interesting."

4

A New Recruit

EPHORAH

With her suitcase packed, her clothes tight and professional, and her enchanted gloves on her hands, Ephorah marched through the marketplace of Hadesh until she reached the mercenary guilds' circle. Here, mercenary companies rented out their services for a variety of purposes. Smaller mercenary outfits, such as Ironwood Company, would protect people's lands from bandits or perform policework. Some, like the Salamanders, specialized in fighting monsters like the Greymarch. All of the mercenary companies offered internships for wizard students.

The mercenary guilds' circle sat at the end of a brick road surrounded by company houses. Each one would have a manager for signing off contracts and a recruitment office where she could check for an internship.

"For Hearth and Home!" A roar of men from a nearby company house chanted their salute. It was a slogan Ephorah knew all too well.

A troupe of Tin Men stormed out of the company house with some new recruits. Ephorah averted her eyes, but she caught a glimpse of one of the new mercenaries. She couldn't resist turning to stare at the young Empyrian marching with his new armor, bearing the Tin Men's crest; a flat-topped enclosed helmet with a sword and pistol behind it.

"Traitor," Ephorah muttered as she dragged her suitcase along.

"Excuse me," one of the Tin Men pulled away from their group and approached Ephorah. "You wouldn't happen to be considering mercenary work, would you? Are you perchance a wizard looking for an internship?"

Ephorah held her tongue for a moment, pushing down the anger welling up inside. "No, thank you." She grabbed her suitcase and walked away.

"Despite the name, the Tin Men recruit women as well," the mercenary called after her. "Especially those who know magic. We hire from all walks of life."

"Do you now?" Ephorah rolled her eyes. "Still not interested."

The Tin Man shrugged and rejoined his fellow soldiers as Ephorah looked around at the other company houses.

Ironwood Company was a smaller policing organization that mostly served the city of Hadesh and the neighboring towns, driving out bandits and dealing with common criminals. Ephorah considered it, but she wanted to get away from Hadesh for a while and put some distance between her and her parents.

The next mercenary house she came to was the Blue Eagles. Their hall was adorned with white flags featuring a blue bird of prey holding three arrows in one claw and a small anchor in the other. The Blue Eagles exclusively patrolled the skies and waterways and fought against air pirates, or the occasional airborne monster in their sky frigates. They might have use for a theurgist, but they'd want air elementals to resupply the ships with helium, and Ephorah didn't have any of those at the moment.

Ephorah paused at the third company house. The Salamanders had a reputation enduring long before the war. They had barely participated in the war at all, only being called in during the midway point when the Empyrians were winning. Ephorah's father never told her stories about the Salamanders, other than that they usually didn't fight humans in the first place. Their company crest, a red lizard with an open flame behind it, stood invitingly above the company house door.

Peaking inside, Ephorah saw a man sitting at a reception desk in the middle of a large, dimly lit room. The only light inside came from lamps hanging from the ceiling, and they were not enough to illuminate the large hall. She stepped inside, dragging her suitcase, and made her way to the desk.

The receptionist was surprised to see her, but quickly took out his ledger and started entering a new log. "Hello miss. What can the Salamanders do for you today? Is there a town in trouble, or a farmstead you need us to protect?"

Ephorah shook her head. "I'm actually looking for your recruitment office."

The man's pencil tip snapped off as he glanced up from the ledger. "I'm sorry, what?"

"I'm a student at the Institute of Theurgy. I wish to apply for an internship."

The receptionist eyed her over. "Girlie, do you understand what we do here? The Salamanders aren't a normal mercenary company. We don't fight petty bandits or thieves."

"I know." Ephorah nodded. "You fight the Greymarch."

"...Yes," the receptionist conceded. "We fight the Greymarch. And the Hisham, and the occasional lilim, or other monsters, but mostly, we protect people from the Greymarch. Do you...do you understand what that is? What those things really are?"

"Yes," Ephorah replied. "They destroyed my hometown, and are the reason my family moved to Hadesh."

"So, you've seen them, and you have some idea of what they can do." The receptionist looked down, not at his ledger, but to focus his thoughts. "But you can't possibly know the full story. The Hisham will kill you. Dragons, ogres, and lilims may eat you. But the Greymarch doesn't do any of those things. Wait!" He slapped his palm against his face. "I'm not supposed to tell you that!"

"I've seen someone turn into a Greymarcher." Ephorah replied. "Just show me the recruitment office."

The receptionist sighed. "You don't know the half of it. Just...take the stairs on your right. Leave your suitcase here. I'll take care of it."

Ephorah left her luggage with the receptionist and marched up the stairs. At the top, a door with a small sign read "recruitment."

Pulling the door open, Ephorah stepped into a small office with an open window in a vain attempt to fend off the hot weather. A man in his early thirties sat behind a desk looking through paperwork. In front of the desk was a small wooden chair for interviews.

The recruitment officer looked up at Ephorah. "Miss, are you lost?"

"No." Ephorah sat down in the chair facing the officer. "I want to apply for an internship here."

The officer's jaw slackened from shock, but he did his best to keep his composure. "You're a bit…young, don't you think?"

Ephorah locked eyes with the man. She couldn't pinpoint why the receptionist and this recruitment officer would be so reluctant to have her work for them. Was it because she was a girl? Or because she was Empyrian? Or was it really because of the Greymarch, and the fact that she was young for a mercenary intern?

"I've already survived a Greymarch attack," Ephorah replied. "And I was here in Hadesh when a dragon spawned an undead army in the middle of the city. If I wasn't too young to handle those things, I'm not too young to work for your company."

"I see." The recruitment officer examined the fifteen-year-old girl in front of him. "Tell me, what is it you wish to learn from our company?"

"Learn…" Ephorah hadn't prepared for this question. "I guess…I…"

"You're not here to learn at all, are you?" The recruitment officer leaned in closer. "Then why are you here?"

"I need to get away from Hadesh for a little while," she replied. "I need to put some distance between myself and my family and work for myself for a change."

"Oh, so you are here to learn." The officer smiled. "You're here to learn how to stand on your own two feet. I can work with that, however…" The recruitment officer dug out some papers from his desk. "There are a few things you need to know before I can hire you. You say you've seen what the Greymarchers do, but you still don't know the whole story."

The recruitment officer stood from his desk, closed the door to the room, and folded his arms behind his back. "What I'm about to reveal to you is not a secret, but you must not tell others outside this room. There are things that normal people do not want to know, and you won't be welcome in polite society if you go about telling people what I'll tell you now."

The officer showed Ephorah a book containing images of various monsters, all of which the Salamanders were renowned for fighting. Pages were tabbed for certain creatures, and one listed the Greymarch. One of the marchers depicted had tattered skin exposing muscle beneath, but the body was intact enough that you could believe it would still move on its own. They were not like the undead puppets that stormed the arena during the Grand Wizard Tournament.

"We've spoken to priests of Osiris and Anubis, begging for information about the fate of those who become Greymarchers. The gods refused to answer, clearly because they think we can't handle the truth. Eventually, Anubis slipped, and let us know that he had collected the souls of the marchers we'd just slain. That's when we knew: the soul of a Greymarcher is trapped within the person's body until something kills them."

At first, Ephorah's mind didn't register why that was such a problem. Then, memories of Aklagos came back to her, and the image of the boy who had fallen to the Greymarch returned to her mind. The marchers whose flesh was tattered, the boy whose nose came right off. Most people thought the Greymarchers couldn't feel pain; at least, they never showed signs of it. But Ephorah couldn't imagine that everyone turned into a Greymarcher was willingly attacking every non-infected person they saw. If their bodies moved against their will, perhaps they were in excruciating pain with no way of showing it.

"That's..." Ephorah struggled to find the words. "That's horrifying! That's so much worse than death!"

"That's why we we're so selective about who we recruit." The officer placed his hand on her shoulder. "Especially when it comes to people as young as you. There are plenty of other mercenary companies who don't work in this field. Join the Tin Men—"

"No!" Ephorah jumped to her feet so quickly she startled the recruitment officer. "I mean, no, thank you. I don't want to join the Tin Men. I'd be honored to help you in fighting the Greymarch, especially now that I know what the Greymarch can do. Let me work with you as a summoner."

"We could always use elemental support." The recruiter smiled. "And I'd feel better if you could work with us without having to fight directly. Can you travel?"

"Yes," Ephorah nodded. "In fact, I'd prefer it. I came pre-packed."

"Eager and prepared," the recruiter chuckled. "That's what I like to see. Let's get you shipped out today."

5

The Joys of Job Applications

CYRUS

In the middle of the Empyrian Quarter, inside a hospital named Light Beacon Medical Center, Cyrus crossed his fingers and passed his credentials over a counter to a hospital clerk. A sliding window separated the alchemy student from the clerk's office.

"So, you're looking to become a medical alchemist?" The clerk looked over Cyrus's papers. "We could always use more of those, and these are some pretty good grades."

Cyrus glanced around the building, which looked like it hadn't seen a coat of paint since before he'd been born. Sounds of vermin whispered from cracks in the walls, and the chairs in the waiting room looked like they could give out under the weight of the next person to take a seat. Several patients in the lobby sat in various states of dishevelment. Three burly men stood near a woman that had found one of the more stable chairs and sat with a sick, sleeping child in her lap.

All of the patients were Empyrian, and Cyrus felt their eyes and scorn fall upon his blond hair.

"So, why are you applying here?" The clerk looked up from Cyrus's papers. "If your grades are this good, and you have former experience working with Ironwood Company and ghoul research, why are you looking for work all the way out here? Why not someplace...more familiar?"

The first rule of job interviews was not to lie. And so long as potential employers throw out applications immediately for things applicants cannot control, that rule will be tossed out the window.

"I am trying to broaden my horizons." Cyrus leaned in closer to the clerk and faked a smile. "Exploring medicine in different walks of life, treating different kinds of injuries." He tapped the back of the clerk's hand with his finger. "Let's be honest, how many people living in the Garden District get regular workplace injuries that need treating?" He traced a circle on the woman's hand with his fingertip. "I think there's a lot more to learn here than in some ritzier hospital, don't you?"

The clerk raised an eyebrow. "...Right...So, let me just ask what you did during the Grand Wizard Tournament? That should have gotten you enough attention from recruiters to land a place already."

To Cyrus's horror, the clerk pulled a list of results for the Grand Wizard Tournament out from under her desk. Flipping through the results, she pointed to a name on the list.

"Cyrus Levitch. That's you, isn't it?" The clerk looked confused. "If you were in the tournament, then why don't you–"

She stopped at the results for the Combat Arena. "Oh, that's why." She looked up at Cyrus with a dry smile. "You won the Combat Arena by stomping on a girl two years younger than you." She tossed Cyrus's paperwork back at him. It scattered onto the floor. "So how many other places have you applied to?"

Cyrus closed his eyes and gritted his teeth. "I've lost count. It was more than twelve."

"Mm-hm." The clerk nodded. "Well guess what? Just like everyone else, we don't need you that badly. Not this year, at any rate. Give it a year, people'll forget about you. Then you can get yourself a job in some glittery, Garden District hospital."

"Wait!" Cyrus scrambled to collect his paperwork off of the floor. "If I don't get a job, an internship, or something on my resume, I'll have a hole in my work history for this year's off-season. Do you have any idea what a setback that would be?"

THE JOYS OF JOB APPLICATIONS

"You should've thought of that before you jumped on a girl's back and cracked her ribs. Get lost." The clerk closed the sliding door.

Holding his papers in a wadded-up mess, Cyrus backed away from the counter and into a man behind him standing a good ten centimeters over his head.

"Hang on a minute," the Empyrian man glared down at Cyrus. "If memory serves, the last fight of the Combat Arena was between an Empyrian girl, and you. That right?"

"Um." Cyrus gave up on keeping the paperwork uncrumpled and tucked it under his left elbow. "I didn't get a chance to check."

The man turned to the other large men in the room. "Can you believe this blond bori trash? He stomps on one of our daughters, snatches the final trophy away from her, and then has the gall to come into one of our hospitals with his stench."

As the two other Empyrian men moved to encircle Cyrus, the alchemy student clapped his hands together and raised his palm. "You can let me leave peacefully, or the police can scrape what's left of you off the floor."

The first man looked like he was about to accept Cyrus's challenge, but one of the others spoke up. "If he's an alchemist, all he's gotta do is touch you."

A spark of magic flickered between Cyrus's fingers. The Empyrians backed off, but their rage-fueled expressions didn't change.

"Guns and magic," one of them spat. "Your kind are weak, but you hide behind spells and weapons."

"You think you can go wherever you want and get away with it," another growled. "And you'll kill us if we're in your way."

Cyrus thought about responding, but it didn't matter. He knew these were not reasonable people. His palm raised, he backed out of the hospital and left.

Out on the streets of the Empyrian Quarter, he debated going home and calling it a day. It was late in the afternoon, and if a rundown hospital wouldn't take on a medical alchemy intern, no one else would.

On the other hand, going home empty-handed meant facing his parents. He could already hear his father dismissing his failure in a flurry of "I told you so's" and smug satisfaction, while his mother would stay quiet, but in some ways that was worse, because Cyrus could feel the disdain coming from her, but he never knew what she was thinking.

Unwilling to face them just yet, Cyrus made his way one more time back to the College of Alchemy. It was nearly on the opposite side of the city, and Cyrus couldn't justify paying autobus fare, so by the time he reached the Academic District, he had less than an hour left before the student services office would close for the day.

Climbing up the steps to the office, Cyrus knocked on the door. A woman Cyrus was becoming all too familiar with opened it.

"Oh, it's you again," she frowned.

"Hello, Mary." Cyrus forced a smile.

She shook her head. "Look, I don't have anything else for you. There's nowhere left in Hadesh. Right now, you're too toxic for anyone to handle."

"What about outside of Hadesh?" Cyrus asked. "Maybe someplace where they didn't watch the tournament?"

"People from foreign nations came to watch the tournament." Mary looked through some papers. "Nothing's guaranteed outside of Hadesh. You'd be taking wild shots in the dark."

Cyrus peered at the papers she was handling. "What are those, exactly? They don't look like job postings."

"They're not." Mary held one up. "This is just a news report congratulating Doctor Raphael Monroe for developing a new serum to help victims of taint poisoning out east. He says he's going to use the award money to work on treatments for lung cancer in Dihorma. And before you ask, he doesn't take on apprentices."

"Dihorma, huh?" The wheels in Cyrus's head turned. "Mind if I see the report?"

"Sure," Mary handed Cyrus the paper. "Sorry about your job search. Like I told you before, people will forget about the tournament by the time next year rolls around."

"Yeah, of course. Everyone says that." Cyrus looked through the report, which detailed Doctor Monroe's work with the sicknesses caused by the tainted water in Harlak. At the bottom, it showed the doctor's permanent home in

THE JOYS OF JOB APPLICATIONS

Dihorma, where he'd returned after completing his work out east.

"Thank you," Cyrus passed the report back to Mary. "I'll just be on my way."

Rather than return home, Cyrus took the north exit from the college, right across from the University Line Rail Station. Checking train times, one was leaving for Dihorma at 10:55, stopping in Baltithar along the way.

Cyrus sprinted back to his parent's house. Two years ago, before he joined the College of Alchemy, he'd spent the mornings of the off-season running five kilometers every day at Thoth's instruction to build up his endurance. Now, that endurance training paid off as he raced home as fast as possible.

Pausing at the front door to catch his breath, he braced himself for any questions as he went inside. His older sister, Eina, was in the kitchen preparing dinner with their mother, while his other siblings were either relaxing after a hard day's work, or doing homework.

Most of Cyrus's brothers were already part of his father's carpentry business. Chorev Levitch was a well-renowned carpenter in Hadesh, and nine of his twelve children had joined the business in some form. Eina worked in the business side of things, while all of Chorev's sons had inherited the talent and developed the woodworking skills to follow in their father's footsteps. All, that is, except for Cyrus.

"How was your search?" Cyrus's mother didn't look up from the stew she was preparing.

"I've got to catch a train in a few hours." Cyrus scrambled up the stairs to his room and dragged out his suitcase. Packing it full of clothes, toiletries, and notebooks for research, Cyrus fastened it shut and carried it down the stairs, ready to leave.

"Do you have time to stay for supper?" His mother asked as he reached for the front doorknob.

Cyrus paused. Technically, yes, he had time to stay for stew. He had time to eat. He did not have time for a lecture from his dad. He had enough money on hand to pay for access to a dining car on the train, but he could also save a lot of cash by eating at home.

A growl from his stomach settled the debate. He sighed, set his suitcase down and sat at the kitchen table.

His mother poured him a bowl of chicken and turnip soup. It was a simple, pleasant dish that reminded Cyrus of when he was a child, and still got along with his father. Back then, there was no pressure for him to be a carpenter, or to move out of his parent's house, or to succeed at all. No bad grades, or years held back in school. Just a happy family with eight brothers and three sisters.

Tasting the soup, Cyrus realized how absurd his actual plan was. He was preparing to jump on a train and travel half-way across the empire to ask for an apprenticeship from an alchemist he didn't really know anything about, other than the fact that he didn't take on apprenticeships. It was a terrible idea, born out of desperation. Was it really so necessary for him to find work experience during this off-season?

Cyrus's father came inside the house from the backdoor. "I checked the shed. Everything's set for tomorrow." He turned to see Cyrus eating his stew. "You're back. Any results?"

This was it. The moment of truth. He either had to admit he had no prospects, or go with his crazy plan.

"I'm taking a train to Dihorma in a few hours," he blurted out. "I'm going to be studying with a medical alchemist over the off-season."

"Oh," Chorev didn't bother looking at his son. "I guess that works. As long as you get results, you're not my problem anymore."

Cyrus had expected his father to rebuke him, criticize him, berate or abuse him. But instead of the booming, furious bombardment of insults for which he'd prepared, his father's words landed softly like dust or sand on a hardwood floor. There was no anger, no accusations anymore. When he'd first come home from the college holding a report card with high marks, his father had exploded with rage, calling him lazy for never applying himself before, or deliberately leeching off of his parents. Now, all of that had melted away and was replaced with indifference.

Finishing his soup, Cyrus grabbed his suitcase and bolted for the door. He no longer cared if his plan was terrible; anything was better than staying in that house.

6

The Dragon Archive

NAMID

Restricted to the grounds of the university, Namid took her brother's advice to explore the campus library. Already she was regretting it.

"Right here, we have relics from the age of the unicorns," the librarian showed her a display case containing colorful fluffy underwear, a blue and purple hoodie, a ruined fuzzy plush toy, and a strange, pink, conical device with the words "ice cream cone maker" on one side. A picture of a horse with a horn sat in the middle of the display.

"These creatures were once so common in this area, the Ancients were able to make all sorts of products from them." The librarian pointed to a pair of women's underwear that had a picture of the horned animal. "But they went too far, and eventually, the unicorns were hunted to extinction to make underpants and ice cream cones."

"Right..." Namid tried to sound enthusiastic.

"And over here we have our collection of relics from Celtic wizards," the librarian explained. "These people knew almost nothing about thaumaturgy, so their version of magecraft mostly consisted of finding things to snort up their noses."

"Yes, that's...wonderful." Namid rolled her eyes. "Is there anything in here that's a bit more...relevant? To people who are still alive, and have access to better magic schooling?"

"Um, well..." the librarian looked upset. "It's all relevant to the scholarly. Uh, we have several translations of Latin writings from the Roman Empire."

Namid sighed. "Where's my brother?"

Amri had told Namid that there was a restricted section on necromancy that the librarian had shown him, but neither of them had been granted full access. Unlike the ancient Celtic snort-wizards, it actually sounded interesting, but the librarian wasn't letting in tourists.

"I think your brother was looking through our section on dragons," the librarian replied.

"A dragon section?" Namid raised an eyebrow. "And you introduced this after the display of ancient nose-hair trimmers?"

The librarian showed Namid a large room filled with stone slabs with strange writings and sheets of paper that had charcoal rubbings of the writing. A few display cases showed bone fragments, and a lone skull of a dragon hung from one wall. Amri stood looking over a stone tablet and reading from a book, occasionally glancing up to look at the stone.

"Okay," Namid looked around. "I was expecting more dragons, and a little less paperwork." She took in just how massive the room actually was; it held; enough bookshelves along one wall to be a library all by itself. "This is a *lot* of paperwork."

"Grand Spire is proud to host the largest archive on dragon culture in the known world," the librarian beamed. "We've got everything: details of different dragon species; peace negotiations between clans; contracts with human cultures; festivals, songs, everything."

"You mean all of these things were written by dragons?" Namid looked closer at the stone slabs. The writing was old, but it looked like it had been carved by a claw. "How does a claw carve so deeply into rock?"

"By heating it with dragonfire," the librarian explained. "This is from Albion, carved by the white razor-chested dragons once native to the east coast of that island." He pointed to another carving. "And that was created by the red razor-chests of the same island, along the west coast."

"Uh-huh." Namid went over to her brother. "Watcha reading?"

"An old poem translated from Draconic," Amri read from the scroll.

"*Oh, bound Orochi, slave of the eastern gods, you break from your chains, knowing you will surely die.*

Oh, free Orochi, rebel of the eastern gods, your stomach never fills, for no god will keep you alive.

Oh, hungry Orochi, anathema of the eastern gods, you bargain with demons to fill your stomach, they split your head in eight.

Oh, eight-headed Orochi, terror of the eastern gods, with eight mouths, you devour all in sight.

Oh, dreaded Orochi, fallen servant of the eastern gods, your mind is shattered, split between your heads.

Oh, mad Orochi, scourge of the eastern gods, you devour maidens in your endless hunger. Susanoo's blade glistens."

"What on Earth is all of that about?" Namid peered at the carving. "And how does anyone know what this thing says?"

Amri pointed to a passage in the book. "Well, there's a note at the end that says 'be thankful we are born free, and do not have to serve gods obsessed with toilet humor just to survive.' There's other writings here that refer to the dragons of the western continent as 'freeborn,' and the dragons of the east as 'slaves.' Not sure what that's about."

"Dragons of the west evolved naturally from dinosaurs," the librarian explained. "Dragons of the east were created by the gods." He showed them a tapestry that depicted an eastern dragon, which was almost like a really long snake with front and back claws, a head with scraggly, beard-like set of scales along its chin, a mustache of sorts, and an expression that could have been read as wise, or exhausted.

"Of course, no creature like that could survive in nature," the librarian pointed to its long, serpentine body. "These things were said to be so massive that they could span the gap between the heavens and earth. No creature that large could consume enough calories to sustain themselves, and notice how it has no wings? They flew purely by magic provided by their gods. In fact, their divine patrons took care of all of their bodily needs through their magic, but only as long as the dragons served their creators. Service or death; those were their choices. Dragons of the west detested that kind of lifestyle, and cherished their freedom as natural creatures."

"Okay," Namid looked at another tapestry showing a red razor-chest dragon. "But are you really going to tell me that these dragons evolved naturally? They've got six limbs – two wings, and four legs. I thought no vertebrate had more than four limbs?"

"We used to think that, too. But then we found this:" the librarian showed them a stone fossil that depicted some kind of dinosaur with wings and four legs. "This creature, the 'rhamphorhynchine pterosaur,' has a pair of wings supported by cartilage that ossified away from the forelimbs. The fossil was found far away from here, but it wasn't the only one of its kind."

The librarian brought out several drawings of dragon skeletons. "None of the skeletons we've ever found had more than four limbs, but a lot of them had joints; places where wings could have gone. No bones for such limbs were ever found, and now we know why." He gestured to the fossil. "They were related to him. And just like that, six-limbed vertebrates are back in fossil record."

"Okay, but they're still huge." Namid eyed the drawings of skeletons. "How did they survive?"

"They're no larger than the dinosaurs from which they evolved," the librarian explained. "Those creatures could handle Earth's gravity, and find enough food. Dinosaurs are now extinct, and so are most of the western dragons." The librarian raised an eyebrow. "Why the sudden scholarly interest?"

"Our hometown was attacked by a dragon only a little more than a month ago," Namid replied. "Well, dracolich, actually. Do you know of any dragons that speak human languages?"

"That was extremely rare," the librarian pulled out a ledger and showed her lists of various dragons. "Dragons that developed the vocal cords to form words like ours only show up in a few places around the world. Ironclaw Drakes in the east, several different wyrms in the far northern islands, although those might have had their evolution influenced by the Norse gods, and the Sky Tyrants that were once native to this peninsula."

"Can you think of any reason such a dragon would attack a city?" Namid asked.

The librarian stroked his beard. "Not off hand. Dragons didn't usually eat humans in cities. They'd use some kind of lure, or bait to draw humans to their caves."

Amri raised an eyebrow. "Why would they want to do that?"

"Dragons discovered at some point that humans will come from outside of their environments and bring in extra calories to the dragons' diets. A long time ago, a dragon discovered that gold was soft enough to sleep on and didn't catch on fire when his hay fever acted up. When word got out that he was sleeping on a mound of gold, treasure hunters came looking for it, and the dragon ate them all for lunch. Other dragons learned that they could order take out this way, and started hoarding their own treasures and setting traps to make human-eating easier."

"They would set traps?" Amri asked. "For dragon-slayers?"

"Indeed," the librarian nodded. "But gold is only valuable because it's rare. There simply wasn't enough gold on the planet for every dragon to lure in humans this way. That's why many dragons switched to kidnapping noblewomen. Princesses are a renewable resource."

"How do you know all of this?" Namid asked. "How did you even translate all of these scratches?"

"Oh, that was due to the Titillation Thesis Tablet!" The librarian beamed. "Our Rosetta Stone! An entire dissertation between dragon clans arguing over whether to strip the maiden nude, or leave her with just enough tattered clothing to leave the naughty bits up to the imagination of any would-be dragon-slayers. The entire thing is written in Draconic, Latin, and Gothic."

The librarian showed them a massive hunk of stone, with claw marks that clearly carved the same language on the other tablets, but below that were two passages with much more human-like words, and beneath that were crude drawings of two girls tied to posts. One was clearly naked and had an 'X' over the picture. The other had enough torn rags to cover her chest and loins and wore a tiara on her head.

Namid frowned. "Dragons had an entire theory on this?"

"Indeed," the librarian pointed to the crown in the picture. "They would kidnap one noblewoman, and then recycle her tiara and place it on the heads of peasant girls they kidnapped afterwards. The idea was that a wannabe hero wouldn't risk his life to rescue a commoner, but would gleefully challenge a dragon for a chance to marry into royalty. So, they'd dress lower-class women to look like nobility, and from a distance the knights, peasants, and other heroic types couldn't tell the difference. And then dinner was served." The librarian pointed to another stone slab. "This here is a cookbook on ways to serve tinned knights, although the author definitely had a thing for horseradish."

"Why Latin and Gothic?" Amri asked. "Why would a dragon know those languages?"

"The tablet was found here, on this peninsula," the librarian replied. "We believe that the tablet was written by Sky Tyrants, a species that had connections to both the Roman Empire, and later the Visgoths. The Sky Tyrants got their name from the fact that they could speak Gothic and would set up next to human towns, demanding fish and livestock as 'protection money,' and occasionally other goods. They would have learned these languages in the process."

Namid looked up from the tablet. "Could we ask one of them why a dracolich attacked Hadesh with an undead army?"

The librarian shook his head. "They're all gone. They were hunted to extinction sometime after the fall of Rome. All dragons capable of speech that we know of, apart from the Wyrms of the far north, are extinct."

"Hunted?" Namid paused. "Who hunts their trading partners to extinction?"

"Not sure," the librarian shrugged. "We don't have enough historical records from that period. Lots of confusion from different writing systems, due to the area being conquered by invaders from the sea."

Namid left the library with her brother that evening. It wasn't easy to see the sun in Grand Spire, mostly because all levels but the top had a ceiling, but the place was lit by lights that ran on electrical energy from a generator — recovered technology from the Ancients. Now, the lights were dimming, a sign that it was sunset outside the spire.

A yawn forced its way through Namid's mouth. "Okay, that was more interesting than I thought." She checked her watch. "We spent four hours in a library, for goodness' sake."

"Some supper, and then bed?" Amri offered.

"If the dining hall is still open," she agreed.

A pair of full stomachs later, the two returned to the guest dormitories for the evening. Once they were prepared for bed, Namid crawled under her sheets.

"Okay," she yawned. "I'm ready."

Amri sat in a chair that came with the dorm room as part of a desk. "Where were we?" He flipped through the pages of their book. "Here we go, 'The Curse of Erysichthon.' Devotees of the harvest goddess Renenutet were worshipping in her sacred grove, when they were interrupted by several loud woodcutters. 'Leave this place!' Erysichthon roared. 'I want this wood for my new palace!'"

As Amri read about a king eating himself from hunger, Namid nestled into her sheets and drifted off to sleep.

7

Desert Storm

DAURGO

The road to the Sumerian underworld was never meant to be traveled in reverse. What little resistance remained from when Daurgo crawled down into the craggy depths now made feeble efforts to stop him from leaving, but they stood no chance. A few guardians simply gave up and let the dracolich pass, knowing they couldn't stop him.

At the entrance to Irkalla, Daurgo stepped out of the Spirit Plane and averted his eyes from the sun. All undead are weakened by sunlight, even if it doesn't kill them. Nevertheless, the dragon lowered a set of shades on his helmet to ease his vision as he walked into the dry lands now known as the Blasted Wastes.

A barren, merciless environment, Daurgo remembered when this land had been a fertile paradise. He was certain that this place had once been Anatolia, with domed cathedrals, farmlands that stretched to the sea, and fortified citadels to protect the populace from slavers from the south and the seas.

Now, it would be charitable to call the Blasted Wastes a desert. Deserts have life of their own, but this place was as barren as the surface of another planet. Taint storms occasionally raked the land and would bring toxic rain, poisonous to the living and corrosive to metal and machines. Daurgo didn't dare bring his mobile fortress in such a destructive place.

"Looks like Kur damaged the logic engine on my armor," Daurgo checked his gear. "I can't fix it from here, which means no long-range teleportation. Well, that's what wings are for."

Daurgo stretched out his ghostly wings and took to the skies. In this desolate wasteland, the dragon remembered when he'd first tried to fly after becoming a lich. His wings needed a lot of magical help to keep him aloft, since they rotted away and were not really there anymore. Strangely, they still needed air beneath him in order to fly.

A gust of wind drove him back to earth. The wind was so forceful, it felt unnatural, like it was warped by the same toxins that filled the wasteland. A storm appeared to be brewing in the skies above.

"Okay," Daurgo checked a compass on his armor and made certain he was heading the right way. "I can still teleport to places I can see."

Aiming for a cracked hilltop in his line of sight, Daurgo folded the space around himself and the wasteland, appearing on the hill, where he was immediately struck by a bolt of arcane energy.

"Hm?" Daurgo felt the heat of the blast ripple through his armor. He'd insulated his equipment, and the energy had almost no effect, but a spell like that didn't come from nowhere.

Turning to the source of the blast, the green lights where his eyes used to be locked onto the goddess Isis, who had a curved wand drawn and was preparing another spell.

"Aw, how quaint." Daurgo examined the goddess as she raised both hands to the sky, her hands making a motion like pulling ropes from the ground.

The earth beneath Daurgo rose up and mud tentacles wrapped around his body. He struggled against the bindings, but Isis' spell was so strong that even a dragon couldn't break free.

The ground beneath the lich turned into mud, and combined with the chains he was completely trapped. Earthen bindings forced his head into the mud. Enraged, Daurgo pumped as much heat from his mind into the mud, the chains, and his armor. The armor was carbon steel, but the bindings were made of rock. The steel could handle the heat, but the stone chains turned to magma and melted off of him.

Isis tried to harden the magma and pin Daurgo to the ground with re-solidified rock, but the dragon leapt from the molten stone and tried to pounce on the goddess. Another gust of extraordinarily powerful wind blew him away from her, and now Daurgo was certain these gales were not natural.

"That's enough of you!" Daurgo tore a hole in the air above Isis to the Spirit Plane, opening a portal to the river of the Duat. Water came pouring out and drenched the goddess before she could attack again. Daurgo then focused on a sun disk in the center of a crown on Isis' forehead and willed the water to freeze around this point, encasing her in ice. Before she could cast a spell to break out, Daurgo smashed the frozen goddess into pieces with his tail.

Frozen chunks of goddess scattered everywhere. The pieces began to thaw, but it would be a while before she could regenerate.

Isis was one of the most powerful magicians in the Egyptian pantheon. Her only equal was Thoth, and unless he showed up, the rest of these immortals wouldn't be too much of a challenge for him. Daurgo scanned the wastes for the ibis-headed god, expecting him at any moment.

An angry hissing sound like a cat in heat came from behind the dragon. "Right on cue," Daurgo muttered as he pierced Sekhmet with the blades on his tail.

Shaking the war goddess off his tail with a flick, the lich scanned around for the next assailant. "Why aren't they all attacking at once?" He asked.

A wounded Sekhmet coughed up golden ichor. "It's called a distraction, smart guy."

Daurgo had just enough time to realize what was looming over him before the meteorite came crashing down. It was small enough not to cause trouble outside of the wastes, but the blow was enough to smash the dragon's armor, ripping the riveted steel apart and crumpling it like tissue paper. Any and all remaining steam came flushing out. Sparks flew from what was left of the tesla coils. In the last instant before the meteorite pulverized him into the ground, Daurgo used every last speck of his mind to will his bones not to break, strengthening the necromancy holding his skeleton together as much as possible.

The explosion left a crater large enough to fit a lake. Daurgo managed to keep himself mostly intact, but he was sprawled along the base of the crater with his skull spinning. His armor would need to be rebuilt from scratch, as all that was left were tattered sheets of burnt metal. "I'm sending someone a bill for this," he struggled to his feet.

Before the dracolich now stood a man with the head of a falcon. Unless Daurgo was mistaken, this must have been Horus. Probably the source of the unnaturally strong winds.

"A dragon," Horus spat. "A necromancer, and to top it all off, a foreigner. You killed Thoth: the wisest and smartest of us all. For that, you will be punished!"

"Killed...?" Daurgo glanced around, and realized that he was now surrounded by gods with a petting zoo's worth of different heads, but the god of knowledge wasn't among them. "Thoth is dead?"

"Yes!" Horus snarled. "And you killed him!"

"Strange," Daurgo stalled for time. "That sounds like something I would do, but I don't remember doing it. When was this?"

"What?" Horus' beak hung open in shock. "One month ago!"

"A month ago?" Daurgo looked up, as if trying to remember something. "Doesn't sound right, but my memory's not what it used to be. Where did this happen?"

"It–" Horus struggled with his temper. The king of the Egyptian pantheon was used to being taken more seriously than this. "In Hadesh! During the Grand Wizard Tournament!"

"I remember fighting Marduk, but I don't remember killing Thoth," Daurgo stretched out his forearms and twisted his right claw, as if it were a normal stretch one does after being struck by a meteorite. "Are you sure it was an Egyptian god?"

Horus looked around to the other gods for support, clearly out his comfort zone. "Yes!"

"One month ago? Near Hadesh?" Daurgo asked.

"YES!" Horus fumed.

Daurgo paused. "I did not kill any Egyptian gods one month ago near Hadesh during the Grand Wizard Tournament."

The Egyptian gods glanced at each other, visibly trying to follow the dragon's wordplay. The falcon-headed god was clearly not convinced. He waved his arms, and a bit of light glowed in the sky, as if a bolt of lightning had just begun to the form, but wouldn't come down.

"I'm going to guess that you felt the need to distract me from the meteorite," Daurgo mused, "because you already knew I can stop time."

Horus' face may have been avian, but you could still see his confidence fall as he realized his lightning bolt wouldn't be coming down on the dracolich anytime soon.

"You see, your spells need time in order to take effect," the lich sneered as he leaned his skull closer to Horus. "And as it turns out, when neither of us have magic, you're basically just a bunch of humans who look like they're dressed up for one of Emperor Nero's creepy fetish parties, whereas I'm still a dragon."

Daurgo bit the sky god's head off before he could react. The other gods tried to draw their weapons, but every arrow, javelin, or sling launched was suspended in air. The dragon spat out Horus's head at the now regenerated Sekhmet and slashed her in half with his claws.

Another cat-headed goddess tried to attack his ribcage in a flurry of claws and blades, hacking away at the skeletal dragon's bones.

"Seriously?" Daurgo picked Bast up by the scruff of her neck, spun her around like a ragdoll, and hurled across the wasteland.

Sobek, the crocodile god, tried to hack away at the dragon's right leg as if he were trying to fell a tree. This might have worked, but Daurgo stretched out his wings and lifted off the ground, knocking Sobek aside with his feet. Meanwhile, the dragon locked his eyes onto a fleeing god and teleported on top of him.

As Daurgo phased on top of the fleeing god, he allowed time to return to normal. The lightning bolt, which Horus had summoned and was still aimed at Daurgo's previous location, came down and struck Sobek instead. The thunder was so loud that it disrupted the remaining gods as Daurgo leapt into the air again. Upon reappearing above a fleeing ram-headed god, he landed with enough force to crush the deity into the cracked ground below.

The remaining gods either hadn't realized that time had unfrozen and they could use their magic again, or were too terrified to care. In previous exploits, Daurgo never liked to pick fights with gods unless it was on his terms; you had to do your research, learn their strengths and weaknesses, and which ones were omniscient. Clearly, this pantheon failed to realize Daurgo was struggling with direct sunlight now that he had lost his armor, was out of gadgets, kilometers away from any corpses he could animate to join him, and had been caught completely off guard. If they'd stop running away, they might realize how unprepared he was to fight an entire pantheon of gods at the moment.

"Okay," Daurgo thought to himself. "Now that they're running around like disoriented chickens, I just need to leave like they're not worth my time fighting anymore."

Stretching his skeleton up to his full height, Daurgo strutted westward towards the place where he'd hidden his mechanical fortress.

A strange sense struck him, like the feeling one gets when they know something is fast approaching from behind. He had just enough time to teleport to his left to avoid the incoming ball of wind.

The ball was like four folded winds pushing in different directions tumbling together as a single mass. Having missed the dracolich, the winds turned and aimed for Daurgo again. Once more, the lich teleported, this time aiming behind the ball. Once he reappeared, the ball of wind changed course again. This time, it caught up to Daurgo and scattered the bones of his ribcage.

"What on Earth are you?" Daurgo pulled his ribcage back together with necromancy.

Somehow, in following the distracting ball of wind, the lich hadn't noticed the amount of sand that had built up in the air around him. He was now standing in a cloud so thick his dragon eyesight couldn't see more than a few meters in any direction.

"What the−?" Daurgo felt another attack incoming, but this one was too fast to dodge. A heavy blow from what felt like a mace shattered his eye sockets of his skull, blinding him.

"That mace!" Daurgo didn't want to believe it, but there was only one god in the area who wielded a mace and moved at this speed. "Marduk, what are you doing here?"

"Thoth was based on Nabu!" Marduk drew back his bow and a bolt of lightning appeared instead of an arrow. "My son, whom the mortals forgot. Did you really think I would take his death lying down?"

Marduk released the lightning. The bolt whizzed passed Daurgo's head, but the sheer force of thunder from lightning that close was deafening. Confused, deaf, and blinded, Daurgo felt Marduk appear behind him, almost as if the god had grabbed hold of his own lightning bolt and ridden it behind the dragon's skull.

Another strike from Marduk's mace cracked the back of Daurgo's head. Dragon bone is strong, but not indestructible. Daurgo felt that back of his skull collide with his teeth as pieces of his head filled his mouth.

"He's got me on the defensive," Daurgo thought. "I have to switch things around!"

Daurgo concentrated his will to blast all of the air around him away, giving him a vacuum bubble. Lightning and sound from outside wouldn't be able to get through, and Marduk would have trouble just breaching the spell, let alone moving within it.

With a short respite, the lich focused his necromancy to repair his skull and recover his eyes. Once his vision returned, he could see Marduk standing outside of the vacuum bubble glaring at him. The god knew he probably couldn't breach the bubble, and wouldn't be able to do much if he did, but he also knew Daurgo couldn't maintain the vacuum for very long.

Immortals seldom duel to the death. Marduk probably had plans to imprison Daurgo, and punish him for the death of Thoth. The lich was immune to any kind of physical torment Marduk could inflict, but there were other ways of punishing him.

Trying to come up with a plan, it dawned on the dragon that he probably wouldn't be able to outrun Marduk. It didn't look like he had his chariot, which the lich had smashed in their last fight, but if he really could ride his own lightning bolts, and Daurgo couldn't teleport— or could he? As a lich, there was one place he could always go, because his soul was already there. But if Marduk followed him, he'd find Daurgo's phylactery. Then Marduk would be able to destroy his soul jar and kill Daurgo for good.

"When you're short on courage, empty bravado is better than cowardice," Daurgo thought to himself. He ended the vacuum spell and roared as air surrounded him again. "Let's go, Marduk! Round Two!"

The king of the Babylonian gods paused. He probably knew Daurgo was up to something, but he wasn't certain what. Marduk held up his fist, and the dust surrounding the god and the dragon settled. Above them, storm clouds spun and started to form a vortex. Daurgo remembered from their last encounter that Marduk could summon tornados.

"Not this time." Daurgo raised a claw and willed time to slow down. The storm clouds froze, but Marduk drew back his bow and launched another lightning bolt.

As soon as the bolt was released from the bowstring, it slowed, a shaft of heat and light aimed at the lich, bright as the sun, but even though it barely moved at all, you could tell that it wasn't completely stopped.

"You can slow time," Marduk smiled. "But you haven't stopped it. You're either too tired, or that trick isn't as powerful as you make it look."

Daurgo sidestepped the oncoming lightning bolt, but he knew he didn't have much fight left.

Marduk knew it too. He dashed to Daurgo's legs and struck his kneecaps with his mace.

"That's it," Daurgo thought. "Take the bait."

As Marduk knocked out Daurgo's legs, Daurgo positioned his ribcage to land on top of him, turning it into another kind of cage altogether. A surprised god tried to break Daurgo's ribs away with is mace, but as he swung and cracked one off, the rib suspended in air, frozen in time.

Daurgo reached inside of his ribcage and grabbed Marduk by the leg. Shaking the god like a rag with his left claw, the lich opened a portal with his right.

"End of the line, Marduk." Daurgo tipped his head and aimed for his new portal.

"What?" Realization spread across Marduk like water on a hardwood floor. "No!"

Daurgo knocked his own skull off of his neck and sent his own head hurtling through the portal. As his skull spun around between the planes, Daurgo got one last look at Marduk scrambling out from under a pile of dragon bones crumbling to dust without Daurgo's magic, only to reach the portal just as it closed.

8

Necrocracy

AMENHOTEP

The High Tomb Lord clasped his bony, bandage-wrapped hands. "What schemes do you have for us today?"

Sekhet, the sage of the Tomb Lords, and Amenhotep's primary expert on the people of Kemet, stepped before her godking's throne and bowed her head. "With Thoth out of the way, our efforts should be able to go unnoticed, at least for now. There was an empire that ruled Egypt, the Middle East, and most of Europe after we were forced back into our tombs. They called it Rome, and it was so powerful, it could not be destroyed from the outside, much like the empire that troubles us in the north. Instead, they rotted from the inside, and their empire destroyed itself. I intend to reverse engineer their collapse among the Borealan Empire."

Amenhotep tilted his head. When he was alive, there had never been a known case of an empire destroying itself. "Do you now? How certain are you that you know how to do this?"

"All of the conditions are right." Sekhet bowed again. "A wealthy empire with no external threats, only occasionally concerned with fairly normal problems, like the Greymarch. The dracolich was even more of a blessing than I could have imagined; the people of Hadesh are running around in fear for the first time in generations. Fear is our friend."

"I see." Amenhotep leaned forward on his throne. "What are these 'right conditions' of which you speak?"

"We used weapons forged from jealousy to kill Thoth," the sage answered. "That jealousy didn't come from nowhere. There's a lot of it, and as the empire embraces its false sense of safety, it will be easy to stir the pot a little further. I'll begin by seeking out the most brutish people burning with anger. The key is to do enough damage to their infrastructure that their army won't be able to fight."

Armies. The Borealans had somehow built up an army so great and so powerful that the best military of Kemet couldn't hope to compete. It used to be that endless hordes of undead warriors would demoralize and crush any enemy as their fellow soldiers joined the ranks of zombie puppets, but things had changed. The Borealans had ships that sailed through the skies and could drop weapons that exploded, wiping out whole legions of skeletal minions. The undead formed no proper ranks, had no real organization, and could never hope to outmaneuver the living. Their best weapon was fear, and the Borealans had gotten so used to fighting the mindless hordes of the Greymarch that the undead no longer scared them. In a straight fight, the armies of the godking stood no chance against the Borealans.

"Very well," Amenhotep dismissed his sage. "Continue your plans. I have a scientist to address."

"Of course, my godking." Sekhet lowered her head, but she didn't hide the sadistic glee in her voice at the thought of what was coming to the scientist. She had never liked Pausiris, and didn't try to hide that fact. Behind her, a throne with four kneeling slaves awaited her and carried the sage away once she returned to her seat.

Amenhotep ignored her and signaled to a slave to send for the scientist to bring in his new inventions.

After the Calamity, new technology and strange machines made it immediately clear that the Tomb Lords couldn't just rely on magic anymore. Pausiris had joined their ranks long before the Liminal Bridges had closed, but his skills were more important now than ever before. The fact that he was so single-minded in his goal of furthering his science made him fairly easy to command, and Amenhotep never had to worry about him trying to usurp the throne; Pausiris couldn't be bothered with ruling anything. But the scientist also lacked anything resembling guile.

Pausiris's throne entered the room. It was not carried by a team of slaves, like Sekhet's, or the other Tomb Lords'. This throne belched smoke as mechanical legs similar to a scarab scuttled along the ground and transported the engineer towards the godking. Behind it, four mechanical warriors marched in step. Each had feet of brass like a bird of prey, a torso filled with clockwork, and four metal arms carrying weapons. Some carried one-handed scythes, an ancient traditional weapon for the armies of the region, but two of them carried large, round maces, similar to the kind used when Amenhotep was alive to fight armored opponents.

"I have managed to find a solution to the production problem." Pausiris threw a lever to stop his throne and bowed before Amenhotep. "I stole an idea from Borealan factories, and have arranged something called an assembly line to streamline the production process. It even uses the slaves you wanted, so the automated systems do not quell your...desire, for forced labor."

Amenhotep eyed the scientist, ignoring the mechanical soldiers. "Tell me, have you learned yet why slavery is so important to us?"

"No," Pausiris shifted in his throne. "I could replace every one of them with more machines, or have undead servants."

The godking of Kemet clasped his hands. "Pausiris, the commoners need to believe that everything they have is a gift from their pharaoh. Their lives, the air they breathe, and any rights or freedoms they are fortunate enough to have. In order for this to work, they need an example of what life looks like when their godking does not deign to grant them these things. I do not take anything away from the slaves; I simply never gave them privileges of freedom to begin with."

"...I think I understand that," the scientist was still visibly trying to work something out. "But could we not find something less...obtrusive for them to do? Digging holes and then filling them back in? Something that doesn't get in the way of my production machines?"

"I'll tell you what," Amenhotep snickered. "You think of something nice and public for the slaves to do, and I'll consider implementing it for the masses.

Although, I like the idea of them working in your smoke-filled factories. Even clean air is a gift."

"I'll...get right on that." Pausiris looked down as if trying to come up with a solution on the spot.

"Excellent work with the sentinel production," Amenhotep gestured to the soldiers. "Build me an army of these things. What of your research into intelligence? Have you found a way to reverse this...evolution problem?"

Pausiris had previously informed the other Tomb Lords that humanity was continuing to evolve without them. Someday, and that day may be very soon from the perspective of a lich, humans would be too smart to still rely on a godking to lead them.

"My research is not exactly...conclusive," the scientists fumbled with some of his notes. "I need more time, and more people on which to test my experiments. Both in a laboratory setting and outside of it."

"Very well then, run your findings by Sekhet. And make sure someone who actually respects you, like Arkeon or Djedefre is present as well." Amenhotep leaned back on his throne. "Now I take my leave. I have a matter that requires my personal attention."

Amenhotep gestured for the slaves by his own throne to lift him up. Directing them to a room in the palace where new recruits for the godking's special police were trained, the godking raised a mummified hand to instruct his throne bearers to stop.

The High Tomb Lord rose from his throne and entered a large chamber where a half dozen of the Necrophytes had recently graduated from their training. All of them froze and bowed as their godking entered the room.

"Good morning, gentlemen." Amenhotep smiled. "Rise."

The Necrophytes stood up and saluted, maintaining a militaristic bearing that was visibly fueled by terror.

"At ease." Amenhotep approached one of the Necrophytes as they dropped the salute, but still held their bearing. "What is your name?"

"Mando, your most illustrious majesty," the Necrophyte replied.

"Please," the pharaoh chided. "Just call me godking."

"Y-yes, my godking."

"Tell me," Amenhotep glanced at the upside-down ankh mark magically branded on the new Necrophyte's head. "How are you taking to your new powers?"

"Um..." Mando was visibly sweating from his forehead. "I am most grateful to my godking for letting me use his powers through his mark—"

"No, no." Amenhotep chuckled. "Not that. I mean the other powers; the opportunities that your new office grants you, among the populace."

"The populace?" Mando paused. "You mean in terms of identifying traitors, punishing criminals, and maintaining order in Kemet?"

"Of course." Amenhotep nodded. "But there are many other opportunities that come with your position. You can do whatever you want. Zombies, skeletons, they will obey you, thanks to my mark. Normal citizens will have no choice but to let you do as you please, or face the wrath of the undead."

Mando raised an eyebrow. "Whatever I want?"

"Whatever you like." Amenhotep patted him on the shoulder. "No one other than I can tell you 'no.'"

With that, Amenhotep bid the Necrophytes farewell, and took his leave. Let the other Tomb Lords have their schemes. He had his own.

9

Buying Money

ROSTAM

Near the docks of Gangryros, several moneychangers had booths setup along a wide stone road. These booths had signs of currencies listing exchange rates, which varied slightly between booths so as to compete with one another.

"Okay," Rostam examined the moneychangers' booths. "And you say the masonry companies won't accept Ioseps?"

"Well, they might," Captain Nadia held up a silver Iosep in her hand as if to examine it. "But they won't like it. Merchants want to know that our money is actually worth what we claim, and they might overcharge us just to be on the safe side."

Rostam raised an eyebrow. "How do you show that money is worth what you claim?"

"Without an alchemist, or someone else who can ensure how much precious metal is actually in a coin, you can't." Nadia held a Iosep up to Rostam to look at the image of Emperor Iosep Charvette. "That's why people use coins with markings in the first place. The markings are supposed to be an assurance that the coin is worth a specific amount of silver, like a brand name that people have come to trust. If people can trust the government that mints the coins, they will trust that the money has value."

Looking at the face on the coin, something bothered Rostam. "I've seen older coins from before the war. They're not used anymore, but Borealan coins back then were minted by private markets, not the government. How did people work with coins that weren't backed by the government?"

"Same way," Nadia pocketed the silver Iosep. "A private mint would buy silver, make them into coins with their brand logo, name, or other identifiers, and then, in the same way some people make a living selling gold to people as an investment, mints would sell coins that were more convenient for doing business."

"But how do you make a profit selling silver coins?" Rostam asked. "Isn't a coin worth what it's made in metal? It's the same amount of silver, but with extra work put into shaping it into a coin. The imperial government can do that because it doesn't need to make a profit, but what private mint could stay afloat making coins at a loss?"

"Simple, they don't sell it for a loss." Nadia patted a purse full of coins they were about to exchange. "Imagine if we did business with unmarked gold bars instead of coins. How do you know that a bar that's supposed to be solid gold isn't really a bar of worthless lead with a thin layer of gold plating? Checking to see if the gold is genuine means going to an alchemist, and that takes time and money, which makes the cost of doing business much more expensive. But what if those gold bars have a stamp or signature that's difficult to counterfeit and comes with a reputation for quality? Business runs smoothly, and that means people will pay the mints more than what they're worth as precious metals, because the reliability has its own value."

Rostam ran this through his head to make sure he understood. "So, there's an...abstract value to the coins?"

Nadia nodded. "I think it's called 'arbitrage' – the value that comes from how something performs its job, not just what it's made of or what it cost to make." She gave Rostam a nudge. "You know, eventually we're going to need a new quartermaster. If you can keep track of all of these things and develop a mind for numbers, you could find yourself filling my old job very soon."

That thought shot through Rostam's head like a lightning bolt. He'd thought about getting promoted at some point, but hadn't set his mind on a position yet. Becoming the ship's quartermaster was a big deal; they were the ones who took over the role of captain if the current captain was unavailable. Nadia had become captain when Zaahid died in the wreck of their previous ship.

"Now, let's exchange some coins." Nadia led Rostam to a moneychanger's stall. "Hello. We are from the Borealan Empire. We wish to exchange silver Ioseps for Hexdrachubes."

A moneychanger from behind the stall stroked a full but well-trimmed beard. "How many?"

Nadia pulled out a slip of paper where she'd written down her requirements. "I would say, twelve Hexdrachubes. That should cover our cargo."

"Hm," the moneychanger checked his lists of currency rates. "That's a smaller currency to a larger one. How many are you offering?"

"I could give you twenty-five hundred Ioseps for the cubes," Nadia offered.

The moneychanger looked at his charts again, then shrugged and smiled. "You know what? That's a fair deal. I'll buy twenty-five hundred Ioseps from you for twelve Hexdrachubes."

After an exchange of coins, Nadia held a bag of Meditian money, which she gave Rostam to carry. Rostam examined one of the cubes. They were a silvery-gold colored piece about two centimeters on each side, and each face held different images. One had a picture of a Meditian king whose name was written in a language Rostam didn't know. Another had a picture of a column, and the other four had symbols Rostam didn't recognize.

"What are these made out of?" Rostam asked.

"Electrum." Nadia looked down at the bag. "It's an alloy of silver and gold. Very valuable, and easy to work into complicated shapes like that, so it's good for making coins."

Returning to the docks, Nadia purchased enough stone, mortar, and lumber to fill the ship's cargo hold, and *the Endurance* set sail back to Hadesh. Silverstack Docks came into view, and Rostam looked over the city he had called home.

A lot of buildings were still damaged or ruined by the dragon's attack. The Academics' Arena was still clearly the epicenter of the damage, but Rostam noticed that the Garden District had mostly been repaired. Ritzier places always seemed to get fixed quickly. The neighboring Imperial District was still under repair, but apart from the Imperial Palace, most of the government buildings were well behind the wealthy homes of the Garden District in terms of mending. The Southern Residential District has seen some homes restored, but was still roughly the same as it was when they left. Fortunately, they hadn't been hit very hard.

But the Empyrian Quarter was no better than it had been on the day after the attack. In fact, from the looks of things, it might have gotten worse. People whose homes had been badly damaged by the dragon's artillery fire had setup tents and tarps to keep out the rain, but none of the buildings had seen any repairs, and while Rostam was no expert on home construction, it looked like the insides of the houses were suffering from exposure to the elements.

As the ship came into port, Rostam monitored the ballast valves to steady the vessel. Once the docking clamps deployed, Nadia checked in with a port authority and checked for details about where to sell their cargo.

"Excuse me," a man waved for Rostam's attention. "Are you carrying building supplies?"

"Uh, yes," Rostam examined the man. He didn't look like a merchant who worked with a construction crew, but any offer was worth reporting to Captain Nadia.

"Oh sir, would you consider donating them to our organization?" The man begged. "It's been so hard on our city since the undead attacked, and we cannot get supplies to fix any of the buildings—"

"That's not my call," Rostam interrupted. "I'm not the captain, just part of the crew. You'll have to talk to our captain."

When Nadia returned, the man came up to her to beg her to give him their cargo.

"No." Nadia replied. "We are not doing well enough financially to be giving away handouts."

"But please," the man begged. "There are so many needy people who are living in shattered homes right now!"

Nadia raised an eyebrow. "Which needy homes, exactly?"

"Well...the needy," the man stammered.

"Yes, but which ones?" Nadia eyed the man up and down. "Which organization did you say you worked for again?"

"Ah...I didn't," the man admitted.

"Okay, mind telling me the name of the charity you're working for?"

"The...um..." he stammered. "The Needy...Homes...Charity."

"Never heard of them," Nadia turned back to her ship. "Don't know if they're a reputable group. Might just be a scam to collect donations of construction materials and resell them to a construction crew. Now, if you'll excuse us, we have a buyer who is offering to pay us for the goods, and time is money."

As the man scurried away, Rostam and the other crew loaded the cargo onto trolleys and rolled the materials onto a massive elevator that scaled the side of the city's wall. At the bottom, a construction crew waited eagerly to receive the goods.

The leader of the construction crew smiled and handed Rostam a large bag of money to carry. "Three thousand, five hundred Ioseps," he turned to Nadia. "And thank you, so much. We've got so many demands, and so many contracts to fill. Every little bit helps."

"A pleasure doing business with you," Nadia shook the man's hand.

Rostam turned to Nadia after the construction crew hauled away the materials. "What now? Should we transport more construction materials?"

"I'm not so sure," Nadia checked her pocket record book. "We made a nice profit, but I've got one of those gut feelings...Something about that man from before, the one scamming people into giving donations? It doesn't sit right with me." She checked her pocket watch. "Besides, other people with the same idea are going to drive up the prices of stone and lumber in Meditia, and we might end up buying materials on our next run for a high price and end up with a load of cargo we cannot sell when we return to Hadesh. The demand might be gone by then. Let's check the nearby job boards for delivery contracts."

Some airships transported goods for specific companies, but independent airships like *the Endurance* either took jobs through speculation, or by contract. Speculation was when the airship captain spotted an upcoming demand and gathered cargo to meet that demand. A contract, on the other hand, was when a private party had a specific need they wanted filled, and would hire ships to bring them the goods they need. Generally, contracts had lower profit margins than you could make through speculation, but they were also less risky.

At the base of the elevator, right at the ground level under Silverstack Docks, where the Whitecoast Railway line traveled overhead through a tunnel midway up the side of the city wall, several job boards held postings for contracts, each listing money offers, the weight of the cargo that needed to be carried, and other details about the work.

"Thre's a lo' here tha' we canna' car'y," Tarchus looked through the listed contracts. "Nee' a bi'ger ship."

"Wait, what's this?" Nadia picked up a contract from the bottom of one of the boards. "The Abbey of Truth?"

"What do they want?" Rostam looked over Nadia's shoulder at the contract.

"They want a delivery of goods out to Harlak." Nadia read the details aloud. "Copper pipe delivery to a water purifier project. Need a transport ship to deliver supplemental materials."

"Supplemental?" Rostam scanned the paper.

"It means they ran out partway through the project."

"I get that, but why did they run out?" Rostam asked. "Did they underestimate how much they needed for this water thing?"

"I'm not sure." Nadia stared at the paper for a while longer. "I'm trying to think. If we went to Harlak, we could probably drop off the copper pipes and pick up copper ore from the nearby mines. We could haul that to Dihorma–"

"Wait, do they need someone hauling copper pipes to a place that already sells copper ore?" Rostam asked. "If Harlak already has the copper, why aren't they making pipes there?"

"There's very little industry in Harlak," Nadia explained. "It used to be the capital city of the Empyrian Empire, but now it's mostly surrounded by subsistence farmers in the neighboring regions, copper mines, and a few other natural resources like sheep and cattle. They live near the Whispering Sea, and the water is salty and filled with poisonous taint from the Calamity. Not a ton of clean water readily available."

"Guess that explains why they need a water purifier." Rostam pointed to the contract. "Four hundred Ioseps. They aren't offering a lot, but we don't have to buy the cargo. Apart from travel expenses, it's all potential profit."

Nadia raised a quizzical eyebrow. "Do you know what those expenses will be?"

"Well, it will take us about seven days, and that means seven days of supplies, which is about forty-two Ioseps. Then there's monthly salaries for Tarchus, Simon, Joseph and me, which come due in about five days, that's another hundred, and we always like to assume fifty in other costs for things like repairs or other problems. That'd leave us with two hundred and eight in profit."

"Very good, future quartermaster." Nadia smiled as she pocketed the contract. "Let's pay the priests at the abbey a visit, and then we'll set off for Harlak."

10

Welcome to Dihorma

CYRUS

The train pulled into Dihorma at six in the morning. The sun was just starting to come up as Cyrus gathered his luggage and stepped off the coach car into the station.

Immediately, Cyrus was struck by the shear amount of filth on the station tiles. In Hadesh, the station floor might have an occasional drink spill, or a pigeon dropping that the janitorial staff hadn't gotten to yet, but on this station, you couldn't go more than a meter without finding some sort of trash. There were paper food wrappers, moldy leftover food waste, a metal blade from a broken knife or pair of scissors, and a garbage can that had been knocked over.

Back in Hadesh, the floor of the train station was so clean you could eat off of it, except that the janitors would scoop up any food spilled on the pavement so quickly it would be gone before you could try. The sight of so much filth on arrival was a shock, and Cyrus already suspected it was a taste for things to come.

As if to confirm his suspicions, once Cyrus exited the rail station and got his first look at Dihorma, his nose was immediately assaulted by the smells of a city full of garbage. The smell of pollutants was one thing; Cyrus could ignore the acrid smoke of houses and exhaust from factories. These were things you occasionally found in Hadesh when the wind blew in from the west and brought the smog of the Industrial Zone. But what you didn't find in Hadesh was the sweet and sour stink of old food waste. It wasn't compost; that was a smell alchemists got familiar with in the biology lab because of how useful it was for farming. This was more like people threw all of their food waste out onto the streets to lure in as much vermin as possible.

Sure enough, more than a few gulls and rats scampered around the streets, avoiding Cyrus's footsteps, but they would return to feed on whatever garbage they could find. Cyrus instinctively lifted his suitcase and slung it over his back, rather than let it roll over whatever filth lay along the ground.

As he ventured further into the city, Cyrus noticed a sign stuck on the inside of several buildings. It showed a picture of a fire extinguisher with a pair of threatening eyes above it and a black silhouette of a house behind them. The sign read "This building is insured by Jasper and Jaime. They're always watching. Arsonists beware!"

In another window, another sign read "Have a home? Thank Jasper." And next to that, a third sign read "The Council wants to get rid of Jasper. Because they don't care if your children burn."

As he read the signs, Cyrus was surprised to hear a voice behind him.

"Are you a Maskil, or a Moron?" The voice was an audio recording on some sort of gramophone device. Behind Cyrus, a pair of animatronic puppets on strings acted out a skit.

"Maskil doesn't need the city council to tell him what he should or should not do." The first puppet, a dapper looking young man who must have been Maskil, was lifted up on a pair of strings and a light shone on him. "He knows that just because it's legal to ride a unicycle on his roof while drinking three beers, doesn't mean it's a good idea." The light switched to the other puppet, who was raised in place of Maskil. This puppet looked like a dope, his clothes were disheveled, and he had both his legs in a cast. "Moron can't ride his unicycle anymore, because he fell off the roof and broke his legs. Don't be a Moron! Be smart, and don't wait for the government to protect you from you!"

"What the actual hell?" Cyrus backed away as the puppet show stopped. Around him, the city was starting to wake up.

"What are you doing standing outside my shop? No one's open at this hour!" A man shook a fist at Cyrus. He wore a burlap apron and thick glasses, looked to be about sixty, and had a wiry gray beard as the only hair on his head. "Holding a bag like you're looking to loot the place! I'm warning you, I'm armed!" He drew a pistol and held it aloft, although he didn't aim it at Cyrus.

Cyrus realized he was the only one out on the street, and that the threat was aimed at him. "Excuse me, do you know where I might find a Doctor Raphael Monroe?"

"Doctor Monroe?" The shopkeeper's aggression dialed down. "What would you want with him?"

"I just got off a train to meet him." Cyrus hoped telling the man about the train would justify him being out on the streets so early in the morning. "I'm going to work with him."

"Didn't think that guy was looking for apprentices," the man stroked his beard. "You an alchemist?"

Cyrus nodded. "I've got his address, but I don't know where the road he lives is."

"Uh, it should be...let's see, I think I heard he lives on Sandybrick lane, and that's outside the city wall, over on the west." He pointed down the road towards the center of town. "If you go to the center of the city and turn right, you'll find Westborough Street. It'll take you in the right direction."

"Thank you!" Cyrus waved. "Oh, and...are you having trouble...with looters or something?"

The shopkeeper paused. "You really don't know, do you? Lucky kid. Keep your head down. Dihorma's not like Hadesh."

Keeping that in mind, Cyrus made his way down to the city center. The closer he got to the middle of the city, the more the trash built up until he reached the very heart of town. In the very center, a city hall sat made of stone and marble. It was well kept, had no trash on the sidewalks surrounding it, and seemed to be the only clean building in the area.

Cyrus also noticed that the lawn around the city hall was well kept and mowed, whereas what grass or lawns could be found around the other lawns was overgrown, brown, or in other states of neglect. Spotting a road sign for

Westborough Street, he followed it to a large wall that encircled the city.

The wall was similar to the one in Hadesh, but unlike Hadesh, this wall looked more worn down, like it was somehow older than the wall that encircled the empire's capital, despite the fact that Dihorma was built after the Empyrian War, and the wall around Hadesh still had battle damage from Sattar's Last Siege. While this wall wasn't as well maintained, it was still in better shape than most of the rest of the city. Cyrus hoped this city didn't skimp on military spending when it came to things like the Greymarch.

Cyrus reached a checkpoint at the base of the wall, where a man in a kiosk opened a sliding door to greet him.

"Trying to get outside of the city? So early? Are you looking to beat the morning traffic?" He asked.

"No, I just got off a train." Cyrus dug through his luggage and pulled out his identification records. "My name is Cyrus Levitch. I'm an alchemy student from Hadesh looking to get some work experience before school starts again."

The man looked over his papers. "Interesting choice to come here. Still, everything seems to be in order. Go on through."

The man handed back Cyrus's papers, and a guard at the city gate opened a normal sized- door that was part of the much larger gate itself.

Cyrus continued on his journey along Westborough Street, all the while looking for the Sandybrick Lane the shopkeeper had mentioned. Small satellite towns surrounded Dihorma's wall, with people who would rush inside of the city in the event of a Greymarch attack. The housing was more affordable here, and Cyrus noticed that the filth of the city was absent.

He passed several intersections and got further and further away from the city itself before he started to wonder if he'd missed the road. Finally, he came to one last intersection with no buildings nearby, where Westborough Street kept going off into the wilderness, and the last crossroad with no signs of life nearby had only one sign: Sandybrick Lane.

Cyrus looked around and spotted a house located on a hill a long way from the intersection. He was tired from walking straight from the train station, but he wasn't going to stop now. Besides, high stamina was part of being an alchemist. Marching the rest of the way to this house, he checked around for any signs of other life. There was a recently ploughed but currently unseeded garden in front of the house, a wooden fence made up of rough wooden poles that seemed meant to deter intruders more than anything else, and a mailbox by the road read "Dr. Monroe." This was the right place.

Forcing away any signs of fatigue, Cyrus walked up to the front door of the house and knocked.

At first, there was nothing. Then there were sounds of someone shuffling around inside. Finally, a man opened the front door.

Dr. Monroe was in his late thirties and must have been close to two meters tall. He had black, straight hair, a stubble that suggested that he shaved, but often forgot to do so, clear brown eyes that seemed to be locked in a perpetual frown, and wore a labcoat that had probably seen better decades.

"What do you want?" The man's tone was calm, but there was a hint of threat buried beneath it. "I'm not interested in buying whatever you're selling."

Cyrus felt his throat swell up. This was the part he'd been dreading. As his voice failed, he tried to force the words out. "I'mheretobeyourapprentice!"

The doctor paused, as if trying to parse what Cyrus had just said. "Not interested."

As the doctor turned to slam the door shut, Cyrus held it open with his hand. "Wait! I came all the way here from Hadesh! I couldn't find an internship or apprenticeship anywhere else so I came looking for you."

"Oh really?" The doctor smirked. "No one else would take you? Now why would that be?"

"Because of how I won the Grand Wizard Tournament," Cyrus paused for a breath. "Well, just the Combat Arena. I–"

"Wait a minute," the doctor opened the door again and locked eyes with Cyrus. "You won the Combat Arena? Alchemists rarely participate. You're telling me you won?"

"Yes. I..." Cyrus hadn't wanted to show the doctor this, but something told him Monroe could sense a liar, and Cyrus wasn't a good liar to begin with. He took out a newsletter and showed the doctor the headline. "Here."

"Alchemist Swipes Victory from Young Girl Through Brute Force." Doctor Monroe read. "Alchemy student Cyrus Levitch, a dark horse candidate in this year's Combat Arena, recently claimed the first-place medal. However, his last fight against first-year theurgy student Ephorah el-Sabat showed questionable sportsmanship." He looked up from the paper. "This is you?"

Cyrus nodded. "It wasn't like they're saying. I did jump on her back, but only as a reflexive move after she tried to tackle me. It wasn't even an illegal move."

"How did you make it to the last round?" The doctor asked.

"I...defeated every other opponent." Cyrus struggled to remember every fight. "I made up for the fact that alchemy doesn't offer much in the way of ranged attacks by using cover to close in on the other person. Made dust clouds, that sort of thing. When that last girl had me outnumbered three-to-one with her summoned spirits, I deconstructed the sigil engraved in one of her elementals and let him loose, so he turned on his former master."

"Your last fight was a three-on-one?" The doctor examined the paper again. "Oh, wow. They even admit that while trying to paint you as some kind of brute."

"Yes," Cyrus went on. "And now, after trying everything I can to become the best alchemist I can be, and repay Thoth for taking me under his wing, no one wants to hire me for an internship because of how this last fight looked."

The doctor's eyes widened. "You worked with Thoth directly? And now... because of the idiot masses..."

"I have no idea what I should have done differently." Cyrus rubbed his forehead, finally letting the questions he'd had since the tournament bubble to the surface. "Should I have thrown the fight? Should I have refused to participate? Would that have been better, or would it have been disgraceful?"

"From the sounds of it, you didn't do anything wrong." The doctor handed back the newsletter. "You just did your best in full view of humanity's worst. Fools; morons...sheep who think with their emotions at the expense of greatness." He paused for a moment, staring off into the distance at the wilderness outside his house. "Geniuses must accept that the world isn't made for us. Life is built for the average, and the average person is not, by definition, a genius. They don't like what they don't understand, and they think everyone should vote on what's right or wrong, as if their collective idiocy was just as valid as your intelligence." He finally looked down at Cyrus again. "This isn't just about finding an apprenticeship, or keeping your resume from having a hole this season, is it?"

"No," Cyrus admitted. "I was there when Thoth was killed, and part of the reason he died was because he was protecting me. I want to make sure I take everything he taught me and become the best alchemist I can be. To the Abyss with what everyone else thinks."

The doctor laughed. "Oh, wow. I couldn't have said it better myself." Sighing, he opened the door and waved inside. "Come in. We have work to do."

11

Fire and Darkness

EPHORAH

"We'll be arriving at the last known sighting soon," Sergeant Chertok checked his watch. "When we get there, how quickly can you conjure up that water spirit of yours?"

Ephorah clutched the railing along the side of the battlewagon and gritted her teeth. Unlike a train car on a smooth railroad, the battlewagon made sure its passengers felt every bump in the uneven ground as they traveled on steel wheels driven by a steam engine at the back of the vehicle.

"It only takes a few seconds," she called back. "Why do you need a water elemental again?"

"We're here to deal with a Hisham spotting," the sergeant answered. "The Hisham can only be killed by fire and sunlight, but fresh water weakens them and stops their regeneration. They aren't always hostile, and we can settle for driving them away from the locals. Of course, if that doesn't work..." He held up a hand-held flamethrower. "The fuel we use for this sort of mission doesn't worry about whether the target is wet, at least when the Hisham are concerned."

The battlewagon slowed down. It was a clear night, sky full of stars, and chilly. The sergeant's weapon, a magically warded device designed to fire a spray of diphosophane, some chemical that could burn water, was common for the Salamanders. Other soldiers had similar weapons, along with pistol sidearms with incendiary bullets and grenades that coated an enemy in flaming oil when they hit. The uniforms that Ephorah and the mercenaries wore were made of some flame-retardant material, but still held the same general style and appearance of military fatigues. The only thing Ephorah noticed was missing were melee weapons; only the sergeant carried an officer's sword, and it was clearly just for show.

"I must admit, I was surprised to see an intern this year," the sergeant said over the rumbling of the battlewagon. "The Salamanders tend to get two kinds of recruits: people who want to hunt monsters for a living, and people with...certain fascinations."

Sergeant Chertok gestured to one of the other men in the wagon, who was holding up a lit match with eyes full of wonder and a smile full of glee. Ephorah got the message.

Once the wagon came to a stop, the mercenaries, six in total, got up and opened a half-door on the side of the wagon to hop out. Ephorah followed them and took a look back at the battlewagon. The vehicle was about eight meters long, two meters wide, with a cabin for an engineer and a driver stoking a furnace to propel it forward. A box of coal at the back of the machine took up a meter of the vehicle's length, with another meter reserved for the driver and engineer. Only the cabin had a roof; the rest of the vehicle was open-topped so that the soldiers could breathe easily and fire from the sides at any enemies who got too close.

In the night air, Ephorah couldn't see very far, and had no idea if there were any of these "Hisham" out in the plains. She took out her statue of an elemental; an icon of the upper half of a woman bursting out of a crest of waves. "Aquaria, come forth."

A tear between the material world and the Duat opened up, and a humanoid tidal wave flowed out into the open air. The elemental had arms and a torso like a normal woman, but the lower half was less distinct, as if she was wearing a skirt that concealed her legs. Her face, on the other hand, was almost human, apart from the fact that it was made out of water.

"Aquaria," Ephorah addressed her elemental. "How well can you see in this light?"

The elemental turned, as if scanning the area. "I cannot see very well. But I can feel the flow of air shift around me. There is...something, in the darkness. Something that doesn't like the light."

"The Hisham are here," Sergeant Chertok checked his weapon before turning to Ephorah. "You ever see one before?"

Ephorah hadn't even heard of the Hisham before applying for this internship. "All I know is that they're supposed to be a cursed tribe from the east, who angered all the gods at once. They don't like fire, sunlight, or fresh water, and that last one is more because of Sobek than anything else."

"Yeah, not sure what the crocodile god has against them." The sergeant gazed out into the darkness. "They don't look very human anymore. Have you got a weapon?"

Ephorah held up her fists, wearing her arachne silk gloves. "These give me the punching strength of ten men."

The sergeant shook his head. "That won't kill them. You need one of our weapons." He handed her a flamethrower.

Ephorah did her best to hold the weapon up, but it was far too heavy. Her arms could take the weight, but not her back.

"Strength of ten men?" The sergeant raised an eyebrow.

"Only my arms," Ephorah winced. "Good for punching, not lifting."

"Ah. Then at least take this." He handed her a glass orb filled with liquid. "It will at least allow you to fend off one of the Hisham if they get too close, and it might scare off the others."

Ephorah took the grenade and stuck it in her uniform's belt. "Are the Hisham normally this active? I thought they didn't usually approach towns."

"Normally, they don't," Sergeant Chertok replied. "Ever since the Empyrian War, they've been getting more active. It was small at first, barely noticeable for decades, but in more recent years, they've gotten to the point of attacking fields and cattle. They'll kill a person they meet wandering alone at night, but they seem to be targeting people's food sources. The Hisham don't seem to eat, or if they do, they don't seem to need to. They can't die of hunger; we know that."

"If they used to be human, couldn't we...ask them?" Ephorah offered. "Ask why they've started attacking farms and pastures?"

The sergeant shook his head. "The Hisham don't talk. Or if they do, no one has ever heard them and lived to tell about it." He adjusted his flamethrower and held it in tactical position. "We need to move out."

Ephorah and Aquaria followed Sergeant Chertok into a large pasture where Ephorah could make out a number of shapes along the ground in the moonlight. These shapes weren't moving, and she couldn't tell what they were until she got closer, at which point she gasped at the gory sight in front of her.

A cow, or most of it, had been torn to shreds. A few of its limbs were missing, and blood pouring out from the wounds had left the ground soft and muddy. The skin of the cow had been cut by something jagged; the marks were like that of a claw, which punctured the skin, dragged it until it gathered into a bunched-up mess, and then released and repeated the process. These wounds resulted in the cow being mostly flayed, but few cut deep enough to sever the limbs or kill the beast without bleeding it out. The missing legs had completely different wounds, like the skin and torn muscles were stretched out, and the limbs had been ripped or torn off, not cut off.

"What in the Abyss did this?" Ephorah couldn't take her eyes off the corpse. "Did a human do this? Are the Hisham super strong?"

"Normally, no." one of the other soldiers examined the corpse. "It's not unheard of, but most are no stronger than a human. This one looks like an exception. Or a pack of them working together."

"Stay close," the sergeant ordered. "We'll sweep the plains together. The girl's elemental says the Hisham are close, so keep your guard up."

"Aquaria, can the Hisham actually do anything to harm you?" Ephorah asked.

The elemental shook her head. "I doubt it. If these creatures are weakened by fresh water, they cannot touch me. I do not believe they have any weapons that can hurt a spirit."

"Then travel in front of us for now," Ephorah ordered. "Let us know if you detect anything."

Aquaria flowed across the ground ahead of the squad as they searched the plains for further clues. Some of the men held lanterns to shed light on the field, but the light only went so far, and it made the darkness of the night seem darker. One soldier spotted a trail of blood from the cows that lead to the edge of the pasture.

At the end of the field was a fence, with a section that had been taken down. Several tracks suggested some of the cattle had escaped through the hole.

"Why would the Hisham do all of this?" Ephorah asked.

"Don't confuse the Hisham with mindless monsters, like the Greymarch." Sergeant Chertok took a lantern and held it closer to the damaged fence. "They aren't. I guarantee that they're actively trying to hurt the food supply of people nearby. They know we know they're weaknesses. They know they can't just slaughter people they want to hurt. So, they're doing something indirect."

"Something is out there," Aquaria pointed off to the left, outside of the fence. "There are many. They seem to be retreating."

The sergeant turned to one of the soldiers. "Return to the battlewagon. Don't let them leave us stranded. Take the girl with you."

Ephorah scowled. "Why am I getting left behind?"

"Because the rest of us are going to be running." The sergeant waved for the rest of the men to follow him as he went off in the direction Aquaria had pointed. The soldiers followed.

"Go with them," Ephorah ordered Aquaira. The elemental flowed after the mercenaries.

"Not a bad idea, but let's hope we don't need her." The remaining soldier took Ephorah's arm. "Let's go."

The soldier pulled Ephorah back to the battlewagon. She thought about struggling, and she might have been able to do so with her enchanted gloves, but she knew it would look bad on her internship report if she resisted a direct order from the sergeant.

Once they returned to the battlewagon at the edge of the pasture, the soldier checked on the driver and engineer. The engineer pulled up a pintle-mounted flamethrower from a storage compartment on the back of the battlewagon, setting up a field of fire along the back of the vehicle.

"*Empyrian...*"

The voice came from behind Ephorah. It was so soft, so raspy she wouldn't be able to hear it were it not so quiet out. Ephorah didn't check her pocket watch, but she was almost certain it was around midnight. Slowly, Ephorah turned to look over her shoulder, dreading whatever just spoke.

"*One of us...*"

Ephorah couldn't tell if this was a statement or a question. As she squinted in the night without a lantern, she couldn't make out anything apart from the flicker of yellow lights in the dark. Then she noticed the pattern of those lights; they were all in pairs, most of them at eye level. They had...well, not pupils, exactly...but something like them.

"*Smells like...possibly...*"

"Hello? Can I get a lantern back here?" Ephorah called. She heard either the driver or the engineer fumbling around in the battlewagon.

"*No...contaminated...*"

Ephorah couldn't tell where the voices were coming from, and finally one of the crew members brought a lantern over to the front of the wagon. At long last, Ephorah could see the Hisham in the light. They had surrounded the front of the vehicle.

They were like living shadows, but they were visibly solid. They were shaped like figures, but by a clumsy-handed craftsman. Some walked upright while others walked on all fours. Some hunched over and were semi-erect. One had three arms, with two growing out of the same shoulder, while another had backwards-facing hands. All were skeletal, like they were just skin and bones, but none had any visible mouths; perhaps they were all on the brink of starvation. But the eyes; now it was perfectly clear to Ephorah that these yellow lights couldn't be anything other than eyes, because in the light of the lantern she could see these creatures studying her. They couldn't have looked less like humans, but it was obvious that they used to be people.

"*Impure...unclean...*"

"Wait, what?" A sense of dread settled into Ephorah's brain. "I thought you said I was one of you!"

The creatures stumbled towards her. One of them swung a massive, mishappen arm and grabbed at her throat. She was able to sidestep it, but the creature grabbed the side of her torso instead and lifted her up. The thing only had two fat fingers on its hand and a wide thumb. She felt them squeeze into her side to keep her from squirming.

With her opera gloves extending all the way up her arms and filling her with enchanted strength, Ephorah rammed her elbow into the monster's arm and shattered it, making it drop her.

The creature howled as something inside had snapped, but it didn't sound like a broken bone. The shattered limb hung limp, then made a horrible sound as it twisted itself back into shape. In seconds, the arm was as good as new.

"*Destroy...impure...*"

Ephorah reached into her grenade belt and pulled out the bomb the sergeant had given her. "Stay back!"

"*Cleanse...purify...*"

Ephorah hurled the bomb at the monster that had grabbed her. It burst open and engulfed the creature in oil that instantly caught fire. It let out an inhuman shriek, but the liquid fire reduced it to ash in seconds.

The other Hisham looked at each other in silence, as if communicating with each other what they just saw. Then two of them lunged for Ephorah and grabbed her arms, lifting her up so her feet couldn't touch the ground. Each pulled as hard as they could against her arms, as if trying to rip her apart. She tried to struggle, but even with her magical strength, her arms couldn't break free while her legs were off the ground.

A slim crack crept along another Hisham's face and became a mouth. It unhinged its jaws and opened a maw wide enough to bite off Ephorah's head and torso.

"*Erase...impurity...*"

Before Ephorah could react to the giant mouth filled with small teeth like jagged pieces of flint, she heard a shout above her as a flame coated the creature in front of her. The engineer hollered something to the remaining soldier who used another flamethrower to drive off the remaining beasts that had encircled the front of the battlewagon.

The confused monsters holding her arms lost their grip and Ephorah's feet were able to touch the ground. Once she had some traction again, she swung her right arm all the way around at the creature on her left, and rapidly pummeled the beast with her fists until it looked like a steak that had been tenderized with a meat mallet.

Before the creature could regenerate, Ephorah bolted for the door of the battlewagon and climbed aboard. The soldier and the engineer had taken the pintle-mounted flamethrower from the back of the wagon and hauled it up to fight the Hisham. Ephorah took the opportunity to go through the wagon's supplies and pulled out two more firebomb grenades.

"Sorry it took us so long," the engineer called to Ephorah as she hurled one of the grenades at a Hisham trying to climb into the battlewagon.

"I've never seen so many in one place before!" The soldier's flamethrower sputtered as it ran out of fuel. He hurled a grenade at another monster before trying to refuel his flamethrower. "I need to reload!"

The engineer fired blasts of flame in short, controlled bursts, killing one Hisham at a time, but it wasn't keeping them at bay. The Hisham tried to rush the wagon, scrambling over each other to climb aboard the vehicle. Ephorah threw a grenade at the growing mound of mangled bodies trying to board the wagon. The flames killed some of the monsters, but the mound kept growing.

Ephorah ran to the front of the wagon where the Hisham mound was highest and tried to punch any beast that tried to climb aboard. A Hisham caught Ephorah's arm. Then, the vehicle lurched to life and started slowly moving forward, ramming into the mound of creatures and releasing Ephorah from the monster's grip. The driver must have started up the engine, in the hope of running them over. Instead, the Hisham were sliding underneath the battlewagon and were threatening to overturn it.

The driver threw the battlewagon into reverse, trying to get the vehicle away from the mound of Hisham, but they had already grabbed hold of the vehicle by the wheels and tried to stop it from getting away.

"We should've brought a demolisher tank!" The soldier struggled to aim his flamethrower underneath the battlewagon at the Hisham, but to no avail.

"Aquaria, return to your mistress!" Ephorah called to the void.

A tear in reality appeared as Aquaria returned from the field to Ephorah. "Yes, mistress?"

Ephorah pointed down at the wagon. "Drench those things!"

The water elemental drifted beneath the wagon and splashed water on each of the Hisham, flowing through them like a wave breaking over jagged rocks in the ocean.

The Hisham howled as the fresh water touched their flesh. Steam that stank of sulfur billowed out from under the wagon as it broke free and backed away from the monsters.

"What happened to the rest of the squad?" Ephorah asked the elemental when she returned.

"Dead," Aquaria replied.

"Dead?" The engineer cried. "Did the Hisham—"

"No," the elemental shook her head. "They took their own lives, before the Greymarch could get them."

"What?" The soldier, who had finished reloading his flamethrower, glared at Aquaria. "The Greymarch are here?"

"Yes," she nodded. "The Hisham lured them here."

12

How to Save a Life

CYRUS

"Bawk!"

Cyrus shoved the squirming chimera into its hole in the garden and surrounded it with dirt, but not enough to prevent its beak from getting air. He then went to the next spot and planted the next chimera.

"Bawk!" The creature, which Doctor Monroe called a "poultrato," was his attempt at combining plant and animal DNA into a new breed of...well, a boneless chicken, but one that could be grown in the ground like a potato.

"Bakawk!" The third chimera tried to bite at Cyrus as he packed it into the dirt, but the pathetic creature couldn't really move much. Instead of limbs, it had tubers, which were not really mobile.

"Okay, I understand the appeal of trying to make a plant that's part animal, and vice-versa." Cyrus looked up at Doctor Monroe, who was watching his progress from the side of the bed. "But why chickens? Why not something less complex, like an insect, or a crustacean?"

"Well, growing lobsters out here would be extremely difficult because of the terrain." Doctor Monroe gestured to the plains that had little natural water. Even his garden was supplied with pipes from the rivers that surrounded Dihorma. "I have an aquarium for storing animals like that, but they wouldn't survive in this heat. Chickens are the next best thing; they have a chimeric acceptance factor of 5.0, the highest of any species known to man."

"Chimeric acceptance factor…" Cyrus had heard something about this. Some animals responded better to being turned into chimeras than others. A domesticated animal had a better chance of becoming a chimera that could reproduce than a wild animal, and some creatures, like jackals, had such a low acceptance factor that they would die of cancer in weeks if turned into chimeras. The more an animal was used to humans, the more it could accept alchemical modification.

"Humans have already turned these birds into walking balls of meat with tiny heads," Monroe explained. "And that was before applying any magic. That's why there's so many mutant chickens running around these days. But the truth is, I'm also hoping to get something that works as a food source that I can eventually sell. You'll learn this later; research materials are expensive, and you'll need to pay bills somehow. We know the market for boneless chickens, and if I can create a protein source that can be grown in the same environments as the hardy potato, we'll have a new, easily marketable crop that we can sell the patent to a larger company." He held up an ordinary potato for examination. "These things will grow *anywhere*. If I can transfer that trait to these boneless chickens, and get them to survive like that, it'd be a massive leap for chimera research. And best of all, they can't move on their own, so there's no chance of another Birdopus Incident of 852."

Monroe explained to Cyrus that a chimera's chances of survival depended on the similarities between the organisms and the traits you were trying to graft. "Since chickens and potatoes don't have a lot in common, the DNA strands can't get an easy foothold, which is why I've had so many failed attempts for these chimeras."

Besides the chickens, Doctor Monroe kept a small flock of sheep that seemed to produce steel wool, and an even smaller pen of pigs. Very few people in the empire kept swine; the doctor told him they were there to consume medical waste. He also hired a caretaker named Hatem from the local area who tended the animals each day. It was clear to Cyrus that the doctor preferred to be alone as much as possible.

Once Cyrus had planted the last clucking poultrato, he came back into the house and washed up. After he was clean, especially his hands, he joined

Doctor Monroe in the laboratory located on the main floor.

Doctor Monroe's house was fairly large. It didn't look particularly big from the road, but on the other side of the hill, a corridor leading away from the main home lead to a research laboratory with a greenhouse, an operating room, and a small library filled with books on alchemy, some of which were from foreign nations. There was also a locked cellar where the doctor performed more delicate experiments that had to be kept out of the sunlight, but he'd told Cyrus he wasn't ready for them yet; they were too delicate to handle without proper training.

Monroe was waiting in the operating room. Unlike the hardwood floor of the rest of the house, the operating room had a floor of marble that was kept completely sterile, along with everything else in the room. A table for working on patients was setup in the center, and shelves of sterilized tools, cabinets filled with flasks of anesthetics and disinfectants, a sink, and in one corner, an icebox magically warded to keep whatever was inside cold enough to stay fresh. The doctor stood over the operating table with a small aquarium that he must have brought up from the cellar. It contained a number of different types of fish, including starfish.

"I don't think you're ready to understand how I'm trying to merge plant and animal cells." Doctor Monroe took a starfish from the aquarium and placed it on an aluminum operating tray. "But soon, I'll show you how I created sheep that grow steel wool. What have you learned about medical alchemy so far?"

"I can heal surface level injuries." Cyrus remembered escaping with other contestants from the Grand Wizard Tournament. One girl had been shot by an arrow in the leg, and while Cyrus tried to heal it, his work came undone and she had to be treated by Thoth. "I'm not good at healing what I can't see."

"Ah, of course." Doctor Monroe selected a scalpel from a line of sterile-looking medical tools on a nearby table. "We all start somewhere. Have your classes taught you about DNA?"

"The blueprint for the cells?" Cyrus remembered reading about the double-helix structures in his textbooks. "Yes, though only in theory. I don't have much practice with it."

"Well, then you're going to learn today." The doctor cut an arm off of the starfish with the scalpel. "Come here, and feel the severed limb of the animal."

Cyrus poured some rubbing alcohol on his hands and approached the table. He put his index finger on the stump where the limb was cut off from the rest of the starfish. It was somewhat smooth; the cut wasn't clean, but nothing like a cut from a claw.

"Clear your mind, reach into the cellular tissue, and feel the DNA inside the cell," Monroe instructed.

Closing his eyes, Cyrus tried to connect with the severed starfish's DNA. He could feel the same magic that flowed through his soul to power his spells seep through his fingertips and trickle into the starfish. Something, some information was definitely recorded there, like a program. It was so long, so complicated, and so detailed that it felt...designed. Cyrus's soul was connecting with the record like it knew the language, the dialect, and even the author. And that author knew how to arrange every molecule in every cell of the animal, and wrote it all down for anyone curious enough to read later. Cyrus couldn't understand what it said, but he could still feel it deep within.

"I feel...something." Cyrus opened his eyes. "It's definitely there."

"Then heal the starfish." Monroe smiled. "Don't worry about getting all of the matter in exactly the right place; let the DNA tell you what to do, and let it tell the cells where molecules need to go."

Cyrus clapped his hands and allowed his body to form a circuit of energy. He then touched the severed limb to the rest of the starfish and released that energy, still connecting with the instructions written into the cell. It was a strange thing. Cyrus let go of controlling the magic and allowed the script to direct the spell from the starfish to the severed limb. He felt less like the spellcaster and more like a conduit.

As he moved the limb closer to the starfish's body, the limb reattached to the starfish, fully restoring the animal. The limb twitched as the starfish became reacquainted with its appendage, and the doctor returned it to its tank.

"Very nice," the doctor congratulated him. "Of course, a starfish can heal from a wound like that on its own, but you'll get to practice with other animals later. Let's hope you don't have to work on a human until you've had some more practice."

"Wow." Cyrus looked at his own hand for a moment. "But, if I'm letting the DNA direct the matter, that means I can't make any changes. You cannot create a chimera with this method."

"No, you cannot," Monroe agreed. "Most chimeras are made by moving material in the animal around, or by placing new matter from another animal and encouraging the material to combine. Fusing cellular tissue between two animals together is very advanced. Most medical alchemists never go that far with chimera research. The only reason I do is in my efforts to create better treatments." He pointed to the starfish in the tank. "These guys can regrow severed limbs over time. I've been working on a serum to temporarily apply that ability to humans; something a non-alchemist could keep in a jar and use when an alchemist isn't around to heal them. You wouldn't even need it all the time; it could be a take-as-needed kind of thing."

Cyrus and Doctor Monroe put together some soup for lunch, and as they ate at the doctor's table, the seasoned alchemist took the opportunity to question his new apprentice.

"So, how are things going back at the college?"

Cyrus paused to take in everything that had happened since the tournament. "Have you heard what happened to Thoth?"

The doctor paused. "News travels out here, but I had hoped it was only rumor."

"I saw it with my own eyes." Cyrus shook his head. "He was killed by the Tomb Lords."

Monroe raised an eyebrow. "Reports said he was killed by the dracolich."

"They used the dragon as a cover. In the wake of the destruction he caused, the Tomb Lords made a surgical strike to kill Thoth. They planned it out ahead of time."

Doctor Monroe rubbed his eyes with his thumb and index finger. "Strangely, I'm not all that surprised that the Tomb Lords wanted Thoth dead. They might have a non-aggression pact with the empire, but they're still a bunch of authoritarian fiends ruled by an ancient tyrant. Despotic rulers don't want science that isn't shackled to their authority, and Thoth was the god of all who seek truth, not just those that seek what their despots desire."

"Wait!" Cyrus nearly choked on a mouthful of stew. "You mean you actually believe me?"

Monroe paused. "I do. This dracolich, from what I heard, engaged Marduk in the city and several other gods, but didn't kill any of them. It doesn't sound like the dragon was trying to kill gods, unless he went to all that trouble to kill Thoth specifically. But what would he have to gain from that? The Tomb Lords, on the other hand, have a clear motive. The chaos of the dragon's incursion would have given them the opportunity. And some of them are among the most powerful wielders of darker, unholy powers. It wouldn't surprise me if they had the means to kill a god of their choosing as well."

It was the first time someone had heard Cyrus's story and believed him. For an entire month, he'd been stuck with the knowledge of what had truly happened to Thoth, and unable to share or reveal it to anyone. He had been truly alone.

"I think...and I can't prove it, but...I think the dragon was actually a distraction." Cyrus remembered hearing about the Philosopher's Stone, and how it had been on display in the college but was stolen after the events of the tournament. "I think the dragon was working with someone who stole the Philosopher's Stone from the college. That would explain why the dracolich didn't seem to want anything other than to cause chaos and fight gods in the middle of the street. The city gates were forced open to allow people to escape from the attack. Perfect for someone to sneak out with the stone."

"The college had the Philosopher's Stone in their possession?" Doctor Monroe had clearly lost interest in the dragon. "Did they...did they at least learn anything from it before it was lost?"

Cyrus thought for a moment. "They might have learned not to put things like that on public display."

Monroe sighed. "That stone could have taught us anything. It might have even shown us how to make more philosopher stones."

"I didn't think those were something you could make," Cyrus replied. "The stone was gifted to humanity by Thoth."

"But how did Thoth make the stone?" The doctor's eyes brightened. "He told us some of the details, did you know? The ancient alchemists from long,

long ago. To make a philosopher's stone, you must have no desire to use it for material gain. Of course, no one likes that requirement, so every attempt has been made throughout the ages to find another way of making the stone."

Cyrus had finished his stew and leaned back in his seat. "I had never heard of this. The college never brings it up."

"No, they wouldn't." Monroe shook his head in dismay. "The college doesn't value the old history anymore. They'd rather repeat it than learn from it. Did you know, alchemists were once the only real scientists in the world? And some of the fields of alchemy refined today used to be practiced, if ham-fistedly, several millennia ago?"

Eyes widening, Cyrus shook his head. He'd never heard any of this.

"Every alchemist should know the history of their craft." Doctor Monroe got up and went over to a bookshelf along one wall.

He returned with a thick volume, which he opened and showed to Cyrus. It was written in a language Cyrus couldn't read, but Monroe had made his own notes all over the page. The center featured a humanoid figure with bat-like wings. It had two heads, one male, the other female, with the sun shining behind the male and the moon behind the female. In his notes, the doctor had labeled it a "rebis," and wrote "alleged perfect being" on the side.

"These ancient alchemists thought that this hermaphrodite, a being with all the powers of masculine and feminine energy, would be a perfect being capable of acting as a living philosopher's stone," Monroe explained. "In effect, they tried to create a philosopher's stone by combining elements of the soul. A philosopher's stone made out of people, in effect. They believed that the human soul was the only thing that such a stone could truly be made from, and in a strange way, they might have been partly right."

"It sounds horrifying." Cyrus continued to read the doctor's annotations. One listed something called "putrefaction" and "purification."

"Probably," Monroe agreed. "They may have been right about the ingredients, or at least somewhere in the ballpark, but their methods were completely off the mark. We have no evidence of them actually succeeding in creating such a creature, but it would almost certainly be a human chimera, with two heads constantly at war with each other. In nature, two-headed animals are often Siamese twins, and unless they're human, and sometimes not even then, they are usually not long for this world."

Cyrus studied the page in bewilderment. "How in the Abyss was this supposed to actually work?"

"Well, first, the alchemists were supposed to remove all of the impurities of the two to be joined through the processes of putrefaction and purification," the doctor explained. "The thing is, while those terms usually refer to what happens to a human body after death, the ancient alchemists wanted to apply them to the human soul. They believed that if you could draw the worst, most vile sins of a person's soul, and separate them by pouring them into a new vessel, such as a homunculus, what would remain of the person's soul would only be their virtues."

"A homunculus?" Cyrus looked up from the book. "What is that?"

"Depends on who you ask," the doctor chuckled. "They are either monsters, an alchemist's artificially made servants, ghosts kept in sealed flasks, or the philosopher's stones themselves. The homunculi as vessels were supposed to be artificial humans made in a laboratory, by an alchemist who somehow found a way to create life."

Cyrus frowned. "Alchemy cannot create life. No mage, no matter how skilled, or what school they follow, can create life."

"The ancient alchemists didn't know that," Monroe continued. "Some of them even used to think that you could create life by placing a cow's corpse in a cave overnight."[2]

"You mean a cow already full of bacteria that are decomposing the corpse?" Cyrus snickered. "The secret formula for creating life from inert matter was to put life into it?"

Monroe chuckled. "Yes, well...they didn't know about bacteria then, either. Anyway, some homunculi were meant to be physical beings that either were living philosopher's stones themselves, or could serve as a vessel to pour sins from putrefaction of a rebis philosopher's stone made out of human souls, but

---

[2] This is a process once known as Takwin, a mostly Islamic study of creating life, although the cow thing was originally Greek.

another, radically different type of homunculus was purely smoke; alleged to be a living being made entirely out of gas and ether. They were supposedly made, almost entirely, out of...semen."

Cyrus tried not to picture ancient alchemists trying to mold a living creature out of that. "Why would...what was the thought process behind this?"

"Well, the alchemists a long time ago believed that male sperm actually contained fully formed human beings, and that male human beings of this sort had their own human beings inside of them, and so on, so that one could predict the end of the world if they had a microscope powerful enough to see how many generations were left like this. Some alchemists got it in their head that if they could extract the spirit of one of these "future people" and bring it to life in a flask without a body, the resulting homunculus could then reveal knowledge it knew from the future, things like the Grand Panacea, a mythical elixir of immortality, and, of course, the secret to making your own philosopher's stone. Without following Thoth's selfless method, of course."

"I take it no one ever got that to work, either?" Cyrus rolled his eyes.

"Not really," replied the doctor. "There was a book regarding something called "*The Scrying Ghosts*," which allegedly were seen by several people, but apparently none of them thought to ask them the questions about any of these big mysteries. Or maybe these "ethereal homunculi" weren't really interested in answering them. Just because you pulled someone's undeveloped soul from the future and stuff them in a flask, doesn't mean they're going to cooperate."

"What is the point behind all of this, anyway?" Cyrus asked. "If Thoth's method of making a philosopher's stone is the only way that works, but you must have no desire to use it to make it, why would anyone who has that level of enlightenment bother making one in the first place?"

Monroe blinked. "Isn't it obvious? To share it with others."

A loud and panicked knock on the front door shook both of them from their conversation. The doctor opened the door to a hysterical woman, her son, and an unconscious man that the son had struggled to carry somewhat upright.

"Doctor, help!" The woman begged. "He passed out at work. His friends brought him home, but he won't wake!"

Monroe pointed to Cyrus. "Get him to the operating room, now!"

Cyrus grabbed the man's legs and led the son, who still held the man's shoulders, to the back room and laid him on the operating table. Instinctively, Cyrus checked that every tool the doctor would use was properly sterilized.

"He's had a heart condition for years—"

"I know, Mrs. Kalb. I've worked with his heart before." Doctor Monroe entered the room and pointed to the cabinet where he kept the anesthesia. "Give him one shot, and be ready in case he needs more."

Opening the cabinet and taking out the anesthetic, Cyrus prepared a needle and filled it with heroin. Dipping a clean rag in a flask of alcohol, he sterilized a spot on the unconscious patient's arm and injected it with a controlled dose of opium.

"I've tried multiple treatments with his heart before. There's only one thing left I can do." The doctor went to the icebox and started rummaging through packages inside. "His blood type is B negative." He held up a tan package; it was a bag made of incredibly smooth treated sheepskin. It was probably sterilized both inside and out. The bag contained some sort of lumpy object inside, and was labeled "O negative."

"This will have to do." The doctor went up to the unconscious patient and looked up at Cyrus. "Get them out of here."

The young alchemist ushered Mrs. Kalb and her son out of the room. They didn't need to see what was coming next. He could still hear the sound of the doctor using alchemy to open the man's chest and clear a path to operate on his heart.

"Cyrus, back in here!"

Motioning for the patient's family to stay put, Cyrus ran back into the operating room, where the patient was writhing in pain. A large hole had been made in his chest where the doctor had opened a path to work on his heart, the missing chunk of his chest placed on an aluminum tray to the side. The patient wasn't really waking up, but he was clearly able to feel the doctor working on him.

"He needs more anesthesia." Monroe gesture to the container of heroin. "Give him a half shot. Not too much."

Cyrus prepared another needle and gave the patient a half dose of opium. As he did, he saw the doctor open the tan bag and reveal what the lump was: a freshly preserved heart, that Monroe had been keeping in the icebox.

"Where did you get that?" Cyrus's jaw dropped. Horrifying thoughts of what the doctor might have done to get a spare heart, or how many other organs were kept in the icebox, filled his head.

"I'll explain after the surgery." Monroe pointed to the man's chest. "I need you to sever his arteries and remove his heart. It'll make it easier for me to attach the new one."

Cyrus nodded. Clapping his hands, he commanded the tissue to release its bonds on the man's heart, which already was beating irregularly. He removed the severed heart from the body while the doctor attached the new heart to his arteries. Cyrus could see blood flowing into the new heart, but it didn't beat.

Doctor Monroe put his hands together, and a spark of electricity flowed between his fingers. He put his palms on the man and zapped his chest with electricity. The new heart started beating, and his breathing returned to normal. As he appeared to stabilize, the doctor reattached the missing chunk of flesh from his chest with alchemy and sealed up the wound.

"Looks like he's going to be okay." The doctor washed his hands in the sink. "Let's get cleaned up, then let his family know."

Monroe told the woman that her husband would be okay. He needed to stay home from work for the next week, but afterwards, he should make a full recovery. When they had left, he returned to the operating room, where Cyrus had just finished cleaning up.

"So...where did you get a spare heart?" Cyrus finally asked.

"Look inside the icebox," Monroe instructed. "Tell me what you see."

Cyrus opened the box. Inside were packages sorted by blood type, with some labeled "kidneys," "livers," and "hearts."

"By the gods!" Cyrus stepped away from the box of spare parts. "Where did you get all of these?"

"Do you know that what we just did to save that man's life is technically illegal?" The doctor asked. "Have you read the prohibition act on human chimeras?"

"Well, yes," Cyrus remembered reading the legislative act in class. "But all transplants are illegal on paper. The person receiving the transplant has the donor's DNA inside of them. That makes them a chimera. Human mixed with another human—"

"But these organs didn't come from a human," Monroe interjected. "Do you know why I keep a herd of swine outside? They aren't just there to dispose of medical waste."

"You..." Realization struck Cyrus like a bolt of lightning. "You mean we just put a *pig's heart* inside that man? Are you— why would you—"

"Because he was dying," Monroe replied. "And now he will live. He will never know that the donor for his new heart wasn't human. I have perfected this process; he will suffer no side effects."

"You mean he isn't going to grow a snout and a curly tail from this?" Cyrus asked. "How can you be so sure? You implanted pig DNA into that man."

"When a person receives a transplant from a human, do they mutate to resemble their donor?" Monroe countered. "It doesn't work that way. The pig's heart will serve as a perfect substitute for the original. He'll never know."

"But..." Cyrus looked for another reason why this was wrong, but he couldn't find one. "Why are we hiding it from him?"

"Most people in the empire think pigs are unclean animals," Monroe explained. "Not suitable for eating, or even getting too close to. Understandable, given their role as garbage disposals and getting rid of filth, but in this case, it is unnecessary. I guarantee you that Mr. Kalb and his family are better off not knowing about this. He's alive, and without my work, he wouldn't be. Isn't that what matters?"

Cyrus chewed on the doctor's words for a moment. "...Yes. Thoth once told me that each human life was precious. I...there is no good reason *not* to use a pig's heart. Not when the alternative would be to kill another human."

Monroe patted Cyrus on the back and smiled. "You understand. Most people don't. They can't let go of stupid, silly sentimentalities. It's the same reason they turned on you for winning your tournament. It should have been seen as an accomplishment, in which you had rightfully achieved a goal for which you worked hard and tried your best, but instead they focused on the fact that your last opponent was a girl. A girl who had previously beaten her other opponents to reach the final match, and had a pair of elementals to fight you with; a three-on-one fight. Why should the public decide what is right or wrong, when they base their decisions on things as trivial as old sex stereotypes? Who are the masses to stand in the way of greatness, progress, achievement? And to what end? What does it benefit the world to let their prejudices dictate anything?"

Cyrus didn't know what to say. He remembered what Thoth told him about the weapons used to strike him down; that they were infused with envy, and that envy was poison to logic and reason. He couldn't shake the feeling that Doctor Monroe was right.

13

A Brief Examination

NAMID

"So, we've got two days left before our visitation ends," Amri looked through details of some of the projects that the Grand Spire University of Thaumaturgy had available. "Did anything catch your eye?"

Namid rubbed sleep from her eyes and squinted in the early morning light. Well, ten o' clock in the morning light, but that was early for her on a Saturday. "Hand me that list again," She mumbled.

Amri handed his sister the brochure, and she sat up to look it over. "There's not much on a Saturday," she noticed. "But there's something here about telepathy. Something about identifying skillsets and amplifying them. Don't see anything else that looks worthwhile."

"Alright," Amri looked at the program. "Wait, that starts in two hours. What were you going to do until then?"

In response, Namid tucked herself back under the sheets. "Wake me in an hour."

A nap, a shower, and a short brunch later, Amri and Namid wandered into a laboratory for telepathy research on the campus. The room wasn't too different from a large classroom, but with a large open space and various tools used for experiments. A brass armchair with purple velvet padding sat in the middle.

"Oh, hello." A woman with gold-rimmed glasses eyed the pair as they

A BRIEF EXAMINATION

walked into the room. "I am Professor Sanchez. Can I help you?"

"Could we take a look at your work?" Amri held up the brochure, showing the telepathy page.

"Of course," she smiled and gestured to the armchair.

Namid took a seat in the chair and peered at the tools lining the wall. "So, what is it you do, exactly?"

"I am going to connect to your nervous system," the professor washed her hands and dabbed rubbing alcohol on Namid's forehead. "And then I'm going to tell you which parts of your brain see the most activity." She pointed to a large chart on a scroll hanging on a chalkboard. "Bring that over here," she said to Amri.

Amri pulled the chart in front Professor Sanchez. "We've been working for decades to map out the human brain and identify which parts are connected to certain skills." She gestured to the chart, which showed a cross-section view of the human brain with a variety of labels. Namid wasn't familiar enough with the Spiran written language to read them.

"Alright, set the chart over here," the professor pointed to where she could see it while working. "And bring me that packet of papers over there."

Amri did as instructed and brought her a stack of papers, the first of which had some kind of inkblot that didn't look entirely random.

"Alright, Amri, I want you to show your sister some cards, and Namid, I want you to say what you think the picture looks like to you." Sanchez put her fingers on Namid's head. "I'll be reading your brain activity as you respond to each image."

Amri drew a card and showed Namid the picture. "Here's card number 1."

Namid looked at the card. "It's a snarling, hungry wolf."

The professor blinked. "Huh. Interesting. Can you draw another card?"

"This says 'number 6.'" Amri glanced at the back of the card. "Are these out of order?"

"They might be," Sanchez replied. "It won't affect the study."

"It looks like a dead animal hide," Namid examined the middle of the picture. "Something split it down the middle."

"Oh," Sanchez cocked an eyebrow. "That's…a little more common. Next card?"

"Number 2," Amri held up the new card. This one was a little different. There were red shapes in addition to the black shapes.

"Two men giving each other high fives," Namid said.

"Ok, good." The professor smiled. "Very...wait, you're certain you see people?"

"Yes." Namid tried to ignore the concerned tone in the professor's voice. "Uh, next card?"

Amri drew another card. "This is number 3."

"Two bald women reaching into a large pot of money to grab some of it." Namid replied.

"Women..." the professor clicked her teeth. "Are you sure you don't see a tool, like a pair of brushes, or some garden implements? Maybe a pair of gloves?"

"No, they look like women," Namid reaffirmed. "Except without hair."

"Right..." the professor took her hand off of Namid's forehead. "Well, your neocortex gets a lot of activity. That's the part of the brain associated with visual-spatial function and analysis. Yours is unusually large for a young woman, but not in any extreme way. The same can be said for your left and right frontal areas. These are great for a career as a sorcerer, but..." she glanced at the inkblot picture Amri was still holding. "The part of your brain that gets the most activity when you see images of people isn't your communication or socializing areas. It's the part associated with tool use."

"What?" Namid raised an eyebrow. "What does that mean?"

"It means you see people the same way normal people see a hammer and a saw," the professor examined Namid coldly. "Except your brother, strangely enough. That's probably a good thing. Here, let me demonstrate a healthy response. Amri, would you please switch places with your sister?"

Amri took a seat and the professor put her fingertips on his forehead. Namid drew a card and showed him the inkblot.

"Card number 4," Namid held it up for Amri to see.

"It's a woman in a flowing dress standing over me," Amri replied.

Professor Sanchez paused. "That's not a normal...let's try another card."

A BRIEF EXAMINATION

Namid held up another image. "This is number seven."

"Uh...I'm not really sure what to say it looks like. A cloud, kind of?" Amri squinted at the image. "A chaotic, sometimes stormy cloud, that's occasionally peaceful?"

"A cloud?" The professor tilted her head with a pained expression. Things were clearly not going according to her plan. "Next card?"

"Number 5." Namid held up the last card.

"It looks like an open hand coming in for a strike," Amri replied. "But it's mirrored. There's a hand coming to land a blow on either side."

Professor Sanchez sighed. "Okay, bad example of a healthy brain." She turned to Amri. "You have an overdeveloped fight-or-flight response, you know that? With odd triggers."

Amri rubbed his forehead where the professor had connected to his brain. "Is that bad?"

"It's not the fight-or-flight response itself that's bad, it's whatever caused you to end up like that in the first place." The professor gathered her cards and looked through several notes. "Your triggers tend to be feminine. You had strong responses to cards associated with femininity, responses that connected women to violent acts of aggression."

"Is that not normal?" Amri looked at Namid for help.

Namid shrugged. "I don't know. Why are you asking me?"

"It isn't," Professor Sanchez replied. "Women rarely show aggression in the form of violence. There isn't enough research as to why, but female aggression tends to be more indirect, like reputational damage or even verbal abuse. The same things that would make a man angry enough to get physically violent usually don't manifest the same way in women."

A thought wormed its way through Namid's mind. "Is that because women are afraid the person they hit might hit back harder?"

"Possibly," the professor flipped through pages in a notebook. "In domestic abuse cases, an abusive husband is more likely to use violence all the time, but women are more likely to use physical abuse against children and other forms on their husbands. If they do get physical with their husbands, they're more likely to grab a weapon. What bothers me more, however, is your sister displaying some of the signs of an antisocial personality disorder."

Namid straightened her back and locked eyes with the professor. "What is that, exactly?"

"A narcissist, sociopath, or psychopath," Sanchez explained. "It's impossible to tell, because you don't show all of the signs of any one of them."

"Oh really," Namid rolled her eyes. "And what symptoms do I show?"

"You lack empathy," the professor replied. "Not to the point of having none at all, but nowhere near a healthy human being. You see people as if they were tools, seem to view the world in a sense of 'kill or be killed,' and if I were to plot out what I read from your brain activity, it would probably show that you have little to no idea of what you *should* do, and are ruled almost entirely by your sense of what you *need* to do, with a bit of room for things you *want* to do."

"What's the difference between 'should' and 'need?'" Namid asked.

The professor's jaw slackened in shock. "...that...might have been the best possible illustration of what I'm talking about." She shook her head. "Still, it's highly unlikely you have an antisocial personality disorder. They're almost unheard of in girls and young women."

Amri raised an eyebrow. "Why is that?"

"One of the defining characteristics of antisocial personality disorders is aggression, especially narcissism and psychopathy, and women rarely display the violent personality traits that we associate with these disorders." The professor cleared her throat. "In all of our studies, women make up only ten percent of persons with narcissism, two percent of psychopaths, and a tiny minority of sociopaths."

Amri frowned. "But didn't you just say that women don't normally display aggression through acts of violence? What would happen if you included those other kinds of aggression in your studies?"

"Uh..." Professor Sanchez froze. "Under the orders of Princess Elvia Valiente, and in the interest of not having our funding cut, we do not ask questions like that."

"Uh-huh." Namid nodded. "Figures."

Later, with their final day at Grand Spire's university nearing its end, the siblings walked to the campus dining hall for their last dinner before going home tomorrow. Namid walked with her arms folded behind her head and a satisfied smile on her face.

"Hey, are you at all worried about that telepathy thing?" Amri walked beside his sister with his back hunched and arms by his sides. "Any of those results bother you?"

"Not really," Namid shrugged. "You can't trust someone who says 'we don't ask questions that upset our royalty' when it comes to stuff like that."

"But..." Amri paused. "What about that whole 'no sense of what you should do' thing?"

"Yeah, probably because I have a firm sense of what I need to do." Namid smirked. "There's no real difference. It's just your state of mind."

"How can you say that?" Amri asked. "What about morals? You don't *need* to do the right thing, but you still should."

"Amri, morals are a bunch of social rules made up by various authority figures to get you to behave and do what they want. You *need* to follow them, so you don't go to jail or get punished. And when there isn't a law involved, you still *need* to do what society says, or you'll get judged by public opinion."

"What about when there's no one around?" Amri asked. "What if there's no one who can judge you, because they can't see you?"

"Then anything goes," Namid replied. "Think of the princess for a moment. She's so powerful in this country that she can do whatever she wants. She doesn't need to follow social mores about treating guests well, or being polite. No one can punish her, or even judge her. If people so much as spread any bad rumors about her, she can have them thrown in jail. That's why you shouldn't put so much stock in these rules; they aren't made by some reliable, infallible judge. They're made by people in power who want to stay that way."

"So you're just going to follow the rules when people are watching, and ignore them when people aren't?" Amri asked.

"Not *just* that." Namid frowned. "Remember the Combat Arena? How my last fight ended?"

"Yeah," Amri nodded. "You impaled your opponent."

"Right, but I won the fight." Namid finally lowered her arms from behind her head. "And even though I followed all the rules of the match as they were written, I still had to withdraw from the competition, and we still ended up coming here instead of an internship. Sometimes, the people who set the rules don't follow them, and will still seek to punish you even when you obey them to the letter. Sometimes, following the rules of society isn't enough. Now, let's get some food. We aren't going to get shellfish like this back in Hadesh."

14

Messaging the Divine

AQUILA

When a woman says that her face is "so beautiful it's a curse," she's usually bragging in a way that makes her sound humble. When a thief says it, she's telling the truth. Unless they're trying to distract their target so they can pick his pockets, a thief wants to go about her business unnoticed. Beautiful women rarely go anywhere unnoticed. Hence, the curse.

Aquila had one of those faces that looked good with little effort. Not necessarily like a theatre starlet or a model for an artist, but each morning, she needed only a shower with no makeup to look her best. Some of this was due to the exercise she got from her job, some was due to the fact that the alternative to regular bathing was walking around with a noticeable stench, which didn't help to stay out of sight. And some was due to her parentage and upbringing.

To compensate for this, Aquila kept a large collection of disguises that she could swap out to avoid recognition. Her room contained a chair and dresser with a mirror along the back. The dresser had a cabinet for different wigs, some of which weren't even natural hair colors, such as pink, and a makeup kit she could use to make a different face each day. But the true masterpiece of her disguises was a pegboard featuring a wide variety of clip-on nose rings.

Aquila was too squeamish to actually get her nose pierced, but the clip-on rings gave her the ability to wear one in public and, if she needed to change her disguise quickly, remove the ring and have a remarkably different face in seconds. The key was in how ugly or disturbing the rings actually were; she had one that featured a pair of round metal balls that would hang from her nostrils like an extremely visible pair of boogers. Wear a ring like that, and people would remember the nose ring and nothing else about your face. Perfect for someone who wants to slip through crowds incognito.

At the moment, Aquila was trying on a thick, stainless steel, clip-on ring like the kind farmers would use to control cows. Then she heard a bony hand knock on the steel door of her quarters.

Putting away the clip-on, the thief got up from her chair and opened the door to confront the skeleton behind it. "Something went wrong?"

"Not at first," Daurgo's voice projected from the skeleton like an echo of the dragon's speech. "Everything went fine going into the underworld and even on my way out, but once I reached the surface, I found an entire pantheon of gods waiting for me."

Aquila rested her hand on her hip and tilted her head. "You sound surprised. What did you think was going to happen after your stunt at the Grand Wizard Tournament?"

"Oh, I knew the risks, make no mistake. But this is only a temporary setback. My skull was able to return to my phylactery, and in time, my body will regenerate." The skeleton gestured to itself. "Unfortunately, that leaves me with little other than whatever puppets I already have setup to work with until I grow a new body, and that will take a few months. After which, I'll have to travel all the way from my soul's hiding place back here, where the Egyptian gods will likely be waiting for me."

"Wait, Egyptian gods?" Aquila blinked. "Why them? It was Marduk you turned into a chew-wad in the wizards' arena. Why are the Egyptian gods so keen on hunting you down?"

"They think I killed Thoth, their god of knowledge, alchemy, reason, etc." The skeleton gestured for Aquila to follow him. "Funny; I didn't even know he was dead. I will admit that I may have killed a god or two by accident in the past, especially when I still thought that was an accomplishment, but I didn't bring any weapons to that fight that could have slain an immortal. Funny you should mention Marduk, he actually showed up to join the Egyptian gods, and he believed I killed Thoth as well. I thought he was able to see everything, or something to that extent."

"Well, he can be fooled," Aquila interjected.

The skeleton paused. "What? How does that work, and how would you know?"

"There's an old myth." Aquila wracked her brain for memories of her school days. "Nergal, the god of storms and plagues, told Marduk that his clothes were shabby, and that no one would respect a king so poorly dressed. Marduk replied that he couldn't leave Babylon unattended to go get new robes, so Nergal offered to watch the city for him while the king went to a tailor. Then Nergal trashed the city with storms, and the other gods had to get involved. Point is, Marduk can be distracted, at least if the distraction starts with something true, like the fact that he needed new clothes. And if he's distracted, he can be tricked."

Daurgo paused, his skeletal eyeholes clearly examining Aquila closely. "I never knew you'd know about older, more obscure myths than me. I do a lot of research before engaging potential adversaries. How did you know all of this?"

"Oh, well..." Aquila averted her eyes and scratched the back of her head. "I had a very...extensive education growing up."

"Hm," the lich seemed to drop the subject at that, but it was obvious he knew there was more Aquila wasn't telling. Well, too bad. He had his secrets, she had hers. He'd kept his species hidden from her for almost a year. He could stand not knowing where she got her schooling.

Shambling like a marionette, Daurgo's puppet skeleton entered the main command bridge of his fortress and sat at a large desk with a typewriter.

"So, what are you going to do?" Aquila asked.

"Isn't it obvious?" The skeleton took out a sheet of paper and began typing. "I'm going to write the Egyptian gods a strongly worded letter."

"What?" Aquila gaped as the skeleton typed. "You're not serious."

"I'm deadly serious," the skeleton continued. "And very dead, which is why as soon as I'm done, you're going to help me deliver it."

A day later, the thief found herself wandering the streets of Hadesh next to a cloaked skeleton in a bronze mask and thick black gloves, trying to figure out where in the city she was supposed to deliver a letter to an entire pantheon of gods. The temple district made the most sense, but which temple? Should she ask a priest? She didn't really want to be associated with whatever Daurgo wrote; some gods had a nasty habit of shooting the messenger.

When Aquila first started working with Daurgo, she knew he was a necromancer, but was under the impression that he was human. He then told her last year that he was a lich, but she had always assumed he was a human lich. She only learned he was a dracolich just before his attack on the wizards' arena. Her gut reaction to learning that her boss wasn't even remotely human was to finish the job and then seek new employment as soon as possible.

Except…Daurgo's money was good. And the work was the right mix of exciting and achievable for her. And she got her own room on Daurgo's fortress while working for him. And there was something to be said, for a young woman working in the criminal underworld, to having an employer who wasn't the least bit interested in sleeping with human women.

"Remind me again why I'm delivering a letter if you're coming too?" Aquila whispered to the skeleton. "I have no idea how to do this."

"I'm dead," the lich replied. "My soul is tucked away in a jar, and my real body can't pass for human in one of your kind's cities. In order to mail the letter, you need a soul, or at least, you need your real body tethered to your soul. That's a must in order to send offerings to the gods."

"Ah, so it's my soul you need." Aquila looked around the temple district. "How in Peppi's unhinged jaws are we supposed to mail a letter to the Egyptian gods without drawing more attention to ourselves?"

"You draw quite a bit of attention just as you are."

Aquila looked over her shoulder and saw a tall man with a black beard in sausage curls, wearing what appeared to be a jasper-green suit made of fish scales and a hat that looked almost like he was wearing a fish on his head, the mouth opened upon his crown like it had tried to swallow his scalp. Looks wise, he was a handsome man, but there was something…off about him. Aquila did not want to be in a room with this guy without adult supervision.

"A girl like you probably gets eyes on her all the time," the fishy man grinned.

Aquila raised an eyebrow. "Right, and you are?"

"Why, where are my manners?" The man beamed. "I am Enki, god of intelligence, crafts, seas, lakes, male fertility, and magic!" He stroked his beard with a devilish smile. "And also mischief. From time to time. Perhaps you've come seeking a boon?"

Aquila tried not to roll her eyes. "Great, look I need to deliver a letter–"

"Wait, you're actually here." Daurgo examined the god. "I see you too. You're not just a psychic projection that my associate sees; you're actually standing on the steps of your own temple, shilling your own worship. Have you nothing better to do?"

"Honestly?" Enki shrugged. "There's no major storms, we're entering the dry season, and fish farming is taking my job away as commercial fishing becomes more industrialized. My main job now is teaching people sorcery, and they've just gone into their off-season. So no, I have nothing better to do then campaign for more believers."

Aquila stepped towards Enki. "Would you be interested in helping us deliver a letter?"

"Keep your distance." Daurgo's skeleton placed a robed arm between Aquila and the god. "He's from a different pantheon," he whispered to Aquila, before turning back to Enki and wagging a finger on his other gloved hand, he pointed at Enki's fish hat and scaly suit. "And I know you're a pervert under that animal getup."

Mortified that he would be so rude to a literal god, Aquila gasped. "I am so sorry! My associate is incredibly rude–"

"No, no." Enki grinned sheepishly. "He's right. But if you're looking for help with mailing letters, all rivers and waterways listen to me. For the right offering, I can make sure your mail gets–"

"Thanks, but I don't think that will work." Aquila stepped back from Enki.

"Ah, well…" Enki clearly was scrambling to put together another sales pitch. "I could–"

"Sorry, but we don't have time for this." Aquila walked away from the god and headed for the Egyptian temples. Once they were away from Enki, she turned to Daurgo. "Were the gods always so...pushy?"

"No." Daurgo replied. "They used to be more distant, more...mysterious. They liked to keep their hands off of mortal lives whenever possible. But ever since they discovered they could be forgotten, and that they need mortals as much, if not more, than mortals need them, they've had to adopt new tactics. Now, many of them are constantly shilling, trying to garner worship and support so they won't lose their powers. My soul isn't even here, and I was able to see him; that means he didn't even check to see if the people he was pandering to could actually give him the worship he desires."

Aquila looked up at a temple to Horus and gritted her teeth. "Okay, how do we do this without exposing ourselves?"

"This isn't just about sending the gods a letter; it's about sending a message. We need to let the gods know just how *not*-omniscient they really are by slipping something right under their noses." Daurgo pointed at a priestess trying to convince people about the important protections that Horus offered.

"Horus is always watching, and his eye can be looking out for you, too, if you ask." The young priestess made a gesture with her arms. "He offers protections from many illnesses, of the flesh, the mind, and the spirit."

"Okay, here's the deal," Daurgo pointed at the priestess. "We need to convince that rube that the letter you have contains something you could sacrifice to Horus. Perhaps a paycheck? A will and testament from a wealthy family member? What kind of important documents might you have that'd be a sacrifice to give up?"

"I might have an idea." Aquila ran her plan by Daurgo.

"All of this for a deed to a pasture?" Daurgo yelled loudly, ensuring the priestess heard.

"You don't understand!" Aquila protested. "This pasture has been in my family for generations! I grew up on that land, held celebrations with calves fattened off those fields, met the man I thought was the love of my life at a party. The land is precious to me!"

"The man you thought was the love of your life?" Daurgo scoffed. "He left you at the altar for some trollop from the village! You call that love?"

Aquila glanced at the priestess, who was completely bewildered by their display. "He held me by the hand, promised me the world, and made me feel things you'll never understand!"

"Ha!" Daurgo's skeleton held its gloves up to the mouth of its bronze mask. "FAAAYYKE!"

"It was love!" Aquila went on. "And now my heart is ruined! Now that I know what broken, empty promises are, my innocence is tarnished!"

"Oh, no!" Daurgo turned to several onlookers. "Her poor, precious ignorance!"

"My unsoiled idealism!"

"Her childish naivete!"

"My beautiful dreams!"

"Her complete lack of anything resembling common sense!"

Aquila gritted her teeth. "My feelings. My feelings, dammit!"

"Um, excuse me," the priestess interrupted. "Is there a reason you're here, having this conversation...in public?"

"Well, if you're *that* nosy," Daurgo scoffed. "Being that we're already here, my fiancé just received a plot of land as inheritance from her recently departed grandfather. A pasture where she apparently has some fanciful memories of men who are most certainly *not* her fiancé. I want her to be rid of the thing. Give it to the gods, to bless our union, but she won't let it go."

"You don't know the memories of a young girl!" Aquila turned to the priestess. "You understand, don't you?

"Uh..." the priestess looked incredibly uncomfortable. "I'm not sure if I'm the best person to settle this."

"Look," Daurgo's robed puppet stepped up next to the priestess and Aquila. "I know the land has a lot of history with you, but I want to build a new history, and that means letting go of the old. I'm asking for a demonstration of your commitment to go down this road with me." Daurgo extended his gloved hand towards Aquila. "Will you let it go for me?"

"Oh, I suppose you're right." Aquila turned to the priestess and handed her the envelope. "Give this to the gods, and ask them to bless our new life together."

"Uh..." the priestess took the envelope. "Certainly. I can do that. Deeds are...unorthodox offerings, but I should be able to toss this into the offering brazier and the gods will receive your devotion. Many blessings on...the two of you."

The pretend couple bowed and walked away from the priestess, who seemed relieved that they were going and grateful for such a large offering.

"As long as the priestess believed that you did, in fact, give her the deed to a large plot of land to sacrifice, the letter should be delivered as planned," Daurgo turned to Aquila once they were out of earshot. "You're certain that she bought it?"

"Oh, trust me," Aquila smirked. "That girl wouldn't have noticed if I'd picked her pocket."

"Please tell me you didn't actually pickpocket the priestess while we were trying to convince her that we were making a charitable offering."

"No, don't worry." Aquila held up her palms. "I don't steal from gods, their clergy, or their temples. They tend to retaliate to things like that, especially when the god in question is usually symbolized by an ever-watchful eye."

"We just tricked that ever-watchful god into accepting a letter from his enemy," Daurgo countered. "Assuming things went according to plan, you just helped me scam a god."

Aquila smiled. That was another thing about working with Daurgo. From stealing the Philosopher's Stone from the College of Alchemy, relieving Tomb Lords of their ancient, irreplaceable books, and now conning the gods themselves, she was quickly working her way up to becoming the greatest thief in the world.

15

Pryomania

EPHORAH

"So, let me get this straight," Colonel Strauss of the Salamanders looked at Ephorah and the remaining mercenaries from the previous Hisham fight. Their commanding officer had ordered a full retreat and got out before the Greymarch could overwhelm them; protocol was to return to the main force and report to the Colonel. "You believe that the Hisham lured us here and drew the attention of the Greymarch, all on purpose, so that they could get us to fight?"

"That's about right," the battlewagon engineer replied.

"Do we have any idea what reason they would have for doing this?" The colonel asked.

"Could be anything," the battlewagon driver said. "Maybe they think of us both as enemies, and wanted us to fight each other. The Hisham aren't mindless monsters; they're as smart as people. They can scheme, and they might even know our company are the ones who are usually called to deal with them. Maybe they want to thin our numbers, or maybe it's a coincidence. They might want the nearby hamlets destroyed, but they don't want to risk their own lives to do it, so they're getting the Greymarch to do their dirty work."

Ephorah raised her hand. "Why would creatures who can regenerate from anything except fire worry about being killed by civilians who don't carry flamethrowers?"

"Maybe they don't think they can get the entire area sacked in one night," the engineer answered. "The sun will burn them, too."

Colonel Strauss shook his head. "This is just great. I can't believe they caught us so unprepared. Four men, forced to choose between suicide and joining the Greymarch. I've sent word to Hadesh to send us reinforcements. They'll likely be able to dispatch a few vehicles by this afternoon. Air support might take longer, depending on what's available."

The sun was only just now rising. Ephorah thought back to how the Greymarchers had attacked her hometown of Aklagos, and how quickly they moved. They might not have until sunrise to wait for reinforcements.

"We have to evacuate as many civilians as possible," the colonel continued. "In the daylight, the Hisham will have retreated underground. They won't be able to give the Greymarch any more direction in the light, so if we can keep them distracted, we might be able to buy the locals some time." He pointed at the engineer and driver. "Take your battlewagon and perform the 'Loud Escapee.'"

The engineer smiled. "Yes, sir."

"Loud Escapee?" Ephorah asked.

"Don't worry," the driver winked. "We'll show you."

Ephorah followed the driver and engineer back to the battlewagon. The engineer stoked up the wagon's furnace and filled it with coal, while the driver held the brakes down until the engineer could load the rest of the wagon with barrels of gunpowder. Once the vehicle was filled with powder and fueled to go for a while, the driver and engineer hopped off and let it start rolling out into the plains, in the direction that the Hisham had been earlier that night.

"When that thing runs out of fuel, those barrels are set to go off," the driver explained. "Should be enough to draw the attention of any Greymarchers, and by that point the wagon will be far away from the nearby village."

Ephorah watched the wagon drive off full of fuel and explosives. "Aren't those wagons expensive?"

"Yeah, but we'll be paid handsomely for this mission." The driver waved the wagon off like he was saying goodbye to an old friend. "We were only paid originally to deal with the Hisham, and normally wouldn't get paid to deal with additional problems, but we've got a deal with the government; a sort of, everlasting agreement. If the Greymarch show up, and we're around to deal with it, if we fight, we get paid. Extra, if need be. Now, come with us, we've got to prepare."

The Salamanders spent the morning in two teams: one to make fortifications around the nearby village, and one to get civilians to evacuate. The fortification team grabbed shovels and started digging holes in the ground where the Greymarch was expected to approach. The soldiers explained that because the Greymarchers were little more than mindless zombies, something as trivial as a hole ten centimeters deep would cause them to trip and fall, thereby slowing them down, and possibly even cause the marchers behind them to stumble. This might not seem like much, but it would allow the mercenaries extra time to shoot as many of them as they tried to attack.

Ephorah was primarily assigned to the evacuation team. Her job was simply to go to each house she could find and instruct people to flee.

Knocking on a door, she waited on a house porch. The owner, a middle-aged woman, opened the door and frowned at the sight of Ephorah. Ephorah wasn't sure if this was because the woman was grumpy, didn't like company, or didn't like Empyrians. She tried to ignore it and repeated the lines Colonel Strauss had given her.

"Ma'am, I am with the Salamanders mercenary company," Ephorah began. "We have reason to believe that the Greymarch are approaching this town. We have setup an evacuation route, and would ask that you quickly gather your friends and family and follow the evacuation route to safety. This is just a precaution. You are not–"

"The Greymarch?" The woman shrieked. "Here? How?"

"–Ma'am, that's not…we do not have all the details on how the Greymarch would have come here, we only have reason to believe that they are on their way."

"Idiots," the woman spat. "Incompetent buffoons. Isn't this what you're paid to do? To keep us safe from monsters? You were hired to deal with the Hisham, and somehow, you've dragged the Greymarch into this!"

Idiots. A common stereotype the Borealans had made about the Empyrians was that they were idiots. Ephorah wanted to give this woman a piece of her mind, but she had a job to finish. "If you would just follow the evacuation route—"

"I heard you, I heard you." The woman shook her head. "I don't know why I'm supposed to trust that your 'evacuation route' is supposed to help when you've shown nothing but incompetence so far."

"—Ma'am, you are not required to follow the evacuation protocol," Ephorah tried to hold back a snicker. "We can't force you. If you'd like to stay here—"

"Don't talk back to me, you spoiled brat!" The woman snapped. "I'm not going to stay here with idiots *and* Greymarchers!"

"Thank you, ma'am," Ephorah bowed to hide the smirk growing on her face. "I'll be off, then."

A few more houses with varying degrees of hostility later, and Ephorah returned to the other Salamanders to report in to Colonel Strauss.

"Nicely done." The Colonel oversaw several flamethrowers the infantrymen were preparing for the upcoming fight. "You can check on the fortification team, see if your elemental can help. Turning the ground into mud might make the marchers even slower.

Ephorah went out to the field, summoned Aquaria, and ordered her to help the soldiers make the ground harder for the Greyrmarchers to traverse. Then she turned to one of the other soldiers who was taking a break from digging holes to rest.

"Hey," she asked. "Have the Hisham ever spoken before?"

"Hm?" He had leaned over against his shovel to relax, but looked up to address Ephorah. "The Hisham? I don't think so. I've never heard of them talking before. Doesn't mean they can't, though."

"One of them spoke to me last night," Ephorah tried to remember the voice she'd heard. "Well, at least one of them. Maybe more."

"Huh," the soldier closed his eyes for a moment. "I hate to say it, but you might be the first person to hear them speak and live to tell about it. At least, first I've heard of."

"The battlewagon had three other people in it. The engineer, the driver, and another soldier." Ephorah went on. "I don't think any of them heard the

Hisham."

"Well..." the soldier eyed Ephorah and was clearly being careful about his next words. "Legend has it that the Hisham were some noble Empyrian family. Maybe only Empyrians can hear them. Or maybe the Hisham only let people they want to hear them."

"I think...they did say something about me being one of them." Ephorah wasn't sure how that made her feel. One would think that a bunch of hideous monsters recognizing you as one of their own would make you feel insulted, but...there was something almost wholesome about it. "Except, then they said I was impure, and tried to kill me. That wasn't so fun."

"Hmm," the soldier scratched his chin. "Any idea if you might have Empyrian royalty in your family tree? Maybe some distant relative of the Hisham tribe?"

"I don't know." Ephorah didn't mind the possibility of being Empyrian royalty, but it didn't explain why the monsters had called her "impure."

After thoroughly ensuring that the ground surrounding the local area would be difficult for the Greymarch to cross, the Salamanders rejoined Colonel Strauss to finalize their plan as reinforcements finally arrived, including a pair of battlewagons, a demolisher tank, and some kind of artillery tank.

Ephorah had heard of bulldozers before; they were large, steam-engine-driven machines with big steel scoops to push mounds of dirt and even rocks out of the way. The demolisher tank was like someone had taken the scoop of a bulldozer and mounted it onto a battle tank. The rest of the vehicle was an armored personnel carrier. Two flamethrowers larger than a man could carry were mounted on either side to deal with attackers from the flanks, while two smaller flamethrowers poked out from two small holes in the bulldozer scoop, as if designed to ignite enemies caught in the blade in addition to shoving them out of the way. Finally, a much larger flamethrower sat on a turret towards the front-center of the tank.

"Do you guys ever try using weapons other than flamethrowers and fire-bombs?" Ephorah asked a vehicle engineer.

"Never," he shook his head. "You see that other one? The one with the artillery gun? That's called a volcano mortar. It launches globes of napalm mixed with propellant, coating the ground in liquid flame. It doesn't just burn our enemies; it also ignites the ground and keeps it burning for a while, making a wall of flame the Greymarch can't cross."

"Uh-huh." Ephorah eyed the mortar tank. "And I see you have a flamethrower on each side of it for shooting anything that gets too close?"

"Well, of course." The engineer beamed. "We've gotta have something to deal with enemies at close range. We're not silly. It's like our founder, Jairus Fierstien once said when he gave us our motto: 'when it comes to monsters, everything burns.'"

"Yeah..." Ephorah didn't want to investigate that too much. "It's a good thing the Salamanders only fight monsters."

"Speaking of which," the engineer pointed at the battlewagons. "Those two aren't for fighting. They're for evacuating anyone who hasn't already left by nightfall. I don't know who will be left when the time comes, but if we need to, we'll save a spot for you on one of those wagons. I guarantee the folks in Hadesh had no intention of sending you out here to fight the Greymarch."

"...We can talk with the colonel when the time comes." Ephorah couldn't explain why, but for some reason, she had no desire to leave. She knew it was dangerous, and she knew fighting wouldn't benefit her, personally. The Greymarch may have destroyed her old home, but she didn't miss it that much; she had her whole family living in Hadesh, and she wouldn't have been able to attend the Institute of Theurgy and study wizardry if she were still living in Aklagos. And how could you seek revenge on a mob of mindless, tortured souls?

And yet, despite all of that, some part of Ephorah didn't want to leave. Maybe she just didn't want to turn tail and run; she had her faults, but cowardice wasn't one of them. But there was something else; a desire to see this through to the end. Ephorah didn't want to leave until the Greymarch and Hisham were beaten.

Approaching Colonel Strauss, Ephorah overheard him laying out his battleplans to the other mercenaries around a table they'd set up near a local barn.

"We're going to cut off their paths of entry with the mortar. Once we have them narrowed, the demolisher will crush as many of them as possible. The mortar will continue to thin their ranks while the demolisher does its work. We'll need to keep an eye out for the Hisham. They might not be done with us yet, and while the Greymarch have no anti-armor weapons, the Hisham might have another trick to pull." He turned to each mercenary. "I want the evacuation team to start transporting as many people as possible. Now."

The soldiers saluted and scattered to their positions. A few started going to check on anyone who wasn't able to evacuate yet and loading them up into the battlewagon. Colonel Strauss turned to Ephorah.

"If there's room, we'll save you a spot on one of the battlewagons for evacuation," he assured her.

"No." Ephorah shook her head. "If there's room, let me take a spot on one of the vehicles for the fight."

The colonel raised an eyebrow. "I appreciate your bravery, but what are you going to do when the Greymarch show up? You do not need to stay–"

"I have a water elemental," Ephorah replied. "We can keep one of the tanks from overheating. She can also attack Greymarchers without becoming one herself."

"…That's…that would be useful," the colonel admitted. "But are you certain?"

Ephorah didn't speak, but clenched her fist.

The colonel sighed. "To be young again. I hope your courage doesn't get you killed today. Very well, you and I will join the crew of the demolisher. Your elemental will help keep the engines cool. I might even have you fire a turret-mounted flamethrower, depending on how things turn out."

Nearby, a horn sounded from one of the scouts. The Greymarch were on their way.

"Dammit!" The colonel ushered Ephorah towards the demolisher. "I thought we'd have more time! The sun is still out. Get inside the tank, now! The mortar is in position, but we've got to make sure the civilians get away in time."

Ephorah sprinted for the demolisher tank. A thick steel door on the side allowed entrance, and several soldiers inside were surprised to see her climbing into the tank. Before they could speak, she conjured Aquaria out from the Spirit Plane.

"We need to keep this vehicle's engine from overheating." Ephorah pointed to a massive boiler with a number of gauges and other equipment. "At my, or the engineer's command, you will cool down any parts of the machinery needed. If a fire starts *inside* the vehicle, your first priority is to put it out. Got that?"

Aquaria nodded. The tank engineer fired up the boiler to a low burn, getting the engine running but not enough to start moving. Colonel Strauss grabbed a periscope that allowed him to see outside of the tank from above.

"The volcano mortar has flooded the plains with napalm," he reported. "The Greymarchers are storming the plains; some are trying to avoid the flames, but others are sliding into them. Nice work muddying the ground. Now the mortar's aiming for the marchers themselves. This horde isn't too big; we can win this."

"This horde?" Ephorah thought aloud. "Does the Greymarch split into different hordes?"

The colonel didn't answer. "Okay, it's time. Give us some speed!"

The engineer gave the vehicle more fuel while the driver undid the tank's brakes. Ephorah felt the vehicle lurch forward as the tank roared to life. The engineer directed Aquaria to keep an eye on one of the temperature gauges and make sure the heat stayed inside of the engine and the steam turbine without overheating the rest of the vehicle. If the heat ignited the flamethrower fuel tanks, the entire vehicle would burn and kill everyone inside.

Aquaria seemed to get the gist of this and pulled condensation from the water inside the turbine out of the engine to keep it cool. Ephorah tried not to think of what would happen if the flamethrower fuel caught fire. Unfortunately, the only other thing to listen to was the sound of the demolisher ramming into the Greymarchers.

Ephorah couldn't see it, but she could hear the sound of the bulldozer scoop crunching into the marchers as they tried to assault the tank. The men in charge of the flamethrowers that poked out of the scoop enflamed the mindless horde in front, turning the scoop into a crucible of napalm and liquid flame.

The men on the sides of the tank and the turret gunner opened fire as well, and between the smells of napalm, soot and grease from the engine, and the smell of sweaty men in a hot, cramped vehicle, Ephorah got her first whiff of the smell of burnt human flesh.

"Gunners, we've got marchers trying to climb the aft side!" Strauss shouted.

"On it!" The turret gunner turned his weapon around and enflamed every marcher that had scaled the back of the tank and gotten onto the roof.

Aquaria looked up at the roof of the vehicle. "Something's wrong."

"The roof is going to get a little hot," the engineer assured her. "Just keep it cool, and we'll be fine. I'll lower the engine power for a while; we're already in the thick of it."

"No," the elemental panicked. "There's something wrong with the–"

An explosion on the roof of the tank took everyone by surprise. The colonel took his eyes away from the periscope in shock. "What–"

Another explosion shook the tank, this time from the starboard side. A third and fourth hit the port.

"We're immobilized!" The driver shouted. "The treads are blown!"

The colonel pointed at the gunners. "Then we defeat every last one of them here–"

"My fuel's on fire!" One of the gunners panicked. "That last explosion–"

What happened next was a big wet blur for Ephorah. She remembered Aquaria flowing onto her and engulfing her in water. Then explosions ripped through the tank as the napalm caught fire and triggered a chain reaction. Holding her breath inside Aquaria, the last thing Ephorah saw before passing out was a bright flash as the heat burned everything around her.

16

Lopsided Law

CYRUS

"Alright, I'm running low on anesthetic." Doctor Monroe examined the container labeled "heroin" from the operating room. "I'll need you to go into town and get me some more heroin. Let them know you're doing this for me, specifically; they won't give you trouble if they know you're working with a doctor who uses it for surgeries."

The doctor handed Cyrus a small pouch of money with a shopping list and sent him on his way. Walking past a bed of clucking poultratoes, Cyrus made the long trek back into Dihorma.

Once he had passed inside the city limits, he was immediately greeted with the rotten smells of filth he'd almost forgotten about. Having lived his whole life in Hadesh, he couldn't believe that a city could be this foul.

As he made his way to an apothecary, he passed by a sign that had been put up for Jasper and Jaime's Fire Insurance. This one had an audio recording that played on repeat, with a picture of one of the founders of the company, sitting in a chintz chair and looking directly at Cyrus as he walked by.

"Hello," the recording said. "My name is Jaime Lyons, and with the help of my late partner, I started Jasper and Jaime with a single question: what if the fire department had a vested reason to protect your home? If you are fortunate enough not to remember the Fires of 868, there was a time when Dihorma had its own fire department owned and operated by the public. These firemen were so lazy, so pathetically incompetent, that they merely drove around putting out fires after buildings had burned to the ground, with or without people inside of them, rather than risk getting in harm's way to actually protect and serve. Rather than deal with the arsonists who set people's homes, schools, businesses, and even public offices ablaze, these firemen waited until there was no chance of harm to themselves."

"Jasper and I thought this wasn't good enough. We created our own fire engines, put together our own firefighter crews, and since we could not get paid through government money like the fire department, we sold fire insurance. We will never allow your homes to burn, or your families, because our bottom line will go up in smoke with them. You need not fear losing your livelihood to arsonists, no matter who they may be, who wish to burn your stores, loot your wares, and murder anyone in their way, because our crew will be on the scene at the first sign of smoke. Now, the city council wants me to be removed. They don't like my success; they don't like the idea of a private party doing what the government should have done all those years ago. The government doesn't care if your livelihood is destroyed; they don't care if you cannot feed your family, or if your children are burned to death."

"Imagine inhaling smoke; you try to breathe, and your body fills with poison instead. Your very lungs are on fire, and you feel like you're drowning in air. Now imagine losing your job, your business, your livelihood. Your family is evicted from their home when you cannot pay your rent; your children starve; your spouse is forced to watch. These are the fates your government would rather your families suffer if it means letting Empyrian arsonists run free in Dihorma. Remember that in this next council election, and vote for Jaime Lyons."

Cyrus realized he'd just allowed an advertisement to get him to stand still while he still had drugs to buy for the doctor. Blinking, he continued on his way to the apothecary as the streets started to fill with more people.

Ever since he'd begun working with Thoth to improve his skills in becoming an alchemist, Cyrus had been an early riser. It was normal for him to be up and about before everyone else from his law enforcement work last year, so he noticed people opening shops and starting their days as he walked through the streets. Once he reached the apothecary, he noticed another automated puppet show like the one he'd seen before, this one in the apothecary window.

"Are you a Maskil, or a Moron?" The voice recording began. The Maskil puppet rose, and the spotlight shone on his smiling, dapper face. "Maskil knows he can purchase medicine from the black shelf, but he doesn't use drugs like heroin or methamphetamines when he doesn't have a medical need to. He knows these drugs should only be used by doctors or dentists who have a good medicinal reason." The Maskil puppet went away and was replaced by a Moron puppet who was what medical experts would call "a hot mess." "Moron doesn't need to see the dentist. Moron doesn't have any teeth left, because he sold them all to pay for his heroin addiction. Don't be a Moron! Be careful, and don't use drugs from the black shelf unless you've spoken with a doctor first!"

Cyrus pondered what kind of idiot would use heroin without a medical reason as he walked into the apothecary.

The building had wall-to-wall shelves of various drugs, some in pill form, some to be taken as herbal teas, and others that needed to be injected into the bloodstream. Along one wall, a middle-aged pharmacist stood by a counter, and behind him, a black-painted shelf with several other drugs hung on the wall. These drugs were labeled "methamphetamines," "amphetamine," "morphine," and "heroin."

"Can I help you?" The apothecary had a calm tone, but there was a hint that he was ready to turn the pleasantries off if needed.

"I'm here on behalf of Doctor Monroe." Cyrus took out the list and handed it to the pharmacist. "We're running low on anesthetics."

The pharmacist looked at the list. "That's Monroe's signature, alright." He got out a large paper bag and went around the store, grabbing several drugs on Monroe's list. Apparently, the doctor was running low on more than just heroin.

"Excuse me," Cyrus eyed the puppet show replaying its message in the pharmacy window. "Why do I keep seeing these puppet shows everywhere? We don't have them in Hadesh."

"Those?" The pharmacist looked at Cyrus with very tired-looking eyes.

"The city council had us put those up. It's a bandage on a big problem."

Every doctor knew that a bandage only hides your wounds, and Cyrus was still curious. "What's the real problem?"

The pharmacist sighed. "It's the Empyrians. They're like...like children with adult bodies. They aren't like you or I, who can think for ourselves. They need an authority figure to tell them what they can or cannot do. If the government doesn't tell them not to abuse drugs like heroin or amphetamines, they'll do it. They've been doing it since before the war."

"Before the war?" Cyrus tried to process that. "You mean their old government didn't stop them from doing heroin either?"

"No," the pharmacist looked up thoughtfully. "I think I read somewhere that heroin was made illegal in the old Empyrian Empire a few years before the war. But the Empyrians were still abusing heroin. Most suppliers back then had no idea what the Empyrians were doing with it in those days; they thought there was just a massive shortage that their empire couldn't meet. When they did find out, everyone back west frowned upon continuing to sell the drugs to the Empyrians, but there were no laws against it, or even a government organized enough to put a stop to it, and people who grew poppies and processed them into opioids were driven by an obvious profit. When their empire banned the stuff, it didn't stop the Empyrians from wanting their drugs, so smugglers started sneaking the stuff through customs."

"That's pretty underhanded," Cyrus said.

"Well, people are all motivated by profit in some way. Lots of folks who produce these drugs don't see a lot of profit from these things; not a ton of people use it out west, because of what it does to you." The pharmacist finished picking up drugs from around the store and returned to the counter, where he measured out an amount of heroin to match the doctor's needs. "It wasn't the only reason the Empyrians declared war, but I know it was one of them."

"I see." Cyrus looked at the puppets again. "And even now, the Empyrians are overusing the stuff?"

"Yeah, and a lot of Empyrians commit all sorts of crime to get the money to buy their fix," the pharmacist finished packing the bag. "Their community leaders want us to stop selling it to them; they say we're poisoning their communities on purpose, and every pharmacy was happy to refuse to sell to Empyrians, but the city council passed a new ordnance preventing us from refusing to do business with people based on race. So, we have to sell them the heroin, their community leaders call us heartless, and the Empyrians who abuse the stuff keep committing crimes to buy the drugs, and there's nothing we can legally do. Some of them have even been caught stealing the drugs from hospitals and pharmacies directly. The only other solution people have suggested is for the government to illegalize heroin altogether."

"But that would be horrible for people who need it for treatments!" Cyrus exclaimed. "Just yesterday, Doctor Monroe and I gave a man a heart transplant. His body would have gone into shock without the drugs, his blood rate would collapse – the whole operation would have killed him!"

The pharmacist nodded as he handed Cyrus the bag. "Yeah, a lot of people are going to die if that happens. And they'd be punishing us pharmacists by costing us a lot of business."

Cyrus left the pharmacy with the bag of medicine. As he walked through the city back towards Monroe's house, he spotted a woman in her twenties standing by a street corner next to a lamppost. As Cyrus approached the end of the street, an Empyrian man in brown running clothes ran up to the woman from behind with a knife. Before Cyrus or the woman could react, the man stabbed her in the back several times, and then spun her around and stabbed her in the chest six more times.

Without thinking, Cyrus ran up to the man and jump-kicked the side of the man's head, which collided with the lamppost, silently thanking Ironwood Company for showing him this move. With the bag of medicine still in his left arm, he smashed his fist into the man's jaw, knocking several teeth out of his mouth.

To Cyrus's shock, the attacker burst out crying like a child, dropped his knife, and ran away. Cyrus almost went after him, but then he remembered the woman bleeding out on the ground. Dropping to his knees, he set the bag of medicine down and ripped open her shirt to examine her wounds.

The sight was overwhelming. Cyrus had seen plenty of medical books, but he had no idea what a person stabbed so many times looked like. There was so much blood, so much torn flesh. Out of the corner of his eye, he spotted the bloody knife the attacker had dropped. The blade was serrated and had tangled the ripped tissue and mixed it with thread from her clothes.

Grabbing as many threads as possible and removing them from the wounds, Cyrus had to clean the wounds quickly to avoid further blood loss. Clapping his hands and touching each wound, Cyrus remembered what Doctor Monroe had taught him about DNA. The flesh stitched itself together, but Cyrus had to do each wound one at a time, and she had already lost a lot of blood. As he closed the wounds on the front of her torso, he didn't notice the crowd forming above him.

"What happened here?"

Cyrus allowed himself to get distracted for a moment to glance up at the people surrounding him. A number of them were just gawkers, but one looked like a police officer. Cyrus tried to put them out of mind as he rolled the unconscious woman on her side and peeled what was left of her shirt off of her back. She had three more stab wounds from where the man had attacked her from behind.

"Sir, I asked you a question." The voice definitely came from the officer.

Pointing to the knife that had been left behind, Cyrus didn't look up from his work. "A man stabbed this woman with a knife and then ran away. I'm a little too busy to answer questions right now."

The officer took out a notebook and began scribbling. "A bloody knife lying next to a woman who's been stabbed, and a young man kneeling over her having torn off her clothes."

Cyrus had to stop himself from healing the woman's last wound, or he would have messed up the spell as he glared at the policeman. "You can't be serious."

A number of people surrounding the crowd began murmuring angrily. At first, Cyrus thought they were going to accuse him as well, but then he realized they weren't angry at him.

"You can't arrest someone for saving a victim's life," one man growled.

"We saw the attacker," a woman added. "He was Empyrian, wearing a tracksuit, and he ran away once this kid drove him off."

The officer looked around at the crowd. Cyrus tried to ignore him to finish sealing the last wound, but he could see that the officer was worried about the people gathered around him. They might have actually attacked the officer if he tried to arrest Cyrus.

But the officer showed his badge, and not-so-subtly showed his gun as well. "All of this is for the judge to decide. Young man, you're coming with me."

Before long, Cyrus found himself seated in a simple chair inside a small room in a courthouse with a lone table and a pair of thick lead gloves locked onto his hands by a set of cuffs chained to the table. The lead was so dense and so chemically inert that it would be impossible to use alchemy to get out of them, and they were heavy enough that trying to lift his hands to fight would have been difficult even if his wrists weren't cuffed to the table.

A man in a suit entered the room and sat in a chair opposing Cyrus. "Mr. Levitch," he began reading from a file. "You were found today standing over a woman with her shirt ripped off, covered in blood, stabbed multiple times by a knife found nearby with your fingerprints on it." He looked up from the file. "Got anything to say?"

"The knife had my fingerprints on it because I pulled it out of her stab wound," Cyrus tried to remember the specifics of the situation, but it had all been a blur. "I'm not the one who put it there."

"And who did?" The man leaned forward. "Where did this mystery person go?"

"Some nut ran up to her and stabbed her multiple times. He was tall, lanky, Empyrian—"

"Stereotyping isn't going to help your case, Mr. Levitch." The man made a note in his file. "Blaming imaginary Empyrian criminals is the sort of bigotry the court isn't going to stand for."

"He wasn't imaginary, I knocked some of his teeth out." Cyrus struggled against the chains as if looking for some of the loose teeth as evidence. "Back at the street corner, there's probably still some teeth lying on the ground."

"So, you admit to assaulting an Empyrian and causing them bodily harm?" The man made another note in his file. "Are there any other crimes for which you'd like to confess?"

"That isn't a crime!" Cyrus tried to pound the table, but could barely lift his fists. "He was attacking a woman with a knife!"

"We have no evidence that there was anyone else involved at the crime scene," the man sat back and clasped his hands. "We only have enough evidence to place you on top of a woman with her clothes torn off, covered in blood, and stabbed multiple times by a knife with your fingerprints. And, I might add, a bag of drugs nearby, including heroin."

Cyrus finally realized he was talking to a prosecutor. "I want to speak to a lawyer."

"Of course," the prosecutor nodded. "As soon as one gets here. In the meantime, do you mind if I ask you some questions?"

"Yes, I do. You already asked me several questions I probably shouldn't have answered without a lawyer, and I'm not even sure if that's legal." Cyrus started to sweat bullets. He wasn't quite sure how much trouble he was in, but he knew he was in a lot.

"Oh, very well." The prosecutor nodded. "We'll see how quickly we can get a lawyer in here for you to talk to. Shouldn't be more than a few days.

"A few days?" Cyrus tried not to panic. "I need to deliver the medicine I was carrying to Doctor Monroe!"

"Perhaps you should have thought of that before you stabbed a woman in broad daylight," the prosecutor replied.

Cyrus wanted to argue, but stopped himself. *He's just trying to goad me,* he thought. *There were witnesses at the crime scene. Surely someone will speak up.* "Can you at least send word to Doctor Monroe? I don't know all of my rights, but I do know you have to let me notify someone as to where I am."

The prosecutor sighed. "Very well. We'll send someone to talk to him immediately. We can't have them drop off any drugs; they're evidence now. You might have been planning to sell them to our local Empyrians, after all."

Cyrus spent the next few hours waiting in the room with his hands still cuffed to the table. Every hour that passed, he was certain that someone would come soon. He felt hungry, but he ignored it. He needed to use the restroom, but with his hands encased in lead, he had to hold it. His throat was parched; was that because he was sweating so much? When was the last time he'd taken a drink of water? Finally, he put his head down on the table and tried to get some sleep.

"Wake up."

Feeling someone poking his head, Cyrus looked up at a man dressed up as some sort of officer, probably a bailiff, or something similar. "Is it time?" He asked.

"Time for what?" The bailiff replied.

"Did you get a lawyer? Or get someone to reach Doctor Monroe?"

The bailiff shook his head. "I don't know anything about a lawyer or a doctor. But you need to stay awake."

Cyrus blinked the sleep away and sat up in his chair. He then realized how badly he needed to use the toilet. "Can you take me to the restroom?"

The bailiff paused. "Can you hold it?"

"I've been holding it for hours. Now I need to go."

Frowning, the bailiff uncuffed Cyrus's hands from the table. They were still chained together and locked in the lead gloves, but he was able to stand up for the first time in hours. He could feel his knees creaking and joints pop as he stood up and followed the bailiff to the bathrooms.

With some difficulty, Cyrus managed to do his business and clean up afterwards with his hands still bound. Going over to the sink, Cyrus washed the metal gloves that covered his hands, just for sanitation's sake. Then, when he was fairly certain no one was looking, he stuck his face under the faucet and guzzled down several mouthfuls of water. It was rusty, probably just clean enough to be considered sanitary, but to someone who couldn't remember the last time he'd had a drink of water, it was the best thing ever.

When he was done, the bailiff returned Cyrus to the waiting room. Along the way, Cyrus spotted the prosecutor, who glanced up at Cyrus.

"Ah, Mr. Levitch." The prosecutor kept an urbane tone and demeaner. "Just so you know, we sent someone to Doctor Monroe's house, but no one answered. Still no word on that lawyer."

"Of course not," Cyrus muttered as the bailiff locked his cuffs to the table again. "Probably never sent anyone in the first place. Or even tried to get a lawyer."

Outside, he heard the prosecutor and a new voice arguing. Cyrus couldn't make out what they were saying, but the new person sounded angry while the prosecutor was getting defensive. Before long, a youngish woman with a dark ponytail and glasses wearing a brown suit and carrying a briefcase opened the door to Cyrus's room and sat down across the table from him.

"Good gods, what in Peppi's unhinged jaws are they doing?" She extended her hand to Cyrus before realizing he couldn't shake it. "I'm Leah Kaplan. I'm an attorney who specializes in criminal defense cases."

"You're the one they sent for?" Cyrus asked.

"No," Leah shook her head. "I have no idea if this courthouse sent for a lawyer at all to defend you. I can tell from the look of this place that they're trying to break you into confessing. Legally, they're not allowed to keep you here for more than twenty-four hours without letting you speak to a lawyer. They didn't tell you that, did they?"

"I don't know a lot about these things," Cyrus admitted. "Never been in trouble with the law before. Maybe they thought I should know this already, because they don't even tell me when I can sleep or go to the bathroom."

"That's no excuse. They're obligated by law to read you your rights. Did they question you without an attorney present?" Leah asked.

"Yes," Cyrus admitted. "Then I realized I should have a lawyer, and I refused to answer any more questions."

"Of course," Leah sighed. "These people know their charges aren't going to stick, so they're trying to force a confession out of you, and they're willing to break the rules to get it."

Cyrus's ears pricked up. "They're not going to stick?"

Leah handed him a business card from her briefcase. The card listed her as a defense attorney working under Jasper and Jaime's Fire Insurance. "Before we can continue, you need to know who I'm working for, and why I've been asked to represent you. I'm here on behalf of an insurance company whose founder and executive director holds a seat on the city's council. Jaime Lyons has a political interest in fighting the corrupt interests of some of the politicians in the city, including prosecutors like the one on your case. He has campaign reasons to ensure that people know he's fighting that corruption."

Cyrus looked at the business card. "Are you going to need me to give some public statement? Sign a paper endorsing this guy?"

"No. By law, you cannot be required to repay Jasper and Jaime in any way for supplying you with legal services." Leah took several sheets of paper from her briefcase. "I will, however, need you to sign some forms. The first is to assign me as your legal counsel. The second is a letter confirming that you understand what you're being charged with, and that you plead not guilty."

"Um, I *don't* know what I'm being charged with." Cyrus looked over the forms. He signed the one granting Leah power of attorney, but wasn't ready to sign the second.

"You were charged with criminal assault and battery of a woman with a weapon. A knife, to be exact." Leah clasped her hands and rested them on the table. "The fact that she had no external injuries at the time she was taken to a hospital means one of two things; either someone with medical alchemy knowledge healed her, or she was never actually stabbed. If the latter is true, the charges won't stick, and in the former case, you were the only person who could have treated her. Even if you did stab her, to heal her immediately afterwards shows you had no intention to hurt her. The number of holes in her shirt indicate that whoever attacked her was so vicious they couldn't have calmed down in time to heal her. On top of all that, the reason I'm here is because someone who works with Jasper and Jaime witnessed the scene and reported it to their headquarters. That isn't a ton of evidence, but the prosecution doesn't have anything stronger than that. There's more than enough to get reasonable doubt."

Letting out a sigh of relief, Cyrus signed the second form. "How long will it take to get me out of here?"

"That depends. I have one more form, and whether you sign it or not determines how long it will take for the court to dismiss you." Leah handed him the third sheet. "I cannot encourage or discourage you from signing this. It's a waiver stating you will not press any countercharges against the city of Dihorma."

"Countercharges?" Cyrus looked over the waiver. "What would I charge the city with?"

"Does anything about this seem strange to you?" The lawyer asked.

"Doesn't it seem odd that you were charged at all? Criminal charges like this have to be proven beyond a reasonable doubt; a guy with confirmed medical alchemy knowledge has a good reason to have his fingerprints on assailant's weapon. Why do you think they've been playing games to keep you from getting a lawyer, or depriving you of water and rest? They were trying to coerce you into confessing to something you didn't do. They didn't even read you your rights."

"I did suspect that they never contacted Doctor Monroe," Cyrus looked at the details of the waiver again. "This says that I agree not to countersue the city in exchange for my immediate release."

"That's correct." Leah nodded. "The fact is that the court prosecution could be in a lot of legal trouble if someone with standing and a lawyer supplied by a company like my employer's sued them for misconduct. You'll be out of here by this evening if you sign that waiver."

"So, if I sign this, I'll be free to go?" Cyrus picked up the paper.

"Not quite," Leah shook her head. "There will still be a trial, but the court will get it over and done with this evening. You'll be free to go then."

"But then...why was I arrested?" Cyrus held the pen above the page, almost ready to sign. "Why go through all of this if they knew that I might not sign this and might press charges?"

Leah opened her jaw as if to speak, and then visibly forced it closed. "Answering that question would be considered influencing your decision. I'm sorry. I can't say."

Cyrus looked at the paper again. "I just want to get this over with and get back to my studies." He signed the form. "Is there any chance you could let Doctor Monroe know where I am? I don't think anyone here even tried to get ahold of him."

Within the hour, the bailiff came back and called Cyrus into court. The courtroom itself wasn't much cleaner than the rest of the city that Cyrus had seen, but the pews were swept clear enough that you could find a seat without playing "what am I sitting in now?" Not that it mattered to Cyrus, as he found himself sitting in a wooden booth near the judge's podium. This must have been the defendant's box.

The overall proceedings of the courtroom went completely over Cyrus's head. He was no lawyer, and all he really understood was that the judge and prosecution wanted Cyrus to be guilty, but the judge had to follow rules that Leah Kaplan would cite; each one had some numerical code attached to it that Cyrus couldn't keep track of. Cyrus thought there'd be a jury, but apparently he had waived this with one of the forms he'd signed. Leah acted like this was in his favor; the prosecution tried to bring up statements Cyrus had made before she'd arrived, and Leah objected numerous times. It was clear that the judge and prosecution were uncomfortable with Leah's rebuttals, and wanted there to be a jury of people. Cyrus didn't understand most of these 'magic numbers' for each courtroom rule; how could anyone else, unless they were a trained lawyer? Even weirder, Leah had told Cyrus that lawyers couldn't sit for jury duty.

Legally, everything Cyrus said without a lawyer present had to be thrown out of the courtroom, and while the judge and prosecution knew that the rules had been broken, a jury wouldn't understand why these statements had to be dismissed.

"Mr. Levitch, do you wish to add your own account of the events?" The judge finally asked. "Do you think you can tell us who, if not you, assaulted the woman with the knife?" He pointed to the bloodstained knife, kept in a metal bin and unaltered from the crime scene earlier.

Cyrus looked up at the judge from the booth. "It was a tall Empyrian man in brown running clothes. Stabbed her multiple times in the front, turned her around and stabbed her in the back, then ran off bawling like a baby after I knocked him off of her."

"This story fits the fact pattern, and matches the description from my client's witness." Lean glared at the judge. "Do you have enough for reasonable doubt?"

The judge sighed in frustration. "Very well. Mr. Levitch is cleared. Of all charges." He began stamping some papers before shuffling them together into a pile. "In view of your testimony and the Equal Incarceration Act, this court will not pursue charges against the Empyrian suspect. Dismissed."

The judge brought down the gavel. The case was over. Cyrus was as free as the man who had stabbed the woman in town.

Getting up from the booth, Cyrus went over to Leah and offered his hand. "Thank you, for all of this."

Leah took his hand and shook it. "Don't worry about it. If there's anyone you should thank, it's Jasper and Jaime's Fire Insurance. These courts are corrupt, and Jaime has his legal teams fighting the corruption."

"...I see." Cyrus left the courthouse, picking up the medicine he'd bought for Doctor Monroe along the way. When he checked the parcel, the heroin had been removed. A note apparently signed by the correctional officer stated that "no heroin arrived in police custody." Cyrus glanced up at the clerk who had handed him the parcel, and noticed that the man was Empyrian. A thought wormed into his mind that he had no idea what the correctional officer's handwriting looked like, and how easy it would be to forge his signature on the note, allowing the clerk to keep the drugs for himself. He wanted to push the idea out of his mind, and not just assume the clerk had stolen the heroin, but it made too much sense to go away.

The clerk locked eyes with Cyrus, as if wondering if he would challenge the note, but Cyrus simply put the bag under his arm and left the courthouse. It was almost night. He was certain to get a stern talking to when he got back to the doctor's house.

17

Resignation of a God

MARDUK

In the privacy of the halls of the Institute of Theurgy, a single room is reserved for its patron god. It has no doors, no windows, no entryways, for Marduk doesn't need them. It has a mail slot for earthly paperwork, and a speaking tube allowing the god to communicate directly with the headmistress of the institute. On one wall, there is a framed diagram of a cross-section of the earth, featuring its molten core surrounded by tectonic plates. On the opposite wall, framed portraits of previous headmasters of the institute hung, along with a lectern featuring a large, leatherbound book listing the names of Marduk's favorite students over the decades. Few names had been entered in the last thirty years.

Marduk materialized into this private room and sat in a large, leather chair to think. He had to make contact with the headmistress soon, and he was not in a civil mood. The dracolich had escaped, and some of the things he'd said bothered Marduk; he truly acted like he did not know Thoth was dead, and too many things didn't add up. Twice now, the lich had fought him with nothing but mortal weapons. If he really had killed Thoth, he would have a weapon with him that could actually kill a god. What was more, there was a brief moment in which the dragon acted like he fully expected Thoth to come and join the fight. And there was still no clear motive. What did the dracolich have to gain from killing Thoth?

The more Marduk turned things over in his mind, the more it seemed like he'd been tricked. He could blame the dragon for distracting him, but the reality was that his attention lately had been spread too thin.

Looking up at the picture of the earth's core, Marduk knew what he had to do. "Sometimes you have to let go."

The god pulled a string along one wall that was connected to a bell in Headmistress Aviva Rubin's office. It wasn't long before her voice came from the speaking tube.

"Yes, lord Marduk?"

"I've been looking over reports regarding a spike in ghouls spotted near local cemeteries," the god began. "Demonic possession is bad enough, but there is now information coming out that the people who have gotten themselves possessed are overwhelmingly graduates from the Institute of Theurgy. They're *our* alumni."

Ghouls. Demons. Paradoxical ideas that promised the perks of living someone else's life by eating that person and taking their shape. Eventually, the ghoul would drive their host to dwell in graveyards and eat corpses until it left the host entirely, leaving the person as a permanently mutated husk that hungered for rotten flesh.

"Those demons can only take possession if the person summons them, and then allows the demon into their mind," Marduk continued. "Which means...something about the way the school is teaching students is drawing evil spirits to them, and the students are dumb enough to think they can control them. I've had issues with the way you run the school before, but this is too far."

"The way we teach our students is designed to help them succeed," Headmistress Rubin interjected. "By any means necessary. We warn students that the world does not value their skills as it should. We inform them that there aren't as many jobs for theurgy students as there are for the more math-centric schools of magic, and I suspect that it is the reality of living in a world that does not give theurgy the respect it deserves that is causing some of our students to turn to extreme measures. What are we supposed to do? Lie to them? Tell them that there will be plenty of job opportunities when we know that there won't? Pretend that the world will give them the careers and riches they deserve once they've earned their degree?"

"A degree is not a magic talisman that guarantees you will be employed," Marduk snarled. "And most of your students are not worthy of careers! You have to give people something of value with your work, or they will not hire you!"

"How are the students not worthy?" Rubin countered. "They work just as hard in their classes as in the other schools, they compete in the same tournaments, they can command spirits to do all sorts of useful things; they deserve the lifestyles that sorcerers and alchemists get. How are they not worthy?"

Marduk gritted his teeth. "There is a world of difference between deserving something and being entitled to it. To be worthy, you don't just have to pass tests; you have to develop the skills needed to actually do what people need you to do. You need to be able to provide people with things they cannot get more reliably from sorcerers or alchemists. The students who go into enchanting understand this, at least somewhat. I have warned you multiple times that you need to teach students how to raise other people up; how to lead spirits by example, not just manipulate them by making them small. You do not listen to my teachings, you ignore my warnings, and now, graduates are getting demonically possessed. I don't have the power to stop you, what with free will and all, but I won't enable you either."

"What?" The headmistress' panicked voice quivered over the speaking tube. "What are you saying?"

"I will not endorse this institute's teachings. I will not provide you with my seal of approval. I will not appear at your booth during the Career Festival anymore. I will be cleaning out my office after this conversation. I will not be associated with this disgrace of a school any longer."

"You...you can't!" The headmistress protested. "Our reputation will be ruined!"

"So be it," Marduk growled. "If that is what must happen to protect the students, your reputation be damned, but you will not take mine with you. My pantheon may try to stop me, but when I tell them that you have allowed demons to possess your students, they will understand. You cannot be allowed to besmirch the name of civilization itself."

"Your name?" Headmistress Rubin fumed from the other side of the speaking tube. "Is this all about your name? Your ego is more important than this university?"

"Foolish mortal," Marduk replied. "My name is the name of civilization itself. My reputation is tied to the foundation of order. People have to believe in me in order for society to remain civil. If they don't, they descend into barbarism, or replace me with a less...savory god to represent their culture."

Memories of when the Babylonians replaced him as their patron god with Hadad gnawed at Marduk's mind. The temples, the sacrifices to the Caananite version of the storm god named "Baal." They still didn't leave Hadad near babies without supervision.

"What are we supposed to do without a patron god?" Rubin asked.

"Do what you will." Marduk shrugged. "You've already been operating without my instruction. Now you'll just be doing it officially."

"I meant for publicity!" Rubin hollered. "How do we recruit new students if we don't have a patron god to speak for us at Career Festivals? All the other universities have gods – even the lawyers! We'll be a laughing stock at best and pariahs at worst!"

"You should have thought of this a long time ago." Marduk stood from his chair and with a flick of his finger, packed the entirety of his office into a single briefcase. "I warned you last year that I will not be used to lure young students, mostly young girls, into an expensive education that will not provide them with any useful skills. Goodbye, headmistress.

Before she could respond, Marduk grabbed his briefcase and shifted out of the material plane into the Aether, the spirit world. There were other places he could serve to benefit civilization and continue to do his job; he had one in mind already.

Re-materializing on the abbey's stone walkways with a cloak and mask to keep his eyes and divine aura from giving him away, he strolled into the abbey's library and got to work.

18

The Waters of Harlak

ROSTAM

The Endurance started to slow down. Harlak was coming into sight, and Rostam took to the ballast controls to aid in steering the vessel into port.

It was late in the morning. The ship was loaded with copper pipes from the Abbey of Truth, and their contact was supposed to meet them tomorrow.

"That's...odd." Captain Nadia checked her pocket watch and compass. "We weren't supposed to arrive until tonight. How did we get here so fast?"

Simon examined the ship's boiler. "Looks like our engines are hotter than normal. Not enough to cause any damage, but enough to give us some extra thrust. Check on that fire elemental."

Rostam opened the tank where Cindrocles floated out and sniffed the air.

"Is there coal?" Cindrocles asked. "I was told there'd be coal."

"Knock yourself out." Rostam tossed a lump of coal at the elemental, which passed into the fireball's form.

"Mmmm..." Cindrocles gave off the impression of chewing the fuel as he burned hotter. A smile crept across his face as he did.

"Well, if we're here early, we can drop off the goods early." Nadia checked her map. "No sense wasting time when we can get back in the skies sooner."

With the ship docked, Nadia stepped down and looked for a port authority. Rostam went along, carrying a pistol and dagger just in case.

"Harlak ain' like Hadesh," Tarchus had warned him. "The streets'll gobble you up an' spi' you out if you ain' armed."

Captain Nadia approached a customs house where authorities were stationed. Instead of having officers on the docks checking in ships as they came, in Harlak, ship captains were expected to go directly to the authorities themselves.

"Hate this part," Nadia took out a small purse of coins. "But it's the cost of doing business in Harlak.

As they stepped inside the customs house, Rostam was shocked by the disarray that greeted them. Ship captains and merchants were crammed into a long queueing line, roped off with an old chain. The port officials sat in booths at the end, with three booths occupied by officers and seven booths empty, with signs that read "Next Booth Over."

There was nothing to do but wait in line. Rostam had to wonder if there'd been some mistake; in Hadesh, and most of the cities he'd been to with Captain Nadia or the late Captain Zaahid, everything was organized to allow merchant ships to unload as quickly as possible so as to deliver goods to customers. Rostam imagined one of these ships carrying fish from out west, and how their cargo would likely rot in their ship's hold before they got to the front of the line. He knew enough about running an airship by now to know that this entire setup was a waste of time and money, which spoiled a lot of people's cargo.

When they were almost at the end of the line, the captain in front of them approached an official.

"Do you have a present for me?" The official asked.

The captain fiddled around for his purse, before coming up dry.

"Back of the line." the official pointed to the end with his pen.

The dejected captain left the line and exited the customs house altogether, presumably to return with a bribe for the port authority.

Captain Nadia and Rostam were next. "Here you are," Nadia passed the purse of coins to the official.

He counted out the coins, as if determining whether or not Nadia had bribed him enough to do his job. "What are you carrying."

"Pipes for the Abbey of Truth." Nadia passed him their cargo manifest.

"They ordered replacements for their water project."

"Hm," the official looked over the paperwork. "Very well, everything seems to be in order." He stamped the papers and handed them back to the captain. "Proceed."

The captain and Rostam left the customs house and headed back to the ship.

"What was that?" Rostam gestured back to the office. "You have to bribe the port authorities to approve your cargo here?"

"In Harlak?" Nadia shrugged. "That's just the way it is. You want the police to arrest someone who robbed you, you have to bribe them. You want the police to leave you alone after they've arrived at your house without a warrant? You have to bribe them, or go to jail. Want the local authorities to supply your home with clean water to drink? Too bad, they've spent all the taxes your family paid for water utilities on bribes, and kept the rest for themselves. There's a reason I got out of this city as soon as I had the chance."

"I didn't know you were from Harlak," Rostam glanced at his captain.

"Born and raised," Nadia smiled. "And fled."

Once they reached the ship, Nadia ordered the crew to ready the cargo, but not to unload. "We're going to talk to the folks at the abbey first," she explained. "See if they'll lend us some muscle to keep the cargo safe so we can make the delivery."

Tarchus and the rest of the crew worked on readying the goods, but Nadia ordered Rostam and Cindrocles to come with her. "This isn't a city where I'm going to walk anywhere by myself," she admitted. "And a fireball by our side would be a good idea."

Cindrocles seemed happy at first to get to look around a place other than the inside of the ship's boiler, but quickly wasn't impressed with anything he saw. "This place is a dump."

"You haven't seen anything yet," Nadia guided them to the end of the docks into the city proper.

Unlike Hadesh, Harlak was built on top of a large, rough hill that would have been extremely difficult to climb. There were cliffsides that were almost vertical, jagged rocks at various places, and only a few traversable areas with large gates controlling traffic in and out. The Greymarch would not be able to scale this city's natural defenses. This is why they had no large city wall to keep such threats away from citizens.

What the city did have, however, were large water barrels on top of every house, with even larger reservoirs on apartment buildings. This was in addition to neighborhoods filled with trash, buildings visibly in poor condition, and vermin crawling through the various garbage piles in the streets. Rats skittered through food waste and were pounced upon by wild cats visibly infested with fleas bouncing around the animals. In the distance, a large and formerly glorious palace had been turned into a government building, surrounded by the same decay and disrepair as the rest of the city. This is what had become of the former capital of the Empyrian Empire.

"What are the water tanks for?" Rostam asked. "Do they collect rain water?"

Nadia shook her head. "They used to, but the vermin wouldn't stay out of them. Now they store water from people who've built private water collectors and have ways to keep the filth out, or they import it from cargo ships."

"Why can't they build some sort of network to pump water into people's homes, like in Hadesh?" Rostam asked. "Even in Aklagos, we had water in our house."

"The local government is supposed to do that," Nadia admitted. "They certainly collect enough taxes to pay for it. But the local authorities simply keep the money for themselves, and use a small amount to pay bribes to Viceroy Havez to look the other way. So the citizens have to pay taxes on water that they don't receive, and then pay for cargo ships to deliver other water supplies." Nadia pointed to a facility under construction in the distance, near the Whispering Sea. "That's where we're headed."

Rostam followed the captain to the facility, where he was surprised to see a team of clay golems digging a trench in nearly perfect unison. Each golem dug with a spade one second behind the one to its right, and at the end of the line was a girl making digging motions that the golems imitated. Rostam recognized her from the Grand Wizard Tournament.

"Greetings!" A priest from the abbey approached Nadia, Rostam, and Cindrocles. "You're here early!"

"Yes, well..." Nadia glanced at Cindrocles. "Turns out our boiler can be...

motivated, with the right incentive. But we're going to need some help getting the goods from our ship to your project."

"Not a problem." The priest turned to the girl working in the trench with the golems. "Ariella? Can you come meet our guests?"

Ariella stopped digging in the trench and called out some sort of word that Rostam didn't catch. All of the golems froze and opened their mouths, revealing small scrolls hidden inside. Then the girl climbed out of the trench and joined the priest.

Ariella was fairly covered in dirt, wearing grimy work clothes, but she also had on a smile like she was one of the few people happy to be in this city. Her blonde hair stood out to Rostam. It was a rare trait unique to the Borealans, and he realized she was the first non-Empyrian he'd seen in Harlak; fitting for the former birthplace of the Empyrian Empire, but he hadn't noticed the lack of any other racial groups in the area until now.

"Afternoon!" She offered a muddy hand, which Nadia reluctantly shook. "You guys need help getting the pipes out here?"

Nadia nodded.

"I've got just the thing." Ariella ran off to a nearby tent and returned later with a bag full of small scrolls like the ones in the mouths of the golems. She inserted four of them into a group of golems from the trench, and the four golems climbed out of the trench and followed her, always trying to stay within a certain distance of their mistress.

"You were a theurgist in the combat arena." Rostam remembered a fight between Ariella and Ephorah, in which one of Ariella's golems had been imitating her every move.

"That's right! And these guys are going to help us carry the cargo, while the rest of us worry about defense," she explained.

Ariella followed Nadia, Rostam, and Cindrocles back to *the Endurance*. Cindrocles kept his distance from the theurgist, his eyes, or whatever he had in the flames that served as eyes, kept shifting to watch her in case she tried anything. Given that Cindrocles had been enslaved by a theurgist and put to work in the boiler of *the Dutchess Authority*, Rostam figured it would be a while before the fire spirit lowered his guard around theurgists again.

"Hey, what is this project of yours, exactly?" Rostam asked Ariella. "I know it involves water, but what is it supposed to do?"

"Well, we're hoping to purify the water in the Whispering Sea into clean, drinkable water that can be pumped into people's homes." Ariella glanced at one of the water tanks sitting on top of a home as they passed by. "The Whispering Sea isn't just full of salt, or bacteria; it's tainted. Poison leftover from the Calamity pollutes the water, and you can't get rid of it by simply boiling it. What we're building is an evaporator; we're going to setup a large machine that will evaporate the water and allow it to condense in a new tank. Metals, bacteria, and the tainted poison don't evaporate with the water, so when it condenses again, the water will be drinkable. We've built the machinery, but now we're trying to connect the pipes to some of the apartment buildings around here, as a start."

"What about the other homes?" Rostam pointed to some houses outside of the city. "Lots of people who don't live in apartments still don't have water in their homes."

"Yeah, but the Abbey of Truth is doing all of this entirely on charity," Ariella explained. "Getting this to work for apartment buildings alone is already an ambitious project; getting it to each and every house? That's a bigger project for another day."

"So why did you run out of pipes?" Rostam asked as they reached the ship. "Did you guys underestimate how many you would need?"

"No," Ariella sighed. She extracted the scrolls from the golems as Simon and Joseph brought crates of pipes to the golems. Ariella replaced the scrolls with new scrolls. The golems went to the crates, lifted them up, and then turned to follow Ariella back to the project. Nadia, Rostam, and Cindrocles served on guard duty to protect the cargo as they returned to the water purifier.

"The reason we've run out of copper pipes is because they keep being stolen," Ariella admitted as she guided the golems. "People keep taking them to sell for copper scrap."

"What?" Rostam glanced around at the city, trying to process why anyone would do such a thing. "These people have to pay twice for water, and even then, it's clear that they don't have enough. Why would someone steal parts from a water purifier? Even if you don't live in a connected apartment building, everyone else will still be able to get water cheaper when the supply goes up."

"Well, yes. In the long run, that would happen," Nadia sighed, like she was all too familiar with this sort of behavior. "Someday, if the purifier is finished and clean water is allowed to flow, everyone will benefit in the future. But the person who steals copper pipes and sells them gets a large sum of money in the here and now. And imagine the people who don't steal the pipes and sell them. They don't get clean water or the money from selling the parts. If the pipes will be stolen either way, lots of people will steal and sell the scrap copper just so they don't miss out."

Rostam remembered what Captain Zaahid had taught him about how people will overexploit land that doesn't belong to anyone. He couldn't help but notice the same problem here; if stealing was acceptable in this city, then the pipes of the water purifier were effectively up for grabs to anyone who wanted them.

Several passersby noticed Ariella and the golems. A few simply stared, but more than one held a look of contempt for the Borealan theurgist. Rostam had some experience with dirty looks from Borealans back in Hadesh, but they usually didn't make an issue of it since he didn't stay put in one place for very long. So long as the folks in Hadesh got the goods they wanted in a timely manner and affordable price, they stopped caring about who did the work. Perhaps the people of Harlak didn't feel that way because they couldn't get those things, and needed someone to blame.

"If you've got these golems under your command, why can't you set some of them up as security guards?" Rostam asked Ariella. "They look like they could deter any thieves from stealing the pipes."

"That would be a really bad idea." Ariella kept an eye on the golems to make sure she was still directing them properly. "We can't just threaten these people with violence to keep them away from the project. Remember, the Abbey of Truth is organizing this as a charity program to help people in Harlak. If we start shooting at them when they try to steal from the purifier, or having golems beat them to death, it undermines the whole point of building this facility in the first place."

"She's either extremely brave, or a naïve fool," Nadia whispered to Rostam. "Lots of people here wish death to the Borealans."

"What?" Rostam observed the looks of hate Ariella was getting. "Bad enough that people steal from the water purifier; now they hate someone who works on it?"

"Do you know where most of the copper in the empire comes from?" Nadia asked. "It comes from the mines just southeast of this city. The west coast has no copper mines, and prior to the war, all copper had to be imported either from Grand Spire or Meditia, or occasionally the norther states like Ulri. It wasn't cheap, and copper is the primary mineral used to make water pipes in the empire, since steel rusts and lead...you don't want to drink from lead pipes."

"Oh," things started to click in Rostam's mind. "So once the war ended, the Borealans had a source of copper to work with, and then made cheap clean water pipes."

"Exactly. It only took a few years for the Borealans to discover the rich supply of copper out here, and a few years later to set up copper smelteries in Hadesh and Baltithar." The group reached the purifier, and Ariella's golems continued to follow her to where the pipes would be laid as Nadia continued. "A lot of Empyrians feel like the Borealans have plundered their lands for their own benefit, and rarely do any of the copper products made from the factories in the west ever return to the cities where the minerals came from. Never mind the destruction to the economy of Harlak once their nobility was removed from power." Nadia pointed to the former palace in the distance, still visible from the purifier at the edge of town. "This city's economy before the war was largely propped up by the whims of the nobility, and without them the economy would have collapsed, had mining companies not setup shop looking for workers. It's true that the Borealans benefited from the spoils of war. It is not true that they gave nothing back in return."

"Oh, well bless the bories and their benevolent mining companies!" A nearby old woman who must have been listening mocked Nadia. "Thank them ever so much for replacing our economy after destroying the one we had before! I can't get clean water other than boiling whatever I can fill in the tank on my roof, and not a single piece of copper pipe ever comes back to us after we've pulled it out of the ground, but hey, people are getting paid to work in a dingy hole to bring up the ore, so it's all fine, right?" She sneered.

"Ignore her," Nadia ordered. "She's a fool."

"You don't seem to like the people of this city very much," Rostam noted.

"I don't." Nadia growled. "There's a reason I offered to work with Captain Zaahid at the first opportunity. I got out of this hole without having to sell my body; not many of my childhood friends can say that. The people who live here could choose to build their own copper smelteries and refine the ore here, make their own copper pipes in town, rather than ship it back and forth across the country at an outrageous price. They don't. They could clean the trash that's luring in the vermin off the streets, or build a landfill, or even just dump it off the side of the cliffs surrounding the city. They don't. They could stop stealing the parts for the purifier, or stop buying the copper pipes as scrap which they know were stolen from *they're own frigging public purifier*, but they don't!"

The priest from before joined the two and gave them a large pouch full of money. "Thank you for your help in this project. We wouldn't be able to do this without you."

Nadia accepted the money and thanked the priest before turning to Rostam. "Let's buy some copper ore and load it on the ship. Then we'll get out of this garbage dump of a city."

19

Strong Words

HORUS

In the Duat, the House of Horus was not exactly a "fixed" structure. It was made entirely out of black granite to reflect the king's role in maintaining order, with gold trim adding a sense of regality. Horus was both the sky god and the king of the Egyptian pantheon; the thoughts and beliefs of mortals defined his home. Hathor sat to his right as the royal pair took account of their recent offerings. At a nearby writing desk, Seshat sat ready to read and record the details of the sacrifices that the mortals that sent them.

"We're still getting the usual gifts from the regulars," Seshat reported. Regulars were mortals who made offerings purely out of habit. "Each one is usually offering the same amount as before, but there's been a dip in the number of regulars over the years."

"What?" Hathor balked. "Are they losing faith?"

"No, not exactly." Seshat looked over the records. "But most of the regulars are old, and the younger generations aren't replacing them. The youth are not as dedicated to us; they offer sacrifices when they want something, and ignore us when they don't."

"I feel...like this has happened before," Horus rubbed his head, but he couldn't remember. A god's memories were dependent on what mortals remembered; only a few gods could hold onto memories beyond the consciousness of mortals. Gods like Thoth.

"Something else bothers me." Hathor rubbed her own head, like she was struggling to remember as well. "Neros, the god of atheism...he, she, it, whatever, was born when humanity stopped believing in gods. Neros is the manifestation of the fact that when humans stop believing in gods, they don't believe in nothing; they'll believe in anything, like soybeans. Is there any evidence that the humans have replaced us with something else? Something other than a god that they turn their focus on instead?"

"I do not know," Seshat glanced through her records. "It may be too soon to tell. You are still receiving offerings from people who want protection," she continued. "Especially worshippers seeking protection from disease, and wealthier parents wanting to make sure their kids turn out alright—"

"Then why do I feel like it's losing its effect?" Horus looked at his own palm, as if his powers were contained within his hand. "Do they not know that the act of sacrifice is supposed to be an investment in their offspring? You gave up a cow for this kid, so take some better care in parenting them!"

"Oh, wait, there's something big here." Seshat held up an envelope that had been offered to Horus. "It says it's a deed to a plot of land filled with cattle, offered by..." Seshat blinked. "Offered by... 'Unknown.' Odd." She opened the envelope and frowned. "Uh-oh."

"Uh-oh?" Horus raised an eyebrow. "What do you mean by 'uh-oh?'"

"This isn't an offering. It's a letter that snuck through the offering plate." Seshat read the first few lines. "From the dracolich."

"The one that killed Thoth?" Horus clenched his fist. "Read it."

Hathor tried to calm her husband down. "Are you sure that's wise—"

"READ IT!" He bellowed.

"Um, okay." Flustered, Seshat started reading the letter aloud. "*Dear Over-Glorified Petting Zoo, let me begin by stating that your security sucks, the décor in your palace is awful, and my undead rat found Bast's missing squeak toy under the cushions of the couch by the southern window. Doofus says 'what?'*"

"WHAT?" Horus roared.

"*Ha, classic!*" Seshat read, only to notice her king glaring at her. "I'm sorry, he actually wrote 'ha, classic!'"

"Just...continue," Horus seethed.

"Right," Seshat turned back to the letter. "*While I enjoyed pounding you all into submission like the furries you are, I feel as though there's been a big misunderstanding between us. I am not the one who killed your birdbrained-egghead. I do not know who killed Thoth, nor why, but I do know how to kill gods if the need arises. Should you screw your courage to the sticking place to come after me again, I shall be prepared with the means to pluck every feather from you and any other chicken-headed gods, air-fry you to a nice flaky golden-brown, and feed you in nugget-form to that giant snake monster you're all so worried about. Then I'll grind Hathor and Apis into hamburgers, toss Serket the nature-goddess into a blender and use whatever comes out as engine lubricant, and make certain at the end that there is not enough left of any one of you to mummify.*

Sincerely,
    Your Favorite Cheeky Bastard,
    Daurgo"

"How the hell..." Horus's fists were clenched so tightly they looked like they might burst. "Did that get snuck in with our offerings?"

"What I don't get," Hathor gritted her teeth, clearly not happy with the thought of being made into hamburger. "Is why someone that obnoxious would deny killing Thoth. He seems like the kind of cocky arrogant jackass who would rub that sort of thing in our faces."

Horus paused. "That's...that makes too much sense...It could be an elaborate act of misdirection, but to what end? What does he have to gain from murdering Thoth and then lying about it?" Horus clutched his head, trying to force the missing puzzle pieces into his mind. He knew his vision was incomplete. If Daurgo didn't kill Thoth, then someone else did. Someone who had a motive to murder the god of reason. But his mind was shaped by mortal beliefs, and the mortals knew of no one else who would have had an agenda against Thoth. To a god, reaching for a conclusion that mortals hadn't thought of was like trying to remember an event that you had never personally witnessed. He could assemble the facts with inhuman wisdom once he had them, but he couldn't find them himself.

"Contact Marduk," Horus finally said. "Normally, I would turn to Thoth in times like this, but in his absence, we're completely in the dark. The Babylonians might be able to find the missing clues, and may even know who might have done this if not the dracolich. I can only keep my eye on so many things at once. Send the smiter after the dragon for now; he's still a threat, but I must keep a lookout for other dangers lurking in the shadows."

Hathor nodded. "Always be watchful."

20

A Desperate Enchantment

EPHORAH

Ears ringing. Vision blurry. Everything seemed dark at first, only to slowly come into focus.

Ephorah woke to find herself inside what was left of the demolisher tank. Her last memory was Aquaria throwing herself onto the young theurgist as everything inside the tank was engulfed in flames. Fire. They were fighting Greymarchers, and one of the flamethrower crew's fuel caught fire. There had been explosions outside, along the port and starboard sides of the tank. At first, water filled Ephorah's lungs and she couldn't breathe. Then she was gasping for air through her mouth.

Air. Oxygen. The fire should have consumed all the air in the tank. How was she breathing? Ephorah looked around and realized there was light coming into the tank. Several spots at various places on the floor held sunlight, which meant there were breaches in the tank's hull. That was why she had air.

Ephorah stumbled to her feet and looked around the tank. The smell finally hit her nose. Burnt flesh. The rest of the crew had been burned alive. They hadn't been lucky enough to have a water elemental–

"Aquaria!" Ephorah looked around for her only remaining spirit. She wasn't certain if Aquaria could be destroyed, but if anything could kill her, it would be a blazing inferno.

Ephorah scrambled around looking for the spirit. There were no signs of a woman made of water. There were no puddles, no droplets of water she could have left behind. There was nothing.

Trying to calm down, Ephorah took several deep breaths to get her bearings. As she did, she could now hear the sounds of something clawing at the tank from the outside. Someone, or rather, a lot of someones, were trying to get in. The occasional moan and groan confirmed Ephorah's fears: there were still Greymarchers outside the tank.

Finally, amidst the horrifying sounds outside the vehicle, Ephorah heard a whimper by her feet. Bending down, Ephorah found a small drop of water that was making noise. If she squinted, she could almost make out a face in the water. This was all that was left of Aquaria.

Ephorah dug through her backpack, which had been protected with her from the flames, and pulled out a small glass vial. Scooping up what was left of Aquaria, she tucked the vial into her pocket. In theory, the elemental would recover in time, but she was too weak to even return to the Duat. It would be a long time before she could fight again.

The sounds of Greymarchers continued to seep into the tank. Ephorah looked up at the opening hatch, which was the only way out of the vehicle. The door was still visibly intact, and bolted shut from the inside. There was no way that it could be opened from the outside. But, Ephorah could only stay here for so long, and it didn't seem like the marchers were going to leave her alone anytime soon.

In terms of weapons, Ephorah had only her opera gloves. They gave her fists the punching power of ten men, but punches alone might not be enough against a swarm of shambling monsters. If only one of them vomited the filthy grey crud inside Ephorah's mouth or nose, she'd become one of them. And according to the Salamanders, her soul would be barred from the afterlife until someone managed to kill her. The thought was so terrifying that Ephorah eyed the late Colonel Strauss's officer sword. It wouldn't be much use against the Greymarch, but she could make sure that she didn't end up joining them when she died...

No. Taking your own life was highly forbidden by most temples, and escaping one hellish life for a permanently hellish afterlife was not a solution.

She had to find another option.

The weapons on the tank were visibly too damaged to use, and the tank's treads had been blown before the flamethrower fuel had caught fire. Of the weapons the crew had with them before they'd been killed, only the colonel's sword was in reasonably good condition, and it wasn't even sharp; it was a purely ceremonial weapon.

And she had a water elemental. A humanus elemental, which meant she was fairly intelligent, but she was too weak to manifest as more than a droplet. And she also had materials in her bag for enchanting artifacts, like her gloves.

Ephorah took out her chalk and notebook, which listed all of the words she knew and the symbols to draw them. Drawing a circle on the floor of the tank and the sigil for "*Aqua*" in the center, Ephorah looked at the vial containing what was left of Aquaria. If she used her in an enchantment, Aquaria would forever become an inanimate object. Ephorah had done this once before to create her gloves, using a symbol for idiocy to strip the spirit of its intelligence, and had immediately regretted it. She hadn't known what the sigil would do at the time, and she knew that intelligent spirits didn't like being turned into artifacts. If she turned Aquaria into an artifact, it would probably be a living hell for the spirit, unless she used the idiocy symbol again. But if she didn't create a weapon that could get her out of this, the Greymarch would eventually add her to their ranks, and she'd be the one in a living hell.

"I'm sorry." Ephorah placed Aquaria's vial in the center of the circle and drew the symbol *Incontio* at one of seven sigils along the circle. Idiocy. It felt better than letting Aquaria be conscious of what was about to happen to her.

For the remaining sigils, Ephorah added what she thought would allow her to be able to fight off an army of Greymarchers. She couldn't afford to get tired. She couldn't afford to have any open wounds. She needed strength, protection, and a source of power.

"*Vix*, *San*, *Fiew*, *Petu*, *Wan*..." Ephorah looked over her lists of words. Blood, heal, flow, force, wave. There was something missing. She needed a source of power for the weapon, in light of how weak Aquaria was now.

Ephorah had a chart for symbols she could use. A water elemental was compatible with the table of water sigils, along with primal symbols that all spirits could use. A humanus spirit like Aquaria could work with all but the most powerful enchantments, but none of the words on her list could offset the spirit's diminutive form.

Except...Ephorah also had a few words that were...taboo. Sort of. One of her professors had taught her the word *Tiran* for forcing spirits under her control, under threat of pain. These sigils had been frowned upon in previous decades, but shifts in policy at the institute meant some teachers encouraged students to use them as necessary. One of the known taboo symbols might be exactly what she needed.

"*Fame.*" Hunger.

Grabbing the colonel's ceremonial sword, the only thing available to enchant, Ephorah chanted her sigils aloud and tapped the blade of the sword against Aquaria's vial. The spirit dissipated out of the glass and into the sword, which made a strange sound like wrenched metal as it reacted to the enchantment. The steel blackened and corroded; metal wasn't supposed to look like that.

"What in the Abyss?" Ephorah held the sword up to the light to see what she'd actually made. "Damnit, this better work!"

Holding the weapon in her right hand, she felt the blade pull itself towards one of the corpses of the tank's crew. The sword tried to connect with their bodies like a magnet to a piece of steel. No, not a magnet. It was a hunger. Or a thirst. The sword wanted blood.

Unable to hold it away any longer, Ephorah allowed the blade to bury itself into the nearest corpse. "Disgusting. How the hell am I going to control this thing? It feels like a mindless, hungry beast."

The corpse was pretty dry, but it wasn't like it had been cremated. There was still blood inside, and Ephorah heard a slurping sound from the edge of the sword that was buried in the flesh.

The corroded look of the weapon faded and was replaced with a shiny, fairly ordinary-looking steel blade, but for the red pattern of lines now etched into the blade in the form of the sigils used in the sword's creation. The edge of the blade became sharper than any tool Ephorah had seen before, and at the same time, strength and energy flowed into her muscles through the weapon's handle. Any exhaustion she'd felt was flushed away as the sword's thirst was satiated.

"Well, what do you know?" Ephorah grinned.

Unlocking the roof hatch, Ephorah held a rag over her mouth and face and thrust the sword upwards as she emerged from the tank. The blade skewered a Greymarcher and drained the blood from it. Apparently, Greymarcher blood fed the sword as much as any other, because Ephorah felt more power flow into her as she sliced her way through enemies to climb out of the tank.

Wielding the weapon with her right hand, she could also fend off attackers with her left, which was still wearing her enchanted gloves. Ephorah was vaguely aware that there was usually a lot of skill to swordsmanship, and she didn't have it. Fortunately, neither did the mindless hordes of the Greymarch, and as long as she could land a cut that would draw some blood, she never got tired.

The marchers would try to grab Ephorah, with grey gunk visibly welling up in their throats, but it was surprisingly easy for her to stab or punch each one away. Perhaps if she could get tired, the Greymarchers would overwhelm her, but with each slash of her sword, she felt herself siphon the strength of her foes.

In what must have only been seconds, Ephorah found herself standing around a dozen dead Greymarchers. She looked around, expecting more to be coming, but there weren't any left. Perhaps the tank and its explosion had killed all the Greymarchers except this final group.

Her sword let out a purring sound, like it was finally satisfied. Ephorah grabbed the sheath from Colonel Strauss's body and put the sword away. There was no need to clean it; it had already consumed all of the gore that had gotten on it from the fight.

Ephorah could see the volcano mortar still parked at the edge of the village, but she had one last thing to do before she could try and reunite with the Salamanders. Checking the sides of the tank where explosions had knocked out the vehicle's treads, Ephorah found several burnt Greymarchers that seemed to have holes in their stomachs. The damage made it look like something had exploded out of their bellies, as if they'd been packed with gunpowder.

The sun was starting to set, and a terrible thought struck Ephorah. This fight wasn't over.

Running back to the mortar vehicle, she had to warn anyone still alive before nightfall. To her surprise, the hatch of the volcano tank opened and a soldier poked his head out.

"You survived?" He pointed to the wrecked demolisher tank. "What happened?"

"The Hisham," Ephorah climbed onto the volcano tank and joined the mercenary. "Some of the Greymarchers had been packed with gunpowder, and exploded when burnt. They're too mindless to come up with something like that on their own, but the Hisham are clever." She checked the sun as it finally set beneath the horizon. "This isn't over."

"We've got a pair of infantry flamethrowers, and the vehicle guns," the mercenary called down to the men in the tank. "The Hisham are coming! Look alive!" He turned back to Ephorah. "Are you coming inside?"

"I think I've had enough of being attacked by hordes in a tin can for one day." Ephorah drew her sword. "Hand me a few firebomb grenades, if you've got them. I'm sick of waiting for someone else to slay things for me."

The mercenary handed Ephorah three firebomb grenades. "That's all we've got."

Ephorah peered out into the quickly darkening fields. Already, red eyes were starting to glow and shadows were moving about in the night. "It'll do."

She leapt off of the tank as the mortar prepared to fire at the incoming monsters. Sadly, their aim was not as good in the dark as it was in the daylight; they seemed to hit some of the Hisham, but it was clear that the monsters were able to avoid most of their mortar shells. Ephorah drew her new weapon and prepared for the incoming attack.

It wasn't clear to her how she knew, but somehow, Ephorah knew that the sword could do more than just drink blood and empower the wielder. Perhaps it was because she knew the sigils that she had used to enchant it.

As a swarm of Hisham approached, Ephorah swept her sword across her front. A wave of red crystals flung from the blade, impaling the incoming Hisham. The crystals embedded themselves into the monsters' flesh, and as they regenerated, the projectiles became buried further into their bodies, limiting their mobility.

A Hisham pointed at Ephorah and howled, as if calling the others to focus on her. Their red eyes were visibly filled with anger; some of them looked like they might have remembered her from their previous meeting.

Ephorah took one of the firebomb grenades and cracked it open onto the blade of her sword. Her gloves, being arachne silk, protected her hands as she coated the blade in the flammable fluid, setting the sword on fire.

Anger in the Hisham's eyes turned to fear as they realized what Ephorah was doing, but it was too late. With a burning blade that hungered for victims, Ephorah started hacking her way through the monsters.

It wasn't long before she realized that Hisham don't bleed; they weren't feeding the sword. She could actually feel the weapon's disappointment as it tore through each monster; burning every wound and reducing them to ash. She wouldn't be able to do this forever like with the Greymarchers; she could feel herself getting tired. Still, she didn't need to kill every last one of them. All she had to do was scare them off.

It wasn't long before the Hisham tried to flee. With Ephorah's blood crystals still lodged in some of their bodies, they couldn't move or fight as well, and they had initially attacked her thinking she wouldn't have a weapon that could actually hurt them. Now almost a dozen monsters had been burnt to death, and the rest were routing, with the volcano tank driving up to use their close-range flamethrowers to pick them off.

Ephorah could hear some of the men cheering over the sounds of the flamethrowers as the Hisham fled. She didn't see anymore red eyes; any Hisham left were in full retreat. Out of breath, she let her sword arm drop and looked at the blade. A normal weapon would have been damaged from that kind of fire, but her sword was as shiny and pristine-looking as earlier.

The tank rolled after the fleeing Hisham, trying to finish them off with their flamethrowers, but Ephorah sat down to rest and looked at her sword. The blade's edges had become serrated, like teeth, and she could still feel its hunger. It was like a ravenous beast with minimal thought as to who it was used against.

What exactly had she created?

21

A New Idea

RUBIN

The headmistress of the Institute of Theurgy looked through the stack of papers, as if one might contain a secret answer to her problems.

"Kollek, how many new students enrolled at the last Career Festival?"

Professor Kollek, who was sitting in the headmistress's office, looked over her notes from the festival. "We've got...twenty-six new students!" She beamed brightly.

"Twenty-six?" Rubin's jaw dropped. "That's...that's barely a tenth of last year's enrollment!"

"Oh, yeah," Kollek frowned and nodded. "Without Marduk there, not a ton of people came to our booth. He wasn't there to draw young women in with those...powers of his."

The headmistress massaged her temples. This was too much. The Institute was running out of money, their enrollment was lower than ever before, and the employment rate of their graduates was so dismal that many students dropped last year to cut their losses. Without their patron god, their school was doomed.

Aviva Rubin opened the small cabinet under her desk and pulled out a bottle of arak, an alcoholic drink. Filling a shot glass, she looked up at the portraits of previous headmasters of the institute. Well into her sixties, a doctor would tell her to ease up on the liquor, but Rubin knew that the unchecked stress was worse.

"Kollek, why did you become a fulltime professor?" She drank her shot and poured another. "What were your goals for the school?"

"Oh, well..." Professor Kollek was a bit of an airhead, and getting answers from her about deep questions could be difficult. "I wanted to be a theurgist because I thought it was fun. And when I graduated, there were no jobs available, so I decided I wanted to stay at the institute. It's nice here, you know?"

Headmistress Rubin replaced the arak bottle in her cabinet and drank the second shot. "I graduated from this school forty-five years ago, back when Headmaster Friedman ran this place. He was replaced a year after I finished, of course, but he was the one who started looking into ways of making theurgy easier." She looked down at the empty shot glass. "Back then, only those of means could attend colleges. You either had to be born into a wealthy family or be extremely lucky. My parents were just barely able to send me to school, and when I graduated I had a dream: I wanted a world where everyone could become a wizard, regardless of birth."

"That's nice. I liked the kitty-cat spirits," Kollek chimed in. "And the other bestia spirits. They're just so cute!"

"Truly, you are the perfect confidant." Rubin sarcastically remarked. *Because you never actually listen to anything I'm saying*, she thought. "At any rate, even though college is more affordable than ever, and middle-class families and even some of the working-class have a shot at it, that dream just seems to get further and further away. And now, not only am I going to have to lay off part of the staff, probably lose more students in the process, no guarantee any of them will find jobs...and our patron god has truly abandoned us. I...I think we'll be able to stay open. Maybe. Perhaps...we could open a research division...something dedicated to discovering new ways of controlling spirits."

"Ooh, we could show people how to make elementals into pets!" Kollek offered. "Who wouldn't want a puppy made of fire?"

"I appreciate that you're thinking, but I don't want to deal with the lawsuits that would bring." Rubin rubbed her eyes with her fingers. "There's not

A NEW IDEA

enough booze in my liquor cabinet."

"Perhaps what you need is a new idea."

A girl, who couldn't be older than eighteen, sat on the edge of the headmistress's desk. She had straight black hair that came down to her shoulders, soft hazel eyes, smooth skin like an oil painting, and wore a simple autumn outfit.

"Are you...a student?" Rubin looked at the door to her office. It was not only closed, but Professor Kollek had left a briefcase propped up against it. There was no way this girl could have entered the room without knocking it over. "How did you get in—"

"Are you seriously worried about that?" The girl smiled. "With all the problems you're facing?"

"Unless you're one of our students, I don't see how that's your concern," Rubin replied. "Now—"

"It's not me who needs to be concerned." The girl tilted her head, letting her raven black hair tumble to one side as she looked at the headmistress. "You're the one who has been steeped in troubles. I'm just here to offer you a solution."

"Solution?" The headmistress scoffed. "And what solution does a teenage girl with no real-world experience have to offer?"

The girl snickered at this remark but straightened her smile out quickly. "Isn't it obvious? You need a new patron god."

"A new god?" Rubin clenched her fist. "You speak like they just grow on trees—"

"Don't they?" The girl's smile brightened. "Gods are born from ideas. There's a lot more of them out there than you think, even if you don't know their names. When I say you need a new god, I mean you need a new idea. One to form the basis of your school around. Your curriculum, your treasury, recruitment — everything should be built around a new idea. One that works for you."

Rubin paused. She had already begun to suspect that the girl in front of her wasn't completely human, and she already knew what the answer to her next question would be. "And what god, or idea, do you think we should base our academy around?"

Leaning closer, the girl's smile widened. Rubin finally noticed the almost serpentine shape of her eyes.

"Me."

"And who..." Rubin was getting tired of the mind games. For all she knew, the goddess before her was some sort of evil deity, or a vengeful spirit angered by the fact that she'd been forgotten by mortals. "...might you be? What are you the goddess of, exactly?"

"...huh, you know what?" The girl grinned. "I don't think I was ever given a formal title, and heaven knows I never accepted a job assigned from Marduk." She clicked her tongue as she spoke the god's name, as if hiding her disgust behind a thin veil of civility. "As for my name, I'm happy to just be called 'mistress.' Or, if that's too much, call me 'Misty.'"

"Misty?" Rubin raised an eyebrow. "But if you don't have a title, what idea are you associated with? All gods need belief, don't they? So, what idea do we need to believe in for you to have the power to save our school?"

"I'm something of a special case," Misty winked. "I exist whether people believe in me or not, so long as they act according to the force of nature that empowers me. All I need you to do is believe that you deserve what you want."

The headmistress blinked. "What I want? I want many things. I want my school to stay open. I want my staff to stay employed. I want my students to graduate and find jobs. I want to create a world where everyone can become a wizard. I want my liquor bottle to be refilled. Which of these things do I need to believe I deserve?"

Misty shrugged. "All of them."

Rubin shook her head and looked at Professor Kollek, who shrugged in confusion. "Everything?" The headmistress asked.

"Everything," Misty nodded and leaned towards the headmistress. "I need you to believe that you deserve everything you want."

Rubin leaned away from the goddess. "I don't trust you. Everything about you creeps me out. Give me one reason to believe you."

"Because you summoned me," Misty touched Rubin's shot glass. Dark wine manifested into the glass until it was halfway full. "When you believed that

A NEW IDEA

Marduk was wrong, and that you deserved better. You've been feeding me for some time now; changing how you use spirits, enslaving sapient elementals. I could show you so much more. All you have to do is believe you deserve it."

The headmistress straightened up and mustered as much courage as she could without drinking the refilled shot of alcohol. "Get out. I don't know who you are, or what you really are, but you might as well have 'evil' stamped on your forehead and embroidered on the hem of your skirt. Leave, and don't come back!"

Misty closed her eyes and laughed. It was exactly like the sort of cute giggle one would expect from a schoolgirl. "Of course. I can't force you to accept me. It's not like I need you to make a decision today."

"This is my decision. Now, and forever." The headmistress stood up to her full height, which, at sixty-eight years old, was barely a full centimeter taller than Misty. "We will not worship a goddess who we do not trust."

"You're adorable," Misty spontaneously grew a few centimeters taller and patted Rubin on the head. "But no one ever really rejects me forever. I'll be there, for the rest of your life, waiting for you to change your mind. And when your mortal life ends, I'll be at the ready for your replacement to make her decision. Just as you did today, all you need to do is believe that you deserve the things you want. And when you do, I'll be back."

The goddess vanished, leaving Rubin standing at her desk, only now aware of how much she'd been sweating.

"Huh," Kollek looked at the headmistress. "She seemed nice."

22

Grave Preparations

AMENHOTEP

The High Tomb Lord approached his Necrophytes, where a familiar face stood at attention.

"Wasn't your name Mando?" The High Tomb Lord asked.

The Necrophyte nodded.

"I heard you took my advice, and have started enjoying the perks of your new position."

Mando slackened his jaw as if to respond, but held his bearing.

"It's alright, you can speak," Amenhotep assured him.

"Yes, sir I...I..."

"I heard about the girl you arrested in the marketplace. She's in the cell on the westernmost wall of the prison under our feet right now." Amenhotep mused. "You were quite brutal with her these last few nights. We could hear you from up here."

Mando tried to keep his bearing, but his whole body rattled from nerves. "...I...I mean...I thought–"

"Oh, Mando," Amenhotep placed a hand on his shoulder to calm him down. "You don't need to worry; I wouldn't have encouraged you otherwise. This is a perk of your job; you're owed this. It's your reward for your loyal service to your godking."

The Necrophyte looked like he'd just gotten the wind knocked out of him, but he was starting to relax. "Th-thank you, my godking."

"Of course, her family won't be too happy about it," Amenhotep added. "But, what can they do? They wouldn't dare lay a finger on you whilst you're under my protection. And I kind of like you. You're my kind of enforcer." He patted the Necrophyte on the shoulder.

"Oh...Why thank you, master."

"It's just...I want to protect my loyal subjects, and especially the ones I like..." Amenhotep looked out the window at the streets of Azzitha. "But I have these...terrible visions...they're not really dreams; I don't need sleep. But the thought of what would happen to my most trusted Necrophytes if something should happen to my power structure. I don't think I could keep them safe." He leaned over to Mando, as if whispering a secret into his ear. "It would be...wise, for you to make sure that never happens."

Mando's eyes widened as he realized what he'd actually gotten himself into. "Of course. I will take extra care in my duties rooting out traitors to the godking."

Amenhotep patted him on the shoulder before turning back to Sekhet. "And that's that."

Sekhet, who knew a lot about manipulating people in masses but clearly had more to learn, stood visibly confused. "How did you get him to..."

"Most people have, on some level, a desire to act out some truly immoral things," Amenhotep explained. "I'm sure you already know this, but forbidden fruit is the most tempting."

"Yes, that part makes sense," Sekhet nodded. "It's fun to do bad things. But...you got him to act on those impulses..."

"And told him it was his right as one of my Necrophytes. 'The privileges of service to the godking.'" Amenhotep chuckled. "As for your matter at hand, seek out people on the fringes of society. Find people who can form the core of an insurrection. Tell them that, in the name of some unachievable moral good, it is acceptable, even commendable, to attack people who stand in opposition of this moral goal. They don't have to start with something as heavy as what Mando did. Remember: small steps corrupt. Get them to commit petty acts of vandalism, or even just act foolishly, so that they'd be embarrassed to admit later that they were unjustified. Once they've committed to minor acts in the name of 'the greater good,' you can get them to escalate."

"...And then, when they've either done enough small crimes or one big crime, anyone who suggests that they might not be on the side of good will be a threat to their self-image." Sekhet put the last pieces together. "We won't need that much manpower; the people will enforce our deceptions for us."

"You won't even have to lift a bony finger at that point." Amenhotep smiled under his golden mask. "Do you know where to begin?"

Sekhet paused. "I'll start with bars, pubs, ghettos, and find thugs, lowlifes, and petty bullies. People are always hurt in riots, and no group you target, be they class, race, or anything else, is entirely made up of good or bad people. You have to get the ball rolling by riling up people who don't care that their actions will, at best, harm the innocent along with the guilty."

Amenhotep nodded. "Assuming 'guilty' isn't just a category we made up. Want to ignite a violent revolution? Start with people looking for an excuse to be violent. Now, if you'll excuse me, I need to inspect the new weapons Djedefre and Pausiris want to implement in our armed forces."

The High Tomb Lord took his leave of Sekhet and headed to meet his chief inventor and general outside of his palace.

Standing overlooking the barren, flat land were a number of death knights standing near Pausiris, Arkeon, and Djedefre. Each death knight was a corpse infused with powerful necromantic energies that made them over two meters tall, their withered flesh stretched to cover warped skeletons, so that each one looked like a vacuum-sealed husk of a corpse in full battle armor. One in particular had a shoulder-mounted cannon situated on top of one of its pauldrons.

"Greetings, my godking." Pausiris bowed. "We have prepared before you a presentation of our newest field artillery."

Arkeon directed one of the death knights to hold up a pair of cannon balls connected by a chain. This death knight went to the front of the cannon held by the other and stuffed the balls down the barrel.

"Cannons are effective against large targets and fortifications, but they are slow to reload, do not explode when we want them to, and are fairly ineffective against enemy infantry. Mortars are devastating against infantry, but difficult to aim, and have a minimum range. My solution has been to implement chained cannon balls and reduce the size of the cannon so that it can be wielded by Arkeon's death knights."

Several target dummies were set up in the field. At least a dozen were positioned near each other like a formation. Pausiris turned to Arkeon. "You may fire when ready."

Arkeon was visibly displeased by being told by the inventor when he was permitted to fire, but he gave the death knight holding the cannon the order. The undead behemoth fired his massive gun, and a projectile erupted from the barrel that spun around and whirled like a blade through the dummies before exploding, leaving two craters near the destroyed targets.

"An excellent weapon," Djedefre exclaimed. "A pair of death knights and one of these cannons would be able to devastate entire swaths of the soul-stealing monkeys that constantly try to break through our walls."

All of the other Tomb Lords shared a look. They had given up explaining to Djedefre that the chimpanzees of the Simian Empire were apes, not monkeys.

Djedefre looked at Pausiris. "Didn't one of your scholars report that the Ancients used the word 'spank' to refer to striking an enemy, and hitting them so badly it put them in their place?"

"I believe so," the inventor replied.

"Then with this new cannon, which will surely put the monkeys in their place, these new soldiers will be called 'the Monkey Spankers!'" The general beamed.

"What?" Pausiris flinched. "He can't call them that!" He turned to Arkeon and Amenhotep for help. "Someone tell him why he can't call them that!"

Arkeon snickered while Amenhotep raised a hand. "Perhaps, Djedefre, you could call your own personal guard of death knights this. But for the rest of our armed forces, who will not be anywhere near the border with the Simian Empire, a different name would be more appropriate."

"Hm," Djedefre appeared to be thinking, or something close to it. "That's a good point. Any death knights positioned anywhere else will have no monkeys to spank."

"Make him stop," Pausiris groaned. "Someone, make him stop!"

"Even still," Amenhotep continued. "A weapon like that deserves its place in our army. How many death knights can you equip with these cannons?"

"In a month?" Arkeon ran some numbers in his head. "Twenty. Making death knights takes time."

"Make it so." He turned to Pausiris. "And your mechanical warriors?"

"I have fifty sentinels completed and ready for combat," the inventor reported. "They cannot use ranged weapons, but mixing them with death knights armed with these cannons will solve that."

"Good. Build me an army stronger than anything the Borealans can throw at us." Amenhotep smiled. "Destabilizing their empire is enough to weaken them, but an unstoppable army of tireless warriors will deliver the killing blow."

23

A Reclusive Alchemist

CYRUS

Returning to Doctor Monroe's house, Cyrus delivered the drugs he'd been sent to get and told the doctor about what had happened earlier.

"Just try to get some rest," Monroe rubbed his face with his palm. "It's late, and you've been through enough today. We can talk in the morning."

Between the exhaustion of the day and the questions buzzing through Cyrus's head, he somehow got to sleep on Monroe's couch. In the morning, the doctor questioned him over breakfast.

"He stabbed a woman several times in the front and back, and then you say he cried like a baby when you kicked him off of her?" The doctor stroked his chin. "I wonder. I'm imagining a child who has never been punished for hitting their sibling or taking their toys getting spanked by their parents for the first time. How confused the child would be, if they'd gotten away with their behavior for years and only now has someone punished them for it." He shrugged. "Perhaps I'm wrong."

"Then I was arrested as I tried to heal the woman's wounds," Cyrus explained. "I used the techniques you taught me; I let her DNA do the work."

Monroe's eyes brightened. "Did she survive?"

Cyrus nodded. "They said she was in a hospital with her external wounds healed, and they only charged me with assault and battery. She's probably still alive, or they'd charge me with murder.

"That's wonderful!" Monroe smiled. "You saved her life!"

"...And I almost went to prison for it." Cyrus grimaced. "I was saved by a lawyer working for that fire insurance company. Apparently, the court never tried to get a defense attorney to look at my case."

Monroe sighed. "You know what? You should spend some time thinking about something else. Why don't I show you how my sheep produce steel wool?"

Cyrus followed the doctor to the pasture outside where a dozen sheep were kept in a pen. These sheep had grey, metallic wool like the sort he'd seen in hardware stores. In addition to eating grass, a trough was setup that contained some kind of red paste that the sheep would occasionally stop to eat.

"Okay, how on earth does this work?" Cyrus looked at Doctor Monroe, who had out a pair of thick cutters and began cutting the steel wool off of a sheep one strand at a time.

"Iron is already a common element in various organisms," the doctor explained. "These sheep are producing a steel-like alloy made from the carbon in their own bodies and an iron-enriched diet, which admittedly required me to modify their digestive tracts." He gestured to the trough, which was clearly filled with some sort of meaty paste. "Of course, the meat-nutrient solution is mixed with a number of iron supplements and vegetables. The sheep aren't going to spontaneously become carnivorous just because they need iron; they don't even have instincts on where to get the nutrients they need. At least we don't have to worry about them eating the poultratoes."

Cyrus glanced over at the bed of squirming, clucking chicken-potatoes. Doctor Monroe had placed a layer of bird netting over them to keep predators from eating his new project. They looked utterly ridiculous wriggling around in their field.

"Why don't we go over the formula for the steel wool inside?" Monroe asked. "Making a chimera like this is fairly difficult."

The doctor showed Cyrus a notebook detailing the experiments he went through to create the new sheep. There were over forty-seven failed attempts, with most of them dying fairly horribly. Some of them died of heavy-metal poisoning. A few had the wool grow too thick through their hair follicles and punctured their skin, inevitably causing death by a thousand cuts.

"Wow," Cyrus winced. "These are painful ways for an animal to die."

"Oh, yes," Monroe sighed. "That's the price of progress. Creating a chimera, even a simple enough design like this, requires many failed experiments before you get a single success. Lots of people don't want to think about the process that makes these amazing things. They just want the results. But for every whimsical, silly-looking chimera, there's a large pile of failures that died in the process. In your classes, did they ever show you how to make a yogurt platypus?"

Cyrus nodded. "Made one using the techniques they taught us."

"I guarantee they did not teach you how many animals died to perfect the method." Doctor Monroe rubbed his forehead and smiled weakly as he set a kettle on for tea. "We scientists like to think we can explore anything in the world, look into whatever corners we want and shine a light on whatever we find. But the truth is, we need to pay bills, we need to cover the costs of research materials, and for that, we need to give people things that they want in the moment. It is not enough to tell the public 'I'll have something amazing in ten to twenty years derived from snail mucus; just be patient!' People want results right now, and they don't want to think about where they come from. Caution, cost, animal cruelty, it's all meaningless to the average person on the street. Most people's eyes glaze over if you so much as mention the logistics."

"Take the poultratoes, for example. There are so many better things I could be experimenting on to make a chimera that's part plant and part animal. But could I sell them? Could I make back the costs of my experiments? This new batch is the seventh group of chickens I've mutated into tuberous vegetables, and all of the rest have died horribly. But I skipped working on something easier, meaning I'll have more dead chickens, all so I can get results I can sell sooner." Monroe poured himself a cup of tea and then offered one to Cyrus.

"Have you tried...explaining to people that there'd be less chicken mess and less animal cruelty if you could take your time?" Cyrus took a sip of tea.

Doctor Monroe sat down at the kitchen table. "Tell me, you spend most of your time now at the College of Alchemy, right?"

"Yes," Cyrus nodded.

"I see." Monroe looked down at the table in despair. "A problem with smart people; we spend most of our time in education when we're young, surrounded by other smart people. Then we get jobs based on our degrees where we work almost exclusively with other smart people. We forget what the average person is actually like. It's not just that the majority of people are uneducated; they just aren't like us. They don't enjoy having discussions about how to modify animals to give steel wool, they don't like to think, and above all else, they don't like to be reminded that we're smart and they're not. So when a scientist tries to explain these sorts of things to normal people, and it goes over the laymen's heads; they don't absorb it. They just get mad. We are usually accused of having a complex for knowing too much, or something like that."

Cyrus paused. He wanted to argue with the doctor, but his own troubles with his family stopped him. "Lots of people have gifts," he finally said. "Gifts that separate them from everyone else. People don't rally together and hate *everyone* who has a special talent; they'd be so busy hating each other that they'd never get anything done."

"This is true," Monroe admitted. "A man who stands over two meters high can proclaim that he is exceptionally tall, and most people will simply agree with him, apart from a few short men who will grumble that he is bragging. A woman with an amazing singing voice can publicly acknowledge that she is a talented singer, and the public will cheer for her so long as she sings to them. But genius? Genius is the one thing everyone wishes they had, and hates in others. If a smart kid tells the two-meters-tall man that he just got top marks in all of his advanced classes, the same people who would agree that the tall man is tall will claim the smart kid is arrogant. They will accuse him of thinking he is better than the normal people, largely because normal people think they are superior to idiots, and the average person believes that if *they* were a genius, then they would be superior to normal people."

Doctor Monroe paused and closed his eyes. This was a subject that clearly weighed on him a lot. "They don't understand. Smart men don't think they're superior. Smart men feel small. A genius may have an advantage over the average individual, but normal people outnumber geniuses by a wide margin.

And they vote. And they form angry mobs. They get upset when the 'wrong person' wins their merit-based tournament, or when reality doesn't comply with their ridiculous beliefs. And yet...we depend on them." Monroe noticed the confused look in Cyrus's eyes. "Smart people cannot stand repetitive tasks. Jobs that do not keep our brains engaged are extremely difficult for us to handle. Geniuses make poor farmhands, factory workers, or other manual laborers. Not because we cannot build the muscles, but because our brains will not be quiet and let us focus on the monotonous tasks at hand."

Cyrus remembered his past experiences with woodworking, and how he'd never been able to get the hang of carpentry like the rest of his brothers and sisters. "Every time I tried to pick up the family trade, or help the family business, my mind would wander. Shaping the wood was a slow, difficult process, and at the end it was shoddy work, no matter what I tried."

"Then you've felt it. The disability that comes with genius. A brilliant mind can only stay focused on a task that doesn't engage him for a limited time. It can be especially dangerous if any steam-driven tools are involved." Monroe finished his tea and clasped his hands. "We are specialized for specific purposes, and we depend on normal people for everything else. Normal people who think themselves clever until they meet one of us, and get angry when they realize how far away they are from true genius. They cast us as arrogant for accurately assessing our abilities, and our calling is to help these people who despise us as much as possible; to treat them of diseases, addictions, and accidents, many of which they afflict upon themselves."

Cyrus smiled. "Thoth told me once that each individual life is priceless."

Monroe's face didn't lift as he continued to stare into the edge of his teacup. "I think he's right, but how do you save people from themselves? Were there a medicine that could cure an addict of the horrors he has loosed upon his own body, or a serum to make fatty tissue from poor health choices melt away...They say that the more you understand, the less you can forgive, and I find it's very, very true. And then, you'll find you have very few people left to relate with. The more you understand, the less you can forgive."

"You sound like you really hate stupid people," Cyrus replied.

"No." Monroe's head snapped upright with a stern look in his eyes. "Do not confuse normal people with genuine idiots. Idiots usually know, at least on some level, that they are not very smart; they don't preen and think themselves clever and get mad at folks like us when they realize we're smarter than them. Almost everyone is smarter than an idiot, and so the idiot has no choice but to develop humility, a respectable trait that every scientist should learn. What's more, idiots and geniuses have something in common: the world isn't built for either of us. It's designed for the average, and we're just living in it."

"Oh." Cyrus took another sip of his tea. "Then why do you make it sound like you're afraid of stupidity?"

"It's not stupidity," Monroe explained. "It's stupidity that thinks itself genius, and will attack true genius to protect its own arrogance. You're still pretty young, and frankly, you're naïve, but one day, you will learn just how dumb the average person truly is. And when that happens, you will experience true powerlessness."

Cyrus wasn't sure he understood what the doctor meant, but he gave it his best guess. "Does this have anything to do with what happened to me earlier, or any of the things going on with the court and my arrest?"

"It does," the doctor admitted. "The situation with the Empyrians is incredibly complicated. They commit way more crime than Borealans or Coptics do, and they're not happy that the majority of people in prison are Empyrian. The city council is trying everything they can think of to keep the peace, but nothing they do is working. Most people in Dihorma believe that the best solution would be to give the Empyrians back at least a portion of their old land, let them govern themselves in their own country. Some Empyrians like the idea, because they'd have their own nation again. Some Borealans like the idea, because then the Empyrians could commit all the violent crime they want far away from Borealans, and we wouldn't have to deal with them anymore; no resources from the east are worth this kind of crime spree. But what the government understands, at both the imperial and provincial levels, is that lines on a map aren't the real problem."

"Drawing a border, dumping all of the Empyrians over it, and telling them to stay on their side won't fix anything. The core of the problem is that Empyrians want the lifestyles that most Borealans enjoy, and if they're willing to commit crimes to reach that standard of living, they'll cross some made up line on a map without a second thought. It's like the story of the Ant and the Grasshopper: the ant thinks he's all set for the winter with all the grain he stored up from the summer, and then the grasshopper breaks into his house, beats him to death with his fiddle, and takes all the grain. It doesn't matter if the grasshopper had no skills, or had any opportunity to harvest grain, or if he truly was just a lazy bum; he wants to live, and is willing to kill and steal to do so."

"Back home, I barely ever gave the Empyrians much thought," Cyrus admitted. "They're barely noticed. They have a section of the city roped off for them; I think I heard someone at school say they prefer to stick to their own, so the rest of the city doesn't notice them unless they're making a ruckus. Even I never noticed them until I had an encounter with a girl in the Blue Diamond Market, and it was over before I even learned her name."

"The Empyrians living in Hadesh, or any other cities in the west, are mostly inducted into our culture. They act more like us than like Empyrians out here. The further east you go, the more of their old culture Empyrians still retain, and it's the culture, not the border, that defines how people live. Empyrians believe that cleaning up trash, or other types of work that involve getting rid of filth, are demeaning. They even have a word for it: 'abeed-shughl,' which apparently means 'slave work.' To us, taking care of your community, even picking up trash and food waste, is an act of civic pride that *needs* to be done. People volunteer for this sort of thing, and getting rid of garbage means there's nothing to draw rats and other vermin, which bring disease. Diseases that are expensive to treat. Bear in mind, garbage collectors make good money in Hadesh; it's a respected career in our culture. In theirs? Not so much."

"Why would they call it 'slave work?'" Cyrus asked. "Do they usually have people who've sold themselves into slavery clean up their streets?" In the Borealan Empire, the only kind of slavery that was legally tolerated was when a person had run up such a huge debt that they had to sell themselves to the government in order to pay it off.

"I don't know. If they did, then it was before the war, under the old Empyrian Empire." Doctor Monroe poured himself a second cup of tea. "On paper, it would be really easy to fix this; just find some unemployed Empyrians, teach them to start a garbage collection business, and clean up the trash. That right there would reduce the filth, vermin, and sickness some people have, and would create a healthier environment to raise their kids." He looked up from his steaming cup of tea. "What is a high standard of living if not a healthy life and a clean environment? Do you know anyone rich who lives in filth and makes himself sick? The solution is so simple, but the Empyrians don't want to do it. And to be fair, the average Empryian living in Hadesh doesn't enjoy the same quality of life as the average Borealan, or the average Coptic. Did this Leah Kaplan tell you about Empyrian arson attacks?"

Cyrus shrugged. "Not much."

"Hm. Tensions boiled in Dihorma for a while in the 860s, and it culminated in a breakout of arson attacks used to terrorize local businesses into paying protection money. When the local fire department didn't want to go putting out fires and risk getting attacked by gangs, Jasper and Jaime bought out there old firefighting equipment and sent their men to protect their clients. Jasper was killed by one of the arsonists, and once Jaime became the only surviving owner, he militarized the company. Ever since the fires reached a peak in 868, the firefighters have carried guns with them on patrol, and will shoot any Empyrian they claim to reasonably suspect is planning to set a building on fire. The fires in Dihorma have stopped, for now, but other crimes are still pretty common, and Empyrians are afraid to be outside at night or Jaime's men will shoot them."

"What?" Cyrus balked. "That can't be legal!"

"It is, thanks to a loophole." Monroe clasped his hands and leaned forward towards Cyrus. "Tell me, if you saw an Empyrian man holding a bottle filled with liquid, and a rag on any part of his body, would you assume that he was planning to set a building on fire so that he could either loot a nearby store in the resulting panic, or as an act of terrorism to extort other stores in the future?"

Cyrus blinked. "No."

Monroe nodded. "You are an outsider to Dihorma. It would be silly for you to see a person of any race and assume they planned to set a building on fire.

Now tell me, if you lived in a town where arson was fairly common, and almost every case was committed by an Empyrian, would your answer change? Would it still be reasonable, after years of Empyrian arson attacks, to assume that an Empyrian man holding a bottle of liquid and a rag *wasn't* about to commit another attack?"

Turning the doctor's words over in his head, a sick feeling hit Cyrus's stomach. "No."

"That's the problem," Monroe explained. "According to the law, if a person reasonably believes that someone is about to commit a crime that could potentially lead to another person's death or serious bodily harm, it is legal to use lethal force to stop them, as that is your right to defend others from violence. Arson is a crime that can easily result in another person's death or bodily harm. The problem is the "reasonably believes" part. Should it be based on someone who lives in Dihorma, and knows about the current situation and crime rate? Or should it be based on an outsider, such as you, who didn't know about any of this?"

"If it were based on an outsider's viewpoint..." Cyrus turned the idea over in his head. "Wouldn't that open the door for someone who comes from a town with a worse Empyrian crime rate to be the standard? Someone whose first instinct would be to shoot to kill, even if the person isn't holding a bottle of liquid at all?"

"That's what Jaime argued in court with his company on the line, and so far, he's won." Monroe stroked his chin, his eyes downcast. "The rest of the council tried to propose that the standard be based on a complete stranger who knew nothing of Empyrians or Borealans. Lyons mocked this and called it the 'total ignoramus standard.'"

"But how reasonable can a completely ignorant person be?" Cyrus asked. "Thoth once told me that stereotypes, especially stereotypes that stick, are the result of people recognizing patterns and taking them too far. They aren't entirely true or false, because while patterns among groups of people exist, no one belongs to just one group."

Monroe nodded. "That is sound advice. Yes, that is a good way to put it, but people need to make quick decisions, and they need big issues resolved. I don't know what the right thing to do here is. I'll stick to my research; that seems to be the best way I can help."

Cyrus agreed, but something bothered him. He realized that he'd been looking to the doctor as a replacement for Thoth, whether intentionally or not. But Monroe wasn't a god; he wasn't the physical manifestation of logic and reason that Thoth was. He was an excellent teacher of medical alchemy and chimerafication, but he was not a substitute for the god that found Cyrus when he was at his lowest point and remade him into an alchemist.

24

A Gassy Experiment

AMRI

The transport ship came into the Academics' Wharf in Silverstack Docks. This special part of the harbor was reserved for ships on business with the Academy District in Hadesh, including transports to and from other magical universities.

Once the ship docked, Amri and Namid gathered their luggage and got off, with Amri struggling to carry most of their bags. Amri knew he was not the strongest young man his age, but that often came with being an academic. With his sister's bags hung on one side of his back, his own bags on the other, and dragging his suitcase on wheels, he was able to keep up with Namid on their way home.

"Still can't believe we got sent home early," Namid grumbled. "I'm going to check the academy once we're settled back in to see if there's anything else I can do until the term starts again."

"Do you ever think about slowing down?" Amri asked. "I get it; it's important not to have holes in your resumé. But maybe something a little less stressful, like taking the remaining five weeks off would be good for you."

"Amri, internships, work studies, on-the-job training, these are all openly called 'voluntary' career preparation. Do you know what 'voluntary' means?" She glared at him. "It means 'you will not get a career after graduation unless you juggle these on top of your assignments, but the school isn't required to lift a finger to ensure you actually land any of these programs.' If they were required to make sure students were employed when they graduated, they'd be called 'sponsorships' instead."

Amri cocked an eyebrow. "What about enjoying life in the moment?"

"We had that." Namid frowned. "When we were kids. Now I'm fifteen. Hell, you're sixteen! Time to grow up."

Her brother thought about this for a moment. On one hand, there was no denying Namid was right; companies wanted to take on new hires with spotless work histories; no holes, no vacations, nothing. On the other hand, Amri wasn't sure yet what he wanted to do with his life. He had always been good at academics, so sorcery seemed like the ideal choice for him, but he had no idea where to go from there. Maybe the best thing to do now was to look through his options.

Their aunt and uncle lived in the Garden District, one of the ritziest places in Hadesh. Mido and Panya Seluk were a medical doctor and an Arbiter of Man, and with both of their incomes could afford a sizeable house in a very nice area. Of course, they also had no children, prior to Amri and Namid losing their parents when the Greymarch attacked Aklagos, so that made their lifestyle more affordable as well.

Once they were home, Amri dropped off the bags in the house foyer and checked to see if either his aunt or uncle were home. They weren't. His only friend from school was Rostam, and he was traveling on *the Endurance* delivering goods across the empire. There was no telling when he'd be back in Hadesh. This meant there wasn't much left for him to do, except take his sister's advice.

It was around eleven in the morning, and the streets of Hadesh were not too busy. Most people were already at work, and there were few people in the Garden District even in the evenings. On his way to the Academy of Sorcery, mixed within the quietness of his mind, Amri realized he not only had no career plans, but next to no friends as well.

There were some strange rules about networking. You were supposed to meet new people and make new "friends," but you were never supposed to ask them for job recommendations, or anything else business related. Even if you met at an employer meet-and-greet, and the whole purpose of connecting was to try and expand career opportunities. And because of these strange rules on what you could talk about, how honest you could be with your new contacts, and how you could never discuss your problems, like fears of where to find a job, you couldn't really call such relationships "friendships," either. But Amri wasn't thinking about that right now. This was the off-season of their first year; lots of students did not spend this time working at unpaid internships. He was going to look at types of careers and figure out what he wanted to do with himself.

At the Academy of Sorcery, like any university, there was an office dedicated to help people figure out their careers. This office wasn't staffed at the moment, but it had a number of fliers showing different jobs on a display shelf.

There were ads for aeromancers to work for various shipping companies, who always needed someone to control the winds and currents to keep their ships moving. There were companies looking for earth wizards who could freeze water and maintain it as ice, allowing goods to be transported in cold storage. Another flier showed an aeromancer and an aquamancer working to create liquifacted coal, a process Amri and Namid had already worked on in class before.

The final ad that caught Amri's eye showed a pyromancer monitoring the energy output of different fuels. The drawing on the flier depicted a sorcerer examining different types of fuel that were being burnt and using magic to read how much power each type released. Curious enough to give it a look, Amri headed for the city's industrial zone to investigate.

The Industrial Zone always had traces of soot and smog from the nearby smokestacks. Railroads traveling in and out of the Whitecoast Railway Depot shipped goods throughout the empire. Factories made goods from glass, metal, and chemicals created by alchemists. There were product testing facilities, research centers, and a large industrial park near the Empyrian Quarter. This was where Amri would find the fuel experiments.

The industrial park was, despite the name, a large indoor multiplex with multiple floors, different offices, laboratories, and supply rooms connected around a single courtyard with a lone, large cypress tree in an attempt to make the place feel less like a building dedicated solely to industrialization. Amri checked the copy of the flier he'd brought and found the room dedicated to the fuel testing labs.

The room was a large, somewhat dirty-looking area made from concrete with steel support beams and various machines for testing. A few smaller rooms were set aside for experiments that needed to be kept contained. These rooms had a single steel door and a thick wall of darkened glass for observing the tests.

"Alright, I've got another gas canister ready to go!" He heard a boy his age shout. "Light it up, and see how hot it burns. Try not go blind!"

The boy had short, closely cropped dark hair, a fairly mean and proud look on his face, and held up a steel canister in both hands that another worker at the plant took from him and placed inside one of the experiment rooms. A sorcerer stood near the glass wall and looked at the canister on the other side.

The sorcerer snapped his fingers; a simple ignition spell that could make a flammable object combust. The canister turned into a ball of light; even through the darkened glass, Amri had to squint from the brightness.

"A little over thirty-seven Megajoules," the sorcerer observed, having used another observation spell on the flash to determine how much energy was actually released. "Nearly thirty-eight. Impressive."

"You expected less?" The boy snickered and folded his arms. "I made that stuff purer than any commercial natural gas!"

"You made that stuff?" Amri asked.

The boy noticed Amri for the first time and frowned. "Who are you?"

"Amri Sadi." Amri offered his hand. "I'm a student of the sorcery academy."

The boy glanced at Amri's hand but didn't take it. "Well, I'm Tomek Ascher. And I'm on track to become the greatest energy alchemist that's ever lived. When I'm done, the empire won't need to worry about dwindling coal reserves around the world; we'll be making our own fuel out of waste matter!"

"Oh, so that's what you're doing here." Amri looked at what was left of the canister inside the room. "Could you tell me more about it?"

Tomek was visibly confused, but seemed eager to tell everyone about his

A GASSY EXPERIMENT

great accomplishments. "Well...right now, we're working with natural gas. Not the kind people try to get out of the earth, a...different kind. Methane gas."

"Don't people normally get methane out of the earth?" Amri asked. "I think I heard something about people bringing canaries into coal mines—"

"NOT THAT KIND OF METHANE GAS, OKAY?" Tomek roared. "The kind that comes from...cows. In factory farms."

"Cows make methane gas?" Amri started to put it together. "Oh, farts!"

"Not farts, burps!" Tomek clenched both his hands into fists. "Most of it comes out of their mouths, not— never mind!"

"So how do you get gas from a cow burp?" Amri pointed to a large tank of gas in one corner of the facility, with several smaller canisters like the one Tomek had filled earlier nearby. "How do you get them to burp into the tank?"

"They don't burp into the tank, you idiot! Methane gas is lighter than air, so it rises. You let it float to the top into a collector that fills the tanks."

Amri winced. "Does that mean that tank is full of other stuff, too? Like cow body odor, sweat, and anything else that floats in a stinky room full of cows? Like farts?"

Tomek gritted his teeth, visibly trying not to scream at Amri again. "No. Because I helped design a filter that goes on the roof of the pen where the cows are kept. The filter is made of a polymer. Methane gas molecules are small enough to pass through that polymer. Other things, like the farts, are too big to pass between the molecules of the polymer, so only methane gas fills the tanks. Got it?"

"Alright, so how do you purify it?" Amri asked.

"Well..." Tomek frowned. "The filter isn't perfect. Sometimes...other stuff gets through."

"Like farts?"

"No, not like...well," Tomek's posture finally started to slump. "Kind of."

Amri figured it was a good time to change the subject. "So, what other fuels do you work on?"

"Right now, I don't. I'm still a student at the College of Alchemy. But there're other projects around here." Tomek raised an eyebrow and looked Amri over. "Why are you asking, anyway?"

"I haven't picked a career yet," Amri grinned sheepishly. "Haven't decided what I want to do with my degree once I've got it, and there's no time to decide like the present."

"Hrm," Tomek looked like he was thinking. "Have you checked the guys that make wards yet? There's a glassworks company with a lab rented out to test out new wards for jars. It'd be worth looking into. Especially if you can find anything that keeps methane from leaking out of a gas canister."

Figuring this was as much as he was going to get out of such an angry young alchemist, Amri thanked Tomek and made his way to the glassworks lab. Just as he was about to turn a corner, he crashed into a scientist in a white lab coat coming from the other direction.

"Oh," the scientist brushed herself off. "Pardon me." She towered over Amri. He wasn't tall, by any stretch of the imagination, but this woman was tall by any standard. Like any alchemist, her body was toned and strong, a requirement for controlling alchemical reactions. She looked down at Amri through a pair of thin spectacles. They didn't look particularly needed; like a pair used only for reading, but that wasn't what caught Amri's attention. Behind those glasses, the scientist had a pair of brown eyes with pupils almost as small as pinholes. There was something...disturbing about how narrow her vision could be as her gaze darted about him.

"Excuse me," Amri bowed slightly and moved out of the scientist's way. "I'll be certain to watch more carefully where I'm going, miss..." He squinted at a nametag on the scientist's lab coat. "...Sorry, *Doctor* Talma Malbim."

Doctor Malbim raised an eyebrow at the sound of her own name, but seemed to relax at the sight of Amri stepping out of her way. "Very well, see that you do."

As she walked away, Amri made a note of other labs in the area she could have just walked out of. One room was the glassworks facility, which had no need for lab coats. Another was a tool repair shop for fixing equipment from around the industrial park; again, no need for a white lab coat, and Doctor Malbim looked far too clean for a job so greasy. The last was a pharmaceutical testing facility.

"Must be a pharmacist," Amri noted to himself as he entered the glassworks laboratory.

Inside, he found a number of workers trying various new ways to carve, etch, or mold wards into glass containers. Amri remembered what he'd learned about wards from his magical safety class; the professor who taught the class was completely insane, but he'd still managed to teach Amri the basics. A ward is meant to resist changes, both physical and magical, and a warded container like a glass jar is meant to keep anything inside from changing. If you put nitroglycerin in a flask that's been properly warded, it will keep the solution inside from exploding when shaken, unless you throw it out a window and the glass breaks.

Amri approached a worker in a thick leather apron who was rolling a glass jar in a furnace. The jar was still red with heat, and the worker was rolling it against a steel mold that had some sort of pattern on it. As the jar rolled against the pattern, it pressed lines into the molten glass that formed a new ward.

"Wow," Amri said as he watched the new warded jar being made.

"What are you doing in here?" The man rolling the jar shouted. He didn't take his eyes off of his work, but he was clearly upset with Amri. "You're not supposed to be here!"

"Oh, I was..." Amri took out the flier from before, but then realized it was a flier for the fuel examination project, unrelated to making wards. "I was hoping to learn how wards are made."

"This isn't a show! You're gonna make me screw it up!" The worker roared. "Get lost!"

Amri backed up and bumped into someone else.

"Who are you?" A man asked. He was wearing similar protective gear and a blast protective mask.

"Uh, my name's Amri. I was hoping to learn more about wards. It's the off-season, and I–"

"We don't need you here." The man in the blast mask said. "This stuff is dangerous, and we have to get back to work. We don't have time to explain all of this to some academy student who'll get in our way, or worse, get himself hurt and get us into a lawsuit. Get out."

The man shooed Amri out of the glassworks lab. Amri thought about looking for more labs to check out, but something stopped him. There was no reason to assume that any one the other lab teams would want Amri around; they'd have to take time out of their schedule to explain to Amri what they were doing, and that would bring all of the problems the man in the mask had mentioned. Tomek had probably told him about the glassworks to get rid of him, and probably for the same reason.

Dejected, Amri left the industrial park and started to head home. He decided to take the shortest way through the Temple District along the edge of the Empyrian Quarter. As he walked with his head down by the priests trying to convince people to come and worship their gods, he passed a wall between the district and the Empyrian Quarter that was still mostly wrecked by the dracolich attack two months prior.

"Excuse me," a young man said to him. "You look lost."

"Lost?" Amri looked up at the man. "I know where I am. And I know where I'm going."

"Do you now?" The man smiled. "Because from here, it looks like you're very confused, and struggling to find your way."

"Okay..." Suspicion flared up in Amri's mind. "Is this some kind of pitch to get me to join your cult?"

The man laughed. "No, no. Not yet, anyway." The man held up a trowel. "I'm just laying bricks to fix some of the broken homes around here. You looked like you could use a job."

"Well, yes." Amri admitted. "But I'm studying sorcery. I could use a job that will get me a career in that."

"All careers begin with work." The man countered. "Interested? It'll help."

Amri wasn't particularly opposed to doing dirty work. He was opposed to doing dirty work in nice clothes for job searching, like the ones he was wearing. But there was something about the man Amri couldn't put his finger on. A kind of warmth he just couldn't say 'no' to."

"Sure," he chuckled. "What could it hurt?"

Namid often joked that one day she'd be stronger than Amri. She was probably right, as Amri was not a muscular young man. The man introduced himself as Esfan Dyer, a priest-initiate at the Abbey of Truth, and Amri struggled with everything he showed him how to do. First, Amri tried hauling bricks in a wheelbarrow wherever the priest and several others working on the wall needed them. This had only resulted in a number of people snickering at Amri trying to push the wheelbarrow when it was full of bricks. Undeterred, Esfan showed Amri how to mix cement with a thick stick in a bucket so he and the others could apply it between bricks. Amri only managed to get the stick stuck as the cement started to dry in the bucket. Esfan then gave Amri a sledgehammer to use to break pieces of rubble into smaller chunks to make them easier to haul away. Amri had difficulty just lifting the sledgehammer, and while he managed to make cracks in the rubble and chip pieces off, it took him a long time to break one large section of the old wall into bits small enough to be loaded into the wheelbarrow.

All the while, Amri could hear lots of other men working on the wall laughing at him. He could even make out a few women making fun of him as well. Just as he was about to throw down the sledgehammer, Esfan clapped a hand on his shoulder.

"Don't worry about them. They're the fools for laughing at free help."

At this, Amri went back to breaking rubble. It started getting easier, though not by much, and he was definitely getting tired. He had to let the hammer head rest on the ground and lean on the handle to take a breather for a moment. Esfan looked up at him from where he was laying bricks and gave Amri a smile and a thumbs up. Amri couldn't help but smile back before returning to work.

Eventually, all of the rubble had been crushed, and Amri was given a shovel to scoop the remains into one of the wheelbarrows. After he'd finished, a woman came up to the workers handing out sandwiches and canteens of water.

"Uh..." Amri looked at the sandwich he'd been given. "I didn't come here to bum you for free food."

"Yeah, we know." Esfan chuckled. "That's why it's a gift."

As they ate, Amri looked over the amount of the wall that had been rebuilt. "Have you guys been working throughout the city?"

"Not all of us," Esfan said between bites. "Those of us who are with the abbey have, but the rest are volunteers. Some live in the Empyrian Quarter, and want the wall rebuilt so they have some privacy from the traffic in the Temple District. Others work for the temples, and want the wall fixed so they can get back to business as usual. Nice job with the rubble today."

Amri looked at the area he'd cleared. It hadn't looked like much while he was doing it, but he'd definitely helped the volunteers make progress. "It's too bad things don't work this way in the industrial park. Or in sorcery jobs elsewhere, for that matter."

"I think they might," Esfan paused. "You agreed to help us, and were promised nothing in exchange. Then you were surprised when we gave you lunch. It wasn't a free meal; you earned it. The people working at the industrial park might work the same way, if you try."

"What are you saying?" Amri looked at Esfan. "No one over there was asking people to come over and give them a hand."

"True, true." Esfan nodded. "Not enough people do that. But what if you were to go there again tomorrow, and ask what you could do to help them? What can you do to help a team of glassworkers making wards? What could you have done to help a fiery boy trying to keep methane gas from leaking out of canisters?"

"...Huh." Amri thought for a moment. "Hold on, Tomek said he was having trouble with gas canisters that could store methane gas. If he were working with glass jars, the simple solution would be to ward the jars to keep the gas cool; that would reduce the gas pressure, and cut down on the amount of methane that escapes from the canisters. But, warding a metal methane gas canister isn't the same as warding a glass jar. I wonder if the workers at the glassworks facility would show me their techniques."

"Sounds like you've put something together." Esfan smiled. "Remember, ask what you can do for the glassworkers. And thanks for your help today."

25

Ogre Country

DUARGO

"So, are we finally done filling the gods' mailboxes with spam?" Aquila sat in the control room to Daurgo's base. "It's getting weird."

The skeleton the lich was currently controlling rustled with laughter. "You really don't know how it works, do you? Belief shapes reality. The gods are that belief in the most concentrated form. I wouldn't have lasted so long, come so far, or acquired so much power if I didn't openly defy them."

"How does actively pissing them off help you in any way?" Aquila asked.

"It amuses me," Daurgo's skeleton pulled several levers and started up the base's mobility engine. The entire bastion roared to life, preparing to move on his command. "Plus, it lets them know that attempts at intimidating me aren't going to work. That can buy me some time; some gods don't know what to do with people they can't bully into submission."

Outside, the massive mechanical centipede that was Daurgo's mobile fortress burst from under the sand where it was buried and stood a hundred meters wide and nearly as tall above the Blasted Wastes. As the skeleton flipped switches and set a course, the skeleton made its way towards the outskirts of the Borealan Empire, staying far enough away from any towns so as not to draw attention.

"Let the gods know that I am defiant," Daurgo mused. "I've been defying more powerful forces than gods since I started this journey. First the laws of life and death, then the laws of necromancy itself."

"Wait." Aquila braced herself as the centipede traveled, always a little unprepared whenever the machinery started moving. "How did you break the laws of necromancy?"

"To become a lich, you normally have to be so afraid of death that you'd be willing to give up everything that makes life worth living in order to live," Daurgo explained. "There's a reason the Tomb Lords never leave Kemet to go searching for far off lands. If they advance outside of their kingdom, it is a slow, methodical process that is not meant to raise attention. They don't want to accidentally anger someone or something so much that it might go looking for their soul jars. Me? I just grind things into the dirt and move on. Act like nothing can stop you, and most people will believe they can't."

"Grind things into the dirt?" Aquila thought about how rarely Daurgo took anything seriously. "Maybe when you're done prancing around and coming up with wisecracks."

"Tsk, tsk." The skeletal puppet wagged a finger. "That's called style."

As the centipede traversed the desert, Aquila looked out a porthole to get a good view. "What is your plan, anyway? What's our next move?"

"I need to find a way to collect...souls," Daurgo finally realized what that meant. "Wow, that even sounds bad. I guess it's not the worst thing I've ever done; it's basically just killing people with extra steps. But now I'm holding their eternal souls for ransom in exchange for resurrection. First, I need to find something that can hold a lot of them as some sort of vessel. I'll have to find–"

Daurgo was interrupted by a beam of yellow light striking the skeleton he was controlling, reducing it to dust. Confused, the lich took direct control of an undead rat he kept in reserve on the centipede and gathered a few more to form a swarm. Scampering through the vents of the machinery, they burst back into the control room and searched for their assailant.

There were no signs of anyone in the room except Aquila, who was hiding under a desk and trying to keep something between her and whatever was shooting light beams that could disintegrate bone. But a rat has more than sight to find things; just because an attacker is unseen, that doesn't mean he can't be heard or smelled.

Picking up the intruder's scent, Daurgo commanded his rats to swarm the source, tackling some odd mass in the control room. The lich then redirected his consciousness to control another human skeleton in the room to get a better view of the rats' work.

The thing underneath the swarm tried to shake them off, but clearly whatever it was, it hadn't prepared for this. More yellow beams of light came from the top of it, and Daurgo realized there was some sort of eye underneath all of those rats. The light incinerated one rat at a time, but they couldn't hit all of them at once. One rat bit the person on the eye, getting itself incinerated, but still clearly wounding the attacker.

A yo-yo launched from under Aquila's hiding spot wrapped around the intruder's...well, presumably where their legs would be. The attacker underneath came tumbling forward, landing with their eye facing down on the floor. Several rats chewed through the intruder's legs to make sure they didn't get back up.

The rats backed off to reveal a severely chewed-up bedsheet over a...person? They looked like someone attempting to dress-up as a ghost. All that was visible were their bare feet, but other than that, nothing. They didn't even have armholes in their sheet, or even any lumps to suggest they had arms, at all.

"Who?" Aquila poked the thing with her foot, as if that would give her answers. "What? How did this...thing get in here?"

"Hm," Daurgo rummaged through a toolbox near a control panel and pulled out a flathead screwdriver. He then went up to the battered intruder and shoved the screwdriver through its remaining eye.

The assailant writhed, but made no sound. It tried to get to its feet, but with no eyes, no visible arms, and no tendons left in their legs, they could only roll about on the floor.

"I'm not a hundred percent certain," Daurgo picked up the assailant from the scruff of what must have been a neck under the sheet. "But...they're definitely immortal, shoot beams of energy out of their eyes, and can move about unseen even through my stronghold. I'm guessing this is Medjed, the

Smiter."

Aquila looked over the mangled creature that Daurgo had captured. "The Ancient Egyptians believed in a silent man who dresses like a kid pretending to be a ghost? Who shoots magic beams from his eye?"

"For the most part," Daurgo summoned several more skeletons who picked up the smiter to carry it away. "At least, they believed in a god of the unseen who did those things, but no clue if he was a man. Sex unknown." As the skeletons carried him away, Daurgo glanced up Medjed's sheet to check, and then wished he hadn't. "Sex *really* unknown."

"Okay, so how did he get in here?" Aquila asked. "And what are you going to do with him?"

"Well, Medjed is technically a god." Daurgo ordered his minions to tie up the intruder and keep him secure. "It can probably go wherever it needs to be, and being god of the unseen, it can probably do so stealthily. I'll have my skeletons pop him in the base's incinerator; it might have a powerful eye-shooting-thing, but Medjed's a bottom-tier god with barely any worshipers. It'll be a while before it can recover and try again. But it will try again; that's just how divine smiter's tend to work."

"Will it be stronger the next time he appears?" Aquila asked.

"Probably not, but it's still a problem." Daurgo consulted his cartography table. "To any mortal, that smiter would be a deadly threat. To me, it's little more than a nuisance, but if it keeps showing up here and destroying the corpses I already have raised, it might cause a problem of attrition. I only have so many undead puppets raised at any given time. I'll need more minions if the gods are going to start whittling away at my forces like this."

"Wait," Aquila confronted her boss. "You once told me that you couldn't cast spells except through your real body. If that's still regenerating, how are you going to animate more corpses without your magic?"

"Remember when I told you about the other ancient magical treasures I keep in storage along with the Philosopher's Stone, and I mentioned that the Pair Dadeni was a cauldron of necromancy with instant soup mix?" Daurgo looked up from the cartography table at the thief. "Time to make some instant soup."

"Okay, so where are you planning on getting the corpses?" Aquila had never helped Daurgo commit a massacre before. It wasn't necessarily against her contract, but it would be a first for her. "You going to go find the nearest densely populated area and bombard them with artillery?"

"That would defeat the purpose of trying to lay low." Daurgo looked over the table at a spot on the map where he'd never visited. It had no known cities or settlements, but was still lush with greenery and wildlife. "What is Egark, and who lives there?"

"Oh, no." Aquila shook her head. "We don't want to go there. 'Egark' is slang for 'Ogre Country.' You won't find cities, or people to raise as zombies. Just a bunch of big, lumbering brutes who slaughter anything they think they can eat. They don't even leave corpses behind for you to raise; they eat the bones, too."

"Aquila, stop!" Daurgo raised a bony hand. "You had me at 'big, lumbering brutes.'" The green lights in Daurgo's eye sockets gleamed. Not that they had much choice. "And what kind of government organization do they have over there?"

"They're just savages." Aquila shrugged. "They form little tribal villages that occasionally go to war with each other and try to eat the rival tribes. The only leadership they have is for the biggest, strongest ogre to sit as chieftain and kill anyone who doesn't like it. And then eat them."

"Well, I'm sold." Daurgo turned to the centipede locomotion controls and entered coordinates for Egark. "Ogre zombies. Why haven't I tried something like this before?"

"Wait, what?" Aquila started to panic. "You can't be serious! You just said we don't have enough minions to waste on fighting gods, now you want to fight ogres? They'll eat the bones of your skeletons! You just admitted that you don't have the manpower or the magic–"

"I never said I don't have the manpower," Daurgo finished inputting coordinates and threw a lever to drive the centipede towards their destination. "Or the firepower."

"They're smelly!" Aquila cried. "They're rumored to be some of the smelliest brutes imaginable! They don't have any hygiene, or sanitation, or brush their teeth!"

"Ha!" Daurgo couldn't keep himself from laughing. "This, from one of the most disgusting species on Earth!"

"Excuse me?" Aquila frowned. "Are you calling humans disgusting?"

"Yes!" Daurgo snapped. "You're a bunch a chimps whose hair fell out except for some of the worst places. I can appreciate keeping the patch of fur on your scalp that protects your brain, but why is there still hair on your bottom? What's it doing there, apart from catching loose bits of fecal matter? And then there's the glands; always with the glands! You even have sweat glands *designed* for spilling your bodily fluids everywhere. It's unsanitary! Pigs don't have glands like that, and they get along just fine!"

Upset, Aquila crossed her arms. "Well, ogres are supposedly worse. They're said to abduct human women."

"For what purpose?" Daurgo asked. "As a snack?"

"I think you know what purpose." Aquila huffed.

"Pfft, that's probably just a rumor." Daurgo pulled out a checklist written in his own language from the cartography table to run through the weapons he'd need to bring. "The worst thing about you humans is that you're always trying to romance other species. You probably just projected your own dirty mindedness onto ogres and assumed they're just like you. Just because your species is always game for bestiality doesn't mean the rest of the animal kingdom is, too."

"Oh really?" Aquila glanced at Daurgo's checklist, but then shrugged when she couldn't read it. Clearly written in another language. "Do you even know what ogres are?"

"No," Daurgo admitted. "I literally just found out about them from you. I've heard of different types of ogres from other places around the world, but no two cultures have the same kinds."

"That's because they aren't natural creatures. They're like elementals, dryads, or similar things," Aquila explained. "They didn't evolve naturally; they're born in the Aether out of humanity's primal fears and instincts. My teacher once told me they were conjured by peoples' ancient fears of savage brutes that come to take our women and precious metals."

Daurgo made a mental note that Aquila once had a teacher that taught her things most commoners knew little about. "Hm, so they're a bit like orcs, then?"

"I...I don't know." Aquila admitted. "I've never heard of orcs before."

"They're a race of muscle-bound green and grey brutes native to the far north." Daurgo pointed to a spot on the map just north of Karsite. "The countries that worship the Norse and Celtic gods have them. They look an awful lot like ugly, pig-tusked Neanderthals, are just barely intelligent enough to be malevolent, and usually wield crude weapons with which they raid civilized areas."

"Neanderthals?" Aquila looked like she was recalling some memory from her childhood education. "I've seen pictures of male Neanderthals, but not females. What do female orcs look like?"

"They don't exist. They're an exclusively male race. They only breed by raiding human towns and abducting–" Daurgo realized he wasn't helping his case. "Bad example. Besides, we're going to do some scouting before we engage these beasts."

"I still think this is a bad idea," Aquila huffed as the centipede marched through the desert.

The mobile fortress stuck to the Blasted Wastes as they traveled, avoiding any populated areas. Daurgo had no intention of drawing any more attention to himself, and as useful as a walking bastion loaded with artillery was, it was not good at keeping a low profile.

After two days-time, they approached the Glowing Sea from the north. This was a desert where mortals feared to enter, as rolling storms of taint leftover from the Calamity wreaked havoc through the dunes from time to time. However, the centipede's internal structure was lined with various heavy metals, including a thin layer of lead for extra protection, and so they could traverse the desert without worry. Even Aquila was safe so long as she didn't step outside of the centipede.

On the fourth day of non-stop traveling, the centipede reached the edges of Egark. Daurgo peered through the windows of the control room to examine the kinds of wildlife that lived in such a place. Fully expecting to find normal, albeit somewhat grizzled fauna, he instead saw a number of strangely twisted creatures, some of which looked no more deadly than the average beast in an ordinary forest.

Egark was covered with foliage. This might have been due to the influences of magic or taint, but the place reminded Daurgo of parts of Europe back in millennia long ago when humans were too few and too primitive to cut down entire forests. Some of what he initially thought were trees were in fact towering mushrooms, and the lich decided he would need to take samples of some of these fungi before leaving this place.

Besides massive mushrooms and overgrown greenery, Egark was crawling with strange beasts that looked just familiar enough that you could guess what they were before this strange land mutated them into whatever they were now. The lich spotted fish that crawled out of lakes and ponds on short, flippery-legs to reach other water holes, birds that might have been flamingoes now covered in scales and with beaks full of sharp teeth. A lumbering beast, possibly reptilian, maybe a mammal, with thick plates like chitin all over its body stomped through the brush to eat the smaller mushrooms that grew in the orange-colored grass.

"I guess even a savage land like this needs a fully-functioning ecosystem," Daurgo mused. "You can't have a working environment with nothing but angry predators and aggressive herbivores."

Several of his skeletal minions brought the Pair Dadeni from the storage room of the centipede. Looking at it again for the first time in centuries, Daurgo noted how strange the cauldron was. It was made of pewter, an alloy that had very little magical potential at all. Yet the strangest hints of powerful, dark chaotic powers hummed off of the cooking pot. If one were to only touch the cauldron, they could hear restless spirits inside asking to be set loose.

"Alright, let's start with some scrying." One of Daurgo's skeletons brought him a smooth, polished obsidian ball in a box, another artifact from the base's storage. "Let's see if we can't get some intel on these things."

"What is that?" Aquila asked.

"A trinket I seldomly use." Daurgo set the ball on a brass stand and hooked it up to a number of runes from the same box. "If I recall, I need someone with a soul present in order to use it, so get over here."

Daurgo grabbed Aquila's hand and placed it on the crystal ball. "Okay," the thief raised an eyebrow. "Now what do I do?"

"The reason I barely use this thing is because it needs to connect to a person's soul in order to work." Daurgo pressed several runes into the base of the ball. "I think it should work...now."

Sparks of orange light flickered inside the black orb. Daurgo believed there was a piece of quartz inside the polished obsidian. Eventually, a voice came through from the other side.

"*Han, Göm Børg, De eü, gedeshke dü, ye gö ørk gun de bür dú, Børk Børk Børk!*"

"What?" Aquila asked. "What on Earth is that?"

"Argh, this thing's picking up something in Swedish again." Daurgo let go of Aquila's hand and made his other minions put the orb away. "Now I remember why I never use this thing. Somewhere in the far north, someone else has one of these things, and if two or more are used at the same time, they connect and show only whatever is going on in the vicinity of the others. We're going to have to do this the old-fashioned way."

"You're going to send out a swarm of rats and other undead creatures to scout out the area?" Aquila asked.

"Oh, no." Daurgo shook the skull of the skeleton he was controlling. "Too many things out there who could gobble up the rats I have left. Remember, I need to be sparing with the corpses I have available until I can rebuild my forces. For that, I need bones on the ground."

"Bones on the...you mean you're going to go out there and scout yourself?" Aquila pointed at the pile of dust where Medjed had disintegrated one of the skeletons a few days before. "Aren't your human skeletons worth more than rats?"

"A small group of human skeletons can do a lot more and handle worse problems than a pack of rats." Daurgo mentally summoned the puppets he'd prepared for just this situation. "Six should do, armed to the teeth. I'll be able to take direct control of any one of them I need, and our seventh member will add a second set of eyes and quick thinking to cover my approach."

"Seventh member?" Aquila made a face like she'd just realized she was the only person around besides Daurgo who could think and had eyes. "Aw, crap."

Six cloaked skeletons wearing bronze masks, steel armor, and carrying various weapons strode through the jungle, with Aquila following close behind. The undead wielded things like maces, spears, and swords, mindlessly trailing after whichever one Daurgo controlled at the time. Aquila tried to make sure at least one of the puppets was behind her at all times, and Daurgo assumed this was in case something attacked the group from the rear.

Through the jungle...or was it a forest? Whichever one had mushrooms the size of trees, Daurgo took note of the weird creatures that lived here. There were boars that had six tusks instead of two, with four on the sides of their faces, which quickly fled when they saw such a group of armed people. There were birds in the trees that appeared to have beaks made of fungi; hopefully, they were a new species and not just sick with some horrifying rotting plague. Then there were snakes that crawled through the undergrowth. Daurgo couldn't help but notice that for all the mutations he could see in this place, the snakes seemed completely unchanged.

"Boss, look here." Aquila pointed to some indentations in the mud. "Something wearing crude boots came this way. Well, a crude boot on the right, and barefoot on the left."

"Hm," Daurgo followed the direction of the footprints. "This looks promising. Keep your head down, we must be getting close."

As they approached, Daurgo noticed a large, tall white object that he'd initially thought was a tree, but was actually a tusk taken from some massive animal. Exactly what it could have come from wasn't something Daurgo wanted to meet at the moment, and judging by the carvings and decorations around the object, it was evident that the beast had been slain by the ogres.

"Look!" Daurgo pointed to a tent made of similar tusks that supported strips of hide. "That's got to be one of their dwellings."

"Good, we found one." Aquila turned around and tried to sneak back to the centipede. "I'll just be off—"

"Where do you think you're going?" Daurgo took control of the rear-guard skeleton and stopped the thief. "We have work to do."

"I'm not going anywhere near an ogre camp." Aquila crossed her arms. "If half the stories are true, they'll kill me, eat me, or worse."

"I need as many thinking persons to scout out the camp, and notice anything I might miss by myself." Daurgo dragged Aquila back towards the ogre tent. "You're the only other person here that can help me do that."

"But what if they're like the orcs you mentioned in the north?" Aquila struggled against the skeleton. "What if they're an all-male race?"

"That's highly unlikely. Hold on." Daurgo transferred his consciousness to a different skeleton. "I'll scout quickly and see if there are any female ogres. And if there aren't any, you can go right back to the base. If there are, you can rest easy and we'll get back to work."

Aquila grumbled, not in agreement, but not in disagreement, either. Daurgo figured that was good enough and his lone skeleton set out towards the tent.

Once he got closer, Daurgo spotted several satellite tents that surrounded the big one. These were made from much smaller tusks, bones, and the occasional tree trunk, all of which just slightly larger than a normal human tent for camping.

Sticking to underbrush and large rocks to stay out of sight, Daurgo set himself up in a hiding spot to monitor the ogres.

There were a lot of ogres in plain sight moving about the camp. Each one was easily three meters tall, slightly fat, but also very muscular. They wore pants made of hide and fur, which actually looked more intricate than the simple rags occasionally worn by orcs in the north. Instead of stone clubs and flint axes, they wielded more advanced weapons of bronze and occasionally iron; one ogre carried a club that was a simple wooden pole with spiked bronze rings along it, making it look more like it was designed by a society with limited access to metals but enough knowledge of smithing to make the most with the materials they had. Another had a two-handed axe made of iron; not steel, but even so, iron working was a sign that these were more advanced than orcs.

The ogres also fashioned their hair in various ways. Some had mustaches that were clearly grown out to form handlebars and similar styles, some had their hair in ponytails, braids, or the occasional dreadlocks. However, not one of them wore a shirt, and none of them showed signs of sexual characteristics that Daurgo could use to identify them as female.

Then a new ogre stepped out of the main tent. This ogre also wore no shirt, but did wear a skirt of hide, along with lots of bone jewelry and blue tattoos. This one carried a staff with an animal skull on the end of it and wore a headdress made of black and brown feathers from what was probably some ogre's lunch last week. But the most important feature on this shirtless, shamanic ogre was the massive breasts that she had to sling over her shoulders in order to carry them.

"Gotcha," Daurgo chuckled. "They've got females, so they don't need to procreate the way orcs do. Still have better weapons than I was expecting."

The lich transferred his consciousness to one of the skeletons back with Aquila. "There are female ogres, so you don't have to worry. Well, not about that. They'll still probably try to kill you and eat you if they catch you."

"Great." Aquila rolled her eyes. "That's...better. Let's just go in, do your scouting, and get back to the centipede."

The thief and remaining skeletons approached the camp. The skeletons spread out quietly to surround the tents, allowing Daurgo to take control and scout the ogres from different points. One skeleton stayed with Aquila.

"Okay, they're all in position." Daurgo handed a spyglass to the thief. "I want a headcount, to know if they have a chain of command, and if they have any ability to do magic. A female ogre dressed as a shaman does not prove she's some kind of chieftain, or if there's a leader who outranks her. Nor does it prove she has actual magical powers."

"Do we need to get any closer?" Aquila crept towards the camp. "Because I can—"

As she took another step, a nearby bird let out a shrill cry. Aquila was so surprised by this that she stepped on a twig that snapped loudly. Every ogre in the camp turned their attention in the direction of the thief and the nearby skeleton.

"Oh," one ogre around thirty meters away lumbered towards Aquila. "Hot lady-human walk right up to camp."

"Me get first round this time," a second one said. "You broke last one before I got a turn."

Aquila glared at Daurgo's skeletal puppet. "I hate you so much right now."

"Look on the bright side," Daurgo checked every weapon on this skeleton's body and prepared for a fight. "At least now we know you're not the *most* disgusting species on the planet.

26

Cause of Death

CYRUS

"Alright, the chicken parts are still getting enough oxygen, but it looks like they're converting the carbon dioxide into food for the potato parts." Cyrus made a note in a journal Monroe gave him to study the poultratoes. "So far, very healthy-looking abominations of nature. Now, what else do we have for the day?"

Doctor Monroe had made him a list of things he needed him to do that day. The young alchemist needed to keep the doctor's tools sterilized and orderly, the chimera pens cleaned, and the medical supplies organized. Once these tasks were done, Monroe wanted him to join him in the operating room.

Around eleven in the morning, Cyrus met with the doctor. Upon the operating table, a corpse of a man lay spread out for examination under a sheet. Cyrus stopped at the sight of the body, which was somewhat blue from having been kept cold in an icebox and thawed out recently. He'd seen corpses before, even made a few, but they still bothered him.

Doctor Monroe held a scalpel in a gloved hand. With his other, he gestured for Cyrus to come closer. "It's time you learned how to do an autopsy."

"Um..." Cyrus approached the body. "Where did you get this guy?"

"I have a deal with the local city council," the doctor explained. "I perform important medical services from time to time, and in turn, they allow me to perform important research on special cases."

Cyrus paused. "This guy was a special case?"

Monroe nodded. "Let's see if you can figure out his cause of death. I'll give you a hint. Autopsies are mandated by law for everybody that is forensically significant. All other autopsies require permission from the deceased's family members."

Trying to remember what 'forensically' meant, Cyrus took a look at the corpse. "Let's see, we begin with examination of the external body." Cyrus removed the sheet and examined the corpse. "We need to note the height, weight, any piercings or tattoos, birthmarks, and..." he knew there was something else.

"His age and sex," Monroe finished. "And if possible, his occupation. Don't worry about those, I've already got the details written down."

Cyrus proceeded to carry out the external measurements. The man had no tattoos, no piercings, a birthmark below his right knee, weighed a little over ninety-five kilos, and was one hundred and eighty-three centimeters tall. Monroe identified his age as fifty-six, and his occupation as a factory worker.

"Okay, now what?" Cyrus asked. "That was as far as I knew to do."

"Now, we take a blood sample." Doctor Monroe took a needle and withdrew several vials of blood from the man's right arm. "We need to check for any toxins that might have contributed to his death."

The doctor showed Cyrus how to apply tests to the blood to detect poisons. Trace amounts of sulfuric acid and iron oxides, more than normal, showed up in the man's blood. In addition, the doctor pointed out small traces of mercury as well. Monroe made a note of this, then proceeded to show Cyrus the next step.

The doctor cut a Y-shaped incision from the shoulders to the pelvis of the corpse. Inside, Monroe showed Cyrus the man's ribcage. Removing his gloves and coating his hands in antibiotic fluid, Monroe disassembled the man's sternum with alchemy and pulled the ribcage away from the rest of the body. Cyrus was then able to get a good look at the man's organs, and immediately he knew what was wrong.

The man's heart, stomach, and esophagus looked exactly like they would in a medical textbook. From what Cyrus could see, his intestines were also healthy. But the lungs – dear gods, the man's lungs looked more like lumps of charcoal than actual innards. There were occasional flecks of red among the burnt, soot-covered organs, but everywhere else they looked like they'd been burnt from the inside out.

"According to the next of kin, this man never smoked." Monroe washed his hands and replaced his gloves. "The city council has asked us to identify what could have caused this."

Before getting too caught up in the issue of the man's lungs, Monroe walked Cyrus through the remaining procedures of the autopsy. Each organ had to be weighed, trauma to any bones had to be noted, and especially any signs of damage to the skull. There was, after all, the slight possibility that some external injury contributed to the man's rotten lungs, in the same way stepping on a rusty nail could cause tetanus leading to other health problems.

When nothing else was found, the doctor returned to the lungs.

"Alright, what did we find in the blood samples?" The doctor quizzed his apprentice.

"An unusual amount of sulfuric acid and iron oxide," Cyrus replied.

"And where, do you think such a thing could have entered his bloodstream?" Monroe had a glint in his eye; it reminded him of the way Thoth looked whenever he had tried to make Cyrus figure something out for himself.

"Well, the sulfuric acid was probably sulfur before it entered the man's bloodstream," the apprentice began. "Or, if he breathed it in, it could have been sulfuric oxide. The iron oxide is...well, that's rust. Rusty flakes of metal broken down and entered his blood. He would have some in his blood normally, but an excess of it means he had too much iron inside of him. And then there's the mercury; that's not supposed to be there at all. So, if he wasn't a smoker, these toxins had to have come from a factory, or some other source of smog," Cyrus noted.

"Well, that's difficult to prove." Monroe finished taking notes in his journal. "The city council suspects that one of the factories isn't washing coal properly before burning it. Coal is supposed to be cleaned to remove things like pyritic sulfur, ash, and mercury. The perfect coal is entirely made of carbon, so that when it burns, it doesn't put things like heavy metals into the air. But cleaning coal is time-consuming, and if the imported coal doesn't come precleaned, factories have been noted to skip this step and burn the unprocessed, dirty fuel to save time and increase production. It's illegal, but we'd need proof that he never smoked cigarettes in order for the council to actually convict anyone."

"Wouldn't there be other symptoms from smoking?" Cyrus asked. "If we checked for those, their absence—"

"Wouldn't prove anything." Monroe shook his head. "No symptom is ever guaranteed to show up. Their absence has no legal weight. However, we might have enough to give the city council a search warrant. The factory in question will almost certainly destroy any evidence before they can investigate, but maybe that'll be enough to get them to clean up their act."

"That's...that's not good enough!" Cyrus exclaimed. "If this man is dead, there needs to be some sort of justice, or at least assurance that it won't happen again!"

"Oh, I know." Monroe nodded. "This man isn't an isolated case. But it's not for us to decide. I wanted you to be a part of this so you could learn the medical process; I don't want you getting involved in any legal matters. Not after what happened when you went into town."

Cyrus's gaze fell. "I...I'm sorry about that."

"Sorry?" Monroe balked. "About what? You saved someone's life! It wasn't your fault you didn't know you could get arrested for it or lose the medicine."

"But...you don't trust me to help you with basic trips to the city anymore." Cyrus couldn't shake the embarrassment in his voice. "I won't make the same mistake again!"

"Yes, you will." The doctor locked eyes with Cyrus. "You'd do just about anything to save a person's life, wouldn't you?" He took off his gloves and washed his hands. "I get it; Thoth would agree. Each human life is precious. But what about your own?" He turned back to Cyrus. "Do you understand what would have happened to you if you'd been convicted? You would have been executed."

"That's..." Cyrus blinked. "No, they only execute people who are too dangerous to be kept alive."

"You're an alchemist, who was charged with randomly running up to a woman and stabbing her multiple times. You could kill a person with a touch, if you felt so inclined, and the charges against you painted you as an unstable murderer. If that doesn't count as 'too dangerous to be kept alive,' I don't know what does."

"You mean... I would have been taken out behind the courthouse and shot...if that lawyer lady hadn't stepped in." Cyrus felt a mixture of fear and rage well up in his throat. "What in the actual Abyss is wrong with this city."

"You don't know the half of it." Monroe massaged his forehead. "Cyrus, it's important to understand why the city's leadership is acting this way. If the peace isn't kept between the Borealans and the Empyrians, there will be war. If the Empyrians feel that they are being hunted by law enforcement, or that they physically cannot achieve happiness in this world, they will riot, and there will be blood in the streets. It may seem cruel to put you under, but what is one life weighed against the lives of everyone else in this city?"

"What are you saying?" Cyrus frowned. "That executing me would have been justified?"

"No." Monroe locked eyes with Cyrus, as if willing the apprentice not to get upset before the doctor could explain. "Have you ever heard of 'the Trolley Problem?'"

Cyrus shook his head. "no."

"Imagine that four people are tied to the rails of a trolley track," Monroe began. "There is a trolley coming, and it will kill all four people when it collides with them. But, if you shove a very fat man in front of the trolley, it will kill him, but the trolley will get stuck, and the four people tied to the track will be saved."

"Wait..." Cyrus thought for a moment. "How did the four people get tied to the track in the first place?"

Monroe shrugged. "Does it matter? Someone else tied them there, I suppose."

"Okay, and how fast is this trolley moving?" Cyrus asked. "Could I jump in front of it and stop it with my own hands?"

"What? No, of course not!" Monroe snapped.

"Then the fat guy won't stop the trolley even if I push him, so I'm not going to push him in front of the trolley and get a fifth person killed for no reason." Cyrus said.

"No, the trolley *will* stop if you push the fat man–"

"No, basic physics," Cyrus explained. "If I'm strong enough to push anything in front of the trolley with sufficient mass to stop it, including a fat guy, then I'm strong enough to jump in front of the trolley and stop it with my own hands. And if not, then pushing the guy won't stop the trolley."

Monroe rolled his eyes. "Okay, say that there's no fat person. Instead, there's a lever, and if you throw the lever, the trolley will switch to a different track and will run over a single person instead of the four. The point of the question is, do you allow four people to die through inaction, or do you kill one person and save the other four?"

Cyrus paused. "Four individuals...against one. I think...I think I'd have to throw the lever."

The doctor nodded. "Yes, four lives are worth more than one. I think Thoth would agree. And these are the choices people in positions of power must make all the time. The city council knows that sacrificing a few innocent lives is a terrible thing, but they're weighed against the lives of everyone else in the city. Maybe even the empire. I do not envy their decisions, but we, as medical professionals, have similar problems. Imagine if the lone person on the track had a terrible, incurable disease, and would die in a few months at most, but the other four could live long, happy lives if you throw the lever. How much easier would the choice be?"

"I guess...if we've already agreed that four people are worth more than one, then four healthy people are worth more than one dying person." Cyrus scratched his head, wondering why such a question needed to be asked. "Isn't there a word for this? When you're having to choose between who lives and who dies?"

"Triage," Monroe nodded. "The word you're thinking of is triage. And yes, medical professionals have to make difficult decisions regarding who to save and who to abandon all the time. We can't save them all, no matter how much we may want to."

"I see." Cyrus had never asked Thoth if there were times he couldn't save everyone. Of course there were; but he wanted to hear the god's answer, and how he dealt with such things.

"This reminds me." Doctor Monroe brought out a small wooden box and handed it to Cyrus. An address was written on the top. "I need you to deliver these drugs to this address. It won't require you to go into the city proper. When you get back, go ahead and call it a night. We'll have more lessons in the morning."

Cyrus happily took the package and set off, glad to be trusted with deliveries again, and wanting to get back in time before it was too dark to see what the doctor had planned.

27

The Perfect Citizen

SEKHET

In Kemet, couples were encouraged to have as many babies as possible. Afterall, Kemet needed its future workforce; it said so on the posters plastered on walls throughout the kingdom. About forty percent of infants in the nation died within the first few months due to disease or pollution-related illnesses. After that, another ten died from starvation and malnutrition. And despite this, many people in Kemet still found themselves with too many children to feed, possibly because they couldn't feed themselves. To alleviate this, the Tomb Lords would generously purchase some of the unwanted babies from families who would give them up in exchange for a royal book of food coupons.

Some were sent to the mines, where the boys were raised to work until they died at the bottom of a hole, and the girls were raised to be comfort women from the age of fifteen. Some were purchased by Amenhotep, who would groom a lucky few to become necrophytes. A portion were acquired by Arkeon, who used them in his many bloody rituals. A few were bought by Pausiris, who would hand select those that showed promise to be trained as his research assistants and use the rest as factory workers or to clean his laboratories. And a good number fell into the care of Sekhet, who used them for her own experiments.

Unfortunately for Sekhet, one of her experiments was going incredibly wrong.

"Sit up!" The lich shrieked at the creature sitting in its cell. "Sit properly, for the good of Kemet!"

The creature didn't respond. It had once been a young boy, but had now become some cross between a human child and a pig, still somewhat wearing the boy's clothes, although it was now too obese for them to fit properly. Like an ordinary swine, it chewed a mouthful of its own fecal matter, since there was no other food in its cement room. It glanced at Sekhet with disinterest, then went back to eating its own waste.

"I said sit up!" Sekhet took out a short whip and struck the creature's face repeatedly until it fell over. The thing squealed with pain, then burped with a mouthful of feces before crawling away from Sekhet on its fat-fingered hands and cloven feet. Sekhet couldn't even tell if this creature was still sapient or not.

"No, no, no! Not another failure!" Sekhet dropped the whip in disgust and exited the cell. She was about to call for her slaves to kill the creature and dump the body when she collided with Amenhotep himself.

"Oh my," the High Tomb Lord looked down at his sage. His linen wraps and golden mask hid any facial expression, but Sekhet knew that voice too well. "Having trouble today?"

"I...my godking." Sekhet did her best to stop her withered bones from rattling. "Forgive me, I was lost in thoughts."

"Oh, no. Don't worry about something like that." Amenhotep waved a hand towards several of Sekhet's other failed experiments. "You've had so much on your mind as of late."

"Forgive me," Sekhet begged. "Everything I try – it's these worms! They keep getting demonically possessed!"

"Oh, Sekhet!" Amenhotep chided. "You know better than to blame your test subjects. They're only children!" He calmly placed a hand on Sekhet's shoulder. "Why don't you tell me what went wrong with these three?"

The High Tomb Lord gestured to three different cells. One held a girl whose hair and nails had fallen out, and could be heard begging for them to grow back as a tooth fell from her mouth. Another no longer looked like a boy or a girl, and had been stripped of all clothing to examine the changes in their body in closer detail. Fecal matter now oozed from the subject's loins, while necrosis spread in various places about the child's chest and abdomen.

The third cell contained a creature whose bones had softened until turning to gelatin. With no solid structure to hold them together, they had devolved into a fleshy blob mostly covered in skin, sitting in a short, droopy cone-shape. A piece floating in the mass sort of looked like an ear, while a zig-zagging mouth held a number of teeth that dangled in every direction. A half-melted eye drizzled along one slope of the cone, though the eye was still in one runny piece. Some sort of corrosive fluid oozed from the creature's pores, dissolving the cement from which the cell was made.

"Very interesting, this one." Amenhotep leaned down and examined the flesh-blob closer. "The purpose of this laboratory is to produce the perfect citizens; men and women of Kemet who will give everything to Kemet and ask nothing in return. Was there something about those instructions that made you think you should create things like this?"

"It was the demons!" Sekhet squeaked. "They took possession of the subjects and warped their bodies like this—"

Amenhotep shook his head. "Demons are the product of human belief. They're just like gods, only that they're paradoxes. You were told to work with children because children will believe anything an adult tells them. What did you tell them that got them all possessed?"

Sekhet looked around the research facility frantically. "My notebook. Where is my notebook!" A slave brought a fat notebook over to the lich, who snatched it away and started flipping through pages. "Mostly, I taught them the things you ordered. 'To focus their efforts on the benefit of everyone in their community, and not themselves...that they must work hard to become a part of the community... that all people are equal, and that they must always obey their superiors, most of all their godking. Respect is earned. Always respect their elders no matter what.'" She looked up from the book. "All of these are things you instructed me to teach them. There shouldn't be anything here that would have gotten them possessed by paradoxical ideas."

Amenhotep's expression was completely hidden, but Sekhet had become so familiar with her master that she could read his emotions from the mere tilts in his head. Today, he was in a good mood. That wasn't necessarily a good thing.

"Show me the artifact I made for you," Amenhotep finally said.

Sekhet fumbled into the pockets of her robes and withdrew a bone charm etched in runes. It was a shaped piece of a person's humerus bone, no more than a few centimeters long, and bound with leather made from a piece of the person's skin.

Amenhotep took the charm, approached the child who was leaking fecal matter from their loins, and made a circle in the air with his hand. "*Fame, Orgo, Aurum*" he chanted.

The charm quivered, and a spirit from the bone infected Amenhotep's shadow, filling it with a life of its own. The Tomb Lord's shadow hungrily sniffed around, detected the sick child in the holding cell and pounced on the kid. The test subject broke into a coughing fit as the shadow ravenously drained the life from their body, until the child's skin turned grey and they finally stopped moving.

Having devoured the child's last breath, the shadow continued to look around, sniffing for its next victim. It caught the scent of the other test subjects and tugged at Amenhotep's legs, trying to pull him closer so it could feed on them as well, but Amenhotep squeezed the charm and forced the spirit back into the bones. His shadow returned to normal.

"Do you understand how a talisman like this is made?" Amenhotep asked.

"It's made from the soul and body of a person who was demonically possessed," Sekhet answered. "A ritual, performed on a bone of the victim's body while they are still alive—"

"Yes, yes, that's all well and good," the High Tomb Lord dismissed her. "But how do you get the person to become possessed with the right demons? How do you get the person to welcome in demons of pride and gluttony in the first place? Do you understand the forces with which you work? I'm not convinced you do. Show me the rest of the children under your care."

Sekhet nodded slowly. "Yes, my godking."

The sage guided her master to the rest of the children she had kept in the depths of her lab. Most of them had been mutated in one horrible way or another, most of which either left them devoid of intelligence or with bodies too broken to survive anymore. Some were crying, some screamed in pain from their mutations, others had stopped moving or making noise altogether. While most had been rendered completely pathetic, Amenhotep seemed to examine a few more closely; while they were nothing like the perfect citizens that Sekhet had been tasked to create, the High Tomb Lord appeared to be making note of them; perhaps they could be used for something else in the future.

"Most of these creatures are abominations," Amenhotep finally said. "Truly, a dismal failure...except, aren't there more? You started this project with two hundred test subjects. This seems like...less. Did the others die?"

"No, they're just quarantined," Sekhet explained. "We keep them in a separate room."

"And why is that?" Amenhotep asked. "What happened to them that would make them dangerous to this lot?"

"I will show you." Sekhet braced herself. This would be the worst part. There was no excusing this.

She guided the High Tomb Lord to a large wall of thick concrete. The inside of the wall was insulated so that no sound could pass through from either side. A single thick door stood locked in their path. Sekhet took out her keyring and opened the door, revealing a small room with a second door inside. She motioned for her master to come in.

Amenhotep looked around the tiny room. "This is quite a lot of security. What are you hiding?"

Sekhet closed the first door and unlocked the second. "This."

This second door swung open to reveal a single, large cage filled with about twenty or thirty small children. Some were dead from malnutrition; the rest were in various stages of starvation. Some were deaf and stupid from famine. None of them cried; they had lost the ability. Some bodies were covered with bluish-black pimples the size of peas, filled with puss that burst out like worms from bodies literally rotting alive. Apart from that, these children looked almost normal compared to the hideously mutated things outside. Most of their conditions looked no different than those of the starving homeless on the streets of Azzitha, the capital city of Kemet.

"Okay, what is it you've done here?" Amenhotep's gaze fell on the faces of the starving children. They returned looks of sheer contempt for the lich.

"These are the children who..." Sekhet braced herself for the worst. "These are the ones who will not listen to anything I tell them. They simply call me a liar and refuse to cooperate."

Amenhotep turned his head slightly to confront his underling. "Excuse me?"

"I have done everything I can to keep their dissidence away from the others!" Sekhet panicked. "They have been given no food, and have been told that they will be left to die if they do not change their ways. Some have even agreed to participate due to starvation!"

"You have a portion of your test subjects," Amenhotep's voice was but a whisper, but he might as well have been roaring with anger. "A group of children, separated from their parents, who would believe anything an adult tells them...you have a portion who will not believe the things you say, even under threat of slow death by starvation?"

"I...forgive me, my godking!" Sekhet knelt before her master, unable to stop her bones from audibly rattling.

"Oh, Sekhet." Amenhotep gently placed a hand on her exposed back. "You have disappointed me. Your failure could not be more complete. It is clear to me that you are in need of...lessons."

At that moment, the High Tomb Lord paused. His head shifted; one of his necrophytes was contacting him through the unholy link between master and servant.

"Interesting." He withdrew his hand from Sekhet's back, who looked up at her master.

"M-master?"

"A man...a suicide bomber...has just blown up a factory only a few kilometers away from the palace." Amenhotep paused, then turned to Sekhet. "This is a perfect teaching opportunity." Sekhet could hear him smiling beneath his mask. "Yes, come with me. You have...learning to do."

28

Warded Glass

AMRI

Wearing clothes appropriate for working in a glass factory, Amri made his way to the industrial park once again. Preparing for the worst, and ready to move on to different workshops or labs if he was rejected again, he walked straight into the industrial park early in the morning and entered the glassworks facility on the first floor.

Before any of the workers who had already arrived could say anything, Amri bowed his head slightly and addressed one of the workers who had shooed him out of the facility before.

"Hello, my name is Amri Sadi, and I wanted..." his voice faltered. He'd practiced what he was going to say all night before, but now he couldn't help but stutter. "I wanted to ask...i-if I can help you with m-making warded jars today."

One of the workers chuckled. Another shrugged and looked away. The one who wore a blast mask lifted the thick metal covering, giving Amri a good look at the man's face. "What are you doing here, kid?"

"Uh..." Amri hadn't practiced this part. "I'm trying to learn more about sorcery jobs."

"We aren't sorcerers," the glassworker replied. "We just make the wards. Sorcerers design them, and tell us how to make the patterns in the glass like engineers. Not one of us ever went to some fancy magic school."

"...I see." Amri was about to give up, but something like a muscle refused to let go. "I would still like to know if I can be of any help today."

"What?" The glassworker squinted, like Amri had just spoken some incomprehensible gibberish. "Why?"

"Because I'd like to learn more about how wards are made," Amri answered. "I can learn about designing them in class. But here..." He looked around the room. "I can learn about the actual process of making the wardlines in glass. Not just in theory, but in practice."

The glassworker sighed and scratched a thick black beard that covered the bottom half of his face. "We've got some tools that could use cleaning. I guess if you stay out of our way, you can watch how we etch the glass."

Amri thanked the glassworker and followed him around the workshop, where he showed Amri how the glass cutting tools were cleaned. There were sprayers that used acid to soften or melt the glass into specific patterns that became corroded with the chemicals they stored, paintbrushes to apply glue that allowed workers to stick patterns to the glass before spraying the jars with acid, and of course, steel molds that would get hot in a furnace and would be used to melt the patterns into the glass directly. These needed to be scraped when they were cooled so as to remove loose glass flakes that got stuck to the steel.

As he cleaned, Amri learned from the glassworkers how these different methods worked. The best wards were made with glass jars that were pressed against the steel molds, as these lines contained no contaminants that could stick to the acidic chemicals and get stuck in the wardlines. Contaminants would create entropy, which would produce all kinds of chaotic reactions when the jar was used. However, jars made with the steel molds had to be made carefully; it was difficult to get the glass just right without leaving pieces of it behind on the mold, and this would not only ruin the jar being made, but would require the workers to stop using the mold until it cooled down enough to scrape all of the wrecked glass off of it.

Amri's mind started buzzing with ideas on how to put this to use. Different wards had been designed for the same purposes before. Surely, a wizard who knew how the glass was etched would be able to design wards that were easier for workers to use. Patents were given out to sorcerers with the best ward patterns, with royalties paid by companies who wanted to use their designs.

After a full morning of cleaning glassworking tools, the workers informed Amri they were going to stop for lunch, which meant heading to a local eatery across the street from the industrial park. Amri agreed to come along, and joined the workers as they ate outside at a table in the afternoon sun.

The glassworker who usually wore his blast mask, who Amri now knew as Seanan, asked Amri why he thought about checking how the glass was made.

"Well," Amri cleared his throat and his mind. "It's sort of like...we're always told about how to draw the best patterns in the academy, how to get the best shapes and lines for the greatest resistance. But there's a big difference between the classroom and the factory floor. They never tell us about the stuff glassworkers go through in making the jars, or how slow and expensive it can be to make jars using the steel molds. No one in the academy ever told me why so many people use the acid embossing method when it risks contamination."

The glassworkers all nodded. Etanin, a man with lots of hair that was starting to turn grey, swallowed a bite of his sandwich. "So do you want to work on wards when you finish school?"

"Possibly." Some things were starting to click with Amri about what he wanted to do. "I've discovered that what I enjoy most is researching, but I also want to know how the stuff we learn about is put into practice. I still don't know what I want to work on, but designing wards that are easier to mold into glass, or ones that could compensate for the contaminants that come from acid embossment, would certainly be a good start."

The workers seemed to like this answer as they finished their lunches, the glass workers explained which parts of the wards were always the easiest or hardest to make using the steel mold. The shape and angles of the lines were a big part of it, and placing higher-resistance patterns vertically along the glass was easier than placing them horizontally. There was a risk though, as a vertical pattern could end up with lines that were too thick. Thick lines had less resistance to both magical and physical effects.

"Do any of you know if it's possible to make these kinds of wards in a metal canister?" Amri's mind wandered back to the gas experiments Tomek had been working with earlier.

"Don't think so," said Gedalya, the third worker who Amir had bothered the day before when he'd been working with a glass jar on the steel mold. "Maybe if it were copper, or tin, but most metal materials people work with have a much higher melting point than glass. The reason the steel molds work on the glass jars without losing its own pattern is because the steel can take much more heat than the glass."

"Some people have tried engraving metal before with your typical cutting tools, but it doesn't usually work," Seanan explained. "People have also tried molding hot metal into a sandcast with the exact shape of the ward, but both of these methods usually lead to too many impurities. Embossing avoids that problem, but the best techniques people have found so far to emboss metal always create lines that are too thick for a reliable ward; not enough resistance in a thick line."

"Huh," Amri tried to think of other options. "What about acid? Could you engrave a metal canister with acid?"

"I've heard people try, but it usually weakens the container." Seanan took another bite from his sandwich. "Most of the time, canisters like that are used to store gases that would put too much pressure on a glass object and break the container. If you compromise the metal in the canister by adding the ward lines, you'll end up with the same problem."

After lunch, Amri continued thinking about this problem as he helped the glassworkers. One of the new tasks they asked him to do was to collect the scrap glass from broken or cracked jars. Sometimes, the jars that the men were given to work on came broken from delivery. Other times, the jars might break as a result of the warding process. Amri was asked to go through each crate of jars delivered by a glass factory and find any that were cracked or broken. If they were, Amri was to remove them and place them in a waste disposal.

Picking through the jars, Amri found that most crates were undamaged, but every so often he'd find a set with two or three that were broken in transport. Apparently, this was normal. Using a pair of thick gloves the workers loaned him, he took care to remove all of the broken glass and collect it in a metal bucket for dumping in a bin outside later.

A thought occurred to Amri about the broken glass. If it was going to be dumped anyway, would they mind if he did his own experiments on it?

As the workday came to a close, Amri asked Seanan if it was okay for him to take some of the broken glass for his own experiments.

The glassworker shrugged. "I guess so. We would usually have to pay someone to haul it away, so I can't see why it would be a problem."

Amri thanked him and took the glass with him in a cardboard box, careful not to let any shards fall out that might cut anyone. As he made his way home, he paused by the wall in the temple district he'd helped work on yesterday. The people still working on it were finishing painting the last parts of the wall. Esfan was among the workers with a paint roller in his hands coating the highest layer of the wall.

"How did your second attempt go?" The priest asked.

Amri hadn't even realized Esfan knew he was there. "A lot better. I learned a lot about how wards are made in glass jars, and I've got a theory I want to test. I'll need to make some glass jars of my own, but they gave me this." He held up the scrap glass from the workshop. "They said I could take the scrap glass, and I've read about how broken glass can be recycled, and I think I could pull it off if I had access to the academy's workshop. They usually let students access it with permission during the off-season."

"Good for you." Esfan took a rag and wiped the sweat from his forehead. "We're about done for the day. Tell me, do you know how to make glass into the jars you want?"

"Not yet," Amri admitted. "There's something else I need to get first. A gas canister. I'd be willing to bet that if I could melt the glass around a canister, and roll it flat so as to act as a thin coating over the metal, I could use the acid techniques they showed me in the workshop to apply a ward to the glass, which could keep things inside the canister cool."

"You're planning to melt the glass around the canister?" Esfan raised an eyebrow. "Would that actually work?"

"It will if the canister has a higher melting point than the glass," Amri smiled. "Which it will, if it's steel."

"Sounds like you have a plan!" Esfan congratulated him. "That's great!"

"...Thank you." Amri let a smile spread across his face. "I wouldn't have figured any of this out without your help yesterday."

Esfan shrugged off the compliment. "You were the one who helped me build a wall, despite not having the strength. And you were the one who wanted to grow. The abbey shows people the way, but you were the one who chose to follow it."

"What will you be doing once the wall is finished?" Amri asked.

"Probably move on to whatever the next project the abbey needs me to do. As a priest in training, I am expected to serve the community as a volunteer wherever I am needed so that I can better understand the lives of the people who live here, and how they might need spiritual guidance."

"...Okay...not going to lie, that sounds...odd." Amri shifted the weight of the box in his hands. He hadn't noticed how weak his arms actually were until recently. "You don't by chance know of anyone who is good at shaping glass at your abbey?"

"Probably not," Esfan shook his head. "But that doesn't mean I won't ask around. There might be someone we've helped lately who could at least show you a thing or two. In the meantime, how do you plan to get a canister to try this plan of yours?"

Amri had been trying to figure out a solution to this as well. "I'd start by asking Tomek or his boss if we could use one in an effort to make his gas containment project easier to work on. If I focus on how it will help them, they might be willing to test it on something they don't need. Junk glass recycled to make a coating over a decommissioned gas canister would be a good test on the warding techniques. It doesn't need to be perfect the first time; I just need to figure out if it will work."

Esfan nodded. "I have to admit, I know next to nothing about sorcery or wards, or any of the glass and metalworking you're talking about. But I do know people, and they'll be more cooperative if you start by asking how you can help them."

The next day, Amri got out of bed feeling somewhat sore from the previous day. His back ached from bending down to pick up glass, and his arms were still tired from scraping the workers' tools clean. Still, he got up early in the morning and headed straight for the industrial park.

"You want to do what?" Tomek's face contorted into a snarl. "Are you out of your mind?"

Amri tried not to make the alchemist any more upset. "Are you asking because you don't think it will work, or because you can't part with a canister?"

"Of course I can't part with a canister! They don't belong to us!" Tomek roared. "Why on earth are you trying to do this in the first place?"

"Because you said you needed a way to keep the methane gas from leaking out of your canisters." Amri tried his best not to fumble the words. "And if you could keep the gas cool somehow, like with a ward that kept the temperature low, you could keep the gas inside colder. Cold gas contracts and reduces pressure. Low pressure gas doesn't leak as much."

"He's technically right," another scientist approached the two boys. "Efforts have been made before to use wards to keep gases cold. You could store more gas at the same pressure, or reduce the pressure so as to prevent the molecules from pushing their way out of the container. If it worked, it would reduce, possibly even eliminate leaks."

"Hello," Amri introduced himself to this older scientist, who was probably in charge of Tomek's gas research project. "Is there any way I could get ahold of a defunct gas canister, or anything to test this on?"

"...No," the scientist shook his head. "We don't have any broken or otherwise defunct canisters for you to test your theory. But there might be another way. You just need something about the same size and shape of a canister in order to encase it with melted glass, right?"

"Uh, yeah." Amri nodded. "I wouldn't even need the whole canister. Just a piece of metal tubing made of the same steel long enough to etch a ward into."

"Spare tubing..." the scientist stroked his chin. "That could be arranged."

The scientist guided Amri to another workshop that dealt with metalworking. Metal tubes were cut into smaller, workable pieces, with some leftover bits too small afterwards to cut into usable parts. Most of these tubes appeared to be made of steel, and came in various widths. The scientist from the gas testing plant picked out several pieces of scrap steel tubing and handed them to Amri. "Test your experiment on these. If it can work on scrap tubing and recycled glass, it will work on normal glass and a real gas canister."

As they left the steel-cutting workshop, Amri noticed a somewhat-familiar face. Doctor Malbim stepped out of the pharmacy lab. She paid no attention to the students and scientist holding metal tubing, simply walking with both hands in the pockets of her lab coat.

"Don't pay her too much attention," the scientist whispered to Amri, who realized he'd been staring at her. "That one's trouble. She's a good-looking woman, but she's too old for you, and has a kid–"

"She creeps me out." Amri interrupted the scientist before the conversation went any further down that line. "I don't know what it is, but something about her comes off as threatening."

"Oh," the scientist chuckled. "That's probably best. She's an alchemist, so, you wouldn't want to make her mad."

"I wouldn't?" Amri turned to look up at the scientist.

"Oh yeah." He nodded. "She could kill you with a touch, if she wanted to."

29

What Really Matters

CYRUS

Having made the delivery of drugs to one of Monroe's patients, Cyrus was almost back for whatever Monroe was ready to show him. As he approached the house, he stopped to take a quick look at the crop bed to check on the poultratoes.

Instead of a bunch of silly, clucking potatoes, he was shocked to see a field of sickening, bloody tubers. Branches of meat-like tendrils had grown out of the chimeras, only to rot and die, oozing blood all over the garden. The chimeras themselves had all stopped clucking; their beaks mostly hung open like they had died gasping for breath. One of the steel wool sheep had begun drinking from the bloody garden, until it took a bite out of a dead poultrato, ripping flesh and tuber with its teeth as it chewed.

Cyrus's stomach churned. "Well, I guess we can chalk that one up as a failure. I better tell Monroe one of his sheep has started eating meat."

Opening the door to the manor, Cyrus found the entire main floor to be completely dark. Fumbling around for a light switch, he managed to turn on the gas lamps and light up the foyer.

"Doctor? I'm back. Have you checked the garden? The poultratoes have died. Looks like another unstable chimera."

Looking around, he didn't see any sign of the doctor anywhere. A piece of paper sat on the table in the kitchen.

"Out collecting research materials, be back this evening," Cyrus read aloud. "Huh."

Looking around, Cyrus noticed the door to the cellar had been left ajar. It wasn't just unlocked; the doctor didn't shut it properly. Light was coming from down the stairs, which seemed odd. Weren't the experiments down there supposed to be sensitive to sunlight? Maybe artificial lights like gas lamps didn't have the same effect.

"I probably shouldn't be doing this," Cyrus thought aloud. "But if the doctor left the lamps on while he's out, that's quite the fire hazard. I'd better make sure everything is turned off down there."

Cyrus headed down into the basement where the doctor kept his current projects. The stairs had a polished wooden railing that he could hold to steady himself as he made his way into the basement.

At the bottom of the stairs, only a few lights were actually lit. For the most part, everything looked fairly secure. There was a massive aquarium in one corner of the room, similar to the one Monroe kept upstairs for storing starfish and other sea creatures. On a table next to the aquarium, several large leather-bound volumes of research sat stacked up against the wall, with one ledger lying open. There was a door along one wall to another room in the cellar, but there was no light coming from under the floorboards. Cyrus thought he heard some sort of noises, like an animal lurking in the other room, but if there were no lights, there shouldn't be a fire hazard. Cyrus didn't want to risk letting any animals Monroe had been experimenting on getting out of their containment, so he left the door closed.

As Cyrus turned off the few gas lamps that were on, the growing darkness made the aquarium clearer. It had been too reflective to see inside of it before, but there was some kind of creature swimming around in the tank. It had spines like an urchin, tentacles like an octopus, the main body of a sea cow and a mouth like a cuttlefish. Its head was strangely human-like. Almost a weird mix of cephalopod, and manatee. The eyes were the most unsettling part; they had whites and irises like a human's, and were clearly looking at Cyrus, but when the creature blinked, the eyes closed in a circular motion. Cyrus had seen diagrams of sea animals that had eyes like this, but had never gotten a chance to observe one in real life.

With no sign of Monroe around, and the threat of any fire hazards extinguished, Cyrus indulged his curiosity and started flipping through the open ledger on the table. On one page, a diagram depicted details of a person's arm with osteoarthritis. Next to that, a drawing of a lobster was followed by a long description of how and why lobsters do not age. Along the side of the page, the doctor had written experimental notes.

"Incompatible formula," the page read. "Attempts at adapting lobster's regenerative abilities complete failure. Merger unsuccessful. Chimera unable to produce transferrable cure for osteoarthritis."

Cyrus turned to the next page.

"The naked mole rat cells seem to contain a natural ability to repair themselves when one develops into cancer. Applying this trait to humans, however, has proven fruitless. My latest subject appears to be stable and her infected lungs have completely cleared up, but there appears to be no transferrable cure in this chimera."

"What?" Cyrus flipped the page to see if there was more data, and found a drawing of the chimera the journal described. It was like a man-sized rodent, with hideous folds of skin, clawed hands, and a tail like a massive rat.

"What is all of this?" Cyrus glanced up and saw the massive glass tank in the darkness. The thing inside swam around in the glass; maybe multiple things, as far as Cyrus could tell.

Cyrus flipped through the doctor's research journal with his back to the cellar door, hoping he was wrong; praying he wouldn't find what he already suspected would be written in Monroe's notes. Then he found a page on the ingredients list of an experiment labeled "Needs Further Improvement," and braced himself against the table.

"Regenerative mutation: success. Ingredients: 27 Red Mediterranean starfish, 12 *Strichopus tremulus* sea cucumbers, 1 Human Male, age 29. Survived for 32 minutes before cellular rejection. More testing required. However, subject produced 342 milliliters of a fluid that works as a regenerative serum for human wounds. Once a stable subject is produced, I should be able to make more."

Cyrus looked up from the ledger at the water tank with the aquatic chimera contained within. It was not the creature from the ledger; this was a different experiment altogether.And now, it's inhuman eyes were locked onto Cyrus with two pleading brown irises.

"Who were you?" Cyrus asked the creature.

"A murderer," Monroe came down the stairs. "You really weren't supposed to come down here yet."

"What?" Cyrus turned to face the doctor and gestured to the ledger. "What is this? Is it what I think it is?"

"Probably," Monroe shrugged. "It depends on what you think it is."

"I think it's a ledger full of people you've either killed, or turned into chimeras!" Cyrus growled.

The doctor nodded. "It is what you think, but I promise there was no malicious intent."

Cyrus couldn't believe how callous Monroe was acting. He pointed at the creature in the tank. "Why? What have you done?"

"I turned a man who murdered six people for a golden watch and expensive jewelry into a lifesaver." Monroe approached the tank. "I swear, evolution gave all the potent regenerative abilities to the deep-sea creatures. Starfish, octopi, even lobsters. Well, I've got plans to change that."

"You...you mean that..." Cyrus turned what Monroe said over in his head. "You turned that man into a monster—"

"No, he was already a monster." Monroe peered into the glass at the creature, which swam away from him in fear. "All I did was use him for experiments. I'm going to find a cure for opium addiction, you mark my words."

Cyrus was still trying to let the doctor's words come together in his mind. "Where did you get this man? If he really is a convict—"

"Oh, no. He wasn't convicted," the doctor explained. "He was Empyrian. The city council sends me patients from time to time for medical purposes. I've got a deal with them, remember? They can't convict this man or throw him in jail; the law is perfectly clear about that. Too many Empyrians have already been arrested for violent crime this year, and not enough Borealans or Coptics have murdered anyone to balance the prison books. It's illegal to convict any more Empyrians until some other ethnic groups commit more crime, but there are other ways to get violent murderers off the streets."

"So... you knew he was a murderer before you made him into a chimera?" Cyrus still wasn't certain about this, but he remembered the man who had stabbed a woman and gotten away with it. "It's a way of removing violent criminals and discovering medical cures at the same time?"

"Exactly." Monroe smiled. "I'm glad you understand."

"Except, the courts and police have already shown me that they can't be trusted," Cyrus countered. "How certain are you that this man is actually a murderer, unless you saw it with your own eyes?"

"The courts are only punishing Borealan and Coptics unjustly, and ignoring excess crime committed by Empyrians," Monroe explained. "On top of encouraging more crime from the Empyrians who know they won't be arrested, these practices openly violate the Iron Constitution; they're not supposed to be making laws that are applied on racial lines, when they can't give a clear definition on what 'race' is. The entire city council, and everyone involved could lose their jobs if it comes to light. They know this man is too dangerous to not be in prison; they only send me the crooks they need to make disappear."

"I'm not sure if that fixes the problem." Cyrus crossed his arms. "It seems like the entire issue was caused by the government applying different standards to people based on their race. Turning Empyrian criminals into chimeras as some sort of 'correction' for the problem sounds like 'two wrongs make a right.'"

"It isn't ideal," the doctor admitted. "But as I said earlier, these are the difficult decisions we have to make all the time."

"How certain are you that the local government is telling you the truth?" Cyrus asked. "They haven't exactly been forthright when it comes to getting rid of people they need removed. Unless you actually saw him commit the crimes, how do you know this was actually a violent murderer, and not just someone politically inconvenient for someone on the city council?"

The doctor paused. The slack in his jaw gave Cyrus all the answer he needed. "This man in question had evidence on his body that he lived a violent life. Scars, marks on his bones that indicated he got into regular fights. There was enough forensic evidence to the trained eye to confirm the government's story. I could show you what to look for, if you want."

Cyrus wasn't entirely convinced, but he wasn't completely unconvinced, either. "Okay, let's say he did commit six murders. I'm pretty sure turning someone into a chimera for medical experiments counts as cruel and unusual punishment. I don't even think it's legal to perform more mundane experiments on prisoners who've actually been convicted for murder."

Doctor Monroe's gaze fell, before looking back at Cyrus. "But now a murderer can save lives instead of taking them. It would be a waste not to take advantage of this opportunity."

Sighing, Cyrus nodded. "I understand. I'm not sure if I'm comfortable with it, but I get it."

"That's okay, we'll work up to that point." Monroe pointed to the door that Cyrus had heard noises from earlier. "Let me show you a different project I'm working on. Maybe it'll convince you further."

The doctor opened the door and revealed a room where a different chimera was locked in a cage. This was clearly some mix of human and naked mole rat; it looked like a massive hairless rodent, but was almost able to walk on its hind legs, sniffed the air with a rodent-like nose on a human-shaped skull, and worst of all, had a pair of human-looking eyes, still visibly intelligent and in pain. This was one of the chimeras from the ledger.

"I'm so close to developing a cure for the lung cancers that have plagued people who've inhaled smog from the factories." Monroe patted the chimera's wrinkly, bald head. "It'll even help people who've damaged their lungs from smoking for years. All I need to do is identify how her immune system destroys cancerous tissue and transfer that process to humans."

"This...this is..." Cyrus struggled to find the words. "What did they do to deserve this? What have you done?"

"Saved her life, among other things." Monroe looked up from the chimera at Cyrus. "She would have died of her disease by now were it not for my intervention. And now, more people with her condition will survive."

"But she's obviously in pain!" Cyrus pointed at the chimera's eyes. "There's no way she's happy like this! We're supposed to get informed consent!"

"Informed consent is one of those things doctor's need on paper, but it really doesn't work in practice," Monroe explained. "If a man has been in an accident and is incapacitated, we don't wait for him to die or magically wake up in order to treat him. Even if that means giving him an organ transplant from a pig. And what about the mental trauma that dying causes? Who in this world is truly of sound mind when they're about to die? We don't accept wills and testaments scribbled out by a person on their deathbed when they're clearly insane from the pain."

"Consent isn't something you throw away in theory just because it doesn't always work in practice." Cyrus looked at the creature in the cage again. "Isn't this a violation of the medical oath? To do no harm?"

"Do no harm...where is the harm?" Monroe gestured to the chimera. "She's alive. Were it not for my experiments, she wouldn't be. So where is the harm?" He locked eyes with Cyrus and gave him a stern look. "What would Thoth say if he were here? The only reason you think this is wrong is because you've allowed the false morality of the masses to corrupt your thinking. The layman looks at something like this and thinks only of how she's suffering in the here and now. They don't see the lives we'll save. They don't see her body in the morgue from smoke inhalation. In the grand calculus of human lives, this extension of hers will benefit hundreds; maybe even thousands."

"Wait a minute..." Cyrus ran scenarios through his head. "Why not more? Why wouldn't this solve all the world's lung cancer in the future?"

"Oh, not just lung cancer," Monroe corrected. "All cancer. And yes, that could happen, but it's more likely to be similar to the regenerative serum I developed from human-starfish chimeras," Monroe explained. "Even once I got a working sample that could apply the regenerative properties of a starfish to human cells, I could only get more by extracting it from other chimeras. I haven't found a way to synthesize it yet; the cancer-fighting powers of the naked mole rats' immune system will likely require the same process."

"So even if it works, you'll have to create more chimeras like her eventually." Cyrus's mind started running numbers through his head.

"What does that matter?" Monroe asked.

"How many people have you sacrificed for this project already?" Cyrus asked. "How many more people will have to become chimeras even after you get your miracle cures to work? Will we just continue to make more of these things forever? How would you even market cures like that without going public with how they're made?"

Monroe shook his head. "I knew you weren't ready for this."

"Doctor," Cyrus gestured to the mole-rat chimera. "This isn't about preparation. You're trying to convince me to commit acts most scientists would never consider."

The doctor's eyes lit up, as if a new idea had just struck him. "Maybe you'd reconsider if you knew how the process worked."

Guiding Cyrus to a new room of the cellar, Monroe showed him a new cage, where a man had been bound and gagged. Cyrus's eyes widened as he recognized the man's face.

"Where did you find this guy?" The apprentice fumbled with his own hands as he remembered reconstructing the shredded tissue of the woman in the city square. Now her attacker was tied up in a cage before him.

"Do you believe this one was falsely accused?" Monroe allowed himself a smirk as he turned a light on, making the man's face even clearer. There was no mistake; Cyrus could even see the gaps in the man's mouth where his foot had had knocked out the thug's teeth.

"How..." Cyrus circled the cage to get a better look, as if checking for some evidence that Monroe hadn't grabbed the wrong man by mistake. "There's no way."

"The judge may have told you that they weren't going after him, but that was only in the sense of pressing charges," Monroe explained. "There were more than enough witnesses to put the details together. All we had to do was find someone missing enough teeth who matched the rest of the description. Now, let me show you what I've got planned for him."

Doctor Monroe retrieved a water-tight box filled with fresh starfish, which he placed next to the cage. "Combining different creatures is more difficult than fixing up someone with their own DNA as a blueprint. To do this, we need to combine the traits of the starfish we want to the human DNA strand. The human is the animal we're keeping alive, so most of his DNA needs to be left intact."

"How..." Cyrus had a sinking suspicion he knew what Doctor Monroe was going to do next. "How do you plan to do that?"

"We're going to peel away the layers of his flesh, and add the starfish in its place. I'll explain the technique as I go through it, and when we're done, I'll show you my notes on the formula. Would you like to help?" Monroe smiled and held up a scalpel, passing the handle of the tool to Cyrus. "I could use some assistance removing the skin. It'd keep my hands free to graft the starfish onto the man's tissue."

"You want me to..." It dawned on Cyrus that many chimeras was probably made through a similar process. The doctor was asking him to flay a man alive so that he could turn him into an abomination. "Can't we give him some anesthetic?"

"Look at his arms." Doctor Monroe grabbed the man by the shoulder and forced him to the ground. Rolling up his sleeves, the doctor showed Cyrus the man's arms, with veins that had become so messed up from too many needle injections that there was no way they could insert a new drip safely into his arm. "This man's a heroin addict. We can't give him any more of the drug, but if we act now, the effects of the chloroform will keep him from feeling too much. Take the scalpel."

Cyrus held the blade for a moment. Maybe he was just being squeamish; he wasn't ready to flay a man alive. Something else wormed into his mind, and he realized that if he participated in turning this man into a chimera, he'd be an accomplice. He'd have to be quiet about the source of Monroe's miracle cures forever, and maybe even help Monroe keep it hidden from people. He'd probably have a secure place by Monroe's side, and could take credit for any new medical marvels they developed in the future, but he'd be helping the doctor in surgeries like this, probably for the rest of his life.

"Wait a minute..." A new thought occurred to Cyrus. "Where does the trolley go afterwards?"

"Pardon?" Monroe asked.

"The trolley. Once you throw the switch and it runs over one person instead of four, where does it go after that?" Cyrus pointed at the mole-rat chimera.

"You flat-out told me that you'd need to make more chimeras in the future to keep harvesting a cure for cancer. You talk about these chimeras like we're making a simple choice between forcing one person to suffer and saving hundreds in the future, but what happens after that?" Cyrus pointed to the room with the chimera floating in the tank. "You say that man deserves what you've done to him, and this woman was going to die of her disease, but do you really think people desperate for medical treatments in the future are going to exclusively use dying patients and convicted murderers? I'm not even convinced that it's okay to do this to the sick or imprisoned."

"You can't make an omelet without breaking a few eggs." Monroe gestured to the scalpel. "Work with me. Let's save countless lives together."

For a moment, Cyrus was unable to move. If Thoth were here, would he agree with the doctor?

"Cyrus, we're scientists," Monroe stepped towards the apprentice, standing a good ten centimeters over him. "We have to be smarter than this; we have to think about the big picture! We're doctors, alchemists—"

"But we're not gods." Cyrus had made up his mind and scanned his surroundings. It was obvious that Monroe was ready to get violent if he didn't comply, and Cyrus knew he couldn't take him in a fight. But there were gas lines running throughout the house, and in the basement, some of these pipes were exposed...

Clapping his hands, Cyrus tapped the nearest gas pipe, willing the metal in the pipe to seal itself closed and heat up at the same time.

Monroe's eyes widened. "What did you just do?"

Cyrus smiled. "Fire in the hole."

The doctor bolted for the stairs, with Cyrus hot on his heels. As they ran, the gas in the pipes was building up in pressure, and getting hotter at the same time. They only had seconds before it would ignite.

Monroe burst out the front door just as an explosion ripped throughout the basement. Cyrus dove to the ground and rolled out the door as gas throughout the rest of the house caught fire. A chain reaction of explosions tore the building apart, blasting entire walls to ash, shattering windows, and leveling the upper story.

Cyrus kept rolling away from the house until he was far enough to avoid the damage. When he finally stopped, Monroe's entire house had gone up in flames. Nearby, he could see lanterns lighting in the night from the nearby neighborhoods. Monroe may have lived far away from anyone else, but everyone outside the city walls could have seen and heard that explosion.

When he finally struggled to his feet, Cyrus could see the doctor glaring at him. Monroe was keeping most of his emotions in check, and his face mostly hid his fury, but there was no hiding the rage in the man's eyes.

"What do you think you've done?" He whispered. "Years of research – destroyed! Organ transplanting techniques – gone! Volumes of lab notes – burnt! Live experiments – dead! You even killed the heroin addict. Are you proud of yourself? Do you think you've somehow saved the people that were in the cellar? People you just burned to death?"

"What people?" A voice called out in the dark. It was an older voice, coming from down the road. An older man in front of a large crowd made their way up towards Doctor Monroe's home. These people mostly only carried lanterns, although a few carried crowbars and buckets of water, likely to pry anyone who might still be trapped inside out of the wreckage.

"You had someone in the cellar?" Another person asked. "They might still be down there!"

A pained, struggling noise from the wrecked cellar told everyone that at least one person or thing was still alive down there. It sounded like a cross between a person and some kind of sea mammal.

Monroe looked at the crowd, and even in the dim light of the lanterns, Cyrus could make out the fear in his eyes.

Cyrus slipped further away from Monroe, but the doctor turned back to him with a glare that made the apprentice freeze. Then Cyrus realized what he had to do to get out of this situation.

"Why don't you all take a look for yourselves?" He asked the crowd. "See if anyone is still alive down there."

"No." Monroe tried to step between the crowd and the ruins of his house. "No! You have no right to poke through my house!"

"Something you don't want us to see?" A woman in the crowd asked.

"Shouldn't you be trying to save your patients?" Another woman called out. "We have to see if anyone is still alive."

As the crowd moved closer to a surrounded Monroe and started shining their lanterns on the wreckage of his basement, Cyrus slipped off to the side. They weren't paying attention to him anymore.

Once he'd made it to the road, Cyrus took one last look at Doctor Monroe and the crowd. He saw Monroe create a cloud of dust with alchemy as the mob moved to surround him. Cyrus took this as his cue to run, because if Monroe escaped, he didn't want to be around for the doctor to find him.

Cyrus kept running until he made it to the city walls of Dihorma. Once he'd reached the gates, he finally allowed himself to look back. There were no signs that anyone was following him. He'd escaped Doctor Monroe, and any potential problems with the mob.

The mob. Cyrus finally bent over with exhaustion and clutched his stomach, but burst into a mix of laughter and tears at the same time. He'd called upon a group of people who knew nothing about Monroe's experiments to escape. An ignorant crowd, with no knowledge of what the doctor had done, to whom, and why. None of them were going to sift through the ruins of the house and discover that the mole-rat chimera was a cancer patient, or that the thing in the aquarium was a murderer. And would it matter to them if they did? That mob wasn't going to make a more intelligent decision on these things.

"I don't know what's right or wrong anymore," he finally wheezed. "Thoth, where in the Abyss are you?"

30

The Time to Fight

AMRI

Squatting down and grabbing the handle of the spade with both hands, Amri grunted as he lifted with all his might and pried a rock out of the earth.

With considerable effort, Amri managed to carry a rock larger than his own head out of the lawn of a house the Abbey of Truth had volunteered to clear. The abbey had taken up the task of mowing, weeding, and picking up trash in lawns throughout the Empyrian Quarter. Due to how huddled together most of these homes were, there wasn't a lot of mowing to be done, but there were still things people needed. Most of the abbey's volunteers were working on trash collection, but since Amri and Esfan were the only young men available, they'd been asked to tackle the heavier jobs.

"Those arms of yours are getting more useful," Esfan joked. "We'll make a laborer out of you, yet!"

"Thanks," Amri chuckled. "But I think I'll still stick with my sorcerer plan. By the way, do you know anybody who works with glass?"

Esfan nodded. "Found someone, and they'd be happy to help with your project. A retired glassworker. He's been feeling bored, and a little restless, so he's looking forward to working with your experiment."

"Sounds good to me," Amri joined Esfan at a folding table, where the priest-in-training handed him a premade sandwich. "Thanks again for having me join you."

"You're thanking me?" Esfan laughed. "Thank you for helping us move rocks!"

"Yeah, but..." Amri paused. "It's the opportunity. To do something useful."

"I know." Esfan nodded. "Did you know I was born in Harlak?"

"Harlak?" Amri tried to remember where that was on a map. "Out east?"

"Yeah," Esfan pointed towards the Academic District. "Old Empyrian capital. All the way on the other side of the empire."

"How did you end up here?" Amri asked.

"Wanted to join the priesthood, and came here for my studies," Esfan closed his eyes. "Wanted to start a new life. Something more useful, less troublesome than my old life."

Amri sized up the priest-in-training. "You look you're twenty-six. Maybe twenty-seven. How much trouble could you have actually caused in your old life?"

"Well, for starters, I'm thirty," Esfan chuckled. "But thanks for the compliment. "I grew up in a household with just me, my mom, and my older cousin who ran with a crime gang. My older cousin was the breadwinner of the home, and by that, I mean he robbed people for the money we needed. Then one day, he went out and he didn't come back. He'd been shot in the middle of a home invasion."

Shocked, Amri had no idea how to respond to that kind of revelation. "By the gods—"

"Don't," Esfan cut him off. "Don't apologize, or anything like that. People who live by violence, die by violence. And he could have chosen another path. But...my mother and I depended on him, and if we didn't maybe he wouldn't have felt so much pressure to get money so quickly. My mother turned to me and told me it was my turn now; that I had to take to the streets and be the new breadwinner. So, I ran. I went in the exact opposite direction of my cousin, and never looked back. Left Harlak, left my mom, left that behind."

"Hm." Amri pondered the priest's revelation. "I have a hard time picturing you as the violent type."

Esfan waited a moment before responding. "That's probably for the best."

"How old were you?" Amri asked. "When you left home?"

"Fifteen," Esfan replied. "Same as you are now."

"Do you know what happened to your mom?"

"No," Esfan admitted. "I've sent her letters since then, telling her that she can join us here, in the abbey. That they would find work for her and give her a place to stay. When she sent letters in reply, they only contained pleas for me to send money. When I told her I had none, she eventually stopped sending replies. I still write to her, to let her know that the door is still open, but I haven't heard from her in years."

Finishing up their lunches, Amri and Esfan folded up the table they'd used and loaded it into a horse-drawn wagon, along with the tools they'd used to dig up rocks and remove weeds from lawns. Once the wagon was loaded up, a woman volunteering with the abbey sat up front and drove the supplies off, back to the abbey.

Done for the day, Esfan shook Amri's hand as they were about to part ways. Before he could turn back around, a rock thrown at his head knocked the trainee priest to the ground.

Struggling to get back to his feet, a man ran up and kicked him in the stomach and stomped on Esfan's head, grinding his face into the dirt. Before Amri could react, the attacker swung his closed fist like a backhand and socked Amri in the jaw.

The man then grabbed Amri by the collar of his shirt and shook him, finally giving Amri a good look at his face. He was barely any older than Amri, just the stubble of a beard, and probably not strong enough to take Esfan in a straight fight.

"Hand over your wallet," the boy snarled. "Now!"

A million thoughts flew through Amri's mind. He was a sorcerer, or at least a sorcery student. He knew enough about magic to freeze the fluids in this boy's body, or flush the wind from his lungs. At this range, he could even boil his blood from the inside. No, he shouldn't do anything of the sort. This kid was a thief who'd attacked Esfan, but did that mean he deserved to die? He just wanted money. He probably spotted Amri working with the abbey these past few days and realized he lived in the Garden District.

"I said now!" The boy choked Amri with one hand and punched him in the eye with the other. Amri's vision blurred as he tried to refocus. Memories he wanted to push aside flowed back into his head.

"Clean it up now!" His mother had said after he'd spilled fruit juice on the kitchen floor. He'd been too short to reach the countertops then, or the rags in the drawers above the kitchen stove. He'd tried to grab a towel from the bathroom. Then he'd felt a sharp pain in the back of his skull. Maybe he'd been too slow to get the towel. Maybe his mom didn't want him to ruin the good bathroom towels. He couldn't remember. He just knew that if he fled from his mother, things would get worse. If he fought his mother, things would also get worse. If he thought bad things about her, she'd read them from his facial expression and explode in a violent rage. So, he always froze.

A second punch in the face brought Amri back to the present. The mugger had drawn a knife. If he froze now, Amri would die.

Somehow, he fumbled into his pockets and produced a wallet. The thief snatched it and shoved Amri to the ground. Digging through the wallet, the thief found four silver Ioseps and three copper coins.

"This is all you have?" The boy angrily shook his knife at Amri. "Where's the rest?"

"I don't carry that much on me," Amri coughed.

The mugger brandished his knife like he was about to throw it at Amri, but something caught his wrist. Esfan had gotten up and twisted the weapon from his hand. He then forced the thief down to his knees and took Amri's wallet back.

"You have the count of three to run," Esfan whispered. "Before I call the police."

Whimpering, the thief ran off into the streets, leaving Esfan and Amri alone.

Esfan looked back at Amri. "Good grief, are you alright?" He grabbed Amri's hand and pulled him back to his feet. "You look terrible."

"It's...a bit hazy." Amri said. "Most of my face hurts."

The priest in training looked Amri over. "You're...a sorcery student. And you didn't fight back?" He guided Amri to a street bench and sat him down. "Rest a bit. Then go home and get yourself cleaned up."

Esfan managed to dig around through the Abbey's supplies and found some rubbing alcohol for Amri's face. It stung like a hornet, but felt better a few minutes later. Once that was done, Amri thanked him and the rest of the Abbey's volunteer crew before heading home.

Once he made it back to his aunt and uncle's house, his aunt was the first to freak out when he walked in the door.

"What in the Abyss happened to your face?" She ran over to him, touched the tender skin with her finger, and then ran to the kitchen and dug some ice cubes out of the icebox. Sticking these directly under Amri's eye, he had just enough feeling left to sense how blisteringly cold his skin now was.

"Did you get into a fight?" His uncle Mido came down the stairs of the house to the foyer, mortified at the sight of his nephew. "Who did this?"

Amri shrugged. "Some thug in the Empyrian Quarter. I was working with the abbey to take care of lawns there. He...he just wanted my wallet."

Uncle Mido rolled his eyes and threw up his hands. "Typical! Just typical. A group of priests clean trash off of their streets for free and what do they immediately try to do? Assault and rob them! Uncivilized beasts!"

Amri thought about saying that it was only the one boy that had attacked him, and that they'd been working in the Empyrian Quarter for over a week now, with only this one incident, but he wasn't about to interrupt his uncle when he was ranting. Now was not the time.

"Did they take anything from you?" Aunt Panya asked.

Amri shook his head. "The guy tried to get my wallet, but my friend fought him off."

Somewhere, out of the corner of his eye, Amri caught a look of...something... in Uncle Mido's expression. Was it disdain? Disappointment? Or just more anger? Was it directed at the mugger, or at Amri?

"So, what's all of this commotion?" Namid came from out of her room. Even though it was nearly one in the afternoon, she looked like she'd just gotten out of bed. "Something about wild beasts?"

"Your brother was attacked," Uncle Mido muttered. "His priest friend fought them off."

Namid looked at her brother and noticed his face. Amri hadn't gotten a chance to check a mirror yet, but he could tell from her expression that it was bad. She tried to hide it, though, and looked away.

"Does he need anything else, or just a nap and a flank steak over his eye?" Namid asked.

"I'll be fine," Amri said. "I've got ice cubes, and I'm heading back over to the industrial park in an hour to meet Esfan's glassworker contact."

"You're going back out there already?" Uncle Mido paused. "Right now?"

"Well, in a few minutes." Amri nodded. "That's when I've agreed to meet the glassworker."

At this, Uncle Mido's expression seemed to soften. He went back upstairs, likely to return to work on his medical recordkeeping.

A short while later, Amri made his way back to the industrial park. Once he was there, he met Avroham Kafrini, the glassworker that Esfan had contacted. Just as Esfan had said earlier, he was retired, with a face that was old and experienced, but still kind and polite.

"What happened to your face?" Avroham asked.

"Eh, a thug attacked the volunteer team in the Empyrian Quarter earlier." Amri pointed to the metal cylinder and recycled glass. "Can you really use shattered junk glass like this?"

"Oh, yeah." Avroham nodded. "All glass is recyclable, and it's not hard to shape it again once it's reheated."

Firing up the glass furnace, Avroham got to work shaping the glass. Amri wasn't able to do much for this part, so he got out his ward pattern and found the acid he needed to etch the glass when it was done. The ward he was preparing would keep things inside the glass from heating up, but would also insulate the material from cooling down. Molding the glass wouldn't work, because once the ward was melted into the glass, it would be impossible to cool. That meant it had to be applied using the acid method.

Once Avroham had shaped the glass into a cylindrical shell around the scrap tubing, he set it upright to cool. Amri willed the heat to move out of the glass into the surrounding air, making the glass cool faster. Once it was stable, Avroham handed the experiment to Amri, who began applying the ward.

"Let's see if I've learned enough about etching to make this work." Amri gritted his teeth.

THE TIME TO FIGHT

Using a trick his sister had shown him, Amri drew the ward pattern on a sheet of pattern and wrapped it around the glass shell. This was an effective way to translate the ward from a flat surface onto a cylinder. With some difficulty, Amri managed to etch the pattern into the glass.

"Alright," Amri set the experiment up so that the acid could dry. "Now all we have to do is wait. If this works, and it looks like it did, I might need your help again later to make one with a real gas canister."

"Okay," Avroham offered Amri a handshake before heading out. "Just let me know. I'm happy to help."

Amri shook his hand and both set out to leave. As the old glassworker left, a young child ran smack into Amri's stomach. Amri was short for his age, but this kid could barely come up to Amri's chest. He seemed too panicked to look where he was going, and appeared to be running *from* something.

"Hey," Amri held the kid in an embrace. "Where are you running off to in such a hurry?"

Instead of answering, the boy tried to get out of Amri's arms and escape. Amri realized the child was trembling more than struggling.

"What are you doing?" A voice came from the direction the boy had come. "Harassing these other workers? Didn't I teach you better than that?"

Doctor Malbim stood a few meters away, her arms crossed. Her face was no more threatening than a mild frown, but her eyes...Amri recognized that look in her pinhole eyes. It was one that had given him nightmares for as long as he could remember.

"Sorry if Izaac gave you any trouble." Doctor Malbim smiled and closed her eyes, as if hiding her real expression. "He has a number of problems. Isn't that right?"

The boy, who must have been Izaac, didn't respond.

"Ahem," Malbim took a step closer. "Isn't that right, Izaac?"

"He's shaking a lot," Amri blurted out. Realizing he might have angered the alchemist even more, he tried to recover. "I think he's got the chills! Is he sick?"

Malbim's expression froze for a moment, but then softened. "Yes, that might be it. Maybe he's made himself sick from running around too much. You know how little boys are. Always running around in places they shouldn't."

Before Amri could say anything else, he heard Izaac whisper in his ear.

"Please don't leave."

Amri froze. He knew from personal experience not to do anything to make Doctor Malbim upset. Anything he did to anger her now would be taken out on her son once they were behind closed doors.

"H-hey," he fought a losing battle to keep his voice under control. "This kid has quite the grip. Want us to walk with you to wherever it is you're going?" As soon as Amri said this, he instinctively put his hand on Izaac's arm, which was wrapped around his shoulder. As he did, Izaac reflexively moved his arm away, but not before Amri felt the bandage on his upper arm under his shirt sleeve.

"Did you get hurt?" Amri asked Izaac, a bit louder than he should have.

"You know how boys are," Malbim answered. "Always playing too recklessly. It's a miracle he's still in one piece. I've been trying to medicate some of his problems, but they're just too strong."

"Medicate?" Avroham paused. It was obvious he wasn't aware of what was actually going on. "What sort of problems does he have?"

"Oh, you know." Malbim kept her smile, but her eyes were nearly closed. "He has ADHD, autism, and antisocial disorders. He thinks he's a bunch of things he's not, and if you leave him alone for more than a minute, he'll grab some random object and use it as a weapon. His arm is bandaged because that's where the injections go."

Amri realized she never answered his question. They were at a quiet standoff; Malbim probably didn't want him or Avroham to follow her with Izaac, but Amri was too afraid to pry the boy off of him. If he didn't, and the doctor blamed the awkward situation on Izaac, there was no telling what she'd do to her son once they were alone.

Suddenly, Izaac let go of Amri and ran over to the doctor.

"Oh, hey." Malbim looked down at her son. "Ready to behave, are you?" She turned back to look at Amri, still maintaining the fake smile. "Sorry to bother you with his tantrums. I'll be sure to keep better control of him in the future."

The doctor took Izaac by the arm and pulled him along with her back to the pharmaceutical department.

Avroham looked at Amri. "What was all that about?"

31

Zombie Ogre Soup

DAURGO

As the ogres approached Aquila and the skeleton Daurgo was possessing, the lich focused his best human-acting skills to move this body exactly like a bombastic human entertainer would.

"Halt!" Daurgo raised the right hand. "I come bearing goods to sell."

"Goods?" An ogre grunted. "We like goods. We take goods from you while we eat you."

"Ah but..." Daurgo reached for the first weapon on this skeleton's loadout and found a round glass vial. "Oh, forget it."

The skeleton chucked the vial at the nearest ogre. The glass shattered on the ogre's forehead. At first, the ogre looked confused and annoyed, but then the acidic compound did its work, and the lumbering brute screamed as his forehead dissolved.

The next vial Daurgo threw burst into flames on impact, setting an ogre on fire. The giant screamed and ran around wildly, disorienting the others while Daurgo reached inside the skeleton's hollow chest and withdrew a gun.

Animated skeletons are normally terribly uncoordinated. A necromancer who takes direct control of a single corpse can guide their actions to be more accurate, but the puppet's different body proportions make it difficult for the sorcerer to aim a firearm. A dragon trying to control a human skeleton was like a grown man trying to fit his massive hand into a kid-sized sock puppet and get it to put on a show. This is why Daurgo liked high-spread scatterguns.

The first blast tore through an ogre, splattering his friends with pieces of ogre flesh. Confused, the other ogres noticed the smoking gun just in time for Daurgo to fire another round. This one left two more ogres torn to shreds, and the others started backing away from the armored man in the bronze mask and black cloak.

Daurgo noted his other five skeletons, some of whom had also been spotted by the ogres. One had been surrounded by the brutes, and had released the mustard gas stored in his armor, leaving a pile of ogres gasping for air. Another had not been spotted yet, and had started throwing firebombs and grenades from cover, while a third had simply charged some of the beasts in melee. The confused giants couldn't keep up with the flurry of bladed weapons that tore through them, especially as it moved unlike any normal human, and didn't even seem to know what a normal limb rotation for a human was.

"Magic or no magic, I am still powerful," the lich gloated as he blew another ogre's head clean off. "And no less dangerous."

Realizing he'd lost track of Aquila, Daurgo scanned the area for the thief. Centuries of single-minded pursuit towards his goals had eroded his moral code, but allowing the employee he dragged on this mission to be taken by these monsters might actually bother him. Eventually. For a time.

The armored skeleton found the thief hiding behind the nearest rock with several empty vials near her feet. Small crossbow in hand, she was dipping bolts in poison and preparing to pick off ogres from her hiding spot.

"These things..." she muttered. "Are so damned big, I'm using up all of my best poisons and they barely seem to notice!"

Daurgo looked at one of the vials at her feet. "Aquila, this is tranquilizer. It isn't supposed to kill."

"Yeah, and I'm not supposed to be an assassin." She fired another shot. "What's your point?"

Switching his consciousness to another skeleton, Daurgo whipped out the weapon hidden in this one's chest: a small flamethrower, with fuel packed inside the skeleton's hollow ribcage.

Approaching a terrified ogre, Daurgo pointed the flamethrower nozzle at the brute. "Fun fact number one: if you surrender, I'll let you live."

"I give, I give!" The ogre pleaded.

"Fun fact number two: I'm a liar." Daurgo cackled as he engulfed the begging ogre in flames.

Burning a few more ogres, Daurgo paused to take in the sight of lightly-smoked ogre meat. He wasn't trying to wreck the bodies too much; then he couldn't raise them. He looked up and noticed an ogre who had witnessed his incendiary slaughter and clung to a crude hammer, clearly unsure whether to attack the lich or not. Daurgo turned to the thug and pointed the flamethrower at him.

"Now I know what you're thinking: how much fuel does that flamethrower have left?" The lich stepped closer. "Personally, I'm not sure. Question is, do you feel lucky today?"

The ogre dropped his hammer with a whimper and ran away from the cackling skeleton. The ogress shaman that Daurgo had seen earlier, however, was not so frightened.

"You scare my louts and wreck my camp," she growled. "But you not frighten me. You only resort to scare trick because you out of fire."

"Hm, let's check." Daurgo squeezed the flamethrower trigger. The last noises the shaman made were almost a scream, but for the enflaming fluid entering her mouth and lungs as she burned.

"I guess not." Daurgo finished off the shaman and looked around for remaining ogres.

The entire ogre camp had suffered grenades, gunshots, mustard gas, firebombs, acid attacks, and the inefficient sleep poisons of a number of crossbow bolts. All of the ogres that he could see had been thoroughly slain.

"Was that the last of them?" Aquila popped up from under her rock.

"Looks like it." Daurgo kicked one of the less-burnt bodies to check that it was dead. "Now to bring in the harvesting crew."

"Harvesting crew?" Aquila asked. "What are we harvesting?"

"The bodies, of course! Did you forget why we were here in the first place?"

"Oh, right," Aquila looked over the corpses. "I forgot killing everyone was the point."

A few hours later, Daurgo had brought his base closer to the ogre camp and had some of his human skeletal minions collecting the corpses. As they did, Daurgo had the *Pair Dadeni* brought up from his storage.

The cauldron of rebirth had several cracks that had been welded back together. This thing had been destroyed and reforged multiple times. On its outer surface, scenes of heroes fighting legendary battles appeared on one side, while the cauldron's operating instructions were depicted on the other. Fairly straightforward; fill cauldron with water, place over fire to boil, insert corpse into cauldron A, receive zombie from cauldron. Simple.

Daurgo had checked this thing multiple times. The cauldron was, for all intents and purposes, a necromantic engine. Although the lich had yet to figure out how it worked, exactly, it did grant the person who used it to revive corpses the same control over the undead it created as if they had raised the person with proper necromancy. No special bonding ritual, no drop of blood required from the user; somehow, the cauldron knew and accepted its user's intentions.

Shoving the first ogre into the filled cauldron, Daurgo stirred the water with a large pewter ladle. Pewter was one of those odd metal alloys that was completely magically inert; perfect for handling tasks like this.

After a few seconds of letting the corpse stew, Aquila took a closer look at the cauldron. "So, is this one of those 'wait for it' moments?"

In answer to her question, the ogre's wrecked hand popped out of the cauldron, grabbed the side of it, and pulled itself out of the water. A large, hulking zombie now stood ready at the lich's command.

"Yes," Daurgo replied. "Yes it is."

A group of skeletons pulled up a large drawing board next to the pot. As a new corpse was added to the water, the lich had his skeletons begin drawing new plans for his next move.

"This is a bit of a slow and tedious process," Daurgo explained. "You have to animate the bodies one at a time. While that happens, I need to come up with a way of getting the gods off my trail."

"How do you usually do that?" Aquila asked. "You give the impression that you've done this before."

"I have, but this time is different. The gods think I killed Thoth. I usually avoid killing gods when it isn't necessary, for exactly this reason. It's not just their pride that's hurt; Thoth is one of those extremely rare, universally liked deities. The entire pantheon wants revenge. What's more, I exposed myself as a dragon to these people."

The thief sat down on a nearby rock and watched as another zombie ogre emerged from the pot. "Is that particularly bad?"

"Very. As a necromancer with an undead army, most people think of me as no more a threat than any other practitioner of dark magic. The Tomb Lords are more dangerous than that. But a dragon? Who can talk, and cast spells? Humans only react to that with either terror, obsession, or shame. And their response to all three is to attack with everything they've got."

Daurgo brought up his inventory of weapons and materials. He was running low on ammunition for his artillery, and he needed parts to repair his armor. Fortunately, he still had a sizeable amount of gold and treasure stored up from raiding old tombs, but there was always a shortage of suppliers willing to sell materials to a skeletal necromancer. But there was one person in the area, not too far from Egark, who might have what the dracolich needed. And he might have more than supplies to offer...

"Okay," Daurgo thought aloud as he raised another ogre zombie. "New army of minions: check. Means of acquiring supplies: Maybe? But I need more information, and more than that, I need more time. As long as the gods think I killed Thoth, they aren't going to stop searching for me. They might even make deals with other pantheons if I flee to a region outside their domain. That means I need to keep them disoriented. Aquila!"

The thief perked up from the rock she'd been sitting on. "Yes!"

"Get some paper and a pen," the lich chuckled. "I need you to write some letters."

Several hours later, Daurgo had finished raising the ogre zombies. "Good grief, I want my regular necromancy back. Grab everything and get ready to go, we're heading out."

Once they'd loaded up the centipede, Daurgo took one last look at Egark. It was a strangely beautiful and primitive land, free of humans, and even the strange mutant fauna had a certain charm to it. He might have to return here someday for more experiments.

"Some other time." A skeletal hand put in coordinates for their next destination, and the centipede took off.

"I'm going to drop you off near Madanaj," he told Aquila. "You'll be able to take a train from there to Hadesh. And where I'm going, it'll be easier to negotiate without any humans around."

"Fair enough," Aquila sat in a reclining chair in the control room and leaned back to take a nap. "I have things to do in Taride. Wake me when we arrive in Madanaj."

Once they were as close as they could get without being seen, Daurgo dropped Aquila off and directed the centipede towards the Iron Mountains. He had a genie to see.

The Iron Mountains were not known to have any iron in them. They were named entirely after the genie who owned the mining company there: Mr. Iron.

Crawling up to the base of the mountains, the centipede released a set of drills that allowed it to bury itself into the earth and stay hidden. Daurgo took possession of a skeleton in robes and one of his more diplomatic outfits, and brought four of the new ogre zombies with him.

The main way of entering Mr. Iron's mountains was through the airship dock near the top of the largest peak. However, to certain friends of the genie, another entrance was available at the foot of the mountains.

Daurgo navigated the various ordinary boulders and approached one that looked no different than the others.

"Now, where's that hidden lever again?" Daurgo found a switch that was buried behind this largest rock. Giving it a hard yank, gears could be heard shifting, and another large rock descended into the ground, revealing a hidden passageway. Daurgo and his ogre minions made their way through this backdoor entrance to the genie's office.

The hidden back passage slowly ascended, but only a little, before reaching a hallway that directed him to the main grand staircase where most visitors entered. Once he reached the main hallway, he had one short but very wide and grandiose flight of steps to follow before reaching the bottom of the stairs, where a massive brass door with a vicious grinning mask-like a face of molded bronze smiled at him.

"Daurgo! Welcome back!" The mask greeted him with a deep soft voice. "It's been too long!"

"Yes, well, I've been busy." Daurgo examined the door a little closer. "You told me before that you're a demonically possessed door, but you never told me your name."

"Nope." The door grinned with rows of jagged teeth. "Don't think I did. And I don't think I will. Names have power."

The lich decided it wasn't worth prying. "No matter. I come here to deal."

"Yes, yes. Come right in." The door swung open to allow the skeleton and his entourage to enter.

Behind the door, Mr. Iron's office was a large, round room with a floor mostly made of smooth, black marble, while the walls and ceiling were hollowed out of the mountain itself. Instead of sanding or smoothing these surfaces, Mr. Iron left them jagged, giving them a more natural look.

Mr. Iron himself sat on a throne in the center of the room on a slightly raised circular platform. He was humanoid, with skin that appeared to be made of grey stones, eyes as black and shiny as amethysts. He was muscular, and on his skin were chiseled song lyrics. When Daurgo had asked about them, Mr. Iron had told him it was an epitaph.

"Well, well." The genie leaned back in his throne and smiled. "What brings you here today?"

"I need supplies for my artillery. I also need materials to repair machinery." Daurgo approached the genie and handed him a list of the things he needed. "And, if you have it, I need information."

"Information?" Mr. Iron looked up from the list. "About what, exactly?"

"One of the Egyptian gods was killed, and someone managed to frame me for it."

Mr. Iron's eyes widened. "Killed a god? That's not something you can pull off on a whim."

"Oh, I know." Daurgo's skeleton nodded. "I've killed gods before. But not this one, and yet, someone has managed to convince the Egyptian gods that I did."

Mr. Irons paused. "I...don't know how gods can be killed. Being a spirit myself, mortality is something I don't fully understand. Djinn are closer to mortals than any other spirit, but the fact that humans can just...die, for no reason other than having lived too long, never made sense to me."

"Well, it doesn't usually work that way for gods, either," Daurgo explained. "Killing one requires a great deal of planning. You need to know the god well enough to understand what idea they represent, and how to counter it. The only thing that can really kill an idea, or at least hurt it in any meaningful way, is another idea. Now, if I know people the way I think I do, then the way to hurt the god of logic and reason is with an emotion that makes them throw sense and reason out the window. A strong, vindictive emotion. Something that festers into malevolence."

"Wrath?" The genie offered.

"No, you're a pretty wrathful guy, no offense, but you've always been rational about it. If anything, it makes you better at hurting humans." Daurgo looked around at the genie's throne. "Speaking of, didn't you used to have a couple of cat-girl chimeras before?"

"Oh, them?" The genie shrugged. "My attempt at the DNA bonding process didn't work out as well as I originally thought. The cell division didn't hold up in their bodies after I added cat genes, so they both died of cancer a few weeks ago." He leaned back and smiled, as if savoring the memory.

"Right..." Daurgo wanted to get the conversation back on track. "Well, anyway, I don't think wrath would make someone viciously unreasonable. Neither would greed; it's too self-serving. To attack reason is an act of self-harm."

"Envy!" Mr. Iron bolted upright in his seat. "Envy could do it."

"Envy...given a physical form..." the pieces were starting to assemble in the lich's mind. "I've suspected for some time now that the Tomb Lords were really responsible. They're the only ones I know of with access to the sorts of materials and magical know-how to turn an emotion like envy into a weapon. But I need proof. Both to confirm my suspicions, and to show the humans that

I'm not the one that actually killed their god."

"Why prove it to the humans?" Mr. Iron asked. "Why not just show it to the gods who are after you?"

"Ignoring the fact that the gods already hate my guts, the nature of gods means they only know what their worshippers know." Daurgo realized that even though Mr. Iron was a spirit, he really didn't know that much about how spiritual beings worked. Maybe he just didn't know from the mortal side of things. "The gods are *technically* smart enough to work all of this out themselves. And if the Tomb Lords were worshippers of the Egyptian gods, they would know the liches were responsible because the liches know they're responsible. But Amenhotep banned religions that worship anyone other than himself in Kemet, so that won't work."

"So...what if you just killed all of the humans that worship these gods?" Mr. Iron clasped his hands on his lap. "Wouldn't that force the gods to stop pursuing you?"

"Well, I can't do that," Daurgo chuckled. "I mean, physically I could, but the consequences would outweigh the benefits. And I'm not ruthless enough to slaughter an entire empire just to get rid of one pantheon of gods."

"Tch," the genie scoffed. "I've never understood this about you. Humans thought your species were nothing but monsters to be slain in order to prove themselves heroes. They only negotiated with your kind when there were too many of you to kill, and they didn't have the strength to pull it off. As soon as some foreign army shows up with the means to wipe you out, they genocide your entire species. Why don't you kill every last one of them? You'd be completely justified if you did."

Daurgo paused. "Isn't it obvious? It's because I'm better than them."

Mr. Iron frowned, as if the dracolich had just insulted him. But then he replaced it with a light smile. "Well, if I ever find myself to be the last of my kind, perhaps I'll feel the same way. Until then, I bid you farewell. I'll have your requested materials delivered to your centipede in a few hours."

32

Gaslighting: A Primer

AMENHOTEP

Observing through the eyes of one of his undead crows, the High Tomb Lord of Kemet watched as one of his necrophytes marched with a dozen zombies under his command. Approaching a shoe factory and bursting through the worker's entrance, the necrophyte pointed at a thirty-year-old laborer bent over a sewing machine and shouted.

"There is the traitor! Bring him to me, alive!"

The zombies following him surged through the factory and knocked over anything or anyone in their way. A confused and terrified new worker made the mistake of not getting out of a zombie's way in time; he was slammed against a wall with a loud snapping sound in his neck. None of the other workers were stupid enough to get between the zombies and their target.

The laborer got up from the sewing machine and tried to flee, but the zombies tackled him and pinned him to the factory floor. One roared at him with a rotten mouth dangling with phlegm, but they were under the necrophyte's orders to bring him alive.

"Mr. Asraf Kassis," the necrophyte took out a roll of paper, a warrant for the man's arrest. "You have been accused of treason against Kemet, and the holy godking himself."

"What?" The laborer tried to look up from the floor, but the zombies had his head pinned. "How? Why? What have I done?"

"Suicide bombing a factory, for starters," the necrophyte folded up the warrant and tucked it away.

"What?" Asraf cried. "That doesn't make sense!"

"You will, of course, be given a trial," the necrophyte explained. "If you are innocent, then you have nothing to fear." He pointed to the zombies. "Take him."

As the undead hoisted Asraf into the air and carried him towards the palace dungeons, Amenhotep returned his vision to his body and looked down at Sekhet, who sat terrified before him.

"I hope you pay close attention to things going forward," the High Tomb Lord clasped his hands. "There will be a quiz at the end."

"M-my godking," Sekhet quivered. "What is…why are we arresting a worker for something he couldn't have done? At least, couldn't have done and survived to be arrested for it?"

"I am the morning and the evening star," Amenhotep raised his hands in demonstration. "I am the sun, the moon, and the truth. No crime can be committed in my kingdom without punishment. Someone must pay for blowing up one of our factories."

"But…even the public won't be fooled. Even the dumbest peasant knows that if that man blew himself up to sabotage one of our factories, he wouldn't still be alive to arrest now."

"Tsk, tsk," Amenhotep wagged a finger. "Pay attention. I wasn't kidding about that quiz."

Asraf Kassis was brought down to the palace, where Amenhotep ordered his necrophytes to torture him into confessing. The torture chamber included a wall of one-way glass, allowing Amenhotep and Sekhet to observe the necrophytes' work without allowing Asraf to see them. The prisoner sat with his hands cuffed to his chair, while the two uniformed necrophytes stood over him. Asraf was about as handsome as an underfed thirty-year-old laborer could be, minus a short facial scar where one of the factory machines must have caught his cheek.

"Bring them in," one necrophyte ordered.

A slave dragged a beaten man and woman into the torture chamber, each bound and gagged.

"Mr. Kassis," the first necrophyte pointed at the couple. "Are these your parents?"

Asraf looked at the beaten couple, then shook his head.

"Heheheh," the first necrophyte looked at his partner, who smiled. "Trying to protect them, hm? You know, the crime you committed was so serious, such a horrendous act against the godking himself, we might need to expunge your entire family as well, just to purify Kemet of this treason. It all depends on how much you deny the word of the godking."

Asraf paused, then lowered his head. "They are my parents."

The necrophytes nodded, then shared a knowing glance. "Very well. Take them away. Then bring in the girl."

As the couple were taken away from the torture chamber, a young woman was escorted into the room by a pair of guards. She was in handcuffs, but showed no signs of abuse.

"Tell me, Mr. Kassis," the second necrophyte looked at a clipboard and turned over a page. "This is Maria. Pretty girl, isn't she? Is she your wife, or your girlfriend?"

The man paused, trying to figure out the correct answer. "Wife."

"Are you sure?" The necrophyte asked. "We don't have a record of the two of you getting married. You aren't trying to claim her as kin to protect her, are you?"

"We...we aren't technically married yet, but I've proposed," Asraf replied. "That's...closer to a wife than a girlfriend. I-I believe."

The necrophytes looked at each other in confusion. "Does that count?" One asked.

"I'm not sure," the other one pointed to the guards. "Better err on the side of caution. Take her back to the kennels and feed her to the zombies, same with the other two."

"No!" Asraf struggled against his restraints, but one of the necrophytes punched him in the nose. The other shook his head at his partner.

"We don't need to do that," He said while the woman's screams filled the dungeon halls as the guards dragged her away. The necrophyte turned back to

Asraf.

"You seem to think this is some kind of mind game. It is not." The necrophyte explained. "When you lie to protect your family members, it gets them killed. When you try to give us the answers you think will get them set free, it gets them killed. When you give us what we want, and only then, we will let them go." He looked at the clipboard again. "You have a sister, correct?"

Asraf shifted in his chair. "...Yes."

"And...you wouldn't want the same thing that's happening to your parents and fiancé right now to happen to her, correct?"

"Please..." the prisoner replied. "Leave her alone."

"Well, that's up to you," the necrophyte explained. "You see, to challenge us is to challenge the godking. We arrested you because he says you're guilty. To argue with him is blaspheme, a serious crime in its own right. Confess, and there is no further harm done. That would be the end of it."

Asraf paused. Eventually, he sat up in his chair. "Alright. I did it."

"Did what?" The first necrophyte asked.

"I'm guilty."

The necrophytes looked at each other in confusion. "Guilty of what? Tell us what you actually did."

"I...I blew up the factory. I walked into the building with a bomb strapped to my back and blew it up. I'm the suicide bomber."

The necrophytes looked at each other and frowned. "I'm sorry Mr. Kassis, but I'm afraid you aren't very convincing. You're lying."

"What?" Asraf looked up at the necrophytes in bewilderment. "But I confessed! You said I was guilty, and to deny it was a crime!"

"But you don't believe your own confession," the necrophytes replied. "It's obvious. You think this whole thing is ridiculous; that you couldn't be the suicide bomber, or you wouldn't be alive right now. Lying in court or under oath is also a crime. When you are ready to be honest with us, we will pick this up again. Until then," the necrophytes pointed to a guard. "Lock him up in the deprivation room. You know the one."

The deprivation room. When he was alive, the idea of a deprivation room had never occurred to Amenhotep. The thought seemed counterintuitive. It was, ultimately, a room where the prisoner was placed in a large metal tank filled with water, with a straw strapped to his mouth and nose. He could breathe, and could not willingly drown himself, but the water made it impossible to hear anything, he would lose all sense of feeling after a few hours, and with the tank closed, it was too dark inside for the man to see. The room itself was made so sterile that there was nothing to smell through the tube, either. Total sensory deprivation. No one experienced it for long and stayed sane.

Sekhet shifted in her seat and took out a notepad to scribble something down. Good, Amenhotep mused. *She clearly doesn't understand the importance of this yet. If she already knew what he was trying to teach her, this entire exercise would be pointless.*

The High Tomb Lord busied himself with finance reports until an hour had passed, at which point the necrophytes informed him that Asraf was being taken out of the tank for further questioning. Amenhotep returned to his observation room, from which Sekhet hadn't dared to budge.

Asraf was dragged back to his chair. This time, he had been stripped naked. When placed in the interrogation chair, he was visibly shocked by the feel of the seat on his skin.

The first necrophyte held up a gloved hand. "How many fingers do you see?"

The man squinted against the light, which now seemed to be hurting his eyes, and tried to reach for his ears, but his hands were cuffed to the chair again. "I...there are...four fingers?"

The necrophyte gave a knowing smile to his partner, before holding his hand closer to Mr. Kassis. "One," he wiggled his first finger. "Two, three, four... five." The necrophyte wiggled his index finger on his other hand held behind the first. To Asraf's dulled vision, it must have looked like the necrophyte had six fingers.

"Your senses deceive you, Mr. Kassis," The other necrophyte handed him a piece of paper and a pen. "Can you still write your name?"

Asraf squinted at the paper. "What am I signing?"

"You don't need to sign anything. Spell your name, one letter at a time."

Asraf Kassis struggled to hold the pen in his numb hand, but managed to write out his full name on the paper. The necrophytes took it away from him and checked his writing.

"Mr. Kassis, you've written your name wrong," the necrophyte pointed to the paper. "Your first name is spelled with two 's's, and your surname has a 'y' in it." He handed the paper back to the prisoner. "Is there something wrong with your head, Mr. Kassis?"

"Head's fine," Asraf croaked as he took the paper back. "I spelled my name right."

"Really?" The second necrophyte took a sheet of paper that Amenhotep had stamped with his seal earlier. "According to the godking, your name is Assraf Kassys. Right here."

Asraf looked at the paper in confusion while the other necrophyte leaned closer.

"Perhaps you'd like to write out your confession this time? Maybe you'll be more convincing?"

The prisoner sighed and nodded, taking the pen to write out a new confession. When he was done, the necrophytes looked at the paper again.

"This is so sloppily written, I can't tell what it says." The first necrophyte crumpled the paper up and threw it on the ground. "Back to the tank with you."

As the man was dragged kicking and screaming back to the sensory deprivation tank, Amenhotep turned to Sekhet.

"Do you understand this part?"

"Yes," she nodded. "The man is trying to make sense of his situation with his reason, but the conditions of his confinement are deliberately unreasonable. The necrophytes are robbing him of his sense of reality, and making his own memories unreliable. The purely psychological nature of the torture is...an interesting touch. I...believe the point of using only mental torture is to prevent from leaving physical marks on his body? Something that could reignite his sense of cause and effect?"

"That's the basic point," Amenhotep nodded. "There is more. We are trying to break his mind, not his body. So, we focus exclusively on mental techniques and do not waste time on the flesh. The key is that Mr. Kassis doesn't have any reliable idea of what will happen next, and will soon lose his ability to keep track of what has happened already."

Another hour later, Asraf was brought in again. The process repeated several times. Once, he was reduced to nothing but a sobbing mess for an entire session, and the necrophytes simply put him back in the tank. Eventually, when they brought him in, he immediately begged forgiveness.

"I'm sorry!" He wept. "I killed those people! I blew up an entire factory full of workers – I don't even know how many them there were, or remember their names. I took them away from their families forever!"

Asraf burst into a fit of tears. The necrophytes looked at the one-way glass and nodded for Amenhotep to see.

"The first stage is complete," Amenhotep gestured for Sekhet to follow him. "Now for the second part."

33

Ephorah's Homecoming

EPHORAH

With only a month left before classes started again, Ephorah's internship with the Salamanders ended. She hadn't been able to sleep during the entire train ride home. Rolling her suitcase behind her, she got off an autobus near her parents' house, and groggily walked up to the front door and stepped inside.

"I have returned from hell," she grumbled as she closed the door behind her.

Her mother was in the living room of their one-story home, mending a pair of pants from a pile that their neighbors had hired her to fix. Ephorah's mother had been mending clothes from home with her brother since before they had lived in Hadesh. "Oh, that's...how was it?" She asked.

Kind of a dumb question, Ephorah thought, but didn't say it. "It was...not a lot of fun, and a bit costly. But I learned some new things, and made a new artifact." She held up the sword she'd made in its sheath. For some reason, it had corroded since returning home. The metal wasn't as bad as it had been when she'd first made it, but the blade had tarnished, the handle had started to rust, and the weapon itself showed no signs of enchantment. Only the sharpened, serrated edge of the blade remained of the sword's initial transformation when it started drinking blood.

"Oh." Her mom examined the new weapon, visibly unimpressed. "It looks kind of...um..."

"Yeah, it looked better when I used it." Ephorah put it away. "Where are dad and Aziz?"

"Your father is trying to teach Aziz how to help him with his job." Her mother's tone suggested that her father was trying and *failing* to teach Aziz. "They're in your father's workshop now."

Ephorah took her suitcase and the sword to her room. She examined the blade one more time. She could feel it thirsty again. It didn't cut her, but it would have stabbed her and drank her blood if it could.

Placing the hungry sword on the desk in her room, Ephorah went to her father's workshop. Shaheer el-Sabet was currently trying to teach her brother how to keep track of the different tools he used. Aziz was doing his best to remember where everything went, and he seemed to have a good memory, but problems arose whenever he had to do math involving fractions.

"Okay, let's try this again," her father rubbed his head like he was trying to stay calm.

"A five-eighths wrench is bigger than a one-half wrench. So where does the three-quarters wrench go?"

Aziz looked at the wrenches on his dad's table and picked up the three-quarters wrench. "Maybe...between the one-half and five-eighths? Three is more than one, but less than five. Four is more than two and less than eight—"

Shaheer sighed. "Maybe we should pick this up again later. For now, just try lining them up from smallest to biggest. See if you're right about the three-quarters wrench."

Ephorah came up to the pair and waved hello. Aziz excitedly tackled his sister in a bear hug, which was a lot cuter when he was smaller, but now that he was ten he was big enough to knock her over.

"Oof!" Ephorah mumbled from in between the floor of her father's workshop and her brother's chest. "Good to see you too."

Their father pried Aziz off of his sister with one hand and helped Ephorah to her feet with the other. "You're back!" He looked his daughter over, somewhat bedraggled, but all in one piece. "How was it?"

"It was...informative." Ephorah admitted. "Although I have more questions now than I did before."

"Ah, what did you learn from the Salamanders?" Her father asked.

"I learned that most people who sign up to work for a monster-hunting mercenary army that fights almost exclusively with flamethrowers aren't the sanest people in Janaan. We fought Greymarchers and Hisham out there."

"The Greymarch?" Shaheer's eyes widened. "They actually brought you out into a battlefield with Greymarchers?"

"Not intentionally." Ephorah instinctively tried to calm her father down. "I was part of a scouting team meant to investigate Hisham attacking a nearby town. The Hisham lured the Greymarchers towards the town as part of their scheme."

"My only daughter..." Shaheer fumed. "My only girl...attacked by those drooling, infectious monsters..." He'd begun to breathe heavily as his fingers started to twitch. "An intern...they took an intern to a fight with Greymarchers..."

"Dad, it wasn't intentional, and it wasn't their fault." Ephorah grabbed his fidgeting right arm and held it with both hands. "The Hisham tricked them, that's all. And I'm here now, safe and sound. So it's fine. It's not like I planned to go into a military career, anyway."

Her father blinked. "Right. Right, you're here now and you're not going back. This was just a...a career building...thing."

Ephorah thought about the reasons she'd done a mercenary internship in the first place. Military work looked good on any résumé, even if it wasn't related to the job they applied to later. Career experience was funny like that.

"Still, I'm glad you're back, all safe and sound." Shaheer hugged his daughter. "And I'm glad to hear you avoided working with the Tin Men."

Returning his embrace, Ephorah let herself enjoy the safety in her father's arms for a moment. Then her mother came into the workshop.

"By the way, your friend Namid wanted to talk to you when you got back," Namid handed Ephorah a letter. "She left this; said you'd want to take advantage of the opportunity."

Knowing that "opportunity" for Namid usually meant money, Ephorah pulled herself away from her father and opened the letter.

EPHORAH'S HOMECOMING

Dear Ephorah,

Amri and I ended up getting banned from a lot of research facilities in Grand Spire by a stuck-up snotbag of a princess. Go figure. Anyway, I found a nice little money-making opportunity coming up this week: ushering a wedding! Some fiasco with the bride and her friends led to the usher volunteers abandoning the wedding, so their hiring replacements. They need two ushers, and we'd be perfect for the role if we signed up as soon as you get back. Let me know if you're ready to make some quick cash!

- Namid

P.S. Wear your strength gloves.

"I guess it shouldn't surprise me that the first thing Namid wants from me when I get back from fighting monsters is help in her money-making scheme." Ephorah folded the note and tucked it into her pocket. "It seems innocent enough, which bothers me, but I should check it out. At least until the other shoe drops."

Ephorah took a shower, put on a fresh set of clothes, and then went over to Namid's house in the Garden District. Originally, her family had been situated in the Empyrian Quarter after their original home was attacked in Aklagos by the Greymarch. Having no house and initially few possessions, the imperial palace rented out their new home in Hadesh, until her father could purchase it once he got his carpentry work back in action. Namid and Amri, however, had family that already lived in Hadesh, and even though their parents were lost in the evacuation chaos, they now lived in a fairly lavish home in the most expensive district in the city.

The front door of the house had an ornate stone archway hanging over a brick porch. The door itself was polished wood, with a fancy glass window above eye-level. It was the sort of window so high up that no one could actually use it to look outside and see who was at the door; it was only there to look expensive.

Using a large brass knocker in the center of the door, Ephorah waited for someone to answer. When a middle-aged woman opened it, she eyed Ephorah and then remembered who she was.

"Oh, Ephorah!" Panya Seluk waved her inside. "It's been a while."

"I was away for my work studies." Ephorah stepped into the foyer and looked around.

The place hadn't changed a bit since she'd last been there. Namid had invited her over many times since they'd moved to Hadesh. The entire house was incredibly fancy; like it had been bought from a family of royalty that had decided to sell the place and move into an even bigger mansion. This house was not necessarily huge, but it had more than enough room for the four people living in it and half of its decorations were worth more than Ephorah's parents made in a year. It finally dawned on Ephorah that back in Aklagos, Namid and Amri had probably been just as poor as her family; no one in their old mining town owned this kind of wealth. While Ephorah had moved from one working class home to another, Namid had gone from being poor to the lap of luxury.

A few minutes later Namid came down the stairs to join Ephorah in the foyer. "You're back!" She beamed. "How was your trip?"

"It wasn't a vacation," Ephorah frowned. "It was an internship."

"Amri and I went to study abroad in Grand Spire," Namid explained. "It wasn't perfect, and obviously we were there to learn, but we still enjoyed the trip."

"You..." Ephorah stopped herself. "I was working with a mercenary company. We fought monsters. Including the Greymarch."

Namid blinked. "...Oh. Okay...yeah, that's...not the same. Well, did you enjoy...no, that'd be silly. Was there anything about it you did like?"

Ephorah paused. "...not particularly."

Nodding, Namid grabbed a wedding invitation from a nearby desk in the foyer. "So, this is somewhat spur-of-the-moment, but I found a way for us to make a quick bag of silver. This woman's getting married, it's a big splashy traditional Borealan wedding, and they're short-staffed. They need people to serve drinks, wait tables, open doors, that sort of thing. They're paying fifty silver Ioseps for each assistant. Interested?"

Looking over the wedding invitation, which wasn't addressed to anyone and presumably was just an unsigned copy, Ephorah glanced at the names and details of the ceremony. "A traditional Borealan wedding? I've heard of those. I think Professor Meir told our class that they were outdated and extremely sexist."

"Oh, that's probably because of the legal stuff," Namid explained. "A traditional Borealan wedding is a marriage before the gods, and *only* the gods – it has no legal weight. Both parties can nullify the marriage at any time, but that won't affect us. If we're just there to bus tables and serve guests, the issues of the newlyweds aren't our problem."

Something about this bothered Ephorah. "Why exactly are you trying to do all of this for fifty silvers? It looks like you've got plenty of money."

Namid noticed Ephorah eyeing the décor of her aunt and uncle's house. "My guardians have plenty of money. I don't, and it's not just about the money; it's about making the most of the short amount of time we have left before school starts. Besides, if you don't want to come, you don't have to. I invited you because I figured you could use the money."

Ephorah looked at the invitation again. "Alright," she sighed. "I guess I could use the extra cash. When is the wedding?"

Namid smirked. "Two days from now."

34

How to Redeem a Bomber

SEKHET

The entire population of Azzitha stood before Amenhotep's palace. They had been summoned to witness justice being done, by the godking's will. They were not permitted to refuse.

Asrraf Kassys was dragged out in public. He had been given a loincloth to wear for decency and was guided by a guard to the crowd. By orders of Amenhotep, his face had been beaten until he was visibly disfigured and hideous to look upon. All the easier for people to hate.

"Remember," Amenhotep had whispered to the guard earlier. "They are not allowed to kill him. His life belongs to me."

Sekhet observed the crowd from a window in the palace. Amenhotep stood next to her, in an unusually cheerful mood. He seemed to think things were going well.

And they were. The sage knew how to work a crowd. This part was her area of expertise. People could be incredibly stupid when they were in large groups.

A necrophyte stood before the crowd and raised a hand. Any murmuring among them stopped as he read the official charges before them.

The necrophyte, whom Sekhet believed was named Mando, cleared his throat and read from a royal decree.

"The man before you is named Asrraf Kassys. He has been tried and convicted of the terrible recent suicide bombing attack."

HOW TO REDEEM A BOMBER

A whisper stirred among the crowd. They weren't sure how to respond.

"By orders of the godking himself, none of you are permitted to kill this man, as his life belongs to the morning and the evening star. However, if there are any among you who lost family members to this man's actions, you are permitted to claim a taste of vengeance."

Several guards offered boxes of small, round stones to the citizens. None of them accepted the rocks.

"This isn't working," Sekhet stared at the crowd. "Groupthink makes people stupid, but these people are still acting as individual—"

"Silence," Amenhotep stopped her. "Sometimes a mob is just a bunch of individuals. I've had this crowd repeating the claim that Asraf committed the bombing for three days now under pain of death. Just watch."

"Whether you agree to throw rocks or not, you are all to join me in reading this man's list of crimes." Mando read the script from his decree. "Shame, Asrraf the traitor!"

"Assraf the traitor," a few people in the crowd murmured unconvincingly.

Mando held his hand to his ear. "Sorry, couldn't hear you."

"Shame, Asrraf the traitor!" A few more people replied.

"Murderer!" Mando continued. "You have slain twenty-seven lives!"

"Murderer!" A few more voices joined in.

"Terrorism!" Mando continued. "Thanks to this man, many workers are afraid to do attend their jobs, and production falters!"

A larger murmur swept through the crowd. Dead factory workers, the public could ignore. Stalled production, not so much.

"Vandalism!" Mando read. "Your destruction of a shoe factory has left even more citizens of this great nation forced to go without footwear!"

Grumbling shifted amongst the crowd. Sekhet noticed that a good number were, in fact, barefoot.

"Saboteur!"

Mando looked up from his decree. "I didn't say that. That's not on my list—"

"My child has hookworms, because I can't afford shoes for her feet!" A woman in the crowd grabbed a rock from one of the guards and chucked it at Asrraf. The stone bounced off him with little effect, but the act had surprised

Mando completely.

"Um," Mando looked back at his list. "Blaspheme—"

Another peasant took a stone and threw it at the convicted man. Then another. More and more peasants joined in, until they were pelting Asrraf with small stones. Some called him a murderer, or a killer, or a traitor. To Sekhet's surprise, some even called him a suicide bomber.

One woman handed a stone to her daughter. "Don't ask, just throw! Quickly!"

Terrified, the child threw the stone and hit Asrraf in the cheek.

"Amateurs use propaganda to convince groups of people to believe things that aren't true, and then get them to speak and act accordingly." Amenhotep tilted his head towards the crowd. He was clearly enjoying this. "And sometimes, that works. But experts know better. Anyone whose mind can be changed that easily can be changed back just as easily. A master of propaganda knows how to get people to say things they *know* aren't true, and then having them act on these falsehoods. This gets people committed to the lies, like a thousand little cuts on their souls as they submit to the deception. Then...they become emotionally invested. That's when they will believe the deception internally. They will not simply repeat the lies until they are no longer being watched; they will accept them, embrace them, *live* them."

He turned away from his handiwork and faced Sekhet. "Tell me, a man blows himself up in a factory, then lives to be convicted for it. Would you call that a paradox?"

"Yes," Sekhet nodded.

"And wouldn't that paradox, if accepted by enough people, manifest itself as a demon?"

Sekhet looked out at the crowd again. Arkeon had taught her a number of tricks that allow a sorcerer to view spirits that are just out of sight of mortal eyes. As she opened her alternate sight, her proverbial "third eye," sure enough, she saw a large, writhing mass of eyes and tendrils, just outside of reality, latched onto the angry mob. Each tendril had a lamprey-like sucker that had hooked onto the peasants, feeding the demon from their anger and making it grow larger.

"A demon is a paradox, and a paradox is, in effect, a demon." Amenhotep explained. "Some demons are harmless. Some have no concept of malice. But wherever you get people convinced to believe in a paradox, you get a demon. We cannot prevent the demon from being formed. But we can shape it. This beast will not warp the bodies of its hosts into the abominations in your lab; it will only turn them into monsters in a metaphorical sense."

"I see." Sekhet bowed. "Thank you, my godking."

"Some say the mind is a plaything of the body. This is true, but it's a two-way street. When people believe things that are inherently contradictory, it pulls the mind in different directions, trying to reconcile the chaos it produces. If it doesn't have an outlet, it will seep into the body, and warp the person's form to match their disjointed mind. I guarantee that's what happened to most of your test subjects; the cognitive dissonance had nowhere to go. Do you understand?"

"Yes, my godking."

Once the crowd had thoroughly pelted Asrraf with stones, the necrophytes stood between them, along with several zombie enforcers. The peasants stopped the attack and dispersed by the necrophytes' command. The palace guards proceeded to drag Asrraf's beaten but still alive body back to the palace dungeon.

"Okay," Amenhotep stepped away from the window. "That's it for stage two. Now for stage three. My favorite part."

Sekhet followed the High Tomb Lord to the palace dungeons. She did not understand what he was planning here, but she knew more now than she had before.

"You will follow me into the prison cell, but do not speak. You need only observe," Amenhotep explained. "Now you must learn about lies people want to believe, even when they know they're false."

Amenhotep led the way to the palace dungeon, where Asrraf had been shackled to a wall.

"Greetings," the High Tomb Lord said politely. "You have had a hard time this past week, haven't you?"

Asrraf didn't respond. His body was covered in small bruises, and he could barely lift his head to look at the lich.

"Isn't this terrible?" Amenhotep said to Sekhet, who didn't dare respond. "An innocent man, brought so low, all because the necrophytes brought in the wrong laborer."

At this, Asrraf's head bolted up. He immediately winced from pain in his neck, and lowered his head again, but Amenhotep lifted his chin with his linen-wrapped fingers.

"Yes, completely innocent," he pronounced. "I am the morning and the evening star. Whatever I say is true, and I say that this man is not a suicide bomber."

Bewildered, Sekhet stood still, trying to maintain an air of legitimacy to her master's claims, but she had the instinctive urge to take notes on what was about to come next.

"I don't understand," Asrraf wheezed. "I blew up the factory. I remember it now."

"Oh, but memory can be faulty." Amenhotep signaled for a guard to unlock Asrraf's shackles. "Please forgive my servants. The culprit who destroyed the factory was so crafty. He planted evidence that pointed to you before fleeing north to the Borealan Empire. It fooled my best necrophytes, but not me."

"I...I..." Asrraf was clearly trying to put the pieces together, but his mind was so broken he couldn't do it anymore.

"You were set up as someone else's patsy," Amenhotep explained as the guard unlocked Asrraf's cuffs. "Someone who bombed a factory, and left you so traumatized from the deaths of your fellow factory workers you even believed you had done the deed."

"Fellow...workers?" Asrraf coughed. "Did...I work...at that factory?"

"My duties as the ruler of this nation prevent me from going to the Borealan Empire and bringing the perpetrator to justice," Amenhotep snarled. "The empire has spies everywhere, and they would see my investigation as an opportunity to ravage the country while I am away. But you...you could be an instrument of justice."

Asrraf was slightly taller than Amenhotep, but still seemed to be looking up at him, somehow. "I could?"

"Yes," Amenhotep placed an arm around Asrraf and held him close. "You will have to go north, where the traitor takes refuge. From there, you will have to kill the turncoat in his new home. I will grant you the tools you need, the weapons, and even means to enter their empire. All you have to do is accept my offer. Can you be a hero of your country?"

Mr. Kassys struggled to stand up straight. "Yes. Yes! If...if it means bringing the bomber to justice, and avenging my friends at the factory, I will gladly be your agent. I would give my life to see this man punished."

"Excellent," Amenhotep placed a hand on his shoulder and leaned towards his ear. "I am your truth now," Sekhet heard him whisper.

Guards came to take Asrraf away, this time leading him to the palace baths to clean himself up and prepare for him for his mission.

Amenhotep turned to Sekhet. "So ends stage three. Now," he clasped his hands. "What have you learned?"

35

Market Crash

ROSTAM

"Alright, that's thirty kilos of ore," a salesman finished filling out a contract. "Just sign here."

As Nadia finalized their contract, Rostam glanced around the mining company house. It was about as filthy as anywhere else they'd visited in Harlak, but the building gave off the feel that they had attempted to make the place nice at some point. Probably before Rostam was born, but at some point.

Once Nadia had finished paying for the copper ore, she and Rostam left the mining house and followed the salesman to a mineral storehouse. If this were Hadesh, there would be a team of porters ready to load *the Endurance* with the goods, as part of the contract. But in Harlak, no such hired help were available. Instead, they were greeted with a number of locks on the storehouse to keep anyone from stealing the contents inside, a feature that would be unnecessary if porters were around keeping watch on the storehouse wares.

The salesman unlocked the storehouse and brought out a small cart and scale. Apparently, Nadia, Rostam, Simon, and Joseph were to weigh out thirty kilos themselves. After about thirty minutes of lifting heavy rocks, the four of them had packed a box full of copper ore, which Simon and Joseph loaded on the ship's own cart and started hauling the goods to the ship.

"Wait a minute," a scratchy voice called. "Are you going west?"

Rostam turned and looked over at an old man in disheveled clothes. He might have been homeless, or just escaped from the nearest asylum. Or a retirement home.

"That's the plan," Rostam replied. "Sell the copper to processing plant in Taisha."

"Be careful out there!" The man cried. "You seem like a good young lad. Stay away from the heroin!"

"...Okay," Rostam glanced at Nadia, who shrugged in confusion. "Wasn't planning to go near any."

"It's a poison!" The man raved. "A drug the bories use to turn us into monkeys, and lock us up like animals in the zoo!"

"...Right." Rostam nodded. "Are there any other drugs you've been...exposed to lately?"

"Listen to me boy! It's no joke! I've seen the stuff turn good lads like yourself into feral apes always looking for their next hit. Stealing from their own families, robbing anyone on the street to get money to buy more! Little more than beasts, these men!"

"Oh, I get it," Rostam said. "You don't mean *literally* turn us into monkeys."

"It's all a plot, you hear me!" The man leaned close to Rostam, filling his nose with bad breath. "The bories want you to become some sort of degenerate beast so they have excuse to throw you in prison where you won't do no harm to anyone else. That's after they've turned you into a violent ape with their poison!" The geezer gritted both of his teeth. "You stay away. Don't let them fool you into thinking it's got any medical uses. That's how they get you hooked, and before long, you're behind bars like my nephew getting fed peanuts and bread by the bori guards!"

"Okay," Rostam looked to Nadia to give him an excuse to get away from this man. "Look at the time! I've got to get back to work. You know how us good young lads are. Always be punctual, that's the deal!"

He slipped back over to the copper hauling crew before the old man could respond. "Think he's gonna leave us alone?"

"Let's hope so," Nadia replied. "Poor fellow."

"Think so?" Rostam asked. "I know he's nuts, but that happens to lots of people when they become senile."

"That wasn't senility, that was grief." The crew reached the docks and started loading the cargo into the ships hold. A man in a shabby-looking uniform approached Nadia.

"Going somewhere?" He asked.

"Yes," Nadia replied. "Funny, there were no port authorities waiting for us when we arrived. We had to go to the customs house to get landing clearance."

"Well, we'll have to see to that. Someone should have been here," he licked his thumb and index finger and flipped to a new page in a notepad. "Now what is it you're planning to load your ship with there? Copper ore for the bories? That could take a while to get authorized."

Nadia groaned and reached into her purse. Once she'd handed the man who might or might not have been an actual law enforcement agent a sizeable bribe, he tipped the filthy hat of his uniform.

"Thank you for your business. Come back to Harlak soon." He chuckled and strolled away.

"More bribes, huh?" Rostam watched the man leave. "Do we even know if he's actually a public servant?"

"Not exactly," Nadia admitted. "Technically, every port authority we've ever done business with could have been a fake. In Hadesh, we trust the officials because they're usually dressed for the part, and because they see us when we arrive and perform the important services of clearing our cargo even when it doesn't benefit them, we trust that those same authorities are legitimate when we pay tariffs to depart. The primary reason you don't trust that guy is because he only shows up to collect money when we're ready to leave."

Rostam cocked an eyebrow. "Then why pay him?"

"Because in Harlak, if you want to be left alone, you have to pay for it." Nadia rubbed her forehead in frustration. "It doesn't matter if it's a mugger, or a guy claiming to be working for the government, or a customs house. Pay, or be ready to fight. To the death, in some cases. The entire city is held together by bribes."

Once the cargo was loaded onto the ship, Nadia took the wheel. "Let's get out of this city. Now."

MARKET CRASH

The crew took their positions as the ship's furnace roared to life. Cindrocles hadn't bothered coming out of the ship since they'd first docked, and Rostam could tell from the feel of the ship that he was as interested in leaving as everyone else.

Rostam took to the ballast controls and aided Nadia in steering the ship out of port. They were off for Taisha.

Once they were set on a course for the city, Nadia took a step away from the wheel. "That old man...he mentioned a nephew who got addicted to heroin. Back when I grew up in Harlak, there were a lot of people who thought they were gonna make it big. Get some job, make a lot of money, and get out of that hellhole. But then there's heroin. Bought and sold at your local market, right next to the first aid supplies and the headache tonics. Or go to an apothecary. Pretty cheap, too. The more people buy it, the higher the demand, and the more the stuff gets imported. Soon, the whole town is flooded with that trash. And anyone with big dreams gets snuffed out once they're hooked. A criminal record later, and they're in jail, where they're probably safest. That poison should be banned; I won't carry it aboard my ship."

Rostam didn't respond. This was beyond him. He had fond memories of growing up in Aklagos. His parents had never mentioned heroin to him; it never came up. Perhaps a small mining town wasn't a place where heroin salesmen plied their wares. No, that couldn't be right; every hospital in the empire used the stuff to treat patients. So why were there no addicts in Aklagos? A mining town would have plenty of people looking for a pain killer.

"So, we're bringing copper ore to Taisha. What do they usually produce?" Rostam asked.

"Taisha's a port town," Nadia replied. "Right at the mouth of the waterfront. Naval ships that can transport larger loads than any airship take goods out east and bring things back. We'll take a look at what's been brought from the east, likely things such as spices, silk, and porcelain or glass products. Trade with the east can get a bit touchy; the cultures out there are pretty different. Some of them have no trouble buying and selling human beings as property – and not the kind who have wracked up an insurmountable debt."

Rostam let that sink in. "Uh...that seems pretty bad. Why do people in Taisha trade with nations that buy other people?"

"Unfortunately, the further east you go, the more of that you see," Nadia admitted. "To the northwest, we find many countries that find chattel slavery abhorrent. But if Taisha were to ban all trade from any nation that practice slavery to the south or to the east, they might as well not have bothered building a port city in the first place. There's only a few nations in the southeast who reject the practice, and their neighbors are regularly trying to attack and enslave their populations. As for the empire...it's unusual for the Borealans to try and police what people do outside their borders. I've noticed..." She paused; memories of loss visible on her face. "The Borealans seem like a very reclusive culture. Unless there's business involved, they want to leave others alone, and be left alone. And they naively everyone else is the same way."

Unsure if he should respond to that, Rostam kept quiet as the ship sailed on. He'd noticed in Hadesh that greedy merchants were welcomed, celebrated, even. But dishonest merchants were punished severely by the law if the public didn't tar and feather them first.

Taisha was on the opposite side of the empire from Harlak; it would be a long trip. Eventually, cities and towns started coming into view below the ship. Rostam knew a little bit about the settlements that were so close together. Ariram, a bit south of Taisha, was a military harbor, in which the imperial navy forged ships of wood and steel. Across the inlet, Zarash was a smaller fishing community, and further up the coast was Gadot, which was mostly a military outpost near the border of Kemet, keeping an eye on the sea. The Tomb Lords seldomly allowed trade between their nations, but the imperial government maintained a trading post to promote peaceful relations. And it also maintained a fleet to further promote such relations.

Rostam manned the ballast controls as the ship prepared to land in Taisha. The sun was high in the sky; it was right around one in the afternoon. When the ship finally docked, he got a sense of being back in a city where you didn't need to worry about being mugged every time you stepped out to get the newspaper.

"Nadia, do you mind if I take Cindrocles out to explore?" Rostam asked. "He spent the entire time in Harlak hiding in the boiler. I don't blame him, but he probably wants to get out for a bit."

"That's probably a good idea." Nadia nodded. "But be back by this evening. We'll need to take off again soon."

Rostam went up to the boiler and unlatched the box where the elemental powered the ship. "We've landed again. Different city. Want to come out?"

Cindrocles took in some of the air. "Oh, this is nice. Air here is more oxygen than human waste. Much better."

The fireball floated out of the boiler and looked around at the airport. "Kinda windy." His flames flickered as a cool breeze blew by. "We must be near the sea."

"Yup," Rostam nodded. "The airport is built right on top of the seaport below."

"Hm, that means we're up high." Cindrocles floated away from the ship and looked down below. Gaps between the dock and the vessel allowed him to see all the way down to the seaport. "I'd like to go down. Higher altitude means more wind, and I'm curious what's down there."

"Apparently, lots of ships carrying cargo from nations to the south, and to the east. Captain Nadia says I should take you exploring."

"Well then, we'll just have to do that." The fireball floated next to Rostam as he found a staircase to descend.

From the bottom of the stairs, Rostam was able to get a better look at the ports themselves. The seaport was made almost entirely out of sandstone reinforced with timber, with a number of pulleys and cranes that descended from a ceiling made of reinforced steel, wherein the cranes hung from chains connected to tracks that rolled along the roof above the ships they were unloading.

The airport above was mostly sandstone as well, but with more steel supports to balance the weight of the building. Elevators cranked by large, stone golems brought loads of goods up and down between the two ports.

"What's all this?" Cindrocles floated towards a bazaar. "Can we go in here?"

"Hm, maybe if we stick to the open-air parts." Rostam pointed to the flammable curtains that separated the interior parts of the bazaar from the outside. "Don't want to get in trouble, you know?"

The boy and his sapient ball of fire took a look at some of the stalls set up in the bazaar. Some sold magical artifacts made from other nations. "Ephorah would love to see some of these," Rostam whistled. Others displayed various garments and foreign fashions made from silks out east. Rostam had seen arachne silk garments before, but these were different. They came in colors other than white, which meant they could have all sorts of intricate designs printed on them. Most of the garments were for women, ranging from blouses to dresses, and the shopkeeper looked unnerved by having a living open flame so close to their wares, so Rostam decided to move on.

Most of the other shops had things that were mildly interesting, such as porcelain products that were embossed with new designs. Some even depicted images of dragons, heroes, and gods worshipped by the people these items came from, but Rostam was looking for something that wasn't just a different culture's version of things he could find at home.

"Exotic medicines!" A man called out. "We have medicines from the nations of Fen, Qiu, and Xun!"

"I have never heard of any of those places," Rostam replied.

"Ah, they are nations that border the sea in the far east," the salesman explained. "There've been a number of wars between the neighboring states, and many kings seek to unify the region into a single grand empire. Most scholars agree that before the Calamity, they were unified into a massive world power. Many of the people living there have been trying to return to their roots and awakening old traditions. This includes ancient medicinal techniques and treatments, like acupuncture, and some of the medicines I have for sale today."

"Oh, so what kinds of stuff do their traditional medicines help you with?"

"Well, this entire shelf–" he gestured to a large stand that took up about half of his market stand. "–Contains everything a man could possibly need to help him get an erection."

Rostam almost choked with surprise. "Uh, I'm a little young to be having trouble with that."

"What's an erection?" Cindrocles asked.

"It's something only men need, my blazing asexual friend." The salesman winked at the elemental. "And even if you're too young to struggle with such problems, it makes a nice gift for an uncle, grandfather, or any other family member who could use a little help in his romantic life."

"Uh-huh," Rostam wasn't convinced. "And...how do these things work, exactly?"

"Well, most of my selection involves various powders that can get a man ready when he snorts them up his nose," the salesman took a small, ornately carved wooden box and withdrew a paper packet of powder. "Here is a sample of ground-up tiger bones. Or, if you're looking for something stronger..." he pulled out another box containing different packets. "We have powdered rhino horn."

"Okay...it's probably a bad idea to ask this," Rostam frowned. "But what if an older man has trouble snorting things up his nose? How is any of this supposed to work for him then?"

"Glad you asked!" The man reached for a lower shelf and pulled out a third box, this one containing an intact rhino horn. "It's more expensive, but we also have unpowdered rhino horn, for the gentleman with sensitive sinuses."

"But...that's just a solid rhino horn!" Rostam pointed at the box. "How are you supposed to put that up your nose?"

"You don't!" The salesman explained. "It's a suppository!"

"That's it, I'm leaving." Rostam walked quickly away from the stall.

Cindrocles looked at the horn for a moment longer. "Still don't get it," he finally said before following Rostam through the market.

"Okay," the airshipmate looked around. "There're some exotic-looking food stalls around. Might not be a bad place to check for supper later."

"I don't understand what most of these things are for," Cindrocles admitted. "Like, why is that guy selling live animals? Don't you humans usually only eat dead ones?"

Rostam glanced in the direction he was looking and spotted several animal cages and carrier boxes. "That's a pet shop."

"Pets?" Cindrocles floated closer to the shop. "I thought humans only kept safe animals as pets. That guy's selling dragons, like the one that attacked Hadesh, only smaller."

"Dragons?" Rostam walked closer to the shop and read the sign on the door. "Darcy and Pippa's Dragon Emporium?"

"Greetings!" A pale-skinned man with dirty-blond hair and a stylish beard stepped out from behind a large green curtain. "Are you interested in purchasing a new dragon companion?" He had a very thick accent, and Rostam could tell that Borealan was his second language, but he was still pretty good at it. "I see you're already comfortable with a fiery pet!"

"I am not a pet," Cindrocles huffed.

"Oh, my apologies!" The man bowed. "I am Darcy, and my wife and I breed dragons!"

"Uh-huh." Rostam looked around at the cages, which were all empty. "Do you...have any?"

"Of course!" Darcy beamed. "These are dragon carriers for when your little friend needs to be taken to the vet. Dragons are easily spooked, so we keep them inside. Come take a look! Don't worry about your friend. Fireproofing is an important part of taking care of dragons."

Rostam looked at Cindrocles and shrugged before following Darcy behind the curtain. Inside, he and Cindrocles were met with the sight of hundreds of lizards of various sizes, some hissing, slithering, or otherwise investigating the newcomers. And the smell...you could tell which dragons could breathe fire by the smell of sulfurous gases alone.

One shelf held terrariums with holes for air, and serpents inside labeled "Swamp wurms." These creatures occasionally exhaled some kind of green spray, which corroded the soil and dirt in the serpents' living space. These came with a warning label that read "level 5 danger rating – for experienced dragon tamers only!"

Next to this, another shelf held rainbow-scaled snakes. These had the very fitting label "Rainbow Serpents," and below that a card that explained more about them.

"*Rainbow Serpents do not have traditional digestive tracts. Instead of defecation, they digest their food and vomit the remains as a green sludge. This sludge is a powerful fertilizer, used by many farmers who know how to care for their dragons.*"

"Okay," Rostam looked around. "I would really like to–"

"Well, hello there!" A short blonde woman with skin as pale as Darcy came up to Rostam. "You look like you have questions."

"Uh, hi." Rostam remembered the sign on the front of the emporium. "I take it you're Pippa?"

"That's me!" She beamed. "Do you see anything you like?"

"Well, I don't really know much about dragons," Rostam admitted. "And I was kind of hoping I could learn more."

"Then let me show you around!" Pippa offered. "This wall is mostly for more advanced dragon owners. Probably not a good idea if you're looking for a first-time dragon pet." She walked him to another shelf of terrariums, this one featuring winged-lizards with beard-like flaps of skin around their throats, all around thirty to forty centimeters long. "These are a first-timers' favorite! The Bearded Chimera!"

"Chimera?" Rostam looked closer at one of the little dragons. "These are chimeras?"

"Uh...what do you call them..." Pippa paused. "They're a chimera species that can breed like normal animals and have healthy babies. Successful chimeras, that's what they're called!" Pippa smiled again. "They were originally wingless lizards, commonly known as 'bearded dragons,' which were technically just an ordinary type of lizard, but alchemists decided to tinker with their genetics and made the name a bit more literal." Pippa reached into one terrarium and carefully scooped one of the bearded lizards up by the belly.

"Always be gentle picking these ones up. Their scales are only meant to be stroked from one direction. They like humans, love attention, and especially like to perch on their owner's shoulders." Pippa set the dragon on her shoulder, but it immediately crawled up her head and rested on top of her scalp.

"Except this girl prefers my head, apparently."

"Uh, isn't it dangerous to have a fire-breathing lizard on your head?" Rostam asked.

"Oh!" Pippa's eyebrows rose. "You were looking for a fire-breathing dragon?"

"These don't breathe fire?" Rostam pointed at the lizard on Pippa's head.

"No," Pippa admitted. "They're just flying lizards."

"Not a big deal," Rostam stroked the bearded chimera, who was just below his eye level on Pippa's head. The dragon purred noisily.

"Let's put this girl back in her terrarium for now." Pippa scooped the dragon up again and put it back. "And let me show you the others."

Rostam looked over at Cindrocles, who was investigating some larger monitor lizards with Darcy. "These are called 'Komodo Dragons.' Naturally existing, even before the Calamity. Be very gentle with them, because they can keep track of which humans have been nice to them and which have not. They have their own venom, so it's wise to keep a bottle of antidote on hand."

"What's venom?" Cindrocles asked.

"Uh, it's poison that an animal makes," Darcy looked shocked that Cindrocles didn't know what venom was. "Their blood plasma contains a powerful antibiotic peptide, so some people use them to make antibiotics."

"What's blood plasma?" Cindrocles asked.

"Alright, these might be the kinds of dragons you're looking for." Pippa drew Rostam's attention to a shelf of dragons slightly smaller than the bearded chimeras. Their heads were like miniature versions of a crocodile's, and their tails had small spikes. These dragons looked like they might leave claw marks if you let them perch on your shoulder.

"Our homeland doesn't have dragons like this," Pippa explained. "These Shoulder Wyverns originally came from a small family from the far north brought down by some of our trader connections. They're a smaller variety than anything left in the wild, but much more easily domesticated."

"They look like they'd take chunks out of your shoulder if you let them use you as a perch," Rostam noted.

"Ah, but we also sell shoulder perches." Pippa showed him a leather harness that went over her head and came with two thick pads for her shoulders. Straps on the pads kept them in place. Each pad had a short, thick-wooden bar that a dragon could latch onto. "Wyverns can be taught to rest on these so they don't hurt their masters. And they're all housebroken, so you won't have to worry about dragon droppings on your back."

"Oh, that's a relief." Rostam looked at one of the dragons, which seemed to be investigating him from inside of its terrarium.

"These little guys are really popular with young ladies. Especially the adventuring types who like to explore in parts unknown." Pippa took the dragon that had been curious about Rostam out of the container by grabbing its back and supporting its stomach at the same time. She placed it on one of the perches on her shoulder pad. "There's just something about a small, fire-breathing lizard on a girl's shoulder that makes her feel brave."

"Okay, if I had a woman I wanted to impress, I'd have to keep you guys in mind," Rostam stuck his finger close enough for the dragon to reach it. It investigated the finger, sniffed it, and then decided Rostam wasn't as interesting as first advertised. "So, do any of them talk?"

"Talk?" Pippa blinked. "We don't have any talking dragons, unfortunately. We've tried to get our hands on some Yellow-Scaled Parrots, but they're extremely rare, and would be pretty pricey even if we had a few."

"Parrots?" Rostam paused. "You mean they just imitate speech, they don't… you know, converse?"

"Converse?" It took Pippa a minute to realize what he was getting at. "Oh! Oh, you mean intelligently!" She tilted her head in a mostly friendly yet somewhat condescending manner. "For starters, we don't sell any intelligent dragons as pets. We uh…come from a country where you don't own sapient beings. And second, intelligent dragons are extremely rare these days. Apart from the ones that are servants of the gods in the northeast, my husband and I haven't actually encountered any. I think most of them might be extinct. And not only that, but legend has it that the ones that were intelligent couldn't speak human words. Most of them, anyway."

"But…I've seen a dragon that could talk." Rostam remembered the way the dracolich attacked Marduk, and exchanged quips before that as he dropped canisters of zombies and raised an undead army in the middle of the arena. "He was pretty snarky about it, too. While he was casting spells."

"…Huh." Pippa was visibly at a loss for words. "That's…I would very much like to meet something like that. What was he like?"

"Well, he was a skeleton," Rostam admitted. "So, maybe he doesn't disprove your extinction theory."

"How did he talk if he was a skeleton?"

"He was a lich," Rostam explained. "I don't know much about necromancy, but he certainly did. Raised an army of zombies and attacked the whole city. Supposedly killed a god in the chaos."

"What!" Pippa's eyes widened. "I mean, it's a shame about your city, and the god, but...that's the sort of thing people like Darcy and I dream of meeting. A talking, spellcasting dragon – one that must not be a creation of the gods, like the northeastern dragons, or he wouldn't be able to slay one. Wait...was he big?"

"Uh, how big do you want with a dragon?" Rostam asked.

"Was he larger than a bird? Could he fly?"

"Y-yeah. He might have been ten meters long, and half as tall." Rostam hadn't exactly measured the dracolich during the attack. "And he definitely flew."

"Fascinating!" Pippa exclaimed. "There are so many theories about dragonflight, with so many different species using different propulsion methods!" The woman reached for a bookshelf and pulled out a large tome that Rostam noticed had a price tag. "There's a lot of research on how dragons developed the ability to fly, and why they use so many different forms. Some of the little ones are just like birds. Those wyverns we have are smaller breeds of a larger species that uses lighter-than-air gases to get extra lift. Most of which is flammable hydrogen, hence the fire-breathing. Another genus in the steppes of the far north uses fart propulsion."

"I'm sorry, did you just say 'fart propulsion?'" Rostam asked.

"They're related to a larger species of ground dragon called 'the quodhog,' which uses flammable gas from its rear as a defense mechanism, and lights the gas by striking its steel-like claws against flint and other stones."

"But...fart propulsion?"

"Yeah, like the rocket hwacha batteries used by northeastern militaries," Pippa went on. "But none of the dragons that can fly, apart from northeastern god-serving dragons, are larger than an ox. And even then, they're not exactly 'graceful.' It's more like they jump and glide long distances instead of actually flying. No one I know has seen any massive flying dragons, and any physicist would tell you that a creature of the size you saw wouldn't be able to fly at all, unless...it used magic."

Rostam realized what she was implying. "You think the dracolich could fly, not because he had wings, but because he was a wizard? Then what are his wings for?"

"Well, human wizards can't fly," Pippa smirked. "Maybe having the mind, the soul, and the body working in tandem is part of the trick. Even dragons that don't use their wings for lift use them for steering and gliding support."

"Interesting." Rostam eyed the book's price tag. "You know, I find myself learning so much about dragons, and I'm more and more certain that I wouldn't be able to take care of one without more information. What other books do you sell here?"

"Ah!" The mention of commerce brought Pippa's mind back to the store. "If that's what you'd like to start with, let me show you this." She handed him a copy of a book titled "Caring for Dragons."

"And if you're interests are more scholarly, there's this." Pippa presented a much larger, thicker leather-bound tome. This one said: "Dragon Taxonomy: A Primer."

"How much?" Rostam asked.

"Six Ioseps," Pippa replied.

Rostam handed her the money. "Thanks. If I ever find myself in your shop again, you'll be my first choice for exotic pets. But first, I've got some reading to do."

Remembering the fire elemental he'd walked into the room with, Rostam looked around for Cindrocles, who was apparently arguing with Darcy.

"Fire is too an element!" The elemental fumed.

"Uh..." Darcy didn't seem to know how to calm him down. "You asked me how the dragons breathe fire, and I'm trying to answer you. I don't know what you want me to say."

"Cindrocles, I think it's time we head out," Rostam came up to the elemental. "I need to grab some food before we head back to the ship."

An upset fireball followed him out of the shop. "A reaction! He said fire was a reaction! The nerve of some people!"

"Don't worry about it." Rostam didn't want to argue this point, especially since he wasn't sure about the science behind it himself. "Maybe we can check and see if they've got any exotic flammable stuff for you. Have you ever burned incense before?"

Cindrocles' mood brightened up. "No, but I wouldn't mind trying it."

"Well than let's see–" Rostam stopped as he saw a man in a nice but not too conspicuous cowl and cloak shambling around in the bazaar streets. He had a face wrap that had been covering his features until now, but it was clearly having trouble staying on his head, likely due to a lack of practice wearing such a garment. The man had a very girthy waist; or at least, he looked like he did under his robes, but in the short time his face was visible Rostam could tell that this man was not well-fed. He was about as handsome as a man in his early thirties could be without a decent meal, minus a short facial scar where it looked like a machine had caught his cheek. The man seemed to notice that Rostam had seen him, and adjusted his face wrap to hide his undernourished body. What was he hiding under his robes to make him look overweight if he was so malnourished? Why was he so starved in the first place? And if he couldn't afford food, where did he get such nice-looking yet ill-fitting clothes?

"Cindrocles, something's not right," Rostam felt a twinge that told him to pursue the man, but the rest of him screamed to run away. "I think we need to head back to the ship. Now."

"What–" the fireball grew quiet and looked at Rostam. "Something wrong?"

"Just a hunch, but I don't like the look of that fat man in the blue robes up ahead. Let's–"

A flash of light, a loud explosion, and the next thing Rostam knew, he was lying on the cobblestone walkway of the bazaar, facing the sky. At first, he thought everyone had left the bazaar, and that everything had gone quiet. Then the ringing in his ears faded, and his hearing came back.

There were screams of panic, cries of pain, and howls of grief. Rostam's whole body felt like gelatin, but he managed to get to his feet. Puddles of blood ran in the streets. Severed limbs and appendages had been scattered around the market. People tried to get lifeless bodies to wake up. Other corpses in the streets were so badly burnt, they were unidentifiable. Rostam looked around for the blue-cloaked man, but there was nothing left to be seen except for a few scraps of tattered blue cloth near an extremely burnt body.

"Cindrocles!" Rostam looked around for the fireball, but he was nowhere to be found. Shattered stalls and wrecked shops were everywhere, many of which were currently on fire. Trying to find one fireball among the other flames was impossible.

The wind was starting to cool down. Tarchus had told Rostam that wind moves to areas of low pressure, and now that the bomb had gone off and blown so much air away, the air had been flowing back into the area. Bullets and bomb shrapnel couldn't hurt a fire elemental, but if Cindrocles was smothered by wreckage or blown out by the force of the explosion, he could die. Would he leave anything behind for someone to find? Rostam checked under overturned stalls and shelves, and while he found a few people who were still alive and grateful to be uncovered, there was no sign of the elemental.

Finally, in a pile of shattered wood, Rostam spotted a small, flickering flame clinging to the debris and cowering from any remaining wind. As he knelt down closer, he could see two small, terrified eyes in the flames, using the dry wood as fuel to stay alive.

Rostam grabbed a thick piece of wooden debris and tied a torn piece of cloth around the end of it. Looking through his pockets, he found his tinderbox, and dabbed a bit of oil from it onto his makeshift torch. Dipping it near the flickering elemental, he let what was left of Cindrocles climb onto the oiled cloth.

"We need to get back to the ship," he whispered.

Cindrocles was too small and weak to respond, so Rostam made his way carefully back to the airport.

36

Blowing Hot Gas

AMRI

Holding a rake, Amri stood over a lawn with sticks, dead leaves, and other things leftover from damaged trees and plants to be picked up. He was supposed to be raking these things up, but his mind had wandered off from his body. He couldn't let go of the boy and the pharmacist.

"Is everything alright?" Esfan came up to Amri and waved a hand in his face, as if checking to see if he was awake or sleeping standing up.

"Hm?" Amri came back to his senses. "Oh, yeah. I was just...thinking."

Esfan raised an eyebrow. "Something on your mind?"

"Not something I need to burden you with." Amri began raking the lawn. "I know you have your own troubles."

At first, it seemed like Esfan had accepted that answer and let the subject drop. Then when it was time to stop for their lunch break, the priest-initiate brought it up again.

"Amri, do you have someone in your life you can talk to about important things?" Esfan passed him a pre-made sandwich.

Amri paused. The obvious answer to avoid further questioning was "yes," but something told the sorcery student not to lie to a priest who worshipped the abstract concept of truth.

"I saw something terrible yesterday, and I don't know what to do about it," he admitted. "At the industrial park, I ran into a pharmacist and her son. I can't prove it, but that kid was clearly terrified of his mom. He couldn't show more signs if he wanted to. He literally begged me not to leave him with her."

Esfan perked up. "Did he have signs of abuse? Any bruises, or marks?"

"He had..." Amri paused. "He didn't have any visible injuries, but he had bandages on his arm under his sleeve. Doctor Malbim said that's where his medication injections go, but I think she was covering something up."

"What did you do?" Esfan asked.

"Mostly, I just tried not to upset her." Amri looked at his sandwich, but he had no appetite. "I was more afraid of making her mad than anything else."

"Really?" Esfan eyed Amri. "Why was that your main concern?"

"Because if you make a mom like that angry, she'll take it out on the kid once they're alone." Amri could see Esfan putting the problem together in his mind. It didn't matter.

"I see," Esfan finally said. "And, what kind of harm do you think this woman was inflicting upon her son?"

Amri closed his eyes. "I don't know. I just..." Amri struggled with this. He didn't want to admit it to himself any more than to Esfan. "I don't...I don't think..." Amri shuddered. He looked around, as if expecting someone to strike him. "I don't think a kid should be afraid of his own parents."

Esfan paused before responding. "I don't think you had any better options. I couldn't help but notice how you reacted to that mugger yesterday. Aren't you a sorcerer? Couldn't you have done something to stop him?"

"Like what?" Amri asked. "Burn him? Freeze his blood? Shock his heart? There were lots of ways I could have killed him, but not many that would have stopped him without violence."

"Amri, the thief was the one that made things violent." Esfan's face darkened. "When a man grabs you and threatens you for your money, he has already broken the rules of civility. After that happens, the only ways things go is that the violent person gets what they want at the expense of their intended victim, or the victim fights back. That's it."

Unsure how to respond, Amri looked back at the lawn they'd been clearing. It had been a productive day; they'd gotten a lot done. How many of these lawns would actually look better if Amri or Esfan pummeled their way through a gang of thieves? Would there be any point to all of this volunteer work if they beat up the people that lived here?

"My mom used to tell me," Amri paused. "When I was eleven, she told me that it is always better to be hurt than to hurt others."

"I see." Esfan raised an eyebrow. "And did she follow this advice herself?"

"...Not at first," Amri admitted. "But as I got older, more and more she became less physical. People can change, you know? She learned her lesson over the years, and then passed it to me."

"...Huh." Esfan didn't sound completely convinced. "And before that, she was more...physical?"

Amri nodded.

"And...you're sure she didn't just notice you were getting bigger?" Esfan asked. "She didn't just dial back the violence when she realized you might start hitting back, and then call it off entirely once you were stronger than her?"

Amri opened his mouth to answer, but stopped himself. He wanted to say that his mother had changed, that Esfan didn't know what he was talking about. But there was something about Esfan's tone, and how non-judgmental the priest-in-training sounded. Like he wasn't trying to correct Amri, but just to get him to think harder about what he'd actually experienced. Had his mother changed?

"I...I don't..." A thought struck Amri. "Antisocial!"

"Um, what?" Esfan blinked. "Your mom was antisocial?"

"No, Doctor Malbim said her son was antisocial!" Something Amri had known wasn't right was finally clicking in his brain. "But the kid had no problem running up to strangers, hugging them as tight as possible for a five-year-old, and then begging for me not to let him go. Does that sound like antisocial personality disorder to you?"

"No," Esfan admitted. "But it doesn't disprove anything, either. If he had just been injected with drugs, he might have been acting different from how he'd usually behave."

"Maybe you're right." Amri leaned back in his chair, defeated. "Maybe I'm jumping at shadows. Maybe Izaac's just a kid who doesn't like shots. It's just…none of it felt right, you know?"

Esfan clasped his hands and thought for a moment. "Perhaps. But that doesn't mean it was wrong for you to be on alert. For now, try to put the problem out of mind. You won't help anyone worrying about something you can't control."

Amri thanked Esfan for the meal and the advice before heading home to clean up. Then he headed off to the industrial park, where he'd get to show the alchemists what he and Avroham had made the day before.

"Let me see if I've got this straight." Tomek gritted his teeth. "This ward of yours is designed to keep things inside of it at a stable temperature. As in, they won't get any colder than they were once they go into a canister with this ward?"

"Right, they won't get colder, or warmer." Amri smiled. "So the gas won't get hotter in the sun or the midday heat—"

"THE GAS IS HOT WHEN IT COMES OUT OF THE COW, DUMBASS!" Tomek squeezed the dummy glass so hard Amri thought it might crack. "It needs to be cooled down once it's inside the canisters!"

Amri looked at one of the gas canisters for a moment. "What if you could cool it before that? What's the filter you're working on made of?"

"It's a ceramic polymer." Tomek crossed his arms. "I can't show you the details or the chemical composition. My supervisor would kill me."

"Is it heat resistant?" Amri asked. "Could one side be cold while the other is warm from the animals and their gases?"

"Well," Tomek made a face like he was running scenarios through his head. "Heat is basically molecules vibrating so rapidly that they bump into other molecules at higher velocities. So, yeah, technically, if the polymer is designed to keep most particles from passing through, it'll block the heat energy as well. That'll reduce the heat of the gas somewhat, but it won't even bring the methane down to room temperature, and a factory farm in the middle of a sunny day is going to bake the gas in-between the filter and the canisters, so even if we're using the filter as insulation, it's still going to be pretty hot when the gas reaches the canisters."

"But you could then make that area into an insulated cooling room, right?"

Amri grabbed a nearby notepad and drew a picture. "You could put some sort of cooling device between the filter that the gas passes through and the gas canisters. That would make the methane cool down as it floats up, and once it's inside the canisters, the wards will keep it from getting hot in the sun. A series of copper pipes with water inside would absorb most of the excess heat, making the gas colder. It doesn't need to be ice cold; the point of this project is to collect *some* methane gas from cows and turn it into fuel. Someone in the future could make it more efficient."

"You might have a point..." Tomek looked like he was getting frustrated at not being able to find something to get angry about. "Methane gas is less dense than air, so even if it isn't hot, it will still float up into the canisters. But the water will get hot pretty quickly, making the whole thing only workable for a short while."

"I think you can make it last longer if it's salt water." Amri tried to remember what he'd learned about water and states of matter. "Water with something mixed in it, like salt, needs more energy to heat up. It's not like anyone needs to drink this water."

Tomek frowned. "That'll buy a little more time, but it would need to be changed out so regularly that no farmer will want to install something like this above their cow pens."

"What if the water was pumped through the pipes?" A new voice added. It was the scientist Amri had seen before; Tomek's supervisor, who had shown him where to get scrap pipes. "What if we installed a pump that drove the water in and out of your 'insulation chamber' and ran through the ground outside of the stable? The earth could absorb some of the excess heat, and you wouldn't need to dig that deep to cool the water down. Ten centimeters would be enough, at least for a trial run."

"But a pump requires something to run it," Tomek countered. "We don't want to use fuel to make fuel. And there's no way this project is going to generate enough power to keep the pump going and collect enough gas to be worth all of this."

"What if the pump was run by a windmill?" The scientist offered. "Or a waterwheel. We don't need that much power to at least run our tests, and it doesn't even need to be that reliable, since the water pump doesn't need to be running constantly to take effect. It's like your friend said; someone else can make this process more efficient in the future once we get it to work."

Tomek cast a side glance at Amri. "We're not friends."

Ignoring that comment, Amri looked up at the scientist. "Is there any way we can test this ward? Something that will give us grounds to try it on a real canister?"

"That should be easy enough." The scientist took the pipe and its glass ward and placed it inside the testing chamber. "Let's see...Some piece of scrap metal on each end..."

The scientist clapped his hands and touched a flat piece of steel to one end of the canister. The metal fused itself to the container, and the scientist repeated the process on the other end, leaving just enough of an opening to pump gas inside of it.

"Didn't know he was an alchemist," Amri whispered, trying to ignore the enraged shock on Tomek's face.

"Okay, now we just put a cork stopper here..." the scientist finished his modifications. "There, good enough to store methane long enough for us to run some tests."

Amri looked at the test canister. The cork stopper would only slow the gas from passing out of the container, and not by much. Still, it would hold the gas inside long enough for a sorcerer to measure the temperature and at least test if the prototype ward worked.

Tomek took a hose and pumped some gas into the container. "You'd better get outside for this part," he grumbled. "This thing could still blow."

Standing safely outside of the testing chamber, Amri observed as Tomek corked the container and exited the chamber himself.

"Okay," the scientist held out a hand and snapped his fingers. Amri now realized he was the same sorcerer whom he'd seen testing fuels with Tomek on his first day visiting the industrial park. "Let's see if this works."

The gas ignited inside the canister. A low flame was visible coming from the opening that had been left behind. The scientist recorded his findings in his notes.

"The gas is mostly staying at a constant temperature inside the tank, but not outside. That's why we get such a low flame coming out."

"So, you're a sorcerer, and an alchemist?" Amri asked.

The scientist nodded. "Not a very advanced one. I did some independent studies on alchemy in order to expand my abilities as a wizard, but it was purely by reading books in my own time rather than attending alchemy classes." As the gas burned out, he took a closer look through the protective glass of the testing chamber. "It looks like your experiment works."

Once they had cleaned the experimenting room, the scientists gave Amri a real gas canister. "Do you think your ward project will work on an actual canister?"

Amr nodded. "Are you sure you're ready to try it with one of these?"

The scientist chuckled. "If it breaks, just tell anyone who asks to blame me."

"Um," Amri was embarrassed to ask his next question. "What was your name again?"

"Dobias," he replied. "Head Researcher Dobias."

Amri thanked Dobias one last time before taking the canister up to the glass workshop. He would have to ask Esfan to get ahold of Avroham again, and so there was nothing else he could do with the gas canister for the day.

Ready to head home for the evening, Amri exited the glass workshop, only to step back inside the room once he saw Doctor Malbim leaving the pharmacy lab.

Not wanting to anger the doctor with another confrontation, Amri ducked out of sight, but allowed himself to watch her leave. She was dragging Izaac along with her. The boy wasn't resisting, but Amri realized Malbim wasn't holding Izaac's hand. She held him by the arm; the same part of the arm where he received his injections. Even if he hadn't received any new shots today, that had to be painful.

"Try to ignore it," Amri told himself. "Follow Esfan's advice; you don't know anything about them for certain."

Once they were out of sight, Amri exited the workshop and walked by the pharmacy. Looking at the door of the medical lab, Amri paused. It occurred to Amri that he could enter the pharmacy and look for information on what

Malbim was giving Izaac. "No," he muttered to himself. "That'd be insane. I don't know what's going on, and I can't just dig through someone's records."

Making his way home, Amri went up to his aunt and uncle's bathroom to clean himself up. He didn't speak much to his aunt or uncle, or to his sister. He simply washed, ate dinner, and then sat in his room, trying to take his mind off of the pharmacist and her son. He had so many other things to think about: classes would be starting soon; the glasswork project was coming along nicely; and he had to figure out what it was he wanted to do with sorcery once he'd earned his degree.

Eventually, Amri tucked himself into bed and tried to get some sleep. Somehow, he fell unconscious immediately, as if drawn into sleep by a supernatural force.

He found himself standing on a flat rock large enough to call an island. But instead of being surrounded by water, the rock floated in an endless dark sky. Strange clouds floated both above and below the rock, and light from an unknown source reflected off of them, giving the void just enough illumination to make out some of the shapes that floated in the darkness. This was not the only island in this place.

"Some sort of dream?" Amri looked down at his hands, which seemed normal in this strange world.

"You may call it that."

A figure materialized out of smoke in front of Amri. He was tall, and had black, lightly tousles hair, firm, handsome features, and an air of authority. He wore a formal business suit, a golden watch, a pair of reflective glasses that concealed his eyes, and a stern, disapproving frown. He had a permanent stubble on his chin, like he couldn't grow a proper beard. Amri had seen this god once before.

"Marduk." Amri wasn't sure if he should kneel, bow, or flee before the king of the Babylonian gods.

"Yes," the god seemed...well, not pleased, exactly, more like he was less disappointed that Amri knew his name. "And you are Amri Sadi." Marduk spoke calmly, but at the sound of Amri's name, his face shifted like he'd just eaten something bitter, and was trying not to look repulsed out of politeness.

"We have a mutual friend. One who thinks you need my protection in the coming days. However, I am not convinced you deserve it."

"Um..." Amri wasn't sure how to respond to that.

"This is what I mean." Marduk gestured to Amri's mouth. "You are weak, in every way imaginable. You are too old to be a boy, and too weak to be a man. You are not a child, but you are not dependable like an adult."

Thinking that Marduk was talking about Amri's lack of muscles, he raised up his palm and froze the air in front of him, creating a small pocket of frost in his hand. "There are many ways to be strong."

"And you have none of them," Marduk replied. "Many people in your life will tell you that it is okay to be weak. A false civility. A mockery. When danger strikes, and people need someone to save them, they will turn to strong men to protect them. And you will be unable to answer their call. Then, even the people who have told you that it is okay for men to be weak will call you useless. And they will be right."

Amri had no answer to that. "What is it that you want?"

"Want?" Marduk crossed his arms. "From you? You have nothing that I want. I am only here because I was asked to be."

"Then, can you offer me guidance?"

At this, Marduk's expression softened, but only slightly. "Speak with your friend who is training to be a priest. He will teach you what you must do to earn my favor."

Before Amri could ask what he meant, Marduk flung him off the rock into the void below. Amri felt himself flailing in the air as he fell, only to wake up in his own bed.

37

Settlers of Canasta

ROSTAM

By the time he'd returned to the ship, Cindrocles had grown large enough again to be the size of a small ball. He had gone from a flicker back to a low flame, and Rostam had kept him supplied with flammable pieces of wood and kindling to keep him burning.

Once he came in view of the ship, Captain Nadia took one look at Cindrocles and freaked out.

"What in the Abyss happened? Why is our ship's fire elemental half-extinguished?"

"There was an attack in the bazaar," Rostam explained, shielding Cindrocles in case frantic air from the captain might blow him out. "Some sort of suicide bomber."

"What?" Captain Nadia's face froze with horror. "Suicide bomber...that's... why? Who would...? What would they have to gain?"

"I don't know, but I think people are going to rush the docks if they haven't already." Rostam climbed aboard the ship and put Cindrocles inside the boiler, which had a thick tin dish where the boy put some charcoal briquettes for the fireball to feed on while he recovered. "I think we should get out of here as soon as Cindrocles is ready. Do we have cargo in the ship yet?"

Nadia nodded. "There's enough trade goods from the imports here to bring back to Hadesh. And you're probably right. First opportunity, we take off and leave before people flee in a panic."

After a few minutes, Cindrocles was strong enough to produce enough heat to raise the ship. It wasn't a lot, but it was enough to get *the Endurance* moving out of the port while other vessels had yet to take off. The boiler had the added bonus of keeping him sheltered from the elements, in case a strong gust of wind might put him out.

"Back to Hadesh," Nadia called as Rostam manned the ballast controls.

"A suicide bomber," Tarchus shuddered. "Tha's gonna git peo'le riled up."

"Don't worry about that now," Nadia ordered. "We can't be focusing on things we don't control. Just worry about getting us back to Hadesh."

Rostam tried to follow orders, but the thoughts of that man in the strange outfit kept coming back to mind. What motivates someone to kill themselves like that? To take out so many innocent people in the process?

Unable to focus on anything else, the crew stayed fairly silent on their way to Hadesh. The trip was thankfully only a few hours.

As the ship came into port, Rostam wanted to think of all the things he'd tell his friends about on his adventures. He wanted to tell them about golems building water plants, conspiracy nuts thinking that the government was using drugs to turn teenagers into monkeys, people using unpowdered rhino horns as suppositories, and dragons that fly using fart propulsion. But now, all he could think about was the sudden, senseless death in the bazaar.

Then Rostam realized: the bomber wasn't targeting anyone specific. They weren't an assassin trying to kill someone important, or an angry lover avenging their cheating partner. They were just trying to kill as many people as possible while taking themselves out in the process. Were they always suicidal? Or was that just a cost of their method of attack? Did they have some political motive? Or were they just trying to hurt as many people as possible?

Once the ship docked, Rostam stepped off the deck of *the Endurance*, and for the first time, he was in no rush to meet his friends. He found himself walking slowly, aimlessly, passing time more than actually walking. He looked around at places in the city, which were almost recovered from the dracolich attack. How odd was it that a crazy undead dragon with a zombie army was less devastating to him than a single man with a bomb? But no, it wasn't odd at all. The dragon had wanted something; there was a purpose to his attack. This was different. It was undirected, and unprovoked. If it could happen once, it could happen again. Anywhere.

Rostam made his way to Amri and Namid's home. It was the only place he could think to visit while in port. When he arrived, only Namid answered the door.

"Oh, you're in town." She opened the door wider. "Well, come on in. Amri's out acting like a lunatic."

"Like a lunatic?" Rostam asked as he stepped inside the house.

"He's become inducted by a group of religious volunteers." Namid shook her head in distrust. "Religious organizations that shower you with love and honeyed words, then get you to do stuff for them for free? Sounds like a cult scam. Other than that, he's been working on a project at the industrial park involving gassy cows. That one might actually lead him to a job someday, so I can get behind that."

"But you can't get behind charity for charity's sake?" Rostam raised an eyebrow.

"It's not for charity's sake. I could almost understand that." Namid sighed. "No, my brother thinks he's making friends of people who are just using him for free labor. That's what I'm worried about."

Rostam realized that of all his friends, Namid might be the best equipped mentally to handle the news about the attack. "There was a suicide bomber. In a bazaar in Taisha."

Namid's eyes widened. "What?"

"I was there, really close to the blast," Rostam admitted. "I saw at least a dozen people dead or injured, and there were probably more."

"This...people are going to go nuts." Namid sat down in a living room chair. "There's going to be panic. And soon."

"Maybe," Rostam replied. "Maybe not. At least, maybe not here. The attack might be written off as a one-time incident, or a local thing that only happens in port towns."

"You work on an airship," Namid scowled. "Every town is a port town."

"...yeah, you're right." Rostam nodded.

"Did you get a look at the attacker, by chance?" Namid asked.

"Actually, yeah. He was Coptic. He had a scar on his face like he'd been caught in a machine. Looked to be about thirty."

"Coptic." Namid gritted her teeth. "Maybe they won't make a big deal about it, but that doesn't sound good for us."

"You think people will turn on the Coptics?" Rostam asked.

"I don't know. If an Empyrian did this, you'd bet that people would be talking about the race of the bomber. They might be worried about backlash, there'd definitely be people grumbling about angry Empyrians, and if it had been a Borealan who had done it, you would never hear the end of it from Ephorah."

"You're right." It was Rostam's turn to sigh. "I've always known that Ephorah's...attitude on race was extreme, but not uncommon. After this last trip out to Harlak, she kind of seems tame by comparison."

"That bad, huh?" Namid grinned.

"Yeah," Rostam chuckled. "I've seen people accuse the government of creating painkillers just to turn their sons into mindless criminals so they could lock them up. And the way they said it, it almost sounded convincing. And I met people who *really* hated a Borealan girl who was volunteering to build a water purifier. Seriously; her only reason for being there was to build them a source of clean water for free, in a city where they have to collect rain water on their roofs, and they still wanted her gone."

"That's messed up," Namid shrugged. "I can understand hating someone because you think they stole your land or robbed you, personally. But hating someone for providing you with free water? That's a special kind of stupid hatred."

"You know, I wanted to work on an airship because I wanted to see the world." Rostam forced a light smile. "And I do get to. I've seen all sorts of amazing and wonderful things. And yet, now I'm seeing all the ugly parts, too. I used to think Ephorah was nuts. She's obsessed with race; I know she gets it from her dad. But a thought occurs: what if she's normal, and people who try to avoid her kind of thinking are the crazy ones? What if all the Empyrians lock arms like that, and I'm the only one left out, and the Borealans don't see me as one of their own. They at best see me as a tolerable civilian, and at worst see me as another troublemaker?"

Namid paused for a moment. "I don't know, but I could use a drink."

While she poured herself a glass of wine, Amri came home.

"Rostam, hey!" He smiled and shook his friend's hand. "Welcome home."

"Hey," Rostam smiled. "What have you been up to?"

The two exchanged stories about their previous exploits. Amri told Rostam how he'd been working on a project at the industrial hub, and how he enjoyed his time working on broken buildings and meeting the priest-initiate.

"A guy from a family of thugs turned priest?" Rostam smirked. "Kind of cliché, no?"

"He says that there's only so many jobs they can go into," Amri replied. "It was the priesthood, the military, or the police."

"Eh, that makes sense," Rostam admitted. "He chose the nonviolent one."

"Actually, he's still pretty violent when he needs to be. I saw him take a would-be mugger apart. Only difference is that he doesn't turn around and demand the attacker's wallet afterwards."

"...Okay. So not a pacifist priest?"

"Maybe a defensive-only priest," Amri offered. "He's not someone who picks fights or engages people, but he will use violence to defend himself or me."

"Ah." Not exactly the actions of someone who's just using Amri for free volunteer labor, Rostam thought. But then, maybe Namid's just wrong about the priest guy. Has she even met him? Or does she just assume that because the man is getting something of value from Amri, he must secretly be playing some angle?

"Any word on how Ephorah's doing?" Rostam asked.

"Eh, heard she's on some sort of internship with a mercenary company," Amri replied. "Kind of scary, if you ask me. She should be done soon, since we've only got two weeks left until internships end, but...mercenary work is dangerous stuff."

Rostam nodded. "I've heard. That alchemist who beat her in the arena...the announcers said that he must have had some kind of real-world experience.

He knew not to hesitate. Which company did she join?"

"I think she signed up with the Salamanders. Which just makes me even more worried about her, since the Salamanders only fight monsters."

"The Salamanders?" Rostam tried to remember what he knew about them. "Aren't those guys the pyromaniacs?"

"Yep," Amri shrugged and smiled. "Legend has it that over a century and a half ago, their founder, a guy named Jairus Fierstien, overheard a soldier say that you cannot make an army entirely out of flamethrower units, and he replied: 'hold my beer.'"

"Monster hunters...that sounds even more dangerous than normal mercenary work. Why choose that company?"

"Well..." Amri paused and looked away for a moment. "It would have been nice if she'd picked the Tin Men."

"Oh, yeah," Rostam rubbed the back of his head and winced. "The Tin Men. Not going to happen. Not Ephorah."

Amri frowned. "I don't know why Ephorah thinks Empyrians should stay away from the Tin Men. I just know she doesn't trust them."

"It's actually because of Taisha," Rostam admitted. "Or, rather, the Battle of Taisha during the war. From what they tell you in history books, Taisha was the first settlement the Borealans tried to build beyond the Jagged Divide to venture into the desert. At the time, the land didn't technically belong to anyone, and there were a lot of property disputes when the Empyrian government found out about it. A whole settlement on land the Empyrians believed was there's, even though no one lived there, no one staked it out, marked it, or anything of the sort. The settlement was built before the two peoples made their first contact."

Amri nodded. "I think I read somewhere that there's laws about that. You can't just declare that you own everything all the way to the sea that you've never actually seen; there's a whole bunch of stuff like 'not wanting to waste land' and how people who've built on the land and actually turned it into something useful when you neglect it have a stronger right to it."

"Yeah, the Borealans will tell you it was their land by right of adverse possession, or something. The Empyrians would disagree. I think Captain

Zaahid told me 'always keep your weapon handy, because there's always someone who says he has a right to what you think is yours, and when negotiations fail, the biggest gun wins.' Anyway, during the war, the Empyrians sent a massive army to take the town. The Borealans didn't really have an organized army, like they do now, so the majority of the fighting was actually done by mercenaries. Most mercenary companies don't have a very long lifespan; only the Tin Men and Salamanders are still around, and the flameheads didn't get involved in the war until the last two years."

"Because they don't like burning people." Amri winced.

"Yeah, that. So, the Tin Men are the only mercenary company that's still around for the Empyrians to aim most of their anger at, but the Battle of Taisha was different. The Tin Men don't act like a normal mercenary company. Mercenaries aren't supposed to care about honor, or bring a chaplain with them into battle, but the Tin Men are...different."

"To be fair, the religious stuff and company reputation for honor are probably why they're still around," Amri offered. "They're so old, they don't even remember the name of their own founder, and can't even pinpoint when they got started."

"Probably," Rostam admitted. "But have you heard about how they acted at Taisha?"

Amri shook his head.

"My dad rarely fed me the kind of angry stuff Ephorah's dad feeds her, but this is one story that gave him the creeps." Rostam shook his head. "He told me to never trust a Tin Man after what happened at Taisha. Mind you, even with all of their weird stuff aside, the Tin Men are still supposed to be mercenaries. Fighting for a living is their job, and the Empyrians should understand that. But the point of a job is to go home at the end with your pay and enjoy your life with the money you've made. The Tin Men at Taisha didn't do that. A hundred mercenaries were able to hold off the Empyrian army that attacked the city. There were supposedly ten thousand Empyrians, but a small force of a hundred men holding off such a large army isn't hard to believe if they're defending a well-fortified area. That's happened throughout history quite a bit, actually. But then the Empyrians suffered so many casualties that they started leaving the city, and rather than just let them go, the remaining Tin Men inside opened the gates and ran out to attack again."

"What?" Amri asked. "Why? What purpose would that serve?"

"No idea." Rostam shook his head. "There was only about twenty Tin Men left at that point, so they were crushed by the remaining Empyrians. Then the Empyrian army realized that Taisha had no defenders left and its gates were wide open, so they rushed in and took the city. So not only did the Tin Men throw their own lives away in a fit of senseless bloodlust, they even threw away a victory and went back on the whole point of their contract just to kill more Empyrians." Rostam looked outside the living room window for a moment. "It's not that my dad thought the Tin Men hate us, specifically. It's that he thought there was something wrong with them. Like their religion makes them some kind of fanatical cult, or maybe they take some sort of ritual drugs before battle that make them insane."

"That…wouldn't surprise me." Amri shuddered. "I wouldn't trust a company that threw away their pay, their lives, and even a city they were supposed to defend like that."

"Hey, lovebirds!" Namid came out holding a card game. "Let's stop talking about terrible things and old history and have some fun instead."

Both boys smiled and joined her at the kitchen table for cards.

"Alright," Rostam looked at his hand. He was short-suited in clubs and diamonds. "I'll open."

Namid looked at her cards and smirked. "I'll raise."

Amri took one glance at his hand and folded.

Rostam looked at Namid. "I raise to forty."

"Forty-five," she replied.

"Fifty." He countered.

Namid shrugged. "It's yours."

"Spades is trump." He laid down his hand. "I have a settlement and a city in trump, that's worth fifteen points."

"Wait," Namid glared at his hand. "You have three wheat in spades?"

Rostam fanned out his cards further so she could see. "One to make the settlement, and two more with three ore to make the city."

"Well, I've got the longest road." Amri gestured to the number of brick and wood piles he had in front of him. There was one in each suit, and an extra in both clubs and diamonds. "That's worth ten points."

"Dang it," Namid looked at her hand. "I've got two settlements, but they're not in spades. They're only worth two points each."

"Let's just see if Rostam can take enough tricks," Amri winked.

Several hours later, the three of them had played three games of Catanichle. They had had so much fun that they hadn't noticed Amri and Namid's aunt calling them for dinner, or that the sun had set. And as his friends' eyelids started getting heavy, Rostam realized that for all the amazing adventures he might have exploring the wonders of the world, his happiest moments were always back here, with his friends.

38

The Brown Wedding

NAMID

Waiting by a bus stop, Namid checked her watch. They only had half an hour before they needed to be at the wedding pavilion. Ephorah had better be there soon, or Namid would start without her.

The two girls had spent yesterday preparing for the ceremony; running through any and all rules they needed to follow, making certain they knew how to address each guest, and recognizing which drinks were which. It was unlikely that either of them would be assigned to bar duty, due to them both being very young, but they would likely be taking coats, waiting tables, and handling other tasks like cleaning up emergency spills.

Namid had done her background check on the bride and groom. Tobias Einhorn, a wealthy owner of multiple steel mills, was marrying Karmina Posner, a socialite from Baltithar. He had been the one to select a traditional Borealan wedding, under the threat of canceling the marriage altogether if Karmina refused.

This was a touchy subject for a lot of women in the empire. If Tobias died, his kids and wife would inherit his property. But if the two separated or got divorced, Karmina would get nothing, because the marriage wasn't legally binding. But it wasn't just a legal issue; there were...traditions at a traditional Borealan wedding. That was the whole point of it being "traditional." Some of these traditions could get...complicated.

THE BROWN WEDDING

Karmina had elected to wear a white gown for her wedding. To many people, this was a sign of purity; it marked her as a virgin. For most people, it was only a symbol; lots of women who were not virgins wore white dresses anyway. But in Borealan tradition, the white dress was serious business.

An autobus rolled up, and Ephorah got out right on time. She was wearing the same uniform as Namid; a black blazer and slacks with a white shirt, bowtie, and a shiny brass nametag.

"Ready to go?" Namid asked.

"Yeah," Ephorah sighed. "Let's go serve a bunch of snobby rich bor—"

"So help me, if you use any ethnic slurs today, I'm going to pretend I don't know you." Namid took Ephorah by the hand and dragged her towards the wedding pavilion.

The wedding was taking place in a large, outdoor pavilion in the Garden District. Elegant, lace-white wooden trusses surrounded the main structure, which was a marble gazebo with sandstone columns and a domed roof. Very fancy, expensive to rent out, and not cheap to staff, either.

Nearby, a large wooden platform held the wedding band, playing music written from before the Empyrian War. Opposite the platform, there was an outdoor bar where Namid ended up assigned to serving drinks, much to her surprise, and next to that was a table where guests dropped off wedding gifts. This being an upper-class wedding, there were a variety of presents wrapped in boxes, but a number of them were simply placed on the table with a nametag from whomever delivered the gift. These unwrapped gifts were things like a set of gold-trimmed wineglasses, a pair of expensive-looking earrings, several necklaces, and a very fancy jeweled choker.

Once they reached the outdoor bar, Namid let go of Ephorah and prepped herself, making certain her uniform was immaculate before entering the building. Already, guests were starting to mill about and mingle, chatting to one another before the ceremony began.

"Can't believe they haven't done something about that dragon yet," one whispered.

"I know. It's been several months now, and it's like the emperor wants us to all forget about it."

"I want to see that monster's head in a parade," one grumbled. "After what he did to the academic's arena. It's a shame on our entire city."

Namid stood at attention to serve drinks to the guests and resisted the urge to roll her eyes. She'd really hoped that people would have moved on from the dragon problem by the time she and her brother had come back from Grand Spire. The dragon had clearly gotten what he wanted and left, or it would still be raiding the city, but people weren't letting go of that sort of thing.

Dragons in general get people's attention, but if it had just been the mindless, deadly beast kind, people would let it go like any other animal attack. But this was the thinking, spellcasting, snarky kind that had some sort of goal. In that way, it was no different than any other criminal, and even *that* would be old news by now. But there was something about mixing the two that left you with an event that people just wouldn't let go of. According to one rumor, this was why they had to find new staff for the wedding under such short notice, to the point where Namid had been reassigned to the bar despite her age; employees had canceled and moved to completely new cities. According to another rumor, this wasn't the only reason so many staff had refused to work for Karmina's wedding.

"Miss, can I get a glass of Gernret Dulce?" One woman asked.

"Of course." Namid smiled while pouring her a glass of sweet wine. "Here you are."

"A glass of brandy for me!" Another guest said.

"Any preference?" Namid asked.

"I want a Java Tonic."

Namid checked the liquor bottles and poured the man his drink. "Your funeral," she muttered.

"I'd like a cup of coffee."

Looking up at the latest guest, Namid took in the features of a thirty-year-old man with a well-trimmed beard. One look in his eyes confirmed Namid's suspicions about how this wedding was going to go.

"Of course," Namid smiled. "Brew it right up."

A few drinks later, Namid looked over at Ephorah, who seemed to be handling her task of greeting people at the front entrance well enough.

THE BROWN WEDDING

"Please don't call the Borealans any names," Namid whispered under her breath.

"Attention!" An announcer stood in the middle of the reception area. "We will begin the ceremony in about five minutes."

All of the guests made their way towards the gazebo and took their seats in white wooden chairs, ready for the procession. Namid spotted three gentlemen speaking to an usher, whose face turned pale before nodding after a while and gesturing them to follow him. One of the gentlemen was the man from earlier who had ordered coffee.

"No stopping that," Namid eyed the gift table. "Might as well be ready for the fireworks."

Before long, the groom was in the center of the gazebo with a priest, who stood by a wooden altar, which held a book that likely contained some ceremonial purpose. No longer required to serve drinks, Namid stood in an attentive pose, partly ready in case guests needed anything, and partly ready for when trouble would strike.

The band across from the bar switched to a slow, processional song for the wedding ceremony. Namid didn't know the tune; it was an older song from Borealan tradition. But she understood the meaning; a bride would be arriving soon.

Namid clenched her fists, ready for things to get ugly. "The turd-flinging procession," she whispered to herself.

Karmina, who wore a white gown and a veil crowned with a tiara, looked like a snow-princess as she walked down the aisle. Two flower girls stood behind her, leaving petals of white roses as she walked.

Once she was about halfway to the altar, the man Namid had served coffee to earlier stood up and threw a ball of mud at the bride's dress. Everyone, including Karmina, froze. The band stopped playing. The groom's eyes widened. The priest looked around like he had no idea what to do. This was a tradition no one expected to see played out.

"You..." Karmina stuttered under her veil. "How dare you! What are you doing here?"

She was interrupted by a second man standing up and throwing a ball of mud at her back. Namid hadn't noticed this man before, but his well-groomed hair and beard gave off a look that would have seemed formal, but for the fact that he still had mud on his right hand.

Karmina turned around to face her new attacker, only for a third ball of mud to strike her in the face. This time, the entire wedding gasped; Namid had read about the turd-flinging procession, and aiming for the face was against the rules.

Murmurs between the guests started as whispers, but in seconds they became a roar. Some pointed fingers at the bride, others at the men who had thrown the mud. The priest was stuttering, as if trying to think of something to say to get the wedding back on track. The only person Namid saw who was silent was the groom; his face was so full of rage that he couldn't speak even if he wanted to.

Tobias swept the priest's book off the altar and stormed out of the pavilion without another word. At this, the guests who had arrived on behalf of the bride started attacking the nearest men who had thrown the mudballs, and the groom's family ran to their defense. Fists started to fly. Somewhere in the scuffle, a guest grabbed a chair and smashed it over another's head.

Namid was already inching towards the gift table as the fight got worse. Checking on Ephorah and making sure no one was looking at her, she swept a few handfuls of gifts into her pockets and made a beeline for the nearest exit, grabbing Ephorah by the sleeve and yanking her along as she went.

"What in the Abyss was that about?" Ephorah gawked at the scuffle.

"The bride's ex-boyfriends showed up," Namid explained. "We need to get out of here."

Ephorah thankfully didn't ask any more questions until they were near the bus stop. But once they were in the clear, she couldn't hold them back.

"What was with the mud?" Ephorah pointed at the pavilion. "Who brings mudballs to a wedding? Why..."

"It's called 'the turd-flinging procession,'" Namid explained. "By Borealan tradition, a woman who wears white to her wedding is claiming to be a virgin. If she doesn't wear white, then the turd-flinging isn't permitted. But if she does, then any man who has ever slept with her can come to her wedding and

THE BROWN WEDDING

throw a ball of mud at her dress." She glanced at the pavilion before turning back to Ephorah. "I hear the 'turd' part used to be literal, but they stopped it for sanitary reasons."

"Why in the world would you include that in a wedding?" Ephorah fumed. "What's the point?"

Namid paused. "I think I read somewhere that the tradition has to do with honesty. The Borealans hate liars, and wearing white when you aren't a virgin is kind of like lying. I think the other men need to provide some kind of evidence that they actually did sleep with the bride, but it doesn't have to be much. A place and a date, along with any description of any discernable markings, like tattoos, is usually enough."

"But why did the groom leave?" Ephorah asked. "Why didn't he defend his fiancé's honor?"

"Maybe he believed the men who threw the mud," Namid shrugged. "Maybe he already suspected Karmina was lying, and this was the final straw."

The autobus arrived. Namid and Ephorah got on board and continued their conversation.

"So he just cancels the wedding, over that?" Ephorah looked back at the pavilion through the bus window. "Why is it so important that his wife be a virgin?"

"Don't know, don't care." Namid sat back in her seat on the bus as it drove off. "He isn't my fiancé, he isn't my problem. Though, to be fair, lots of men are like that. Especially rich men who own lots of steel mills. So, if I am being honest, I'm staying chaste so I don't have Karmina's problems somewhere down the line."

Ephorah scowled. "Don't you think it's wrong to discard her like that?"

Namid shrugged. "No. What's it to me?"

"The fact that lots of men agree with him," Ephorah frowned. "If lots of men are like that, then it does affect you."

"Not if I refuse to have sex until marriage," Namid chuckled. "If that's what it takes to get a husband who's loaded, then that's what I plan to do."

Ephorah eyed Namid like she was examining a dog that wouldn't go fetch a ball that had been thrown. "But why would you want a husband who needs you to be a virgin? Do you think a man as rich as that 'Einhorn' guy is staying chaste? Why should you?"

Namid thought for a moment. "Think of it like this. If I want money, and a rich man like Tobias wants a virgin bride, and we both have what the other wants, who cares if I'm not also rich or he's not also a virgin? I don't give a rip how many women he's slept with, as long as he isn't spending all his money on kids he's had with ex-girlfriends."

"But doesn't it bother you that he has such a rule in the first place?" Ephorah asked. "You wanting a man with lots of money makes sense. It's selfish, but at least I understand it. Why does he care how many men you've been with in the past?"

"Ever hear of the golden rule?" Namid countered. "The one who has the gold, makes the rules?"

"But the rules they make aren't fair!"

Namid frowned, starting to get annoyed with Ephorah. "Who told you that mattered? Lots of rules people make aren't fair. Why should this be special? It's a good day when the people in power can be made to follow their own rules. If they make enough sense for folks to follow them, that's as good as you're usually gonna get. Be grateful the guys like Einhorn are being honest about what they want, and not giving you a list of conditions they *don't* care about while keeping secrets about the things they do. I guarantee you, that's what one or all of the guys Karmina was with before did." Namid clapped her hands and lowered her voice as much as she could. "Oh, Karmina! You're so beautiful! I promise to marry you after we have fun tonight!"

"Wait a minute..." something in Ephorah's head finally clicked. "Namid...did you know the wedding was going to flop? Did you know she had ex-boyfriends who were going to show up and ruin the ceremony?"

"Well..." Namid shrugged. "I had suspicions, but I couldn't say for sure until they actually arrived. If they didn't, we would go in, do our jobs, get paid, and get out. But if things went poorly..." She pulled some of the loot she'd grabbed from the gift table and examined it. "We've got...a very nice and probably expensive watch, a pair of earrings with what I think are real sapphires, a silver amulet, a pretty choker, and a set of combs. The kind you put in your hair as decorations."

"What is wrong with you?" Ephorah almost stood up, but the autobus was still moving. "You stole gifts from the wedding?"

"Well, we're not going to get paid for the jobs we've done; not after that fight between the families." Namid handed Ephorah the watch and the choker. "Here. Pawn these, and they should be worth twice what you would have gotten if you'd been paid for the work you did."

Namid dropped the gifts into Ephorah's hands. Ephorah paused, as if trying to decide whether to accept them or not. "You knew there would be a fight," she finally said. "You knew it was going to get violent."

"No," Namid corrected. "I had no solid proof. I only suspected it."

"You *wanted* the wedding to fail," Ephorah gritted her teeth. "Your goal was to make a profit. That's all you cared about. That's all you ever care about!" Ephorah pocketed the items, but her anger didn't let up. "I might keep these things because I won't get paid for my work, and my family always needs money, but you? Your family is rich. You live in the Garden District. Ever since we came to this city; my family moved from one working class home to another, but you moved into a mansion. And you're *still* obsessed with money!"

Namid rolled her eyes. "And your point would be?"

"You brought me to a wedding that you knew could get violent. Even if you 'weren't certain,' you were counting on it so you could rob the place and get away with it. You didn't think to warn me that the families might start fighting in the middle of the procession, or that I might not want to be a part of a wedding that would devolve into throwing mud at the bride or your scheme to rob the gift table."

"You were never in any real danger," Namid scoffed.

"You. Didn't. Know. That." Ephorah clenched her teeth, trying not to yell so loud as to draw the attention of everyone else on the autobus. They didn't need people asking questions about the stolen goods. "'Wear my strength gloves.' That's what you told me in your letter. Wear my enchanted gloves that give me superstrength. There was no need to move anything heavy or do anything else at that party involving superstrength. You told me to bring them in case we needed to fight. You wanted a meat shield in case you got into trouble, but you never thought to tell me what to expect."

"You take things too personally, you know that?" Namid maintained an air of calm, but she knew Ephorah was right. Namid realized Ephorah had a good reason to be angry, but if she conceded the point, that meant Ephorah might lash out even worse. Namid needed a distraction.

"If you're really so upset, then hand back the watch and the choker, and wash your hands of my 'schemes.'"

Ephorah didn't answer, but her eyes burned with anger. As the autobus pulled up to a stop that was still many blocks away from her home, she took the watch and choker from her pockets and dumped them into Namid's lap.

"Fine." Ephorah got up and got off the bus, leaving Namid alone with her loot.

39

Family Feud

NAMID

Alone. On a bus full of people. By herself.

Namid could do things on her own when she planned for it. She was not good with abandonment.

The bus had been a short distance from her aunt and uncle's home to the wedding, but now took the long way around the city back to the Garden District. This meant that Namid had to sit by herself on a bus for quite some time before she'd be safe at home.

Eyeing the other people on the autobus where Ephorah had left her, Namid took stock of what she could do if they started trouble. She had at least one knife that was easy for her right arm to reach in a fight. She opened the window behind her so as to have more air to work with to create a pressurized breeze to keep people away from her. A pressure-sealed container could cause all sorts of problems with aeromancy, but with at least one open window, she could blast someone with enough air to slow them down and slash with her knife.

Next, she examined the other passengers. There was a woman with her daughter further down the bus. An older couple across from her seemed to be watching the woman and her child with longing. A crusty old gentleman sat at the end of the bus grumbling about things you couldn't get anymore and "the good old days." A pair of shifty-eyed men sat a few seats up from Namid.

There were more people further up towards the front of the bus, but they were likely to be too far away to cause trouble. There was just the old couple, the woman with her kid, the shady men, the grumbling curmudgeon, and the cute blond guy with his forehead resting on his clasped hands.

Namid blinked, wondering how she'd missed this guy before. He had mostly straight blond hair, lightly bronzed skin, and a face too deep in thought to have been paying attention to anyone else. He looked to be slightly older than Namid, but his bookbag suggested he was also a student. He had the build of a young man that could be useful in a fight, but wasn't interested in picking one.

"Excuse me, is this seat taken?" Namid asked the brooding boy.

"Hm?" He finally broke his concentration, but not his frown. "Oh, no. Go ahead."

He leaned back and sat up straight, making him look even better. Namid tucked the loot she stole from the flopped wedding into the pockets on the left side of her clothes and sat with the boy to her right. As soon as she did, she got to brush up against the boy's arm and noticed the muscles.

"You...do a lot of heavy lifting for a living?" She asked.

"Huh? Oh, not exactly. Alchemy requires lots of stamina, and controlling chemical reactions requires force of will. And since the mind is shaped somewhat by the body, building muscle mass is useful for the craft." The boy gestured with his hands as he spoke, giving Namid a better view of his arms in his short-sleeved shirt.

"Holry bishops..." Namid had to close her mouth to keep from drooling. "And you're an alchemist? That sounds pretty smart. What was your name?"

"Oh, yeah. I'm Cyrus. And you?"

"Namid," she leaned a bit closer.

"Nice," he nodded, but still frowned. "Can I ask you something?"

"Sure," Namid inched her hand towards his.

"Where does morality come from?"

"What?" Namid recoiled her hand.

"Does it come from the public? Do people as a collective decide what's good and what's not? Is it like the gods, where belief makes it real?" Cyrus turned his face to finally meet Namid's. "Or is it set in stone somewhere, like the laws of nature, where it doesn't change no matter what people believe?"

"This is what you wanted to ask me..." Namid cocked an eyebrow. "Uh-huh."

"I mean, if the public decides what's right or wrong, does it change based on people's attitudes? If it all comes down to cultural baggage, can something like sacrificing a few handfuls of people to cure cancer be considered good? But if it's not flexible like that, and saving as many people as possible is the highest good, then wouldn't it follow that curing cancer at the cost of a few dozen lives would still be the right thing? So why does it feel so repulsive?"

Namid could understand that Cyrus was droning on about this, and caught the gist of what he was saying as she drifted off to sleep. At some point, she was vaguely aware of a strand of drool hanging from her mouth as she woke herself up with her own snoring.

"–but then, is it really okay to let countless people suffer from cancer when you could have done something about it?" Cyrus went on, oblivious to Namid's disinterest. "Don't their lives matter? And if you add them all up, who gets priority? Do you do it by numbers, or do you let fate sort it out?"

The autobus came to a stop.

"Oh, this is where I get off." Cyrus got up from the bus.

"Wha–? We're getting off now?" Namid got to her feet without really thinking and followed Cyrus off the bus. Once she was on solid ground again, she came back to her senses. "Wait a minute, this isn't my stop!" She glared at Cyrus. "I blame you for this."

Cyrus responded by pointing at Namid's chin. "You've got a little drool..."

Namid wiped her chin and scowled. "Completely ridiculous. That's it, I'm out." She turned around and was about to start walking before realizing that she was still a long ways from home, and so she just sulked waiting for the next bus.

"Sorry," Cyrus shrugged as he carried his suitcase across the street. Apparently, his house was right across from the bus stop.

Continuing to glare at him for boring her to the point that she got off at the wrong bus stop, Namid watched him enter what must have been the home of a larger family, because after a few minutes, multiple voices could be heard shouting at each other.

At first, Namid wanted to ignore it. Loud arguing between parents and their sons returning from internships were not exactly her problem. But then the sounds of hands slapping against tables and splintering wood followed, and this became more than just eavesdropping on a family fight.

"Um…" Namid rubbed her forehead as she heard what sounded like a table snapping in half. "What's my duty of care in this scenario?"

Finally, an armchair was thrown out the second story window of the house and crashed onto the lawn. Cyrus wrenched the front door open again and stormed out of the house in a huff, still carrying his suitcase.

Namid let her mouth hang open in confusion. "What the…?"

Cyrus made his way to the side of the road, checked both ways, then quickly walked back to the bus stop. "Mind if I join you?" He was doing his best to keep his calm, but he was obviously on the brink of losing it.

"What on Earth was that?" Namid asked. "Did you just kill someone?"

The boy looked at her in bewilderment before finally letting out a tiny laugh. "No, didn't kill anybody. Did some property damage, though."

"I heard furniture smashing!" Namid pointed to the wrecked chair in the yard. "And saw it, too!"

"It's…well," Cyrus sighed. "It's my dad. He never wanted me to become an alchemist, and now that I've had to come crawling back home from… something pretty bad, he's using this to justify why he's right that I shouldn't have gone to the college in the first place."

"Seriously?" Namid raised an eyebrow. "You seem nerdy enough."

"Well, I wasn't." Cyrus looked back at the house. "I used to be bad at just about everything. Except baking bread, oddly enough. We're a family of carpenters, and I was the one that didn't fit. Even before I went back to school."

"So…who threw the chair?" Namid asked.

"Oh, that one was me," Cyrus admitted. "That's…well, it's my dad's handiwork. He's so proud of his woodworking, and I just really wanted to hurt him…I don't think it worked." He turned and looked back at Namid. "I'm sorry, I know that probably sounds insane, but I swear I wasn't going to hurt him *physically*."

"Eh, it doesn't sound that crazy." Namid had once blackmailed her father with evidence of his affair with a florist. She wasn't going to cede the high ground to Cyrus by admitting it, though. "So, what now?"

"Now, I need to find a place to stay until the school season starts again." Cyrus looked down at his suitcase. "I...can't live with them right now. I'm not welcome."

"Do you have another place to go to?" Namid asked.

"Well, once classes start again, I can pay for room and board on campus. It wouldn't be hard to reduce the costs by getting a job at school. The problem is what I'm going to do until then."

Namid toyed with a thought in her head for a moment. She had no real obligation to help this guy, and it probably wouldn't benefit her in any way, and yet...an idea popped up that came at no cost to her.

"Listen, I...might have an idea." Namid really hoped she wouldn't regret this. "If you're an alchemist–"

"Alchemy student," he corrected. "Don't know if that matters."

"Right, well, I know someone who works on an airship. They...might have use for an alchemist for a while. What kind of alchemy do you do?"

"Medical. I'm studying to be an alchemical doctor."

"A tall doctor, got it." Namid shook the thought out of her head. "So, a guy I know works on an airship. They might be able to give you a place to stay, for a discount, for the remaining week and a half until the semester starts again."

"Okay," Cyrus raised an eyebrow. "What's the catch?"

"The catch is, when I say 'for a discount,' that's probably if you offer to work while you're with them."

"Okay," Cyrus smirked. "But what's the catch?"

When the bus arrived, Namid and Cyrus rode to the stop near Silverstack Docks, where she brought him to the crew of *the Endurance*.

"Hey, Nadia!" Namid smiled. "You remember me, right? From the zombie attack a few months ago?"

"I don't think...no, wait, I do remember. Your friends with Rostam, right?"

The captain looked at Cyrus. "Who's this?"

"Another..." Namid realized she wasn't sure what to call Cyrus. "Person. He needs a place to stay until the semester starts again, and he's an alchemy student. Can you hire him for the next week and a half?"

Nadia scoffed. "Hire? What do you think this is? A charity boat?"

"Well, hire means I'd be working for you for the time, so it's not really charity." Cyrus corrected. "Does your ship need a medic? Or a cook? Or an extra pair of hands?"

The captain laughed viciously. "Extra hands? You've never handled a ship in your life! What could you do to help keep a ship in the air?"

Cyrus pointed to a hole in the ship's hull. "Hunting incident?"

"That's..." Nadia sighed. "We had a run in with some pirates. What's it to you?"

The boy clapped his hands and touched the splintered wood. In a flash, the planks disassembled themselves and reformed as if they had never been punctured. "Organic chemistry. Most of my studies on fixing people will work for other organic matter, too. That includes wooden ships and things like rope." He gestured to the captain's pistol, which was showing signs of rust. "But there's also a simple transmutation to reverse oxidization and get rid of rust."

Nadia paused, running things through her mind for a moment. "A week and a half. We do have a job we're getting ready to do starting tomorrow. We'll probably be back here a day earlier than you need...you could repair a lot of stuff in that time..." She finally sighed. "Alright...if you agree to fix whatever you can, including us if worst comes to worst, we'll have you back here in about ten days. Take it or leave it."

"Deal." Cyrus shook the captain's hand. "And thanks," he whispered to Namid.

Namid shrugged. "Don't mention it. Especially if this goes south."

Waving bon voyage to Captain Nadia and the cute but nerdy blond boy, Namid made her way back home, taking the bus for a third time, but with a mental checklist of people who would owe her favors in the future.

Once she finally got home, she settled into her room, changed out of her wedding uniform that she'd inevitably have to return, and put on some casual clothes. As she did, her brother came out of his room in work clothes.

"Going back to that cleanup crew again?" Namid scoffed.

Amri looked down at his clothes. "Why are you acting like I'm not dressed for the job? Old, worn shirt, worn out pants, this is what I should be wearing to clear out building wreckage."

"Oh, no. You're dressed for it. But that's the problem. You're dressed to go out fixing broken buildings. For free. I get why you're doing the glassworks thing; that might open up options for you to get a job later. But what are you hoping to get out of this volunteer project?"

"I'm making friends." Amri checked his pockets and made sure his wallet was somewhere it wouldn't get stolen.

"Friends?" Namid scowled. "They're just using you to help them clean up dragon wreckage! If you weren't useful to them they wouldn't give you the time of day!"

Amri paused. "Maybe that's what I need. Maybe being useful to someone is what I'm getting out of this. What if that is what I want?"

"That's ridiculous." Namid shook her head. "Your ambition is to be someone else's servant. Please tell me you're joking."

"What if I'm not?"

"Then you're insane. What on Earth would make you want that? No normal person would think that way."

Amri looked down for a moment before responding. "I'm not normal, sis. You can have your 'normal' ambitions. You didn't ruin anyone else's lives when you were born."

Namid rolled her eyes. "Don't tell me you still feel bad about mom. After everything she did—"

"Who said anything about mom?" Amri asked. "Okay, yes, I do think she could have turned out better if she hadn't gotten pregnant. Maybe she would have been a better person if she hadn't lost all of her dreams at once. But what about dad? He never did anything wrong. Why should he have to marry a violent woman and have such an awful marriage?"

"You were truly blinded, weren't you?" Namid snickered. "Not me. Dad didn't dote on me like he did you. And guess what?" She got up in Amri's face and glared at him. "He was just as responsible for that trash bin of a family as mom was."

"What?" Amri cocked an eyebrow. "No, he wasn't—"

"Mom might have been drunk when she went to bed with dad, but dad chose to take a drunk girl to bed. Why her? What was he thinking? Where was his sense of caution? His duty to his future kids?"

"That's..." Amri fell silent.

"He chose her," Namid hissed. "Even if it was just a moment of lust, that was his choice. And for that, he was just as responsible for everything mom did as she was."

Amri didn't respond. After a few moments of silence, he simply put on some working gloves and headed out.

40

The Institute's Salvation

EPHORAH

Climbing the stairs to the Institute of Theurgy, Ephorah was surprised to see how empty the place was. Of course, classes would be starting again in a little more than a week, so there wouldn't be a ton of students on campus. Even still, it was odd to see the building so empty.

At the institute's main office, Ephorah checked in with the school security, who balked at the sight of the sword she was carrying.

"This is an artifact," Ephorah explained. "I need to speak with Professor Massouh about it."

The head of security sighed and handed her a slip of pink paper. "Stick this notice on your sword, and don't take it out of its sheath until you find him."

Ephorah attached the slip and made her way to the enchantment and artifacy classroom. Professor Massouh was the teacher who showed her how to infuse spirits into artifacts. If anyone could explain to her whether the sword was dangerous, it was him.

Once she reached his classroom, she found the door locked. No schedule had been posted as to where he would be instead. Was he not on campus during the break?

"Excuse me," Ephorah popped her head into a nearby classroom, where a professor was going over her lesson plan. "Do you know where Professor Massouh is?"

"Did you check his classroom?" she asked.

Ephorah nodded. "He's not there."

"Did you check the women's changing room?"

"Uh, was I supposed to?" Ephorah asked.

"...Never mind." The teacher got up from her desk and checked a calendar. "The schedule says he's on campus somewhere. Run down to the headmistress's office. They'll find him for you."

Ephorah thanked her and made her way to Headmistress Rubin's office. As she approached, she could hear what sounded like two faculty members arguing. One sounded slightly drunk.

"You mean to tell me she just 'appeared' in your office and offered you everything we need, and you told her to leave?" Ephorah recognized that voice. It was Professor Dorin Meir, teacher of spirit capture classes.

"Just because we're in a bind, doesn't mean we go around trusting a goddess who might as well have had 'evil' embroidered on her hankies." That was the headmistress. Ephorah could almost hear the alcohol on her breath.

"Uh, excuse me." Ephorah knocked on the door to the office. "Can anyone tell me where Professor Massouh might be?"

Professor Meir opened the door. When she looked down at Ephorah, her face appeared to be stuck in a permanent scowl. Ephorah had once thought that Meir could have been a natural beauty, between her curly black hair, fair bronze skin, bright green eyes, and slim yet curved figure. She even had one of those bodies that looked good in any dress she wore. But somehow, she always looked so angry that it didn't matter. Her expression made her look like a beautiful princess who wanted to destroy everyone in front of her.

"Did you check his classroom?" She asked.

Ephorah nodded.

"Did you check the women's changing room?"

Ephorah looked behind her at the headmistress. "What's this thing about the women's changing room?"

Instead of answering, the headmistress looked at a large schedule on her desk. "I've got a note here saying that he's working on an experiment in one of the labs on the...second floor, north wing. Try there."

Ephorah stepped away from the headmistress's office and hurried out of there before the two women resumed whatever bitter conversation they'd been having before. It was only after she made her way to the labs that she realized there were about a dozen labs with different projects, and she didn't know which one Massouh would be working in. If he had stepped out for a break, she might check a room, not see him, and end up missing him.

Near the labs, the school had a research material supply room. Quartermaster Idrees el-Farah sat behind a desk mumbling something over his notes. He had a wiry white beard and hair, a bushy mustache, and a face that you could look at and immediately think 'curmudgeon' without missing a beat.

Ephorah was always careful around the supply room. The first time she'd been in here, she had almost been killed by a homicidal flying carpet that someone had let out accidentally. She still didn't trust any rugs she saw in rooms unless they were pinned down by a coffee table.

"Excuse me," Ephorah approached the quartermaster. "Can you tell me where to find Professor Massouh?"

"Um," el-Farah snapped out of his mumblings. "Massouh? Did you check his classroom?"

"First place I looked," Ephorah nodded.

"Did you check the women's changing room?"

"No," Ephorah sighed. "And I'm really starting to worry about why everyone thinks I should."

"Never mind, I just found him right here." He pointed to a detailed timesheet of all the labs and when people had signed up to use them. "He's in lab 2E. Second floor, third on the right."

"Ah, thank you!" Ephorah was about to leave.

"And what's with the sword?" The quartermaster asked.

"Research project!" Ephorah called back as she left.

Making her way through the halls, Ephorah found lab 2E. The door was open, and thankfully, Professor Massouh was inside. He was clearly in the middle of a binding ritual of some sort between a mirror and a spirit in a jar. Ephorah didn't dare disturb the ritual process.

After a few moments, the professor touched mirror to the spirit jar. The being inside was pulled into the artifact, completing the process.

"Nice!" Professor Massouh laid the mirror down on a table. "Show me Professor Meir's office."

Ephorah stepped up towards the professor. "Uh, excuse me?"

"Ah!" The professor covered the mirror with his hands. "Uh, dismiss," he whispered to the mirror. "Um, welcome, miss! What can I do for you?"

"It's Ephorah," she stepped up and placed the sword on the table next to the mirror. "And I need your advice. This artifact..." she drew the officer's sword from the scabbard. "Well, I don't know if I can trust it."

"Don't trust it?" Professor Massouh looked at the blade with curiosity. "Where did it come from?"

"I made it," Ephorah admitted. "But it's...evil. I think."

Massouh examined the sword. The metal was as corroded as when Ephorah had first enchanted it, with a tarnished steel blade and crusty, rusted handle. The professor tried picking it up, and touched the stained metal with his finger. He immediately dropped it back on the table and stuck his finger in his mouth.

"Ow," he winced. "This thing's sharp, even where it shouldn't be!"

A few drops of blood had dripped from his pricked finger and landed on the blade. Where they had fallen, the corrosion cleared up, revealing a shiny, polished black surface instead.

"Oh, so that's how it works." The professor leaned closer. "It's hungry."

"That isn't good, is it?" Ephorah asked. "For an artifact to want blood?"

"Hm," the professor returned the blade to its scabbard. "I'm not sure. It doesn't seem to be able to move on its own. Did you have any problems carrying it here?"

Ephorah shook her head.

"Then it's safe as long as it stays in its scabbard."

"But..." Ephorah looked down at her creation again. "It has a hunger of its own. And possibly a will. But no sign of a mind in there. I don't think it cares from whom the blood flows, only that it gets its fill."

"So, it's like literally any ordinary beast," Massouh replied. "It's no more evil than a lion. Comes with using bestia spirits, although if it can clear corrosion that quickly, it must have been a very powerful spirit. It almost looked like a work of a humanus elemental."

"It was," Ephorah admitted, and then wished she hadn't.

"Wait, what did you say?" Professor Massouh's eyes widened. "That sword showed less signs of any free will than a typical bestia spirit. Did...did you do something to a humanus elemental to make it more compliant?"

"Um," Ephorah backed away. "I...uh, it was an emergency. I was on an internship, with the Salamanders. We were attacked by the Greymarch—"

"The Greymarch?" The professor blinked. "How did you...did that sword... were you able to fend off the Greymarchers with that thing?"

"Um, maybe. Possibly, I uh..."

"This is amazing!" Massouh clapped his hands. "Do you have any idea what this means?"

"Uh, sorry?" Ephorah raised an eyebrow.

"That sword is an incredibly powerful artifact. If it really did help you survive a Greymarch attack, and can clear its own corrosion so quickly, it might be able to help save our school. Think about it; an artifact is only as powerful as the spirit bound to it. But the most powerful spirits we've ever been able to capture are humanus level elementals. Professor Meir is extremely good at subjugating them, but getting them to cooperate once they've been turned into an enchanted artifact is a lot harder. You've seen what can happen when an enchanted artifact gets out of control. And now you've found a way to make powerful spirits more docile? More cooperative?" He locked eyes with Ephorah, and his expression softened. "You might very well have saved our school."

"...I did?" Ephorah looked at the sword again.

"What command sigils did you use to make this?" Massouh pointed to the sword.

"Well, I used Fame. That's why it hungers for blood. It's a water elemental, so that's why it works with fluids. Then there's Vix, San, Fiew, Petu, Wan..." Ephorah was dreading the last. "And Incontio."

"Okay," Massouh seemed to be running those sigils in his head. "Incontio. I don't know this one. What does it mean?"

Ephorah struggled to find the words, but more than the fear of what would happen if she told him about the sigil and where she learned it, she feared what would happen if she refused to tell Massouh the truth.

"It means…idiocy," Ephorah admitted. "I've only used it twice, and the second time was only in an emergency."

"Idiocy," Massouh turned the idea in his head for a moment. "I need to consult with Professor Meir about this. She would know more about what to do with this. Come to think of it, weren't you the one who made really powerful gloves for Combat Arena? Was that your other usage of this sigil?"

Ephorah nodded. "That…wasn't against the rules, was it?"

Professor Massouh shook his head. "Nope. There's nothing in the rules against using creativity and ingenuity to get an edge in the tournament. In fact, it's encouraged. Well, most of the time," the professor admitted. His expression drooped a bit. "To be frank, the headmistress has been trying to restrain the use of creativity in the tournament, because it gives creative students an unfair advantage over less-creative ones. But I think she was mostly just trying to stop the sorcery and alchemy contestants from using it against our pupils. Let's go see if we can talk to Professor Meir and find more about this new sigil."

"She's with the headmistress," Ephorah followed the professor out of the lab. "At least, that's where I saw her a little while ago."

"By the way, where did you learn this new sigil?" Massouh asked.

There was no way that Ephorah was going to admit that she learned it from a woman who was probably a Tomb Lord, so she made up a lie. "I saw it in an old book once. One my parents used to own back when we lived in Aklagos. Lost it in a Greymarch attack."

"That's a pity," Massouh said. "We could have used it to find out more about it. By chance, was the book from the old Empyrian Empire? Maybe they discovered it a long time ago. That would explain why I've never heard of it."

"…it might have been." Ephorah didn't want the lie to get any larger. "I can't remember."

The two reached Professor Meir's classroom to check if she was in. Sure enough, the professor had finished her argument with the headmistress and had returned to her room in a huff. She appeared to be cleaning out her desk into a large leather bag.

"Oh, it's you again," she addressed Ephorah. "Massouh, I recommend you start looking for new employment. The headmistress has decided to drive this school into the ground."

"We need your advice," Massouh showed Professor Meir the sword. "This student may have found a way to save the institute."

Meir paused, but her expression softened ever so slightly. "I find that hard to believe. What have you got?"

"She's found a way to make artifacts out of humanus elementals, and make the spirits cooperate with their user." Massouh showed Meir the sword. "She did this once to make the gloves she used in the Combat Arena, and now she's made a powerful sword that hungers for blood, but can be kept safely contained in a scabbard like this."

The spirit capturing professor looked at Ephorah for a moment. "I do remember the gloves you used in the arena. I thought they were unusually powerful for a bestia spirit. And you got them to obey?" She looked down at the sword. "And it wasn't just a one-time thing. If you did it twice, then..."

Massouh nudged Ephorah and handed her a notepad. "Can you show her the sigil you used?"

Reluctantly, Ephorah drew the sigil on the paper and wrote the word "incontio" below the image. She then handed the notepad to Meir.

"Idiocy..." Professor Meir seemed to be working something out in her mind. "This...this could save us. This could save our school!"

"I know, right?" Massouh smiled and clapped a hand on Ephorah's shoulder. "You might be the golden beacon of hope we've been looking for."

"Oh..." Ephorah forced a smile. "Great."

"We need to study this further." Meir looked at Ephorah. "Have you ever been to the Duat to capture spirits?"

"Uh, twice," Ephorah admitted.

"Then you're coming with me to collect some spirits. We need to do some experiments." Meir packed a bag with a dozen warded glass jars for spirit capture. "Are you doing anything right now?"

"Uh...not really."

Meir handed her the bag of jars. "Then we're going now."

"Oh, can I come?" Massouh smiled.

"No," Meir scowled. "You stay here. And stay out of the women's changing room."

41

A Simple Trip to get Wine

NAMID

Lying awake in bed, Namid was upset. For starters, it was only six thirty in the morning. Usually, she was still asleep at this time, but not today. And part of that was because she hadn't slept well the night before.

Reliable people were hard to come by. Ephorah had abandoned her on a bus. Rostam was flying away with the airship. And Amri had...well, it was strange. Namid was certain that she had won her argument with Amri, and yet...he was still going to that volunteer thing every day, and then working on his glass-cannister-ward-thing. He'd read her a story the night before as normal, other than that, he acted like their conversation didn't matter. It was like winning the argument hadn't actually gotten her anywhere, except alone, lying awake in bed, with nothing better to do than get up at a reasonable hour.

Groggily, Namid got out of bed and looked around her room. It was a nice room in an upper-middle class house with a bright window, a view of the Garden District, a full-size bed, and a number of nice furnishings such as her dresser and nightstand that matched the overall fanciness of the house.

And it was a mess. Namid would be the first to admit that she did not keep her room remotely clean. There were dirty clothes all over the floor, a discarded shirt hanging on the doorknob, her sheets hadn't been washed in a month, and the attached bathroom was even worse. In the interest of not getting yelled at by her aunt, Namid scooped up all the dirty clothes and tossed them in a laundry basket. That should keep any lectures to a minimum, at least.

Namid then cleaned herself up in the bathroom and got herself dressed. She thought about putting on something casual enough for sitting comfortably around the house, but then a thought occurred. Ephorah's birthday was coming up soon, in less than a month. She might be able to smooth things over for her by preparing a nice enough party. She was pretty sure she could throw something together and planning it would give her something to do for the day.

Putting on some clothes that were nice enough to go out in public with, Namid ran a number of possible options in her head.

First, she needed to get her a proper gift. The more Namid thought about it, the more she realized that Ephorah was one of those people who had a long list of things she didn't like, but not a lot that she did. She liked pomegranates, and...

"Is that really it?" Namid thought aloud.

No, there was something else. Ephorah liked power. She liked having it in the form of control over her spirits; she liked having it in artifacts that she could use to threaten anyone who got in her way. She liked money enough to do a side-job with Namid working at a wedding. The problem was, you couldn't wrap power. Or could you?

"It doesn't have to be a gun, or a fist, or an enchanted artifact." Namid grinned. "Power is in being able to get others to do what you want. Power is in getting boys to do what you want. Some new outfits that'll make girls in her classes jealous and boys ask her out on dates. I'm pretty sure her dress size is the same as mine, just ten centimeters longer."

Namid would make a trip to the Hanging Bazaar and ask a tailor to whip up some new clothes. They should be done before Ephorah's birthday, and after that, she would make a stop at a winery at the edge of the Garden District and see if they had anything pomegranate-related.

The trip to the Hanging Bazaar was fairly straightforward. Namid was able to pawn the items she stole from the wedding and find a tailor who could work with Ephorah's sizes, and design three new shirts, a pair of skirts, and shorts to go underneath the skirts for Ephorah. Namid thought about asking her to make a dress as well, but decided against it. The last time she brought Ephorah to an evening club where a fancy dress would be appropriate, it didn't go well.

Once the plans for the new clothes were laid out and Namid paid for the work with most of the money she had gotten from the things she'd pawned, she turned her mind over to plans for party beverages.

"Okay, so Ephorah's turning fifteen," Namid thought aloud. "I know she can't handle her liquor, so I'll get her something not too strong for her party.She's got a sweet tooth, too. So, less wine, more like slightly alcoholic juice."

Only a few buildings were permitted in the Garden District that weren't residential. They mostly had to be things that served some sort of utility, like a cistern, or were directly approved of by the people living in the district. Namid spotted a winery opposite the main cityscape. The place looked like they grew some of their own grapes on the spot, which would explain the city permit. "Perfect," Namid thought as she went to check the place out.

Stepping inside, she heard a mumble of hushed voices before a woman stumbled out of a backroom behind a counter wearing a white medical mask over her mouth. "Uh, welcome to the Risen Zombie Coffeehouse. There's no zombies here, only sandwiches."

Glancing around at bottles of wine shelved on each wall, she raised an eyebrow at the woman. "This is a winery."

The woman's milky-white eyes didn't move. "...So it is. But we're actually closed now, due to us being sick. Please come back later."

Namid looked at the "OPEN" sign on the door. "The sign says you're open 8-5. And that you're open right now."

"Oh, well, y-y-yes, but...um..." The woman's head tipped slightly, like something wasn't quite right with her neck.

"Look, I just want to pick up something for a friend's birthday."Namid approached the counter."She's a lightweight with the pallet of a five-year-old. Do you have anything sweet, preferably pomegranate, with a low alcohol content?"

"Uh...not in stock, but we might be able to order some and have it delivered."

The woman didn't right her head, giving her an uncanny appearance.Namid noticed that the woman's eyes didn't seem to blink.

"Um, maybe I could come back another time—you're bleeding!" Namid pointed to a red spot growing on the woman's shirt.

"Oh?" The woman bent her head in an unnatural manner to look at her shirt. "No, that's red wine. Yes, that's perfectly normal in a winery."

As she said this, her entire head fell off. Her surgical mask slipped off her face, revealing a broken jawline with rotten gums and missing teeth with the same dead eyes as before.

"Yes, perfectly normal." The voice continued from the woman's head, but her mouth wasn't moving.

Namid screamed and tried to run and grab the door, but a bony hand had her by the collar before she could escape. She looked over her shoulder and saw a golden mask on a body wrapped in linens. When she was little, the Tomb Lords had just been stories to scare little girls into eating their vegetables. They couldn't really be here in Hadesh, could they? But lots of things turned out to be real if enough people believed in them. Were the stories about them taking kids who fed their stewed veggies to the dog true?

"I promise to eat my squash!" She squeaked. "Just let me go!"

The lich dragged her back behind the counter into the winery's cellar. There, two other Tomb Lord's waited next to a pile of bodies. One had magical wards woven throughout their robes, while the other wore a tool belt with an assortment of mechanical contraptions and had gauntlets equipped with various implements. The bodies next to them must have been the winery's real employees.

"We have a problem." The lich who'd caught Namid threw her at the feet of the other two. Her voice sounded female. "The puppet came apart in front of her. I couldn't get her to leave."

"She's not part of this building's staff." The lich with wards looked at Namid. This one sounded male. "Young, pretty, probably either a student or some young man's girlfriend. They'll be looking for her."

"We kill her and leave the body to burn with the others." The first lich said. "No one will identify her body. And we already have enough problems to cover up today as it is."

"That'll just raise suspicion when people investigate this place." The second lich glared at the first. "We don't want people asking questions, like why there's a body in the ashes that shouldn't be here."

"Then we kill her, and drop her body in a dumpster where it will be found by the garbage collectors." The first lich raised a palm and aimed it at Namid like she was about to cast some spell.

Namid curled into a ball on the floor and tried not to whimper. She thought about fighting, but how do you fight three undead wizards who are virtually immortal?

"Then the police will want to know how she died." The warded lich interrupted the first. "Killing her with necromancy is stupid; it's a murder weapon that'll send the whole city on high alert. Even without it, they'll probably start searching the entire city to identify the murderer. We've already lost this contact point to let your spies into the city because one of the winery workers came down while the runegate was still active before we could hide it. This isn't Kemet, or even Harlak. Homicides are rare in this city; they're treated like a travesty."

"What if we just let her go?" The third lich with the tool belt leaned in close to Namid for a better look. Another male, but with a deeper, echoing voice. "She's what, fourteen? Fifteen? What's she going to do, tell the authorities that liches from Kemet burned down a winery in the middle of Hadesh? Does she even know of our other plans? Do you realize how ridiculous she'll sound if she reports us? She won't have any evidence, and the fire will look like an accident, anyway. They'll just think she's a young girl pleading for attention and tell her to scram. We won't have to hide a body, or worry about anyone asking where she went, because she'll be running around in broad daylight making a fool of herself."

Namid's eyes widened as she looked at the mechanic lich and nodded furiously in agreement.

"And when she does tell the authorities," the first lich turned to the mechanic. "If, by some chance, they decide to investigate, and ruin our godking's plans, we'll be certain he learns that letting her go was your idea, Pausiris."

The lich mechanic, who must have been Pausiris, paused. "Never mind. Forget I said anything. I'll leave you to sort this while I prepare the fire."

"Yeah, you do that." The female lich turned back to Namid. "Now, that leaves us with the option of taking her with us. No extra bodies in the ashes of this building means the local authorities won't connect her disappearance with the fire."

"Wait a minute." The sorcerer held Namid up by the scruff of the neck. "Nice hips, cute face, shapely curves...why kill her when she'd be more useful alive? The slaves who toil in our mines are always more manageable when supplied with comfort women."

An icy chill rolled down Namid's spine as she realized what the sorcerer was suggesting. She did her best to hold her composure, but the thought of being passed around by a bunch of smelly miners crept its way into the front of her mind.

"Hang on," the female lich grabbed Namid's chin and looked closer at her face. "This girl looks a lot like Mereshank did when she was alive. She's getting close to needing new flesh, and she'll definitely want this girl."

"Oh," the sorcerer cackled as he held Namid up to his golden face mask. "Tell me, which fate sounds better to you? Live out your days as a comfort girl in the mines, or hacked up for spare parts?"

Namid tried to think which sounded better, but it was impossible to choose in a dark cellar surrounded by liches, especially when one meant instant death and the other a life of hell.

"I'm just kidding," the sorcerer chuckled. "We're not really giving you a choice. Mereshank would never let us hear the end of it."

The female lich turned back to the mechanic. "Is everything ready?"

"The building is ready to burn, and your spies have orders to use a different drop-off point in the future." The mechanic turned to the others. "We should leave."

The sorcerer and female lich dragged Namid towards a runegate that had been hidden behind a wall in the winery cellar. The female lich pressed several runes to activate the portal, while the mechanic lich joined them.

"Fire's lit. Let's go."

The portal showed what appeared to be a room made entirely of black bricks. The liches dragged Namid through the gate as it closed behind them.

"Wait," Namid squeaked. "If you let me go I promise not to—"

The mechanic responded by aiming his right gauntlet at Namid. A narrow nozzle on a bulkier part of his arm sprayed some kind of sticky black substance over Namid's face, covering her mouth. She tried to scream, but her lips were stuck together, and she could only barely breathe through her nose.

"What was that?" The other male lich asked.

"Synthetic arachne silk," the mechanic explained. "I tinkered with the chemical composition, so it will biodegrade in about an hour, just in case I spray something that I don't want permanently stuck together." He looked down at his wrist, and then at the black gunk he'd plastered over Namid's mouth. "That's also why it isn't white like the real stuff."

"I want one of those," the other male lich muttered as he looked at Namid's glued mouth.

"Enough of this." The female lich grabbed Namid's forehead. "Sleep."

Namid felt drowsiness wash over her mind like a liquid pouring over her brain. The last thing she heard was the female lich's laughter as her world went dark.

42

The Origin of Elementals

EPHORAH

"So, do you have different gates to reach the spirit plane?" Ephorah followed Professor Meir, carrying her bag of spirit capture jars.

"Yes, and in our case, we'll be heading to an area filled with fire spirits, so put this on." The professor handed her an amulet with an orange gemstone in the center. "It will give you a degree of protection from the heat."

Ephorah put down the jars to slip the necklace on while Professor Meir donned a pair of gloves that looked a bit like oven mitts, but let her move her fingers more freely. Wardlines in the fabric indicated that they were protective as well. Finally, Meir showed Ephorah a runegate in the southern wing of the institute. The gate was an archway about the size of a normal door, supported by two columns covered in wards.

"This should take us to a place where fire elementals like to roam." The professor activated several sigils on the gate. Magical energy arched through the columns and powered a portal that appeared between the school room and the spirit plane. On the other side, Ephorah could see a dry, barren landscape with burning trees and flickering ash in the sky.

"Don't worry, it's breathable." Professor Meir stepped through the portal and gestured for Ephorah to follow. "Just be careful to avoid–" Light could pass through the portal, but not sound, so once the professor was on the other side, Ephorah couldn't hear her. Hoping whatever she just said wasn't important, the student stepped through the archway.

"—so that you don't spontaneously combust." Meir pointed at fumes coming from natural vents in the ground. "Did you hear me? Don't come into contact with those fumes."

"If you say so." Ephorah looked around at the landscape. The ground was a barren, cracked, arid wasteland. Flames erupted from the ground in places, but according to Meir, the fumes without flame were even hotter; those were gases too hot to burn. Various fire spirits lived here. Some looked like serpents made of lava, slithering in and out of cracks in the land. Base elementals that looked like stones dotted the landscape and could probably be mined in a place like this. And on closer inspection, Ephorah realized that the burning trees were actually made of embers and were elementals themselves.

"We're looking for something more intelligent than snakes and rocks." Professor Meir scouted the land. Ephorah couldn't help but grin at the odd sight of the professor wearing a flowing red dress in such an inhospitable wasteland. "Do you know where people think elementals come from?"

"Uh, they come from here." Ephorah gestured to the fiery landscape they were standing on.

"No," the professor scowled. "I mean how they're born. What gives birth to an elemental spirit in the first place?"

"I...don't know," Ephorah admitted.

"The dominant theory is that they're born from humans giving inanimate objects the traits of living things," Meir explained. "Say that a child sees a toy bear sitting by itself, and thinks the bear looks lonely. Of course, a teddy bear can't actually be lonely. But if the child thinks its lonely, she's ascribing emotions to it. If she asks it a question, and imagines it giving an answer, she's ascribing an intellect to it. Even if the teddy bear's 'answer' is wrong, that just shapes the intellect further. And if she makes the teddy bear answer with snark, or an attitude, she gives it a personality. And when the toy is eventually destroyed from wear and tear, or lost in the trash, the pile of beliefs the child has formed do not disappear; they end up in the spirit plane. This is how most wizards believe elementals are born."

"Really?" Ephorah tried to imagine all the toys she used to play with, and the times she imagined them thinking, feeling, or responding. No wonder there seemed to be an endless supply of elementals; every child's imaginary friend alone would keep the spirit plane populated.

"An object or flame that gets lots of use but not a lot of attention becomes a base elemental," Meir continued. "No intelligence, no instincts, no feelings. Like a favorite pen you use every day that feels comfortable in your hand. And if a gardener viewed a flowerbed like a coworker, or teammate in the process of growing flowers, he might treat it like an intelligent being. And that's what the flowerbed will become. Understand?"

Ephorah remembered a spirit she met during the wizard tournament, one who had flowers growing out of his back before Ephorah captured him. "Yeah, that actually makes a lot of sense."

"Good. Now follow me." The professor lead further into the infernal place. "Step where I step. We're going to go find some spirits who are particularly difficult to control. Ones that will need your new sigil to make use of their powers."

Professor Meir led the way through the landscape. Eventually, they entered an area with sharp rocks rising out of the ground in strange formations. Ephorah could hear things that sounded much more vicious than lava snakes and flowerbeds. Things that sounded angry, or hungry, or worse lurked in these lands.

"Okay." The professor found a spot in between five stone columns. "This looks like a good place. Somewhere nearby, there's a not-so friendly spirit we're going to capture."

"Alright, and how do you plan to do this?" Ephorah looked around. Something was definitely nearby.

"Most of the humanus spirits you've encountered in class do not understand the concept of violence. At least, not until we teach it to them." Meir drew a large magic circle with chalk on the ground. "That's because most of the spirits we have an easy time summoning were originally brought to life by children. Kids will believe in anything and will assign personalities to inanimate objects all the time. Since kids don't give their imaginary friends violent temperaments, the spirits they create are usually fairly docile, at least until betrayed or turned into an artifact. But here, we're going to capture a spirit born from a child's nightmares."

Before Ephorah could ask if that was really a good idea, a rumbling from behind told her something was coming. It had found two humans in the spirit world and was coming to 'get' them. It occurred to Ephorah that it might not even know what 'get' entailed.

A spirit of fire and possibly steel crawled over a hilltop and roared at the two theurgists. This thing looked like some twisted furnace in the bottom of someone's house; the sort that kids always think are really a monster hiding in the basement. With a mouth like a grill filled with flames, and two metallic claws that dragged its flaming body along the ground, the spirt crawled towards the wizards with soot and ash pouring out the back of the metal hull of its body.

"Uh, professor?" Ephorah glanced at the circle Meir had drawn on the ground. "Is that going to hold this thing?"

"It will if you stand in it," Meir dragged Ephorah over to the middle of the circle. "Hold right here until it gets close."

The professor then hid herself behind a column and got out a large tablecloth from the bag she'd had Ephorah carry. Ephorah wasn't stoked about being used as bait, but she realized this was probably the best way to trap such a potent spirit. The elemental moved surprisingly fast for a large house appliance crawling on two limbs. Once it was within a few centimeters of the circle, Ephorah backed away from it.

The creature stopped just short of the capturing circle that the professor had drawn in the dirt. It looked down, clearly recognizing the trap before it, and smashed one of its mechanical claws onto the ground, digging the edge of the circle away. Once the trap was thoroughly broken, the spirit continued to pursue Ephorah, who had started running away from the broken trap.

Ephorah ran towards the column where Meir had hidden, the spirit hot on her heels. As Ephorah reached the rock column, Meir threw her tablecloth over the spirit. Ephorah got just enough of a look at the unfolded cloth to spot another capture circle embroidered into it in a different colored of fabric.

The spirit bucked and struggled against the cloth, attempting to burn its way out of its new prison, but the professor had clearly thought of that. The more the creature struggled, the more the wards and spells on the cloth constricted its movement, until it eventually collapsed from exhaustion.

"Nice start." Professor Meir took out a warded jar to finish the capture. Unscrewing the lid, she pointed the opened jar at the spirit, which forced the fiery monster to become a smokey haze that was sucked inside the jar. "We're going to need more, though."

Ephorah and the professor managed to capture four more ill-tempered elementals from the region before the professor called it good. One was something like an angry ball of lightning with eyes, while the other three looked like different versions of the same nightmare furnace. How many kids were scared of their own basements?

"We'll start with these for now." Meir placed the jars in her bag and carried it back to the runegate. "Let's see if this miracle word of yours is as powerful as Massouh thinks."

Once they had returned to the institute campus, Professor Meir led the way to her classroom and drew a chalk circle on the floor. "We need something to enchant." The professor went to one of her storage closets and pulled out a bullwhip, which she placed in the center of the circle.

"Uh...why do you have this?" Ephorah pointed at the whip.

"None of your business," she muttered as she drew sigils around the circle. "*Sape, Jules, Torma, Poten, Thun, Irem,*"...She checked the sigil Ephorah had drawn earlier. "*Incontio.*"

Meir withdrew the thunder elemental from her bag and placed it in the center of the circle. When the ritual was complete, the thunder spirit was bound to the whip, which now cackled with electricity.

Holding the new artifact in hand, Professor Meir took it to one of the testing labs on the north wing and located a large, straw practice dummy. Electric artifact in hand, she snapped the whip and struck the dummy, which burst into flames and collapsed.

"Nice," Meir admired the whip. "I've always wanted something like this."

Ephorah tried to put her choice of sigils together in her mind to figure out exactly what the professor had created. "Doesn't *Torma* mean 'pain?'"

Meir ignored her. "But once isn't really enough to prove anything. We need to test these other spirits. Maybe...the boiler."

"What boiler?" Ephorah asked.

"Theurgists have been trying to make a boiler that can power an airship with no chance of the spirit inside breaking free." Professor Meir rubbed her chin. "Bestia spirits just don't have the power to drive an airship, at least not fast enough to sail against the winds and air currents to be reliable. Humanus spirits have always been necessary to power airship boilers, but there always needs to be a theurgist on the ship to keep the spirit from breaking free and attacking the crew. Turning the boiler itself into an artifact powered by a fire elemental never fixed the problem, because the spirit would be enraged immediately and try to burn the entire ship right away. But if we could use your new sigil to control it."

Ephorah's heart sank as she finally realized what she'd unleashed. Professor Meir wasn't just talking about using the sigil to make a few unruly spirits of household appliances that used to terrify children. She wanted to mass-produce artifacts powered by lobotomized spirits; an entire nation of airships fueled by humanus elementals deprived of their intelligence. Ephorah wasn't sure if Meir understood how bad the spell must have been for the elementals, and she feared Meir was the kind of person who wouldn't care even if she did.

"Should we look for any..." Ephorah struggled for an excuse. "...possible side-effects? Things we wouldn't want to get out of hand?"

"Hm?" Meir looked at Ephorah with a raised eyebrow. "That's certainly possible. We'll need to do more testing before we can start selling artifacts like these. But if this works..." She looked down at the whip and smiled. "We theurgists might get the respect we deserve. No more limiting how powerful our enchantments can be, no more dangerous artifacts that can hurt the users. And no more lawsuits. Especially no more lawsuits."

Ephorah knew she had let something terrible out of control. She still remembered the look on the earth elemental's face when she used the incontio spell to make her strength gloves. These beings knew what the sigil did to them, and they feared it. But there was no covering its effects up now.

"Is there..." Ephorah paused. "Are you sure...what if..."

Meir scowled. "Spit it out already."

"Do you understand what the incontio sigil does to the spirits?" Ephorah asked. "It doesn't just make them docile."

The professor shrugged. "It's the word for 'idiocy.' I imagine it makes the spirit an idiot."

"Ah," Ephorah shuddered. *So, she knows, but doesn't care.*

"Look, there's nothing else we need you to do today." The professor put the whip back in her closet and locked it. "That'll be all. Go home now."

43

Weakness

AMRI

"So, what made you decide to get Marduk involved?"

Amri was wiping a window that had just been installed on a shop that had been looted during the dracolich attack. Esfan was putting calk on another windowpane next to it.

The priest in training chuckled. "He's not being subtle, is he?"

"He said he was in my dreams on behalf of a mutual friend." Amri inspected the glass to make sure he'd gotten all the smudges off it. One smear remained. "It was pretty obvious who he was talking about."

Esfan calked another edge of the window. "Well, after everything you said about the pharmacist and her son, it sounded like you could use some divine guidance, or maybe a little protection."

"Fair enough," Amri admitted. "It's not that I don't appreciate it. But what I don't get is, why would your abbey be involved with him in the first place? Isn't he a rival god of a completely different religion?"

"Rival..." Esfan looked up from the window sealant and paused, visibly turning the word over in his mind. "Marduk has a...complicated relationship with Truth. Not like he's a liar, or anything, but...it's...complicated. Most gods don't really like talking about the One at the Heart of All very much, but Marduk and a few others, like Thoth, are exceptions."

"Why do other gods not like your Truth?" Amri asked.

"Well, it's not *our* truth. It's everyone's Truth." Esfan finished the last edge of calking and used a curved tool to wipe the excess sealant off the glass. "The abbey worships the abstract concept of truth; reality itself. Since gods are the products of humans believing them into existence, their connection to reality is...shaky at best. But Truth exists regardless of what we believe. The abbey believes that Truth actively ordered things in the universe to ensure humans would exist; that the human soul is a piece of Truth inside of us that allows us to bend the rules of reality. This is what you sorcerers and wizards do whenever you cast spells. But unlike humans, who are wanted, the gods are simply...tolerated."

"Tolerated?" Amri looked up from the window and its frustratingly persistent smear. "You mean the...thing you worship... I'm not sure it belongs in the same category as 'god' if it can dictate whether the others are allowed to exist...it doesn't care about the gods at all?"

"I wouldn't say that." Esfan paused. "Truth allowed the gods to exist in ancient times before communicating with men, because we weren't ready to understand just what Truth is. He wouldn't remove the others from existence if He didn't care at all; it's just that they're at best a tool and at worst antagonistic. Many gods don't like the fact that something greater than them can snuff them out at any time and have tried to rebel. And because the gods are created by men, and men are flawed, the gods are flawed, and some are outright evil."

Esfan looked down in a moment of thought. "Have you ever noticed that people in general have very little piety? No one comes to temples anymore just for the sake of going to temples. They offer sacrifices to gods when they want something, or to maintain the powers of the gods so that they'll keep everything running smoothly, but no one just burns a cow or a goat just as a show of thanks anymore."

"I guess...I haven't been paying attention to that sort of thing." Amri didn't want to admit that he'd never set foot inside a temple in his life.

"That's because, after the Calamity, the gods may have woken up and offered to fix the planet, but the proverbial jig was up," Esfan explained. "No one could be fooled into thinking the gods created us; we created them, and that makes them less than divine, undeserving of spontaneous worship. Today, it's just a trade; almost as mundane as paying your water bill, just with burnt offerings instead of money. But Truth, Veritas, the One at the Heart of All – He's a different story. He existed before time, He existed before us, and He *is* worth worshiping, just because you can."

"So, what does any of this have to do with Marduk?" Amri was about to give up on the last stubborn window smudge. "If he's a god like the others, he only exists because he's allowed to, and he has every reason to dislike Truth–"

"He doesn't." Esfan shook his head. "Marduk has never opposed Truth and has been used by Truth on more than one occasion." Esfan looked up, as if piecing together his thoughts in the sky above. "The abbey believes that Marduk is what humans come up with when they try to connect with the One at the Heart of All, the source of the human soul, and invent something that is not quite the real thing, but actively trying to be. Marduk tries to be everything that Truth is, and that includes taking care of his subjects as a king, even submitting to a better one when possible." Esfan paused. "Be careful talking about this with him. The fact that he's supposed to be the perfect king but knows he can never be what humans made him to be...it's a bit of a sore subject for him."

"Hm." Amri gave the windowpane one last wipe before conceding to the smudge's victory. "I'd rather not make him mad. As it stands, he doesn't seem to like me. He thinks I'm not worthy."

"Yeah, about that." Esfan's tone shifted, as if trying to be extra diplomatic about what he would say next. "The only way to convince him that you are worthy is by showing him you have traits he admires."

"Like strength?" Amri asked.

"Eh...that'd be a start," Esfan admitted. "But you'd need a bit more than that. Marduk would tell you that being a strong bully is better than being a wimp, but only a little. He wants to see things like diligence, or responsibility. Maturity, or self-control. Humility, or courage."

"I told him there were different kinds of strength, and he said I had none of them." Amri's face fell. "Is...do you think that's true?"

"I'm not sure." Esfan paused. "With that thief that attacked you – what would you have done if he tried to kill you? Would you fight?"

Amri didn't answer. Esfan looked like he already knew the answer.

"There is no real difference between being unable to fight and being unwilling to," Esfan explained. "Whether you lack the ability or the will, you will still be easy prey for anyone trying to kill you."

"But fighting has never solved anything," Amri replied. "Whether it's a bully in school, or someone at home, even if you beat them, you'll just be in even more trouble."

Esfan raised an eyebrow at Amri, but he didn't speak for a moment. "It seems fighting never helped you when you were younger. I understand; if you fight back against a bully in school, you get punished just as harshly as the bully. If you don't fight, you can hope that the teachers or other faculty members step in and do something about it. But I have seen how these things play out; your typical schoolteacher has no interest in stopping the aggressor. They don't like conflict and will pretend it doesn't exist just so they don't have to do the job of protecting their students."

"Well, yeah." Amri nodded. "Most adults don't really care about kids. It's not like they're ignoring their own kids getting hurt."

"That's the sort of attitude Marduk can't stand." Esfan capped his bottle of window sealant and gathered up his tools. "Of all the ideas that make up his personality, the strongest and most important is the idea that rulers should dedicate themselves to those they rule, and that parents, by extensions, should take care of their children. Marduk has been known to lay all manner of curses and punishments upon those that wield authority over the small and abuse them with it. It's part of the reason he's never very popular with older generations."

Amri and Esfan sat down at a picnic table with the rest of the volunteer crew for lunch. They were having salad, which Amri wasn't particularly fond of. In fact, he really disliked cold vegetables. But he knew better than to complain about the food scrounged up by a volunteer force, and he wasn't there for free meals, anyway, so he ate without complaint, doing his best to hide his disgust at the taste.

After a moment of eating, Esfan looked up from his salad at Amri. "Do you know what moral courage is?"

Amri was having too much trouble convincing his throat to swallow the bite of what might as well have been lawn clippings in his mouth to answer, so he just shook his head.

"Imagine that there is a building in a warzone, and inside the building is a small child," Esfan explained. "One hundred soldiers stand outside the building, and there is artillery fire incoming. A cannonball might hit the building at any moment and blow it to smithereens, with the child still inside. Out of the one hundred soldiers, seventy of them, on average would run inside the building and try to rescue the child, knowing that if the building gets hit, they will die along with the child."

"That's moral courage?" Amri finally managed to swallow.

"No," Esfan answered. "That's physical courage. Now imagine that there will be no artillery fire for another hour. The cannons are all being reloaded but will resume shelling afterward. Plenty of time for a soldier to run in, grab the kid, and get out alive. However, the child is the son of an enemy officer, and any soldier who runs inside to rescue him will be immediately branded as a traitor if he does. This is moral courage; being brave enough to do the right thing not in the face of physical danger, but under threat of societal repercussions. In the second scenario, one soldier out of the hundred *might* run in to rescue the enemy officer's son. Most of the time, none of them will."

"I see." Amri enjoyed the break from trying to stomach the raw veggies. "And I take it you're trying to tell me that what I lack is moral courage?"

"Eh, kind of." Esfan paused for a moment. "It's hard to say you lack something that most people just don't have. The reason most people when attacked don't defend themselves is because they fear that the law won't respect their act of self-defense. They're afraid of what their neighbors will think of the violent individual who beat up a man just because they tried to steal from him. They fear the damage defending themselves will do to their relationships more than they fear the immediate danger posed by the attacker." Esfan gestured to the other volunteers, and then around to the community that they'd been working to rebuild. "We're social creatures. If cut off from the rest of society, most people wouldn't survive. I think that's what you're afraid of. Your brain is running calculations in your head and thinks your chances of survival are better if you don't defend yourself."

"That...might be it." A thought gnawed at Amri's mind, like there was a piece the priest in training hadn't found yet. "But there's one other thing. Did that thief the other day really deserve to be burned? Or have me freeze his blood? There are many ways a sorcerer could fight back, but not without causing some permanent damage. Did he truly deserve that? Is my wallet really worth more than his life?"

"That was his choice," Esfan replied. "The thief decides what his life is worth when he tries to take other people's money by force. He's the one risking your life and his own for your wallet. He's the one that decided your money is worth the gamble of both of your lives."

Amri winced. "Yeah, but...it's also my choice how I react. If I just go about killing or maiming people to protect property, isn't that a terrible thing to do?"

"If you allow thieves to go unpunished, it affects all of society." Esfan clasped his hands and leaned forward across the picnic table. "Trust me; when petty thieves discover that they can steal with no repercussions, they don't just take one wallet or mug one group of people. They start making a career out of it. You are doing them no favors by letting them spiral further into a life of crime."

Once they'd finished lunch, Amri headed home to clean up and then went to the industrial park. Today, they were going to encase a proper gas cylinder in an insulation ward.

On his way to the glassworks, Amri deliberately looked away from the pharmacy. He owed it to the people he'd brought in his cannister warding project not to get further involved with Malbim or Izaac.

Even as he walked by the pharmacy lab, he could overhear voices from inside.

"Just hold still, and this won't hurt at all." That was definitely Doctor Malbim's voice.

"Ignore it," Amri told himself. "You have no evidence—"

"Stop!" Izaac cried. "I don't want to do this anymore."

"Hush!" Malbim's voice sounded like she was trying to yell quietly, somehow. "Someone will hear you! I don't want to hear it, anyway."

"These make me feel sick," Izaac replied. "They make me itch all over."

"You're being too sensitive," Doctor Malbim snapped. "I'm your doctor and your mother, and I know what's best. I'm fixing you! So you won't be such a pest anymore."

A thought clicked in Amri's brain. He didn't have anything solid, but he had enough evidence to get the police to at least investigate the doctor and her son. If they couldn't get a warrant, they could at least keep an eye on them. That might be enough to scare the doctor into stopping whatever she was doing, at least for a while.

It wasn't hard for Amri and Avroham to recreate the ward on the gas cannister. Within an hour, a newly etched layer of glass coated the cannister, and Amri brought it down to the gas lab to show Tomek and Head Researcher Dobias.

Finishing up for the day, Amri took a detour from home and stopped by the mercenary guilds and checked into the headquarters of Ironwood Company. These were the mercenary policing agency that was in charge of maintaining order in Hadesh. Under the rules of the Iron Constitution that governed the empire, the imperial government was not allowed to have its own police force. All police work had to be done by private parties, such as mercenary companies like Ironwood.

Stepping inside the headquarters lobby, Amri walked up to a desk where a clerk with short black hair in a white button-down shirt sat making notes on a typewriter.

"I need to report a case of child abuse," Amri said to the clerk.

The clerk looked up from her typewriter. "Uh...okay, let's...hold on, they gave me a form for that."

She opened a drawer in her desk and pulled out a number of papers, one of which must have been the form she was looking for. "Alright, so here's the process. We need the name of the child, the name of the alleged abuser, and a location where we could go to find and interview them both. If the interview shows that there is something worth investigating, we'll put a request in to a judge to get a search warrant."

"All right," Amri smiled. His plan was working. "The child is Izaac Malbim.

The mother...I'm sorry, I don't know her first name. She's a doctor, though. An alchemist who specializes in pharmaceuticals."

"Okay." The clerk wrote these details down on her form. "Keep going."

"Right," Amri cleared his throat. "They've both been in the pharmacy lab in the park over in the industrial district every day lately. You should be able to find and interview both of them between noon and five o'clock."

"Great," the clerk finished another part of the form. "Now I just need the name of the person you suspect is committing the abuse, and where our agents can potentially meet him for an interview."

"Uh...It's the mother." Amri paused. "Doctor Malbim. I'm sorry, do you need her first name? I never heard her say it."

The clerk gave Amri a quizzical look. "No, no. I need the name of the abuser. Who are you accusing of committing the abuse? Or, wait–" she looked back at her form. "Did I fill this out wrong? Did you mean Izaac was abusing Doctor Malbim?"

"No." Amri was confused, trying to figure out why the clerk wasn't understanding him. "Doctor Malbim is abusing her five-year-old son, Izaac. She's performing medical experiments on him and injecting him with drugs against his will."

The clerk looked down at the form again. "...oh," she finally said. "I'm sorry, we'll...we'll get someone..." The clerk tapped her pen against the desk, as if trying to think of the next thing to say. It was enough to tell Amri that something was wrong.

"You're not going to send anyone, are you?" Amri asked.

"...no, I'm sorry." The clerk threw the form she'd filled out in a trash bin. "This isn't a case we work with."

"I see." Amri's heart sank. "Could you tell me why not?"

"No," the clerk shook her head. "Please leave."

"Can't you tell me–"

"Leave," the clerk replied. "Before I call security."

Not wanting to be dragged out of the company headquarters by any armed mercenaries, Amri left the building and tried to figure out what had gone wrong. He had his suspicions that the clerk wasn't allowed to file a form for a case in which the abuser was a parent, or maybe it was because the abuse involved pharmaceutical drugs instead of simple beatings. After all, Doctor Malbim was a pharmacist. Maybe the mercenaries weren't qualified to check on a case where drugs were being misapplied to a child. Then again, the standards for simply filling out a report weren't very high, and interviewing the kid and the parent didn't require the kind of evidence needed for a search warrant. What really bothered Amri was the fact that the clerk wouldn't just tell him why she couldn't file the form.

Dejected, Amri went home to his aunt and uncle's house, only to find them both in a frantic panic.

"Where have you been?" Aunt Panya asked on the verge of tears. "Where is your sister?"

"I was with the glassworker at the industrial park." His aunt's words finally hit Amri's mind. "Wait, where is Namid?"

"She's run off again!" Uncle Mido roared. "She went out to get something for her friend's birthday party, and that was this morning! She hasn't been back since!"

"What?" Amri slumped against a wall in the foyer of the house. A little over a year ago, Namid had run off when an airship had crashed in the middle of the Career Day Festival. Uncle Mido had taken Amri out onto the streets in the evening to go find her, and they'd had no luck. Namid had come back home on her own, but Amri had hoped she'd learned her lesson by now. Apparently not.

"Do you have any idea where she would have gone?" Panya asked.

Amri shook his head. "I didn't even know she'd left. I went this morning to join the volunteer crew, and I didn't know she was gone when I came back to get ready to go to the industrial park."

Uncle Mido slammed his fist against a wall. "I'd go after her. If I had any idea where she was!" He glared at Amri. "Why don't you know anything about what she was up to? Do you at least know the friend she was trying to buy things for?"

"I'm sorry," Amri stammered. "I just don't know."

Mido threw up his hands and stormed out of the room. Amri could feel the rage aimed at him. Sure, not all of his uncle's anger was aimed at Amri, but he could tell from his face and voice that Mido wanted Amri to be able to solve this, somehow.

Amri gave up trying to figure things out and went up to his room. There was no point going out in the night air to search for his sister; they had no idea where to look.

Unsure of what else to do, Amri locked his bedroom door and tucked himself into bed. He didn't know what Mido would do if he found him trying to get some sleep, but he didn't want to find out.

Once again, Amri found himself floating in Marduk's void in his dreams.

"Curious that you would turn to the police over that boy," Marduk stroked his chin, which held barely a stubble, but no proper beard. "And now, your sister is missing."

"I don't know what to do," even in his dreams, Amri's voice was dry. "About either of them."

"You are the older brother. That makes you your sister's keeper." Marduk's frown never lightened. "Your uncle isn't just upset that she's missing; he's upset that you are useless to help."

"Am I supposed to keep her on a leash?" Amri asked. "Like, a literal leather strap around her neck? How do I keep her out of trouble without restraining her?"

"You don't," Marduk admitted. "And, let's not pretend that your uncle is innocent. He has as much responsibility to monitor his niece's whereabouts as you, if not more. It seems that no one in your family kept tabs on where Namid was going, and no one made sure she traveled with a chaperone."

"A chaperone?" Amri asked. "Is that really necessary?"

"Apparently, yes!" Marduk hissed. "She wouldn't be missing, would she?" Marduk turned to face the infinite void and clasped his hands behind his back. "A person can be free, or they can be safe. It is the role of men to keep women safe. Maybe it's a wife, or a daughter, or a sister, or someone else. It is his job to keep her protected. But she isn't free if she's safe; if she is free to roam as she pleases, she is not protected. And even if she claims she wanted the freedom to go where she wants, you will still be responsible if she ends up in trouble. Wise men do not give women this much freedom."

Amri glanced in the direction Marduk was staring before looking back at him. "That's a bit sexist, don't you think?"

"Irrelevant," the god replied. "It is sexist to expect men to always protect women. Has that ever stopped anyone from placing the burden upon your shoulders? Did you ask to be your sister's keeper? To be held responsible when your sister chooses to run off by herself and goes missing? No, you didn't, and yet the responsibility was assigned to you all the same. Power without responsibility is tyranny. Responsibility without power is slavery. If you are accountable when your sister disappears, you should have the power to keep her from going missing in the first place."

"Well, I had no power to stop Namid from running off, which she did, and now I'm being held partly responsible," Amri replied. "Is there anything you can do? Can you see where she's gone, or help me find her?"

"Do you realize that I'm the god of civilization?" Marduk turned to face Amri again. "Do you know how much I do to maintain peace and order on a daily basis? Keeping demons from attaching themselves to the minds of mortals, watching for invaders of both a mortal and supernatural kind? Searching for a dracolich that needs to be punished? And now keeping watch on a boy who's not enough to be a man, who is also asking me to watch for his sister?"

Amri raised a hand in defense. "I get it. You're busy. I'll ask the police for help."

"I didn't say I wouldn't keep an eye out." Marduk replied. "Nothing escapes my vision over your city. If she's anywhere in the empire, I should be able to find her."

"Thank you," Amri bowed his head before Marduk. "I tried asking her for help before with the Malbims, but she wasn't interested."

"Why do you keep poking around with the pharmacist?" Marduk asked. "What evidence do you have of wrongdoing?"

"The doctor says her son has several personality disorders, but they don't line up with his behavior." Amri tried to close his eyes to remember, but instead ended up pulling the memories into view in the void. Apparently, memories work differently in dreams. "The very first time I met Izaac, he grabbed onto me and held on so tight, I thought he'd break his fingers."

The memory of this event played out in the clouds in the void, and Marduk's expression changed from his usual frown to light shock at seeing the boy clinging to Amri.

"The only thing he said to me was 'please don't go.' Then he went off when his mom when he realized she was just getting more upset with him."

Marduk examined the memory and his face sank. "It seems you have been paying attention, at least to this. These are not the actions of a happy, healthy child, or a caring mother. And I can tell from your own memories that these are signs you've learned to detect from experience. But tell me, why is this boy important to you? He isn't family, like your missing sister, you have no responsibility to help him, you went to the authorities already and they've refused to act. You have nothing to gain, but if you continue to get involved, you might lose everything: your chances at a career, your studies as a sorcerer at the academy, your reputation, possibly even your freedom, since you could be arrested if you break the law to continue getting involved."

"I know," Amri admitted. "But he reminds me so much of me when I was his age. I always had my dad, who would take me away from my mom when she was particularly violent to his tool shop, and he'd show me how to tinker with the mechanical devices he was working on. I think that's why I like taking things apart and figuring out how they work. But Izaac doesn't have a father. He's alone with the doctor all the time. I know I have no right to get involved, but no one else will."

Marduk's face softened a little, but his frown returned. "Noble. But I repeat: you have nothing to gain, but could lose it all. You are too weak to stop the pharmacist; you lack the will to even step between her and her son in the first place."

Weak. Lacking the will. Amri was all too familiar. "I know."

44

The Eternal Boiler

EPHORAH

Inside another lab in the Institute of Theurgy, Professor Massouh examined the whip Professor Meir had made.

"Fascinating. Far more power than any bestia elemental can provide, and yet..."

The enchantment professor struck a wooden dummy in the experimentation room with the whip. As Ephorah had seen before, the dummy burst into flames before falling over.

"Amazing." Massouh handed the whip back to Professor Meir. "I think you're right. We should try the boiler again. Ask the quartermaster if he can get some golems to bring one up."

Meir rolled up the whip and slung it over one shoulder. Then she went off to the quartermaster, leaving Ephorah and Professor Massouh alone.

"Professor, is this...is this really a good idea?" Ephorah asked. "The incontio spell...I only used it once when I didn't know what it was, and then again in a life-or-death scenario. Using it on spirits for personal gain, with full knowledge of what it does, seems...wrong."

Massouh sat in a chair and looked up at the ceiling for a moment, then smiled at Ephorah. "Do you remember when we first met? In the quartermaster's storehouse?"

"...yes," Ephorah winced. "There was a violent rug that tried to kill me."

"Well, that artifact was made by a reckless wizard wanting a faster method of travel," the professor explained. "The thing is, lots of people have been looking for ways of keeping spirits from getting hostile like that. Most of our society relies on fuel in some way or another. You think we'd be able to feed as many people as we do without industrialized farms? There are always people who think that if the energy cost is too expensive, we should just stop burning fossil fuels, or relying on fire elementals. They have no idea how many people would starve if we actually did that."

"Uh... How does this relate back to the homicidal carpet?" Ephorah asked.

"Do you know where we get most of our fuel?" Massouh asked.

"I believe we import it?" Ephorah replied.

"That's right!" Massouh smiled. "There are no coal mines throughout the entire empire. We have never been able to dig deep enough or find any kind of fossil fuels in the old Borealan or even the pre-war Empyrian lands. Some of the post-war expansion colonies have tried to find deposits, with trace amounts of success, but none could provide power to the entire empire. And think of the damage that kind of mining does to the planet." He held the whip in his hands like he was cradling a compass. "We've been relying on fire elementals to transport goods, in both our airships and most of our trains, but a theurgist must always be present to keep them under control. Do you know how many human lives are lost each year to elementals escaping from their machines?"

Ephorah shook her head.

Massouh sighed. "Death by fire is considered one of the worst ways to go, in almost every culture known to man. Over a hundred people meet this fate from rampaging elementals each year in our empire alone. Don't just think of all the lives this new spell will save in our borders; think of the people in other countries who won't be burned alive by hate-fueled spirits."

Ephorah grimaced. "But–"

"The eternal boiler is a project we've been trying to solve for two decades. And think of what it will mean for the empire. Do you know the most common reason why nations go to war? It's resources. It's always been resources." The professor leaned back in his chair, relaxing over the promise this project held. "The empire has been importing from countries that could use our dependency against us. It's been projected that a resource war in the near future is inevitable if things don't change. You might very well have given us the secret to prevent such a war for generations." He held up his hands in resignation. "I don't pretend this will stop all war or prevent some other shortage in the future. But maybe someone generations from now will build off your discovery and find a solution then. Can't you relax a bit? The lives we'll save will greatly outweigh any harm we cause."

Glancing at the whip, Ephorah rubbed her forehead to come up with another argument. "Why can't we just use bestia spirits for jobs like this? A pair of fire elementals of the bestia class wouldn't need sigils like this."

"Don't you remember from my class?" The professor looked disappointed. "The power output of a spirit goes up quadratically with each category step, not linearly. Bestia spirits only have a fraction of the power of a humanus spirit. If your gloves had been made with a bestia spirit, or even a pair of spirits, they wouldn't give you half as much strength as they do now. Imagine if every airship needed four or five boilers, how much more weight they'd add to the ships. And it's not as if bestia spirits are tame. They're often wild, and less predictable than their cognizant cousins. Having four of them on the same ship would put the crew at even more risk than they face now."

Ephorah wanted to argue, but the truth was, if Professor Massouh wouldn't budge, she wasn't going to convince anyone else. She certainly wasn't going to get through to Professor Meir or Sayegh.

"I think this is a wonderful development."

A girl with black hair down to her shoulders leaned against a wall of the lab next to the nearest doorway. She must have come in while Ephorah and the professor were talking, because neither of them had heard her come in.

"I'm sorry, who are you?" Professor Massouh asked. "Are you one of my students?"

"No, actually." The girl smiled. She had impossibly smooth skin, and eyes that...were they always green? "I was hoping you might become one of mine."

"Um...I don't think that's how universities work." Professor Massouh cocked an eyebrow.

"Your school...how do I put this?" The girl gave a playful smile. "You don't have a patron god anymore. A discovery like this...that would certainly help your school from collapse, but it only forestalls the problem. You need a goal; something you all value. You need...a central idea."

The girl left the wall and approached the professor. Playfully, she traced the handle of the whip with her fingers, and all the warning bells in Ephorah's mind told her this girl wasn't human. She couldn't prove it, but there was something...off about her.

"Uh...well..." Professor Massouh smiled nervously as the dark-haired girl got close. "What are you...uh...offering?"

"You need a new patron god," the girl replied. "Or perhaps, a goddess. Some of the faculty already follow one, even if they don't know it yet." She traced the stubble on the professor's chin with her finger. "I want you to make it more...official."

"Who are you?" Ephorah interrupted. "I have a funny feeling you're the goddess the faculty already follows."

The girl laughed. "Guilty." She stepped closer to Ephorah. "I could save this school, and I could even help you, if you let me."

Up close, Ephorah got a really good look at this goddess. Her features were flawless; she looked like the perfect ingenue. She wasn't overtly sexy, but had the sort of unkempt beauty that only a handful of women could pull off. And yet, this close to her, Ephorah could smell something on her breath masked by traces of perfume that almost covered it up. Her breath smelled like carrion.

Ephorah coughed and backed away.

The goddess shrugged. "Well, I don't need you to serve me. Not yet, anyway." She looked up at the professor. "But what about you? Are you ready to follow a goddess who will save your school, your job and everything else you care about?" She leaned in closer to him. "Professor Meir and Professor Sayegh are already devout, even if they don't realize it yet."

"Professor Meir, you say?" Massouh stuttered. "And...what exactly are you the goddess of?"

"Technically? Nothing." The girl replied. "My nephew never had authority to give me an assignment. But for you? The only idea you need for me to work wonders in your lives is to believe that you deserve it."

"Deserve what, exactly?" Ephorah asked.

"Everything you want!" The goddess smiled as she stepped closer to Ephorah. "I know you have desires," she whispered in her ear. "Things you don't dare say out loud. About your goals. Your dreams. Your enemies. How many wishes could be granted if you only had the courage to ask?"

Ephorah brushed the girl away from her with her hand, and glared at the goddess's now-blue eyes and ivory face. "I don't trust you."

The goddess gave a soft smile. Then her neck grew longer, like a serpent. It stretched out and surrounded Ephorah like the coils of a snake. The goddess' head, still human, still impossibly beautiful, crept up close to Ephorah at the end of her horribly long neck.

"Smart."

The goddess recoiled her neck and resumed her previous, inconspicuous form. Professor Massouh looked like he hadn't been able to see anything she'd just done, and was instead looking at something in the window of the lab.

"Are those bats? But it's mid-afternoon." He walked up to the window and tapped on the glass. The bats hissed in response, making him jump back.

"Anyways, I'll be around." The goddess slinked away from Ephorah and made her way to the door before turning back to the both of them. "We'll meet again. I promise."

As she left, the bats bolted away from the window, scaring Massouh again.

"That was…a thing." He tried to pretend he wasn't scared.

Ephorah reached into her bookbag and put on her gloves. She was going to start wearing them more often now, she decided.

45

Ancient Tyrant

AMENHOTEP

"So, to clarify," Amenhotep clasped his hands. "One of your spies was seen exiting a runegate hidden in a winery cellar, the workers in the winery noticed this and tried to report it, and you had to respond by immediately killing everyone in the winery and destroying the gate?"

"Yes, my godking," Sekhet tried to remain calm. This wasn't really her failure, but she couldn't afford to give Amenhotep any more ammunition. "I plant within all of my spies a mark of my power, similar to your necrophytes. It lets me see through their eyes, gift them the stillness and stealth of a corpse, and has a sort of...self-destruct. A wave of necrotic energy that will kill the spy and anyone in the immediate vicinity. No witnesses escaped."

"About that..." Amenhotep tilted his head. "You took a...what, a hostage?"

"Someone who entered the building after the self-destruct had already gone off," Sekhet replied. "She saw too much while we were cleaning up, and Arkeon noted that she'd be perfect for Mereshank."

"Hm," Amenhotep paused for a moment. "Very well, but there is still the matter of the lost runegate. I understand that there are other gates in Hadesh, but those routes through the currents of the Duat took centuries to chart. The loss of one is costly. Make sure your spies understand this."

"Yes, my godking," Sekhet backed away from Amenhotep's throne and left, allowing Pausiris to approach next.

"Here is my latest report." Pausiris presented a dossier to his master. "It seems poverty plays some role in the intellect of a population, but only objective poverty. Relative poverty doesn't matter."

"Relative poverty?" Amenhotep skimmed the documents.

"A person's brain development is impacted by things like not getting enough food, or access to clean drinking water," Pausiris explained. "But once they have enough to keep survival needs at bay, more wealth doesn't have much impact. A child who doesn't get enough to eat won't develop their full potential. But if the basics are covered, it doesn't matter if they're at the bottom of society; the existence of rich merchants with their own fleets of airships doesn't make the poor dumb, or make the rich any smarter, any more than stuffing a child with extra food can make them grow taller. They just get wider."

Amenhotep couldn't help but snicker at the thought of overstuffed peasants. "You know, this is the sort of research that your original people would have killed you for. I do hope you still appreciate that."

"I do," the scientist bowed his head. "And at this point, I assume an angry mob of people will form around any discovery. It just takes the right bought of insanity, or politics."

"Let Sekhet handle the politics!" Amenhotep laughed. "She knows tricks that didn't exist in my day."

Outside the liches' administrative center, a man wearing a government jumpsuit put up a new poster on a wall of a grey housing building, using a roller to slather it with glue. When he was done, the wall held a large image of Mereshank, clad only in wraps that covered her chest and loins, arms outstretched with the message: "Suffering is Heroic, Disunity is Strength, Ignorance is Bliss" in an icon of a scroll between her hands.

Next to the poster of the scantily clad Mereshank, another poster was setup displaying an obese, bald man with a crooked nose, bushy grey eyebrows, and an unkempt beard, along with a shirt encrusted with bits of old food. This disgusting-looking ugly man was surrounded by smaller-print complaints about Amenhotep and the Tomb Lords, such as "The liches have stripped your lives of meaning!" "The necrophytes have been given free-reign to assault your daughters!" and "The populace starves while the necrophytes live in luxury!" Below this, in larger, bold lettering, the poster read: "Will you listen to the lies of the Empire?"

"According to Sekhet, the commoners will ignore or cringe at a true statement made by an ugly person, even convincing themselves that it's wrong just because the person saying it is unappealing, but will heartily accept an obvious lie when it comes from a nearly-naked woman." Amenhotep turned away from the window back to Pausiris. "But...you already knew that, didn't you?"

The scientist nodded dejectedly. "It is an insanity beyond words. Whoever said that man is a rational animal was a fool." After a moment, Pausiris looked up at Amenhotep again. "Now that we have the insecorite that Sekhet worked so hard to create, why can't we arm our soldiers with the cursed metal and kill any gods that get in the way of your plans?"

Amenhotep had to remind himself that the scientist's lack of understanding of how gods worked was an asset and not a liability. "Pausiris, it wasn't simply the metal forged from envy that killed Thoth. That was just a physicality; an act to finish the task. What really killed Thoth was the poison Sekhet cultivated in the minds of mortals living in Hadesh, starting with their Institute of Theurgy, and among the Empyrians. While I would argue she simply made use of embitterment already present, the point is that the people of Hadesh and elsewhere throughout their empire have been turned away from reason. As above, so below. The insecorite weapons wouldn't have worked if we harnessed resentment from a far-off nation and then stabbed Thoth with those. Yes, that's probably why he didn't try to flee. He knew his fate was already sealed."

"Hm," Pausiris nodded in understanding. "I see. My other report." Pausiris presented a second dossier. "Arkeon has assisted me with his sorcery to scan the brains of my test subjects. We have detected specific cells in a person's brain that appear to be responsible for empathy. The more you have, the more you can understand other people, their pain, their motivations, their goals – all of it. Everyone is born with a certain amount to start with, and it's possible through upbringing to make a person grow more."

"And?" Amenhotep looked at the scientist expectingly.

"And...there doesn't appear to be any way of getting rid of them," Pausiris admitted. "I can take a baby born with few of these 'empathy cells' and raise them to grow more, and become empathetic, but once the cells are there, they don't go away. Even if you hit them on the head to kill the brain cells, they grow back."

Amenhotep took a long time mulling this over before responding again. "And...you said there was some relation between intellect and empathy?"

"There was, but not what I originally thought," Pausiris flipped through his notes again. "It's easier for smart people to develop more empathy if they weren't born with it, just as it's easier for them to learn anything, but there is no relationship between the number of empathy cells a person is born with and their intelligence."

"...I see." Amenhotep stood from his throne and clasped his hands in front of his belt. "You may go now."

The scientist, wise enough to know that was a command and not a suggestion, grabbed his things, left his research dossiers behind, and quickly exited the throne room.

The High Tomb Lord, now alone, drummed his fingers on the folder containing Pausiris' research on empathy.

"Intelligent people are just more clever animals," he murmured. "But this... this is new."

46

The Research Facility

CYRUS

"Alright crew, this is Cyrus." Captain Nadia gestured to the new boy on the deck of *the Endurance*. "He'll be fixing stuff around the ship for the next week or so. Including us, if we need him to."

"Uh, how is he going to fix us, exactly?" One of the crewmates asked.

"I'm an alchemy student," Cyrus explained. "And while I know enough metallurgy to repair metal objects, my primary focus is medical alchemy."

"Cyrus, the guy who just spoke was Joseph. Next to him is Simon." Nadia pointed to the older man with the spyglass. "The spymaster's name is Tarchus; you won't see too much of him because he'll be up in the crow's nest. And the last of the deckhands is Rostam."

Rostam looked to be the closest to Cyrus's age. In fact, many of the students in the College of Alchemy were Rostam's age.

"So, do we have a job?" Rostam asked.

"We do, and ironically, it comes from the College of Alchemy." Nadia held up a sheet of contract paperwork. "They've asked us to deliver supplies to a research project near Domasa, and to bring back a report on how their project is running. Apparently, they haven't sent word back in over a month, and that's unusual."

Kind of, Cyrus thought. Some scientists have a habit of losing track of time. "So, what supplies are we bringing?"

THE RESEARCH FACILITY

"Mostly just food, water, and other necessities. Most of the equipment and research materials they need are already on site. They just need us to drop off provisions." Nadia pointed to the lower deck. "Most of which are better-tasting than the dried rations we'll be eating. I'd like you to do your thing with some of our utensils in the kitchen below deck."

"Sure thing." Cyrus climbed down to the lower deck of the ship, where a small galley served as the kitchen. A quick look at some of the pots and pans showed they were almost in need of replacing. The metal had tarnished, some of them were permanently stained, and many of them were bent out of shape. Fortunately, none of these things were difficult for an alchemist to fix.

Clapping his hands together, he touched the corroded edge of a cast iron skillet and willed the metal to revert back to its untarnished form. Cracks in the metal sealed together, and the skillet became shiny enough for Cyrus to see a reflection in it. It wasn't his own.

The head of an ibis, which morphed into the face of Thoth, appeared in the polished metal. Cyrus almost dropped the skillet, but turned it over instead. Thoth was dead. He'd seen the Tomb Lords kill him with his own eyes.

"Just need to focus on the...the..." he looked around at other things he could mend and grabbed a wooden spoon that was cracked and stained. "Less reflective things."

An hour later, Cyrus had made most of the cooking utensils good as new. And as a result, he was getting tired. With the last of the cookware restored, Cyrus sat down in a nearby chair and took a break.

"So, how's it going?"

Cyrus looked up at Rostam, who was inspecting the repaired cookware. "You did all this in an hour?"

"Yup," Cyrus yawned. "Burns up my stamina, though. Takes about as much energy to repair metal like that as if I had done it the normal way. It's just faster to do it with alchemy, but now I'm drained."

"Oh," Rostam turned back to Cyrus. "So, when did you decide to become an alchemist?"

"Heh," Cyrus smiled as he remembered his first encounter with Thoth. He had literally bumped into the god's booth at the Career Festival. "I met the god of alchemy in person, and he helped me when I was at my lowest point. I'm from a family of skilled carpenters, and all of my brothers and even some of my sisters inherited my dad's talent for woodwork, but everything I tried to make turned to junk. And it wasn't just a lack of skill; I never had the patience for it, either. Staying focused on a project was tough, and I've recently learned that smart people have trouble with tasks that don't keep our brains occupied."

"Uh-huh." Rostam's smile fell slightly, just enough for Cyrus to notice. "So, what do you think of life on an airship?"

"It seems nice here." Cyrus looked around the ship. "I can see why some people wouldn't like it. Not having a permanent home would bother people. But lately, I definitely don't mind the change of pace. It's good to be able to wander, you know?"

"Hm," Rostam's gaze fell, but he kept his smile. "All of my friends from mandatory school went on to magical colleges. I wonder sometimes what they think of my job."

"Was one of them the girl with the Coptic bob cut?" Cyrus asked.

"Yeah," Rostam's smile widened into a smirk. "That's Namid."

"She's the one who introduced me to your ship. After, well, listening to me fight with my parents and throw a chair out of our house." Cyrus grinned sheepishly.

"What in the Abyss?" Rostam's eyes widened. "Um...you don't do stuff like that on airships, do you?"

"No, no." Cyrus shook his head. "I was mad at my dad, so I threw his handiwork out the window. He...doesn't approve of my choice to go into alchemy, so...we don't get along very well."

"Why would he not approve of..." Rostam paused. "I've never heard of someone working in a skilled trade getting upset at their kid for going into higher education."

"Happens more often than you'd think." Cyrus gave a light smile. "Parents not liking their kids going into different lines of work is pretty common. Some people like it; their son or daughter is going on to a potentially higher-paying line of work, and thus a higher class. But for most people, it's 'this kid isn't like the rest of the family,' and 'now he thinks he's better than us.' That sort of thing."

"Do you think you're better than the rest of your family?" Rostam asked.

Cyrus thought for a moment. "Yes. But not because of alchemy. If I had a kid who struggled for years to find something he was good at, and then discovered a talent for a profession he could make into a career, I would never get upset about it. I'd be proud that he'd found a way to...not be a loser anymore."

"I see." Rostam looked like he was stuck in his thoughts. It was clear to Cyrus what was wrong; Rostam's friends had all gone off to college, and Rostam either suspected they thought they were better than him, or they had told him so.

"Do you like what you do?" Cyrus asked.

"For the most part, I do," the airshipmate nodded. "I get to see the whole empire, and most of the time, I get to see the best parts. Lately, I've run into some of the uglier things, too."

"Yeah." Now it was Cyrus's turn to let his gaze fall. "I got to see some pretty terrible things lately, too. From twisted laws, to crooked justice, and outright horrifying medical experiments."

The two sat in silence for a moment, but they shared an understanding. Words can only say so much.

After a few days, the ship came up to the outskirts of Domasa. Cyrus had repaired as much of the ship's woodwork as he could find, and had also managed to clean some of the ship's ballast pipes, which started to corrode as a result of the saltwater inside.

Domasa was a small hamlet on the outskirts of the empire's furthest possible border with the Tainted Desert. Markers had been placed with many warnings about venturing out into the sands. No one knew why, but the desert had been drowned in so much taint from the Calamity that the entire area was uninhabitable, not just for humans, but everything. Since the taint didn't seem to affect metal objects, especially things made from lead, researchers had tried using long lead poles to place things within the boundaries of the Tainted Desert to determine its effects. Even bacteria couldn't survive in a place like this.

Much more bizarre were the reports of "taint storms," which were apparently cases of hostile weather that rolled across the desert and pelted the ground with glowing green rain. Lightning was said to bear unnatural colors, and rumors of things that wandered the desert in these storms would spread, telling stories of hideous abominations that crawled out at night to drink the poisoned rainwater.

If you could avoid the storms, the Tainted Desert was passable via airship. For some reason, the effects of the taint only traveled so far up, and would not harm you if you were more than eighty kilometers above the ground. Not every airship could fly that high, but merchants with smaller ships swore that somewhere in the desert, there was an entire city hidden in a safe spot where the poison couldn't reach.

What had started as a research station many years ago had grown into the town of Domasa. The neighboring farming community of Herez supplied food, and the discovery of minerals in the hills north of the village brought miners looking for work.

"We won't be stopping in Domasa itself," Captain Nadia pointed to a remote location about five kilometers away from the town. "That's the research facility we're delivering goods to."

Simon, Joseph, and Rostam went inside the lower deck of the ship and, using a system of cranks and levers, dropped a set of landing gear for the airship. The landing gear mostly consisted of a large, fluffy set of cushions that dropped from sections of the ship's hull, spaced out so that they would keep the wooden belly of the vessel from scraping against the dry ground below. Were they to land on sand, the landing gear probably wouldn't be necessary, but the area around the research facility was dry, solid, and a bit rocky in places.

When the ship finally dropped, Cyrus waited for Captain Nadia and Rostam to lower a rope ladder and climb down before joining them.

"You don't actually need to be part of this," Nadia told Cyrus.

"It's an alchemy research station. Probably interesting stuff." Cyrus glanced up at Nadia, who didn't look impressed. "If you'd rather I stay behind—"

"It's no big deal either way, but we won't be here long enough for you to go through their science projects." Nadia gestured for Simon and Joseph to lower a crate of provisions from the ship's hold. They deployed a pair of pulleys to

THE RESEARCH FACILITY

bring the goods down carefully. "Still, I won't make you stay behind."

"You'd be surprised what you can learn in a short meeting." Cyrus pointed at the provisions. "Need another pair of hands?"

"We're fine."

The crew dropped down from the ship and carried the boxes of provisions. The ground was too uneven to bring out a cart, but each box was apparently light enough that Rostam, Simon, and Joseph could grab one each. Tarchus stayed up in the crow's nest, spyglass trained on the Tainted Desert. No doubt, he was watching for taint storms. They were never supposed to travel outside the desert sands, but the spymaster didn't seem like he was ready to count on that.

A final crewmember that Cyrus hadn't even noticed before joined the others on the ground. A living fireball, the size of a man's head, with what appeared to be eyes flickering in the flames, floated along next to Rostam.

"Has...there always been a fireball?" Cyrus pointed to the spirit.

Rostam smiled. "He powers the ship. Good to see you've recovered. Say hello, Cindrocles."

"Hello." The elemental had a voice that sounded a bit like you'd expect from a middle-aged accountant. "Who are you? You're not a wizard are you?"

"Uh..." Cyrus cleared his throat. "Sensing hostility. I am a wizard... student–"

"Are you a theurgist?" The fireball asked.

"No." Cyrus shook his head. "I'm an alchemist."

"Okay." The fireball became less aggressive. "Just as long as you're not a theurgist." He floated away towards the captain, and then turned around and glared at Cyrus again. "And fire is totally an element!"

"It really isn't," Cyrus whispered to Rostam.

"I heard that!" Cindrocles fumed.

The group made their way to the research facility, which apparently was a small brick house in the middle of nowhere. The building was barely any larger than a toolshed; Cyrus had no idea how any projects were supposed to be done inside. Then Captain Nadia knocked on the door, only for it to swing open at her touch, revealing a spiral staircase that descended deep underground.

"Okay..." the captain examined the door frame. "It wasn't even latched. What on Earth?"

"Maybe some scientist got too engrossed in his work," Simon offered.

"That could be it," Cyrus admitted.

"Then we're going down, and finding out what they're up to." Nadia led the descent into the depths below. Cindrocles followed close enough to light the way, while the crewmates followed behind. Cyrus brought up the rear, and instinctively closed the door behind him.

The staircase itself was dimly lit, but at the bottom, gas lamps illuminated a large, hollowed out laboratory. Rather than a dirty, dingy hole in the ground, the floor was made of flat dry wood. Nothing you'd want to walk on with bare feet, but definitely better than uneven earth shoveled aside. In some places, stone tile had been put down, creating an even more level surface for alchemists to do their work. Several cauldrons sat at the ready to be used for holding concoctions. Tables lay setup with research journals, alembics, mortars, Bunsen burners, and several lumps of various rocks that must have been taken from the nearby soil.

The only thing missing from this alchemy lab were the alchemists themselves.

"Where is everyone?" Nadia poked her head down a hall dug into the soil. "Hello? Anybody down there?"

"What's this?" Rostam approached a table with a lab notebook lying open. "Okay..." His voice filled with confusion. "I know what some of these words mean."

"Where the heck would everybody have gone to?" Joseph put down his box of provisions. "Did they run out of supplies and head to the local town for supper?"

"Cyrus, take a look at this journal and see if you can read this jargon." Nadia pointed to the lab notebook Rostam had found. "Maybe it'll give us a clue."

"That might need to be a last resort," Cyrus replied. "Some alchemists can get...persnickety about people reading their lab research. They're all afraid someone's going to steal their work, you know?"

Nadia put her hands on her hips. "How worried are we about some reclusive alchemists getting upset that we read their research notes?"

"How worried are you about these alchemists refusing to pay you over a breach of research confidentiality?" Cyrus countered.

The captain sighed. "Okay, that's a good point. Let's just look around and see if we can find anyone."

Cyrus went up to the table, flipped the notebook closed, and checked the cover for a name. "Dr. Eliot Rosenberg. I have no idea if that was the head researcher, or someone else who just happened to work here, but keep an eye out for any diplomas hung on walls anywhere. Some alchemists lug those sorts of things to hang wherever they find themselves working."

"Um, guys?" Cindrocles made a sound like he was sniffing the air down the direction of a tunnel. "I feel air moving in and out of this tunnel. It's slight, but there's definitely more oxygen going in than coming out."

Making a mental note that the fireball could detect when someone else was using up oxygen, Cyrus walked down the hallway, Rostam and Cindrocles followed close behind.

The tunnel had a few branching points, which didn't go very far, but held various supplies for different projects. "Sulfur." Cyrus noted the ancient alchemical symbol for the spirit hanging above the door of a small closet. Another had the symbol for the body. "Salt. Hey, Rostam? Don't touch anything shiny and liquid."

"Okay," Rostam nodded. "Why not?"

"Because it's probably..." Cyrus spotted a closet with the symbol for the mind. This one had been left open. "Mercury." Checking inside the closet, he noted that several vials of mercury were shattered all over the floor. "What were you guys doing here?"

A wheeze from further down the tunnel interrupted his thoughts.

"Someone's still down here." Rostam pushed ahead of Cyrus and made his way further down the halls. Cindrocles followed, with Cyrus right behind.

They reached a dark room where the gas lamps had gone out. Cyrus wafted the air above a lamp towards his nose, and confirmed that no gas was flowing to these lamps. The lines had been cut. "Strange," he muttered.

"Oh, no." Rostam pointed.

They had found a room filled with kennels. By the looks of them, the kennels had contained dogs, judging by the bits of shed hair and animal bowls. But now, all of them were empty. Except for one.

A single Labrador sat huddled in a corner. It clearly hadn't eaten in a while. Which was odd, because there was plenty of dog food available in several bags nearby.

Rostam poured a bowl of kibble out for the remaining dog and brought it near the last kennel. Placing it in front of the kennel door, he slowly let the animal out so it could get to the food. It lapped the stuff up cheerfully, wagging its tail, and thanking Rostam afterwards with a happy bark.

"Why wouldn't they feed their dog?" Cyrus looked around at the other kennels. Clearly, there had been more animals here until recently. Then, in the light cast by Cindrocles, Cyrus noticed a large, thick metal door with a warning label on it. "Hey, where do you suppose we are?"

"...In an alchemy lab," Rostam replied. "Obviously."

"Well, yeah, but I mean..." Cyrus looked up. "I got turned around when we came down here and went through all of those tunnels, but I wonder if we're right under the edge of the Tainted Desert. If we haven't crossed under it already. This door looks like it's made of the kinds of metals that would keep the taint out. So, I'm thinking..."

"You think this place was testing the effects of the taint, and how far down into the soil it could travel." Rostam looked at the other kennels. "Poor dogs."

"It's a messy business, but testing on animals to protect human life is pretty normal for scientists." Cyrus pet the Labrador. "It isn't fun, but most of the medical breakthroughs we make wouldn't be possible without testing on something. Using them on people would be far worse than testing them on animals."

"Yeah," Rostam stroked the dog's ears. "Still a shame, though."

"So, if this guy was sitting here alone for a while, then my guess is..." Cyrus looked around the room for any evidence that might prove him wrong. "The researchers are dead."

"That doesn't sound right." Cindrocles seemed to be sniffing the air again. "I don't smell dead humans."

THE RESEARCH FACILITY

"You can smell dead humans?" Cyrus blinked. "Can you smell live humans?"

"Yes, but...right now, there's two in this very room. I can't distinguish between the different humans, just how stinky they are from being dead for a while."

"Right..." Cyrus looked to Rostam. "How good are you with animals?"

"Eh...I can manage. Maybe. Why?"

Cyrus patted the dog's head. "Because this guy might be able to find some of the research crew. If you know how to get him to lead us, because I don't."

Rostam bent down and rubbed the sides of the dog's head. "Hey, buddy. Can you help us find one of your masters?"

The dog made a grumbling noise, but then scampered down the tunnel back the way they had come.

"I hope that's what he's doing," Rostam whispered. "Let's follow him."

The three made their way back to the main cavern of the underground lab. Nadia, Simon, and Joseph were still there.

"Follow that dog!" Rostam pointed at the Labrador.

As the others pursued the dog, Cyrus stopped at the research journal and flipped it open, too curious to ignore now. "Unattended lab animals, no signs of life. I think now qualifies as a last resort."

Dr. Rosenberg's journal began with details of preparing for leaving Hadesh, on June 23rd.

"*Departing from the college today. Odd assortment of crew. The college didn't recommend anyone, so we took volunteers. I don't think the college is giving the program much thought. They either don't believe this project is worth investigating, or they have a lot of faith in my abilities. I choose to believe the latter. By some twist of fate, I find myself reunited with Kaniel Wadermann. I haven't seen him since we were in mandatory school, back when we lived in Petryan. How he's changed...*

Still, it is nice to see a familiar face amongst all these strangers."

From July 1st:

"*We've managed to get the lab setup faster than I'd thought. The locals must have found a crew willing to dig out these tunnels. The only place that still needs digging is the area that will stretch under the Tainted Desert. Not surprising. They* wouldn't have the proper equipment for that, and by proper equipment, I mean the golems we brought with us. They seem to be immune to the effects of the taint, and if not, they're expendable.

Sad to hear how things have turned out for Kaniel. He was never a top-marks student in school, but he wasn't dumb. Yet he's wound up as a golem operator. Not a bad job, but not the one he wanted. I am surprised he went into theurgy at all. I remember him bragging in mandatory school how he would become the greatest sorcerer ever, but I guess his weight made that impossible."

From July 12th:

"The golems have finally finished digging their tunnel and have erected two thick doors of lead to prevent any possible contamination from affecting the research team. It seems that the golems have picked up trace amounts of taint but show no signs of damage. It seems our original suspicions that the golems were immune, and that the taint could seep down into the earth, were correct.

The golems shouldn't have taken this long. Kaniel has been a dick uncooperative. He spends most of his time grumbling about the tunnels, the work, being underground, everything. He's been complaining a lot about having grown up in some sort of slums, in some sort of one-room hovel, and that this is why his life has turned out so poorly. Has he forgotten that we used to have sleepovers at his home? How we would tell each other scary stories in his bedroom, on the second floor of his house? I don't argue with him; I'm afraid that'll make things worse. But I'm worried that bringing him along was a mistake."

"Strange," Cyrus thought aloud. "This says that there were golems at work here. We haven't seen a single one. Or any elementals, for that matter."

Cyrus looked up from the journal and realized that he was now standing alone in the chamber. The others must have followed the dog.

"I have no idea which way they went." Cyrus turned back to the notebook. "Might as well stay put, so I don't get lost."

47

Courage of a Hundred Men

AMRI

Stumbling out of bed, Amri cleaned himself up and took a shower. He needed to go back to the police and report his sister as missing, and then make sure the cannister he'd been working on at the industrial park had set and was ready to show the alchemists. The abbey volunteers had finished cleaning up the mess made by the dracolich, so they wouldn't need his help today.

Amri ran his plans by his aunt and uncle before grabbing a bagel for breakfast. His aunt thanked him for stopping by the police station while his uncle said nothing.

Hopping on the first autobus with his dry bagel in hand, Amri ate quickly and prepared himself for what he would say to the Ironwood receptionist. He was aware how awkward it would be for him to come in with a missing person report after being dismissed the day before with a child abuse complaint.

When he entered Ironwood Company's headquarters again, a different clerk was sitting behind the desk. This one looked up at him and smiled politely, as if people came into the policing company's headquarters with good news this early in the morning.

"I'd like to report a missing person," Amri stated. "Do you have a sketch artist on hand?"

The clerk called a man over who took Amri's description of his sister and made a fairly accurate drawing of Namid after a few tries. It was surprisingly simple to finish the missing person's report, and within an hour after entering the headquarters Amri was ready to head to his next stop.

Without any volunteer workers to join that morning, Amri had some time before he needed to be at the industrial park. From the Mercenary Guild's Circle, he walked to the Imperial Palace district and stopped by the courthouse.

Inside, Amri looked around for the court library. Hadesh was renowned for its universities of engineering, architecture, and wizardry, but there were no law schools in the city; most lawyers studied in either Baltithar or Dumiabet. That meant the only legal library that Amri could browse was the one in the imperial courthouse itself. Hopefully, someone there would be able to show him where to find what he was looking for.

At the courthouse, there was a library containing law books on every subject in the empire lining a sea of bookshelves. This library was said to only contain the basics, with a larger collection kept inside the palace that wasn't available to the public. Even still, Amri had no idea how to search through these books for what he needed, so he went up to the front desk and looked for a clerk.

Behind the desk stood a girl slightly older than Amri with straight blonde hair – common enough for Borealans – staring down at a magazine propped open on the front desk. The first thing Amri noticed about her was that her nose and entire face were aimed down at her magazine so that she couldn't possibly see him approaching. The second thing he noticed was the utterly massive chest she sported underneath her face, as if her downturned nose were pointing at the windowful of cleavage in her outfit. A shiny brass pin that read "Theurgy Grad" drew the eye to the window even more.

Amri tried not to stare – and not to think about what went through this girl's head when she prepared for her job in the mornings – and tapped on the desk. "Hello? Miss?"

"Hm?" She looked up from her magazine, revealing a shapely face with full lips and brown eyes. Sadly, said eyes showed no signs of intelligent life.

"I need help finding something." Amri turned his words carefully over in his mind. "I'm looking for the laws about child abuse."

"Um...oh," the girl responded as though she were not expecting to actually have to do her job today. "Uh...hold on...let me see."

She flipped through an old ledger and pulled out some sheet that must have listed where books in this library were kept. At one point, she stopped, turned the sheet upside down, and began reading again, nodding as if the words made more sense this way.

"Okay, right this way." She guided Amri to a bookshelf and pointed to one row. "Here's what we've got. If you need anything else, let me know."

Before Amri could ask if she had any recommendations on which book to start with, the girl had already walked away. He glanced at the library desk, and sure enough, she was back to reading her magazine.

Ignoring the library ditz, Amri examined the legal tomes that had been placed along the shelf and picked one titled "Child Protection Laws."

"Alright," Amri muttered to himself. "Let's find out if Malbim is actually breaking any laws."

Amri found a table and sat down with the book, pouring through the table of contents. There were all sorts of details regarding physical abuse, starting with signs regarding bruises, burns, and other types of wounds that were usually hidden out of sight. Recommendations on how to find these wounds without upsetting the child were also disclosed, as well as details on how and when the authorities were to get involved. However, there was nothing in the research about physical abuse regarding medical treatment, so Amri turned to another book.

The second tome detailed psychological abuse. This one was more helpful, as it detailed forms of abuse that Amri hadn't considered. One chapter said that controlling a person to an unhealthy extent was listed, although it was difficult to identify in children, as parents were expected to control their kids. In fact, one page discussed how most controlling or manipulative abuse was built around treating the victim like they were a child. There were limits to this, but they were almost impossible to distinguish between normal parenting behavior. The primary purpose of the chapter was to identify abuse in elders and in relationships.

Another type of mental abuse that caught Amri's eye was shaming. Again, this was aimed more towards elder and relationship abuse, and wasn't particularly useful in identifying abuse in children. That said, the techniques that could result in an elderly person being taken out of another person's care by law could in theory apply to a child if they were extreme enough.

Even with this new information, Amri wasn't finding what he was looking for. What he really needed were laws about abuse around medical treatment, but there didn't seem to be any kinds of laws about such a thing. If anything, it was like the government hadn't gotten around to the subject or even defined it.

Amri was about to go back to the girl at the desk to ask for more help, but as he stood up and looked over at her, he realized from across the library that her shirt had popped unbuttoned, her bra was completely visible, her chest was hanging partially out of her clothes, and she somehow hadn't noticed any of this while filing her nails. Amri was not prepared for the awkwardness of that conversation and decided to try his luck finding books on his own.

Looking through the bookshelves, Amri found a shelf dedicated to medical law. He grabbed a book about ethical practices and took it back to the table.

Most of the contents detailed issues Amri didn't understand. There were chapters about reasonable fees for charging customers, ethical practices for various procedures, but Amri wasn't certain enough about the nature of Doctor Malbim's treatments on Izaac to know which chapter to start with.

Then he noticed a chapter regarding conflict of interests. Flipping through it, one passage caught Amri's eye:

Doctors are not normally supposed to accept immediate family members as clients. Some doctors have been able to successfully challenge this law in cases of extreme poverty, but due to the fact that most doctors have sufficient means, they are not allowed to diagnose, treat, or medicate their own spouse, children, or parents.

"Well, well." Amri smiled. "So, she is breaking the law, even if it's only a technicality."

The book contained an explanation of the law stating that there were issues of conflict of interest when medical professionals work on their family members as clients, and might refuse to acknowledge a problem or misdiagnose a patient based on their personal attachment to the client. As he read, Amri realized that this law wasn't just a technicality; Doctor Malbim was violating the law for the very reason the law was put in place.

Amri brought the book up to the front desk and was about to ask the clerk if he could borrow the book from the library when he noticed the stain on the clerk's shirt. She had thankfully realized her shirt was undone and fixed her attire since he'd last seen her, but then she'd gotten a glass of water, managed to dunk both of her breasts into it, dripped water all over several law books on the desk, and her wet shirt made the outline of her chest even more visible than before. She didn't seem to notice any of this and was now leaning back in a chair with one foot propped up on the desk next to a stack of books.

"You know what?" Amri muttered to himself. "I don't need to borrow this. I know all the legal stuff I need now."

Leaving the book on the table, Amri walked out of the courthouse and headed for the industrial park, hoping that judges and lawyers at the courthouse never needed help finding things in that library. It wouldn't be long now before the folks working with the gas would want to see the new cannister.

The fact that Namid was missing was still weighing on Amri's mind. Of course, she probably just stayed at a friend's house without telling their aunt and uncle beforehand, but it still bothered him. Nevertheless, he'd made the police report; that was all he could do for now.

In the center of the park, Amri took a moment to examine the tree in the middle of the courtyard. In this part of the facility, it was easy to forget what the park was for; the tree was so large and sat surrounded by tables where researchers and engineers took their lunch breaks. It ran all the way up above the roof of the facility yet had been given so much space that none of the branches touched the walls of the offices and laboratories.

Amri snapped himself out of focusing on the out-of-place nature and made his way up to the glassworkshop. The finished cannister had dried, and was ready to be brought down to the gas cannister lab.

As he was about to retrieve the cannister, Amri heard a crash in a nearby lab. Sighing, he mentally told himself to ignore it. He knew which room it was, and he could tell from the sound that someone small was thrashing around and had knocked over a glass object; probably something like a beaker, or other pharmaceutical equipment.

"You have to ignore it," he whispered. "Wait until later, then report her for breaking the law regarding medical practice on her own kid."

A thought wormed into Amri's head that the industrial park authorities, like the police clerk at Ironwood company, might not actually take any action against the doctor. Ironwood company ignored the abuse of a child, but park authorities weren't like a policing company, were they? Surely, they wouldn't ignore someone blatantly violating the law, right?

More sounds of a struggle came from inside the pharmacy lab. Izaac could be heard squeaking as he tried to get away from his mother.

"It's illegal to get involved," Amri told himself. "I can't just but my nose in where it doesn't belong. I have to let the law run its course. I just need to tell someone she's breaking the law–"

And then what?

The question popped into Amri's head so fast he wasn't even sure if it even was his idea.

What happens after you tell the authorities? Does she go to jail? Does she stand for trial? Will she argue that, as a single mother, she is too poor to hire a pediatrician for Izaac? It doesn't matter if it isn't true; if the jury believes her, or the judge takes pity on a 'poor single mother,' does any of this really matter? What's the point in notifying the authorities?

"To save that kid," Amri argued against the voice in his own head. "To do the right thing."

Why can't you do the right thing now? The voice countered. *Because it's illegal to grab Izaac and get him far away from that woman? If it's illegal to do the right thing, why are you trusting in the law to settle this?*

Amri paused and checked the pharmacy lab door. It was cracked open this time, stuck only on the doorknob latch that hadn't closed properly. Amri quietly slid the door open and peeked inside.

The pharmacy lab was divided into two sections; one side contained a sink, ceramic counters and shelves, and a series of cabinets with glass panes revealing the chemicals stored inside. Other tools were on display, and Amri noticed a small scalpel on a tool rack on one wall. The other side of the lab featured a pair of tables, another sink, and chairs where patients would sit while being treated. A sliding window overlooked a fire escape in case of emergencies.

Doctor Malbim had tied Izaac's arm to a metal yardstick, presumably to keep him from moving it away. She had bound his legs to the feet of a metal folding chair in the patient section, and his torso to the back of the seat. She looked somewhat exasperated but was now getting out several jars of chemicals. One jar had been shattered on the floor near where Izaac was sitting.

"This, right here," Malbim huffed as she prepared a syringe. "Is why I'm doing this. All these tantrums, all of these little fits of yours. The point of this medicine is to make you behave." She filled the needles with a measurement of chemicals and held it up to the light of a nearby window to check that she had the right dosage. "Now hold still, so I can fix you."

"What to do, what to do..." Amri hadn't been seen yet. Malbim was focused on the dosage in her syringe, and Izaac was looking away from the lab door. Amri was torn between knowing he wasn't allowed to be here and not wanting to leave. If he tried to stop the doctor now, he'd probably be committing one or two misdemeanors, but more than that, he'd be breaking the trust of everyone he'd worked with since weaseling his way into the industrial park and putting this cannister project together. But now that he'd seen what the doctor was really up to, he couldn't just walk away.

Stepping into the laboratory proper, he went up to a countertop in one corner of the room behind the doctor and dropped his bookbag loudly on the ground. The doctor turned and her narrow eyes zeroed in on Amri, but then tried to hide the syringe behind her back.

"Another day, another...wait a second," Amri looked around, pretending to be confused. "This isn't the right lab." He turned to look at Doctor Malbim as if just now noticing her. "Oh, hello again! I'm sorry, I didn't interrupt anything, did I?"

The doctor tried to conceal her rage and play along with Amri, probably hoping he'd just go away. "Not much. Just private matters that you really shouldn't be a part of." She managed something of an angry-looking smile to try and sell this, and if the situation wasn't so unnerving, it would have been funny.

"Ah right, privacy and all that." Amri nodded as he picked his bookbag back up and slung it over his shoulder. "Say, you're not your own son's pediatrician, are you?"

Malbim opened her mouth but paused, stepping towards Amri before speaking. "I might be. Now, why would you ask?"

Amri squinted, as if remembering some esoteric rule he'd heard of a long time ago but wasn't really sure about. "Isn't there some law or ethics thing that says you can't practice on your own family? Something about a conflict of interest?"

The doctor took another step towards him. "Interesting. I'll have to double check that. Can I ask which lab you thought this was?"

"The…uh…glass…chemical lab." Amri started walking towards the door. "I heard broken glass and came in here by mistake to clean it up."

Doctor Malbim nodded, but her eyes told Amri she wasn't buying it. "Right."

Amri barely knew anything about alchemy, but he knew alchemists touched their hands together to cast spells. As Doctor Malbim set the syringe on a counter and clasped her palms in front of her chest, Amri knew what it meant, even if she was trying to pretend she wasn't about to get violent.

Before she could get take another step, Amri conjured a blast of air in her face to throw her off her guard and tried to bolt for the door. In response, Malbim touched the ground with her finger. The floor disassembled itself at her touch and reformed, enveloping the bottom of the door with tile, making it impossible to open.

Amri responded by snapping his fingers and aiming his magic at a number of chemicals he spotted in a glass cabinet behind the doctor. Unsure what he'd actually set on fire, several chemicals in glass beakers started to burn, boil, evaporate, and expand into the cabinet.

Doctor Malbim had just enough time to dive to the ground while Amri snatched the scalpel from the tool rack mounted on a wall and ran over to Izaac.

The cabinet exploded, sending smoke and hot chemicals everywhere, and soon the heat set off a chain reaction with similar chemicals around the lab.

Doctor Malbim couldn't possibly know what each of these things did when heated, and stayed low to the ground with her hands covering the back of her neck while beakers continued to shatter and burst.

Amri cut the cords binding Izaac and pulled him towards the window. Sliding it open, he guided Izaac towards the fire escape and started climbing onto it himself, but he caught a glimpse of a furious pharmacist glaring back at him.

"Izaac," Amri panted. "I need to know: do you want me to get you away from her? Your mom...what she's doing to you is illegal."

"There's nowhere I can run where she won't find me." Izaac's face was filled with fear. "She'll hurt you worse now."

"I know a guy who works on an airship," Amri found a ladder on the fire escape and pulled a latch to release it. The ladder dropped down to the ground below as he pulled Izaac away from the window. "I can get you far away."

Before Izaac could answer, the entire fire escape rattled beneath them. Rust and corrosion crawled along the metal bars and the entire structure creaked. Parts of the railing fell off entirely, and Amri looked back at the window and saw Doctor Malbim's hand grasping the fire escape; the corrosion radiating from her finger. She was too tall and too curvy to easily slip through such a small window, but she wasn't letting them get away so easily.

The rusty fire escape bucked and swayed. Amri grabbed Izaac and jumped off of the collapsing structure to an adjacent fire escape that was close enough to step over to, but wasn't physically touching the rusty, corroding metals. Amri looked through the window of the room attached to this walkway and realized he was right outside of the glassworkshop.

Inside the workshop, a confused looking Avroham peered out the window at Amri, who waved and gestured for the glassworker to open the window.

"What on earth are you doing with Doctor Malbim's kid?" Avroham slid open the window and let the two inside.

"She's gone nuts," Amri panted. "I caught her in the act of something illegal, and now she's out for blood."

As he spoke, one wall's plaster started to rapidly age and flake off. Mortar turned wet and lost its ability to keep bricks from being knocked out of place. In seconds, an angry alchemist forced her way through what was left of the crumbling wall.

Amri had to think fast. "She tried to attack me with alchemy." He pointed out the window at the fire escape. "And then she tried to kill us both by making the fire escape rust."

"That wouldn't have killed you," the pharmacist smiled and stepped closer. "It would have only taught you a lesson."

"Uh..." Avroham's eyes widened as he looked at the doctor. "Did you actually corrode the escape while they were on it? That's...that might be taking it too far."

"It's nothing you need to worry about." Doctor Malbim kept her smile up as she approached Avroham, who instinctively stepped between her and Amri to defuse whatever situation was going on.

Amri had a sense of where this was going and looked around the room for options, but before he could act Malbim touched her hands together and put her finger to Avroham's nose.

Where Avroham had been standing, a red burst of blood and viscera now rested upon two legs, which slumped to the floor. Everything from Avroham's waste up had been ripped apart; his legs, completely unaffected, lay lifeless at the alchemist's feet.

"How..." Amri froze. "Alchemy...it's not supposed to be that fast!"

"Destroying without creating," Izaac whimpered. "She told me it was reckless, harder to control, but faster. You don't have to think or tell stuff what to do once it's broken."

The pharmacist turned to her son and Amri, her labcoat, shoes, and even the bottom of her face covered in blood. But she managed another simple smile again, and spoke as if nothing was wrong. "Izaac, do you see this? This man is dead because of you and your friend. Do you really think you should be playing games with him?" She pointed to Amri.

Izaac pulled away from Amri, but he didn't let go of his hand. "No."

"Right." Malbim extended her bloody hand to Izaac. "So, what do you think you should do?"

Amri felt the boy's hand pull against his. It was obvious he wanted to go with her. Then all of this would be over, and the pharmacist would stop, or so

Izaac probably thought. But Amri knew better.

"Y-you are truly as awful as they come." Amri gripped Izaac's hand tighter.

"Oh, now that's not a nice thing to say," Malbim tilted her head. "You should apologize."

"No, you are truly pathetic! You blame your son, your *five-year-old son*, for your decision to murder a man in cold blood! All because he knew too much about what you tried to do to Izaac and me. Because he and I both knew that what you're doing to your own flesh and blood isn't just illegal, it's outright evil! And you smiled, you bitch! You smiled while you gruesomely murdered an innocent man in front of your own son and blamed him for it!"

"You and him both knew not to get involved in my business," Malbim replied.

"All of this comes down to *your* decisions, *your* actions! Izaac never chose to have you as a mother, but you choose to have him! Every blame you lay on him is your doing!"

The pharmacist paused, her smile finally fading. She knelt down next to Avroham's legs, looked at the bloody mess for a moment, placing her hands together on the dead man's shin. Then she gave Amri a somber look.

"I bet you thought that would really hurt me."

She touched the ground, and tile of the floor tore itself apart and reformed, creating spikes that shot up from under Amri and pierced the backs of his shins from an angle. Izaac was unharmed, but Amri was in so much pain that he would have fallen to his knees if the spikes weren't holding him in place.

"But it didn't." The pharmacist rose to her feet and approached Amri. "You should never have stuck your nose where it doesn't belong."

"Wait!" Izaac grabbed his mother's hand. "If I come with you, will you let him go? Will you promise not to hurt him if I be good?"

"He's seen too much, sweetie." Malbim smiled down at her son. "If I let him live, I'll lose you forever."

Amri struggled to break his legs free, but even if he ignored the pain, it was a slow process. The spikes weren't smooth cuts; they were jagged, with chunks of tile floor lodged into his flesh. He didn't have time to break loose or escape. He had to try something else.

"You're a sorcerer, right?" Malbim clapped her hands together. "You could kill if you wanted to, but you don't have it in you. But for me? All it takes is a touch."

As the alchemist brought her hand closer to his face, Amri instinctively leaned backwards. Before she could get closer, he raised his own palm to his chest and willed the air in front of him to ignite.

It wasn't enough to burn her; he'd learned that in sorcery class with Professor Datz. But he hoped that the flames that erupted from his hand would be enough to buy him some more time.

As soon as the fire made contact with Malbim's palm, she withdrew her hand in horror, but sparks erupted from her own fingers. Her own alchemy reacted to the flames unpredictably, and her entire arm turned black as her hand ripped itself apart. Layers of skin, muscle, and sinew peeled away and became ash as her alchemy backfired. The reaction made its way up her arm to her elbow, only stopping at the joint. But what was left of her forearm was little more than blackened bones with some burnt flesh in between them.

Malbim screamed and clutched her hand. It was more a cry of horror than pain. Amri vaguely remembered hearing that you can't feel pain if you haven't any nerve endings, and hers were definitely gone.

"How the hell?" Amri wrenched one of his legs free. "That was just a simple fire spell. That shouldn't—"

"Destroy without creating," Izaac whispered, stepping back away from his mother. "You're not supposed to do it for a reason."

The alchemist gestured to her destroyed arm. "Look what you've done to me, you bastard!" She placed her left hand on her destroyed right hand and made a new circuit of alchemical energy. She was about to try and kill Amri again, probably being more careful of his arms this time, but with one leg free, Amri was able to twist the leg still pierced and, with great pain, dodge her attack and trip her over his stuck leg, grabbing her from behind with his arms and hurling her over his pierced leg.

Malbim went tumbling onto the mangled floor she'd rearranged earlier. None of the jagged edges were able to really hurt her, but her face and good hand were scraped. Instead of having another alchemy backfire, once she touched the floor, the tile became dust that quickly started filling the room. The effect expanded through the tile until Amri found himself trapped in a cloud that was too thick to see through. Outside, a bolt of lightning struck nearby, so close it almost knocked Amri off his feet.

She'll probably attack me from behind. Amri thought as he slipped to his side. *But this is still the glassworkshop.* He tried to think of anything in the room that could help him against the alchemist. He knew his way around the room; she didn't. Maybe he could use that.

Amri held his breath as the chalky dust filled his lungs. His legs were still bleeding, but adrenaline shut off the pain as he wrenched his other leg free and tried to think.

All she needs to do is touch me once, and I can't see her. he looked towards the wall where the workshop window should be behind all the dust. Somehow, despite the haze, Amri could make out some sort of flames outside. Had the lightning struck the tree in the center of the park? It didn't matter. If he wanted to live, he needed to clear the air.

Focusing the air in the room into two points, Amri forced as much of the air as possible towards the workshop window, blasting through the glass in a torrent of chalk-filled wind. When the dust cleared, an angry alchemist was standing barely a meter away from him, her one remaining good arm nearest Amri.

Malbim clapped her hands and tried to touch Amri immediately, but he had enough time to slip behind her arm and grab her wrist and shoulder. In a fit of adrenaline-fueled strength, he twisted her arm and forced her down to the ground, holding her wrist away from his hand like a poisonous stinger.

Malbim continued to struggle against Amri. He tried to keep her pinned, but she had more than a few extra kilograms on him. Even with just her legs, she would throw him off soon.

The image of a poisonous stinger flickered in Amri's mind, with instant death waiting for him if her hand managed to touch any part of his body. The doctor's arm was the stinger tail. If he couldn't keep the scorpion pinned, then the only way to avoid being stung was...

Just as Malbim bucked against Amri enough to slide her legs under her stomach and force him off her shoulder, Amri twisted her left arm straight, elbow facing up. Taking his right knee from her shoulder, he brought his foot down and stomped on her arm.

The sound. It was like two sections of a damp tree branch joined at a knot breaking, but not fully severed. A fairly normal sound one might hear when walking through a forest and stepping on a large twig.

It was also the sound of a person's arm being broken at the elbow.

The doctor screamed, this time in a blood-curdling cry of pain as her left arm hung limp from the elbow up. She tried moving it, and her upper arm still worked, but the rest hung with a jagged piece of bone visibly shifting against the flesh at the joint. She cried out again, and rolled over onto her back, trying to bring her arms together to cast another alchemical spell, but with both arms wrecked, she couldn't make a circuit.

"AAHH!" Malbim screamed again, trying to move her broken left arm. She turned to her right arm, as if hoping the flesh had grown back since the last time she'd checked. In her desperation, the shock and blood loss must have caught up to her. Amri felt the adrenaline run out in his own body as exhaustion and pain took hold of him. He barely saw Malbim slump to the ground before passing out himself.

Drifting in the endless void, Amri floated on his back until his head bumped into something. He looked up in the sunless, dark sky and saw Marduk standing over him.

"Why have you done this?" The god's normal frowning expression was gone. All that was left was a look of sheer bewilderment. "What did you think would come of it?"

"What have I done?" Amri stirred groggily. "What are you talking about?"

"You could have ended up dead, or in prison for interfering with Talma and her son." Marduk waved his hand and shifted the clouds in the void apart. "Were it not for my involvement, no one would be coming right now to retrieve you, the boy, or the pharmacist while the evidence of her crimes is still fresh."

In the clouds, an image formed of the tree in the middle of the industrial park. A bolt of lightning, which Amri had heard before and now realized came from Marduk, struck the tree and set it on fire. People throughout the industrial park scattered to get out of their offices and workshops as someone called for the fire department.

"Even now, the police and medics are coming up to the room where your body and hers are lying on the floor," Marduk explained. "They will find Avroham's corpse, they will know that only an alchemist like her could have killed him, and his blood is literally on her hands. The police will have no choice but to let you go and arrest her for her actions today."

"Oh." Amri's voice had somehow dried up even in his dreams. "Thank you–"

"Otherwise, you would have gone to jail for this!" Marduk grabbed Amri by the scruff of his neck and hoisted him up to his eye level. "What were you thinking? Your life, your freedom, your career; why risk it all for this boy? You had nothing to gain and everything to lose!"

Amri paused, and somehow, the answer finally clicked in his brain. "When I was a kid, no matter how bad things got between me and my mom, I always had my dad. Izaac...he has no one."

Marduk's jaw hung open as he set Amri down and gazed off in the distance. Amri had never seen anyone, mortal or god, so taken aback before. He wasn't sure how to break the tension.

"You..." Marduk finally whispered. "You have the courage of a hundred men."

Amri tried to understand what Marduk meant, but he felt a pair of hands he couldn't see grasping his torso, under his shoulders. Another pair grabbed hold of his legs.

"Find me, in the waking world," Marduk finally said as Amri drifted away. "In the abbey where your priest friend works."

A bright light hung above Amri as he opened his eyes. He kept them closed, and the warmth told him it was the sun.

"Hey, you're waking up." A woman's voice waved a hand in front of his face. "How many fingers do you see?"

"Uh..." Amri's cracked his eyes open, but his vision was still blurry. "Six?"

"Okay, you just rest now." The woman stood behind Amri, who realized he was lying down, and started rolling him away. He must have been on a stretcher, or something similar. "You're going to be fine, you've just lost some blood. And you have holes in your legs. Filled with floor tile pieces."

Amri tried to lie down and rest, but a roar of an all-too-familiar voice woke him up. He bolted upright to face the source of Malbim's voice, but once he saw her, he started to relax.

Doctor Malbim had been strapped with thick leather restraints to a stretcher of her own and was being rolled into a medical wagon to take her to a hospital. A pair of police standing nearby indicated that she wouldn't be going free when she got out.

"Let me go!" She squirmed against her restraints. "Where is my son? Don't leave mommy alone! Let me—"

A nurse shoved her into the medical wagon and shut the door behind, where her screams became muffled noises. The nurse latched the door and gave a signal to the driver to take off, hauling her away to the hospital.

"Since you're conscious," the nurse beside Amri handed him a clipboard. "Do you have a preference as to which hospital we take you to?"

Amri looked over the clipboard, listing the names of several medical centers. One name stood out among the others.

"Can you take me to the Abbey of Truth?"

48

Mereshank's Palace

NAMID

A bump shook Namid awake. She could feel herself in some kind of moving vehicle, riding on a very rickety road. She wracked her brain to remember where she'd been when she fell asleep, and how many roads in Hadesh were this poorly maintained. Then she recalled the Tomb Lords dragging her through a runegate. She wasn't in Hadesh anymore.

Light from above came through a pair of opposing windows with bars. She was in some sort of carriage, being hauled by something that seemed to be rattling as it walked. Images of skeletal horses came to mind as she pulled herself up to the barred windows. She needed to get a look at her surroundings.

The sky was filled with various kinds of smoke. Some came from steam released from various boilers, others were smog billowing out of a few factories in the area. Although it was clearly daytime, the sky was so clouded that you couldn't really see the sun. Namid had heard rumors that the undead hate sunlight, even if they aren't directly harmed by it. Maybe this smokescreen was deliberate.

There were people shambling about in the streets as well. Each one looked like they were halfway starved. Namid clenched her teeth as the carriage bounced again. A look down at the road showed that it was made of bricks, but there were a lot of pieces missing, and it almost looked as if someone had gone through and stolen bricks here and there from the road.

Filth dotted the streets, both in the road proper, and on the sidewalks. Namid at first wondered why there were no vermin picking through trash to eat, until she saw a man trying to roast a rat raw over a trashcan fire. Even the vermin weren't safe here.

The buildings all looked identical, like they had literally been measured out by the same architect and deliberately made to be the same grey and brown concrete structures. There were windows in the same place on each wall at the same height and location. There was no architectural aesthetics; the buildings were simple, flat, concrete slabs stuck together in the ugliest ways possible. There was no art at all.

There were, however, posters glued to the walls of buildings. One showed an image of A royal looking woman wearing only enough clothing to cover her private areas raising her arm to the sun, with words below that read "Venerate the Morning and Evening Star. Honor to the Godking!"

Another depicted a fat man having tied up a child on a plate and holding a knife like he was about to cut him up for dinner, but the fat man timidly looked over his shoulder at a golden mask lined with black onyx and bright glowing eyes. This poster read "Kemet needs its future workforce! Eating your children is high treason!"

Namid bit her tongue hard as the carriage hit another hole in the road before finally coming to a stop. The sound of boots landing on the ground and keys rattling told her they'd arrived.

Okay, Namid thought to herself. *I haven't been handcuffed. If what I heard from the liches earlier is right, then maybe they're trying to avoid damaging my body. I don't think they know I'm a sorcerer yet. That could be my ace in the hole.*

A door to the carriage opened on the right side, revealing a line of a half dozen zombies standing in perfect attention. One could almost mistake them for normal soldiers in a line, but for the fact that some of them were missing pieces of flesh or attracting flies. A woman in a closely-groomed haircut and military uniform stepped out in front of her.

"It is time," the woman said. "Move."

Now's my chance, Namid thought. *I'll blast this woman across the street once her back is turned and make a break for it. I can handle a few zombies with a whirlwind.*

Then Namid stepped out of the carriage, and realized there were more than a few zombies waiting for her. An entire showing of guards armed with guns stood along a black stone fence with steel bars that encompassed a massive moat filled not with water but undead hounds that barked hungrily for someone to fall in, all of which surrounded a palace made of black marble. Black was supposed to be the color of order to the ancient Egyptians, as opposed to red, but even with that context, under the smog-filled sky, this place couldn't look more like an evil lich's castle if they tried.

But beyond the bastion, the fence, and the moat, the thing that got Namid's attention was the steel gate that closed behind the carriage, locking her and everyone else inside another wall outside the other defenses. Even if she tried to fight her way through these guards and walking corpses, even if she avoided the other defenses, she would still be locked inside the outer wall, and more guards would surely come to restrain her. There was no way she could fight her way out of this.

The woman in the military uniform shoved the barrel of a gun against her back. "Move!"

Namid started walking towards the castle, instinctively putting her hands up. A mechanical drawbridge of some sort of dark metal extended from the base of the castle to make a path over the moat of hungry undead animals.

"Got good shoes on?" The woman snickered.

"Uh...they're...they're nothing fancy," Namid replied.

"Got any holes in them?" The military woman asked.

"No."

"Good." She poked Namid with the barrel of her gun again. "Walk. Don't touch the bridge with your bare skin."

Namid started to cross the bridge. As soon as her shoes hit the dark metal, a cold feeling seeped through the soles and made her feet feel as if something were trying to pull her through the fabric. The gun against her back made her keep walking, but she could feel this bridge trying to drain something from her as she walked across it.

When they reached the end, they were greeted by a marble statue of a woman

Namid recognized. It was the same woman who had been shown on the poster before; the one reaching for the sun and praising their "godking." And she was wearing about as much clothing; Namid was almost certain the sculptor had included her nipples, but covered them with almost enough fabric for decency.

"Gaze upon the glory of your new owner, Mereshank, Princess of Kemet!" The military woman saluted the statue before pointing her gun to Namid's back again. "Keep walking."

The woman guided Namid to a dungeon in the palace where two large guards in thick metal armor waited.

"Oh, this is a good one." one of the guards eyed Namid. "Haven't seen such a good-looking girl in my life, much less one that looks so much like the princess."

"This new slave is descended from traitors who fled to the north," the military woman explained. "She was captured recently by Sekhet and Arkeon."

"Really?" The second guard smirked at Namid. "Sucks to be you. Welcome to the special dungeon, where we keep ladies in waiting."

"Ladies in waiting?" Namid shuddered. "Waiting for what?"

"To be used to keep the princess's beauty intact, of course." The first guard opened the steel door to the dungeon. "This way, please. If you need anything, just call."

Namid stepped into the prison expecting that last line to be a sick joke, but was greeted with a room that was stocked with fresh fruit, excellent ventilation, and even workout equipment. There were five other girls already there; all of whom looked healthier than anyone else Namid had seen since arriving in Kemet. None of them looked happy to be there, however.

"So," one of the girls sitting on a couch looked at Namid while the others looked away. "Where are you from?"

"I'm..." Namid wondered if she should lie; people of Kemet clearly didn't like Coptics that had escaped to the Borealan Empire. But maybe that wasn't necessary here. These girls looked like they had given up hope, and honesty might work in her favor. "I'm from Hadesh."

"Seriously?" A girl who was looking out the window glanced at Namid for the first time. "You were brought here from the Borealan Empire? I thought people were safe up there."

"I don't think they usually do." Namid sighed. "I simply walked into the wrong store at the wrong time. They talked about sending me to the mines as a comfort girl, but said they had to bring me here because of my looks."

"So…" one girl tilted her head. "You don't know if your case is unusual, do you?"

Namid's eyes widened as realization hit her. "No. I don't."

"I've been here for three years," the girl sitting on a nearby couch replied. "I've been here longer than anyone else, and I've never met anyone from the north before. So maybe it isn't common. But maybe most people that get snatched up like you don't look enough like Mereshank to be brought here."

"I know that this is a stupid thing to ask," Namid looked around the room for ideas. "But have any of you got ideas of escape?"

The girl by the window snickered pathetically, but the girl on the couch didn't even change her expression.

"Wow…" the girl on the couch folded her hands. "Is that…hope? I can't remember a time when I ever felt that. Not here, not before I was selected to be brought here, not when I was with my parents. That is…" She looked at the wall for a moment, but her expression showed her mind was elsewhere. "I can't even wrap my head around hope anymore."

A knock on the door broke their conversation. A guard entered the room.

"Good news!" He smiled. "Princess Mereshank has recently had…an accident with her thigh. Which means one of you has the glorious opportunity to give of thine self to preserve her beauty."

"I volunteer." A girl who hadn't spoken to Namid yet jumped up from a chair by a bookcase. "Take me."

"Just like that?" The guard asked. "Usually we make you draw lots. You do realize that by 'good news,' I mean you're about to die, right?"

"Earlier today, from the windowsill, I watched a man living on the streets trying to sell his fingers and toes as food to passersby," she explained. "Then I saw a group of zombies eat him alive, and a necrophyte barking accusations at him for selling meat without the proper license. I'm ready to meet Osiris now."

"Oh," the surprised guard shrugged. "Well, this'll be great for you then. Right this way."

The girl left with the guard while Namid turned to the one on the couch. "What's a necrophyte?"

"The woman in the military outfit that led you here," she replied. "She was a necrophyte. Amenhotep's military police. He gives them the power to command his undead minions, and they hold the highest rank possible in the Kemet police force. They've pretty much got the authority to do as they please, so long as they achieve their godking's goals."

Namid sat next to the girl on the couch. "Have you got a name?" It was a genuine question. It wouldn't surprise Namid if she didn't.

"I think I did at one point..." she blinked. "But the only people who used to call me by it were other girls in here, and that makes it harder to say goodbye."

Namid hushed her voice. "Well, my name is Namid, and now it'll be harder to say goodbye to me. Listen, I am not going to give up so easily. I want out, and I'd rather die making those liches suffer than waste away slowly in here, waiting to be skinned alive."

"You don't get it," the girl shook her head. "It's not just that there's no way out of here, although that is part of it. It's that there's nowhere to go. Even if you somehow escaped, you'd just be on the streets of Azzitha, with nowhere to hide by nightfall. When the necrophytes find you, they might bring you back here. They might not recognize you, and have their zombies eat you alive if they decide there's too many homeless people on the streets for their quota. They might accuse you of being a spy, and have you dragged off to a private dungeon, where they'll do things to you that'll make you wish you'd stayed here. And if you escape Azzitha, you'll be out in the desert, with nowhere to go. If you headed north, there's only the sea, and no boats you could take to return to your lovely Borealan home. If you went south, best case scenario, you die in the desert. Or you make your way to the Simian Empire, where some ape murders you and tries to steal your soul. Head west, and you'll only find Vakraz. If Arkeon and his minions find you, he'll drag you right back here. And if you head east, there's only the Nile."

"What's so bad about the Nile?" Namid asked. "I'm not a competitive swimmer, but if I absolutely had to, I could make it across without drowning. Are there crocodiles?"

"Not anymore," the girl admitted. "All the wildlife along the Nile is long gone. And you cannot drown in the Nile River; no one can, not anymore. But you can die of asphyxiation from the fumes."

"Okay," Namid made a mental note of this. "That means I don't have to worry about many things trying to follow me through." She leaned closer to the girl and whispered in her ear. "I have a way to cross the river."

"You can't." The girl shook her head. "You couldn't have even known the river was polluted until now. The Tomb Lords do a pretty good job keeping that a secret from the empire."

"But I'm a sorceress," Namid whispered. "I haven't graduated yet, but I have enough magical training to make a bubble of breathable air big enough to make it across. We'd have to be quick, but I could do it. I'd have a better chance of succeeding if you came with me, and I might be able to get the both of us to safety."

"Seriously?" The girl looked Namid over. "A wizard?"

"Shh!" Namid put a finger to her lips. "I don't want anyone else to know. It's my one ace in the hole."

"Can you...prove any of this?" The girl asked.

Looking around to see if any of the other girls were paying attention, Namid directed a current of air to flow through an open window and blow up the skirt of a girl who was slumped against a piano. The girl looked down at her exposed underwear, shrugged, and then went back to moping on the piano.

"That's all I'm willing to do right now," Namid whispered. "I can't save all of them, and I don't want to reveal myself to one of these girls who might sell me out in exchange for freedom."

"And how do you know I won't sell you out?" The first girl asked.

"Because you lost hope a long time ago," Namid replied.

The girl chuckled. "...Yeah. I have. But I guess you haven't."

"Will you help me?" Namid asked. "Will you come with me?"

"...Yes."

"So, can I get a name?"

"You can call me...Rana," the girl replied.

49

It Came From a Lab Down Under

ROSTAM

The crew followed the dog down a long, dark tunnel that broke off at several points. Rostam spotted a bedroom chamber, a lavatory, and a kitchen, among other things.

"This doesn't look like the way to any experiment rooms," Rostam called back to the others.

"So?" Nadia called back.

"Don't you think that's a little odd?" Rostam asked. "Can't find signs of the researchers, and the dog is heading away from the research stations? If the team isn't here right now, why is it taking us further down the tunnel away from the exit? If something went wrong, and the research team is dead, wouldn't they be near their laboratory? This seems more like the living quarters."

Before the captain could respond, the dog stopped near an entryway to another chamber. Instead of going in, the animal whimpered and crawled back to Rostam.

Having grabbed a small amount of kibble to bring with him, the boy gave the dog another handful and pet its head. "What's wrong? Is there something down there?"

"I don't like any of this," Simon whispered. "Everything about this project seems wrong. The taint doesn't kill people and leave no bodies behind to find.

What in the Abyss were they up to down here?"

"I feel like we're walking into a trap." Joseph approached the chamber entryway and pressed himself against the wall, trying to peek inside the new room without making himself too visible to anything inside. "It's dark in there. Looks like they never finished digging this room out. It doesn't even seem to have gas lines running to it yet."

"I've heard stories about miners who dug too deep, and woke up something they should've just left alone." Simon inched away from the entryway. "Maybe that's what we should do. Leave it alone."

"You're all just being silly," Nadia whispered. "There's not going to be some horrible supernatural thing in the bottom of some hole in the ground."

"I'm a supernatural thing," Cindrocles muttered. "I'm at the bottom of some hole in the ground."

"Shut up," Nadia replied.

The Labrador continued to whimper and huddled against Rostam. He was not going into that chamber.

Rostam patted the dog's head. "He thinks there's someone in there from the research team. Or, at least, what's left of them. If someone's in there who needs help, well...you know. And if they're dead, we should at least confirm it."

"What if the thing that killed them is still in there?" Simon countered. "Maybe this opening isn't big enough for it to get through."

"Well," Rostam swallowed. "We have a wizard with us."

"Do we?" Nadia looked around. "Where is Cyrus?"

"I think we left him behind in the main chamber," Joseph admitted. "Think he was reading the lab notebooks to get some sort of clue. Something about it being time for 'the last resort.'"

"Okay," Nadia gritted her teeth. "He's not even part of our crew. He's a customer. Sort of. We can't just leave him unattended in the bottom of a hole. Even if there aren't any stupid monsters running around down here."

"You don't know that," Simon muttered.

"I know a lot of spiritual monsters only exist if people believe they do," Nadia snapped. "And if you'd stop believing in them, maybe they'd go away.

Regardless, Rostam – I want you and Cindrocles to go back the way we came, find Cyrus, and drag his ass back here."

Rostam nodded. "On it."

As he left, and Cindrocles followed behind, Rostam couldn't help but overhear Simon one last time.

"I am not going in there if the wizard *and* the fireball aren't coming with us."

"I second that," Joseph added.

"Would you two stop it!" Nadia huffed.

Rostam and Cindrocles made their way back down the tunnel to the main chamber. Cyrus was still there, reading the doctor's journal.

"Oh, hey there!" He waved. "Sorry for getting separated. I thought there might be some clues in here."

"Are there?" Rostam pointed at the notebook. "Clues, I mean?"

"Of a sort." Cyrus turned a page. "He talks a lot about problems with the research crew. Especially someone named Kaniel Wadermann, who was in charge of some golems here that dug out the tunnels near the lab. It sounds like Kaniel and the doctor might have been friends at one point, but...Dr. Rosenberg went off to become a successful alchemist, and Kaniel...well, you can see where the doctor has some unpleasant things to say about him, but then crosses it out and tries to be more polite. In his own private research log, mind you."

"Was this...Kaniel guy a problem?" Rostam asked.

"I've been looking at that, hoping there might be some sort of clue, or signs of trouble ahead, but so far it's just a record of Kaniel griping a lot. Whining about how it's not fair that he's fat and the doctor is thin, or how he ended up a theurgist instead of a sorcerer because his poor health made direct handling of magic too dangerous for him. Dr. Rosenberg says that he blames his genetics a lot for his poor health, and claims to have grown up poor and have to live in a multi-generational home just to make ends meet. It apparently started upsetting the other members of the research team, because some of the porters live in multi-generational homes, and they felt insulted by this guy's grumbling."

"But...nothing dangerous?" Rostam asked.

Cyrus shook his head. "Don't think so. If this Kaniel guy was actually capable of being a threat, Dr. Rosenberg never noticed it. And from the sounds of things, he was too out of shape and weak in spirit to actually be a threat to anyone."

"Alright, then come join us with the others." Rostam gestured back down the tunnel where the Labrador had led earlier. "We've found some chamber that the dog won't enter, and the rest of the crew is too spooked to go inside. How good are you in a fight?"

"I'm an alchemist. Comes with the territory." Cyrus cocked his head. "Why?"

"I want you to tell Simon and Joseph you could kill a monster with a touch if you had to. Hopefully, that'll get them to stop hiding from a half-excavated room."

Cyrus gave a sideways glance, and for a moment, Rostam wondered if he actually could kill something with only a touch. *So what if it turns out to be true?* He thought. *That makes it even better.*

"Right," Cyrus tucked the lab notebook under one arm. "I'm just bringing this along for safety's sake. I haven't read it all, but there might be something in here that could tell us where everyone went."

The alchemist, the airshipmate, and the fireball made their way back down the passage towards the unfinished chamber. As they passed the door to the sleeping quarters, Cyrus stopped.

"Hold on," Cyrus knocked on the door. "Let me just check something."

There was no response from inside. Cyrus swung the door open and checked the lab book again. "It says in here that one of the doctor's students he brought with him on an internship found some odd hole in the corner of this room. They boarded it up, but why was it dug out at all?" He turned to the fireball. "Cindrocles, that's your name, right? Can you give me some light in here?"

"Sure." The fireball floated into the sleeping chamber, and spotted a corner of one wall that had been covered with wooden boards. "That's odd."

Rostam poked his head into the room. "What is it?"

"They didn't seal the hole up, or even secure these boards. In fact..." Cindrocles floated closer and examined the covering. "These were moved.

Regularly. Dust builds up on things that don't move on their own and get left in a room full of humans. This isn't dusty, dirty, or anything like that. I think someone was moving these wooden planks regularly." He sniffed the air for a moment. "And there's more air flowing in and out of the cracks between the planks then there should be, at least when I'm here to soak up the oxygen from inside. If it was a small hole, it wouldn't be noticeable, but I don't think this is 'small.'"

Rostam came up to the boards and wrenched one away from the wall. It came away easily, having been set there inside a rut that had been dug into the floor and side of the hole. Someone had covered this hole, but intended for a person to still be able to get in and out of it.

"Okay," Rostam peered into the darkness of the hole. "Definitely deeper than you'd expect. Almost a hidden room. Cindrocles, can you light it up?"

The fireball floated into the middle of the room. Cyrus came up next to Rostam to see what they'd found. Now it was clear why this room had been hidden.

The room was about five meters, almost a square, and a little over two meters tall. In the middle, on the floor, someone had drawn a dark pentagram on the ground, which was almost perfectly flat, despite having been dug out of the solid earth. Several candles had been setup around the pentagram forming a circle, now half-melted. Someone had used this room for some kind of ritual.

"What the?" Cyrus sniffed the air. "Sulfur? How did I miss that smell before?" He got down near the pentagram, but held his hand back to Rostam to keep him away. "Don't touch this. I think..." He squinted at the circle in the dim light. "I think this was drawn with mercury."

"What?" Rostam looked around the room. Several chunks of sulfur were lying in one corner. "Why would someone do that and risk getting poisoned?"

"Mercury is the element alchemically associated with the mind," Cyrus explained. "If one were to try and bring something from the astral plane, such as a spirit, or some other kind of entity born out of human thoughts, then mercury might make the connection stronger. The sulfur..."

"What's sulfur associated with?" Rostam asked.

"The body, for starters," Cyrus got up from the ground. "But that's not all. Some alchemists used it to denote hell, or base human instincts. The body without the soul or the mind is just an animal, so sometimes sulfur is associated with animalistic behaviors that a human descends into when he lets go of his reason or conscience. In a ritual like this, they're using the mind and the body, so maybe..." Cyrus grimaced. "I'm not a theurgist. I'm not sure why someone would do any of this. My best guess is that someone tried to summon something from the plane of the mind and give it a form. But where is the salt? They used alchemical reagents in their summoning ritual, but why would they leave out the salt? They left out the spirit..."

Rostam took one last look around the room, and a chill crawled up his spine. "We should get back to the others."

"Yeah," Cyrus nodded. "This just...bothers me."

Cindrocles gave the secret room one last sniff and shuddered. "Something wrong about this place. Everyone out."

The two boys stepped outside of the room, only for the fire elemental to float to the center of it and erupt into flames. The fire was so hot, Rostam dove to the ground while Cyrus ducked behind a wall. When the heat finally died down, the boys looked at the hidden room again. Cindrocles was still in the center of it, looking over the ground that he'd burnt in confusion. The soil had been roasted, the candles had melted away to wax puddles on the floor, but the pentagram was untouched.

"Alchemy guy," the elemental turned to Cyrus. "What happens when you get mercury really hot?"

"Uh...it burns." He looked at the shiny pentagram, still intact in the room. "It turns into a red powder."

"See any such red powder?" The elemental asked.

"No," Cyrus peered at the pentagram. "There's something wrong about all of this."

The three left the strange hidden room and rejoined the others at the unfinished chamber.

"What took you guys so long?" Nadia asked.

"We found...clues," Rostam looked at Cyrus and Cindrocles.

"That's one way to put it," Cyrus agreed. "There was more than one magical research project done down here, it seems."

The Labrador whined and huddled against Rostam's leg. It looked up at him, as if begging the boy to take him out of this place.

"Sorry boy," Rostam rubbed his head. "We've got to go in there."

"Great, I'll lead the way." Nadia stepped up to the entrance. "Cindrocles, we need you to fly the ship, so stay out of reach if something goes wrong."

"Got it," the fireball...well, not really nodded; he was more like a floating head without a neck. But the shaking of the fireball looked sort of like a nod.

Nadia stepped into the room, using a makeshift torch for light. Rostam and Cyrus followed, with Cindrocles, Joseph, and Simon bringing up the rear.

The chamber was fairly large; about thirty meters long on the one side that had been finished, and the earth had been dug into by about fifteen meters on the sides. A shattered stone golem lay in pieces on the ground near the undug section of the room. It almost looked like a statue that had fallen over, but nobody worked particularly hard to make the face look human, and the torso had been broken like someone had tried to shatter it. A spherical hole in the center of the torso told Rostam that someone had retrieved the golem's core, possibly to salvage it, or to just get it to stop moving.

The Labrador whined even more now, avoiding corners of the room. Heaps of rubble from the excavation lay everywhere. A seemingly intact golem sat lifeless in a corner, stone hands caked in dirt. Cindrocles did his best to light the place up, but there were too many nooks and crannies formed by the remaining dirt to light the whole room.

"What was this room for?" Joseph asked.

As if in answer, a mumbling sound came from a pile of dirt. Realizing that someone was under it, Rostam started scooping earth off the pile until a human hand was visible. The fingers flexed, curling into a fist and then back into a palm. Then pointed down to the pile as if gesturing for Rostam to dig him out.

Cyrus, Simon, and Joseph joined Rostam in unburying the owner of the hand. Soon, a disheveled, muscular man in a lab coat and soiled clothes was freed from all the rubble.

"Thank you," he wheezed. "Do you have any water?"

Rostam handed him his canteen. The man drank it greedily, then sat up on the pile of earth.

"Who are you?" He asked.

"We're the delivery team come to resupply you with provisions," Nadia replied. "Who are you?"

"Ah!" The man jumped to his feet and stood up straight. "I am Doctor Eliot Rosenberg! Pleased to meet you all!" He extended his filthy hand to Nadia and beamed.

"Uh, great." Nadia reached into the pocket of her shirt and stuck a piece of paper in the doctor's outstretched hand. "Here's our invoice. We'll need you to sign this."

"Oh," the doctor looked at the sheet of paper. "Right. I'll get right on this. Soon as I get cleaned up."

"Excellent," Nadia nodded. "Once you do, we'll get out of your hair."

"Oh, ah..." the doctor winced. "I...am going to need to charter your ship."

"Our ship?" The captain raised an eyebrow.

"Yes. To return to Hadesh. This research program has...failed."

"Where is everyone else?" Rostam asked. "We haven't found anyone else except this dog." He rubbed the Labrador's head, but now more than ever, the animal was trying to get away.

"Oh, that is rather disappointing," Dr. Rosenberg shook his head. "They wandered off one night to the local town for late night drinking, and never came back. I was in here when part of the ceiling collapsed on top of me, and was stuck for what must have been hours before you arrived. I'm very lucky you came when you did."

"Only a few hours?" Cyrus asked. "That's pretty lucky. But then, what were you doing in this room when the ceiling collapsed?"

"I was arguing with our golem operator. He was the one digging this tunnel out. When the ceiling collapsed, I think he ran off. I know he had at least two golems left so he could have dug me out, but didn't."

"Huh," Cyrus looked down, as if putting together pieces of a puzzle. "What happened to Kaniel?"

"Uh..." Rosenberg's eyes widened. "Didn't know you knew his name. He must have run off. Left the research station altogether."

"That seems like a dick move." Cyrus crossed his arms.

"...I refuse to comment," Rosenberg replied.

The Labrador whimpered again, and Rostam realized that the dog was trying to get away from Dr. Rosenberg, specifically. "Why don't you go get cleaned up?" Rostam asked. "Then you can sign the invoice, and we can give you passaged back to Hadesh."

Dr. Rosenberg locked eyes with Rostam for a moment. "Certainly."

He went down the passageway back to the living quarters. Joseph and Simon followed.

"Hey, get this." Joseph pointed to Simon with his thumb. "This guy thought you and your research crew had dug too deep and woken up some ancient evil, and that was why we couldn't find you guys."

"Oh really?" The doctor grinned. "That's kind of funny."

As the two laughed at an unhappy Simon's expense, Rostam turned to Cyrus.

"Why does that guy give me the creeps?" He whispered.

"Because there's something very wrong about his story," Cyrus replied. "Other researchers all just wandered off into the desert to get drunk? The only person who sticks behind is the guy that the doctor notes is always complaining?" Cyrus held up a page of the doctor's notebook. "I want to see how this guy signs his invoice."

"Why?" Rostam asked. "Okay, so the doctor is acting kind of shady. How would that change his signature?"

Cyrus looked around to make sure no one else was in earshot. Nadia had left with the others and taken the dog with her, but Cindrocles had stayed behind. "Alright. Fireball, come closer. You should hear this too."

The elemental floated closer to Cyrus.

"Okay," the alchemist whispered. "Do either of you know what a ghoul is?"

"Hm...name's familiar, but no," Cindrocles replied.

Rostam shook his head. "Heard of them, don't know anything about them."

"They're shapeshifters," Cyrus explained. "They can take the form of anyone they've eaten."

"Eaten?" Rostam's eyes widened. "You mean like...cannibals?"

"Exactly like cannibals," Cyrus went on. "They're demons. They possess human bodies and use the human as a puppet. I don't know how someone gets possessed, but I've seen the husks these ghouls leave behind. They aren't pretty."

"And you think Dr. Rosenberg is possessed?" Rostam asked.

"I don't think that's Dr. Rosenberg at all." Cyrus held up the notebook and pointed to the signature. "But I could be wrong. Let's get him to sign the invoice. If the signature's don't line up, we won't tell the ghoul we're onto him. We can play along with him until we're on the ship, high in the sky. Then we throw the demon overboard."

"Uh..." Rostam leaned away from Cyrus and looked him over. "You just suggested we kill someone."

"A demon isn't a person," Cyrus replied. "And if you think a cannibalistic ghoul who has eaten at least one person doesn't deserve to die, then you are a very forgiving person. For all I know, ghouls eat everything; bones and all. Maybe the rest of the research team didn't just wander off into the night like idiots and not come back like even bigger idiots. Maybe they're in that monster's stomach."

Rostam grimaced. "But...they're possessing someone. You said it yourself: they're using the human as a puppet. Throwing them overboard kills the host and the demon."

Cyrus paused. "I have seen what a human who has been possessed by a ghoul that leaves looks like. It's...not pretty. All that shapeshifting warps the body into something horrible, and they crave rotten human flesh so they can incubate more demons inside of them. But maybe the host isn't that far gone." He closed his eyes and sighed. "Okay, we'll try to exorcise the demon and save the host. *If* I'm right and the doctor actually is a ghoul in disguise. Do you have any idea how to do this?"

"...No idea." Rostam shook his head.

"None of this makes any sense to me," Cindrocles chipped in.

"I know demons hate salt, silver, and gold. And the one alchemical reagent that the summoner didn't use in that secret room was the salt." Cyrus pointed to the unfinished chamber's entryway. "Let's see if we can stock up and prepare a trap. Best part? If he's not a ghoul, this won't hurt him."

As they made their way to the alchemical reagent storage, questions popped into Rostam's mind. "Why does salt hurt demons?"

"Because a demon's paradoxical nature makes it inherently chaotic, and they can't stand things that preserve or purify, like salt. Depending on the nature of the demon, certain household cleaning supplies have been known to hurt them, though not to the same effect as salt."

"Okay," Rostam nodded. "I've heard that silver is a curse to the cursed, but why would gold hurt demons?"

"Oh, it's not that silver is a curse to the cursed," Cyrus explained. "It's actually the alchemical properties of pure silver and gold. Those two elements are so non-reactive you can occasionally find them in their pure elemental forms in nature. Pure silver, not sterling silver, but the pure stuff, never tarnishes, and the same is true for gold. Demons hate things that can't be corroded."

"Huh." Rostam looked at the axe he kept hanging from his belt in case he got in a fight and took out a few coins from his belt pouch. He wouldn't assume that silver coins would be more effective against a demon than an axe. Then again, the coins weren't pure silver. But pure silver was supposed to be really malleable; you couldn't make a weapon out of it. Even sterling silver couldn't keep an edge.

As they passed by the living quarters, they noticed Nadia leaning against the wall while sounds of a shower could be heard inside. The Labrador was nowhere to be seen.

"Where are Simon and Joseph?" Rostam asked.

"They went back to the ship," Nadia replied.

"Maybe...you should wait for the doctor in the main entry chamber," Cyrus noted. "The doctor seemed a tad...eccentric. Probably from being buried alive for several hours. He might need some space."

"Hm. Probably right." Nadia made her way back to where they'd first entered the facility.

"Don't want your captain to get eaten when we're not looking," Cyrus whispered to Rostam, who nodded in agreement.

50

Basic Training

AMRI

Waking up in a surprisingly itchy bed, Amri opened his eyes and realized he didn't recognize the ceiling. Turning his head to the left, he squinted as his vision cleared and showed him a hospital room filled with beds. The infirmary was very clean, but you could tell they did not have a lot of money for things like the sorts of fabrics Amri slept on at home.

That's right, Amri thought. *I asked to be brought to the Abbey of Truth.* The entire event between himself, Dr. Malbim, and Izaac came back to him. And so did a sharp pain in both of his calves. He winced as he realized that he'd been given some kind of painkillers, but they were definitely wearing off.

The rest of Amri's body didn't feel too bad. Apparently, he'd been sleeping long enough to get over everything except where Malbim had punctured his legs. He sat up and looked around at the room.

There were twelve beds in the hospital, including Amri's. Three other beds were occupied, and while Amri couldn't see two of them due to their heads being covered by sheets, he could tell that the third was old, and looked like he might have been homeless.

"Not really surprising," Amri tried to take his mind off the pain in his legs. "They would be the sort to give homeless people medical aid."

"Hello there." A nurse with a cute haircut about Amri's age and wearing a surgical mask over her mouth, approached his bedside. "Good to see you

BASIC TRAINING

awake."

"Thanks, uh..." he squinted and read a nametag on her lapel. "Sarah."

"You are welcome." Her voice was fairly sweet, but Amri could hear the bedside mannerisms in it. Definitely, she treated all her patients this way. "How are you feeling?"

"Legs hurt." Amri looked down at his feet. "Everything else is fine."

"Yeah, your legs are going to need time to heal." The nurse was looking over some sort of chart. "We don't have a medical alchemist on hand who can help with that sort of thing, just whomever happens to be volunteering with us for a while. Like me."

"You're a volunteer?"

"Yup!" Sarah was clearly smiling behind her mask. "Almost anyone working here is. Except the priests."

"Can you tell me what happened to a boy named Izaac?" Amri leaned up and realized he was still very woozy. "He's about five—"

"He's fine," Sarah replied. "The police took him into custody and have already sent him to live with his paternal grandparents. They live in Petryan, and he's on a train to meet them soon."

Amri nodded. It was over, then. "Um...Is it possible for me to get out of bed?"

"Yes, but not by walking." Sarah retrieved a folding wheelchair from a nearby closet. "Your legs need more time to heal before you can put weight on them again, so if you want to get up, you'll have to use this."

Sarah helped him get into the wheelchair. "Do you guys have a bathroom or anywhere I can get cleaned up?"

The nurse nodded. "We have a communal bathroom. Separated by gender, of course. Want me to wheel you to the men's room?"

Amri nodded, and noticed that he was wearing a hospital gown. "Thank you. And do you by chance have any clean clothes? Mine stink."

"Of course." She pushed the chair to one end of the infirmary room, where a short hallway broke into two bathrooms. "Will you be able to roll yourself from here? I'd rather not enter the men's room if I don't have to."

"I've got it." Amri found the handles on the wheels and managed to drive himself forward.

"I'll be back with some clean clothes." Sarah left.

Once he managed to steer himself into the bathing area, Amri found a large room with a round basin like a swimming pool. Several other men were already bathing there, and there was a small changing room nearby. The other men in the basin seemed to be using nearby pitchers that held some sort of oil instead of soap for cleaning; Amri had heard of this. The oil was made from the same sorts of animal fat used to make soap, but could be laced with scents, herbs, and aloe, making them useful for treating infections and injuries.

Amri stripped off his hospital gown and, with some difficulty, lowered himself into the water. Grabbing a nearby pitcher, he rubbed the oil onto his injuries first. It stung a little, but not as much as he'd been expecting.

He proceeded to scrub all the stinky parts of his body, hoping to smell better by the time he saw the cute nurse again. He'd heard his sister mention once that she'd rather date an ugly guy who smelled good than a handsome man who stank of body odor. Amri made certain to really grind the oil into his armpits and onto his chest before scraping it off with a tool that came attached to the pitchers.

Once he was satisfied with how he smelled, Amri sat on the edge of the basin and pulled himself up onto the wheelchair. Towels were available in cubbies along one wall, and after he dried himself off, Amri found a set of clothes folded and waiting for him outside the bathroom.

When he'd gotten himself changed, Amri rolled the chair back to the infirmary, where Sarah had begun checking on the other patients.

"Am I allowed to leave the infirmary?" He asked.

"You can, but there are some limits. Your injuries are not healed enough for us to discharge you, and we have to ask you to stay in the main square of the abbey." Sarah directed him to a window and showed him the main courtyard of the abbey. "Stick to the hospital, the chapel, and the library for now. Do you want me to get someone to accompany you?"

"I don't think so." Amri wouldn't have minded having Sarah give him a tour of the place, but he suspected he needed to visit the library alone. "I should be fine."

BASIC TRAINING

Letting the nurse get back to her work, Amri rolled himself out of the hospital building into the main courtyard. The chapel was pretty easy to identify, thanks to the religious spires and icons on it. The library must have been the other, much more plain-looking building. Several steps lead up to the library entrance. Thankfully, a wheelchair accessible ramp ran along the left side of the staircase.

Once inside, Amri took a look at the library shelves. There was a front desk, as one would expect, but there were several other desks as large as the first. These must have been for monks and priests to study their texts. Other than that, it looked similar to your typical library, but there was a different attitude here. Even though many books were probably not read by the monks, they were not ignored like the dusty old tomes of the less-visited shelves Amri had seen in the library at the Academy of Sorcerers. Old books in that library were often falling apart, with pieces of pages flaking off from time to time. These books were meticulously cleaned and cared for, almost like their religion required it. Maybe it did.

Rolling up to the middle of the library, Amri noticed the floor was entirely done in blue tiles, with a strange pattern in the middle walkway that he hadn't noticed he'd been rolling over. The floor held a massive image of...a tree? Maybe? It was kind of shaped like a tree, but it was made entirely out of circles connected by branches. Each circle contained a word written in a very old language that Amri couldn't read.

Unsure of what the tree meant to the abbey's beliefs, he decided to chalk it up to some sort of religious symbol and moved on. Looking around at the people in the library, Amri spotted six other persons. Five of them appeared to be monks reading some of the books, likely for monastic study. The sixth sat at a desk with a stack of books to one side, and was making some sort of list. Unlike everyone else in the library, this person was dressed in long robes that concealed their body, a hood that covered their head, and a metal mask that hid their face.

Amri rolled towards the masked man as he made his list. "I had a feeling I'd find you here."

"And so you did," Marduk whispered through the mask. "And you came alone. Good choice. We have much to discuss, preferably in private."

"Can I ask what you're doing?" Amri pointed at the books Marduk had stacked up.

"Documenting, organizing, compiling." Marduk gestured to the tomes. "I have not always been a god of writing, but I was always associated with the written word. Babylon, the first city to make me their top god, installed my cult at the same time their mortal king drafted the first code of laws, and the literacy rate of a civilization feeds into my power. So, like other gods associated with writing, I can remember everything mortals have recorded in writing. Here, I go through the things mortals have written, and organize the more important ones in ways that humans today can find what they need."

"Have you always been working with this abbey?" Amri asked.

"No," Marduk admitted. "Thoth used to do this, but in his absence, I am the only god left who remembers everything written. Even Horus, who's cult derived a lot of influence from me, didn't make this connection. Gods who do not have a close relationship to the written word can only remember what mortals remember."

"Wait, aren't some of you supposed to be omniscient?"

"Not as you would think of it. We know what the collective consciousness of humanity knows, and only the humans who worship us. That means we know everything you know, and it's impossible for humans to hide things from us, but we don't know what humans don't know, and most of us can only remember what humans *currently* know."

"Huh." Amri found the thought fascinating, and could see himself asking Marduk questions about the subject for days, but knew the god had called him there for a reason. "So, what—"

"There is nothing wrong with your curiosity," Marduk interrupted. "It is good for you to want to know more about the ideas that your culture have made manifest. And yes, as part of our ability to know everything mortals know, I can see into your mind. At least, I can detect the thoughts you are thinking right now. And the reason I summoned you here is because you are in need of the wisdom of older generations."

"Wait," Amri blinked. "Are you saying I don't listen enough to my elders?"

"No," Marduk sighed and stopped working on his book project altogether. "Listening to your elders is probably the reason you don't have their wisdom. Do you know why I cannot seem to grow a full beard?"

"Uh, no," Amri shook his head. "What does that have to do with anything?"

"The reason I cannot grow a proper beard anymore..." Marduk stroked his chin under his mask. "...is because mortals who have read my stories lately have focused so heavily on my status as the youngest god of my pantheon. Well, maybe not the youngest, but the last generation. And I became king of my pantheon by slaying the chaos born of my elders' mistakes. Many mortals believe me to be some sort of upstart who took advantage of the situation to take power away from elders that I did not respect, and the result is that I am now stuck with a permanently nineteen-year-old body."

"Oh." Amri frowned. "That doesn't sound good."

"It's not so bad." Marduk shrugged. "All of my eyes are located on the front of my head this era, and that's nice, because it makes it easier for me to read."

Amri realized something. "Wait, if you're shaped by human belief, then why aren't you more of disrespectful punk, or something? You seem plenty respectful to people you interact with."

"That's because certain elements of a god's personality cannot be changed, without them ceasing to be the same god. The fact is, I am civilization made manifest, and that means that I respect people who deserve it. It is foundational to civilization that people are not granted reverence for things... hm, how to say in this language. Immutable characteristics? Civilization is at its best when people are not simply granted honor and respect for things they were simply born into. Class, sex, race, and of course, age. Everyone who wants respect must earn it, and that applies to elders as well. This is why so many old people don't like me."

"Class?" Amri raised an eyebrow. "Aren't you a king? People are born into the role of princes and kings. Are you telling me kings aren't entitled to respect?"

"No, they are not," Marduk replied. "And to be frank, this is why many mortal kings do not like me, either. But all authority should be questioned. Regularly. Kings must be ready to explain where their authority comes from, and why they deserve to sit on their thrones. If they can't, it's time to abdicate."

"A king of gods who wants people to question him?" Amri felt a streak of cockiness in his mind, and he figured he might as well ask if Marduk knew the question anyway. "Okay, so where does your authority come from?"

"Hm...how to explain so that you would understand?" Marduk paused. "A king of gods is not like a king of men. Different rules apply, but there are some similar ones. To begin, I am an idea, and you mortals have decided that you like being ruled by civilization rather than other ideas. So, in part, my authority comes from the consent of the people over whom I rule. However, it is not the same as how your current society votes for elector counts, who then decide if the emperor can keep his position."

"So, if that's true, can people choose to replace you as the king of the gods?" Amri asked.

"Absolutely. Not every civilization in Janaan, or in ancient Sumeria, believed the same creation myth, or that I was the rightful king of the gods. Although, there is a reason why Babylon's version ended up being remembered the longest. But the Assyrians worshipped Assur, a version of Enlil with a new name and the older personality traits shaved off. The Empyrians worshipped the god of patriarchs directly as their top god as well. And that's just Enlil; Anu has lead the pantheon as king, as has my father, Enki. The point is, what you humans value, rules you."

"Huh." Amri turned that over in his head for a moment before asking another question. "Any goddesses ever take the throne?"

Even behind his mask, Marduk's expression somehow darkened. "Yes, and the less said about her, the better. Some ideas should never rule you. Let's just say that the queen of the gods before me was so awful, the Babylonians picked a minor agricultural[3] deity and reimagined him as their new king just to get rid of her. Now, to the matter at hand, do you know why I had no respect for you until recently?"

---

[3] Marduk was a minor deity of farmhands before Babylon remade him into the king of their pantheon.

"Um…" Amri tried to remember exactly what Marduk had said before. "Something about me being pathetic. Not having any strength. Things like that."

"Indeed." Marduk nodded. "Truly, you are one of the weakest boys I have ever met. Completely lacking anything resembling strength, either of mind, or of body."

"Uh…thanks?" Amri wasn't sure how he was supposed to respond to something like this.

"And yet, you showed me you have some strength of character." Marduk clasped his hands and leaned forward. "Genuine courage. And not only that, when your life depended on it, you were able to break that woman's arm. This tells me that for all your faults, you still have potential."

"Breaking a woman's arm…is potential? To the god of civilization?" Amri wasn't sure if he wanted to hear much more of what this god had to say.

"Indeed." Marduk nodded, visibly aware Amri's concerns. "Civilization can only stand as long as its guardians are willing and able to deal with evildoers. Regardless of age, race, and sex. If a person tries to kill you, it is not only right, but good, to use force to stop such a person, so that they do not harm others after they're done reducing you to a corpse. Doesn't matter if it's a woman. So, yes. It is a good thing that you were able to snap that woman's arm when she tried to kill you," Marduk leaned his head closer to Amri. "I also know about the mugger who attacked you and Esfan. The one you were unwilling to use your sorcery to fight him off. Always remember: someone who attacks you, who initiates the act of violence, has chosen to endanger your person as well as their own. They have forfeited their own rights to avoid harm in doing so. Civilization depends upon the belief that the people who instigate violence can and will suffer, while the people who are innocent can do anything they must to protect themselves."

Amri relaxed a bit at this but remembered the issue at hand. "So, what is it you want me to do now?"

"Come with me." The god rose from his seat and guided Amri out of the library to a small court behind the building. This court had a single metal pole, which had a hook up top to hang a rope for a tetherball, or mount a hoop for other sports. The rest of the court was mostly black pavement, cracked in some places, but previously drawn chalk squares showed that people used this court from time to time.

"Why does the abbey have this?" Amri asked.

"Physical rehabilitation," Marduk replied. "What they can afford, anyway." He pointed to a pair of metal double doors along the library building wall. "They keep various equipment inside. Some of which, we're going to use to build up your body."

"Okay." Amri rolled up to the door and tried the knob. It was locked. "Got any keys?"

"No," Marduk replied and walked through the door. Literally, phasing through the metal like it wasn't there. Amri then heard the lock unclick from inside and swing open. Marduk dragged out a set of poles and sandbags. If he were mortal, Amri would have wondered how he could carry so much weight.

Setting the equipment down on a reasonably flat piece of the blacktop, Marduk assembled a pullup bar from the equipment. "We're going to start by getting you to literally pull your own weight."

"Uh...I have never been able to do a pullup before," Amri admitted.

"I know. That's why we're doing this." Marduk gestured to Amri's injured legs. "We can't exactly work on your leg strength right now."

"But, how am I supposed to do a pullup if I've never been able to before?"

"Today, you won't." Marduk grabbed Amri by the shoulders and lifted him up to the bar. "Grab on."

Amri grabbed the bar as if he were going to do a pullup. "I've tried this before. It's not going to change anything–"

"Slowly, allow yourself to drop. This will tear the muscles you would normally use to pull yourself up."

Doing as he said, Amri felt his arm muscles ripping against the strain as he allowed himself to fall. Once his arms were fully extended, he hung limp from the bar, still unable to pull himself up.

Marduk grabbed his shoulders and lifted his head above the bar again. "Repeat."

Amri let himself fall again, slowly ripping his arm muscles even further.

They were already on fire, but Marduk made him repeat the process ten more times before returning him to the wheelchair.

"That was called a 'reverse pullup.' Do these regularly for several days, and it won't be long until you'll be strong enough to do a real pullup." Marduk held out a device to Amri. It was a hand gripper, used to buildup strength in one's fingers. "Use it. Fifty times in each hand."

After the first ten reps with the gripper, Amri had to struggle to close his hand. Marduk, who Amri could feel poking around in his brain measuring the physical limits of his mortal body, allowed him to stop at thirty-eight reps with his right hand and thirty-four with his left.

"We've got a long way to go." Marduk examined Amri again. "But...we have some time."

51

The Demon in the Tunnels

CYRUS

Rostam, Cindrocles, and Cyrus reached the alchemical reagent storage they had seen earlier when they had first found the kennels. The mercury and sulfur closets had been plundered, but hopefully, the salt supply was still—

"What?" Cyrus opened the salt closet door. "Where is…why?"

All of the salt had been removed. There weren't even grains of the stuff on the floor of the closet, or white powder left behind where bags of salt might have spilt. "What happened? Where would all the salt have gone?"

"Is it possible that the demon knows that salt can hurt it?" Rostam asked. "Could the demon have gotten rid of it?"

"Maybe," Cyrus admitted. "But salt is matter. It doesn't just disappear. Unless the ghoul is possessing an alchemist, it would have to go somewhere."

"What if he dumped it in a big bathtub full of water?" Rostam asked. "Then it would dissolve."

"Dissolution is a physical change. The alchemical properties of the salt would stay the same. But—" Cyrus smirked. "If the demon isn't possessing an alchemist, then he might not know that. And there's only one place around here that might have a water source like that. Let's check the bathroom."

"What if the demon is possessing an alchemist?" Cindrocles asked. "There was a whole alchemy research team here. Even if it didn't hop into the head alchemist, it could be in one of the assistants."

Cyrus paused. "Dang. That's...actually a really good point. If that's true, they might have broken down the salt into something else. Maybe. I don't actually know if a demonically possessed alchemist can still touch things that would harm the demon."

"What did you say earlier about pure silver hurting demons?" Rostam took a few silver coins from his purse. "Could you purify the silver in these?"

"Yes..." Cyrus looked over the coins. "But pure silver is as soft as gum, and wouldn't make much of a weapon."

Rostam held up his axe and pointed to the steel head. "What if you put a coating of silver on this?"

"Silver-plated steel..." Cyrus thought for a moment. "That could work. Bring it back to the lab where we found the kennels. There should be a table I can work on there."

In the kennel room, the three found a large wooden table. Not a particularly well-built table; it actually looked like something Cyrus once put together. But it would do. Rostam set the axe onto the table along with a handful of silver coins.

"This is going to be expensive," Rostam muttered.

"It's what we've got." Cyrus clapped his hands and touched the silver coins. The metal melted off the disks and poured over the head of the axe. With a bit of work, he was able to keep the overall shape of the axe head, but coated with a thin layer of pure silver. A few pieces of junk metal were all that remained of the coins.

"All right," Cyrus handed the axe back to Rostam. "Let's hope this is enough. Maybe we'll get lucky, and I'm wrong about the doctor being a ghoul in the first place."

The three returned to the main chamber where Captain Nadia was still waiting.

"Uh...where is Doctor Rosenberg?" Rostam asked.

"He's taking too long," Nadia replied. "Hasn't even signed our invoice yet."

Cyrus looked at Rostam. "Without salt to sprinkle on him, or a signature to check against his handwriting, I don't know how to prove if he's a ghoul or human."

Rostam held up the axe. "We've got the silver."

"What are you going to do?" Cyrus asked. "Hit him with the axe and check if his flesh bursts into flames after you maim him?"

Rostam frowned, and didn't reply.

"Why don't we check on the good doctor?" Cyrus asked Nadia. "Captain, we'll just see if he's ok. He was buried alive for a while, after all. Maybe he had some unexpected problem."

Nadia shrugged. "Fine. Just hurry it up. We've been here longer than we were supposed to already."

Rostam, Cyrus, and Cindrocles exchanged looks. They were ready.

Once they'd reached the living quarters again, Rostam cupped his left ear with his hand. "I don't hear any running water. He's not still taking a shower."

Cyrus opened the door to the locker room near the baths. There was no sign of the doctor. "He might have eaten the other researchers," he whispered to Rostam. "If that's the case, he could take their forms. Don't trust anyone you don't recognize."

A thorough search of the locker rooms and bathroom showed no signs of the doctor. The trio checked the changing rooms as well; nothing.

"Okay..." Cyrus looked around. "Where'd he go? Is he hiding?"

Rostam poked his head in the sleeping quarters. "Hey, anyone in here?"

"Woof!" In response, the Labrador they had found back in the kennels crawled out from under a bed and bounced up to Rostam. He was far more energetic than before; maybe he had learned there was nothing to fear, or maybe it just really liked the humans and fireball that had rescued him from starvation.

"Well, hello again!" Rostam smiled as he rubbed the dog's head. "I was wondering where you'd gone off to. Can you show us where Dr. Rosenberg went?" He lifted the silver-plated axe and slung it over one shoulder. "We just need to talk to him."

"Woof!" The dog headed back down the tunnels towards the unfinished chamber where they had originally found the doctor.

"I guess he went back that way." Cyrus checked down the hall. "I wonder if they found something important in that excavation site after all."

THE DEMON IN THE TUNNELS

Rostam looked uneasy, but Cindrocles started following the dog before he could say anything. Cyrus glanced at Rostam, but decided to follow the fireball.

As they made their way down the tunnel, Rostam tapped Cyrus on the shoulder.

"Hey, how much do you know about ghouls, exactly?" He asked.

"Uh...only what I've seen," Cyrus admitted. "Why?"

"Well, do you know...can a ghoul take the shape of any *person* they've eaten, or any*thing*?"

Cyrus thought for a moment. "I'm not sure. I don't even know how a ghoul gets possession of a person to begin with. I do know that they can change their size even without changing their shape, but I don't know much outside of that."

As they reached the end of the tunnel, Rostam looked down, visibly puzzling something out. He finally looked back at Cyrus.

"I'm just worried that—"

Cyrus didn't hear what Rostam said next. Or rather, he wasn't listening. He was too frozen in terror at the thing looming above them.

A dog, which still looked a bit like a black Labrador, now stood tall enough for its head to graze the ceiling. It looked down at them, just as happy as before, with a bright smile filled with sharp teeth, each the size of a man. And above that, two bright yellow eyes looked down at the three. Eyes filled with a malevolent glee.

"Hi," the beast said.

"Run!" Cyrus tried to dive for the entrance, but a massive black paw slammed down in front of it.

"Figured me out, did you?" The beast lunged with its snout and tried to gobble up Rostam, who managed to roll out of the way. "Then I'll add you to my disguises!"

Rostam managed to roll into a corner of the room where the dog's snout was too big to fit in and get him. The ghoul laughed and shrank himself slightly, getting closer to the boy to try and snap him up.

Rostam swung with the axe. Cyrus watched its effect on the ghoul's flesh; it was a bit like watching a slug shrivel when sprinkled with salt. The ghoul howled in pain from the blow as it cauterized the misshapen flesh. It tried to swat at Rostam with its other paw to keep its face away from his axe.

Now, Cyrus thought. With one paw being used to attack, the beast wouldn't be able to stand if Cyrus took out another. He clapped his hands together and touched the ghoul's leg that had blocked the entrance.

Instead of breaking the leg off or turning it into ash, the furry mass quivered under Cyrus's touch. The alchemist felt his power go out of his palms, and then return into his hands with no effect. "What?"

"Alchemy starts with comprehension, right?" The ghoul snickered. "You don't have a clue what I'm made of, do you?" The beast switched away from attacking Rostam and tried to claw Cyrus to death with his paw. Cyrus clapped his hands together and superheated the air in front of him with his palms. The boiling steam seared the ghoul's flesh and made him recoil, buying him a few seconds. Cyrus then ran between the giant dog's legs, hoping it would either have to shrink down or change shape in order to fight him while he looked for a way to attack it from behind.

Instead, the ghoul's head pulled into its body and reemerged from its rear. Cyrus realized how many laws of nature this thing violated; no wonder it didn't react to alchemy.

As soon as it tried to bite Cyrus, it let out a pained howl. Rostam had started hacking at its front leg like the trunk of a tree. The silver was like a hot steak knife through melted butter to the demon; within three swings, the leg was severed from the paw.

In response, the ghoul pulled all of its mass into the limb near the entrance and morphed into a human shape. At first, it looked like an amorphous blob-like person, before taking the shape of the researchers. Cyrus didn't recognize the ghoul's new face, but the body and build was the same he'd had when pretending to be Dr. Rosenberg.

The only thing different about the demon's muscular torso was that the right hand was missing; only a bloody stump remained. The ghoul let out a howl, it's face contorting into impossible shapes as it raged at the loss of its hand.

"Hold on a minute," Cyrus squinted at the rest of the ghoul's torso. *He likes the muscular build. That might not have even been Dr. Rosenberg's original upper body.*

"You know, an alchemist can't do magic without one of his hands," Cyrus called out to the ghoul. "It's a real shame." This wasn't true; an alchemist needed only form a circuit of power. There were stories of alchemists who had lost both hands and still managed to perform spells. But if Cyrus was right, the ghoul wouldn't know this."

"You!" The ghoul's jaw hung open too far to be normal, but its fury was all-too human. Then, a portion of the stump on the monster's wrist regenerated. The ghoul looked at his recovering arm and let out a laugh. "Ha! This will heal in a few minutes, and then I'll–"

"–take over Dr. Rosenberg's life?" Cyrus interrupted. "That was your plan, wasn't it? Eat the successful alchemist and replace him?"

The ghoul frowned, contorting into Dr. Rosenberg's face. "What's it to you? You're about to be dead, anyway. In fact...a young alchemy student...maybe I should take your identity instead."

The ghoul's muscles twisted into legs and arms long enough for it to walk on while still maintaining a human-ish shape. Its hand finished regenerating and contorted into a claw as it lurched towards Cyrus, but as soon as it did, a fireball floated up and bombarded the monster's head with flames.

"I couldn't do this when you were big and furry." Cindrocles aimed a ray of his flames at the ghoul's face, who cowered and tried to shield his eyes from the heat. "But now that you don't have all that damp fur to keep the heat off–"

If the elemental was going to say something else, he was cut off by the ghoul swiping at him with one of his limbs, forcing the fireball against a wall. Cindrocles struggled against the crushing blow, but the ghoul morphed its hand and tried to seal the elemental against the surface of the cavern to cut him off from the air. Rostam took the opportunity to hack off another one of its limbs. This was slowing the creature down, but they needed a way to exorcise it. There had to be a way to separate the demon from the host.

Salt, Cyrus thought. *That would do the trick, but where did the ghoul hide it? He couldn't have transmuted it if he wasn't an alchemist, so where...*Then a thought hit him. He could make new salt out of nearby materials if he could find the right ingredients. There was enough metal equipment in the research station that finding a metal agent would be easy enough; the problem was finding a halogenic element like chlorine or fluorine. The trace amounts in the air wouldn't be enough.

I need to search the living quarters. Maybe there's something there I can work with.

Cindrocles had managed to escape from the ghoul's palm. Rostam drew his pistol and shot the monster in the torso, which didn't kill it but seemed to slow it down.

"Buy me some time!" Cyrus called to the others.

Hearing this, the ghoul turned its head to face Cyrus and looked like it was going to focus its attention on him, but as soon as Rostam saw an opening, he hacked off another one of the monster's limbs. Roaring in pain again, the beast contorted its hands into claws and dug into the ceiling, crawling along the roof of the cavern while its dangling legs regenerated.

"Damned alchemist!" The ghoul roared. "Get back here!"

Cyrus heard the sounds of more flames trying to hold off the ghoul, but he was certain that the monster wanted his blood. Scrambling for the living quarters, he looked over his shoulder several times and spotted a pair of yellow eyes following him.

"Come on, come on…" He made his way to the living area and started tearing through cabinets. "There's got to be something here…protein bars? Trail rations? A banana that's been sitting too long? Ew…Didn't they bring any cleaning supplies?"

At last, Cyrus spotted a first aid kit. Dashing for it, he tried to ignore the sounds of the ghoul scampering closer as he ripped the kit open.

"Pleaseohpleaseohplease–" he rummaged through the kit and found what he was looking for. "Yes!"

A large, clawed hand yanked him across the living quarters and slammed him against the tunnel wall. The alchemist clung to a small brown bottle he'd found and tried to get his bearings. The last thing he saw before his body moved on its own was a human-like mouth opened too wide for a human with teeth too long to fit in a normal person's jaw.

Cyrus remembered clapping his hands in front of his face and thinking "heat" before the air in front of him became a superhot wave. The ghoul recoiled enough for Cyrus to find the bottle he'd dropped on the ground. Now he just needed something to combine it with.

"Damned alchemist!" The ghoul spat. "Why? Why did you come here to ruin everything?"

"Tell me, who's in control?" Cyrus asked.

"What?" A pair of yellow dog eyes widened in the dim light of the tunnel.

"Which one of you is in control?" Careful not to draw attention, the alchemist felt along the ground behind him. There was something soft and squishy by his hand. "Is it the demon, or the theurgist?"

The ghoul's face wasn't really human, but still gave a recognizable frown. "How in any of the hells did you figure that out?"

"Read the doctor's lab journal," Cyrus stalled. *Is this...a mushy banana? That's right. Somewhere in the cabinets, there'd been food items that must have been thrown around. Well, that's lucky.* "He mentioned you a lot, actually. Kaniel, was it? Something about you having been friends in mandatory school? You even had sleepovers on your second-story bedroom at your parents' house at some point. Except, he says you were going on about how your life turned out terrible because you'd grown up in a one-room hovel. I don't know which of those stories is correct."

"You're right," the demon growled. "You don't know. And you're not going to. You're going to die down here, and I'm going to add your face to my collection."

"See, now I know who's in control," Cyrus alchemically combined the banana and the brown bottle of iodine behind his back. "Because the demon wouldn't care about these stories." The alchemist frowned. "He was your childhood friend."

"He had the life I always wanted!" The ghoul slammed a fist along an unnaturally long arm against the ground. "I should have been a sorcerer! I should have been respected! I should have been rich! I should have been good-looking!"

"Of course. Knew that wasn't the doctor's original upper body," Cyrus muttered.

The ghoul lashed at Cyrus and dragged him up close, bearing a set of massive fangs and foul breath in his face. "What did you say?"

"Open wide." Cyrus poured the new contents of the brown bottle down the ghoul's throat.

A part of Cyrus couldn't help but take scientific interest in what happened next. The rest of him just wanted to get away from the writhing, furious monster that was lashing out every direction it could. A bottle of potassium iodide probably wouldn't have done much damage to him on the surface, but to have it inside of him; it was the difference between sprinkling a little bit of salt on a large fat slug, and tricking the slug into eating the salt.

Pus burst from the pores of the ghoul as it tried to re-putrify itself, but the salt inside him sapped the demonic influence. The massive, contorted body of the ghoul shrank as whatever mass-conservation-defying powers the demon had shriveled away. Before long, all that was left was a fat, thirty-year-old man with the deformities Cyrus had seen before among ghoul husks. Kaniel didn't have it as bad as the subjects he'd worked on almost a year ago at the college; maybe he could still get better.

"What have you done to me!" Kaniel got to his feet and felt his newly mangled face. Even in the dim light of the tunnels, it wasn't pretty. One eye was now higher than the other, his jaw had become crooked, and the skin on his forehead had turned a different color than the rest of his face. Still nowhere near as bad as the ghoul husks Cyrus had seen before.

"Purged the demon," Cyrus replied. "You should thank me. You still sound somewhat sane. You don't have any cravings for rotting human meat, do you?"

"I'll kill you, you little bastard!"

"Yeah, you don't have any of those shapeshifting powers anymore, so I'm not–" Cyrus's eyes widened as Kaniel grabbed a revolver from a nearby closet. "What? Where did– Why was there a loaded gun in there?"

"Wasn't loaded." Kaniel pulled a quick-loader from the cabinet and shoved six bullets into the gun. "Now it's loaded."

Cyrus heard a gunshot, but it hadn't come from Kaniel's weapon. The man screamed as blood poured from his right leg. He turned to look over his shoulder, where Captain Nadia stood with a smoking gun.

"What?" Kaniel cried in horror at Nadia. "Where did you–"

"Who in the Abyss are you?" Nadia growled. "And why are you pointing a gun at my ship's passenger?"

"Did you mean to just wound him?" Cyrus looked at Kaniel's leg. From what the medical alchemist could tell, the bullet only hit some soft tissue. "That'd be impressive if you did."

"Eh, I was aiming for his chest," Nadia admitted before pointing her gun at Kaniel again. "Surrender now, or I'm going to make sure the next one hits something more...vital."

Kaniel lowered his head, but his face still held a scowl. His eyes darted back and forth between Nadia and Cyrus, as if unsure who was the bigger threat. Cyrus looked around the living quarters and noticed that Rostam and Cindrocles had reached them as well. Rostam's silver-plated axe wouldn't be much help now that the demon was gone, and Cindrocles couldn't really set a human on fire very easily; Cyrus had seen how the ghoul was able to smother him earlier. But maybe...

While Kaniel had his attention on Nadia, Cyrus reached along the ground and looked for more material to work with. Nadia seemed to catch on and kept Kaniel's attention on her.

"I know what you're thinking." Nadia gripped her pistol with both hands. "I can fire this gun faster than you can aim yours at me. But maybe, *maybe* you can swing it around and shoot at the same time. Maybe the bullet can reach me before mine finds you. Maybe if you duck, roll, or do any fancy maneuvering of the sort, you can take me out. But maybe you can't. Maybe a forty-five millimeter bullet sends you straight to the afterlife. I kinda like those odds. Do you?"

Looking around, Kaniel's expression looked like he was torn between fear, rage, and self-pity. "Heh. Heheheh." Kaniel forced a laugh as he held his gun by the barrel with two fingers as if to drop it. Nadia eyed the weapon and didn't notice Kaniel reach into his pocket and pull out a ring with his other hand.

"By the way," he cackled. "I'm a wizard too."

Whispering some curse too quiet for Cyrus to hear, a wave of dust erupted from the ring and swarmed Nadia. It didn't appear to hurt her, but she fired her gun blindly in the cloud while Kaniel threw the quick-loader at her head. It smacked her in the forehead and knocked her on her back while the theurgist whipped his gun around to point at Cyrus.

"Catch!" Cyrus threw a handful of newly-made yellow clumps at Kaniel, which splattered onto his face and shoulders and shattered harmlessly into powder.

"The hell?" The theurgist looked over down at the yellow powder. "The salt trick won't work again, you idiot!"

"That wasn't salt. That was phosphorous." Cyrus looked at Cindrocles. "Light it."

The fire elemental shot a beam of flame at the theurgist. The resulting blast sent Kaniel in pieces across the room. The largest piece landed against a wall. His head was badly burnt, his torso was now much lighter than before, and his arms were missing several fingers. His legs were somewhere else around the room.

Kaniel twitched painfully for a moment. "I don't...wanna die..."

The theurgist stopped moving.

Cyrus ran over to Nadia. She had a nasty gash on her forehead, but otherwise looked alright. Clapping his hands, he was able to heal the gash but left the rest of her head as it was.

"Hey, can you fix headaches?" Nadia wheezed. Her mouth was starting to drool a little as the alchemist helped her to her feet.

"It's better if heads be allowed to heal naturally." Cyrus propped her up onto his shoulder. "Better if I don't take your skull or cranium apart and try to put it back together. I repaired the skin so it won't scar, but you should just get some rest back on the ship and let me take a closer look. That's the best way to heal injuries like this."

"Okay." She slumped against Cyrus's shoulder. "I'll take that nap now."

Rostam helped carry Nadia up the stairs to the surface. They were just in time to watch the sunrise.

"Didn't realize how long we were down there." Cindrocles looked up at the big ball of flame in the sky. "Always liked sunrises."

"Hey, Cindrocles?" Rostam looked over at the fire elemental. "Why couldn't you set the ghoul on fire before? Was it because of the demon?"

Cyrus shook his head. "That might have made it harder, but I don't think so. There's a pretty basic combustion spell that every sorcerer learns early on. All they need to do is point at a thing they want to burn and snap their fingers, but you never see them use it on human beings, not even for warfare or self-defense. That's because human bodies aren't very flammable. We're mostly made of water. And even if human flesh does catch fire, it won't release enough heat energy to create the kind of chain reaction you see when you burn a dry log."

"Um…okay." Rostam's face suggested he didn't understand all of that. "So, what you're saying is, I don't have to worry about some wizard snapping his fingers and setting me on fire?"

"Nope," Cyrus shook his head. "Not going to happen. The only part of a person's body that's flammable is the fatty tissue, and I've never heard of a wizard being able to target that specifically."

"Okay…I don't really get it, but I'll take your word for it."

A shocked Joseph and Simon lowered the rope ladder for the boys and the captain to board the ship.

"What happened to our captain?" Joseph pointed to Nadia slumped over Cyrus's shoulder.

"She just needs some rest." Cyrus handed her over to Joseph, who carried her to the captain's quarters. "Dr. Rosenberg was really a ghoul in disguise."

Rostam and Cyrus filled the two in on what had happened in the research station.

"Now what do we do?" Simon asked. "We don't even have someone to sign the invoice. We can't just return to the college and tell the alchemists that their entire crew is dead; we don't even have bodies to prove it."

"Actually, we have this." Cyrus held up Dr. Rosenberg's journal. "And there is one body left down there. Well, most of one. We should pack up what's left of him, return the provisions back to the college, and gather up any other evidence we can bring back. I'm going to make a detailed diagram of the summoning circle we found in that hidden room. That should at least get us something to prove our story about the demon."

"And can we bring the dog?" Simon's eyes brightened. "I liked that Labrador. We should come up with a name for him. He can be our ship's mascot."

Cyrus looked at Rostam. Both of them frowned. "He...ran off. Maybe if we find him again, we can keep him."

"That's a shame," Simon looked disappointed. "I would have named him Scavy. He's a survivor, just like the ship itself."

"Yeah..." Rostam nodded glumly. "That would have been a great name."

52

The Good Enough Escape

NAMID

"Okay," Rana whispered to Namid. "Before we do anything else, you should know what will happen if we're caught."

Namid looked around at the other girls locked in the fancy room. "What should I be worried about?"

"If we escape, there is no guarantee that the necrophytes will be notified. None of the Tomb Lords ever want people realizing that their property can leave, so they might keep quiet. That means they might not be told to look for us," Rana explained.

"Isn't that...good?" Namid raised an eyebrow. "For us, at least?"

"No. Because if the necrophytes find us, they might think we're fair game to do as they wish. There's a curfew strictly enforced in the cities. We'll have nowhere to take shelter, and the two of us combined are better-looking than half the women in this entire nation, just from getting three meals a day alone. I shouldn't have to spell out what the male necrophytes will do, and that'd be a mercy compared to where the females will send us if one of them catches us outside at night. If you think being made into a comfort girl at the bottom of a mineshaft sounds bad, you have no idea. Either way, we end up as shambling corpses."

"...oh," was all Namid could say.

"There's a reason the other girls aren't going to try this."

"Okay, but one thing at a time." Namid gestured to the window. "How do you want to get out of here?"

"Well, the window might not be our best option." Rana looked at the sky outside. "We're on the second floor, and before you suggest making a rope of bedsheets, there's a moat full of undead animals right below us, and they'll tear us limb from limb."

"Do you know anything about the building layout below us?" Namid asked.

"If you listen carefully, you'll hear people moving back and forth at various times of the day. I think it's a hallway, and there are guards who patrol at different times of the night."

"So, we drop down, and swing into the hallway below." Namid looked out the window and pretended to be looking down at the city outside the palace, but was really looking at the zombie hounds in the moat. Sure enough, there was a window in the hallway below. "If we went during the day, we could probably avoid the night guards and have a better chance of avoiding curfew patrols..."

"No," Rana shook her head. "We don't want to sneak out while the rest of the girls here are awake. They'll alert the guards."

"Why?" Namid looked around at the other girls, who mostly looked bored and spent their days trying to use entertainments like the piano or drawing supplies to distract themselves from where they were. "What would they have to gain by ratting us out?"

"Ever see crabs in a bucket before?" Rana asked. "No one in Kemet has any real shot of bettering their lives. So, if anyone makes an earnest go of it, the one joy people in this nation have left is to drag others down."

"Then why are you helping me?" Namid asked. "Why should I trust you?"

Rana locked eyes with Namid. "Because you gave me your hope."

Not good with sharp responses like that, Namid turned her mind back to her plan. "Okay. We leave after lights out. We drop down to the floor below and open the window. Then we need to make our way through the inside of the palace and open the front gate."

"You can't touch the gate." Rana shook her head. "It's made of stygian iron. It'll drain the life and soul from your body if it touches your skin."

"So that's what I felt when they marched me across the drawbridge." Namid gritted her teeth and looked down at her feet. Her shoes had been confiscated earlier. "But if I was wearing shoes, I could cross it with minimal problems."

"If you can lower it," Rana replied. "That's just it; the gate is also the bridge. We need to lower the bridge and make sure we have something to protect our feet."

"That necrophyte woman had thick boots on, and she didn't seem to have a problem," Namid whispered. "If we could grab two pairs of boots, we shouldn't have any trouble with the bridge. There's gotta be a mechanism to lower it. That'll happen after we get proper footwear."

"And how are we getting proper footwear?" Rana asked.

Namid shrugged. "If it's at night, then some of the guards will be asleep. We sneak in, grab what we need, and get out. Make sure you don't grab two left boots."

"Wow, you're really winging this, aren't you?" Rana chuckled.

"It's less 'winging it' and more 'working with what little I've got.' If I had better intel, I could probably make a better plan."

That night, after the other girls had gone to sleep in their separate beds, Namid got up and tiptoed between the slumbering girls. Fortunately, Mereshank splurged on the girls' beauty sleep, and the beds were so comfortable no one was waking up if they heard someone sneaking around. Namid had planned around this and drank so much water before bed that her bladder would wake her up regardless of the hypoallergenic sheets.

Once she'd relieved herself in the bathroom, Namid made her way over to Rana' bed and shook her awake.

"Erm..." Rana opened her eyes and looked at Namid. "We doing this?"

"No time like the present," Namid replied.

Rana got up and threw the sheets off of her bed to reveal a rope of laundry she'd tied together. "Denim jeans," she whispered. "The guards will supply us with whatever clothes we want if we claim it's good for our skin. Mereshank apparently does something similar with her own clothes."

"An entire rope made of denim?" Namid looked at the jeans tied together. "Nothing else?"

"Strongest stuff I could get." Rana yawned. "Let's hope it holds our weight. If it snaps while you're dangling over the moat of undead dogs—"

Namid shuddered. "We'll make it work."

Quietly creeping to the window, Rana tied one end of the rope to the foot of a fainting couch. Checking that it was secure, she gave a thumbs up to Namid. It was her turn to act.

Undead monsters don't need sleep, and are usually stronger at night when there is no sun, anyway. The only way to keep them from howling at the two tasty-looking girls trying to climb down was with a distraction. Namid took out a piece of fabric she'd torn off a shirt and let it fall from the open window. As it fell, a few undead hounds turned their eyes on the fabric. Namid commanded the wind to keep the scrap of cloth afloat in the air and directed it with her magic to float away from the window where they stood.

The monsters in the moat chased after the cloth. Namid could hear the scrambling sound of clawed feet, but they became quieter as she directed the cloth further away, until she made the wind bring it down right on the edge of the moat, far enough away from the girls' window that the hounds wouldn't notice them climbing down.

"Okay," Namid checked that the coast was clear. "You first."

"Oh, hell no." Rana handed Namid the denim rope. "You're the wizard. You drop down and open the window. You might need magic to pull it off."

Namid wanted to argue, but the truth was, she might have been right. Sulking, Namid climbed onto the windowsill and dropped down.

The sound of dogs barking suddenly filled the night air. It was almost like a normal dog, but...wrong, somehow. Only just. Namid froze and nearly fell from the rope. She looked over her shoulder at the undead hounds, who were howling at the scrap of cloth that hadn't fallen into the moat.

Lights inside the palace came on as several guards came to the source of the noise. Namid tried not to think of what would happen if they caught her hanging from the windowsill like this, but that didn't happen. Instead, the guards that rushed to the sound ran towards the barking dogs and hung lanterns out to find what they were barking at. No one was coming anywhere near the window with the girl hanging out of it.

THE GOOD ENOUGH ESCAPE

"Keep going," Rana whispered.

Namid climbed her way down the side of the palace, propping her bare feet against the black granite walls as she struggled to keep herself up with the rope. She wasn't exactly setting any records for upper arm strength; Amri was stronger than her, and Amri wasn't exactly "strong" by any metric.

Once she'd reached the first floor window, Namid grabbed the outer edge with one hand and tried to pull it open. Instead of opening, her hand slipped off of the glass and she nearly lost her grip on the rope. Hanging from just her left arm, she found herself dangling away from the window as the rope swung back and forth. Trying not to panic, she felt herself loosing what little grip she had on the rope as she swung back towards the window.

Grabbing the window again, she tried to hold one pane and push against the wall with her foot, hoping to wrench the window open. Instead, her grip on the glass slipped again and the added force of her foot sent the rope further away from the wall than before.

"Oh no," Namid gritted her teeth as her left hand gave out and she lost her grip on the denim. She tumbled from the rope and landed on the ground with a soft "pluff!" Sand made its way into her nose and mouth.

Fully expecting the undead hounds to be upon her at any moment, Namid jumped to her feet and prepared for a fight, ready to use explosive spells to take a few of them down with her.

But they hounds weren't coming. Because Namid hadn't landed in the moat; the denim rope had swung so far that she'd landed on the other side of it. She looked over at the black palace; the massive door of Stygian iron that doubled as a drawbridge. Across from it, a mundane looking gate stood with a simple gatehouse, occupied by a single guard that was looking at the road.

Namid shrugged. "Okay then. Plan B," she muttered as she looked back up at Rana and waved for her to drop down.

It occurred to Namid that, if Rana wanted to rat her out, here and now would be the perfect time to do so with no chance of Rana being caught. After all, Namid was on the grounds of the palace across the moat, while Rana hadn't left the room yet. Namid had prepared herself to draw all the air out of Rana' lungs if she tried such a thing; she was pretty sure she could pull it off from this distance, too.

But instead of calling for the guards, Rana simply crawled out the window and made her way down the rope. Swinging towards Namid, She jumped off the rope and crash landed on Namid, who had been ready to try and grab her if she missed her jump and landed in the moat.

Tumbling through the sand, Namid realized Rana was even lighter than her. They were both about the same height, with Namid being better fed. Of course, Rana enjoyed the luxuries and pampering that Mereshank gave her prisoners; couldn't let hunger spoil their beauty. But Namid got a good feel of Rana' arms and realized they were even scrawnier than hers. If they got into a fight, it was over.

Rana spat out some sand and got to her feet. Looking around she pointed at the gatehouse. "Only way we're getting out of here without raising an alarm is if we can take him out quietly."

"Leave that to me," Namid whispered as she crept towards the gatehouse.

The guard inside was dutifully paying attention to the road outside the palace wall. Had he been paying that same attention to the girl inside the palace grounds, he might have been able to shout for backup before all of the wind in his lungs was pulled out, leaving him blue and unconscious on the floor of the gatehouse.

Namid opened the door and gestured to Rana. "After you," she smirked.

Rana looked down at the guard, whose face looked like a ripe plum. "Is he going to be okay?"

"Probably." Namid shrugged. "I think. I wasn't planning on sticking around to find out."

The gatehouse had a second door that lead outside the palace walls. This one was locked, but the blue guard had a ring of keys hanging from his belt. As Namid bent down to grab them, she could see the guard moving air through his mouth and starting to regain consciousness. Grabbing a pair of handcuffs from his belt, she bound his hands behind his back and rolled him onto his belly. She then took off one his socks and stuffed it into his mouth, while putting on his boots and using his belt to keep him from spitting out the make-shift gag when he woke up.

"I can confirm that he'll recover from my spell," Namid muttered as she unlocked the door to the gatehouse. "No guarantee about when his master's find him, though."

And with that, the girls escaped Mereshank's palace and made their way into the streets of Kemet, where necrophytes and zombies hunt for anyone out past curfew.

53

The Root of the Problem

AMRI

After a long day of working with his dad, Amri followed him through the front door of their small, one-floor house. Smoke from a hookah filled the living room. The walls were stained yellow, and the floor hadn't been swept in ages. Clothes and sheets had been piled up in various places for so long no one could remember if they were supposed to be clean laundry that hadn't been folded yet, or dirty clothes that still needed to be washed. Filth covered every surface.

Inside, Amri spotted a lump on the couch along one side of the living room, where his mother lay slumped on the couch under a few blankets. Several empty bottles were strewn around the floor beside her. She stirred at the sound of her husband and son coming home, but simply put a pillow over her ears and grumbled back to sleep.

Across from the front door, a hallway led to two bedrooms; one for Amri and Namid, and the other for their parents. Having heard Amri and their father come home, Namid poked her head out from behind a corner of the wall at the end of the hallway. Tiptoeing across the floors, she made her way through the living room.

Their father ignored her, taking off his shoes and heading to the kitchen sink to clean himself up from the day. Amri quietly took off his own shoes and would have used their bathroom sink near their bedrooms, but the thing on the couch stirred again.

Namid's eyes widened as she looked at their mother. Between the empty bottles, the coffee table, and other bits of filth in the living room, there were only so many places one could walk, and so Namid would have to get close to the couch if she wanted to reach her brother.

As quiet as possible, Namid crept around the coffee table towards the foyer. Knowing what she was trying to do, Amri stayed perfectly still so as not to make any noise.

Then a hand reached out from beneath the blankets and grabbed Namid's arm. She let out a yelp as their mother pulled her in and dragged her onto her lap.

"Oh, hey," their mother's gravely voice sounded like it was coming into focus. "Namid. You decided to come out and…and be social today, huh? *Hic.* You shouldn't…you shouldn't avoid me so much, but I forgive you. Gods know, I forgive every one of you, every day. It's a…it's a virtuous cycle."

Namid feebly attempted to wriggle herself free from the arm holding her in her mother's lap, but she and Amri both knew that if you put up a genuine struggle, you made her mood worse.

Her resemblance to Namid was uncanny; on one hand, you could tell where Namid got her looks, but between their mother's unkempt hair, her glazed-over eyes, blotchy, unwashed skin, sallow expression and poor posture, she looked nothing like Namid anymore. All that remained of her former beauty were her cheekbones.

Grabbing the nearest bottle, their mother took a swig, only to find it empty. Looking around the room at the piles of sheets and clothes, she examined the bottle and let it fall to the floor, clattering against the rug before spinning under the couch.

"How did…how did things get so bad around here?" Their mother rubbed her eyes with her free hand. "You know, sometimes I almost feel awful about the things I…" She paused, her eyes moving in and out of focus. "Well, I just feel awful."

Namid tried to wriggle herself free from her mother, and the woman simply held her tighter.

"Girls like you and me," she murmured. "We don't really live. We just... survive."

Namid finally got one arm loose and reached for her brother. Amri almost grabbed her hand to pull her free, but their mother's gaze turned and locked with Amri's. The boy felt his blood run cold as she stared at him. Time itself froze as her eyes pierced through his.

"Hey, you haven't cleaned up yet?"

Amri felt his father's hand on his shoulder, shuffling him towards the hallway to get washed up. The boy had to stop himself from tripping over a pile of clothes his father nudged him towards.

"We spent all day in the shop. We probably smell a little funky." His father seemed to move effortlessly through the junk and filth of the room, stepping over piles of clothes and overturned furniture. "You should never make people smell you when you don't smell your best."

"How in the Abyss does this guy smell anything in this house other than alcohol, hookah smoke, and dust?"

It was a voice Amri recognized, but it didn't belong in his old house. Old house. The one he lived in back in Aklagos.

"That's right," Amri realized. "I don't live here anymore. My parents...I don't know what became of them. I live in Hadesh now with my aunt and uncle."

"This is your mind?" The familiar voice came again, this time more clearly. "It's a dump!"

Amri looked around at the couch, but his mother and sister had disappeared. Even his father was gone. Marduk stepped out from the kitchen and scowled at the living room.

"What the...what are you doing here?" Amri asked.

"Where, your mind, or your old house?" Marduk pressed his hand against one wall and pushed, as if testing to see if the wall would give way and reveal more filth. "You're dreaming. Or, maybe remembering. Your body's asleep, and your mind is replaying old memories. Apologies for the intrusion, but it didn't seem like a pleasant one."

The god took a brass cudgel from his belt and tapped it lightly against a wall, pressing his ear to the surface as if trying to hear something Amri couldn't. "You know this place is infested, right?"

"With termites?" Amri winced. "I hate those things. Or was it something else, like cockroaches?"

"Demons," the god replied. "And I was talking about your mind, not this old house."

Marduk picked up a pile of old bedsheets and tossed them aside, revealing something that kind of looked like an extremely fat worm underneath that was growing through the floorboards. It was as wide as a man's neck, its body like that of a grub, but the head was some horrible mishappen thing that almost looked human, if a human head had been shaped from clay that hadn't baked right. The thing shrieked at Marduk, who grabbed it in his hand, stomped on the floorboards and ripped the creature out by the root.

"Ow!" Amri clutched his head. It had been as if someone had painfully torn brain cells from his skull. "I think that was attached!"

Flames engulfed the creature as it struggled in Marduk's hand, until the monster was nothing but ash and a bad memory.

"If I thought your mortal mind could handle it, I'd comb through this place with a garbage bag." He looked around at the yellow-stained walls again. "Or maybe a whole dumpster."

"Not that I don't appreciate you ripping demons out of my mind," Amri winced as his head still felt like it was missing something. "But why are you here?"

The god paused. "I was going to put you through some mental training in here, since your body is currently resting. But now I see I need to diagnose your problems better before we can get to work."

He eyed the door to the master bedroom with a scowl. Amri suspected that there was something Marduk could see in there that a mortal couldn't, and the god wasn't certain how to fix whatever was back there.

Finally, the god turned back to Amri. "Rest for now. Strengthening your body will have to do until...until I have a plan for your mind. And try to dream of something other than this place; I don't know, dream about...puppies or something."

The god walked up to the edge of the living room that bordered the master bedroom and, rather than go around and use the door, phased through the wall.

Amri found himself waking up in the hospital again. His legs hurt, but this was somehow comforting. He looked outside and saw that the sun was starting to rise.

Climbing out of bed, Amri took two steps before realizing that he still needed the wheelchair. Sarah had shown him the rehabilitation plan; he should stay off his feet for two more days.

Once he'd gone through his new routine and was ready to head out, he rolled up to the infirmary door, where he bumped into Esfan.

"Oh, hey!" The priest-initiate smiled. "I was just coming to get you."

"I'm able to get out of bed now, even if I can't walk." Amri's stomach rumbled. "Don't suppose I can get breakfast around here?"

"Of course, come out to the picnic table. We have eggs and toast for those who are here." Esfan grabbed the handles on the back of Amri's wheelchair to roll him out.

"Um, I'd actually prefer if you'd let me do this myself." Amri grabbed the round handles on the wheels. "I need to be able to."

"Of course." Esfan clapped him on the shoulder.

Outside, a picnic table was lined with members of the abbey and a few volunteers. A few were working over a make-shift stove serving scrambled eggs and toast, while the others enjoyed their meals and discussed the day's plans.

"I was told to include you in today's volunteer work," Esfan said as they reached a table and got some plates. "Something to keep you busy, and also as medicine for your soul."

"My soul?" Amri raised an eyebrow. "What about my soul?"

Esfan paused. "I've been...advised, that your mental state needs help."

"Marduk." Amri's eyes widened. "That's right, you're the one who asked him to look after me. You've been talking to him?"

The priest-initiate nodded. "He says your body will heal on its own, but your mind and soul need some help. Charity work like what we have planned today will be a good place to start."

"Charity work..." Amri thought for a moment. "You mean we're going to go door-to-door, asking for donations for the poor, or something like that?"

"Oh, no." Esfan shook his head. "The abbey does that from time to time, but you're in no condition to go knocking on doors. I mean something you can do on the abbey's grounds, since you haven't been discharged yet."

"What kind of charity work do you do here?" Amri took a bite of toast.

"All sorts," Esfan retrieved a pitcher of water from the other volunteers and poured them each a glass. "You've already been doing charity for the abbey before; clearing away rubble, cleaning lawns, picking up trash. Charity doesn't mean giving, that's just one type."

"It doesn't?" Amri tried to remember any time in his life when he'd heard anyone refer to cleaning things as charity work.

"Charity just means taking care of your fellow man, without expecting a reward." Esfan explained. "Giving people money is the most visible and simplistic way of doing that, but it's something that should be done sparingly. Give money to a family on the verge of bankruptcy, and you keep them afloat for a while. Give money to an alcoholic whose run out of beer, and he might just drink himself to death. That's why the project we're working on today is about feeding people."

"Wait," Amri looked down at his half-eaten breakfast. "Did I miss something?"

"That just comes with being a patient," Esfan laughed. "No, later on we're going to make dehydrated soup."

"Um..." Amri tried to imagine a soup without water.

"Don't worry about it," the clergyman laughed some more. "It'll make sense later, just eat your breakfast."

Once they'd finished their meals, Esfan showed Amri a washing basin for his hands, and then had him put on a set of gloves made of thick papyrus.

"What are these for?" Amri looked at the gloves. "Too thin to protect your hands from thorns."

"No, but they've been treated with wax that keeps germs away," Esfan explained. "Perfect for handling food for other people."

Amri followed Esfan to a pair of burlap tents that had been setup on the grounds of the abbey. A set of folding tables had been laid out underneath, with several stations arranged at each table. There were a number of temple staff and volunteers in work clothes packing items into jars at each station, and at the end of each table, the jars were loaded into crates and carried off onto a wooden pallet for temporary storage.

"This is a soup cannery." Esfan pointed to the stations. "We've gathered a lot of dehydrated ingredients; dried vegetables, chicken, powdered chicken broth, and even some spices. We pack them all into little glass jars, seal them tight, and then you have dehydrated soup ready to store." Esfan picked up a jar and showed it to Amri. "These things last a long time, and all you need is hot water in a pan to turn it into a meal for a whole family."

"Oh, so that's how it works." Amri examined one of the glass jars. They were about the size of a soup can. "You're sure these can feed a whole family? They're pretty small."

"They get bigger when rehydrated," Esfan explained. "We have outposts throughout the empire, especially the eastern cities, and we're going to load up a whole train with these jars and hand them out there. Not as a traditional soup kitchen, mind you. We give the folks who arrive a jug of water and jar of dehydrated soup, and they can take them home to feed their families there."

"Alright," Amri looked around at the stations. "So, what do you want me to do?"

"Right now?" Esfan pointed to the end of the tables where the jars were being packed into crates. "You'll be pouring powdered broth into the jars after they've been packed with everything else.

The task was pretty simple. Amri only had to measure out the powdered broth and pour it into the jars as they came down the line. This was the last ingredient that would go into the jars before another member of the abbey would pack them into a box. A large wagon pulled by a pair of horses drove up near the station, and a pair of volunteers would pack the boxes of jars into the wagon. By the end of the morning, they had over fifty boxes with twenty jars each loaded. As the horses drew away, Esfan came up to Amri.

"How are you feeling?" He asked.

"Physically?" Amri flexed his toes. "My calves still hurt when I move too much down there, but it's a dull pain. Mentally? This has been a good morning."

"Good," Esfan nodded. "I had worried you'd feel like I had forced you into this, since you couldn't easily avoid it. Simple acts of kindness like this...do you feel it?"

Amri paused. When he closed his eyes, he could see the grub-like demon Marduk had ripped from his mind. "Yes, oddly enough. I don't know how, but...I do feel like I'm making progress, somehow."

"Smoke, mirrors, and flashy lights," Esfan mused.

"Flashy lights?" Amri cocked his head.

"Oh, just thinking about something I was reading earlier," the priest-initiate sat down at a picnic table next to Amri. "There's a theory that sorcerers and some other magicians only need to use physical arm movements to make people think that's part of the magic. Some mages, including some sorcerers, can cast spells while remaining perfectly still. Some rely on chanting incantations. There's a lot of different types of magic around the world, and they all somehow get the same effect without agreeing on how. The theory is, none of the wand-waving, dancing around, or ominous chanting is actually necessary. It's all just a mental shortcut to make yourself believe that what you're doing will work, even though it logically shouldn't. Same way a fake magician uses smoke, mirrors, and flashy lights to distract people from his tricks."

"Okay..." Amri frowned. "How does that have anything to do with what we were doing here today?"

"Because it means real magic happens all the time, you just don't think of it as magic," Esfan replied. "No loud noises, or strange mumbo-jumbo. The real magic is the stuff you take for granted every day. Some of it shouldn't even work, but somehow, it does. You know..." Esfan gave Amri a sideways look. "Marduk wants me to teach you about belief, faith, and the gods."

"I'm not really a religious person," Amri replied.

"He wants me to teach you about the concepts on a scholastic level," Esfan continued. "Whether you choose to worship any of them, that's another matter. This is also something he wants me to do to help me with my training." He winked. "Part of the job of a proper priest once I take the oath."

"I don't see how this is important if I'm not going to join the church." Amri watched the remainder of the abbey's volunteers dissipate and head to other tasks.

"It's not a problem if you aren't religious," Esfan smiled as he stirred his own cup for a moment. "But there are things you should know, and things I should practice teaching people. Faith plays a role in your life in one way or another. Knowing how it works allows you some control over it. To begin: do you know the difference between faith and belief?"

"I wasn't aware there was one," Amri admitted. "I imagine faith has more to do with religion, and belief is more about the mundane."

"Well...no," Esfan shook his head. "Not really. Belief is the acceptance of things you are told but cannot prove. For example, you are told in school many things about history that you cannot confirm, because you can't go back and see the events unfold themselves. You believe that they are true, but you don't do anything else with these ideas. Faith, on the other hand, is when you are committed enough to a belief that you take risks. Sacrifices. And neither one of these things is limited to religion."

"Are we talking about burnt offerings?" Amri asked.

"Sometimes," Esfan shrugged. "Whether they actually work depends on what you're trying to do. On the surface, burning a fattened calf as an offering to a god looks like a really stupid thing to do. You're giving up something you have an actual use for, in the hopes that a deity you might not even be able to see will receive it and reward you for your 'gift.' If the world were purely material, these sorts of things would never have caught on; people who kept their livestock would have stayed fed and happy while the ones making sacrifices to gods that didn't exist would have inevitably been underfed and starved. But the ideas they worshipped have real power."

"Right, but isn't that more of a bargain than an act of faith?" Amri rolled himself back and forth in his chair. The pavement around the abbey was not exactly even. "When you make a sacrifice to a god, you're trying to make a deal, aren't you?"

Esfan shook his head. "No, because a deal is where both parties agree to the exchange beforehand. When you make a sacrifice, you're handing over your 'payment' with no confirmation that the other party will even receive it, let alone reward you. The god might be stingy and keep the sacrifice for himself. He might reject your sacrifice, and you'll have given up your offering for nothing. That's the difference."

"Okay, but I've got a confession to make," Amri's gaze avoided the priest as he rubbed the back of his head. "I've never made an offering to the gods in my life. I've prayed before, when I was a kid, but the gods never came, and by the time I had money to buy things to sacrifice—"

"Oh, yes you do," Esfan smirked. "Sacrifices needn't be burnt animals. Imagine if humans were like boats, floating in the ocean at night. We all want to find a port, so we pick a star in the sky and try to sail towards it to find the shore. Some of us have better navigation skills. Some have sea charts. But one way or another, we all try to find some kind of stability so we don't drown." Esfan paused. "What do you know about Neros, the god of atheism?"

"The...what?" Amri cocked an eyebrow. "There's a god of atheism? I thought atheists couldn't have any gods."

"Well, no one worships Neros directly," Esfan poured himself another glass of water from the pitcher left out earlier from breakfast and offered Amri one. "But in a way, he's a perfect embodiment of what a god is. As bizarre as the idea may be."

"...How?" Amri asked.

"Because, as the idea of atheism, Neros is the result of people believing with enough fervor that there are no gods. Except, the idea of atheism has changed somewhat." Esfan handed Amri his glass and poured another one. "It used to be that atheism simply meant you didn't believe in gods at all. No one's really like that anymore, not since the Calamity and the reawakening of the old pantheons. Today, an atheist is someone who refuses to acknowledge the gods as beings worthy of worship."

"How does the abbey know so much about ancient history, anyway?" Amri had been wondering about this for some time. "You can tell me details like records and quotes from people who had already been ancient before the

Calamity, and even tell me what people believed all the way back in times when humans were first building cities, but you can't tell me anything about what happened in the century or two before the Calamity happened? What's up with that?"

"Ah, that's because of the Mystery of the Tablets," Esfan smiled and pulled out a strange device from his pocket. It was a rectangle, about the size of a stone tablet, but even corroded, it was clear that it had once been perfectly formed. No human hand or even power tool could carve such a perfect shape. It had rounded corners, one side had been cracked and appeared to be made of broken glass, while the opposite side had a picture of an apple with a bite taken out of it.

"What is that?" Amri asked.

"This is one of the Tablets." Esfan placed the rectangle on the table. "Legend has it that these things could store an entire library worth of information, and yet you could carry them in your pocket. The Ancients stopped writing things down on paper and actually destroyed many of their old records once they were transferred onto these things, likely to save space, or something." He held the Tablet in his hand and turned it over in the light of the late morning sun. "But...no one can get them to work anymore. So even if the library is still in there, we can't get to it." He returned the Tablet to his pocket. "But paper, paper still works. The Ancients kept a lot of old books and documents in their original forms partly as historical artifacts as much as for their records. These books, which detail Ancient Rome, Athens, Egypt, and even Babylon...these have survived."

"Huh." Amri was still trying to imagine what it would look like to have an entire library crammed into a Tablet, and then try to carry it in his pocket.

"Anyway, I was telling you about the new atheism. There were actually a number of atheist rebellions a few centuries ago, from here all the way to the frozen north."

"I heard something about that." Amri nodded. "Something about getting rid of all religions to starve the evil gods of faith?"

"Yeah, not every god that humans believe in or choose to empower is good," Esfan admitted. "The Red Serpent threatens to devour the sun and destroy the world. Loki in the north is said to one day bring about Ragnarök. Zeus was a serial sexual predator at best, and when his pantheon wasn't brought back, the Meditians got along just fine without them. So, the rebels' logic wasn't unfounded. What they didn't realize was, rather than actually cut the gods off from their believers, they just made the people who worshiped them more faithful; try to ban something, and people just cling to it more. And in their crusade, understandable as it was, they just ended up making a new god."

"Do atheists understand this?" Amri tried to imagine militant atheists realizing that they'd brought a new god into existence. "I can't imagine they'd willingly bow down to Neros."

"They don't, and that's probably exactly how Neros likes it," Esfan replied. "You see, atheists are just like everyone else; they've picked a star, and set their sails towards it. Zero is still a number; the belief in nothing is not the same as not believing in anything. And to some, the promises that Neros makes are too tempting to ignore."

"Promises?" Amri frowned. "How does the idea of nothing promise anything to people who don't even know they're being faithful to it?"

"Nothing holds a lot of promises," Esfan smiled. "Not the same as other gods, but that's the point; if you wanted their benefits, you would worship them instead. Neros doesn't offer you miraculous healings, but he does promise never to take your burnt offerings and refuse to answer your prayers. Tithing is unnecessary when there are no gods to receive it, no unanswered requests. Neros also promises to never drag you into a holy war in which men kill each other for no real reason, and on a less-noble note, Neros promises atheists the feeling of superiority over people who still bow down to gods created by men."

"But wait a minute," Amri turned that idea over in his head. "You just told me about rebellions all the way from here to the frozen north where atheists fought a war to get rid of religions. Also, they're still making sacrifices to their ideas, just different ones than burnt animal offerings. And if they're technically feeding another idea that's become a god, aren't they still bowing down to a man-made god? Sort of?"

"Well, Neros is a flawed god, like any other created by men." Esfan gave

Amri a knowing smile. "He doesn't always keep his promises."

Amri raised an eyebrow. "And the thing you worship does? What makes Truth different from other gods? A lot of atheists would argue you're an atheist too; they just believe in one fewer gods than you do."

"Because what we believe in is objective truth," Esfan replied. "The abstract concept of reality itself. We don't claim to *know* the truth; we admit with humility that we can't. But the universe existed before we did; the didactic principle; the idea that the universe can only exist if there is someone to observe it, is wrong; there were dinosaurs that walked this planet long before us, and before that, other creatures predated them. Truth, the One at the Heart of All, exists regardless of what we believe. Truth is not a god made by men, but one that legitimately made us. That is why we worship Him."

"Okay," Amri leaned back in his seat. "So, what does Marduk want me to take away from all of this?"

"Whether it's your time, your money, or your consciousness, you are always making sacrifices. Marduk fears that the things you devote yourself to, even if you don't think it's religious, are the wrong things."

"Uh…" Amri smiled. "A god thinks I'm worshipping the wrong things? He's not exactly an unbiased source."

"Haven't you been listening? The irreligious haven't gotten rid of gods. They just slapped a new label on an old concept." Esfan dug out a silver Iosep from his pocket. "Why does the abbey encourage people to tithe? It isn't because Truth needs money. It's because willingly giving up a portion of your money takes self-control. Do this, and you are in control of your gold; it doesn't control you. What you put your trust in, what you choose as the star to follow, that is your god. It can be gold, glory, women, men, government – anything. Why do you think so many religions around the world depict at least the top god of their pantheons as a man in the sky with a beard?"

Amri shrugged. "I think I heard somewhere that if horses drew gods, they'd draw them to look like horses."

"Well, maybe," Esfan admitted. "But to a child, the bearded man in the sky is god. You just didn't call him that; you called him 'dad.' That's the person most people trust to guide and take care of them, at least when they're kids."

"So," Amri thought for a moment. "What you're saying is, Marduk is worried that I've started turning to worship things that are bad for me?"

Esfan nodded. "He believes that you have allowed falsehoods to cloud your judgment. Things that cannot be true; paradoxes, that will form into demons if left unchecked."

"He told me my head was infested," Amri admitted. "But don't demons usually warp the body or mutate a person horribly? I don't seem to be having that problem at all."

"A demon can disfigure a person physically, but that's not the only way they can warp a you. Some distort your mind. Some will leave you a bitter, empty shell. A demon is any idea so inherently false that it will take over your mind and cut you off from the Truth."

Amri gave the priest-initiate a skeptical expression. "I take it that's your church's interpretation?"

"I suppose so," Esfan admitted. "Marduk is the idea of civilization. Though he rarely admits it, there is room for him inside of Truth."

"Why would Marduk have trouble admitting that?" Amri asked.

"Well, gods in general don't like The One at the Heart of All. And in return, He only tolerates them for now, He won't always. Marduk assists us at the abbey because he believes we're the best tools at his disposal for maintaining civilization, and I think on some level, he respects Truth, but he knows the feeling isn't mutual." Esfan leaned closer to Amri, and checked if anyone else could hear them. "Between you and me, I believe Marduk became the god that he is as a result of ancient humans trying to connect with Truth, but only being able to make Marduk instead. There was a point when he was worshipped by the Babylonians almost to the point of monotheism. He seems like a sort of...prototype."

Amri didn't know what to say to that. He couldn't shake the thought of some incredibly powerful king who wouldn't give a loyal servant the time of day, and intended to squash him like a bug when he was no longer useful.

"At any rate, Marduk has told me that your mind is tangled with a mess of conflicting ideas. Some of which you almost broke out of during your fight with Doctor Malbim."

"Okay..." Amri wanted to approach the subject carefully. "Such as?"

"You seem to be torn between the knowledge that how your mother raised you was abusive, and the belief that she did nothing wrong." Esfan clasped his hands in front of himself. "Those cannot both be true."

Amri opened his mouth to reply, but nothing came out. He had no response.

"Marduk hasn't shared all the details with me, but he has told me you were raised by a violent woman who blamed you for ruining her life. He tells me that at some point, she stopped being physically violent, and told you that it was better to be hurt yourself than to hurt others. Is this correct?"

Amri tried his best to keep a poker face.

Esfan tilted his head. "Is any of this true?"

"My mother did tell me that it was better to be hurt yourself than to hurt others," Amri answered. "That is true."

"And did she follow her own advice?" Esfan asked.

"Stop. Stop asking that!" Fear pulsed through Amri's brain. He covered his face with his hands so he wouldn't show anything that looked like discontent. Then he noticed his breathing; he'd been panting, like he'd been running laps around the academy's track. He rubbed his eyes and tried to calm down.

Esfan said no more, but he was clearly studying Amri. "I see." He held his glass in one hand and tapped his fingers against the side of it. "Let's stop for today. We need to keep you up to date on your physical training. Come on, it'll take your mind off things."

54

The Underground Market

AQUILA

The city-state of Tarida sat on its own island, where many ships traveled into and out of their vast port. The people who lived in this wealthy trading hub spoke the same language as the Borealans, were roughly the same ethnic group, and shared most of their customs, but had never joined the empire. They held an open-border policy, but they did not submit to imperial taxes or laws.

This meant, of course, that the imperial navy could not patrol their waters, or guard the island's shores. Perfect for thieves, pirates, and other scoundrels to setup a black market, just out of sight of Tarida's own, flimsy security. Most people in Taride knew there was an entire city under the city; they just didn't know how to access it. Or bring it up in polite conversation.

Aquila entered a bar known as *The Drunken Conger*, with a wooden sign hanging above the entrance, a picture of an ugly fish painted on the side, jaw slackened in a stupor. Inside, a clean-shaven bartender looked up and smiled at the thief.

"What'll it be today?" He asked.

"I'm waiting for friends to celebrate," Aquila answered. The first stanza of the password.

"Oh?" The bartender replied. "And what will you be celebrating?"

"My boss's new promotion."

"Of course," the bartender nodded. "We have a table waiting for you in the private dining room. And, might I recommend the brandy we have today: 542, a fine year."

Aquila headed for a door opposite the front entrance, where she found a private room with a large table, clearly meant for hosting parties. A fancy-looking man-sized cabinet stood along one wall, matching the style of the table and armchairs, all very posh. The cabinet had a pair of doors with a numbered combination lock built into one panel. Aquila entered 542 into the lock and heard something inside the cabinet click.

Opening the cabinet, she found it empty, with two bare shelves. Aquila lifted up these shelves, which slid out of place easily, and pressed a small button on the bottom corner of the cabinet's back wall with the toe of her foot. Difficult to see if you didn't know it was there, and impossible to activate if you didn't enter the combination.

The back panel of the cabinet retreated a few centimeters, and then slid to one side, revealing a ladder that descended deep below the tavern. Aquila climbed down into the depths, into the undercity, as the secret entrance closed behind her.

This was Aestival. The locals had all agreed to give it a name that wouldn't sound ominous, or draw the attention of any local authorities who heard it on the surface. There were some people who made their permanent homes down in this sunless space. These were the folks that ran some of the shops where illegal goods and services could be bought.

At the bottom of the ladder was a dumbwaiter that ran all the way back up to the tavern. Most likely, the bartender had a deal in which Aestival provided him with illegal goods on occasion, and in turn, he kept quiet about the hidden entrance.

Aquila couldn't help but browse a bit at the shops hidden in the sunless city, lit entirely by gaslamps. There were, of course, more mundane things, like merchandise smuggled out of distant shores without passing through customs, stolen goods, and items that were legal to acquire in the empire, but contraband in other nations, such as heroin.

Then there were the things that were illegal everywhere. This was what

THE UNDERGROUND MARKET

Aquila always wanted to browse. Tell a man that something is forbidden to even have, and he'll pay a hefty price just to get a good look at the thing.

"Good morning," a familiar, scratchy voice came from a shop Aquila always passed by when she entered the underground market. "Any chance there's someone who's caught your eye?"

"It's after lunch. And I'm not interested, Alceste." Aquila didn't bother looking at his wares. He only ever had one thing, in different varieties.

"Oh, don't tell me there's no one on the surface you'd like to impress," he smiled. "Though, I guess, a girl like you might think she doesn't need any of my love potions..."

"I know the stories about that stuff," Aquila snarled. "Some alchemist in her late thirties cooks up some cocktail of pheromones hoping it will make the men around her go mad; override all their normal logic or inhibitions once they get a whiff of her. Then the first six guys she ran into assaulted her. Everyone involved went to jail. Those things are too dangerous to be properly illegal; governments don't want to acknowledge they exist. You don't sell 'love potions,' just lust in a bottle. No thanks."

"Suit yourself," Alceste smiled.

The next place Aquila passed was Dimitris' pet shop. Of course, he wouldn't be selling his pets down here if they were the sort Aquila could handle.

"Aquila!" Dimitris beamed. He had dark, curly hair and a closely shaved chin. "Always a fine day with you around. Any chance you're looking for an animal companion?"

The thief paused, closed her eyes, and allowed herself to smile. "Got anything that isn't venomous?"

Dimitris whipped out a logbook and looked it over. "Not venomous...not venomous... Well, spitting acid isn't technically the same as venom..."

"I'm not allowed to bring any pets around my current lodging," Aquila admitted. "I'm always a little curious, but my employer won't allow it."

"Ah, your...employer." Dimitris held his grin but gritted his teeth. "You know, rumor has it that he wouldn't be out of place among my wares."

"Oh?" Aquila frowned. "You sell sapients, do you?"

"No, no." Dimitris shook his head. "You'd want to talk to the Di Francos for something like that. What I meant is, there've been rumors that you were involved in the stealing of the Philosopher's Stone from the College of Alchemy in Hadesh—"

"I can confirm that those rumors were true." Aquila crossed her arms and smirked. "And I stole from the Abbey of Truth's chapel library. And conned a god. And robbed a Tomb Lord."

Dimitris swallowed, gingerly approaching the topic. "Right...and those are definitely going to get you up the ranks in the Thieves' Guild leaderboard, but...there was a dragon of some sort involved in the theft of the stone, wasn't there?"

"What of it?" Aquila asked.

"Aquila...you haven't sold any of us out to a monster, have you?" Dimitris' handsome features darkened. "I'm not talking about Aestival. I mean... everyone. Out there, on the surface."

"My employer is..." Aquila paused. She couldn't say he wasn't dangerous; that couldn't be further from the truth. He just wasn't dangerous to anyone who wasn't in his way. At the given moment. Which meant anyone in the hidden city. "My employer is not a threat to you, or anyone you know."

Dimitris nodded. "Right...I...hope it stays that way."

Aquila bid him farewell and continued her way through the market. To her left, there was a stairwell that led down to the Delvers' Cove, a place she never dared to go. In the lower depths of Aestival, the Delvers had dug out an underwater lock where they kept a handful of submarines. They would then go down and bring things from the murky depths, some of which came from monsters that didn't exist in any known almanacs. The cheapest things they sold were whale bones with odd, entropic powers, but they also brought back strange gold, curious gemstones that the delvers swore were made just like pearls, ivory from the beasts below, and stories about what lurked beneath.

Daurgo once bragged to her about how he had earned the respect of half his dragon clan by slaying an entire pod of whales. Apparently the other half wasn't impressed, because he used his magic to pull it off. But the dracolich had a bizarre, irrational fear of sperm whales and dolphins, whom he insisted had their own magic, and always muttered about things like "heralds of the deep elder things" and "minions of the ancient ones" whenever she broached the subject. If he was afraid of these things, then Aquila didn't want to know what was down there. The dracolich said things that lived down there couldn't handle the low pressure of the surface. That was enough for her.

Beyond the Delvers were a few satellite markets that sold various illicit goods and services, most of which were little more than a stall offering a variety of drugs and illegal weapons, but a few larger ones sold materials for sorcerers and enchanters that could only be acquired through...grisly means.

An old man with a mop and a wash bucket cleaned the streets, and while some of the local thugs and crooks paid him no heed, the ones who knew better gave him a wide berth. In the distance, nestled into a cavern on the edge of the undercity, was the Super-Secret Society of Elderly Janitors. Staffed by old men from all over the world, each dressed in rags, unassuming, and as non-threatening as possible. They could go anywhere they wanted, because most people don't even notice a feeble old man who comes around your castle at night to clean the floors. Old women who cleaned up evoked feelings of kind old grandmothers that needed to be hugged regularly and helped down the stairs. Old men, on the other hand, were barely even noticed, let alone approached.

And of the ones who do notice, most don't bother to question it, since the guy who does the cleaning is probably *supposed* to be there. And if they did question it, they'd stop as soon as the old man pretended to be senile. No secrets were safe from the janitors, no battle plans could be kept from the enemy, no scandal stayed hidden. And their services did not come cheap.

Further into the undercity was the Di Francos' Slave Market. A large burgundy tent held cages of captives, but a few were out on display. There were humans for sale, of course, but the slavers exhibited other sapients as well, including a caged lamia, an arachne whose mouth was bound with bloody cotton to show that her fangs had recently been removed, and even an adult male naga, the strange snake people from the east. Aquila couldn't help but look closer at this one, since she'd never seen one of his kind before. She'd heard they were snake people, but always assumed they were mostly human from the waist up like lamia, but this creature was entirely reptilian. He had scaly green skin all over his body, no hair, no nipples, and slits where his nose would be. His four arms were toned and muscular, and while he wore no clothes, he appeared to have nothing to cover.

"So that's what they look like," she whispered. Aquila hurried passed the slave market and avoided looking any of the slavers in the eye. She wanted nothing from them, least of all their attention.

Across from the slave market sat a shop that sold illegal healing potions. Long ago, an alchemist at some point figured out how to create a tonic that could cause an injured person to regenerate from even the most grievous wounds. The potion accomplished this by overclocking the body's natural healing to regenerate lost tissue, but came with horrible side effects. Aquila glanced at one of the red potions. Even in the criminal underworld, they came with a bright warning label:

WARNING: Ingesting so much as a drop more than needed of this potion can cause cancer! Super, horrible, mega cancer! That's literally what happens when you grow extra cell tissue that you don't need. It's...probably still better than bleeding out on a battlefield, though.

The final building on her way to the Thieves' Guild hall was an ore and metalworks shop. The merchants sold stygian iron ore, pitch-black rocks that absorbed the light around them known as "soul amber," blocks of sulfur at bargain rates, and other minerals drawn up from the depths of the underworld. How these things were mined was a trade secret; Daurgo had told her that a necromancer could send his soulless minions to acquire these things from the banks of the Duat, and that soul amber came from the edge of the Abyss, the endless pit where Peppi the Red Serpent was said to lurk at the bottom to regrow his head every night.

In addition to the ores, the merchants also sold stygian steel, which was stygian iron alloyed with sulfur, along with the processed forms of these unnatural minerals. Unless her boss had a request to pickup materials, Aquila had no interest in their goods.

Finally, Aquila came to the thieves guild. A fairly ordinary-looking brick building the size of a townhouse, the poor-lighting of the underground city still gave the place a menacing appearance. Aquila opened a pair of plain-looking double doors and stepped into the den.

The idea of a thieves' guild is something most law enforcement agencies scoff at. After all, thieves are supposed to be too chaotic and short-sighted to organize. What they don't realize is that, while the average *thief* could never plan out such an organization, there are many parts to any guild. Not all merchant guild members are traveling merchants themselves; the same works for thieves.

Aquila entered the hall and climbed a flight of stairs to a balcony that encircled the second floor. There, she approached the office of one of the guild's rooks, a title they picked for the office in case someone was eavesdropping on communications. The rooks' job was to receive word from thieves returning from longer missions, and to send them on their next assignment. They were the workhorses of the guild's organizational staff, and they hardly ever left the castle.

"It's been a while," a rook looked up from his desk as Aquila entered the room. He was a very simply-dressed man; formal, but not too showy. He wore a plain set of spectacles, had a closely groomed beard, and short, dark hair. "There have been rumors that reach me faster than you did."

"Some of them are probably even true," Aquila smiled. "I am the one who stole the Philosopher's Stone."

It was the rook's turn to smile. "We know."

"I stole a book from the Tomb Lord Sekhet's personal collection as well." Aquila showed the choker Daurgo had made for her to repel magical attacks. "My employer crafted this anti-magical necklace to protect me from the lich's powers. I also stole from the priests of the Abbey of Truth, and lately I've been part of my employer's scheme to swindle the gods themselves." Aquila held up a packet of letters written by Daurgo. "I actually have to make this a short stay, because I have more letters my boss wants sent to the gods through his deceptions."

"Right..." the rook looked away, as if pondering how to approach a subject. "This...employer of yours. We're pretty certain that he is the dracolich that attacked Hadesh earlier this year. Is that the case?"

Aquila paused. Rooks were not people you lied to. "It is."

"Not human, and never was." the rook shook his head. "Working with a monster that used to be human, like one of the Tomb Lords, would be bad enough. Lots of our employers are human 'monsters' in a metaphorical way, such as a psychopath. But this is a creature with an inherently inhuman way of looking at the world. Throw in the fact that he practices dark magic, and you have reason for concern."

"I've told Daurgo before: if he wants me to kill someone, the assassins' guild is down the road from our hall. Other than that, he mostly just sends me out to steal things. Some of those things aren't far removed from the things other thieves steal."

The rook drummed his fingers against his desk. "The thieves' guild is particular about taking contracts from outside employers. When Daurgo originally contacted us, he approached as a cloaked figure with a brass mask. Nothing too out of the ordinary; lots of clients protect their identities. But he deceived us into thinking he was human. If he fooled the entire guild, there's no telling what he could be up to next. If you are to continue working with him, we want you to keep us up to date. Deliver updates to our dead drop locations, and someone will retrieve them. All of the letters you have from him? Give them to the knights in the basement. You can have them back once they've steamed them open and resealed the envelopes."

Knights. The forgery experts of the guild, who bypassed defenses in unorthodox ways. No surprise the guild would want tabs kept on what Daurgo was planning. The dracolich might not take kindly to being spied on.

"I'll see what I can do," Aquila glanced at those letters. "Make certain those are resealed properly. I don't want him to know someone's going through his mail."

The rook nodded. "We'll see to it he doesn't."

Aquila saw herself out of the office and recomposed herself. She wouldn't be having anyone convince her to terminate her current contract. Not until she topped the leaderboards and got promoted.

Descending the stairs back to the main lounge of the thieves' guild, she strolled up the leaderboard to check the rankings. A thief could always earn the guild's interest by stealing things of great value and bringing back a lot of gold, but that was only one method. A high-profile theft, and especially one where the thief got away without being identified, could boost your ranking as well. After all, everything was worth what it's purchaser will pay for it, and the more famous an item was, the more likely that some collector was willing to part with a fortune for it.

"Feast your eyes!" One thief beamed as he held up an ornately carved box full of jewels, some as large as a fist. "Vito the Sly always pulls through!"

"You call that a score?" Another thief scoffed and held up a well-shaped tobacco box. "These are from a research lab where sorcerers try to enhance their powers. A wizard smokes one of these, and he gets an hour of enhanced arcane powers."

"Got any proof that those actually work?" Vito sneered. "Gold is always valuable. Your fancy tobacco is only worth something if you can prove it."

"I bet they have side-effects," another thief grumbled. "Stuff like that always does."

"Pretty baubles and experimental drugs..." a sultry voice came from the upper balcony above. "Such simple, basic things."

A curvy, Meditian woman in a backless satin dress descended a nearby flight of stairs slowly. Aquila clenched her fist. Of course, she'd be here.

"Your shiny gems are so commonplace, every jewel you steal cheapens the last." The woman gave Vito a dismissive look before turning to the other thief. "And a new product that you can't even say if it works? Come on, you really thought that was impressive?" She gestured to a massive tapestry kept in a case brought in for display by two pawns, workmen from the guild. "I give you *the Apocalypse Tapestry*, fully restored by expert alchemists, hand-woven millennia ago, and hand-stolen by yours, truly."

"Who'd you seduce to get that?" Aquila snickered.

The woman paused, but didn't frown. Isabelle's composure didn't crack so easily. "I see you've returned, Aquila. Tell me, are the rumors regarding your latest heists true? That you stole the Philosopher's Stone itself?"

"Among other things," Aquila smirked. "Like the *Grimorium Verum* from the personal vaults of the Tomb Lord Sekhet herself. Lately, I've been involved in a scheme to con the gods by filling their mailboxes with spam." Aquila paused as the other thieves snickered. "Okay, that sounds kind of ridiculous when I say that out loud, but it's not an easy thing to do. It's all in the performance."

"Oh, of course," Isabelle nodded. "I know exactly what you mean, but tell us...who hires you to steal an old book from the Tomb Lords? *The Apocalypse Tapestry* has great historical and artistic value, previously owned by an aficionado of such things, but not some evil sorceress who would come after the next owner to show it off in their private collection. Who do you work for that is either brave or foolish enough to steal from a lich?" She tilted her head in a way that shifted her long, black curls slightly, but in a way that Aquila knew had been practiced. "Another lich, perhaps? One who was never human to begin with?"

"Does it matter?" Aquila held her ground. "Have you never worked for anything that wasn't human before? A naga, or an arachne? There's lots of things out there that aren't human that will pay good money for an ancient tome or forgotten artifact."

"Perhaps, but how many of them pick fights with gods and win?" Isabelle tilted her head. "A foolish employer is fine; they're easy to steal from. You can loot their coffers after they bite off more than they can chew. But this is different. Your dragon-boss seems to be exactly as powerful as he thinks he is. Giving him the means to upset the laws of heaven and earth is a terrible idea."

Mumbling from the crowd of thieves told Aquila they were leaning in Isabelle's favor.

"How many people here can say they've never stolen something on behalf of a tyrant, a slaver, or some other villain?" Aquila asked. "We all take jobs for unsavory figures if the money is good enough. What makes this so different?"

"Don't the gods of Janaan have some sort of...Red Serpent to deal with?" Isabelle slinked towards Aquila. "Some monster...I think the Ancient Greeks called him Apophis, and you're too terrified to say his real name? If he offered you a continent's worth of gold to steal the eye of Horus, would you do it?"

"No," Aquila replied.

"So then," Isabelle paused and measured the tension in the room. "What makes *this* any different?"

Aquila crossed her arms. "My employer isn't threatening to destroy the world. That's where he keeps all his stuff."

A few of the other thieves chuckled. Isabelle almost frowned.

"You know what I see before me?" Aquila sneered. "I see an aging harlot who slept her way to the top, and now she's upset that someone else is climbing up the ranks without lying on her back."

A few thieves gasped. One of the pawns who had brought in the tapestry winced and started inching away.

Isabelle's face finally dropped. Then she started to chuckle, before bursting into raucous laughter. "This bishop thinks she's ready to be a queen." She looked at the other thieves in the guild hall, who nervously laughed with her. "Think you know how I operate so well? Perhaps I should shadow you on your next heist. Maybe you could teach me a thing or to."

"Oh, no," Aquila snickered. "You wouldn't last five minutes. You'd be a Tomb Lord's drooling mindless zombie by the time I've escaped with the loot."

"You don't get to tell me 'no.'" Isabelle stepped closer to Aquila, close enough to her face that Aquila could smell her perfume. "I'm a queen. I move as I please. I don't need to contract with an employer like a bishop. If I see something I wish to steal, it's mine for the taking."

"If you can get your skanky little hands on it, that is," Aquila spat.

Isabelle's eyes narrowed. "To think someone like you used to be nobility."

"Enough, both of you."

The rook Aquila had met with earlier stood at the second-floor balcony and held up the letters he'd confiscated from her. "These have been checked by the knights. They say there's nothing in here we should be worried about. They're weird as hell, but not dangerous to us. You can take them and your leave, before the two of you start an actual fight."

"Thank you," Aquila turned from Isabelle and climbed the stairs to the balcony. As she took the letters back from the rook, he leaned in closer to her.

"That dragon is insane," he whispered. "Beyond words. Watch yourself."

55

Crossing the Nile

NAMID

In Hadesh, there were parts of the city that never slept, because bars, clubs, and other businesses were open for nightlife activities.

In Azzitha, the living slept, but the dead did not.

Instead of the sounds of people cheerfully drinking and dancing the night away, the capital of Kemet was flooded with the patter of undead paws as hounds patrolled the streets, followed by the shuffling of zombies that lurched behind them.

Namid had always expected zombies to moan, or make some kind of vocal noise, but these corpses were silent as they marched. Namid had seen the Greymarch before, and they made the sorts of sounds you expected from zombies. But they were rumored to be "not quite undead." From inside of a large, wide garbage can full of soot, she and Rana were hopefully able to disguise their scent.

"Once dawn breaks, we'll have a new problem," Rana whispered. "Walking around in the daylight as we are won't be less of a hassle if people can recognize us."

"We stay put until we see some people leave their homes and go to work," Namid replied. "Once the coast is clear, we're going to break into a house and take what we need for disguises."

Rana looked at Namid half-heartedly. "You really want to steal what we need? That's your first plan?"

"We're trying not to die," Namid replied. "Stealing isn't as important as getting out alive."

"...you adapt to this place pretty quick." Rana looked out from the rim of their garbage can. "Okay, what happens if we break into a house after we see people go to work, and there's someone else still there? An elderly person, or a child? Someone who would call for help? What then?"

"You've seen how quickly I can silence people," Namid replied. "We don't have to kill them, when tying them up and gagging worked well before."

"Truly, you are like a fish in water here. But, what if there's a grandma and her grandchildren in the house? How many people can you take out at once with your magic?"

Namid thought for a moment. "Reliably? Just the one."

"Then can I suggest a different plan?" Rana wiped some of the soot off of the inside of the can with her fingers and smeared it across Namid's forehead.

By morning, the two girls were covered in enough grime and filth that anyone looking at them would assume they had been dead for a while. Namid had even torn some holes in their clothes to enhance the illusion.

"Got to see if I can do a convincing moan like a zombie," Namid muttered.

Rana shook her head. "Zombies don't moan."

"Why not?" Namid asked. "In stories, they moan all the time."

"Well, in real life, there's no reason for a zombie to breathe, so they wouldn't moan unless the necromancer controlling them commanded them to. If you start moaning in the streets, people will either think that we're feral zombies, or that we're a pair of girls pretending to be zombies."

At around eight in the morning, a large bell rang out through the town, and doors to homes opened, allowing people to step out into the cloudy streets of Azzitha. As they did, the girls crawled out of their garbage can and made their way east, shambling around in their best attempts to imitate the zombies that still patrolled the city, although they were slower in the daylight that trickled through the smog above.

Lurching their way through the crowds was easier than Namid originally thought, because people did their best to give the fake-undead girls a wide berth. Even better, people seemed to avoid making eye-contact with them, which made it easier to keep them from noticing the obvious signs the girls were still alive.

"You're breathing too much," Rana whispered once they were away from the larger crowds. "Take light breaths through your nose. Don't let your chest rise and fall. Keep the movements of your arms to a minimum, and when you've got to move them, make them jerky."

Doing her best to follow Rana' instructions, the pair made their way towards the city limits. Thankfully, people continued to avoid looking at the "zombies" out on patrol, which made the illusion possible. When the edge of the desert finally came into view, Namid held in a sigh of relief. They had almost made it.

"Hey," a male voice came from the girls' left. "Those two zombies..."

"What about them?" A different man's voice replied.

"Those have to be the best-looking girls I've seen in months."

"But...they're zombies."

"Yeah, which is what makes it so weird. The one on the right has the nicest butt I've ever seen."

Realizing he was talking about her, Namid resisted the urge to look at the source of the voices and kept shambling towards the desert. *Don't react. A zombie girl wouldn't react to things like that.*

"That...is odd," the second voice added. "Those two look well-fed. Not fat, just...not missing any meals. And if they've been dead for a while, aren't the meatier bits the first things to go? I haven't seen a rack like that on a living girl in ages."

"...well...she doesn't look that dead to me," the first voice had a joking hint to it that sounded less like an actual joke and more like a suggestion. "If you know what I mean."

As they made their way to the edge of the city, Namid realized that they couldn't just wander off into the desert with people watching. They needed to act natural, or at least undead, until these two left them alone.

"That's...kind of messed up," the second voice added. "That's a walking corpse you're talking about."

"What?" The first voice snickered. "They're dead! It's a victimless crime."

"When have you ever cared about victims?" The second voice asked.

"True, but then there's even less reason to worry about it." The first voice sounded like it was walking closer. "There's one for each of us."

"You know whoever's controlling them is going to be mad if we interrupt their tasks," the second voice replied.

"Hm, you've got a point. They're obviously in the middle of...actually, what are those two doing?" The first voice came closer. "There's nothing out past the edge of the city."

"We should check and make sure they haven't gone feral." The second voice was a lot closer now. "We might be held responsible if they killed someone."

Namid's eyes turned to look at Rana as they shambled onwards. Rana didn't turn her head, but Namid could see her close her eyes in defeat.

Footsteps approached the girls from behind. A hand waved in Namid's face. She couldn't stop herself from blinking.

"Wait..." came the first voice. "She reacted. She blinked! They're alive!"

The other voice grabbed Rana and spun her around. Rana let out a squeak as her eye lid was held open and eye examined.

A firm hand gripped Namid's arm and pinned her against the owner's chest. Namid could feel the buttons of a shirt, possibly a uniform, against her back.

"Just where do you think you're going?" An angry man's voice filled Namid's ear, while breath that smelled like old ham clouded her nose. "We're going to have some fun with you!"

More than ever before, Namid wished she still had her knives. "Let go of me, or I'll call the authorities!"

"Seriously?" The face of a man only a few years older than her sneered down at her. "We are the authorities!"

"Oh, screw it!" Namid closed her eyes and pulled a gust of wind full of dust and sand into her attackers face. Once he was distracted with eyes clenched, Namid elbowed him in the stomach and wriggled out of his grip.

Turning around and facing the two men for the first time, she was surprised to see them wearing the same uniforms as the woman who had first walked Namid into Mereshank's palace; the one Rana had called a necrophyte. The first one was somewhat taller, and Namid had recognized his voice as the one that had originally been interested in the girls when he thought they were zombies. The other held Rana in a headlock.

Both men had some kind of marks on their foreheads. Namid could tell instinctively that the black sigil of an upside-down ankh drawn on their skin had some kind of supernatural connection, but she didn't know what. She only knew they weren't normal tattoos, and even that was less because of their appearance and more a gut feeling the images gave off.

"You dare attack one of the godking's military police!" The one that had held her captive withdrew a pistol from his belt. Namid aimed for the gun and snapped her fingers.

The necrophyte must have instinctively realized that Namid had cast a spell, because he had just enough reaction time to throw his pistol off to his right as the powder in the gun exploded.

"A wizard?" The other necrophyte gaped, loosening his grip on Rana. "How did you learn to do that?"

Rana tried to take advantage of the distraction and escape from the man's grip, but he held on tight.

"We need backup!" The first necrophyte raised his arm with his hand facing down, fingers curled like claws. "Come to me and restrain this worm!"

Namid didn't need to ask what he was doing. The patter of rotten feet stumbled through the street as a group of zombies came crawling from the city patrols to join the necrophytes.

"Bring her to me," he snarled and pointed at Namid. "Alive!"

"To Peppi's maw with this!" Namid willed a stream of wind to flow down the other necrophyte's nostrils and mouth. He had a brief period of horror as he realized what she was doing, but couldn't even scream as the pressure burst his lungs. Rana slipped away from him as he gasped for air but choked on his own blood.

The other necrophyte covered his head with a pocket handkerchief and barked orders at the zombies. "Get them! Kill them if you have to but bring me the bodies!"

Namid pointed to the desert. "Time to run!"

Rana scurried after her as a dozen zombies scampered behind them. The girls reached the desert; if there had been more sand, Namid would have made a dust devil and tried to shred the corpses. Instead, the ground was hard, rocky, and dry. Good for running on, but not so good for whipping up a sandstorm.

Stomping her foot on the ground, Namid summoned a jagged pillar of earth that punctured one of the zombies in the stomach. As it flailed about trying to pursue the girls, another one ran into it and ripped itself in half through the collision. Namid made a mental note that zombies don't know how to restrain themselves from self-harm like humans do and kept running.

"I thought this was a desert!" Namid yelled to Rana. "Where's all the damned sand?"

"Used..." Rana panted. She wasn't as athletic as Namid, and was only wearing rags she'd found to tie around her feet instead of shoes. "Factories... glass...exported..."

"And they used up all the sand? That's ridiculous!"

"Not...the...time," Rana panted.

The zombies were gaining on them. Namid realized that she could easily outrun Rana, and the zombies and their necrophyte might be satisfied if they caught just her and filed a report, even if Namid escaped. On the other hand, Rana clearly knew more about Kemet, and could have be crucial to reaching the border. And there was no guarantee that if the necrophytes caught her they'd give up chasing after Namid.

Of course, not abandoning Rana meant having to deal with the zombies. The undead never tired, and Rana was already out of breath and on the verge of collapse. Turning to face the shambling corpses, Namid looked around for something she could use to fight them.

The earth-pillar trick was too slow to work on all of the zombies. But there were other spells Namid knew for manipulating dry, hard earth like this. Focusing on the ground a few meters in front of her, Namid put her left foot out front and slid it horizontally, keeping her focus on the earth between her and the zombies.

As her foot slid, a jagged fissure cracked its way through the earth. It was only a few centimeters deep, but it pushed the ground out into jagged edges, like a gash that had started to grow a scab, only to crack open again.

The zombies closed the distance with the girls, but as they reached the fissure, their feet snagged on the jagged pieces of rock jutting out of the ground and they stumbled against the hard earth. Many of them ripped their own bodies apart in the process, with no signs of pain or hesitation as the broken corpses still tried to attack the girls.

Rana managed to chuck a small rock at one of the zombies. The blow broke its rotten skull, and the corpse stopped moving. Namid stomped on the ground and made more pillars, deliberately creating jagged stalagmites that puncture the zombies and pinned them in place. Once all of the corpses were too broken to chase them or skewered by a sharp stone formation, Namid grabbed Rana and propped her up on her shoulder.

"Let's keep moving! We've got to reach the river!"

"Zombies...won't be stopped by...river," Rana gasped.

"Maybe, but we might lose that necrophyte!"

Namid and Rana made their way through the landscape. It could no longer be called a desert; a desert had sand, and life of its own. This was nothing more than a wasteland. Namid looked around for the Nile, the river they needed to cross, but all she could find was a long field of greenish-brown sludge that stretched out to either side of the girls, blocking their path and view of the river.

"Where in the Abyss is that Nile?" Namid looked around frantically.

"This is it," Rana caught her breath. "This is the Nile."

"That's..." Namid paused, and her mind flooded with a number of things she'd learned in school about the Nile. Allegedly, it had once been the breadbasket of the ancient world. One of the first civilizations had been built on top of its fertile waters, and an entire people learned how to develop a written language simply to convey how to plan around the floods which made the plains so fertile. Now, all that was left was a river of sludge. Namid suspected that she could walk across the top of it, so long as she held her breath. "What on Earth happened here?"

"The Tomb Lords insist that there is nothing wrong with the Nile." Rana glanced over their shoulder to see if the zombies were catching up to them. "The water passes through so many kidneys and livers, it must be pure, right?

But everything from sewage to factory waste gets dumped here eventually. There actually used to be squatter camps out here, full of homeless people living in makeshift housing. That was before I was born, though. And before the fumes were so bad you couldn't live too close."

"Apart from the fumes, are you sure it's safe to walk across?" Namid eyed the sludge and tried to pick out a route through the waste.

"Not even a little," Rana chuckled. "No one has ever made it across. Of course, no wizards with air-manipulating powers have tried. That's where you come in."

Namid sighed and conjured up a bubble of air around her and Rana. The bubble was only about a meter in diameter, and only held enough air to keep them going for a little while. They had to be quick.

Another reason to make haste was coming from the wastes behind them. Shambling corpses in various states of dismemberment were still in hot pursuit. Some of them must have just recently broken off of Namid's jagged rocks from before. Some still had sharp pieces of stone stuck inside of their bodies.

Most of the zombies were now missing either some limbs, or had been torn in half from the waist down, and were only able to limp or crawl after the girls. But they would still reach them, if Namid and Rana didn't move quickly.

"Try to take fewer breaths," Namid muttered, "and let's hope this works."

The girls stepped into the brown and green muck. Namid could feel a layer of her sole come off of her stolen boot as she pulled her foot out of the corrosive mud and took another step. Rana seemed to be fairing slightly better, but only just. Their feet would sink into the ground a centimeter or two, and then had to be pulled out forcefully to keep going.

Namid struggled to keep the air bubble around hers and Rana' heads. She could actually watch the fumes stain their clothes brown as they made their way across the river. She remembered reading that, around the city of Azzitha, the Nile river was around two kilometers wide. They had a long way to go.

By constantly rotating the bubble, Namid would normally be able to let some of their carbon dioxide out and let fresh air in, but the problem was, all of the air around the girls was entirely made of poison. Even still, a volume of air like the one she'd made should last them a good half hour.

The girls struggled to pull their feet through the mire. Namid could hear the undead trying to pursue them through the muck, but she had to focus on maintaining the spell. If she let herself get too distracted, her spell would wear out long before they ran out of air.

Zombies waded or crawled through the sludge to chase the girls. Namid didn't dare look back, lest she see something so horrible it broke her concentration, but Rana did.

"Can you tell me what you see?"

"Their struggling through the chemical waste," Rana replied. "The sludge is eating their flesh like acid. They're dead, so maybe the stuff reacts different to them, but we might have trouble with our skin later. Let's hope we don't have trouble with that before we reach the other side."

"Great..." Namid tried to focus on the spell. They probably wouldn't have to worry about the zombies because the toxic waste they were wading through would kill them first. "Maybe we'll get to the other shore, and we'll still have some of our hair left."

Rana giggled. "Just keep thinking about how we'll get out of this place."

The two pushed on through the toxic river. Namid started to feel her legs burn; there was something wrong with her feet. They itched, then stung, then hurt like hell. Namid had no idea how close they were to the other side; she had to focus entirely on maintaining the spell, while Rana guided them through the muck.

Just as she thought her spell was about to give out, Rana pointed towards something in the distance. There, through the haze of fumes and poisonous clouds, was the other bank of the river.

Namid held her breath to keep from using up their remaining air in excitement. The bubble was already hot enough and had very little good air left. A few minutes later, and her foot touched solid ground again.

The girls resisted the urge to check on the damage done to their legs until they were a good ten meters away from the poisonous river. Once they were far enough away from the shoreline so as not to inhale anymore fumes, Namid dispelled the air bubble and took in as much fresh air as her lungs could hold.

"Good gods, that's never been so amazing!" Namid exclaimed. She finally knelt down, lifted her skirt, and examined her calves.

An entire layer of skin had been burnt by the chemicals in the river. Her feet were slightly better, having been protected by her boots, which were now mostly mush. Even still, it hurt to walk on them anymore.

"How in the Abyss do people usually cross the Nile anymore?" Namid looked over the scope of the polluted river. There were no boats, no bridges she could see, or any other ways across.

"Rumor has it that the Tomb Lords have a tunnel that goes underneath it." Rana checked her own legs and winced at the damage. "But other than that, people go to the sea and sail around it."

"Do you have any idea if we can find treatment for this?" Namid pointed at her burned legs.

"Not really," Rana admitted as she peeled the wraps off of her chemically-burnt feet. "The next city is Khasoun, and we might not even want to go in there, anyway. The good news is, if you believe the rumors, the chemicals in the river are dangerous to breathe, and corrosive to the skin, but no one seems to get sick beyond that. That could be because no one's ever survived long enough to get sick, but...well, let's hope."

Namid snorted. "I don't like relying on 'hope.' Let's see if we can't find a road. Maybe there'll be an inn, or something along the way to the border."

"About that..." Rana gave a weak smile. "I didn't actually think we'd get this far, so I never made much of a plan. But there's two ways of getting through to the empire. We either try to cross the wall along the border, which Khasoun was largely built to guard, or...we could try to cross the inlet."

"You mean...by sea?" Namid paused. "Is there a port? Could we sneak aboard a ship?"

"...Maybe, but that's not what I had in mind." Rana looked out through the desert, which was now more sand than wasteland. "I was thinking we go further south and try to put together a raft."

"You mean...cross the sea, from the desert, with no assistance?" Namid tried to remember a map of the region. She didn't study Kemet too closely, but their population was mostly made up of big cities and smaller farming communities. You didn't see many towns on a map of the nation. "How do you plan to get across the inlet?"

"I was born in a small farmstead in the south," Rana explained. "There were illegal fishing boats there. They smuggle people through the sea all the time. They might be our best bet."

"Isn't this illegal? By both Kemet's laws and the empire's? What if they throw us back across the border?"

"You're originally a Borealan citizen, right?" Rana gestured to Namid. "And frankly, you don't look like someone who's spent their whole life struggling to get their next meal. They won't doubt you if you claim you were kidnapped and taken from your home in Hadesh."

"What about you?" Namid eyed Rana. "Do you think you'll be able to claim you're originally from the empire, and were simply kidnapped as well?"

"We'll cross that bridge when we get there," Rana chuckled weakly before coughing. "First thing's first: we need to get somewhere we can treat our legs. If we find signs of civilization, we should be able to find some medicine."

The two girls struggled to stand and started crossing the desert. They'd lost their shoes to the Nile, and so Namid tore off her sleeves and made makeshift wraps for her feet. Rana did the same. Her feet were worse than Namid's.

"If we find a village, or a farm, or anything of the sort, they'll have excess medical supplies," Rana explained as they walked. "A few years ago, Mereshank decided that, since doctors make more money than farmers, she would conscript some of the populace to make medical supplies and become pharmacists and surgeons so that her lands wouldn't be so poor, and we're in her lands right now. Then there was a surplus of doctors, most of whom had no idea what they were doing, and not enough people farming the land. The easy stuff, like aloe vera and penicillin that you can grow from a farm, were mass-produced, since that was the only thing the conscripted doctors knew how to make. A few leaves of that stuff, or even just some extract, and something to clean our feet should be all we need to treat these burns."

"What was Mereshank thinking?" Namid ran the lich-princess's plan through her head as they climbed a sandy dune. "Doctors make more money because there's never enough of them to treat everyone who needs to be treated.

And part of that's because most people aren't smart enough to become doctors. What kind of bullcrap economy was she trying to make? Explain how this was supposed to make sense?"

"The explanation is that Mereshank is dumb." Rana cackled. "Oh, man. I can't remember a time when I was brave enough to say something like that."

"Yes, well..." Namid looked back over the polluted river. From atop their dune, she could just barely see over the filth and fumes to get a look at Azzitha from a distance. "I don't imagine you could say such things in her palace."

"Let's keep moving," Rana winced. "We've got to find somewhere to treat our legs."

"How can there be farmlands away from the Nile?" Namid asked. "There's no water, and there's very little fertile soil."

"Well...some of the farms out here aren't exactly...legal." Rana grinned. "They use some unsanctioned methods to grow food out here."

Namid pulled up her shirt and held it over her head as a sunshield. "Uh...how long do you think it'll take to get there on foot?"

"We probably won't reach anyone before nightfall." Rana looked up at the sun, which was high in the sky, but finally starting to tip down. "We'll need water before then. Can you pull water from underground?"

"If there's water to pull..." Namid's least favorite form of magic was aquamancy, but she could probably make enough pressure to force the water up to the surface. "No promises it'll be clean, though."

"Doesn't matter if it's got mud or sand," Rana shook her head. "If it's that or death, that's what we'll do. But we've got to get further away from the Nile first. The pollution seeps into the ground, and we don't want to risk drinking that stuff."

A few hours later, the sun had begun to hang low in the sky, and while Namid was grateful for the reprieve from the heat, her throat felt like old parchment that would flake apart if you touched it. She needed to find water.

Focusing on the ground beneath her, Namid tried to find any gaps in the earth below. She had read about things like water tables and ground water, and finding it was all about locating the pockets of liquid underground. *There*, her soul whispered. A few meters away from where she was standing, a natural reservoir lay within the earth.

Of course, locating the water was one thing. Pulling it to the surface was another. Manipulating fluids had always been difficult for her. Her classmate, Joshwa ben Re'em, had told her during the Combat Arena of the Grand Wizard Tournament that this was because she wasn't flexible or adaptable like the water itself. She could handle pressure, and so aeromancy was no problem, and she could be rigid like a stone, but flexibility? That didn't come naturally to her.

She tried coaxing the water to come to the surface, but it wouldn't move. She tried directing it to flow upwards against gravity, but it didn't respond. Frustrated, she tried to heat it up, so that it would expand like any normal liquid and burst out of the ground from pressure, but it just contracted, and the ground around it collapsed inwards, leaving a dent in the surface.

That's right, Namid thought. *Water is weird. It expands when it freezes and contracts when it boils. So then, logically...*

Focusing on the dent in the sand ahead of her, Namid focused on the water again, now willing it to cool as much as possible. *Become like stone*, she thought. *Become ice.*

The water resisted at first, but then the ground around the water started to rise. After a few minutes, chunks of ice poked their way out of the sands.

"There," Namid panted. "Water."

Grabbing an ice shard that had extruded from the ground as long as her arm, Namid kicked the base of it with her foot and snapped it into smaller pieces over her knee. Popping them into her mouth, she let the cold wash over her while the ice melted into throat.

While she was enjoying herself, Namid felt a nudge from her right and glanced over at Rana, who had her hand out. Namid's first instinct was annoyance, but then she remembered how useful Rana had been so far; she knew her way around Kemet. The plans for escaping were hers, not Namid's. And if they were to find any sort of help to get back to the empire, Namid still needed Rana' guidance. She had made the right call in saving her from the zombies earlier.

Namid shattered another piece of ice and handed it to Rana, who tucked it into her cheeks. As she did, Namid knelt down and gathered together enough sand to form a sort of bowl. Forcing the sands to heat up, the bowl became a dark glass basin half a meter wide. Namid broke off several more chunks of ice and placed them in the bowl to melt, for when they needed water quickly later. She then decided to make a second basin for Rana. Theoretically, they could carry these basins with them, though they wouldn't hold enough water to get them very far. They had best drink as much water as they could tonight.

A growl roared through Namid's ears. It took her a moment to realize it had come from her stomach. They could go without food for a while, but sooner or later, they needed to find something.

"Heh," Rana chuckled. "With an empty stomach like that, you'll fit right in with the rest of Kemet." She leaned against the dunes and shuddered. "You know, the desert gets pretty cold at night. You don't happen to have any way of keeping us warm, do you?"

"I might," Namid groaned. "But, I'm running out of strength. The more spells I cast, the more I'm going to need food."

Namid performed the same crude glassmaking spell as before, but this time, she made a wall of rugged glass in one of the dunes. Sand drifted away from the new structure, and Namid shaped two more walls to the side. "I can't make a roof," she finally said.

"Walls to keep out the cold might be enough." Rana leveled out the sand and lay down. Standing up, Rana was taller than the walls Namid had made. She started stacking sand along the opening between the walls to keep out the cold in that direction. "Not exactly big, but it'll do."

Namid crawled in next to her. Her stomach was empty and the skin on the bottom of her feet ached, but she was completely exhausted. It wasn't long before she fell asleep.

56

The Source of Authority

AMRI

After three days of physical training, Amri was still a bit embarrassed that he couldn't do much in the way of actual pull-ups. "I'm...getting there."

"Marduk waited to tell me about what happened at the industrial park until you were feeling better." Esfan frowned. "That wasn't the kind of danger I was worried about."

"It found me anyway. Wait," Amri cocked his head. "What kind of danger were you worried about?"

"The kind in which a young man drifts aimlessly with no goals and ends up wasting his life," Esfan replied. "When I first met you, you had no goal, no ambition, and no idea how to fix yourself."

"Did I really seem that broken to you?" Amri asked.

"Seem? Oh no, you still are," Marduk answered. "No past-tense about it. But there is progress."

"Gee, thanks." Amri rolled his eyes.

"See, that level of snark right there suggests you almost have the courage to start standing up for yourself," Marduk explained. "Not enough to really do much, but progress is progress."

"It's not okay to be weak;" Esfan explained. "Whether that's weakness of the mind, weakness of the body, or of the spirit. Sooner or later, you will find yourself in a situation where people around you need you to be strong. Anyone who would simply allow a person to mug them without resistance is too weak to be of help to anyone, and like it or not, that's the quickest way to make people not want you around. If you had continued on the road you were on, you would have ended up alone, with no friends, little-to-no family, few job prospects, and no real hope. And that's the best-case scenario; worst-case, you could end up bitter, angry, and looking for a way to lash out."

"That happens more often than people like to think," Marduk added. "Fortunately, most people who end up in that situation by their own faults are either too lazy, ignorant, foolish, or selfish to be an actual threat to society. It is rare that someone gets so fired up in the desire to destroy that they become successful at lashing out. Most don't even get off the couch; they just drown themselves in whatever hedonistic pleasures are available that don't put any risk to themselves."

"What if someone ended up in a terrible situation like that, and it wasn't their fault?" Amri countered. "What if someone did everything right, and still ended up jobless, alone, and hopeless because of bad luck?"

Marduk's face darkened. "Bad luck alone can rarely do that. Keep your guard up; there's almost always some sign you can watch for to prevent that sort of thing. But it is possible for poor education, which is never the fault of the student, bad parenting, or a society with broken or corrupt laws to sabotage a person. A civilization that is no longer civilized can have that effect. But you should never count on excuses should things fall apart. As a man, you will be expected to be someone people can rely on to get things done. It goes back to the days of hunting and gathering; the hunter who doesn't bring home meat has failed. The people who count on him for food don't care if he has an excuse; they either get to eat, or they don't. Those ancient stone age responses never went away. Even people who would use every excuse to cover their own failings will still expect you to be faultlessly dependable."

Amri wanted to argue, but he'd noticed that even his own family expected him to be more reliable than he was. His aunt and uncle hadn't visited him once when he was in the hospital, and Uncle Mido still expected him to find his sister.

"But every now and then, you do end up with people who truly do suffer for no fault of their own," Marduk admitted. "The ones who studied, put in the work, took initiative at every opportunity, and still failed. Those people are much more dangerous than the ones who have lost by their own shortcomings, since they have a motive to lash out, and may have the skills, knowledge, or the physique to actually be dangerous. A lazy bum who is bitter and unemployed will never be as dangerous as a man who worked hard for years and then lost everything due to bad luck or poor treatment from others."

Amri let that sink in, and finally realized something. "You're more afraid of people who've done everything right and failed than you are of people who just never got their act together. But...how can a civilization be 'uncivilized?'"

The god paused, then leaned closer to the boy. "Amri, do you understand how fragile civilization really is? What it really is?"

"Aren't you the embodiment of civilization?" Amri asked. "It's 'incarnation,' or something? You're supposed to be the strongest of the Babylonian gods. How can civilization be weak if you're not?"

"I wield the full power of a civilization oriented towards the good of its own populace," Marduk answered. "All the powers of such a nation are mine to wield against anyone who would threaten its citizens. But that's physical strength. I'm talking about the strength of the idea itself. How easily it can be broken. Do you know why I'm a god of magic? Why I was asked to be the patron of the theurgists for so many years?"

Amri shook his head. "I just figured it came with your powers."

"No," Marduk replied. "I'm a god of magic because civilization is a pile of spells stacked on top of one another. The kind where things are the way they are purely because people believe them to be. You cannot walk down the street with an axe and hack people to bits. Why? Because people in society believe violence is wrong. That isn't the case in the rest of the animal kingdom. People get jobs where they work for eight hours expecting to be paid at the end of every other week. Why do their bosses pay them? Because they believe in their contracts, and they believe in things humans made up like honor and duty. Things that would dissipate in a heartbeat if people stopped believing in them. Do you understand?"

"I...I actually think I do," Amri replied.

"Good." Marduk nodded. "Then you must also realize that civilization can break if people decide they don't like these ideas anymore. Remember when I told you my authority comes from the consent of the people I govern? What do you think happens if people decide they don't want to be governed by the idea of civilization anymore? Other gods will try to take the throne, and they've succeeded from time to time. Heck, that's how I got the throne from my ex-wife in the first place."

"But what does that mean?" Amri frowned. "What does it mean to be governed by civilization? And what would make people want to get rid of you and replace you with something else?"

"Hm." Marduk handed Amri the strength gripper. "Use this while I try to explain. Civilization is, at its core, the idea that right makes might. The belief that the strong should use their power to lift others up. The idea that the powerful have a duty to make life better for the weak. That trees should be planted by those who know they will never sit in their shade. That violence should never be used to simply take what you want, or force others into obedience, but only to protect. It's a powerful idea, if I do say so myself, but it's an idea that many powerful people don't want to live by."

"Oh," Amri nodded. "I get it now."

"Indeed." Marduk smiled a bit. "Enlil is a prime example. He is...perhaps the best way of imagining his idea is that might makes right. The elders demand respect and obedience from their descendants, and back this up with threats until they comply. Then they wonder why these kids stop 'respecting' them when the children get old enough to leave, so the elders must place the curse of 'respect your elders, or you're a bad person' on their children so that they don't just stick them in a retirement home and forget all about them. As long as the youth believe in the spell, it haunts them unless they continue to care for their curmudgeon parents. Enlil is tempting to many people because he offers an easy way to get respect; just bully your own children when they are small into doing whatever you say. When the kid gets bigger, rely on seniority so that the child-now-an-adult doesn't throw the parents' own 'might makes right' mentality right back in their faces. No need to live by your own rules or lead by example; just use your offspring for your own ends."

Amri's jaw hung open for a moment. "When I turned ten, my mom started to mellow out. She didn't hit me as much and got a lot better at keeping her anger under control. I always thought she was making progress, but...that wasn't it, was it? She was afraid of me, wasn't she?"

"Yes," Marduk admitted. "This is a classic tactic. Physical abuse while a child is small; manipulation when the child grows big. And when parents raise children along these lines, it becomes very difficult for them to accept the ideas that make civilization work. Why would a child who was always raised in a home where might made right become an adult who believes the opposite? Who would even teach such things to them?"

"This is part of the reason why the church keeps Marduk in good graces," Esfan added. There're other ideas people try to replace civilization with; Enlil is just one of them."

"And it is also why I want youths like you to become strong," Marduk placed a hand upon Amri's shoulder. "So you can follow my example, and show others you meet how to live by my ideals as well."

Amri nodded. "Okay, I've got a question. Why can't Marduk look women in the eye without them ripping off all their clothes and trying to jump him?"

Esfan gave him a look that read *you actually asked him that?*

"Don't look at me like that. He already knows what I'm thinking." Amri gestured to the god. "I want to know what his effect on women has to do with civilization."

"It's fine, Esfan," Marduk's default frown returned. "There's nothing wrong with curiosity in this place. This abbey is all about sharing truth. And the influence I have on people, not just women, comes from a number of factors. First, it was always the right of ancient Mesopotamian kings to take whatever they wanted. The man who sits on the top of society can have what he wants, including his choice of women. When people say, 'it's a man's world,' they are right; it's not 'men's world,' but '*a* man's world.' Mortals have changed what that looks like, but they never destroyed the concept."

"So, as long as there have been people, one man got to have most of the women?" Amri asked.

"Oh, no, this isn't a 'people' thing," Marduk gave a light smirk. "It's more of an 'animal kingdom' thing. Part of civilization is rising above it. Another reason I have this influence over people is that, historically, people tried to offer up whatever they believed was the best thing they could to their ruler, in hopes of receiving generous boons in return. Most mortals don't see this, but the only women who throw their bodies at me are the ones who think that's the best thing they have to offer. This is especially true of fairly young girls, who don't have much else yet because they're so young. And finally, the fact is that I have the physical power to take whatever I want from this society, but I don't have the right. In order for humans to fully understand the difference, they need to see a man who wields unlimited power exemplify this distinction."

Amri took a moment to figure out what that meant. "You mean, you never actually take the opportunities these women offer you?"

"Indeed." Marduk nodded.

Part of Amri sarcastically thought '*oh, how gracious of you,*' as if to diminish the god's self-control. And maybe if Marduk was an ordinary man, especially a nineteen-year-old like he appeared, he would have said something to that extent. But the otherworldliness of Marduk and the aura he projected drove such thoughts away. There was something about the god that Amri couldn't help but respect, and the fact that he would bear the burden of temperance all for humanity's sake wasn't something you could mock.

"Chastity is a virtue that goes unnoticed in men," Marduk explained, clearly still reading Amri's thoughts. "If a man is not going through women like a box of tissues, people will assume that he just doesn't have the option; no one considers the possibility that he would be chaste by choice. And by far the worst offenders are the women themselves. A man can recognize that another man might have a lot on his mind, might be worried about diseases or having illegitimate children, or that he might genuinely have principles that he wishes to follow.

But women? They have no idea how men think, and they often assume that a man is always willing. So it follows that if he isn't seducing women, he must not be able, which makes him less desirable in her eyes. Ever wonder why women often say that all the good men are taken? They're brains fool them;

they assume that if a woman has taken a man as her husband, he must be a good man. She then believes that the men who are taken are good, and that the men who have not been selected by a woman are not. This is one reason some men who aren't particularly lustful will still consider loose women; it prevents the women he might actually want to date from deciding he is undesirable."

"Then why aren't you affected?" Amri asked. "No one seems to think you're a loser just because you aren't sleeping around."

"Because the effect I have on women makes it undeniable that I have the option. People who see the way women flock to me have no choice but to acknowledge that the king practices chastity."

"Or just accuse you of being gay." Esfan frowned.

"Well, that too," Marduk admitted. "At any rate, kings have been looking for ways of getting around my example since the Babylonians became an empire. Mortal kings are supposed to follow my lead, you see. Ever hear of the old right of prima nocte? It was a big deal long ago; it even kicked off the Epic of Gilgamesh. Old kings of the Fertile Crescent had this right, and so did I, but if I never used it, then mortal kings were expected not to, either. So, you can imagine how much the mortal rulers wanted to get rid of me. My power always came from the ground up, not the top down. That's why I feed off the literacy rate of a populace; the more independent the citizens, the more they question authority and keep it in check. Keeps things civilized."

Amri decided this was a good point to stop asking questions and simply dwell on what he'd learned for now. He finished his daily workout with Marduk and then walked back to the hospital. It was a slow process, but the nurse had given him a cane that he could use to get around until his legs finished healing.

As he approached the hospital, which would probably dismiss him to go home tomorrow, he heard the sound of someone panting heavily as he ran along the side of the abbey library. Amri looked over his shoulder at Tomek Ascher running up to him with a roll of papers in his hand.

"You..." he panted. "Been looking...all over for you."

"What for?" Amri's eyes drifted towards the papers in Tomek's hand.

"I need you to sign this." Tomek handed Amri a first sheet of paper. "It's a patent application for a method of collecting methane gas from cows. And then this." He handed Amri another paper. "Another application, this one for a wardable glass sleeve to encase metal cannisters. You...technically helped invent both of these things, so...we need your name on both inventions. And then..." Tomek handed him one last paper. "There's this. Diamond Energy – a company that produces and supplies fuels – wants to buy the rights to both inventions. They're offering us a total of five thousand Ioseps for the pair, if all of the inventors sign."

Amri looked at each page. Three names were already signed. Tomek, Avroham, and a third name Amri didn't recognize, who must have been working on the project from the cannister lab. All that was left was a space for Amri's name.

57

Raiding a Lich's Laboratory

DAURGO

A submarine emerged from the waters near the coast of Kemet. Swarms of rat corpses and other rodents poured out as the vessel pulled up to the shore. Of the corpses Daurgo brought with him, only a handful were human.

"I am not happy about coming back to this country," Aquila grumbled. She'd just gotten back from her visit to the undercity of Taride.

"You took care of the letters, right?" Daurgo asked. "There should be a few left to mail."

"Yeah, everything seems to be going as you planned," Aquila's eyes darted around the area. "I still hate this place."

"We won't be going into Sekhet's personal bastion again." Daurgo gestured to a large, flat building that sprawled over the sands. "This time, we're going to search her laboratories."

"That isn't much better." Aquila frowned. "Liches don't need sleep. There's no reason to assume she isn't working in her lab right now."

"That's what all these undead animals are for. Now, shall we begin?"

Daurgo's beasts lead the way as they moved through the sands. There were few guards outside the laboratory building, but closer to the front gate, a man in a necrophyte uniform stood on watch.

"I'll handle this," Daurgo whispered as one of his human puppets shambled towards the necrophyte. Dressed in his usual black robes and brass mask, he could pass himself off as human if he concentrated on moving the way normal humans do. Not an easy task for a creature with wildly different limb proportions.

"Who the hell are you?" The necrophyte drew a pistol and pointed it at the robed skeleton. "What are you doing here?"

"Making a delivery, obviously." Daurgo kept the skeleton's hands clasped. It made it easier to avoid moving like a marionette.

"Then show me your papers," the necrophyte snarled.

"Oh, you don't need to see my papers." Daurgo managed to wave the skeleton's hand in front of the necrophyte like he was casting a spell.

"Think you're some sort of wizard, do you?" The necrophyte brandished his gun. "Then tell me, why don't I need to see your papers?"

Before he could react, a swarm of undead rats crawled up the necrophyte's legs and tore him apart like a pack of piranhas. He had just enough time to scream before there wasn't enough left of him to stand.

"That's why." Daurgo gestured for Aquila to join him and made his way to the lab, digging through what was left of the necrophyte for his keys.

Once inside the lab, Daurgo sent out his rats like spies to scour the place for guards. On the main level, he could identify two dozen guards stationed at different points, although most weren't paying attention to their posts. If anything, they didn't think anyone would actually be brazen enough to enter their mistress's laboratory.

Daurgo also learned that there were very few actual experiments kept on the main floor. There was a torture chamber, a holding cell, a guardhouse, and a few offices holding lots of papers that he wouldn't have time to pick through. But there was also a basement, much larger than the part of the building one could see from the outside, and most of the experiments were kept down there. An elevator in the center of the main floor appeared to be the only access point.

"What exactly are we looking for?" Aquila kept her voice hushed. "Breaking and entering doesn't give us a lot of time. If we aren't looking for something specific—"

"We're looking for current projects." Daurgo sent a scurry of rats to the nearest file room and had them start pilfering paperwork to drag back to the coast. "My minions will bring me her files and load up the submarine. But I can't leave until I understand more about what the Tomb Lords are planning. Killing a god is not easy; it takes planning, knowledge, and resources that most people don't have. And most important, it takes an actual *motive*; something that makes the high risk and costs of actually slaying the god worthwhile. I want to know how and why they killed Thoth."

"You sound like you speak from experience," Aquila noted.

"Oh, yes. Yes I do," the lich chuckled. "Wouldn't be worth my attention if they hadn't pinned the blame for the deed on me, but that just raises more questions. Sometimes the goal of killing a god is to prove it can be done, or to gain the notoriety and fear that it brings. But to do it secretly? Something else is afoot."

Daurgo fumbled around inside his ribcage and checked the supplies he'd brought with himself. Aquila was the skilled thief; if lockpicking was required, he'd rely on her primate fingers and hand-eye coordination. He'd brought… other equipment, in case it was necessary. Or just fun.

"The guards are currently not paying any attention, but there appears to be some sort of monitoring alarm that will go off whenever someone uses the elevator when it isn't scheduled." He took direct control of one of his undead rats and chewed through a cord that connected the elevator to the alarm. "Disabling it…now. Let's head to the basement."

The lich was no stranger to stealth, but it wasn't his strong suit. He relied on the eyes and ears of his rats to watch for patrols as he and Aquila made their way to the elevator room. Several steam-filled pistons operated the lift, and a single lever inside of a birdcage-like box released the gears that dropped the elevator into the basement. Gathering a dozen rats and three human skeletons, Daurgo and Aquila climbed into the box and threw the lever.

"This is a big elevator," Aquila noticed. "You could haul some large, heavy equipment in this."

"Indeed." Daurgo examined the walls of the lift. They weren't really walls, per se, but more like a pair of thick steel railings on each side of the elevator to keep it on track. "But what I find odd is this open design. Maybe they're really trying to save money on materials, but this is ridiculous."

"Unless the elevator doubles as an observation platform."

Daurgo's current host skeleton glanced at Aquila, who was looking down through the bars of the elevator cage. Daurgo then peered through the edges himself, where he could see the experiments Sekhet had been performing from above.

The basement itself was so deep, it's ceiling so high, that Daurgo hadn't initially noticed the lights below. Aquila's living eyes needed light to see; his didn't, so it was no surprise she noticed the change before him. Below, cages, terrariums, aquariums, holding pens, and various other enclosures sprawled out holding the Tomb Lord's latest experiments. In these cages were...things. Things Daurgo couldn't identify.

Some of them had too many limbs to be vertebrates. Some had only one or two limbs that didn't come in a pair. Some looked more like mush than actual living creatures, but they were moving around too much to be anything else. A few had growths along their limbs that looked like nothing Daurgo had seen before.

But the worst part about these laboratory experiments was the smell. A lich doesn't need to breathe, so he doesn't *need* to smell things. Which was good, because Daurgo's entire body was wracked with a sense so vile, so awful that even from his current puppet-body, he felt like doubling over and emptying the contents of his non-existent stomach.

"What in all the darkest recesses of the universe is this?" Daurgo had to stop himself from rattling the supplies he'd brought with him tucked away inside his ribcage.

"What are you so upset about?" Aquila looked around as the elevator finally reached the bottom. "What's got you so riled up?"

"Can't you smell it?" Daurgo took off his mask and rubbed the spot of his puppet's skull where his nose would be. "Gah! I don't even have an animus bulb anymore and this stench floods every part of my brain!"

"Animus bulb?" Aquila cocked an eyebrow.

"It's the part of a dragon's nose that smells demons!" Daurgo paused. "Wait, I forget. Do humans have those?"

Aquila shook her head. "Don't think so."

"Oh, that explains it." Daurgo put his mask back on. "Damn, this place is flooded with the foulest energies imaginable! Every one of these things in the labs are demonically possessed. There must be thousands of demons in here. What could..." he paused, and looked down at the nearest creature in a terrarium. Matted hair grew from places it shouldn't, gnarled claws that might have been fingernails, fecal matter that oozed from a hole in the front of its body where the loins should be, and an eyeball bulged from one side of...was that it's head? Another eye seemed to collapse inwards, and both looked eerily human.

"Demons can't possess animals, only things with souls." Daurgo let the true nature of these creatures set in. "So that means... Aquila?" He turned to address the thief. "My kind – dragons would eat everything in sight if we grew too numerous, and like any larger animal we had a long gestation rate; there were never more than a few thousand of us at a time. So, everyone knew each other. We even kept tabs on other dragon species, even the ones that couldn't speak human languages. But Humans are different. You breed like rats and flood the earth in your numbers. Tell me...is life cheap to you?"

Aquila shrugged. "Don't know. Never thought of it. Why do you ask?"

"Because..." Daurgo looked at the creature that used to be a human child, and probably still was on some level. "Wait, do you not know what this is?"

The thief shook her head. "Never seen anything like it before."

"...Right." Daurgo looked around the lab. "Well, the short explanation is that every single one of these creatures is demonically possessed. That's why they're so horribly mutated."

"You mean these used to be animals?" Aquila examined another creature that had bones growing through the skin above its spinal cord. "I don't normally make a big deal about animal abuse, but this is pretty ghastly."

"...Yes. Animals. That's what we're going with." Daurgo made a new mental note that Aquila didn't know how demons worked. "Not my species, not my problem," he muttered. "At any rate, I need to scour this place."

Daurgo sent out his rats to check every nook and cranny of the lab. While they found many nightmarishly mutated abominations, there were very few written reports. No, there was a ledger. A large, fat tome that his undead rodents couldn't carry.

"I've found Sekhet's research notes." The lich recovered his composure. "Let's grab it."

A short trek through the lab of horrors later, and they had the ledger. A leatherbound tome at least five centimeters thick, it must have held some sort of explanation for what Sekhet was doing down here.

Aquila looked around at some of the mutants that were still recognizable. "You sure these are animals?" She paused. "That one sounded like it was trying to talk, and another one almost looked like a little girl."

"Here, carry this book for me." Daurgo handed Aquila the heavy ledger as a distraction.

"Oof!" Aquila struggled to hold up the tome. "Why am I carrying this?"

"Because I'm about to blow this place." Daurgo dug through his ribcage.

"You know, if that's supposed to be a one-liner, it's not very–"

"No, I'm literally blowing this place to hell." Daurgo withdrew several demolition charges from his skeleton and started looking for places to plant them.

"What?" Aquila shifted to keep the book from falling out of her hands. "Why?"

"Because this whole place is a giant cesspit of demons." Daurgo allowed himself to smell the foul air one more time and shuddered. "Even without my real body here, I can sense the walls between the astral plane and reality have worn thin here. I wouldn't be surprised if a demon gained a physical form of his own in this little island of hell and tore a path out of the Aether into the material world. If it hasn't happened yet, soon a number of demons who don't even need hosts anymore will break out of this lab and wreak havoc on anything they can reach."

"Is...is that something that can actually happen?" Aquila glanced at the mutants in their containment cells again. "Demons that don't need a host?"

"If humans pervert the world so much that they prepare a beachhead for them? Yes. That can happen." Daurgo picked a load-bearing column and strapped a demolition charge. "There's only two possible reasons the Tomb Lords would make a place like this. Either it's some kind of demonic battery, to try and harness the unholy energies of these fiends, or it's a weapon of some sort. Or worse, they've done this by accident, and have no way of preventing an outbreak. Either way, I can't let them keep it when I don't know what it does."

"You're not going to try and steal it?" Aquila asked.

"Tempting, but not practical. I've never seen a place as horrible as this, but that makes it novel. Novel is good; it means there are more answers out there in the world, including the ones I'm looking for." Daurgo took control of one his other skeletons and planted their bomb charges at key points around the laboratory. "Don't know if I brought enough. A cave-in might have to suffice. Ooh! A gasline. Perfect."

"Alright," Aquila started lugging the book towards the elevator, her burden now taking her mind off of asking questions about the things in the lab. "I hope you know what you're doing, blowing up your precious secrets."

"Power I can't use is no power at all." The lich finished planting his bombs and set them all to go off in half an hour. "Let's go."

As the thief and the lich rode the elevator back up to the surface, Daurgo handed Aquila a gas mask. "The guards are waiting by the lift entrance. My rats have spotted them."

"Um, okay..." Aquila put the mask on as the lift reached the ground floor, where they were greeted by two dozen guards.

"Hold it right there!" The guards had guns trained on them. Several zombies that must have been waiting for their necrophyte's command to attack leered hungrily at Aquila.

"Is there a problem officers?" Daurgo held something round and shiny in his palm.

"Hands in the air!" The lead guard barked.

"Of course!" Daurgo held up his hands, flashing the shiny object to the guards.

The necrophytes trained their guns on Daurgo. "What's in your hand? Drop it!"

"As you wish." Daurgo released the gas bomb.

Purple gas flooded the hallway.

"Oh, I see." Aquila nodded. "Deadly gas?"

"Deadly? Oh, where's your sense of fun?" Daurgo chuckled. "That was a hallucinogen."

As the guards choked on the gas, some of them started beating each other with the stocks of their own guns, aiming for things they must have thought were crawling all over their comrades. Others attacked their own zombie backup, trying to eat the rotten flesh of their own undead minions. A few clawed at things they thought were on their faces, another rolled laughing on the ground.

After a few minutes of pure madness, the few guards that were still alive were slumped in a wreck on the floor.

"Sure, it's not as quick and efficient as a deadly poison gas, but sometimes you've got to go the extra mile, you know? And it was a perfect chance to test that stuff out. Now, let's get out of here before those bombs go off." Daurgo stepped over the body of a man who had clawed his own face off. Aquila hurried after him.

58

Stranded by the Tainted Desert

ROSTAM

"Has the captain recovered?" Simon asked.

Cyrus took a look at Captain Nadia's head, which had an angry bruise, but was otherwise fine. She'd been resting in bed ever since Kaniel had struck her in the forehead. "She should be alright, but it'd be best if she continued to rest."

"She's the one who steers the ship," Simon grumbled. "Why can't you fix her with your magic already?"

"Alchemy is as invasive as surgery," Cyrus explained. "It shouldn't be your first resort for fixing injuries that will heal on their own. Especially brains. You don't mess with brains unless death is certain. Just keep her lying in bed for now. That's the best way to recover from a head injury like this."

"We're stuck here without her!" Simon grumbled. "By some demon-hole in the ground, in the middle of nowhere!"

"Simon, calm down." Joseph sat on a crate near Nadia's bed, his hands clasped in front of his face. "You know we can't rush something like this."

"We're running out of supplies!" Simon ranted. "We've been here for three days, with no navigator, and no help from Domasa."

"We tried recruiting crew from the village." Joseph shook his head. "None of them were interested.

"We can't keep the ship flying without at least one more pair of hands, and we don't have anyone who can steer!" Simon continued.

"Is the steering really that difficult?" Cyrus asked. "That part doesn't look that hard."

"You try it yourself then!" Simon gestured to the ship's wheel. "You'll run us aground and kill us all!"

"I could probably handle the ship's wheel," Rostam offered. "But then we'd need someone else to handle the ballast pipes."

Cyrus looked up at the crow's nest. "Hey, Tarchus? How well could we fly if you stepped down and handled the steering?"

"I can' han'le tha wheel," came the spymaster's reply. "Steerin's more 'an jus' knowin' 'ere to go. You got 'a keep 'er flyin' agains' tha winds an' storms. It's a youngun's game, an' I...I'm too old."

"We really need him up in the crow's nest, anyway." Joseph looked out at the sky. "It's clear now, but we don't want an inexperienced navigator handling the wheel without someone keeping an eye out for storms."

Rostam had seen Tarchus' books and charts on what to look for in terms of weather patterns. He could tell by the shape of the clouds and where they were moving when a storm would approach. Rostam couldn't keep track even with the book in hand; and Tarchus knew all the signs by heart. Joseph was right; they couldn't afford not to have the spymaster on duty.

"We've got no captain, no navigator," Simon grumbled. "And our fire elemental keeps sneaking away to that creepy lab to stare at the bricks!"

"What?" Cindrocles, who'd been quiet up until now, perked up from his resting place on a piece of dried wood Rostam had found. "I like bricks! Brick chimneys, brick fireplaces, brick furnaces, brick ovens – they're cozy!"

"There's nothing for it," Joseph turned to Simon. "Grab a gun from below deck. While it's still light out, we should see if we can forage some more supplies."

Simon shook his head. "We're too close to the Tainted Desert. Nothing could survive that."

"Then we check to the north," Joseph replied. "It'll give you something to do. Domasa has water from their own wells. We'll see if we can find something out there to trade."

"Do you want me to come as well?" Rostam asked.

"No, stay here and watch the ship." Joseph pointed at the captain. "The alchemist can take care of himself, but guarding the ship is your duty. Grab a gun and stay alert."

Rostam nodded. They'd been changing guard shifts in the past, but this was different. Joseph knew they weren't going to find any supplies in the wilderness; he was trying to keep Simon from going crazy. And Simon was right to be worried; Nadia's head injury wasn't severe enough that she couldn't heal, but they weren't in a good place for her to rest.

Cindrocles stayed above deck to keep watch with Rostam as the others went foraging. Rostam checked in on Cyrus, who had been staying close to Captain Nadia since they'd gotten out of the research facility.

"Need an extra pair of eyes out there?" Cyrus asked.

"You sure you don't need to keep an eye on her?" Rostam countered.

Cyrus shook his head. "Mild concussion. Best thing for her is to just rest and not move too much. She might be ready to fly tomorrow if she takes it easy."

Rostam sighed. "We're going to need more crew. We're running with the bare minimum right now, and I don't know how long that'll last."

The alchemist got up from his seat by the captain's bed and came out of her quarters onto the main deck. He looked over the starboard side at the Tainted Desert.

"A whole area like that, just completely dead." He stared. "Not just dead, but killing anything else that dares to enter."

Something was clearly bothering him. Rostam had a theory about what it was.

"Hey, you know we don't actually blame you for us being stuck here, right?" Rostam came up to Cyrus and leaned against the starboard railing. "Simon's just freaking out because...well, he's like that. But we believe you when you say it's not a good idea to try and take the captain's head apart to fix it."

"Yeah," Cyrus nodded, but he still looked lost in thought.

"Something bothering you?" Rostam asked.

"Something's always bothering me," he replied. "It's funny. I used to fret over finding a job after mandatory school. Then when I started training as an alchemist, it was always 'pass exams,' and 'find an internship.' Now it's something else." He finally turned away from the inhospitable wasteland to look at Rostam. "Have you ever been to Dihorma?"

"I think we stopped there, once," Rostam remembered walking out of the desert from a shipwreck after leaving the Iron Mountains. "Well, we crashed. But we didn't stay long."

"What did you make of the city?" Cyrus asked.

Rostam squinted and tried to remember. "Didn't think much about the city at all. It wasn't as nice as Hadesh, that's for sure. We were mostly just trying to get back on our feet. Didn't pay much attention to the locals."

Cyrus nodded. "What were your parents like growing up? Would they have—"

"I don't like thinking about my parents," Rostam blurted out. "I ended up in Hadesh because of a Greymarch attack, and we got separated in the mess. I don't know what evacuation ship they got on, or where they ended up, or if they were on one of the ships that got lost later. And it bugs me, because I love them both, but there's not a thing I can do to find either one of them."

"Oh." Cyrus's eyes widened. "Right...Sorry I asked."

"Don't worry about it," Rostam shrugged. "Just...please don't bring it up again."

"I did an apprenticeship recently with another alchemist," Cyrus changed the subject. "First time really setting foot outside the west, the pre-war territory." He leaned against the railing next to Rostam. "How much of the empire have you seen?"

"Quite a bit. Best part of my job." Rostam smiled. "It's a big world out there, filled with amazing things. And there's some terrible things, too. The further east you go, the worse the empire gets."

The look on the alchemist's face told Rostam that Cyrus didn't know how to approach the next subject, so the shipmate took the lead.

"When I was a boy, I lived in Aklagos. Quiet mining town, in the middle of nowhere. Got our water from a well, most of the folks either worked in the mines, or supported the miners. My dad was a blacksmith, my friend Amri's dad was a tinkerer, and my other friend's dad was a carpenter. Amri and his sister are Coptic, and their parents moved there from Dumiabet to get away from angry grandparents. My family came from the east, and the town was filled with a lot of folks from different backgrounds. They all had the same goal, though. They all just wanted a job that paid for a roof over their heads, hot meals for their kids, and some time with friends and family. Where they all came from didn't have to matter, if you didn't let it."

Cyrus massaged his forehead and smiled. "Wow. That sounds rather nice. Dihorma...it's a city on the verge of all out war. I saw a heroine addict stab a woman in broad daylight. I saw police too afraid to arrest him because of how the public would react. In the name of peace, they permit violence."

A horrid thought occurred to Rostam. A thought of Ephorah. He'd never been able to put his finger on it before, but he finally understood what bothered him so much about her.

"I mentioned one of my other friends from Aklagos. The one whose dad is a carpenter? I've been noticing something in her. She always had a sort of...thing to her. Like, she always believed that the empire was out to get her, but not just her. Our entire race, specifically. But she's been getting worse. My friends don't notice it, but maybe that's because they see her every day, and the change is so gradual they don't see it. But I'll go off on a ship to the other side of the empire, or to Meditia, and I'll be gone for a month. And when I get back, I see her for the first time in weeks, and if I could..." Rostam tried to visualize what he was thinking in his mind. "If I could take all the days that I've spent with Ephorah and line them up together, I bet it would show a much steeper change in her personality. And I don't like what she's changing into."

"Is it that bad?" Cyrus asked.

"Considering some of the people I saw in Harlak?" Rostam paused. "She could become something scarier than that ghoul."

"I see." Cyrus nodded. "Okay, my turn. You are not dumb."

Rostam raised an eyebrow. "I'm sorry?"

"You are not dumb, just because you didn't do any schooling beyond the mandatory course." Cyrus didn't turn his head, but he locked one eye with Rostam's. "I could tell something was bothering you earlier, too. Back when I was fixing your cookware in the galley. Just didn't know how to approach it."

The alchemist looked down at his own hand. The fingers which could tear things apart and stitch them back together in seconds. "My own family doesn't like me. They didn't like me before I joined the college, but it was different. I was just a failure to them, and they could tolerate that. Now, I'm something... else, and they can't handle that. Especially my dad. And while part of that's because they got so used to seeing me as a failure that they don't know what to do with me now, the problem my siblings have is that I'm something 'other' to them. Even the ones who didn't dislike me before...we can't connect, we don't have any shared interests, or experiences. I can't talk to them about alchemy, or my goals, or ambitions. It'd just go over their heads."

"Yeah," Rostam winced. "Not trying to derail your point, but I don't think we have any common ground, either. If you were to talk about magic to me, I wouldn't understand a word of it. And I can tell from how you didn't know the basics of steering the ship's wheel that you wouldn't get it if I tried to talk to you about sailing an airship."

"But we do have common experiences," Cyrus countered. "We fought a demon in a hole in the ground together. Joseph and Simon can't say that. We've both seen how people live in the eastern cities like Dihorma and Harlak. Your friends in Hadesh haven't. And we both agree that we don't want to live in a world where the problems those cities have come back to Hadesh. We're a lot more alike than we are different."

The alchemist stretched out his neck and sighed. "I don't know anyone else at the College of Alchemy that I could talk to about these sorts of things. Most of them come from families of academics, and they don't spend a lot of time with people who work in a mine, or on a farm. Many have never lived outside the major cities; even the students from outside Hadesh usually come from Baltithar, Tiberias, or Dumiabet."

"Does that matter?" Rostam asked. "Sure, they come from wealthy families. So what?"

"My family isn't poor," Cyrus replied. "Not by a longshot. A whole team of carpenters who can finish projects quickly, get paid, and move onto the next can live well. But the cities are just...different, from the countryside. In my class year, I was the only person to take on an internship with a mercenary company, and one of only three to spend the off-season outside of one of the major cities. There's just something...different, about the folks who never step out from behind the walls."

Rostam turned this idea over in his head. It made sense; if Rostam wanted to fix a part of the ship that was broken, he had to go to the place where the part was located and actually fix it himself. But at the same time, a trader often had to speculate about what goods to bring to different cities. If he could never get the right products to people who would buy them, he'd go bankrupt immediately. And it's not like traders who stayed in business would just guess where to deliver goods and hope they got it right. They'd make an educated decision, based on what kinds of things people needed in the areas where they lived. But then, Captain Zaahid had run up a large debt because he'd made mistakes, presuming a demand for wool when the town he was delivering to had just had a bad crop. There had to be some sort of middle ground.

"Anyway, you shouldn't get any ideas about academics being smarter, or better than you," Cyrus continued. "You know things they don't. You said so yourself about your friend Ephorah, and how your other friends don't see how much it's ruining her."

Rostam looked down and realized how much Ephorah had started to gnaw at the back of his mind. "Yeah. She takes every possible thing in the worst way. She sees something like an Empyrian in an advertisement drawn to look like a fool and her blood starts to boil."

"Does it never bother you?" Cyrus asked. "Seeing things like that, or hearing people say your race is inherently dumb and violent?"

The shipmate rubbed his eyes. "Of course it does. But whenever I hear things like that I always try to give people the benefit of the doubt. There's a lot of ways you could take casual banter. Ephorah assumes the absolute worst in everyone; I think she's more interested in proving that Borealans are evil than she is in actually finding bigoted people. But I also know I have an advantage Ephorah doesn't: I can always get back on the ship and fly away from anyone who spouts stuff like that. She's stuck in that city, and has to deal with that stuff with no escape."

Cyrus didn't say anything at first. No surprise – what do you say to something like that? When the alchemist finally spoke, it was a slow, carefully chosen response.

"I do not know what she has faced, or you," he paused. "But I do believe that you're the kind of person who would find a way to make the most of any situation. In the city or the skies, you'd find a way to make it work. I..." his voice trailed off. "I have to ask, if there were a trolley rolling along a rail, and four people were tied to the track, but you could throw a switch so that the trolley would change tracks and kill one person instead of four, what would you do?"

"Um..." Rostam tried to picture this in his head. "I don't know how to work a trolley rail switch. I know just enough from talking to people who work on rail lines to know that they're more complicated than people think they are. A lot of them have safety stuff so people don't go messing with them."

Shaking his head, Cyrus looked back at Rostam. "Pretend it's a simple switch. One you could throw easily. What would you do?"

Rostam tried to think of the problem again. "Probably throw the switch. One fatality is better than four."

Cyrus nodded. "That's what I figured. I just...didn't have it in me to pull the trigger, I guess."

"You..." Rostam blinked. "I'm sorry, what now?"

"Don't worry about it. I just...messed up an important lab experiment, you know?" Cyrus looked back at the Tainted Desert. "Something big. Curing cancer."

"Woah!" Rostam finally thought he understood what the alchemist was getting at. "You...curing cancer...and it's–"

"It's gone," Cyrus shook his head. "The lab, the research notes, everything. Even the scientist I was working with; he can't fix it."

"I'm...sure it was an accident." Rostam said.

Cyrus didn't respond.

"You can't get too worked up over a mistake," Rostam added. "Sure, some people would be mad that they've lost a possible cancer cure, but that scientist will probably put together a new lab and get the same ideas going again. If it had any real chance of working, I'm sure he can recreate it."

The alchemist slumped against the railing and said nothing. Clearly, Rostam wasn't helping, but he had to try.

"Most people would recognize that you didn't do anything wrong."

"I don't accept that a majority opinion decides what's good and what's not," Cyrus replied.

"Well...hm," Rostam was out of ideas. This wasn't the sort of thing his parents had told him about when he was younger. Right and wrong back then were really clear; you did unto others as you would have them do unto you, and failing that, you didn't do things to other people the stuff you didn't want them doing to you. Rostam's dad never told him what to do if you screw up so badly people didn't get a cure for cancer. But there was something his dad had told him.

"This too will pass," Rostam leaned over the railing so that his face was lined with Cyrus. "Whatever you've done, whatever mistakes you've made, you can't change them, but you can learn from them."

Cyrus glanced at Rostam, but his frown didn't let up. "I'm not sure what lesson I was supposed to learn."

"Okay," Rostam grimaced. "I tried." With that, he got up, and went back to the captain's quarters to check on Nadia.

As soon as he was alone with the captain, he regretted walking away like that. "Stupid." He cursed himself. "Just being around that guy makes me feel stupid. Even when he tells me I'm not."

Rostam paced the quarters and occasionally looked back at the sleeping captain. She never acted like she felt dumb around Cyrus. But maybe she was just better at hiding it.

All of my friends are like that, Rostam thought to himself. *In one way or another. They're all wizards, learning how to do things I could never imagine. Namid can make air explosions, Amri can do the same. Even Ephorah could punch me across a room with those gloves of hers. What is an airshipman compared to that?*

59

Posters

AMRI

The Garden District had always been the most expensive part of Hadesh to own a home. Only people with high incomes could cover the cost, and to afford to raise children here was even pricier. Amri's aunt and uncle had no children. They were well off, but they were not the best paid people in Hadesh. Standing on their porch, it dawned on Amri that the reason they could afford to live in the Garden District was purely because they were childless.

Opening the front door, Amri stepped into the foyer with the cane he'd borrowed from the abbey and prepared for his aunt to be worried sick about him. He had, of course, sent a letter notifying them of which hospital he'd been staying at for these last few days. But they had never come up to the abbey's hospital, and it was not like them to ignore him when he was sick at the house.

"I'm home!" He called out as he took off his shoes.

At first, there was no response. Then his aunt came out to the foyer.

"Hey, I'm sorry I haven't been home." Amri was prepared for her to be upset. "I've been—"

"You were at the abbey, in their infirmary. We know." Aunt Panya nodded. "We got your letter."

"You...did?" Amri blinked. "You never...you didn't visit, write back, or even send word that you got my message."

"Oh, well..." she winced and looked over her shoulder at the staircase behind her. "Your uncle...we've been so concerned with finding Namid we didn't have time. We knew where you were; we still don't know where she is."

"Right." Amri nodded. "I had hoped she would've been found by now, but I guess that was just wishful thinking. Where is my uncle?"

"He's at work for now, but when he gets back, he will almost certainly go out and try to find her some more. He's knocked on the door of every mercenary company and asked everyone we know to try and find her. He even had posters printed. He'll be putting those out later tonight." Aunt Panya showed Amri a sheet of paper with a rough sketch of Namid with the word "MISSING" above it and "1,000 IOSEP REWARD" below.

Amri looked over the poster. "How many of these does he have?"

"He said he had a hundred made. He plans to go to the academies, the market and temple districts, and even the southern residential homes to set them up." Panya leaned in closer to her nephew. "If you are able, he'll want your help."

Amri nodded. "What about our neighbors?" He asked.

"If they see her, they already know to contact us. And they won't be enticed by the reward money, anyway."

"The Abbey is only a short walk from here." Amri took four of the posters and a chunk of sticky tack from a desk near the foyer. "I could go there, drop a few of these off, and be back before uncle gets home."

Panya paused, then nodded in agreement. "Just make sure you get here before he does. I don't want him cross with you."

Amri took the posters and stepped back outside the house. The last time Namid had run off, he hadn't been particularly helpful in helping his uncle find her, and while she did come back home on her own, Uncle Mido never forgot. Amri's legs still hurt, and he could feel the puncture wounds the alchemist had left, but if he didn't help put these posters up, his uncle would never let him live it down.

He could just go straight to the abbey, but there was a city gate to the southeast. It was the only gate along the eastern side of the wall. He could make a short detour there, put up a poster, and then head for the abbey. He'd show Esfan one of the posters, and see if he could rally anyone else to a search party.

About halfway to the city gate, the pain in his legs told Amri he'd bitten off more than he could chew. It had been five days since his fight with Doctor Malbim. He'd read somewhere that puncture wounds like his could take two weeks to fully recover. But a bad relationship with his uncle was something that might never heal.

Amri made it to the city gate and setup a poster along one side of the gatehouse wall, under an overlap of the roof shingles where the rain wouldn't wash it away. Now he just needed to get back to the abbey.

A painful walk later, he made it to the abbey's entrance. It was a slight uphill hobble from here.

The abbey was one of the few places in the Garden District that wasn't someone's home. There was some kind of special setup that allowed organizations like a church to operate in the district, with some sort of requirements. Amri didn't know all the details, but he knew they had to be a non-profit organization, or something like that. The place where Namid and Ephorah had worked for a wedding was another setup that had a bunch of fancy requirements; something about "cultural value in the area," or whatever.

When Amri reached the top of the hill, he sat down at the fountain in the center of the three abbey buildings and took a moment to rest his legs. He rolled up the fabric of his pants to check the wounds that hadn't quite healed. They were already starting to bleed again.

"Didn't we send you home earlier?"

Amri looked up at Esfan who was carrying a sweeping broom. Leaves cluttered the area around the fountain.

"I wanted to bring these." Amri handed the three remaining posters to the confused priest-initiate. "My sis...she's still missing."

Esfan looked at the sheets. "That's a large reward. They're that worried about her." He smiled. "We should all be so lucky to have such loyal kin."

"Can you...show those to people?" Amri clutched his legs. "I don't know if the abbey will let me put them up here, but..."

"Don't worry about it," Esfan rolled up the posters and tucked them under his arm. "Marduk mentioned that he was already keeping an eye out, but now my brothers and I will have a face to look for." He looked at Amri's legs. "You shouldn't have walked all the way back here. Once to your house was enough; the nurse should have told you—"

"I know." Amri raised a hand in surrender. "This wasn't...it wasn't a good idea *physically*. It was just better than the alternative. I just...I just need to rest a bit before I try to go home."

Esfan knelt down next to him. "You could stay another night here. With those injuries, no one would blame you. Especially since you were only trying to take care of your missing sister."

Amri shook his head. "I have to get back." He checked his pocket watch and nearly gasped. It was after five o' clock. It had taken him so long to get to the abbey that his uncle would be home in minutes. If he hurried, and got home before his uncle left the house, he could still go with him to put up more posters around the city.

"I have to go!" Amri jumped to his feet, forcing himself through the pain.

"You have to rest!" Esfan tried to grab him, but Amri shrugged him off.

"I can still make it!" Amri clutched the cane and hobbled back towards the street.

"This is a terrible idea!" Esfan held up the posters. "You've done more than could be asked of you already!"

"You have no idea what's been asked of me." Amri continued down the hill. "Pray to your god for me, if you're so worried."

"I will!" The priest-initiate called back. "I do every day already!"

With good legs, it would take Amri about half an hour to walk from the abbey to his house, or vice-versa. In his current condition, Amri could only move at about half his normal speed, and that wasn't fast enough. The sun was starting to set.

Finally back at the house, Amri pounded on the front door, his left hand using the cane to keep himself up.

Aunt Panya opened the door and sighed. "He's already left."

Amri teetered in the doorway for a moment, trying to decide if he should track his uncle down in the night or simply give up. Before he could decide, his aunt pulled him into the house and made him sit on the staircase in the foyer.

"Show me your legs." She pointed to his wounds.

Amri rolled up his pants, and his aunt felt his calves. When she looked at her hand again, it was lightly stained with blood.

"You shouldn't have gone back out," she sighed. "I know why you did, but...I will talk with your uncle when he gets home. Go bandage your legs. And don't forget to put some alcohol on them."

Shambling to the nearest bathroom, Amri took a jug of rubbing alcohol from a cupboard under the sink and winced as he splashed some on each of his calves. Then he put new bandages on. He was tired. Too tired to stay up.

"I'm going to bed early," he told his aunt as he shuffled to his room.

Sitting in bed and looking up at the ceiling, Amri was torn between trying to rest and listening for when his uncle returned home. Eventually, exhaustion got the better of him, and he floated off to sleep.

He washed his face in the basin in his old bathroom. His parents couldn't afford one of the newer homes with indoor plumbing, so they relied on an old brass jug to fill it. Amri rubbed his hands through his hair and shook out the smell of the workshop where he and his father had been making tools earlier. Most of their work was not exceptionally dirty or grimy, but the shop itself had a sort of...smell, that mother didn't like. All that hardware, plumbing kits, and parts for things in people's homes carried something that made her upset, at least more than usual.

Amri changed his clothes as well and dabbed a new layer of deodorant on. How a person smelled was just as important as how they looked.

Stepping out of the bathroom he shared with his sister, he dreaded the thought of going back into the living room right away, so he instead checked in on his dad, who was in the process of cleaning himself up.

"Oh, hey Amri!" His dad smiled. His face was lathered in shaving cream and he had a razor in his right hand. "Already cleaned up? There's probably more you could do. Hang on, let me just..." he cut the remaining rows of his chin and felt it with his other hand. "That should do it."

Amri never thought his dad an ugly man; not by any objective measure. He had his wrinkles from being middle-aged, but that meant nothing to a boy who was not even a teenager. He was, for the most part, very ordinary-looking, with a smile that usually contained a sunbeam of warmth, a receding hairline he had tried to cover until he just shaved it all off, and the occasional fissure where his skin had started to bleed. This didn't stop him from spending more time in the mirror.

"Here we go," the man applied a coating of wax to his chin and upper lip. "Let's just take care of the rest and then..." He glanced at Amri in the mirror. "You want to try this too? No, ha-ha. You're not old enough yet. But someday."

Placing a piece of fabric against the wax, Amri's dad ripped whatever hair remained off of his face, along with bits of skin. He then took a pair of tweezers and started plucking his eyebrows. "Now, this you should learn how to do. In fact, come a little closer. Let me get a whiff of you."

Amri walked through his parents' bedroom to their bathroom, where his dad winced just a bit with each hair he plucked from his eyebrows.

"You know, our ancestors used to remove all of their hair, everywhere." His dad kept plucking. "They thought hair was unclean, and if you let it get too bushy like this, then they were right."

Once he finished with his eyebrows, he took out a jar of aloe vera extract and rubbed it on his face. "There. That should heal my skin so it looks nice and healthy. Just need to make sure not to use too much, or it could make me break out. How is yours looking?" He turned to look at Amri. "Your skin looks like it could use some work. Maybe start with some exfoliating. I wish I still had my hair." He looked back at his bald head, which occasionally had something of a five o' clock shadow in the places where his hair would still grow. He applied some sort of exfoliating creme to his scalp to keep it shiny and smooth.

"Enough." Marduk's voice echoed through the house and reminded Amri that this was somewhere between a dream and a memory. "I've seen plenty."

A bubbling form of liquid burst from the corner of the bathroom and morphed into Marduk. He stepped up to the mirror, where Amri's father had become frozen in place.

"There is truth to the old saying that 'beauty is devotion,' and when a person does their best to look good for their partner, it can be an act of love, but only when it's reciprocated." The god scowled at the memory of Amri's father. "When it's purely one-sided, it becomes an obsession, and quickly turns to madness."

"Mother always thought she deserved better than him," Amri admitted. "I think...I think he thought that if he could be better, in any possible way, she'd change. Maybe if he were good enough, she'd accept him, and then accept us." Amri gestured weakly to the hall where his sister was presumably still being held in her mother's arms. "Myself, and my sister."

"There is nothing inherently wrong with trying to better yourself for your spouse," Marduk eyed the mirror. "But you should look for signs of positive feedback. If your spouse never shows you any gratitude, or tries to improve themselves, continuing down this road leads to madness. It is a kind of narcissism to believe that you can diet and exercise to make the people around you lose weight. Self-improvement improves only yourself; it can inspire others to do the same, but it can't force them."

Amri looked at the frozen memory of his dad. He wanted to hold onto the idea that his father was the perfect role model, the kind of person that Amri should strive to be like. He was a man who was always trying to make the most of a bad situation, taking on the responsibility of raising Amri and shielding him from his mother whenever possible. But there had always been something off about him. Now Amri could see clearly that his father wasn't entirely sane, and while he may have meant well, some of his habits had made their family worse off.

"I think I understand," Amri finally said. "He...he enabled her. All of her worst traits, in trying to be the man she wanted, he just made her worse."

"That is...part of the problem." Marduk opened the mirror above the sink which, in the real world, contained a cabinet for things like toothbrushes. Instead, this mirror concealed a dark, fleshy hole where another grub-like demon lurked. But this one was different. While the one Marduk had yanked out from under the piles of laundry looked fat and...well, "healthy" wasn't the right word, but certainly not undernourished, this one looked like it hadn't had a meal in days. Bits of its shriveled skin had flaked and turned to ash that would've crumpled off at a touch.

"Demons are like rats that eat garbage in the streets," Marduk explained. "You can shoe the rats away, but so long as the spiritual trash remains, they will return to feast. But get rid of the garbage the vermin eat..." the god grabbed the maggot-demon, who was too weak to resist this time and came right out like a weed without roots. "And they starve."

Amri rubbed his head, and realized there was no pain from this demon being removed. Instead, he felt like his thoughts were somehow clearer than before.

"Hold onto these lessons." Marduk wiped the dusty remains of the demon from his hands. "I fear you will need this wisdom soon. Things are stirring, and your civilization will soon be under threat. From within, and without."

Before Amri could ask what he meant, he heard what sounded like birds chirping, and felt the sun on his face. He opened his eyes and was back in his bed.

It would have been a perfect morning for a run, but with his legs still bound, he grabbed a set of dumbbells he'd bought recently and did a workout with his arms instead. It was too early for anyone else to be up yet; he would have to face his uncle at breakfast later.

Once he heard the sounds of his aunt and uncle moving about, he took a deep breath and prepared himself before heading to the kitchen. There, his aunt was making scrambled eggs over the stove, while his uncle sat at the family table. He had presumably slept the whole night, but he looked up at Amri with very tired eyes.

"Sit." He gestured to a chair. There was no anger in his tone, but Amri kept his guard up.

"Show me your legs," he ordered.

Amri paused. He had not changed his bandages since last night, and he had no idea what his calves looked like this morning. But he unwrapped the linens around his legs and revealed the puncture wounds. They had healed from the damage he'd done to them last night, but no more than that.

His uncle sighed. "You were out giving posters to your friends at the abbey last night?"

Amri nodded. "I also put one up at the gate by the eastern wall."

"It wasn't..." Uncle Mido paused, struggling with his words. "I am not trying...to trade you for your sister. You shouldn't feel like you have to injure yourself to find her."

Amri didn't know what to say. He hadn't prepared for this at all. "Really? You're not mad that I wasn't able to go with you last night?"

Uncle Mido shook his head.

"Why don't we let last night go." Aunt Panya brought over two plates of scrambled eggs. "Have some breakfast."

Amri allowed himself to relax, while his uncle took a moment holding his forehead before touching his eggs, but something still bothered him. What did Marduk mean that civilization would be threatened? From within? From without?

60

Desert Survivalist

NAMID

The feel of something soft and warm.

Namid started to wake up, realizing that she was holding something soft and warm against her chest. She opened her eyes to see she was squeezing Rana like a teddy bear in their make-shift shelter.

"Good morning." Rana opened her eyes.

"Ah!" Namid recoiled and smacked her head against the glass wall behind her. "What? I didn't do anything!"

"It's alright." Rana rubbed sleep from her eyes. "You were probably cold and grabbed the nearest warm thing while you slept. Might have kept us warm enough to survive the night."

"Uh...right." Namid rubbed the back of her head. It dawned on her that she had actually managed to sleep fairly well, despite not having her brother around to read her a bedtime story. "Um...we need to get moving again."

Less of the ice had melted overnight than Namid had expected. That really wasn't surprising, considering how cold it still was in the desert, even with the sun starting to rise. Namid checked the basins she'd made the night before. They were filled with water. Not exactly clean water, but water none the less.

Breaking off chunks of ice to store in their mouths as they traveled, Namid and Rana each carried a basin as they continued towards the sunrise. To the east.

"You know, I've been wondering." Rana sucked on her ice chunk. "What is life in the Borealan Empire like? What is 'normal' to you?"

"Well..." Namid thought about how to explain. "It's frankly better than life here in almost every way. No one sells their own fingers for food because no one is poor enough to buy them. No one is really struggling for water because the Borealans setup water plants a long time ago. There's not really a shortage of food. There's a shortage of food that tastes good, as anyone who's ever eaten Jacob's Kudzu can tell you, but no one is starving to death."

"Anything about your family?" Rana asked.

"I've got an uncle I see in the evenings when he comes home from work, and an aunt who mostly works from home. But my brother's been with me since we had to flee from our old home in Aklagos. He's...hm."

"Cat got your tongue?" Rana asked.

"He's...well, he's...kind of weak," Namid admitted. "Okay, he's a wimp. I've seen him allow another boy to beat him within a hair of his life in a contest where fighting wasn't allowed. He'd rather obey all the rules than defend his own life."

"That's not good. Is he okay now?"

"Physically?" Namid glanced at Rana. "His wounds have healed. But mentally, I don't think he's changed at all."

"Ah." Rana paused before giving Namid a wry smile. "So, got a boyfriend?"

"Nope," Namid shook her head. "Made a go of it, but no success. I was getting close to a boy named Joshwa, but...it didn't work out."

"Did he dump you?"

"No, we never quite reached the 'dating' stage. But we fought each other in the Grand Wizard Tournament, and I won, but...we're not speaking anymore."

Namid didn't want to mention that the fight was literally part of the competition, and that the real reason they stopped talking was because Joshwa had called her a sociopath. And she'd impaled him with an icicle.

"You know something else?" Namid wanted to change the subject. "No one in the empire gets attacked by the police. What in the unhinged jaws of the red serpent was that about?"

"That's pretty common here," Rana replied. "The necrophytes have free reign to do as they will to the common person, as long as order is maintained and the Tomb Lords stay in power. I hear they're even encouraged to take full advantage of young women they find."

"That's messed up." Namid crunched an ice chunk in her mouth. "Why have police at all if they're going to commit crimes for you?"

"The Tomb Lords don't really care about crime," Rana explained. "Or, they don't care about that kind of crime. When a necrophyte does it, it is not illegal. All that matters is that public order is maintained."

Rana paused for a moment. Namid stopped to check if she had a problem, but Rana was staring off into the distance, deep in thought.

"Do you know what I'm scared of most?" Rana finally asked. "The one fear I still have?"

Namid shook her head. She didn't know, and she didn't really care, either.

"Amenhotep...he isn't just evil. He makes everyone around him evil. That's how he keeps them under his control. When I was four, I wanted to be a princess. Then when I was twelve, I was scouted by one of Mereshank's servants, who bought me from my family to live in the palace. I always thought I was terribly unlucky, having been bought to be raised like a pig for the slaughter."

Namid rolled her eyes but didn't let Rana see. She wasn't interested in Rana' life story, but she might as well let the girl ramble.

"But I'd occasionally be let out of the prison when I asked for exercise to maintain my figure, and the guards would let me walk or occasionally run around the palace grounds. I got a good look at some of the children bought by Amenhotep to become necrophytes. They're all twisted beyond belief. Funny, it's not that they have no empathy, or that they have no sense of right and wrong. It's that they have a very *warped* sense of right and wrong, and they don't dare question whether the orders they're given are coming from a monster. Afterall, they tell themselves all the time that torturing prisoners is justified if it's for the good of Kemet. Starving peasants and taking every last grain of wheat away from them? Killing a homeless man for 'dirtying up the streets?' Even rape can be justified if they tell themselves it's for the greater good."

As much as Namid hadn't cared before, she found herself listening more closely than she'd intended to Rana's story. Maybe it was because they were walking in the desert and she was incredibly bored. Maybe it was something else.

"Then there's the people who aren't bought up as children," Rana continued. "The ones who still work in the fields and factories. You know when I mentioned crabs in a bucket back in the palace? Well, the whole of Kemet is like that. No one over the age of ten has any dreams, or hopes, ambitions for any kind of better life. If you did actually rise above the others in your community, whatever you've produced will be taken by the Tomb Lords back to the capital to be redistributed. I think it's called a 'palace economy,' or something like that. So, the only thing that anyone has to look forward to anymore is to see someone else be brought down. Especially someone who tried to climb out of the shared misery of everyone else. In some ways, they're worse than the necrophytes, because they don't even try to justify tearing each other apart by saying it's 'for the greater good.'"

Namid made a mental note to be on her guard when they found signs of civilization again. Now the conversation had her full attention.

"The thing is..." Rana glanced at Namid. "They're a bit like you. Not the part about trying to bring other people down, but...you're...a killer."

"So?" Namid raised an eyebrow.

"You threatened to call the authorities on those necrophytes, like you actually believed the police would protect us. You're not from a place where the police are worse than criminals. But as soon as you learned they *were* the authorities, you exploded the lungs of the guy who grabbed me. I've lived in Kemet my whole life, was born in a hovel, and spent the last few years in Mereshank's holding center. But if I had a gun in my hand when those necrophytes attacked, I don't know if I could pull the trigger."

"Well..." Namid paused for a moment. She was somewhat aware that killing people, even in a situation where it was necessary, was supposed to be something most folks would have trouble with. But she could never wrap her head around why. Why was it supposed to be difficult to kill crooked military police in self-defense? Why was she expected to hesitate? If she had, the two girls probably wouldn't have gotten away from those necrophytes. "It seemed like a good idea at the time," she finally said.

"It was," Rana admitted. "Just...hard for most people."

After an hour of walking through the desert, the sun was starting to beat down on them. They still had water in the basins they carried, but it wouldn't last for long.

Namid stepped on something that was too hard to be sand. In the desert heat, it took her a moment to realize what it was.

"A road?"

Stretching out to their left and right, Namid checked the motion of the sun. They had been heading east, so that meant...

"If we turn left, it will take us south." Rana pointed to the distance. "There will be farms down there, and we'll find ways of getting across the sea to the empire."

The girls did their best to shield themselves from the sun with their clothes. Eventually, some small buildings came into view.

"When we get there, you might need to use your powers to perform some services to trade for what we need," Rana said.

"I hope you mean services involving magic," Namid grumbled. "I've had just about enough of this country's views of women."

Rana chuckled. "Wow. You really are spoiled."

Once they reached the edge of the field, the girls huddled against the first shed they could find and used its shade to take refuge from the sun. Nearby, Namid and Rana noticed a large compost bin exposed to the sun, with water inside.

"How good is your magic at moving dirt?" Rana asked.

"Very," Namid replied. "Why, could I help them by plowing fields?"

"Hm, not likely." Rana gave Namid a light smile. "There's something else they might need you to do."

Rana knocked on a door to a shed and waited.

Namid cocked an eyebrow. "Is this one of those 'wait for it' moments?"

A few seconds later, a man with a terrible stoop and more hair on his chin than on his scalp cracked the door open. "What do you want?"

"We need penicillin and aloe vera extract," Rana pointed to their burned legs. "I know you have some."

"Don't care." The man tried to slam the door, but Rana stopped it with her foot.

"We also know what you have growing down there," she whispered. "Unless you pour water into your compost bin for wasteful reasons, I'm guessing you're brewing nutrient solution, draining into the basement of your shed."

The man's eyes widened, but he held his ground. "There's nothing down there for you."

"What if I told you my friend here is a wizard?" Rana gestured to Namid, who conjured a small ball of wind in her palm as a demonstration.

"Doesn't matter," his face hardened further. "If you're with the necrocracy, show me your badges and be done with it. If not, get off my farm."

"We both know you don't own this land," Rana replied. "That's why you're running an illegal farm underground. We can help you expand it, maybe even grow enough food to feed some of your neighbors, or we can report you to the necrophytes."

The man's eyes flickered back and forth between the girls before checking outside the shed to see if anyone else was watching. "Damn you both. Come inside."

Rana swung the door open as the man went further into his shed. Outside, the building was little more than a barn for storing tools. You couldn't even put livestock in such a small place. But a hatch in one corner lay open, revealing a narrow ladder down into the earth.

The ladder led to a dug out, rocky place with clumsily laid bricks stacked in places to act as supports. A few wooden beams held the ceiling up, but Namid worried that this place could collapse at any minute. The old man had to use an oil lamp to navigate in the darkness. The sorceress was about to ask why anyone would dig this pit, or why they were so secretive about it, but the old man lit a larger fire that illuminated the burrow, revealing six long rows of mushrooms growing through some sort of wooden planter with holes in it that allowed the rest of the fungi to extend down into...whatever they were growing out of.

"Hydroponics," Rana explained. "It's illegal, but they use only about a tenth of the water needed for growing plants in the soil. Most of that water just goes into the dirt and becomes lost. My uncle used to have one of these farms where he grew mushrooms like these." She lightly touched one of the heads of a large, white stalk. "These things are fungi, not plants, so they'll grow down here without any sunlight at all. You can hide your crop from the harvesters."

"Harvesters?" Namid asked.

"Government workers who collect the food the farmers grow and take it to Azzitha. They then divide it up and redistribute it back throughout the country. Problem is, with such poor management of the Nile, no one can use the old farmlands we used to have, and the only water out here in the desert is underground. So, the surface farms never grow enough for the farmers to feed themselves, let alone redistribute their crop throughout the country. Unless..." she gestured to the mushroom farm. "They hide it like this."

The old man handed them a brown earthenware jar. "Here is the aloe extract. And here is a bottle of penicillin. Now what can your wizard do for me?"

"What do you want me to do?" Namid gestured towards the farm. "You want more water? Or more space down here to grow crops?" She looked up at the ceiling. "I might be able to do something about this roof to make sure it doesn't collapse on us.

"I..." the old man paused. "Fortify my ceiling first as payment for the medicine. Then get me more water, and I'll give you what mushrooms I can spare."

Examining the roof of the cave, Namid pulled a pillar of earth up from the ground and pushed it against the ceiling as an extra support. She then took the old man's oil lamp and cooked the dirt into more solid clay, or a rough equivalent. As she did, Rana applied the aloe vera extract to both the girls' legs.

Once the cave roof was solidified and wouldn't collapse anytime soon, Namid reached her spirit into the surrounding earth and looked for water. "The guy probably won't pay me if I find him water that he was already using."

Namid followed the water supplied to the mushrooms to a pipe that lead to an underground well. Only a little bit of water was coming in at a time.

"Alright, so any other source of water should do." Namid walked over to the nearest wall of the cave and started feeling around in the earth for water deposits. Nothing. She tried the other three walls of the cavern. Again, no water.

"Ugh," Namid rubbed dirt from her eyes. She'd been doing her best not to complain, but these last few days had been a big change from her aunt and uncle's home in the Garden District. As soon as she got back, she was taking a long hot bath. With salts.

"There's no other sources of water down here." Namid turned to Rana. "He's already found the only underground water deposit near this cave."

"You were able to find water from the surface in the desert," Rana said.

"I can try looking for water up there, but..." Namid's eye darted around, looking for the old man in case he was in earshot. "If there isn't any to find, what are you prepared to do?"

"Prepared?" Rana asked. "What should I be preparing for?"

"...nothing." Namid shook her head. "You wouldn't have the stomach for it anyway."

Namid climbed back up to the surface and started looking for water. There was enough of an old, poorly maintained fence around the property for her to determine the boundary of the old man's farm. "Farm" being used loosely, as it was mostly just sand and dirt that had been tilled but couldn't grow anything without more water.

Placing her hands on the ground to try and find water, she felt around under the earth, looking for any untapped deposits. Then she was struck by a sudden hunger pain that brought her to her knees. She hadn't eaten anything since the night before they had escaped from the palace, and while she had fought off her own hunger as best she could, it was catching up to her.

She wanted to provide the old man with water and get paid in mushrooms like they'd agreed. She wanted to fulfill their bargain, and not get into any kind of fight over food. She wanted to get food for herself and Rana and then be on their way. She knew Rana wouldn't understand, or maybe she would, but wouldn't approve. But the more she reached out into the earth and searched, the more certain she was that there was no more water to be found under this farm. The old man already had access to the only underground reservoir in this plot of land.

"We're going to starve to death," she whispered to herself. "There's only one option."

Struggling back to her feet, Namid looked around the farm and saw the shack that must have been the old man's house. As she approached the shack, the old man stormed out with a kitchen knife.

"Well?" He asked. "Where's my water?"

As he asked this, Rana came out of the shed where the mushroom farm was hidden. Her eyes widened at the sight of the kitchen knife, but she held her calm.

"There is no more water," Namid replied. "I check your entire farm. There's no underground sources of water you haven't already tapped into."

"Then there's nothing else to discuss." The old man clutched his knife. He didn't actually look strong enough to be a serious threat in a fight. Only because of hunger would the girls be unable to overpower him. "I gave you your medicine in exchange for fortifying my cellar. Now get going! I can't afford to feed you!"

"Wait." Rana's stomach was starting to rumble as well. "Didn't you say you'd see what you could spare? Maybe there's something else we can trade—"

Namid shook her head. "There isn't, Rana. It's not just about what we can offer. The only reason he might have food to spare is if we could give him more water to grow more. The food he might spare now would come out of whatever he's stored up to live off while he grows more mushrooms. If he gives us what he has in storage now without more water to expand his growth operation, he'll starve."

"Then can't you get him more water?" Rana asked. "You found water in the desert."

"Because there was water there to find," Namid replied. "I didn't make the water out of nothing. I just pulled existing water to the surface."

"Then is there really nothing you can do?" Rana pleaded. "We won't make it without any food!"

"There is," Namid whispered. "There always was."

The old man raised his knife. "Stay back. You know I can't afford any handouts. You just explained why!"

Namid opened and closed her fists a few times. This was different than what she'd experienced with the necrophytes. "I know."

Unsure of what she was doing, the old man leaned back against his shack, as if to protect his home from the two starving girls in the desert. This did him no good as the air evacuated from his lungs. Namid looked away from Rana as she pulled the last of the air out of the man's nose and mouth, his face turning blue as he struggled to breathe.

"That's enough," Rana gawked. "That's enough! You don't have to kill him!"

"We don't need to let him live." Namid kept the spell going. "A dead man can't report us. And I told you, if we take what food he has now, he'll starve anyway."

The mushroom farmer dropped his knife and grasped his throat. Falling to his knees and eventually lying on his side, his bulging eyes locked with Namid and pleaded for mercy. She didn't stop the spell until she felt no more air trying to go into his lungs.

"Grab whatever food you can find and let's go." Namid turned to a stunned Rana. "It was him or us."

Rana finally caught her breath. "That was murder."

Namid shrugged. "It was self-preservation."

61

Power Lunch

EPHORAH

"Ah! So many choices!" Ephorah looked up at the menu in awe. "I can't decide!"

"Get whatever you like." Professor Sayegh smiled. "It's our treat for all your help."

Professors Sayegh and Meir had invited Ephorah out to lunch at an outdoor café along the interior wall of the city between the Academic and Garden districts. The headmistress herself would be joining them soon.

In the meantime, they were ordering food, which was no easy task for Ephorah, who did not go to many restaurants. Every item was expensive, especially for lunch prices, and Ephorah hadn't even heard of some of these items before.

Professor Sayegh had ordered a turkey schnitzel, while Meir had ordered the Masabacha with pine nuts, which was apparently hummus with whole chickpeas. Finally, Ephorah noted an option that she was surprised to see available so late in the day.

"Can I get the Shakshouka?" Ephorah asked.

"Of course," Sayegh replied. "Nothing wrong with breakfast for lunch."

Once they'd placed their orders with their waitress, Professor Meir turned to Ephorah.

"Now, about why we've brought you here. The headmistress will talk more when we arrive, but..."

"You've put us in a somewhat awkward position," Sayegh finished. "On the one hand, your discovery of the *incontio* spell may very well be the salvation of our school. On the other hand, we don't currently have the means to reward you."

"Reward?" Ephorah blinked. She'd noticed that neither of these two professors were this polite in their classrooms. Now she knew why.

"Strictly speaking, the discovery of the *incontio* spell is your intellectual property," Sayegh admitted. "And that means we're supposed to either buy out the rights to the spell, or arrange a contract with you regarding royalties. And right now..." the rotund professor sighed. "The school cannot afford to do either."

"We want to talk to you about possible options for any kind of deal we can make," Meir added. "There has to be a way we can work something out."

Ephorah was vaguely aware that Professor Meir was listing other options, but she wasn't listening. Ephorah's focus was now on the advertisement that was playing across the street from the café.

"Do you ever feel dumb when you leave your house without putting on your pants?" A recorded voice played from within an advertisement machine. An image wheel rotated to show a picture of a smart-looking Borealan who was fully dressed, and a confused Empyrian who was standing around in his underwear. *"Studies show that 9 out of 10 people feel stupid when they forget to put pants on before heading to work. So, if wearing pants makes you feel smarter, why not get the most for your money? Try our new SmartyPants! Never leave home without them!"* The image wheel rotated to show the confused, pants-less Empyrian pick up a pair of pants with no idea what to do with them, and as the image wheel rotated, it showed the man put them on and transform into a smart-looking Borealan. *"SmartyPants: put some pants on!"*

Professor Sayegh waved a plump-fingered hand in front of Ephorah. "Hello? Are you still with us?"

"Sorry," Ephorah turned away from the advertisement. "That ad was just so..."

"Distracting?" Meir offered.

"Insulting," Ephorah replied. "Seriously, why does your race insist on portraying mine as stupid? And does anyone actually believe putting pants on makes you smarter? Smart people don't leave their pants at home because they're smart, not the other way around!"

The professors looked at each other for a moment, then smiled at Ephorah.

"Sorry," Professor Sayegh bowed her head slightly. "We forget all about such things. Tell me, is this a big issue for you?"

"What, insulting advertisements?" Ephorah rolled her eyes. "It's normal. My dad told me..." Ephorah stopped herself. Both professors were Borealan, and so was the headmistress. They wouldn't understand.

When Ephorah was a little girl, she'd heard her father tell of Borealans who would call Empyrians "baboons," and would even offer them bananas as an insult. The Egyptian god Babi was the god of angry, violent, horny monkeys, and the Borealans used to refer to Empyrians as baboons to call them violent thugs, and even imply they were savages. Nowadays, the Borealans were too polite to call Empyrians that to their faces, but that was just a different form of insult. 'Oh, we're too good, too advanced, too *evolved* to use such petty language. Unlike you, who still call us bories to our faces.' All the same offensiveness without the effort.

Headmistress Rubin finally came up to their table and sat down. Before anyone could ask what she wanted to order, she held up her hand and tried to catch her breath. For her age, she was physically very fit. It's just that "for her age" meant "passed the point when most people retire," as the headmistress would be turning seventy in a few months. Ephorah wondered why Rubin hadn't retired already.

"Okay," the headmistress recovered. "Apologies, that struck me so quickly. Good afternoon, Ephorah."

"Hello, headmistress." The two professors greeted their boss. "Ephorah had just been telling us about...well," Professor Sayegh glanced at Ephorah. "Would you like to share with the headmistress what you just told us?"

Ephorah rubbed her temples. "It's not worth it. There's nothing any of you can do about it."

"About what?" Rubin asked.

"Ephorah was just telling us how insulting advertisements like the one across the street are," Sayegh explained.

The headmistress looked over at the SmartyPants advertisement. "Oh. Oh! Wow, that brings back old memories."

Ephorah blinked. "It does?"

"Yes. Not of Empyrians being treated like idiots, mind you." Rubin locked eyes with Ephorah and frowned. "Poor people. And women. Back when I was a student at the Institute, we were the first generation where the middle class could afford tuition. Before that, the price was just too high for anyone but the rich to afford to go to school. And so, the rich often mocked those of us from more humble origins for being 'ignorant working-class slobs.'" The headmistress gestured to the advertisement and scoffed. "Second verse, same as the first. Utterly reprehensible." She seemed to calm down, but any anger in her expression was quickly replaced with fatigue. "I had a dream when I became a teacher that one day everyone would be able to become a wizard. You can see how well that's been turning out."

"You mentioned women as well?" Ephorah interjected. "What was that about?"

"Hm? Oh," the headmistress waved her hand dismissively. "Good old-fashioned sexism. Nothing new. It's...better, in some ways. You know how the College of Alchemy and Academy of Sorcerers have barely any female students? Theurgy used to be like that as well. It's mostly thanks to me that things have changed at the institute."

Ephorah had never considered the fact that the culture of Hadesh used to be worse than it is now. An idea wormed into Ephorah's brain.

"Why do you think it is that other schools don't take in more girls?" She asked.

"They'll tell you some garbage about how women don't like math." Rubin rolled her eyes. "Nonsense. Lots of young women are good at math."

"Are you good at math?" Ephorah asked.

"I can manage," the elderly woman replied. "I don't like algebra, and I wouldn't want to make a career out of it, but I can do it."

A waitress brough them their meals. The headmistress had ordered a light sandwich and salad, and the four ate before continuing their conversation.

"I was a little relieved when the alchemists lost their patron god," Professor Meir smirked. "They literally worshipped the god of reason, an idea designed to turn women away. In their view, if something is *logically* true, then it must be *accepted* as true, even if it's offensive, or it denies people the things we rightfully deserve. Reason is nothing but a construct designed to make women feel inferior to men."

Ephorah tried to follow the logic behind the professor's thought process. "Okay, that one made my brain hurt." *Maybe that's what happens when you think reason is bad*, she thought.

"I could never stand the physical requirements." Professor Sayegh wiped some sauce off her cheek with a pudgy finger and stuck it in her mouth. "Absolutely dreadful! If you wanted to be an alchemist back then, you had to be able to run without stopping for three kilometers. And it's even worse today! The sorcerers aren't any better; they expect you to be able to channel the magic through your body without any breaks, and if your heart can't handle it, they tell you to improve your health or leave their academy." The portly professor wiped her finger on a napkin. "Their standards are absolutely barbaric. They're *designed* to keep people with different body types or conditions like anorexia out of their elitist institution."

"Wait," Ephorah looked at Professor Sayegh. "Are you...are you anorexic?"

"Of course!" The professor wiped meat juice that had fallen between two of her chins off with a napkin. "Every time I look in the mirror, I see a fat person."

"...Okay...so what could you do for the Empyrians?" Ephorah tried not to look at Sayegh as she disassembled another piece of schnitzel in her mouth. "Could you offer discounts to Empyrians who are looking to go into higher education? Something to get people to stop treating us like idiots?"

"I don't know if that can happen overnight," the headmistress admitted. "But the rich no longer treat the middle class like idiots for being uneducated. If we could get more Empyrians into higher education..."

"People in academia are smart. Therefore, if more Empyrians went to university, they'd be smart, too," Ephorah concluded. "And the Borealans would recognize that fact."

"Hm," Rubin rubbed her forehead. The waitress delivered the headmistress another cup of coffee, which she then drank. "It might work, but there's a problem. The Institute of Theurgy can't afford to cut tuition costs, even if it means bringing in more students."

"What about the other schools?" Ephorah asked. "Could you convince the sorcerers or the alchemists to lower their tuition costs for Empyrians? Doesn't even have to be a magical education. Architects, engineers, lawyers. Any education would probably work."

Rubin shook her head. "We don't have any sway over the other colleges, I'm afraid."

"Wait a moment," Professor Sayegh paused between bites of schnitzel. "We do have a way to influence the other schools. If we were to turn to the imperial palace, introduce them to Ephorah, and show them her *incontio* spell...and especially if we could produce a working example of the boiler..."

"We could convince the emperor that brilliant Empyrians could invent more things if given the chance." The headmistress looked outside at the advertisement again. "We could get the emperor to setup a government tuition fund."

"The Iron Constitution won't allow it," Professor Meir huffed. "The government cannot pass a law regarding anything they can't clearly define, and no one can come up with a concrete definition of what an 'Empyrian' is. Or race, for that matter. Once again, that blasted document exists to oppress anyone who isn't a rich male."

"Isn't it obvious what an Empyrian is, though?" Ephorah swallowed a poached egg from her meal. "An Empyrian is anyone of Empyrian descent. Simple."

"What if someone has an Empyrian mother and a Borealan father?" Sayegh asked. "Do they count? Should they get the full benefit of the fund, or just half? What if someone's ancestry is even more mixed than that?"

"What about poverty?" Rubin offered. "The government can't define race, but it can define wealth. If the fund were aimed at the poor, rather than a certain race, most of whom happen to be poor, then it could get around the constitution."

"We could even name it after you," Professor Sayegh offered. "The Ephorah Tuition Assistance Fund. Has a nice ring to it, no?"

"Would you accept us doing this in light of not being able to compensate you for your spell?" The headmistress looked at Ephorah with a very tired expression.

Ephorah looked down at her plate for a moment, which now only contained bits of cumin and tomato sauce. This was probably the best deal she was going to get.

"Yes. Let's do this." She looked up at Rubin. "Let's make it happen."

The headmistress sighed with relief. "This I can actually do. All right, I'll make an appointment with the Imperial Palace immediately. I just—"

An owl swooped down onto the table, grabbed the last piece of schnitzel from Sayegh's plate, and flew off before any of them could scream.

"What in the Abyss was that?" Professor Meir seethed.

"Owls?" Rubin looked at the plate. "But it's the middle of the day!"

"I've seen more and more bats around the institute lately, too." Sayegh looked glumly at her empty plate. She clearly wanted that last bite. "In broad daylight, no less."

"I saw those outside a lab when that strange girl showed up," Ephorah added. "The one who's clearly an evil goddess trying to replace Marduk. Think they're connected?"

"It's possible," Rubin shrugged. "A goddess is, effectively, a really powerful spirit. But I don't think she's very powerful, at least not now."

"Why not?" Ephorah asked. "Aren't all goddesses powerful?"

Rubin shook her head. "No. And in this one's case…have you ever seen her grab anything physical? Or harm anyone in a way that lasted after she left the room?"

Ephorah thought back to when she'd seen the girl enter the lab. "No, come to think of it."

"Exactly. A god or goddess can appear in one of two ways," Rubin explained. "A god can always manifest in the minds of everyone who believes in him, wherever they may be. Gods can even be in multiple places at once this way.

But they aren't physically there, and their ability to affect the world is very limited. They can't grab inanimate objects and move them with their hands, because they don't actually have hands in that form. And they can't exist wherever their believers aren't present."

"But if a deity is powerful enough, she can pull a portion of her essence together into a physical body, and in that form she has all the limits and abilities a human body has. Marduk could sit in his office unobserved by anyone and write curriculum plans, and it didn't matter how many of these I used for kindling for the school's furnaces; my belief in his ability to write didn't matter when he was doing this through his own physical body. But I don't think this goddess has enough power to take on a physical form."

"Not yet, anyway," Professor Sayegh added. "But I do suspect that the nocturnal animals are her doing. I wish I knew what she was the goddess of, exactly."

Ephorah frowned. "She told me she wasn't the goddess of anything, *per se*. Whatever that means."

"She told us something similar," the headmistress finished her coffee. "But I saw her at the same time as Professor Kollek, which means there's something that the both of us believe in that this mystery goddess was able to latch onto. Something you and Professor Massouh have as well."

"Believe you deserve it," Professor Meir whispered. "That's what she told me. So I do."

Rubin blinked and snapped her gaze at Meir. "You what?"

"I believe that I deserve the things I'm owed." The youngest professor sat back and crossed her arms. She didn't smile, but her resting frown was somewhat less intense than usual. "Why not? Think of the things you had to deal with when you first became headmistress. Think of how much the economy undervalues our work. Do you think it's a coincidence that when women finally made their way into theurgy, the job market for theurgists dried up?"

Rubin paused. Clearly, she had thought of this, but hadn't made the connection.

"She has a point." Professor Sayegh nodded. "Theurgists never had a problem getting jobs when the field was male dominated. Maybe we do deserve a break. And as for this goddess, what's our alternative? Believe that we *don't* deserve the things we want or need? Is that even a good idea?"

"The only thing I know about that goddess is that she shouldn't be trusted." Rubin scowled.

"I agree with the headmistress," Ephorah winced. The other professors ignored her.

"Does that really matter?" Sayegh asked. "Marduk *seemed* trustworthy, but he abandoned us when we needed him most. A school like ours without a patron god has no plan, no ideals, no fundamental vision for the future. The deity isn't just a figurehead; their the core of the institution. We have to believe in something, or our school will fall apart."

"Why do we need a patron deity?" Ephorah asked. "We aren't a religious institute, are we?"

Meir scoffed, and Sayegh ignored her, but Rubin perked up.

"A god is an idea," the headmistress explained. "So, a patron god is the idea that the school dedicates itself to and gathers around as a focal point. Without a patron deity, a school is just a bunch of people with no connected beliefs; no reason to work with each other. Eventually, something mundane, like money, or just getting a job will take the place of a patron god. And not even a goddess associated with wealth, like Hathor, but literally just the idea of 'get money' will be the only thing holding us together. The alchemists worship Thoth, dead or alive, because they're dedicated to the idea of knowledge for its own sake, and sharing it with anyone who wants it, or something like that. Enki, despite being a perverted trickster in a fish costume, is dedicated to human creativity and ingenuity, so innovation is the motivation of the sorcerers."

"And Marduk?" Ephorah asked.

Rubin sighed. "I can't remember. I know he's the god of a number of things, including civilization itself, but I can't remember why the institute used to follow him. It was a different time, you know? They taught a very different form of theurgy back then. Maybe that was part of why they worshipped Marduk. He isn't necessary for teaching the new theurgy."

"New theurgy," Professor Meir frowned. Or rather, her face returned to its default expression. "Ephorah, you said you found this sigil, *Incontio*, in an old book? Something lost in your old home before you came to live in Hadesh?"

"Uh..." Ephorah remembered the lie she'd given Professor Massouh about where she'd found the word. "Yes...that's right."

"I wonder..." an almost-smile crossed Meir's lips. "Have you ever been to a translator's office?"

"For things like languages?" Ephorah blinked. "No, I've never needed to do that. I don't have plans for traveling anytime soon."

"I wasn't talking about languages people still speak," the professor went on. "I'm talking about a sigil translator. Do you know where the sigils we use in our enchantment rituals come from?"

Ephorah shook her head.

"Then perhaps a field trip is in order."

62

Homecoming

ROSTAM

A good solid wind had *the Endurance* headed quickly to Hadesh.

"Good to be back in the skies again," Joseph mumbled as he went about his work.

Simon grumbled something in agreement as the ship carried on its way. Cyrus leaned against the railing and looked up at Captain Nadia, who was mostly back to her normal self, apart from the occasional headache.

Rostam had locked the ballast system so that the ship would maintain course. He was now free to step away and check the rest of the ship. Which meant checking on Cyrus.

"How are you holding up?" He asked the alchemist.

"Me?" Cyrus blinked. "I'm fine. It's everyone else I'm worried about."

"That's what I meant." Rostam leaned against the railing next to him. "We're back in the air. Everything'll be back on schedule soon enough."

"Back on schedule…how does that work?" Cyrus asked. "You lost three days waiting for your captain to recover from a head injury. How do you recover from that?"

"Adaptability is key to a merchant ship like this," Rostam explained. "There are always changes in the market, and we go wherever there's a demand that needs to be balanced."

"You don't have contracts that need to be filled on a regular basis?" Cyrus asked. "I would have thought you guys had to meet strict deadlines, or something."

"Nah." Rostam shook his head. "Big shipping companies fill demands that are set in advance. Small ships like this tackle demands as they crop up."

Cyrus frowned. "Why not find something stable you can rely on? Say, a town that needs a regular supply of goods?"

"That's not how it works." Rostam grinned. It was an odd feeling, teaching someone else the things Captain Zaahid used to teach him. "Big companies make regular routes like that, supplying people with things they need regularly. But surprise demands? Shortages due to unpredictable weather, or bad crops? A shift in people's tastes, or a sudden dragon attack? That's how small ships like ours make a living, in the corners of the economy where you can't predict things years in advance."

"Okay..." Cyrus looked like he was trying to wrap his head around all of this. "But aren't there things people always want or need? Things like food to people living in the mountains, or fish that can be bought cheaper in a fishing village?"

"Nope, and you know why?" Rostam gestured to the rest of the ship. "Because sooner or later, everything can become worthless. Supply and demand. A fishing village may have cheap fish to sell, but who's going to buy it? If you bring a load of fish to an inland town, they may buy up your cargo, but if you immediately run back to the fishing village and buy more, you'll find that the town won't purchase them again for the same price. They've still got some leftover from your last delivery. Everything, even gold and other things people used to think are valuable can become worthless if you suddenly find yourself with more than you can use."

"Wait," Cyrus raised an eyebrow. "You can have too much gold? I'm talking to a guy who works on a merchant vessel, right?"

"Where are you going to put it?" Rostam asked. "Imagine if this ship were carrying so much treasure that it could no longer get any lift. We'd have to throw some of it overboard. There's a reason people store money in banks. Imagine if you had to rent out a warehouse to store all your gold. How would you keep people from breaking in and stealing it?"

"Okay," Cyrus conceded. "But things like food, which need to be consumed every day – surely you can always find a buyer for those things, right?"

"Nope," Rostam shook his head again. "People can only eat one breakfast, one lunch, one dinner per day. Too much food, and they just ignore it. No way to store it all, so it just rots. Imagine if we brought jars of water to a desert town. They'd need some of it, for sure. But bring too much, more than they can drink in a reasonable amount of time, and they have to find somewhere to store it. Imagine jars of water stacked on top of each other until the weight crushes the jugs at the bottom. Even things people always need and always consume become a problem if there's too much supply and not enough demand."

"Oh, it's like oversaturation!" Cyrus exclaimed.

"Uh, I think I've heard people say something to that extent before," Rostam admitted. "Something like 'saturating the market,' or –"

"No, I mean like in a solution!" Cyrus smiled. "You add salt to water to turn it into brine, right? And the water absorbs the salt crystals and spreads them out evenly through the solute, basic diffusion, you know? But then, you reach a saturation point of the water where it can't hold any more salt crystals, so if you add more salt, it just drifts to the bottom of the container and doesn't become part of the solution."

"...Right." Rostam's eyes widened as he tried to follow the alchemist's metaphor. "That's...that's exactly what happens. Anyway, we're always on the move, traveling between new towns and filling demands as they pop up. It's nice, because if you make too many trips to the wrong customers, they start grumbling about you being a middleman, and the grumbling can turn into violence if you don't move along."

"Middleman?" Cyrus raised an eyebrow. "I know the word, but I don't get why people would get violent."

"In Hadesh, they don't. In some cities..." Rostam winced. "Ships like ours usually charge higher prices to bring goods out to cities like Harlak or Barkina. Captain says we might make a trek out to Sankro one day, across the border, and that'd be nice, but if a ship stops in a place like Harlak too long, well..." Rostam looked out over the edge of the ship. "To people who don't understand how trade works, traveling merchants are some kind of thief. Anyone who doesn't think very hard about it, either because they can't or won't, will tell you that making a profit off of goods you buy in one place and sell in another is some kind of scam. There're even countries with laws against making a profit off 'untransformed goods,' which is a fancy way of saying they've made small merchant ships like this illegal."

"Okay," Cyrus looked like he was putting this together in his head. "I believe you, but how is it not a scam to buy up goods and resell them at a higher price? Grocers are a kind of middleman, aren't they? They buy goods from a supplier, they don't do anything to change them, they just sell them to customers. Why does the middleman deserve to make a profit there? Why can't I just go straight to the producers and buy the stuff I need from them?"

"You can." Rostam smiled. "Just walk, ride, or whatever you can to each supplier of each product you need to buy. Should only take you a few weeks to get to each farm, factory, and packing plant."

"Ah, so it's a time-saving thing?" Cyrus paused. "But don't the producers usually deliver goods to the grocer? Why can't I have them do the same thing to my house?"

"You could do that, too," Rostam replied. "You just have to buy a minimum of five hundred loaves of bread per delivery, or two hundred cartons of eggs. The delivery wagons used to bring goods to a grocer? They aren't cheap, and the grocer pays for each delivery. Every time a wagon has to be sent out, it needs to be filled with as many goods as possible, and it's not like the wagons coming from the produce farm are also coming from the packing plant that boxes up your cereal. Then there's travel time to consider. Imagine if this ship had to choose between delivering a single carton of eggs to your house, or taking a full load of goods somewhere else in the same amount of time. The only reason we'd take the option of delivering the eggs to your home is if we could make more money doing that than we could doing a different job in that amount of time. You'd probably have to be pay us thousands of Ioseps for a single carton of eggs just to make it worth our while."

Cyrus leaned back and grinned. "I love learning new things like this. They'd never teach stuff like that in the college."

"They don't?" Rostam cocked an eyebrow. "This seems...hm."

"What?" Cyrus asked.

"Well, it just seems...necessary." Rostam folded his arms behind his head. "Like, stuff you need to know if you're going to get through life. How do you expect to find a job if you don't know where people need an alchemist?"

"Eh, people always need medical alchemists." Cyrus shrugged. "I've discovered that I enjoy working with organic chemistry, and there's so few people who do that there's never enough people out there becoming medical alchemists, even though medical alchemists are among the highest-paid wizards in the empire, possibly even the world. I guess if there's not a lot of people wanting to do the job, there's never enough supply to meet the demand, right?"

"Sounds right," Rostam nodded.

"Although now that I think of it, organic chemistry is only part of the problem," Cyrus admitted. "Another issue is the stamina. I know a lot of people who have the mental ability to handle alchemy, but can't meet the physical requirements. I think that guy in the lab, the one who had a ghoul in him? I bet he thought he'd be a great wizard one day, but his body couldn't take it."

Rostam scratched his chin. "Is it true that anyone can become a wizard?"

"In theory, yes. No one is born with it, and everyone who has a soul can tap the power of magic and cast spells." Cyrus's eyes furrowed. "But the reality is, not everyone can stand reading about balancing chemical equations. The theory that anyone can be a wizard is about as true as the idea that anyone can be a carpenter. Or an airshipman, for that matter."

"Rostam," Nadia called. "We're getting close to Hadesh. Man the ballast pipes."

Leaving Cyrus and grabbing the pipe controls, Rostam steadied the ship's ballast network until they landed in Silverstack Docks. Home sweet Hadesh.

Cyrus packed up his bags and brought them up to the main deck. "Well, I think this is goodbye. Thank you." He gestured to the entire crew. "All of you, for giving me a place to stay until I could get room and board with the college."

"Thank you for dealing with that demon," Simon muttered.

Nadia extended her hand to Cyrus. "Farewell. Good luck in your studies."

"Thank you." The alchemist shook her hand. "I wish you well in your business and your travels."

With that, he hauled his luggage off the ship and headed off to the docks.

"I know he didn't end up using his magic on my head, but I'm going to miss having a medical officer who can mend broken wood on board." The captain put her hand on Rostam's shoulder. "You might as well take some shore leave. We won't be taking off again for three more days. Got a bone to pick with the alchemists over their supply delivery contract."

Rostam knew that if the captain had something she wanted him to learn from such a meeting, she wouldn't be granting him shore leave. This was going to be the sort of meeting in which Captain Nadia would say and do a number of things she didn't want her impressionable understudy to hear.

This was the last weekend before classes would start again for Amri, Namid and Ephorah. He might as well see if they were up for a final hurrah.

As he left the ship and headed for the elevators, Rostam thought about the things he'd discussed with Cyrus at the edge of the Tainted Desert. There had been a time when Ephorah's eyes would light up whenever she saw him, and he could go straight to her house in the Empyrian Quarter. The problem was, Amri and his aunt and uncle had always told Rostam that their door was open to him; Ephorah's family had never invited him into their home. Rostam knew where she lived, but had never set foot inside.

Rather than show up uninvited at Ephorah's house, Rostam decided to go to the Garden District instead. As soon as he stepped off of the elevator and left Silverstack Docks, he was greeted with a poster plastered to one of the support columns. A sketch of Namid's face smiled back at him, with the words "Missing – Report to Ironwood Policing Company if found" underneath.

"What the hell happened while I was away?" Rostam examined the poster. "She literally saw us off."

Rostam briefly thought of tracking down Cyrus and asking him for help, but then put the thought out of mind. The alchemist wouldn't know anything her family didn't, and the last Cyrus saw Namid, he was with Rostam. No, he needed to talk to Amri right away.

Weaving through crowds in the Market District, Rostam grabbed a ride on the first autobus he could find and took it to the Garden District. There, on the opposite side of the city, he hurried over to Amri's home and knocked on the door, trying to suppress his alarm.

Amri's aunt opened the door. "Oh, Rostam?"

"What happened to Namid?" Rostam asked. "When did she disappear?"

The woman sighed. "Come in and have some tea. I'll tell you everything."

Panya Seluk made Rostam a cup of herbal tea, which he didn't touch as he sat at the kitchen table.

"When was the last time you saw her?"

Panya paused, looking down at her own cup of tea. "It was the morning after you last left. She'd had a spat with Ephorah; something about the wedding they had gone to work for. But she never told any of us where she was going afterwards."

"I saw her before the ship took off," Rostam clenched and unclenched his right hand. His fingers were stiff with callouses, but a rage was welling up inside of him. Problem was, he had no one to aim it at.

"You did?" Panya's eyes widened. "Where? What was she doing?"

"She introduced *the Endurance* and its crew to an alchemy student named Cyrus Levitch. We took him in for the week since he couldn't stay at his house, for some reason, and he...well, he agreed to earn his keep while on board."

"Where did she meet this...Cyrus?" Panya's eyes darted around. "And why does that name sound familiar?"

Rostam tried to remember what Cyrus had told him. "I think they met on a bus, and there was something about someone throwing a chair through a window."

"Of the bus?" Panya blinked.

"No, a house." Rostam realized he didn't remember as many details as he probably should have. Had he known it was the last time he'd see her, or if any small part might have been important...

"Yeah, she didn't tell us anything about this." Panya took another sip of her tea. "She mentioned her good deed of helping some stranger find work and housing on your ship. She left out the part about throwing a chair through a window."

"Where is Amri?" Rostam asked.

"He...went out last night." Panya tapped her teacup nervously. "He shouldn't have done that. He was delivering some of those missing person posters to the folks over at the Abbey of Truth. All that walking opened his leg wounds again, and now my husband had to take our coach to drop him back off at the Abbey to treat the infection that flared up this morning."

"Leg wounds?" Rostam blinked. "What happened to his legs?"

"Oh, right." Panya chuckled weakly. "You weren't here for that. He...got in a...spat, of sorts, with an alchemist. She...uh...tried to kill him. But she's in an asylum now, so everything's alright." She patted Rostam's hand.

"Okay." Rostam gritted his teeth. "Since his life's not in danger anymore, I'm going to table that whole package of what-in-the-actual-hell until I can grill him in person. I'm going to ask Ephorah if she knows anything about Namid."

"You're leaving?" Panya asked.

"Oh, I'll be back," Rostam muttered. "I need to figure out what the hell Amri's been up to. I go away for ten days..."

Rostam thanked Panya for the tea and headed out. He knew he wasn't exactly invited to Ephorah's home, but this was an emergency.

The airshipman had been to the Empyrian Quarter before. He once lived in a common house when he was still in mandatory school, and that had been located on the edge of the Empyrian Quarter. Of course, the Empyrians didn't actually want the common house located within their quarter, so it was located at the edge of the Southern Residential District.

Rostam was aware that, legally, the Empyrian Quarter didn't *have* to exist. Empyrians weren't required to live there, and strictly speaking, people of other races could buy property here. On paper, at any rate. In reality, the Empyrians who occupied the quarter wanted to be around people of their own race, and while they lived in the cheapest part of the town inside the wall, and some of their houses were under a railroad track, the quarter was effectively theirs.

No one of any other race in recent years had tried to buy property in the quarter, and there were rumors that if someone actually tried, the locals would ensure that their new neighbors would be wise to sell their new home and move somewhere else. This had the added effect of keeping the cost of a house in the quarter relatively affordable for anyone who was of Empyrian heritage, and ensured that they were next to worthless as collateral for a loan. Many banks would flat out refuse to lend money to any Empyrians looking to start their own businesses if the only property the borrower could offer up was a house in the Empyrian Quarter.

Rostam had to double check a note he'd left in his wallet a long time ago that had Ephorah's address on it.

"137 Shepherds Lane." He pocketed the note. He'd never been here before.

Walking up to the front door, he paused before knocking. An uncomfortable feeling wouldn't leave him be as he raised the knocker and let it fall.

A few moments later, a woman opened the door and looked at him with suspicious eyes. "Do we know you?"

"Rostam Tar'ik?" Rostam tilted his head hopefully. Ephorah's mother had met him before. It had just been a while. "I was in Ephorah's graduating class in mandatory school. We met back in Aklagos. Remember?"

"Oh, huh." She opened the door wider. "What are you here for?"

"I wanted to speak with Ephorah." As soon as he said this, he realized how she might misinterpret it. "I want to ask if she knows anything about Namid."

"Namid...Namid...Oh! I know Namid." She held up a finger for him to wait right there as she called for her daughter. "Ephorah? Someone's at the door for you."

Soon after, Ephorah came to the front door and looked at Rostam. "Oh, hey."

"Hey." Rostam thought about asking her if he could come in, but something stopped him. "Mind coming out here to chat?"

Ephorah shrugged and stepped out onto the porch of the house. Unlike the Sadis' fancy home in the Garden District, this porch was made entirely of wood planks, some loose enough to see the sandy ground beneath, with tufts of grass loosely visible below. A single railing of round wooden beams that had neither been sanded nor painted surrounded the porch. There was no overhang, and yet, Rostam couldn't help but imagine sitting out here one day, enjoying the sunshine, a glass of lemonade, and maybe a good book. Especially on a day like this.

"Ugh, it's so bright out," Ephorah shielded her eyes with her hand. "What did you want to talk about?"

"Did you know Namid is missing?" Rostam asked. "Her family has no idea where she is, and she's been gone for a while now."

"What?" Ephorah raised an eyebrow. "How long?"

"From the sounds of it, she disappeared shortly after I left on my last journey. She left the house one morning without a word, and never came home afterwards."

"That's..." Ephorah paused. "It's not like her to leave the house without some kind of protection. I know for a fact that she keeps a knife hidden inside her pant leg. And a throwing dart hidden in the sole of her right shoe. And maybe a second one in her left shoe. And there's the ballistic knife she carries in her purse—"

"Namid's weird obsession with knives aside, no one knows where she went." Rostam continued. "Apparently, Amri got hurt at the industrial park at some point, and he hasn't been able to help much in searching for her."

"Eh, that's nothing new." Ephorah shrugged. "For Amri, anyway."

Rostam didn't want to say it, but she had a point. Amri had always been pretty weak when it came to defending his sister. Although, their aunt had told him he'd been out last night trying to pass out missing person posters...

"Maybe Namid angered the wrong person, and it came back to bite her in the rear," Ephorah offered.

"You...you think Namid tried to con someone, or something like that, and they came after her?"

Ephorah nodded. "It's possible."

"Um..." Rostam wasn't sure how to ask his next question. "Are you at all bothered by her being gone? There's literally no telling what could have happened to her. The absolute worst possible things might have actually happened. She could have been abducted. She could have been sold by traffickers. She could be dead for all we know."

Ephorah paused. "When was the last time you spent any time with Namid? Like, just you and her?"

Rostam shrugged. "Last time I was in town, I had a one-on-one conversation with her. About you and Amri, mostly."

"Hm," Ephorah, replied. "And...when was the last time she involved you in one of her schemes? Like, getting you involved with a wedding that she knew could go to hell in a heartbeat so she could use you as a bodyguard while she robbed the gift table?"

"That's...Namid...wouldn't..." Rostam thought for a few seconds. "She would totally do that, wouldn't she?"

"Yup" Ephorah nodded. "She did. And now, I can't bring myself to be all that concerned with her disappearance, because the first thing that comes to mind is the possibility that one of her schemes caught up to her. That's what makes the most sense, anyway."

"...I see." Rostam hung his head a bit. He was disappointed with Namid, and he could understand where Ephorah was coming from. And yet...

"Thanks." Rostam turned to leave. "If anything comes up, either I or Amri will let you know. Now I need to go rake him over the coals for nearly getting killed by a crazy alchemist."

63

The Translator

EPHORAH

"Where are you heading?"

Ephorah looked up at her mom as she packed her bookbag. "Market District. One of my professors is introducing me to a translator's office."

Her mom paused. "You take your gloves with you when you go out by yourself, right?"

"Yes, mom." Ephorah rolled her eyes. No one outside of the Empyrian Quarter had ever made so much as an attempt to harass her, and people who knew she had gloves that let her pulverize granite didn't bother her, either. This didn't stop her mom from imagining the worst.

"What is this translator, anyway?" Her mom asked. "What do they translate?"

"Sigils, old magic words." Ephorah zipped up her bookbag. "Things from old languages. I'm off!"

"Hold on." Her mother went over to her parents' bedroom.

"I really need to meet my professor—"

"Just a second!" Her mother came back with a small book that she handed to Ephorah.

"What's this?" Ephorah asked. The book had a title, but she couldn't make it out. It was small, only about one centimeter thick, and could almost fit in a large pocket.

"Something your father received from his father that was saved from the war," her mother smiled. "It's old Empyrian. When the war ended, the Borealans banned our ancestral language from being taught, and this book itself would have been burned if the government found it. Now, they aren't so worried about these things; they think our culture is entirely gone. But we have things like this. We just can't read it."

Ephorah held the book like it was a secret treasure. A piece of Empyrian heritage that had survived the Borealans' purge after the war. It was risky, but if the translator could handle the job, she had to learn what was in such a book.

Hopping on a bus to the Market District, Ephorah spotted Professor Meir outside of a large building. It was the sort of place that had multiple offices rented out to anyone looking to run a business in a building shared by others, preferably not your competitors. Ephorah spotted the professor and ran up to join her.

Meir wore less of a frown today and more of a light scowl. The more time Ephorah spent with her, the more she started to understand the slight differences in the professor's moods. None of them were pleasant, unfortunately.

"Good, you're finally here." The professor gestured to the building. "Follow me."

Ephorah followed Professor Meir into the building's main floor, then took the first flight of stairs down to the basement. Gaslamps kept the dark rooms barely lit, and Ephorah was shocked someone would setup a business in a place like this.

"This is where the cheaper offices are kept," Meir said, as if reading Ephorah's thoughts. "The woman who runs this business doesn't make enough money to rent one of the rooms above-ground."

Once they reached an office near the bottom of the stairs, Professor Meir knocked on the door and crossed her arms, tapping her foot impatiently. Ephorah noticed a placard on the door that read "Office of Daniela Sachar."

After a moment, the door opened and a thirty-year-old woman greeted them. She wasn't bad looking for thirty, but age was catching up to her, and while she was slightly taller than Professor Meir, she seemed to stoop slightly in Meir's presence, as if cowed by the younger wizard. Her face was coated in a look that read "busy, but come right in," and she swung the door open and bowed as the professor and student entered the office.

Inside were several bookshelves of old tomes, some of which had titles on their spines that Ephorah couldn't read, and every wall space that was available had a tapestry hanging on it. The office itself was large enough to be a living room, and a small kitchen set that had recently been used told Ephorah that the translator might actually live here, but with every space filled with stacks of papers and more books, the cluttered space felt absolutely tiny.

A desk with stacks of paperwork sat along one wall. Sachar shuffled a few stacks aside and smiled at a single notebook with glyphs on it that Ephorah had never seen before.

"Truly, theurgical translations are like poetry," she chuckled as she closed the notebook and tried to wedge it into a shelf where it almost fit.

"Why?" Ephorah asked. "Because it rhymes?"

"No." the translator gave up on finding a spot for the notebook. "Because everything gets lost in translation." She opened the book and showed Ephorah the glyphs. "This is a form of poetry called a 'haiku.' People from Janaan or the northern nations would tell you it's a poem with three lines, the first having five syllables, the second having seven, the third having five again. But to the culture that first created the format, there are so many more rules. Each poem is supposed to contain an observation; a moment of inspiration! These are not rules that translate between cultures very well. Because how do you explain to a completely different culture how to write an observation?"

"How did the original culture write it?" Ephorah asked.

"With pictures." Sachar showed Ephorah the glyphs in the notebook. On one page, the glyphs were written at different heights, and sure enough, the symbols did appear to be drawing...something, but Ephorah couldn't tell what.

"Their written language was pictographic, which further muddies the meaning when one tries to translate their poem format into a purely textual language like ours." Sachar closed the notebook and settled for resting it on a pile of other papers and notes on top of the bookshelf. "Now, you had an appointment regarding a new sigil?"

"Yes, finally." Professor Meir presented a sheet of paper with the sigil for *incontio* drawn on it. "Can you tell us the origin and meaning of this?"

Sachar examined the paper. "Hm. This is...this..." She rummaged through a number of books on a different shelf. Ephorah wondered for a moment how this woman could find anything in this mess, but sure enough, the translator retrieved a tome and dropped it on her desk. "It looks a bit like a hieratic script, but...it's not a hieroglyphic, but I'd swear this had some roots from ancient Egyptian. No, that's too broad. Every language has a root or two from Egyptian, Latin, or Greek if you trace it back far enough. This is...more like something from the original source."

"So...can you tell us what its original meaning meant?" Meir asked. "What was it in the original source?"

"Well, it looks like an Egyptian script, but it isn't a hieroglyphic symbol, so it's probably demotic, or something close to it." The translator poured through several more books on one shelf before flittering over to another. "The thing is, most ancient Egyptian writings were similar to semitic languages, in that they never wrote down their vowel sounds. This makes translation very difficult. We can go from ancient Coptic, which is very different from modern Coptic, and try to work our way backwards to get the pronunciation right, but it gets tricky. The 'o' sound in the middle of *incontio* in particular bothers me."

"Um," Ephorah furrowed her eyebrows. "Why, exactly?"

"Because from what we can tell, Middle Kingdom Egyptian didn't have the soft 'o' sound like we do now. Instead, they used a hard 'a' sound. In all likeliness, the word we're looking at now sounds nothing like its original translation."

Ephorah raised an eyebrow. "But it still works?"

"Of course. If the translation is exact, and the meaning behind it is preserved, the sigil will still work. Speaking of..." Sachar tapped the sigil for *incontio*. "What do you think this word means?"

"Idiocy," Meir replied. "It strips a humanus elemental of its intelligence and makes them docile. Easy to control."

Sachar paused. For a moment, Ephorah thought the translator might protest the use of such a sigil. But instead, she turned back to the image of the symbol and compared it to her notes.

"Okay, this doesn't line up with any known Egyptian symbols or words, but there are other languages from that era we could rely on. The word 'idiot' originates from Attic Greek, an ancient dialect whose texts were eventually studied across the ancient world. But to the Greeks, the word 'idiot' didn't mean 'stupid.' It meant 'private person.' So this sigil..."

"Excuse me," Professor Meir crossed her arms. "But is this something you intend to figure out right now, or are you going to need some time?"

The translator looked up from her cluttered desk. "Sorry, this will take a while. Usually, projects like this take about a week."

"Then we'll leave you to it," Professor Meir turned to leave. "The headmistress gave you all the details, I'm sure you know where to send the bill."

"Uh, one second." Ephorah stepped closer to the translator. "Would you, by any chance, be able to read old Empyrian?"

Danielle Sachar blinked for a moment. "I'm not sure. I can't exactly say either way. Do you have a sample of old Empyrian?"

"I might." Ephorah was about to rummage through her bag, but a thought stopped her. This woman was a Borealan, and the book in her bag was technically illegal to own. It was a law barely ever enforced, but maybe that was just because there were rarely any samples of pre-war Empyrian culture to enforce the law upon. This woman might just be looking for an excuse to send the police to her house. Ephorah thought of her gloves, and the sword that lay corroded in her bedroom, still thirsty. Yes, the Borealans might send a company of mercenaries to her home to arrest her and her parents for having such a book. But if they did, some part of Ephorah felt like she could give them hell.

"Here," Ephorah handed the translator the book. "This is something my parents gave me. I...found the symbol in an old book, so it might help with finding the answer behind the *incontio* sigil."

"Doubtful," Sachar shook her head. "There's too much in common with ancient demotic and other Egyptian dialects."

Ephorah winced "Is there any chance you could translate it anyway?"

"I could give it a try," the translator looked at the book and flipped through the pages. "It's not too different from Arabic. Give me a few months. I'll have to send you my fee upon completion."

"How much do you usually charge for a job like this?" Ephorah worried she wouldn't be able to afford the bill afterwards.

Sachar held out an invoice to the theurgy student. "Going rate is ten Ioseps per page, usually. Then there's adjustments for time and other costs if it turns out to be an exceptionally difficult job. Empyrian has a lot in common with Arabic, so I don't think it will be. Probably."

"I see." Ephorah reached for the invoice. As she did, the translator grabbed her arm and pulled her in close.

"Listen," the translator hissed, eyeing the door as if making sure Professor Meir was already gone. "There's a reason I rent out a dingy office in a basement when the theurgy institute would gladly provide me with a free place on campus and plenty of business. That school has become a den of vipers!"

Ephorah was about to wrench her arm free of Sachar's grip, but she realized the translator wasn't actually hurting her.

"Be careful whom you trust," Sachar whispered. "Especially when they ask you to work on a sigil like this." She held up the symbol for *incontio*.

Ephorah didn't respond. Her eyes locked on the sigil, which she only now noticed looked like some kind of pictograph, but she couldn't figure out what.

Sachar let go of her arm. "Alright, that'll be all!" She smiled as if nothing had happened. "I'll send you a copy when the translation's done. Good luck in your classes!"

With that, the translator shoed Ephorah out of the office and shut the door behind her.

64

Business in Kemet

NAMID

Two girls crossed the desert wearing clothes fit for a mushroom farmer. Each carried a jar of mushrooms and a flask of water from a shack. Neither one spoke.

"Namid," Rana tried to break the silence. She clearly wanted to talk about what had happened back at the mushroom farm, but there was nothing to say. It had been too simple.

"Save your breath," Namid replied. "Talking makes you thirsty."

Continuing along the road that led southeast, the girls made their way towards the sea. They occasionally passed by other farms, but neither of the girls wanted to stop to resupply. Not after what had happened last time. Namid hoped Rana was right about there being an illegal fishing boat they could charter.

Eventually, Rana broke the silence.

"Why do you want to return to your empire so much?"

"That's a stupid question," Namid scoffed. "Because the police here are worse than the criminals. Because the biggest source of fresh water is worse than an open-air sewer, no offense. Because there's so little food and water here that even the stuff that tastes like mud and dirt feels like a feast, no offense. Because this whole nation is a shithole, no offense. And because the people in it act like I'm a weirdo for exercising basic human survival instincts, no offense."

"Rana tilted her head. "Why would I take offense to that last one?"

"Because you're the one treating me like a weirdo."

"Oh, okay." Rana paused for a moment. "But, you get along well here. You don't have trouble killing someone for food. You don't hesitate to get violent when your own life is threatened, and you don't even try to negotiate when you're at an impasse with someone. You might not like this country, but you fit right in."

"Right, but I don't want to," Namid snapped. "So what's your point?"

"Well, is everyone in your homeland like you?" Rana asked.

"I think they are. They just hide it. You can't just come out and tell people you're only in it for yourself, even if everyone is. We all have to do this song and dance where we pretend to care about other people who equally pretend to care about us. Namid Sadi is on Namid Sadi's side, just like everyone else. Just look at the state of this nation. Why do you think the Tomb Lords take every scrap of food and then redistribute it to everyone?"

"Officially, it's to make sure people with excess don't hoard it for themselves, and so that the poor will have enough to eat," Rana replied.

"And how does that actually work out? How many people in this dump of a country are actually getting enough to eat?" Namid found herself yelling now, but she no longer cared. "I guarantee that whatever public-serving excuse they give is just a mask. Do you really think people like Mereshank and the guy who raises all those necrophytes to be sadists actually cares about the people of Kemet?"

"Fair enough," Rana admitted. "But if everyone in the empire was like you, do you really believe the empire would be any better than this place?"

"Everyone in the empire is like me," Namid scowled. "They're just well-fed to the point that it doesn't seem to matter. Lots of people with full bellies offer up table scraps to appear generous. Before I got abducted, do you know what I was doing? I was preparing a surprise birthday party for my childhood friend who was mad at me, all so I could smooth things over to keep her around in case I needed her again. And before that, I helped a tall handsome alchemist boy find temporary work and lodging with another one of my friends so he'd owe me, and so I'd have a medical alchemist in my debt later. Anyone can pretend to care about others in the moment so that you'll feel bad and help them out later if they need it. It isn't charity, it isn't generosity, it's just prudent."

Rana didn't say anything else, but Namid saw her face fall. *Maybe I went too far*, she thought. *If I demoralize her now, she might not guide me to a fishing boat.*

"Maybe the problem is the words," Namid tried to sound like she was only thinking aloud. "People use words like 'charity' and 'generosity,' but what do they really mean? Would it have been generous for that mushroom farmer to give us his food supplies if he knew it would leave him with nothing to avoid starvation? Do you have to give up your own life to be generous? Maybe he would have been more willing to share if he had more food. It's a lot easier to give when you have things to share."

"...I guess." Rana didn't look up.

The girls walked on in silence for a while. Out of the corner of her eye, Namid noticed someone watching them from another farm. They were wrapped up in enough clothes that Namid couldn't tell if it was a woman or a man, and they appeared to be staring at the jars the girls carried.

They can't have them, Namid thought. *These need to last until we reach the shore. I can't kill someone else for food while Rana is watching.*

While Rana was watching. Something about that bothered her. Tactically, she really only needed Rana to think well enough of her so that the one person who could guide Namid to the sea didn't ditch her. But there was something else; something that irked Namid. She didn't just want Rana to stay with Namid out of mutual need; she wanted Rana to think well of her. And after the incident with the old man on the farm, she clearly didn't.

If Rana would just see reason, she'd realize that killing the mushroom farmer was necessary. It was dirty, but it was survival. Surely Rana didn't want to die.

Namid was pulled out of her thoughts by the sound of someone pointing at them from a distance and shouting. A man and his wife were looking at the girls, and while Namid couldn't make out what they were planning, they were not being quiet about it.

"Let's move faster," Namid whispered to Rana, but it was already too late.

The man, who looked to be mid-forties, started running towards the girls.

The woman slipped inside the house and was quickly replaced by a younger man, probably the older couple's son. He started running at the girls alongside the older man.

"You two!" The older man yelled. "Show us your faces!"

"Crap," Namid muttered. "Can I ask why you're accosting us? We're wearing these heavy robes to keep the sun off of our skin. Why do you need to see our faces?"

"There's been an order put out by the Tomb Lords." The older man frowned. "The necrophytes are looking for two young women who have fled from Mereshank's palace."

"Do we look like we came from a palace?" Namid gestured to her clothes. "We're just peasants. Even if we had come from Azzitha, how would we have crossed the Nile?"

"Your clothes don't fit you," the younger man hissed. "I'd bet you stole them as a disguise. Now why would you need a disguise if you are only mushroom farmers?"

Namid sighed and looked over at Rana. "How do you want to handle this?"

Rana said nothing. Her face had fallen again. She knew what was coming.

Namid had taken the mushroom farmer's kitchen knife just in case. She had thought about handing it to Rana so she could defend herself as well, but she knew better. Rana didn't have the stomach for it. But now she had a way of fighting that didn't rely on exposing herself as a wizard.

"Show us your faces already!" The younger man grabbed the wrappings on Namid's face to rip them off, but his arm suddenly hung limp. He looked at the slash Namid had cut across his bicep. A clean cut; he wasn't going to bleed out anytime soon, but he couldn't move his lower arm with his muscle cut.

"My son!" The older man bellowed. "You bitch!"

He was about to lunge at Namid, but she swung the knife around and felt it cut through...something. Blood from the man's hand and a small pink thing in the sand told her she'd cut into his wrist. He yelped and clutched his wounded arm with his other hand.

"Any hands you don't keep to yourselves..." Namid raised the knife to her eye level. "...you don't get back. We're leaving."

The men gave the girls the sorts of expressions that make you think "if looks could kill…," but neither tried to stop them as they hurried away.

"What happened to 'dead men don't report us?'" Rana snickered.

"I didn't kill them," Namid muttered. "I thought you'd appreciate that."

"Have you ever used a knife like that before?" Rana asked.

"Not exactly." Namid took a rag from her pocket and wiped the blood from the blade. "I've taken courses on knife etiquette. Slash, don't stab. Aim for the muscle groups. Don't try to threaten them or give them warnings, just swing with your elbow bent. If they're aggressive enough to get within that range, they aren't going to listen to warnings. If they don't get that close, then that's a better warning than just brandishing the knife."

Rana seemed to be taking all that in. "Aim for the muscle groups?"

Namid drew a line with her finger along her upper arm. "Cut these, and your attacker can't move his arm. The goal isn't to kill him, it's to get away. Don't worry about the jugular; he'll protect that. Avoid aiming for his gut, or other fatal parts. He won't bleed out quickly, and if he realizes he's going to die, he'll probably take you to the grave with him."

"Wow," Rana whistled. "You know a lot about killing people."

"No, I know a lot about fending off attackers." Namid couldn't help but hear a smile coming from Rana. "None of this is meant to kill, just to disable!"

"Then why didn't you do that with the mushroom farmer?" Rana asked.

"Because he was the one holding the knife!" Namid scowled.

Rana chuckled. Namid hid her face in her outfit, but she allowed herself a smirk as well.

As the sun started to set, the girls approached a small cluster of buildings that were too close together to be individual farms. Namid sometimes wondered why none of these sorts of places were on any maps. She knew there were villages that dotted the salty coast across from Zarash, but no one ever bothered drawing them on any charts. Maybe the Tomb Lords didn't think they were important, or cartographers in Hadesh didn't know what to put on those parts of the map.

This cluster of buildings was too small to be called a hamlet or a village. It was more like a handful of shacks, although one looked like it might be an inn.

"It might be dangerous to spend the night here," Namid whispered. "But it might be better than sleeping outside again."

"You don't want to try that ice trick again?" Rana asked.

"I'd need to find water underground again, and there's too many people around. I didn't want to use my sorcery when dealing with those guys before, but if I started making the sand into glass out here in the desert, it'll draw attention. If you don't want to try and find a place to rest here, we need to get further out into the desert."

"No." Rana pointed to the building that might be an inn. "We should at least try to get a place to rest for the night."

"They're probably still on the lookout for two girls who've come in from the desert." Namid thought about the man and his son who had attacked them earlier. "How do you want to handle this?"

"I'm going to go inside and ask if I can sing for the night in exchange for warm meals." Rana drank the last gulp of water from her supply and gargled it in her mouth before swallowing.

"Seriously?" Namid asked. "You sing?"

"Well, that isn't why they're going to give me a shot," Rana admitted. "The truth is, thanks to Mereshank's pampering and your upbringing in the empire, we're better looking than any woman these people will have seen in years. That's why they'll gladly let me entertain guests for the night."

"...I see." Namid offered Rana the kitchen knife. "Want it?"

"...Yes," Rana pocketed the knife.

"I could join you up there," Namid offered. "If you want. I don't normally sing, but I could try telling jokes. There's got to be some I've heard back home no one around here will know–"

"No!" Rana' eyes widened. "Joke telling for a trade is illegal in Kemet. Anyone trying to make a living as a comedian gets eaten alive by zombies."

Namid's jaw dropped. "...what."

Rana shook her head. "Just go in an hour after me and get a room. We don't want to look like we're together. I'll tell them I'm traveling to meet my fiancé in an arranged marriage. There's always someone having to move between villages so we don't end up with too many people marrying their cousins, and my dad was too sick to come with me. I'll come and join you later."

Namid didn't have any money, least of all in whatever they used for currency in Kemet. However, she wasn't going to tell Rana that. Best if she didn't know how Namid planned to get what they'd need.

"Alright," Namid nodded. "Sounds like a plan. Go on in. I'll get a room in an hour."

As Rana went off to the inn, Namid looked around for a mark. Had she thought about it, she would have done a more thorough job looting the mushroom farmer's house for money, but she never found anything that looked like money. Just a few coupons that might have been for discounts on food, or something.

Keeping her face well concealed under the mushroom farmer's wraps and her mushroom jar nestled into the robes, Namid examined some of the people milling about the half-dozen buildings. There didn't seem to be any people who carried coin purses. Where did people keep their money?

Namid decided to blend in with the crowd and just people watch for a moment. Maybe she'd see some sort of commerce to give her an idea of where people kept their money.

A small building at the edge of town seemed to be a general store, or something like it. Namid came up close to it and found a bench that she almost considered sitting on. Except, it looked like it was mostly still standing thanks to the dust and worms it had collected, as if the maggots that called it home were desperately keeping the rotten wood together with slime alone. Instead of resting on the so-called-bench, Namid decided to lean against a wall near the window, and waited to see if she could inconspicuously watch someone come in and do business.

Sure enough, a woman came into the building and approached a counter with a bucket, a box of needles, and a pair of shoes. A man behind the counter examined the goods and held out an expecting hand.

This is it, Namid thought. *What does their money look like?*

Instead of coins, or metal cubes, or anything sensible, the woman took out a book of coupons and ripped a number of coupons from the sheet. She handed them to the man, with no other money to go with it.

What? Namid pressed her ear against the wall to hear what was going on. Fortunately, the walls had been thinned out by termites.

"There's not enough here," the shopkeeper said.

"That can't be right!" The woman complained. "That was enough last week!"

"Price has gone up," the shopkeeper replied. "Not enough production. The needles alone cost two more utility coupons, and the shoes cost twice as many luxury coupons."

Coupons? Namid peeked through the store window again. *Are those coupons the currency? How on Earth does that work?*

"I finally get paid enough to buy what I need, and the price just jumps out of my reach again?" The woman sighed and handed the man more coupons. She walked out with the bucket and the box of needles, but left the shoes. As she left the store, Namid noticed the footprints she left behind in the sand were of bare feet.

"Hmph." Namid wiggled her toes in the boots she'd stolen from the necrophyte back in Azzitha. They were far too big for her, but suddenly that didn't matter as much. Stepping away from the store, she looked back at the inn.

"I have no idea what kind of coupons I'm supposed to use to get a night for us," she muttered as she looked around at the few people still milling about. She couldn't just ask one of them; they might wonder why she didn't know.

Namid walked into the store and looked around. The shopkeeper looked to be about fifty. He stood behind a dilapidated counter with a pair of equally old and sorry-looking shelves on either side of him. One held jars of preserves, while another was heavily laden with clay pots of cooking oil. Namid took note of how heavy these goods looked as she approached the counter.

"Hello, I'm traveling with my friend to escort her to meet her fiancé. We're looking to stay the night in the local inn, but it looks like we forgot to bring the right coupons. Is there anything your store buys from people that you'd be willing to trade for them?"

The man shook his head. "I'm not supposed to give you leisure coupons. Like for like – that's the law."

Leisure coupons, Namid thought. *Now I know what I need.* "I see. Thank you for your—"

"Although," the man made a sly smile. "I might be willing to make a deal. One the Tomb Lords would overlook. If I had to explain how I acquired goods without a record of my transaction, I could be executed. But services..."

"What kind of services?" Namid raised an eyebrow.

"Leisure services for leisure coupons," he smirked.

"No, thank you." Namid entertained the idea of suffocating this man and stealing the coupons she needed, but if she did that, someone would find his body, and in this small community the locals would find her and Rana instantly. She wished she'd learned how to put someone to sleep with telepathy, but that was a more difficult telepath spell.

"Oh, very well," the shopkeeper leaned back and clasped his hands behind his head. "Suit yourself."

Namid examined his expression closely and started heading for the door.

"Of course, you'll have a hard time finding lodging once the whole village learns you're a thief," the man snickered.

"That so?" Namid prepared herself. "And what, pray tell, have I stolen?"

The shopkeeper looked around the store. "Oh, I'm sure there's something missing here. Something a stranger from out of town might have taken. It's not like the folks around here are going to take your word over mine."

Namid sighed. "Yeah, I was afraid you'd say something like that."

Flicking her wrist, she made a small air explosion right in the middle of the shelf to the shopkeeper's right, where the jars of preserves were stored. The two preserves flew off the shelf and crashed down onto the man's head, while the shelf snapped in half. The shopkeeper was knocked onto his back, right underneath the second shelf. Namid destroyed this shelf as well, and heavy pots of oil rained down on top of the helpless man.

Namid came back up to the counter and looked down at the shopkeeper, who now had abrasions on his face, his head gashed not only from the pots and jars, but from hitting the floor as well. His arm reached pitifully to Namid as she dug through his counter and found a book of coupons.

"My, what a terrible accident." Namid checked that the book had leisure coupons and tucked it into her robes. "Pleasure doing business with you."

65

Origin of a King

AMRI

"An infection," Marduk growled from his desk. "You ran around after being expressly warned to rest your wounded legs, and your wounds opened back up and got infected."

"It's pretty minor." Esfan finished bandaging Amri's calves back up after he'd applied a new ointment to kill the bacteria. "We caught it right away."

"That isn't the point!" The god hissed. "He got lucky, nothing more!" Marduk glared at Amri. "You could have lost both of your legs from the knees down. Easily."

"My uncle wanted me to help him put up missing person posters," Amri protested. "She's been gone over a week now."

"You came to this very temple to hand out posters that you could have delivered in the morning after a night's rest." Even as mad as he was, Marduk didn't let his lecture interrupt his work translating the book in front of him. He continued writing new copies of whatever tome he had out in one hand while his other pounded the desk in a fist. "What possible value could there have been in coming back here immediately? Did you think the priests at this temple were going to go comb the city and find her? Do you think their eyes can see things in the dark that mine could not in the past nine days? There was no reason not to wait until morning, after your body had had a chance to rest and heal!"

Amri looked away from Marduk. "My uncle expected me to help immediately. If I told him I couldn't because I was hurt—"

"Are you so desperate for approval that you'd cripple yourself just to please your uncle in the moment?" Marduk bellowed. "Do you think I'm joking when I say you could have lost your legs? There's a hacksaw in the infirmary. That's what Sarah would have used if the infection had been worse."

Amri winced and instinctively rubbed his shins. "But what was I supposed to do? My sister's been missing for over a week! My uncle is right to be worried about her."

"Listen, boy." Marduk lowered his voice, but you could hear thunder rolling in the depths of his speech. "It's about time you learned this. You are a young man. In nature, males are the expendable sex. Women can bear children, and a handful of males of any species with a wider number of females can repopulate a tribe. But the reverse doesn't work, and this is more true for your kind than almost any animal on the planet, since your species has a longer pregnancy term than any other creature of your size. For this reason, if society must choose between saving your life and saving your sister's, it will cast you aside to protect her for the simple reason that she's more valuable. The only way to keep society from throwing you away is to make certain you can provide valuable services."

Marduk's words sank into Amri's mind slowly. Some part of him already knew all of this, but he'd never heard it said aloud.

"So, what you're really saying is..." Amri cleared his throat. "If I hurt myself to help my uncle find Namid, he won't help me if I find myself handicapped and useless."

"In a sense," Marduk nodded. "It's not uncommon for people to take care of their relatives when they are injured as such, but it is rare for them to do so without bearing a grudge. The moment you become a burden on the people around you, that's when they will resent keeping you around. The exceptions are people like those who work in this abbey, but they've all made a conscious decision to perform charity work."

"So what should I do, if my uncle is demanding that I help him find Namid?" Amri asked. "He told me this morning that it is not his plan to trade me for her."

"When he'd had a good night's sleep and was thinking more clearly, yes." Marduk never stopped writing his translated copies. "Last night, he was probably driven by his desire to find his niece, and had you crossed paths, he would have demanded that you help him, able-bodied or not. Consequences that come later mean nothing in the heat of the moment. What you should have done is assess your own condition and put your foot down. Tell him, or your aunt, that you will help them in the morning after a night's rest. That is the way of the king; to know his own limits, and to help when he can, but not overextend himself when it would cause greater problems later."

Amri looked down at his legs, which stung with disinfectant. He'd been thinking purely in the heat of the moment last night as well. He had been so focused on not being chastised by his uncle for failing to help find Namid that he hadn't thought about what his uncle would do with him if he lost his legs to infection. Surely, anyone who would berate him for not helping when his legs needed healing would do much worse to a person who could never walk again.

Marduk looked up at Esfan. "Take him out back and train his arms. Keep him in the wheelchair. There are dumbbells back there he can use. Just keep him moving."

Esfan nodded and rolled Amri back to the paved area where the exercise equipment was stored. He brought out two fifteen-pound weights and had Amri do curls from his wheelchair.

"Urgh..." Amri struggled with one weight as Esfan did his own set of curls with a set of thirty-pound weights. Embarrassed at the gap between him and the initiate, he let the weight drop and thought of something to distract them both with.

"Hey," Amri panted. "Why does Marduk always talk like somebody's dad? I get that he's stuck in the body of a nineteen or twenty-year-old because people think of him as an upstart, but he doesn't have any children, does he?"

"Not anymore," Esfan admitted. "He did have a son, once. Nabu, I think his name was. A god entirely associated with writing, who often was seen as the co-ruler of Babylon before it became an empire."

"Before it became an empire?" Amri tried to remember if he'd heard anything about the Babylonian Empire before it fell. "I don't know much about that."

"Marduk's cult was originally elevated to power when the Sumerian city states started to collapse," Esfan explained. "The evidence we have of the time suggests that a goddess whose name Marduk deliberately wiped from all our records, so, probably his ex-wife, was the dominant power in the region at the time. Her temples held a monopoly on prostitution, and, according to one stone tablet found before the reign of Hammurabi, would loan money to people starting their own businesses, accepting their children as collateral. At some point, they even gained the authority to demand a tithe of young girls as slaves for their temple brothels. Part of the reason Marduk sounds like a dad with a short fuse is because his cult seems to have originally been propelled to prominence by a bunch of angry fathers who wanted their little girls back."

Esfan resumed curling his weights, and Amri realized breaktime was over.

"There were a lot of political shenanigans between Marduk and the old goddess," Esfan said between curls. "A union that made sense on paper to unite the old ways with the new, but was really a terrible match. Remember how Marduk gets stronger the more people become literate? Well, Hammurabi, first king of Babylon, mandated that all citizens be taught to read and write in cuneiform, and that included women and girls. Babylonian law also permitted women to own and operate their own businesses, especially breweries. This led to a lot of women choosing to get jobs that didn't involve sex work, which crippled the goddess's source of financial and political power. And while she was laid low from losing prostitutes to control men and her theocratic laws to force women into the trade, Marduk became bloated with the power of the world's first fully literate kingdom. It wasn't long before he was strong enough to boot her off the throne entirely and take over Babylon as the sole ruler."

"Eventually, he became strongly connected to the concept of fatherhood, and he had a wife, but she never really had a defined personality and never received enough faith to manifest or be seen by mortals. Originally, Nabu was just as powerful as Marduk, but since people like to keep things simple, folks today just assign Marduk the duties of writing that his son used to have and forgot about Nabu altogether."

"Then how do you know about this?" Amri asked.

"Because Marduk told me, and showed me some of the records and stone tablets that confirm Nabu used to exist," Esfan replied. "So, to answer your original question, fatherhood is directly tied to Marduk's nature as the god of civilization, but people forgot about his son, and he's no longer able to manifest as a god.

"Okay..." Amri hadn't expected a history lesson, but it had taken his mind off how sore his arms now were from curling dumbbells. "But...how come I've never heard the name 'Nabu' before? Why don't any of the other gods ever bring him up, if they're from that time period?"

Esfan set down his dumbbell and took a deep breath. "Because unlike Marduk, they can't remember anything if mortals don't. Only a god associated with writing can remember the things people have written down, which means lately, Marduk is the only god who can remember his forgotten son."

Amri took Esfan's relaxation as a cue to put down his own weight and rest his arms. "I once heard that different pantheons have the same gods, just with different names. Even if Nabu has been forgotten, isn't there a similar god in any of the other pantheons? Someone he could point to and make people remember?"

"Well," Esfan winced. "There was. In the Egyptian pantheon, Nabu became Thoth."

66

The Inn at the End of the Road

NAMID

Namid made certain to leave the store as calmly and casually as possible. The shopkeeper wasn't dead when she left, and might even survive. Anyone who saw behind the counter would simply assume that the old rotten shelves had given out, and he'd simply had an accident.

Inside the tavern, Namid could hear Rana singing *To the Field of Reeds*. Namid had heard her father sing this song in the privacy of his home, but his version had been different. When he sang it, it was more about what one needed to do to get to Osiris's afterlife; Rana's song was more about the paradise that awaited those whose heart weighed less than a feather. Which, admittedly, mostly included bountiful harvests and crops that never failed.

Namid was surprised that Rana's voice was so sweet and soft; it wasn't the sort you'd hear from a professional at a music theater, but Namid hadn't expected Rana to be able to sing at all from what she'd mentioned earlier.

Both of the other guests at the inn seemed enthralled by her singing. The main room was fairly large, with several empty tables and a small stage reserved for entertainers, where Rana was singing. The only other guests were an older man huddled over a pint of beer, and a man only a few years older than Namid was finishing a meal of what looked like gruel made from lentils, beans, and a thick white stew.

Namid approached a bar where a man with a balding head and a thick beard did his best to clean a beer glass with a dirty rag. His eyes had been on Rana, but he looked up at Namid as she came up to the bar.

"Hello," Namid flipped open the stolen book of coupons and found a page labeled "leisure." None of these coupons had been used yet. "I need a room for two. My friend will be joining me later."

"I'm going to need five coupons for each of you," the bartender replied.

Namid showed him the book. The bartender ripped ten of the coupons out of the book and placed them in a drawer behind the counter. He then handed her a room key.

"Need anything else?" He asked.

"Actually, yeah." Namid glanced over at the meal the young man was eating. "What have you got on the menu?"

"Right now? Just the gruel," the man replied.

"What kind of gruel?"

"Flour for thickener, lentils and beans for protein. You get a bowl for two food coupons." The man crossed his arms. "And for a third, I'll add some peapods."

Namid checked the food coupons in the book. Unlike the leisure coupons, this section had seen more use, but there were still quite a few pages left. Namid ripped out three coupons and handed them to the bartender. He handed her a bowl of gruel and directed her to sit at a table.

To her surprise, the gruel was better tasting than it looked. Namid hadn't realized how hungry she'd been lately, having told her hungry stomach to shut up and let her focus on the problems at hand. This wasn't just a meal; it was a hot meal. The water used to make the broth tasted rusty, but mixed with the flour and other ingredients, it was surprisingly good. Even the peapods, which Namid normally didn't like but knew she needed the greens, tasted better than expected. Perhaps hunger will do that to you.

Rana made eye contact with Namid, who nodded towards her as she ate. She ripped out a few more food coupons so Rana could see them and know there'd be food for her, too. Then she finished her meal and headed up to their room.

A single bed sat in the middle of the small room. Namid set the food coupons for Rana down on the bed where she could see them and took a look around.

There wasn't exactly a laundry machine available, but there was a washroom and a tub. Namid took a bath and proceeded to wash the clothes she'd been wearing in the bathtub. She then hung them on the curtain rack and left them to air dry. Draping herself in a towel, she checked the rest of the room for any kinds of security threats.

The bedsheets were surprisingly clean…ish. They were a bit dusty, but Namid had expected them to be infested with pests or something. Instead of the substandard motel that she'd been expecting, this place looked like it had once been a fairly nice bed and breakfast that was only in somewhat poor condition due to disuse, and no new insects or parasites had moved into the place without customers. A single lantern sat on an end table next to the bed. The windows had iron interior cross-shaped frames that could probably be opened, at least if they weren't too rusty, and although she was careful not to expose herself in nothing but a towel to the outside world, she made a note of emergency escape routes if she and Rana had to exit through the window.

Outside, the roof tiles looked like they'd tear off if anything heavier than a stiff breeze were to touch them. They were only a single story above the ground, although a fall from this height would still injure the girls if they tried to jump.

Around the room, there was a small, crusty-looking dresser that Namid could slide in front of the door once Rana came in for the night. It might not be enough to hold off anyone trying to break in if the door's lock didn't hold, but it would at least wake them up and give them time to make another escape.

When Rana eventually came up to the room and knocked on the door, Namid confirmed it was her through a peephole and let her in.

"Go grab some food," Namid handed her the coupons. "Then come up, get clean, and wash your clothes. If you hurry, they'll be dry by the morning." Namid's clothes were still wet, but she moved them over to a towel rack that hung on the washroom wall so Rana could use the tub.

"How did you get these coupons?" Rana asked. "Looks like you gathered quite a few."

"I had to take care of some trash in the general store around here," Namid explained. *Close enough to the truth, which she definitely doesn't want to hear.*

"Guess it doesn't matter." She went downstairs for dinner.

When she returned, Rana cleaned herself and her clothes in the tub and hung them up on the curtain rack. Dressed in a towel like Namid, she tucked herself into bed to stay warm. Namid had lit the lantern by the bed; the only light in the room now that night had fallen outside.

"Okay, now I'm dying to know." Namid sat up in bed. "Why are comedians illegal in Kemet?"

"Hm?" Rana dried her hair on one of the smaller towels. "Well, if you believe the legends, that's old magic. Really old. So old, it's not really magic anymore, but something else, like a natural law."

Namid frowned. "What is?"

"Comedy," Rana replied. "If someone can make you laugh, they've got you. They can make you do all sorts of things. They can even change your beliefs. That's dangerous to a god, or to a lich who thinks he's a god."

"Huh." Namid tried to think how jokes could hurt a lich. "Okay. So, how much further do you think we are from the coast?"

"We'll get there tomorrow," Rana smiled. "I never imagined we'd get this close."

"What are you planning to do when we get to the empire?" Namid leaned back in bed. "Do you have any family there?"

"No, but that doesn't matter to me," Rana admitted. "I don't think I have any family left here. When your parents sell you to someone like Mereshank, they forfeit their right to call you their daughter."

"You should come to Hadesh with me. My aunt and uncle will help you find a new home, or a job. They might even let you stay with us." Namid tilted her head. "Come to think of it, my brother was spending an awful lot of time with a priest he'd met at an abbey. They might offer you some sort of sanctuary."

"Maybe." Rana looked up at the shadows dancing on the ceiling in the fading light of the lantern. "What are your aunt and uncle like? Are they a lot like you?"

Namid paused. She knew what Rana was asking about. "Not exactly. My uncle will, on occasion, get angry at things he should get mad about, but I've never seen him actually get violent. He works as a doctor; not a mage, but as a physician he diagnoses patients and prescribes treatments. My aunt is an Arbiter of Man; they're like historians, although they also make these theories about why empires rise and fall. She doesn't like conflict, though, so she mostly focuses on the documentation and not the theories."

"That's the sort of job that would get your fingernails ripped out here," Rana whispered. "There's a forbidden pharaoh, whom we're never supposed to talk about. He's either Amenhotep's son, or one of his other descendants. Amenhotep has done everything he can to remove him from history."

"Why? What in the Abyss did he do?" Namid asked.

"Something extreme." Rana glanced at the door that Namid had blocked with the dresser, as if expecting a necrophyte to come bursting through it at any moment. "Actually, quite a few things. He tried to change all the artwork that previously depicted pharaohs as godlike and perfect and had himself shown with a paunch. He tried to destroy the polytheistic religion of the time and make people worship a single god instead. He even denied his status as a god in human form. We're never supposed to admit it, but everyone knows: Amenhotep is ashamed of this guy."

"Heh, that's why most Arbiter's of Man don't get a lot of work outside Hadesh," Namid nestled further into the bed. "My uncle is definitely the breadwinner of the house. Still, my aunt knows a thing or two about people and how they've lived throughout the ages, and what happens when an empire breaks apart."

"Oh? And what does happen?" Rana asked.

"They eat each other." Namid tilted her head. "Well, not always literally. But people are really only as moral as society allows them to be, or forces them to be. You see this all the time: the people who are rich and don't want to give up their wealth are motivated by greed. The people who aren't rich and demand that the rich give away their wealth are also motivated by greed. Most people's 'morals' are a bad joke. Even Hadesh, which I'll admit has a really low crime rate, at least right now. Just turn off the trains that bring in food to the marketplace, or stop the supply of fuel to the city. Watch how long they stay 'civilized.' How long that crime rate stays so low."

"People can't all be like that." Rana wriggled as she lay in bed, trying to get comfortable. "If they were, they'd never have formed a civilization in the first place."

"Maybe that's true," Namid admitted. "But the people who build them are nothing like the people born into them. The ones that build a civilization already knew how to survive without one. They agreed to work with each other because they knew the wilderness was filled with dangers. In the end, civilization was always about how you can be useful to the people around you. If you aren't useful, you get left behind as a homeless person. Or you get eaten by a rakshasa who then poses as a homeless person. There is something I still don't get though."

"Oh really?" Rana's voice was wry and tired. "What's that?"

"Why do I have to explain any of this to you, of all people? I've got a brother back in Hadesh who doesn't get it, but he's always trying to appease others in a weird way that just confirms everything. But you've spent three years in Mereshank's palace among those other girls. You even told me to be quiet about our escape plans around the other girls there, because they'd expose us to the guards just so that we wouldn't get away. You even compared them to crabs in a bucket."

"Yeah, because they have nothing else," Rana replied. "I've always thought that if people could have their own hopes and dreams, they wouldn't need to destroy other people's. I believe you when you say that people in the empire are more generous because they have more to give; you can't give what you don't have. But then...what's the point of it all?"

"Of what?" Namid asked. "Empires? Wealth?"

"No, life!" Rana rolled over to lock eyes with Namid. "I've watched the Tomb Lords, especially Amenhotep, drain every ounce of morality out of everyone he gets his bony hands on. That lich could turn a sweet innocent princess into a serial killer. And the closer you get to him, the worse it is. The folks who work in the factories or get to live on farms outside the cities have it best; as poor and wretched as their lives get, they still have the chance to make their family's lives brighter, even if it's only in little ways like a kind word now and then. The necrophytes? Their entire lives are dedicated to one horrifying act after another."

"And for all the privileges and better quality of life that they get, their lives have no meaning. The women especially; the male necrophytes seem to view the ugly parts of their jobs as just something they need to do, but the girls? I've seen them command zombies to tear homeless old people to shreds with the hint of a sense of purpose, like killing the helpless is the closest thing they have left to meaning in their lives. As if that were the morality they live by." Rana looked at her wrist and checked her own pulse. "Sometimes I fear that if people in Kemet die and go to some sort of hell, they don't even notice, because it's just more of this place."

"Perhaps you'd fit right in with the people of Hadesh," Namid mused as the last light of the lantern went out. In the darkness of the room, she found herself quickly drifting off to sleep.

She woke to the sound of someone slapping her hand against the mattress. She'd been cradling something warm. Something that was trying to break out of her arms and had resorted to slapping the bed like someone signaling they were surrendering in a self-defense course.

Namid realized that while she'd been asleep, she had wrapped her arms around Rana and bearhugged her to the point that the girl's face was being smothered with her chest. Namid released her, and Rana took in a deep breath, and while Namid couldn't see her in the dark, she had a mental image of the girl's eyes bulging from lack of air.

Several gasps later, Rana's breathing returned to normal. "I know that in the desert, freezing to death was a real thing to worry about. But we're in a warm bed at an Inn. What's with the cuddle-of-death?"

"Um..." Namid tried to think. "Didn't even know I was doing this." She made a mental note that this was the second night in a row that she'd managed to sleep well without her brother reading her a bedtime story.

Her thoughts were interrupted by the sounds of voices in the floor below. Namid couldn't make them out, but they didn't sound like a bartender or innkeeper just tidying up for the night. Then she heard footsteps. Someone was coming up the stairs.

Namid lit the lantern and got out of bed. Still wearing nothing but the towel from earlier, she checked on the clothes that had been hung up to dry in the bathroom. They were still a little damp, but they'd have to do.

"What are you doing?" Rana groggily sat up on the bed.

"Grab your clothes and get dressed." Namid threw her still-damp clothes on. "We need to leave."

Before Rana could ask why, at least two sets of footsteps quietly walked up to the door of their room. If the girls had still been asleep, Namid wouldn't be able to hear them. The sounds of keys and someone fiddling with the lock on the door told her someone was trying to enter the room without waking anyone else. Namid put her finger to her lips and gestured for Rana to get dressed. This time, Rana hurried out of bed and scrambled to put her clothes on.

Once the door was unlocked, whoever was outside in the hallway tried to open the door, only for it to get stuck on the dresser Namid had shoved in front of it. The intruder was trying to open the door quietly, and hadn't yet figured out that the door was blocked from the inside.

Namid checked the window. It was old and rusted from the outside. The staff at the inn had done a pretty good job keeping it clean on the inside, but it was too corroded to open normally. The only way they could escape through this was if Namid blasted her way through with raw force. That would put whomever was outside on high alert; she needed to do it when the time was exactly right.

Rana had finally gotten dressed just as the person trying to open the door started getting more forceful. They started slamming against the door, and the dresser started to shake. It wouldn't hold forever.

"Open up!" A voice called. This wasn't the voice of the bartender from the night before; it was too feminine. It was either a different member of the staff, or someone else entirely.

"Ready?" Namid whispered to Rana, who nodded.

"In the name of the godking," the voice hissed. "Open this door!"

Namid compressed the air in front of the window, then reversed the pressure and made an explosion of air. The blast was enough to shatter the glass, but only bent the metal frame of the window.

"What?" Namid looked at the frame. She hadn't used a big enough burst of air to blow the frame out. With the glass gone, all of the air of another explosion would go straight outside and leave the frame alone. She couldn't try again now.

"What was that?" This was the voice of the bartender. So, he was working with someone else, probably a necrophyte.

"Traitors!" The other voice growled. "You are both traitors who have fled from your mistress Mereshank! I am to drag you back alive, but first I'll punish to the fullest extent of my authority!"

Namid tried to think of a way to get the window open, but Rana grabbed the lantern from the night stand. Removing the glass cover that protected the flame, she held the small fire up to the iron window frame.

"Of course!" Namid touched her finger to the opposite side of the frame and willed the metal to heat up. "Come on, come on!"

The sound of slamming against the door grew louder. The dresser tipped over and crashed into the bed. Its feet were still somewhat blocking the door, but the bartender was able to crack it open. "Come out now! That reward is mine!"

"A farmer and his son told us about you," the other voice snarled. "You injured one of the young and strong farmers that feed this nation. I'll enjoy breaking you both before I hand you over to Mereshank!"

Namid kicked the half-melted window frame. The old, rusted metal broke off and left them with an escape route. "Grab the quilt from the bed!" Namid ordered.

Rana tore the quilt from off the bed and dragged it over to the window. Namid took it and placed it over top the rotten shingles.

"Okay," Namid gestured to the quilt. "We need to get on it at the same time!"

Rana nodded. "On three."

Namid gritted her teeth. "One."

The bartender and the necrophyte smashed the door with enough force to break the legs of the dresser. The door still didn't open wide enough for them to get in, but they were coming through.

"Two."

The next blow from the pair in the hallway ripped the door's upper hinges off the wall. The girls were out of time.

"Three!"

The girls jumped out the window onto the quilt just as the door was smashed to pieces. The roof shingles completely gave out under their weight and tore loose as the quilt started sliding down the roof.

Namid directed the air underneath the quilt like a stream of wind. It wouldn't keep them in the air or carry them away, but she could slow their fall.

The girls fell with a rough bump on the ground beside the inn. They landed on their shins, which were bruised, but other than that they were unharmed.

Angry shouting from the room they'd fled told the girls that the bartender and the necrophyte had figured out that they'd escaped the inn.

"Time to run!" Namid grabbed Rana's arm and pulled her along.

The cluster of buildings that could barely be called a village didn't leave them with many hiding spots. The night sky was clear and filled with stars; there was plenty of light for the girls to see where they were going, which also meant they couldn't rely on darkness to conceal them. They could try to run out into the desert, where there would be no cover or places to hide. Or they could try to find a hiding spot in the few buildings around here and hope they weren't spotted.

Several men in uniforms were standing outside the general store. The old shopkeeper whom Namid had injured earlier had been dragged outside and laid in the dirt by the shop. His face had new injuries that looked like he'd been struck with a blunt object, and he wasn't moving now. Namid yanked Rana away from the men before they could have been spotted. It was a good thing Rana was lighter than Namid.

"In here!" Namid herded Rana into a corner behind a compost bin. "This thing stinks," she whispered. "They won't look too close at something this foul."

The uniformed men were probably either soldiers or military police, because they grabbed a woman who had come out to see what was going on and proceeded to beat her. Local police wouldn't treat their neighbors this way. Probably.

"Where'd they go?" One of the men bellowed.

The woman merely sobbed in confusion. She clearly had no idea what he was talking about. The man held up a rifle and beat her with the stock of his gun repeatedly, but to no avail.

"Dead men don't report on us." Rana's eyes were dull and lifeless.

"What?" Namid hissed. "Be quiet!"

"Dead men don't report...the man and his son who tried to grab us earlier. You didn't kill them. Should've killed them. Would have been...the smart thing."

Namid covered Rana's mouth. "Don't worry about that now, just shut up and lay low."

"You...were right." Rana's mumbled. Her eyes didn't blink.

"Listen," Namid pulled Rana's face to line up with hers. "Nothing that happened before matters now. There is this moment, and nothing else. Except your dreams; your dreams might live on. if. you. survive. You want to see the empire? You want to watch people who stop clawing at each other like crabs in a bucket? Then you forget about what we should have done and get through this moment."

"Heh," Rana smiled, but her eyes were still devoid of light. "Crabs in a bucket. You know what? I don't think I want to get to your empire."

"What?" Namid hissed. She could hear what sounded like smaller footsteps nearby. The military police had hunting dogs.

"I want you to get to your empire." Rana stood up, exposing herself to the guards.

"What are you–" Namid stopped herself from making any more noise, but it was too late. The guards were already pointing at Rana and shouting. Rana gave Namid one last dull smile before running off into the night. She went back the way the girls had originally entered the village, leading the military police away from the road Namid needed to take to continue on her way to the sea.

But Namid was too frozen in confusion to move out from behind the compost bin. She couldn't decide whether to try and flee, chase after Rana, or try to fight off the police. She had no idea how many police there actually were; she could hear dogs snapping at Rana' heels. She knew she should run. She'd stayed put too long; there was no way she could catch up to Rana or the police, and even if she could, she wasn't some archwizard who could go up against a large swarm of armed men and dogs and come out on top. But there was that nagging doubt that said "maybe."

Eventually, as the sounds and lights of the chase were out of sight, Namid realized that there was now truly no way to save Rana. She'd stayed petrified behind the compost bin for too long.

Slowly, she stood up, and shuffled her way towards the road, unable to stand up straight.

67

Nightmares

NAMID

Stumbling through the desert in the night, Namid occasionally looked over her shoulder to see if any of the military police were following her. There was still no sign of them. They must have figured out by now that she wasn't with Rana; it was only a matter of time before they started combing the desert.

Even still, Namid was exhausted. She had only slept so much, and she feared continuing in the dark. If the military police had any undead monsters with them, then they had the upper hand at night. She needed more rest, and she wouldn't get far in the dark.

Bundled up in her clothes, Namid tapped into her magic and created walls of hardened sand like she'd done before. This time, harder ground was available. She couldn't rely on Rana' body heat, but there were slabs of earth she could harden into a roof to go with her walls.

After some tricky spell work, she managed to create a small cubby for her to crawl into. It was too short for her to stand up inside, and had only one opening. Namid was too claustrophobic to climb in head-first, so she instead crawled into her new shelter like a sleeping bag. Wrapped in her clothes, she was able to get warm enough to fall asleep.

Namid awoke to the feel of cold night air on her face. Somehow, she was wrapped in a blanket on some wooden surface exposed to the elements.

Peeling the blankets off, she leaned up and tried to figure out where she was.

NIGHTMARES

She felt above herself to check for a ceiling or a tent, but there was nothing. She knelt down on the wooden surface and felt around for clues. Her right hand caught onto an oil lantern. Fiddling with a knob and igniting the oil with a snap of her fingers, she held up the lantern and looked around.

Somehow, she found herself in a four-wheeled wagon. There was no horse, or driver, or any sign of how she or the wagon got there.

Namid shuddered in the night, but then realized she didn't feel cold. It finally dawned on her that this was the first night she'd tried to sleep alone since being brought to Kemet.

"You really don't know what to do without me, do you?" A familiar voice came from behind Namid. She turned around and confronted her brother.

"You're not really here." Namid turned away. "I know this is a nightmare."

"Maybe so, but why do you have nightmares like this?" Amri crossed his arms. "What if your subconscious is trying to tell you something you don't want to hear? How else can you explain your inability to get a good night's sleep without someone to hold like a teddy bear or read you a story like you're still a baby?"

"Shut up!" Namid threw a fist at her illusionary brother. Her punch turned his face into sludge, which melted and reformed next to where he'd been standing.

"Did you forget you're talking to yourself?" He asked. "It's not like there's anyone else here."

"I am not putting up with this right now!" Namid shook her head, trying to wake herself up. "I've had more than enough to deal with – I've spent the last few days in a literal hell!"

"Last few days?" This time, the voice of her brother came not from the dream of him, but from the sky itself, blending with other voices Namid almost recognized. "No, you've spent the last several *years* in hell! Hadesh, Azzitha, the desert – hell is wherever you go. A prison of isolation you carry with you."

"Isolation?" Namid scoffed. "Don't give me that crap. I've been doing just fine by myself!"

"Think so?" Ephorah's voice came from the air as her face materialized out of the ether. "If you really don't need anyone else, then why do you involve me in your stupid schemes? What do you think the real Ephorah would say if she found out you sent letters to that bride-to-be's former lovers tipping them off about the wedding?"

"Or do you not care, if we're all just tools to you?" A deeper, relaxed voice came out of the night air. Joshwa Ben Re'em was the next ghost to visit her dreams. "You make all these tightly woven schemes, where everyone either plays their part or you find a replacement.

"Do you think I sacrificed myself for you?" Rana' voice echoed through the sky. "What if I sacrificed myself so I wouldn't end up like you?"

She wanted to respond, but there were too many memories hitting her at once. She turned to run away, but wherever she went, another memory haunted her.

"Girls like us don't really live," her mother's voice chided. "We just survive."

Namid tried to back away from an image of her mother that formed in the desert sands and backed straight into her brother.

"What are you going to do when I finish school?" He asked. "I'm not going to stay in our aunt and uncle's house forever. Do you really think that when I get my own place, you can move in with me? What if I decide one day that I've had enough of your crap and don't allow it? Where will you go?"

"You'd fit right in with us." A new voice, this one Namid didn't recognize, came from behind her. Namid turned around and faced a group of necrophytes. Some had faces she recognized from her time here in Kemet. Others were blank faces with no features. "You should come with us."

"No thanks!" Namid tried to turn and run, but her feet kept banging into rocks that stuck out of the ground, slowing her down as the necrophytes caught up to her.

"Come with us," the faceless ones chanted. "Come with us!"

"No! Take a hint already!" Namid tried to make an air explosion in front of her pursuers, but no such luck in a dream.

"You're coming with us," one of the female necrophytes Namid recognized sneered. "Now!"

"NO!" Namid felt hands pulling her upwards. No, dragging her across her back. She woke and realized she was being dragged out of her makeshift shelter in the desert by a pair of military policemen. The necrophyte from the inn sneered as the men cuffed Namid's arms from behind her back.

"You're coming with us," the necrophyte said as she placed a cloth bag over Namid's head.

68

The Ruins of Sekhet's Lab

AMENHOTEP

Six liches stood near the still-smoking ruins of a laboratory. None spoke. Some were too occupied observing the wreckage. Some were too angry to speak. And one was watching the other five, waiting to see how each would react.

"My lab..." Sekhet finally said. "My research." She looked down from the desert into the exposed subbasement of the building, were everything that had been down there had been reduced to ash and slag.

Djedefre twitched under his armor. He scoured the outer perimeter of the building, searching for clues to whatever security breach made this disaster possible.

Pausiris took a staff and poked at what remained of the main floor to see if it was still safe to stand on. It crumbled to dust at his touch.

Mereshank looked slightly bored, and despite wearing nothing more than enough wrappings to cover her loins and chest, scowled at the sun on her bare skin and ordered a slave to shield her with a parasol.

Arkeon circled what was left of the building walls. "This mess has that dracolich's name all over it!"

"How do you figure?" Pausiris asked.

"Literally!" The sorcerer pointed to one of the walls that was still mostly intact.

The other Tomb Lords came around to see what he meant. The wall in question had been covered in graffiti, including a crude drawing of a dragon's skull peering over a wall with "Daurgo was here" written next to it, and other messages scribbled all over it like "Dragons Rule," "Mummies Stink," and "Mereshank Can't Dance."

Amenhotep made a point to look away from Mereshank, and especially the infuriated look on her face. It was unbecoming of a godking to show mirth in situations like this, and he wouldn't be able to hold it back for very long. Instead, he focused on Sekhet.

"Tell me, why do you think the dragon targeted your lab?"

Sekhet looked over the remains of the blasted facility. "Perhaps he thought I was onto something. Yes, that must have been it. I was about to have a breakthrough and he sabotaged my work to prevent me from creating the perfect citizens for you."

"Hm," Amenhotep nodded. "That's certainly possible. However–"

"Everything about this is wrong!" Arkeon cried as he uncovered another graffiti picture, this one depicting a dracolich chewing on Amenhotep like a piece of gum. "This violates the laws of necromancy!"

"How so?" Amenhotep made a mental note to punish the sorcerer for his interruption later.

Arkeon paused, and looked slowly at the other Tomb Lords. "In order to become a lich, a person has to...well, they have to fear death. They have to be so afraid of death that they are willing to give up their actual lives in order to...well, live. All of us...we all know this. None of us ever wanted to meet Osiris–"

"Skip the parts we already know," Amenhotep fumed. "And get to the part we don't know."

"This dragon–" Arkeon pointed to the graffiti. "These are not the works of a person who fears death. This is the work of someone who would punch death unconscious and then rummage through his pockets for spare change. His soul shouldn't be able to bind itself to a phylactery like this!"

The other liches eyed one another. Arkeon knew more about necromancy than anyone living or dead. If he was worried about this...

"The sorcerer raises a good point," Pausiris added. "The dracolich doesn't act like a normal lich. He goes about angering the gods, travels across continents, exposes himself to nations and governments that might rally against him – either he keeps his phylactery with him, making it easier for someone to find, or he leaves it someplace safe and unguarded. No normal lich would do this."

Amenhotep glared at Arkeon. "And I presume you have no idea how he managed to break the rules of necromancy?"

"If I knew, I'd know how to defeat him," the sorcerer replied. "Permanently."

The High Tomb Lord thought for a moment. In his experience, the best way to kill a dragon was to have someone else do it for you, but a dragon who couldn't simply be slain? That was another matter.

"There's an opportunity here," Amenhotep clenched his fist, trying to force the pieces together in his mind. "The dragon already gave us the opening we needed to kill Thoth, and raised a great deal of panic among the commoners in Hadesh. If we can just get him to keep his efforts focused on the empire to the north, we can get the two to whittle their forces down until we're ready to finish off both of them." The High Tomb Lord paused. "Sekhet, weren't there reports that the Philosopher's Stone went missing in the aftermath of the dragon's attack?"

"Yes, my godking." The sage bowed her head, but the anger in her voice at the loss of her lab was still audible. "Since the dragon accomplished nothing else of note during his attack, it stands to reason that he was distracting the gods and the public from an agent of his who stole the stone in the chaos."

"Then he's probably searching for artifacts of power." Amenhotep habitually stroked his chin. "And whatever he's searching for, he hasn't found it yet." The High Tomb Lord turned to the master sorcerer. "Arkeon, what ancient relics of unholy power do you have locked away in a vault? Anything we can spare?"

Arkeon scoffed. "By definition, if they contain unholy power, they can't be thrown away like pieces on a chessboard. And if we used something of little to no value, the dracolich would probably realize it." The sorcerer turned to look

THE RUINS OF SEKHET'S LAB

at his godking. "Because that's what you're planning, isn't it? Bait him with some powerful ancient artifact, then spring a trap to capture him? If we can't kill him, maybe we could bury him and keep him entombed."

"Hm," Amenhotep mused. "That's not *exactly* what I had in mind."

"In my bastion," Sekhet never took her eyes off the ruins of her laboratory. "I have a number of things that might work. Let me get you a list of ancient relics, and…I'm sure there's something we can use to bring that dragon to his knees."

Amenhotep laughed. "Excellent."

A few days later, Sekhet arrived at Amenhotep's palace, just as he was in the training yard, breaking in his newest necrophyte recruits: two girls and one boy, now the only living survivors of Sekhet's lab.

"Now, I know you've all felt the sting of empty bellies with no clean water," Amenhotep placed his hands on the backs of the two girls. "The truth is, food is scarce. There has never been enough for everyone, and while we do usually give fewer rations to the disobedient, my friend Sekhet was…overzealous with you and all the others in your cage."

The girls looked at each other. It was a look Amenhotep knew all too well. They weren't sure what to believe, but they'd each been given small doses of food since they'd arrived at his palace. Their shrunken bellies had started to return to normal, and soon they'd be able to handle full-sized meals for typical five-year-olds again.

"Ah, there she is now!" Amenhotep looked up at Sekhet and waved her over to the three of them.

The girls instinctively tried to run, but Amenhotep gripped their shoulders.

"Not yet, she's coming to apologize," he said, loud enough for Sekhet to hear. "You shouldn't leave without at least giving her the chance."

Sekhet clearly took the hint and got down on her knees, bowing her head before the girls. "I am so, very sorry!" She begged. "Please, can you forgive me?"

Neither girl responded. They were clearly too scared to react.

"Now, children," Amenhotep chided. "She asked you a question. What is your answer?"

Neither child spoke at first, but one finally looked at Sekhet. "Why should we believe you? My friends believed the things you said, and it turned them into monsters."

"My friend's hair fell out, and then her spine collapsed," The other murmured. "Then her...her privates smelled like poo all the time, and every time she threw up, she'd lose more parts from inside."

"Oh, dear." Amenhotep shook his head. "That is simply terrible. But..." He leaned in closer to the girls. "You don't have to believe anything Sekhet says right this moment. You can decide later. Okay?"

The girls didn't speak, but slowly nodded.

"Excellent. Now, whether you decide to forgive Sekhet or not, you should understand the situation that led to her rash decisions." Amenhotep waved for several guards, who directed a family into the training ground.

There was one man, shriveled, bald, with not an ounce of fat and barely any muscle on him, followed by an even more emaciated woman. They had three children with them, all of whom were slightly better fed than their parents, but only just.

"This is one of the families from just across the Nile," Amenhotep explained. "Right in the countryside between here and Khasoun. As you can see, they haven't had a decent meal in a long time."

"Why don't you give them the same beans and gruel you gave us?" One of the girls asked.

"Oh, I will," Amenhotep nodded. "But you see, there's only so much that we have in the palace, and there are far more families out there who need food. Just look at the mother and father." He squatted down next to the girls, so that his gaze was at their eye level, and pointed to the couple. "They're clearly letting their children take the lion's share of what food they have. Such loving parents. Don't they deserve a better life than this?"

The girls looked at Amenhotep with an expression that read "what's your point?" At this, Amenhotep smiled under his golden mask and nodded to his guards again.

This time, they dragged a man into the training yard. He was bound and gagged, and while he didn't exactly have a healthy waistline, he was much

THE RUINS OF SEKHET'S LAB

better fed than anyone else in the yard.

"Now this man, whom we've recovered from the same village, has been ordered to turn over all of his food to feed the poor." Amenhotep placed his hands on both girls' heads and gently adjusted them to make sure they were looking at the bound man. "My agents have told me that there are many farmers out in the desert who keep secret mushroom farms underground, where they hide their food so they won't have to share. So that good people like them–" He pointed to the starved family. "Don't have enough to eat."

The lich squatted down next to the girls. "I need your help," he whispered into their ears. "This man has food that he's been hiding. I've got to make him tell us where it is, but he just won't talk. I've tried asking him nicely, I've tried offering him money, but he insists he doesn't have any hidden mushrooms. How could I make such a selfish man share his food, so that the families don't starve?"

The girls didn't respond right away. "What if he doesn't have any food?" One of them finally asked.

"Hm," Amenhotep stroked his chin beneath his mask. "He does look like he's had more to eat lately than any of the others from his village." He gestured to the malnourished family, then back to the bound man. "Do you really think he doesn't have some secret stash? Some reason why he'd be eating better than an entire family?"

The lich smiled behind his mask. In actuality, he had no idea whether the man had a mushroom farm or not. Maybe he was illegally hoarding food, maybe he wasn't. But that was never the point.

"Could we...force him to talk?" The girl on Amenhotep's left suggested.

"Force him?" Amenhotep feigned ignorance. "Force him how?"

The girl balled a fist and punched her own hand as a demonstration.

"Hm," the lich mused. "You really think you could get him to talk that way? Could you show me?"

The girl paused, then walked up to the man. Pulling the gag down from his mouth, she looked into his eyes.

"Tell us where the mushroom farm is, or we will hurt you."

The man's eyes were visibly forcing back tears. "There is no farm."

The girl slapped him. It probably stung, but getting slapped by a six-year-old girl probably didn't hurt that much compared to what he was used to.

"I don't think you'll get him to talk like that," Amenhotep chuckled as he turned to the girl on his right. "Do you have any ideas?"

Before speaking, the second girl spent a moment looking at how the first girl was trying, pathetically, to slap, punch, and kick the man into talking. "We would need…um…" She was visibly looking for a word that she just couldn't find. "It's like…a string. But longer, and it makes a snapping noise."

"Do you mean a whip?" Amenhotep asked.

The girl nodded.

Amenhotep gave a knowing look to his guards, who produced two bullwhips from the belts of their uniforms.

"Would these do?" They asked the girls.

The two girls took the whips and proceeded to beat the man. Amenhotep could tell from the looks in their eyes that each one was partly whipping him because the other girl was as well, but there was something else. Maybe a desire to be the one holding the lash for a change? Maybe a resentment against the man for having withheld his food? Or was it just a desire to find this man's mushroom farm to feed the poor?

"Excellent," Amenhotep said softly over the man's screams. "Show me your devotion to justice! Show me what you can do to help the people of Kemet!" He finally turned to Sekhet. Her mask hid her face, but her posture was like that of a person who had just seen a conductor lead an orchestra. "Do you understand where you went wrong?"

Sekhet looked at the two girls in awe. "I'm at a loss for words."

Amenhotep paused before answering. This wasn't some confused child. This was one of his closest advisors. Her strings needed to be pulled more gently.

"You were born after I had already died," the High Tomb Lord finally said. "You learned about things like public criers, tabloids, crowd control; you've always been good at manipulating people when they're in a group."

Sekhet bowed slightly. "People become dumb and hysterical when they're in a crowd."

"And your skills at finding ways to reach wide audiences and enthrall them are essential. I could not achieve my plans without them," Amenhotep smirked behind his mask. "But when it comes to individuals, your skillset comes up short. The only children who would resist listening to beliefs you try to instill within them are those who already have beliefs of their own; morals that their parents instilled them with before you got ahold of them. You can't get rid of their existing beliefs, any more than you can erase the grain in a piece of lumber. But cut with the grain, and you can shape them into what you desire."

Amenhotep gestured to the girls as they continued to beat the man for information.

"What about the boy you asked for?" Sekhet craned her neck, as if checking to see if he was elsewhere in the training yard. "Will you promise him the same privileges you offered that other necrophyte, Mando?"

"The license to do as he wants?" Amenhotep chuckled. "That only works on men without morals to restrain them when the law does not. A boy with his own conscience needs a different approach. I will use a method you showed me, in due time, but with my own...adjustments. Now, show me your relic list."

Sekhet produced her list and handed it to the High Tomb Lord. Amenhotep scanned the items in the sage's inventory. His eyes zeroed in on one artifact in particular.

"Is this real?" He asked.

Sekhet nodded. "Yes, my godking."

"And you're certain we can afford to lose it?"

"Yes, my godking."

"Then it's settled." He handed back the list. "Bring me the Ring of Solomon. That dragon won't be able to resist."

69

Escape From Azzitha

NAMID

There are few things that wake a person up like a bucket of cold water to the face. Most of the time, people either wake up satisfied from a long, pleasant rest, or angry at a ringing alarm clock, which they then proceed to smash. Occasionally, some people awake to a rooster crowing at the sight of the sun, which is usually outside and too far away to smash with your first if you want to hit the snooze.

But a person splashed in the face with water doesn't feel satisfied with a night's rest, or angry at their alarm. They don't even make plans for rooster-noodle soup later. The only thing going through a person woken up with a bucket of water is fear.

Namid gasped as she tried to get her bearings, but her eyes wouldn't come into focus. She heard someone putting down a bucket before leaving the room. There was barely any light. She was sitting in some sort of wooden chair, her arms tied behind her back, her feet chained to the floor. Ropes around her wrists, chains around her legs. Probably using different materials to make it harder for a wizard to escape.

Then she heard some sort of switch being flipped, and a bright burning flame flooded the room with light. The difference in illumination was so great that Namid had to shut her eyes, but even that wasn't enough to protect them. She couldn't cast a spell to get out of this if she couldn't see what she was doing.

"A wizard, eh?" A voice came from a speaking tube. Whoever was talking was outside the room. "We should have done a better job screening for that."

Just as Namid's eyes started to adjust to the bright light, a thick metal sheet dropped over the flame and left the room completely dark. *It's probably on a timer*, Namid thought to herself. *They're trying to keep my eyes from adjusting to the room. They might even be trying to keep me from getting my bearings.* Namid kept her eyes closed, but swayed her head slightly, as if dizzy. *If I don't play along, they'll find some way to make it worse.*

"You caused quite a bit of trouble for us," the voice on the speaking tube continued. "You killed a number of necrophytes, you actually made it across the river, and even got pretty far into the desert. Under other circumstances, we'd all be impressed, but...you've also made us all look bad."

Us. We. The voice on the other end of the speaking tube sounded too normal, too natural to be a lich. Who was talking? A necrophyte? One of Kemet's other public servants? It was a man's voice, older than Namid's, but only just.

"What is it you want from me?" Namid asked, her eyes still closed.

"Did I say you could speak?" The voice replied. "I don't think you're supposed to do that. Not in your position. Sekhet doesn't like it. She's the one who owns you now, by the way."

The metal sheet moved again, revealing the burning flame once more. Namid drooped her head to one side, her mouth hanging open.

"Nice try, but you're still thinking of escape, aren't you?" The voice on the tube laughed. "I'll admit, nobody back at Mereshank's palace expected you'd be able to brave the desert at all. But no one gets as far as you have without a strong stomach and a bit of grit. The light trick? That's not meant to leave you debilitated. Just to keep you distracted until Sekhet gets here to interrogate you herself. Which will be any minute now, since we sent word as soon as you woke up."

"What could I possibly know..." Namid rasped. "That she'd want?"

The voice on the other end of the tube didn't respond right away. "Good question. That's...not really for me to know. But hey, maybe I'll be allowed to stick around for the interrogation. Well, probably not. Doesn't matter."

"Why...not?" Namid tried timing how long she had between the opening and closing of the furnace, but it was no good. Someone was throwing the switch manually, deliberately keeping it random.

"Haha! Look at you!" The voice laughed as the furnace opened again. "Trying to get information out of me. You just don't quit, do you? What a waste. If the Tomb Lord's could have gotten ahold of you sooner, maybe you'd be a great necrophyte. You've got the basics down already. Aren't you from Hadesh? I didn't even know there were people in that blasted city who were so ready to kill. You fought like a demon against my colleagues."

Ah, so that's it, Namid thought. *Perhaps that's the string I need to pull to get more out of him.*

"They had names, you know," the necrophyte snarled.

"I know." Namid sat up, dropping the helplessness act. "I called them Corpse-Shagger and Red Balloon."

"Wha..." the voice took a moment to respond. "You..."

"I named them myself." Namid tried to shrug, but her restraints kept her arms held down. "I don't remember killing Corpse-Shagger, come to think of it. But the first thing he tried to do when I and the other girl were trying to escape Azzitha was take advantage of us both. Mind you, we were both disguised as zombies at the moment, and he genuinely believed he was about to have his way with two mindless corpses."

The voice on the tube didn't respond verbally, but Namid could hear what sounded like a person clearing their throat on the other end. The furnace stayed open.

"And then Red Balloon – see, I filled his lungs with some extra air. So much, they popped. And so did he. Just. Like. A balloon."

There was a long pause from the other end of the tube. Then a very forced laughter.

"I get what you're trying to do!" The necrophyte finally said. "You're hoping you can goad me to come down there to punish you, because you think it'll give you some chance at escaping!"

The furnace stayed open. Namid's eyes finally adjusted to the room.

"You got me," Namid admitted, smiling as she took in her surroundings.

She was about three meters away from the furnace. The door to the room was about twice that distance from her chair. Sekhet was supposed to be a powerful wizard in her own right; there was no way Namid could take her in a fight of spellcraft. Could she escape before then?

"But I'm a little surprised you necrophytes give a damn about each other. You make life for civilians a living hell. Sometimes an unliving hell. Why do you care when one gets killed?"

If Namid could turn her chair so that the ropes were closer to the furnace, she could probably use her magic to burn through the bindings and free her hands. But her feet were chained to the floor, and the bolts went into the ground. Steel had too high a melting point to get through without burning her own flesh.

"You know nothing about Kemet," the necrophyte replied. "We are the guardians that protect our society from falling apart. Everything we do, we do for the good of our nation. A man is suspected of treason? Kill him. Better safe than sorry. He hides his wealth, his food, his business from the godking? He has betrayed the whole country for his own selfish goals. Only the necrophytes keep the selfish from destroying our entire civilization; only our organization maintains order. If that means some of us resort to blowing off steam at the expense of a few individuals, it is for the greater good."

"By the gods," Namid paused her planning. "You actually believe it, don't you?"

"The word of the godking is law," the necrophyte replied. "And we are the instruments of his will."

Fine, keep talking, Namid thought to herself. She had a plan, but the moment she cast her first spell, she was certain an alarm would go off. *Oh well. No time like the present.*

Namid stomped her right foot with all her might, focusing her magic into the ground and willing the floor to shatter. Cracks appeared throughout the masonry. The bolts holding her legs became loose. She stomped again, resisting the urge to use both feet. Better to hit one point of pressure, she figured.

The second time, the ground around the bolt holding her right leg crumbled into dust and the chain popped out of the floor. Her left leg was still stuck.

"Hey! What are you doing?" The necrophyte must have caught on, but the furnace stayed open.

He's probably abandoned the switch, Namid thought. *Heading for the door.*

Namid would have loved to tear the man apart and take his keys, but the fact was her arms and left leg were still bound. She needed more time.

The door. Namid stomped her right foot and willed a pillar of stone to rise out of the ground and block the doorway. That would buy some time.

The door opened and slammed into the pillar. Namid didn't know how long it would hold. The necrophyte tried to force the door open for a while, but then stopped struggling. Namid managed to free the bolt holding her left leg from the floor, and then waddled over to the furnace, facing her back to the flames.

Just as she tried to burn through the ropes, the furnace slammed shut, leaving her in the dark. *That necrophyte must have gone back and closed the door*, she thought.

Namid ran through her options. She had freed her legs, at least from the floor, but she still had a chair strapped to her back and her arms tied behind it. If she had something jagged, she might be able to cut the ropes, but she could no longer see in the dark room.

Well, I can at least do something about the chair. It's not like it's some high-quality furniture. Namid stomped her foot through the seat of the chair and snapped it off at the back. With some work, she was down to having her hands bound behind the back of the chair, but no longer had to waddle around with the rest of it.

Footsteps outside. She didn't have long before they would find a way to break through that door. But with her feet free, she had more options with her spells.

With her hands behind her back, Namid jumped and slammed the ground with her feet, pointed at the door. A wave of new columns of stone burst through the ground and reinforced the entrance. Now Namid had a bit more time to think.

In the dark of the room, Namid was still functionally blind. She could try to force one of the walls down and get some light, but she didn't want to have to fight any necrophytes with her hands bound. She could try to force open the furnace, but it was probably still hot, and in the dark it would be too dangerous to try and use.

Namid decided to try her luck cutting through the ropes with a jagged edge of one of her columns. Slowly rubbing her bindings against the stone, she could hear the fibers start to fray. She had no real idea if this would work, but it was all she could think to try.

On the other end of the door, she could hear someone lugging something towards the entrance. They were probably going to try and bring it down with a battering ram.

A few of the fibers snapped, and Namid was able to stretch her wrists a bit further apart. Then a massive blow to the door sent her tumbling away from the stone pillar she was using. Several of the stone pillars cracked and fell over. The largest one that she'd made first still held, but it wouldn't last forever.

Struggling against her bindings, she still hadn't gotten her hands free. She stomped another pillar, this one far from the door, so she could keep working on the ropes, but the ram outside smashed against the door again.

"Almost," she muttered to herself. "Soon as I get my hands free, I'm tearing these guys apart!"

More fibers started to snap as all but the first pillar crumbled against the battering ram. Namid couldn't see, but that gave her an idea as she finally freed her hands.

When the door finally gave out and the last pillar toppled over, the guards found a room filled with dust. One threw a flare into the room to illuminate the darkness, but the dust cloud Namid had made scattered the light.

Namid's eyes readjusted to the dim light of the flare. The guards were as blind in the room as she was.

One of the guards stepped into the room, and judging from the sound of his footsteps, he was wearing combat boots. Probably carrying a gun, maybe a knife.

The guards were trying to be quiet enough to hear where Namid was. But she could pick out their breathing through the dust cloud. The guard in the room took a breath and panicked as his lungs filled with so much air they started to burst. His arms flailed frantically until a sick popping sound came from in his chest, and he slumped to the ground.

The other guards started to panic and began firing their guns randomly into the cloud. But by this point, Namid had already moved over to the same wall as the door; out of their arc of fire.

Gunshots. Loud noises on top of no visibility. If Namid hadn't been ready for this, it would have disoriented her. But she knew these men probably had guns and had prepared herself ahead of time.

Before the guards had finished emptying their guns, Namid focused on the ground beneath the source of the gunshots and stomped her right foot, summoning a new set of pillars from the ground beneath the guards. A few stopped firing. A few grumbled about a block of stone rising up and striking them in the groin. But none said a word about the sudden increase in air pressure around their squad.

Namid reversed the pressure and made the air expand into an explosion. Between the stone pillars blocking them in and the tightness of the corridor where they stood, the guards couldn't move away from the source of the explosion and the blast ripped several of them apart. None of them were immediately killed; there wasn't enough force for that. But the sounds of screams, breaking bones, coughs of blood, and shattering stone told Namid she'd wounded them all.

However, Namid wasn't satisfied with just wounding a squad of armed men. With just enough light to see what she was doing, Namid stepped closer to the door and forced a blast of wind to engulf the guards, hitting them with enough force to shatter more bones and leave any that weren't already dying mortally wounded. They'd be in no condition to stop her from escaping now.

Dashing out of the room, Namid looked around at the corridor. The hall was lined with doors similar to the one she'd just left, likely to identical rooms. The hall went in either direction, and Namid had no idea which way led where.

Then something made its way toward Namid from her right, and she didn't have trouble choosing which way to go. Dressed in white linen wraps, a black shawl, and a golden mask that Namid would never forget, Sekhet made her way down the right-side of the hall. Namid waded through the broken pillars of shattered floor and mangled bodies of the guards as the lich realized her prisoner was escaping and started gliding down the corridor with inhuman speed. Namid had just enough time to summon one last earth pillar right in front of the lich to smack her in the face before turning to run.

Sekhet made angry noises as she smashed the pillar out of her face with her magic. She uttered some curse too quiet for Namid to hear, and the girl glanced back in horror as the lich's shadow sprung to life, viciously attacking what was left of the guards and turning them to dust before hungrily lashing out at any possible living thing that got close.

There was no way Namid could hide from something like that. That hungry shadow would sniff her out from any hiding spot. She needed to lose the lich before she caught her, but between the chains still hanging from her legs slowing her down and Sekhet's unnatural speed, she couldn't outrun her. She had to find some way to ditch the mummy.

With a flick of her clenched fist, Namid made a small blast of air behind her to disrupt Sekhet. The lich merely put her palm in front of her and willed the pressurized wind to flow around her and continued her pursuit.

Namid then rounded a corner and tried to blast the corner wall with air, hoping it would bring down enough of the roof to block the walkway. While she did knock out a corner of the wall and made a significant amount of the floor above collapse into the lich's path, Sekhet simply melted her way through the rubble with magic and kept gaining ground.

As she sprinted along the corridor, Namid rounded a flight of stairs, wherein a confused necrophyte in uniform slammed into her. Namid managed to duck under his arms and kick him down the stairs to get away. The necrophyte tumbled down the steps into Sekhet, whose shadow latched itself onto him and drained his life until he was nothing but cracked skin and broken bones.

Scrambling up the stairs, Namid stomped her foot on the steps and willed them to become jagged, pop up and out of order, with some being forced down too low to reach the next, and some being pushed up too high for a person's leg to reach. Sekhet made what sounded like a snort before waving a hand and forcing the steps back into place, unbroken as if they had never been moved at all.

Trying to find another option, Namid reached the top of the stairs and looked around. She must have been in some kind of basement level before, because this floor had windows that showed a courtyard outside. Somehow, despite draining all the water from the Nile and leaving lots of the country with no clean water to drink, there was a magnificent fountain in the middle of a garden outside, with large stone walls surrounding it. Namid was terrible with aquamancy, so that wasn't likely to be of any help, but she needed more options.

Sprinting as fast as her short legs could go, Namid willed the water in the fountain to freeze. In a burst of adrenaline-fueled power, she felt the water pipes under the ground that flowed under the courtyard and even through the very floor upon which she stood.

Ice burst from the ground behind her. The fountain outside shook as the masonry crumbled, the expensive artwork cracking apart as crystalline shards ruptured the stonework. More frozen spikes burst from the pipes under the courtyard, but the largest ones trailed behind Namid, shooting up from the ground as she ran along the corridor.

Somewhere behind her, Sekhet was impaled by several icicles, and while they couldn't really hurt her, a shard of ice pierced each of her legs. As Sekhet continued to float along the ground, the ice tore her frozen legs off at the knees. The lich tumbled forward, landing on more icicles that pierced her through the chest and arms. She swore, more from frustration and surprise than anything else.

Namid risked looking back at the mummy and focused on the icicles inside of her, willing more water into them. As they grew, they expanded into the struggling lich's chest and tore her apart, leaving her arms and head flopping harmless on the ground. Even her living shadow could no longer hold itself together without her body to block the light.

Sekhet snarled and rolled around with rage, her limbs and ragged remains drifting together to rejoin themselves like dust assembling into a sandstorm. This gave Namid one final idea.

Reversing her earlier spell, Namid willed the ice to melt, which was easier than freezing it in the daylight heat, anyway. The icicles became a river of water that Namid shoved away with a powerful gust of wind, blowing the fluid back down the stairs, and carrying the angry parts of Sekhet trying to reassemble herself down a torrent back into the basement level.

With a moment of relief, Namid raised her fist in triumph as she felt something wet trickling down her upper lip. She wiped her nose, thinking it was water from the burst pipes, and then gaped at the red stain on her arm. She then felt her heart trying to beat its way out of her chest. A sorcerer's use of magic requires arcane energy to pump through her body, and can raise her blood pressure as a result. Namid could handle a bit more magic than the average student, but that had been a lot of power. Combined with aerobics like sprinting, she had gone far passed her limit. She needed a place to lie low and recover.

As soon as she tried to move, Namid was hit with the full force of exhaustion that came from having used too much magic too quickly. She could barely walk, let alone run, and she'd need someplace to recover before Sekhet reformed and made her way back up the stairs.

Limping to the end of the hallway, Namid could hear swarms of guards pouring into the courtyard to investigate the destroyed fountain. Fortunately, they hadn't come from her corridor, but soon they'd fan out and search for whatever caused an ice storm in the middle of one of the hottest cities on Earth.

Scrambling down the hall, more stumbling than anything else, Namid found a large double door she could open and crawl through. Inside was a massive room with a black marble floor, sparkling white walls, and a large conference table in the center, surrounded by a set of ornate chairs. In addition to the black marble floors were black curtains with gold trim, on tracks set into the roof, allowing them to darken the room as necessary to simulate various stages of daylight for their maps.

Namid couldn't help but scoff at the black curtains and floors. Black was a color associated with order, her aunt had told her. Back in the ancient times, it was a color of divinity. The color of fertile soil from which crops would spring forth. The color of life to the ancients of this land. The Tomb Lords' overuse of this pallet scheme meant they might as well have been writing signs with big flaming letters saying "Trust us! We're the good guys!" Although now that she thought of that, some of the posters Namid had seen on the walls of Azzitha from before actually did say things like that.

Footsteps came from another door. Namid had to hide. Grabbing one of the black, exaggerated curtains, she tucked herself behind it. *Take advantage of this time to rest*, she thought. *You can't run, or do any more magic right now, anyway.*

"There's been another incident," an echoing voice came from the other entrance. Namid was certain it was another lich. "The girl in the torture chamber has escaped."

"Sekhet has failed again," a second lich replied. "Was there a reason she kept the girl alive?"

"The girl only got as far as she did because she's a wizard," the first voice answered. They were standing closer to Namid's curtain now. One of them lit a lamp that was bright enough to illuminate the dark room. The black curtain was thin enough that Namid could see them through it, at least a little. The first voice belonged to a Tomb Lord Namid recognized; he had been one of the liches that had abducted her from the winery; the one addressed as Arkeon.

"First, she allowed a leak to slip in her outpost to the local workers, and while she did clean up the mess by burning the entire winery, she then fails to produce the citizens I had asked for, and now…" This other lich paused. He was more regal-looking than Arkeon, although Namid couldn't make out much from behind the curtain.

It was shocking how short most of these liches actually were; now that she wasn't prone before them, it dawned on Namid that these mummies were around her height. Arkeon was barely taller than her, and Sekhet had been around her height, which was about 160 centimeters. Namid was short, even by teenage girl standards, and these ancient tyrants were around her size. But this regal-looking one was an exception. He towered over the others, and was tall for a man of any age. Namid had heard rumors that people back when the Tomb Lords were alive were shorter than they were today, but that among the pharaohs, men were unusually tall, and the women were shorter than the rest of their populace. The fact that many kings of ancient Kemet married their sisters was thought to be the reason.

"After all of her training." Arkeon looked uncomfortable, like he was afraid of how to ask his next question. Or if he even should ask at all. "Do you know how to create the perfect citizen? If it is a failure from Sekhet, and something beyond her abilities, surely—"

"I am a god in human form," the regal lich replied with a slight hint of disdain for the sorcerer. "I am infallible. The reason why I do not craft my perfect citizens, from corpses, if necessary, is because it would serve no point; if I must do everything in my kingdom, there is no kingdom. My subjects must learn to carry out my instructions and pay reverence to their godking. And that goes for you, as well."

"Of-of course. Do you intend to take...punitive actions?" The sorcerer seemed to be choosing his words carefully.

The regal lich paused. "Not yet." He pulled from his robes a single, golden ring. At it's socket, the ring feature a sort of crown, meant for holding a gem or precious stone. "You will all fail me now and then; that is to be expected. And now, Sekhet has provided me with this, which will allow me to overlook her recent setbacks. I—"

The taller lich paused. His gaze snapped around and locked onto Namid's curtain. Even though he wore a golden mask that concealed his face, and the eyes of the mask contained a pair of gemstones that concealed his actual visage, Namid felt as if he were making eye contact with her, as if daring her to stay hidden.

"Is something the matter, my godking?" Arkeon asked.

Godking, Namid thought. *This is the one Rana told me about. The one that rules the entire nation. This is Amenhotep!*

Namid held her breath and tried not to make any signs of movement. It was all she could do to keep them from peeling back the curtain and finding her.

"Where was I?" Amenhotep turned back to Arkeon, as if he'd just completely forgotten his suspicions that the two liches weren't alone. "Ah, yes. The Ring of Solomon. With it, we can command demons themselves to do our bidding. Sekhet should have tried using it earlier; then maybe the demonically possessed mutants in her laboratory could have been put to some sort of use." Amenhotep set the ring down on the conference table. "Chaos has always created monsters out of men; now we have the power of control. With it, the empire itself will crumble."

Arkeon looked at the ring on the table. "Should we...secure it? Or at least, keep it on one of our persons at all times?"

"Hm, I think not." Amenhotep shook his head slightly. "Apparently, the guards found Sekhet reassembling herself from shattered parts in a puddle in the basement just now. Someone is loose in my palace, and keeping objects like this on our person risks them being obtained by the wizard girl until she is found. Besides, if it sits here, in this private room, looking inconspicuous, neither the girl, nor anyone else would even know what it is. Lock it up tight in a special box, and you might as well say 'this is important. Steal whatever is hidden behind this.'"

The sorcerer paused, as if trying to connect what his master was saying. Finally, he bowed in submission. "Very good, my godking. What shall we do now?"

"It appears that the palace guards have not yet captured the escaped prisoner." Amenhotep's voice carried a wry sense of humor, as if his entire palace guard failing to capture a single fugitive was a joke to him. "I will have to assist in the matter of hunting for her personally. I want you to go check the portal network in the citadel and make certain nothing tries to escape through one of the runegates."

Runegates. *That's right,* Namid thought. *That's how I was brought here from Hadesh in the first place.* Runegates were extremely difficult to build; they could open a portal that permanently linked two locations, either in the material plane, or a permanent doorway to the spirit plane. Setting them up took lots of preparation, and they couldn't be built just anywhere; they drained a lot of magical power from the Aether, and relied on stable currents through the Spirit Plane to work; Namid had seen that in Grand Spire. But if she could open one, she could get back to the Borealan Empire. It didn't matter which city; anywhere was better than Kemet, and she could always take a train home if she contacted the authorities. *Just think. Authorities that don't try to assault young girls and actually protect people who need their help.* She missed home.

The two liches left the room. Namid waited a moment more, and felt her pulse. For the most part, she had recovered from her early expenditure of magic. She could run, or she could try to cast her way out of a fight, but probably not both. That was okay; she just needed to be stealthy.

Namid almost passed the conference table without a second thought. Afterall, what did it matter to her what the liches were planning? Surely, taking Amenhotep's ring would get her in more trouble than if she didn't steal it. If she were caught with it, she would most certainly be brutally executed, but if she were caught without it, she would simply be...well, probably brutally executed.

But Amenhotep had looked right at her through the curtain. Surely, he wouldn't have said so much about his plans if he knew someone else was in the room, would he? Afterall, he was an ancient tyrant who thought himself an infallible god...no, okay, he probably would place his special super weapon, or whatever, unguarded in a room where he believed no one would come to find it. If he thinks he's an infallible god.

Of course, it was possible that this was all a trick. Amenhotep had made a point to voice aloud that he thought this ring should be left unguarded to avoid drawing suspicion. Namid held one palm out in front of her and put her other hand to her head, trying to detect any sort of magic on the table, or the ring itself. Anything that could have been used to lay a trap for unsuspecting thieves.

Nothing. There were no signs of magic surrounding the ring, or hidden among the details of the table, or coming from the ring itself, strangely. Namid had expected a ring that can allegedly control demons to resonate with power, but the ring felt...mundane, almost. Like nothing more than an ordinary piece of jewelry.

Gingerly, Namid picked the ring up and examined it. The crown of the golden band featured a strange six-pointed star surrounded by symbols Namid didn't recognize. It might have actually been a piece of common jewelry as far as Namid was aware. But...she'd read enough stories where things that seemed like junk turned out to be more than meets the eye. It was entirely possible that this thing really was some kind of superweapon to the Tomb Lords.

Namid pocketed the ring and quietly made her way to the door she had originally entered through. As soon as she opened it, she came face to mask with Amenhotep.

"Well, well." The lich chuckled wryly. "So, this is the ragdoll that's been causing Sekhet so much trouble? We'll have to fix that."

Amenhotep grabbed a tube on a flexible cable hanging from the wall that Namid hadn't paid attention to before. It looked like a speaking tube, and the lich held it to his mouth.

"Attention!" Namid could hear Amenhotep's voice throughout the entire palace, and she suspected that the tubes were designed to carry his voice further than that. "All of Azzitha! A saboteur from the Borealan Empire has entered the courthouse and stolen an important relic. Whoever brings her in, dead or alive, will receive a reward of three years of wages."

Amenhotep put the tube back on the wall and clasped his hands. "I've seen you fight, and I've seen you kill my necrophytes. Now, let's see you run."

Namid ran for the other door to the room, leaving a laughing Amenhotep behind her. Why didn't he just grab her himself? These weren't questions she had time to ask. *Citadel*, she thought. *There's a citadel with a runegate network. I just need to make it there.*

Bolting out of the room and out into the main palace floor, Namid was surprised not to see any guards there. Perhaps they were still investigating the fountain she'd destroyed? She had a clear line straight for the front gate of the palace. Unlike Mereshank's home where she'd been brought before, this building had no moat, no door made of stygian iron; just a more normal-looking wooden exit. Perhaps she'd been in some sort of administrative center, separate from whatever military building the citadel was.

But as soon as Namid forced a door open and stepped out into the front yard of whatever government building this was, she realized why Amenhotep wasn't worried about catching her himself or the lack of guards in the center of the building.

What might very well have been the entire city's population had started swarming the building's outer wall, surrounding the courtyard, pushing and shoving their way through each other to get to her, all driven mad by the promise of a reward. Some of the people in the front actually tripped from the mass behind them and were trampled to death by the rest of the mob.

The only chance Namid had was that these people seemed to have no concept of teamwork.

As the angry mob clobbered each other while closing in on Namid, she looked around for options and saw that they were actually pouring into a large opening in a black steel fence that surrounded the building. The fence was about five meters tall and had spikes on top, not easy to climb. But it gave Namid an idea.

Rationing her magic, Namid ran along the perimeter of the fence and found a spot where there were no people, far away from the front gate. She stomped her foot, willing pillars of earth to rise up from the ground, making a sort-of staircase she could climb, at least with some difficulty. She panted climbing the steps, grabbed the top of the fence, and swung herself over just as she heard people hollering behind her.

Willing the air beneath her to heat up so it would rise against her skirt, she managed to land without breaking her legs, hobbled to her feet, and tore off running before the mob could figure out how to get to her.

Which way was the citadel? Namid looked around for some kind of signs, but there weren't many around. Namid could only assume that a military building wouldn't be accessible to the public. It would also be the sort of place that had some connection to the larger roads to move lots of military hardware in and out of places.

As Namid heard more shouting and the movement of an angry mob, she decided she could locate the citadel later and find a place to hide now.

Running for the edge of the city, she could still hear the crowd, but they were getting quieter. What wasn't quiet were the few people who lived further out from the city center and weren't part of the mob pointing and shouting at the girl running down the street.

Dead or alive, she thought. *These people would sooner kill me and bring Amenhotep my head than try to capture me.*

One man nearby tried to tackle her. Only the fact that Namid was short and small allowed her to slip away. Two more men and a woman armed with a frying pan tried to corner her in the street.

"Okay, you guys know you can't all claim the reward, right?" Namid remembered how the mob from before had been shoving each other with no concern for their fellows' wellbeing.

"Yeah, but we can split it," one man smirked while the woman with the frying pan struck him in the back of the head. He fell over, face first into the street, with a bloody gash on the back of his skull.

"What the hell?" The other man looked at the woman with the pan. "It'll be months before we can take him to a doctor! If he isn't dead already, you've sealed his fate!"

"Split the reward?" The woman snarled. "My kids need to eat!"

"Then you can join my brother!" The man intercepted her next swing with the pan and tackled the woman, beating her into the ground with his fists as Namid slipped away.

Trying to ignore the pain in her body as she kept running, Namid tried to run down an alleyway, but immediately stopped when it was blocked with more chasers. Namid had just enough time to spin on her heels and keep running as a small gang of civilians came pouring out of the alley to catch her.

It dawned on Namid that the only reason she could outrun these people with her short-legged, skinny body was because none of these people had eaten a decent meal in their lives. Indeed, they were in worse shape than she was, and some of the people chasing her actually appeared to be missing body parts. She could have sworn she'd seen a man on crutches among the alleyway mob, hobbling after her as fast as he could. It'd have been entertaining to watch, if she wasn't running for her life. Beside him, a woman only a few years older than Namid had to stop her pursuit to cough up blood and blackened soot from one of the factories.

Namid realized she was slowing down; her body couldn't keep running at full speed. Fortunately, neither could her pursuers, resulting in what might have been the slowest and most pathetic street chase in recent history.

As she managed to get further away from the center of town, the buildings became shorter, with most of the taller residential apartments being located in the middle of the city. Out here, it was possible for Namid to see the factory smokestacks sticking out above the skyline, flooding the sky with smoke that blocked out the sun.

Strange, she thought to herself. *I still have enough light to see where I'm going, and it's not like smoke like that really blocks out the sun's rays. Could those smokestacks really protect the undead from sunlight?* Maybe the undead weren't bothered by sunlight; maybe it was just the idea of the sun that weakened their magic.

Behind the smokestacks, Namid noticed something else. A large, fortified building made of more black marble. The citadel.

Namid turned and started running for the black stronghold. A new rabble of people rounded a corner in front of her and scrambled towards her. It dawned on Namid that these people were about as organized as the zombies that had chased her the last time she'd tried to escape Azzitha.

"Enough!" She shouted as she stomped her foot in front of her and made a large slab of ground burst out and block the mob. She could hear several people smack into it and get crushed by the horde behind them. Namid made enough smaller pillars to climb and reached the top of the slab, which now walled off the entire alleyway and was almost level with the roof of one of the nearby buildings.

From on top of her newly made wall, Namid got a good look at the crowd below. Some of them threw stones at her, trying to either kill her or knock her off the wall, but most of their throws were pathetic, and the few stones that actually might have given her trouble were easy to dodge as she made her way to the nearby roof.

The somewhat-safer view from above gave Namid a moment to breathe and recover. It dawned on her that these people were so weak but still willing to risk being trampled to death by their own neighbors because the conditions of Kemet were beyond terrible. Somewhere, a utilitarian academic would have argued that Namid should let them kill her, and collect the reward, since her death would have allowed an entire family a chance at a better life, at least for a while. But Namid was not the sort to care about strangers, no matter how poor they were, at least when they wanted to split her head open like a watermelon and present it to a mummy for several books of coupons.

Making her way across the roof, she was surprised by how close most buildings were to one another. On the one hand, this meant that more people could be packed into a smaller area. On the other hand, this also meant that a single fire could take out an entire city block. But it also meant Namid could traverse the rooftops fairly easily to avoid the hordes of people.

It wasn't long before the citadel came closer into view, so that Namid could make out a thick wall surrounding the building proper. She'd need to find a way through.

Skidding to a stop on one roof where she could catch her breath, Namid scanned the outer wall for signs of an entryway. To her right, there appeared to be a main, regal-looking entrance where the Tomb Lords likely entered, but it was crawling with guards. But to Namid's left, there seemed to be a loading entrance for cargo and deliveries. A thick steel door wide enough to allow wagons through stood firmly shut, but the smaller personnel doors weren't so well defended.

Sticking above ground as much as she could, Namid got closer to the citadel until it was right across a wide street. Somehow, there were no people visible on the streets themselves.

Taking one last moment to make sure she'd caught her breath, Namid swore to any gods that were listening that she'd join her brother for cardio in the mornings and dropped down from the roof to the ground, cushioning her fall with a gust of wind, and bolted across the street to the loading area.

The personnel door was a thick slab of steel, not to different from what Namid had expected. Afterall, you wouldn't leave a weak entry point unguarded. Namid was about to try heating the lock on the door to melt her way through the lock, but a ward on the door told her that wouldn't work. She'd seen this same ward before; it was the first one she'd learned in class and would keep the door from changing temperature.

If Namid knew how, she could try something called a shatter-point technique to break the stonework around the door hinges and break through that way. If she ever made it home, she swore she'd study that spell until she could break boulders from a distance with her mind. Instead, she would have to find a way over the wall.

Namid stomped her foot, trying to raise earth pillars to make herself a staircase, as she'd done before. Nothing happened. Confused, Namid put her hand on the pavement below. *No*, she thought. *They couldn't be that paranoid, could they?* But there it was; Namid could feel ward lines arcing with power beneath the pavement. The ground wouldn't budge, either by magical means, or even a low-scale earthquake.

Fine, Namid gritted her teeth. *They can't ward the sky.*

Namid focused a stream of air into the keyhole of the thick steel door and willed the air inside to cool down. Then she kicked herself as she realized the door had become a vessel for the air, and the gas inside of it would be affected by the same ward. She couldn't heat the air or create an air explosion, because the gas would be held at whatever temperature it was when it went into the keyhole.

"Oh, come on!" Frustrated, she looked around for anything she might have missed. The wall was far too high for her to go find a ladder; even if she managed to break off chunks of the masonry for handholds, she wasn't strong enough to scale a wall that high. There were no adjacent buildings for her to try and climb. The only things she had to work with were a few empty wagons with tarps too heavy for her to try and float herself over the wall. She needed another approach.

Hang on a minute, Namid thought to herself. *There's got to be people inside this thing if it's got guards out front.*

Namid climbed into a wagon and tucked herself under a tarp where she'd be out of sight from anyone coming out of the personnel door. Focusing a pocket of air in front of the door to cool until it became a compressed bubble, she quickly heated the pocket so it would rapidly expand in a large blast. The resulting hiss was too loud for anyone near the loading entrance not to hear it.

Pressing her ear against the loading door, Namid heard footsteps after a few minutes coming towards the personnel entrance. She heard locks being disengaged as the door swung open and a pack of zombies swarmed the loading area, looking for the source of the sound. A single necrophyte stepped out behind them, hands behind his back, his gaze looking official as he let the zombies do the searching.

Despite what many people believe, becoming a zombie does not give a person superhuman senses. In fact, most of the time, being undead dramatically reduces any activity that requires higher brain functionality, such as trying to pick out the smell of a particular human in an area where humans regularly frequent, and the creature trying to sniff them out has a (mostly) human body themselves, just smellier thanks to decay and a lack of deodorant. Zombies could see better than the living in the dark, but it was the middle of the day, and the factory smoke clouds only made the sky look overcast. All of this worked out quite well for Namid as she focused on the necrophyte from her hiding place and slowly, carefully made the air around his head thinner.

The necrophyte didn't seem to initially notice that he was having to take deeper breaths for a moment. When he did finally notice, he was stumbling to one side, trying to stay standing, struggling to maintain his composure, and still not aware of what was going on. Either he was too afraid of what would happen if he showed weakness this close to the citadel, or he was too stubborn and determined to maintain his bearing as a necrophyte officer. Either way, he collapsed from oxygen loss after a few minutes, still trying to breathe, fading in and out of consciousness.

The zombies didn't show any signs of noticing that their commander had just fallen. They apparently didn't need him conscious in order to keep searching. Namid counted five zombies. She could try to fight them off with magic, but she didn't like those odds. Instead, Namid focused on a spot in the middle of the street and created another air explosion, this one cracking the pavement in the middle of the road.

Reacting to the noise, the zombies swarmed into the middle of the street, searching for the source of the sound. Namid took her chance to climb out of the wagon, dashed up the steps to the open personnel door, and slammed it shut as the screaming zombies ran towards her. She could hear them slamming the other end of the door as she locked a thick deadbolt to keep it closed.

Okay, she thought. *I'm in the citadel. There's got to be a portal network somewhere.*

Inside the main wall, Namid got a look at the inner part of the loading area. There were several workers who were in the process of unloading crates from a wagon already parked in the area, and a massive door into the citadel itself, where the workers carried boxes in and out. Fortunately, there was another, normal-sized door closer to Namid and away from the workers that she could use to enter the building.

Namid approached the smaller door and quietly opened it, revealing a single corridor inside with another door at the end. Quietly, she walked down the hallway and opened the door, revealing Amenhotep on the other side.

"Hello!" The lich clasped his hands calmly.

Slamming the door shut, Namid tried to scramble back down the corridor, but the entire work crew she'd seen before now blocked her in, brandishing various tools in case she tried to force her way through. They'd been aware of her the whole time.

"My, my. That was fun, wasn't it?" The lich cornered Namid as she backed into him. "Well, I had fun, anyway."

Namid tried to create another air explosion, but Amenhotep simply placed his hand on her head, and in an instant her mind was overloaded with numbness.

"I don't think so," he chuckled. "This was amusing, but...you've caused quite a bit of trouble today. Why don't you come with me?"

Amenhotep hoisted Namid up with one arm and hauled her further into the citadel. "We really can't take our eyes off of you, can we?"

Her head spinning, Namid's eyes weren't able to see clearly, only getting glimpses and flashes of things that passed before her. There were more black floors and white walls, more black drapes and doors that looked like military offices. She caught sight of something in the boxes; something that looked like weapons, but she couldn't make out what they were. A few looked like machinery.

"You know, if half the reports I've received about you are true, then you're one of my favorite kinds of mortals," Amenhotep chuckled. "Killing my necrophytes, siphoning the air out of a farmer...was that storekeeper we found your handiwork, too? My, my..."

A dazed Namid tried to put words in her own mouth, but it wasn't working. Parts of her brain were coming back online, but it was a slow process.

"You know, to animals, humans are like gods." Amenhotep held her up to his eye level, her feet dangling off the ground by almost a meter. "Every animal understands hunting; a human hunter is no different than a predatory lion to a sheep. But a developer? A being who can come into an animal's environment and simply rearrange the entire area to his liking, clearing away swamps to build new houses, rearranging rivers to irrigate farms? Animals don't understand that kind of power. If something had the power to do that to humans, we'd call them a god."

Namid responded by half-heartedly pawing at the lich and wheezing. Amenhotep took this to mean that she was more hammered by that spell than he'd intended.

"Hm, your brain is weaker than I thought." He held one of her eyes open and examined her pupils. "Perhaps you don't understand a word of this. But if you can, I want you to know what kind of being can turn an entire city against you. What kind of person you've tried to defy; I am no mere human. I am a god in human form."

Namid did not know how to fake being barely conscious, but she had heard that drunks couldn't follow a light with their finger or track things well. She did her best to keep her eye as lazy as possible to convince the Tomb Lord that she was barely conscious.

And while she had the lich's attention on her eye, she focused an air explosion right in the space between her and Amenhotep.

The blast wasn't very powerful; Namid hadn't wanted to tear herself to shreds. But it was enough to force the girl away from the lich. Amenhotep didn't let go of his prey easily, and his grip was so strong that his arm tore off his shoulder.

Namid pried the lich's arm off of her, which was still moving and tried to strangle her, but not before she was able to throw it away. An armless Amenhotep managed to maintain his composure while raising his other hand towards Namid. Before he could cast some unholy spell, Namid stomped her foot and raised a pillar from the ground under his right leg, throwing him off balance before she set off another air explosion in front of him.

Perhaps the liches were out of practice fighting other mages. Perhaps Amenhotep was a ruler who avoided direct combat.

The blast from this second explosion sent Amenhotep flying against a wall, disheveled enough for Namid to escape further into the citadel.

The building itself didn't have a lot in the way of markings to show Namid where to go. She didn't even know if the portal network was real, or just another trick by Amenhotep, but she had to try. She found a staircase. Should she go up or down?

Namid didn't know enough about runegates to say where they would be located. Did they need elevation? No, that couldn't be right. Namid had seen runegates at the arena during the Grand Wizard Tournament. They had been level with the ground. Did they need access to open air? Would they be on the roof? Namid had seen the roof; it looked heavily fortified, not with anything like a runegate exposed to the air. And you wouldn't want a mortar battery to come down and destroy your expensive gates, anyway.

Okay, she thought. *Let's try underground.*

Of course, every instinct in Namid's brain told her to never run underground when an angry lich was chasing you, but Namid knew she was dead if she didn't find a runegate out of this city. There was no way she could keep wriggling out of prisons, misdirecting guards, or deceiving necrophytes. If anything, their master was wise to most of her tricks, and if he didn't just kill her, he'd tell his underlings what to watch for.

At the bottom of the stairs was a long hallway. To Namid's relief, there was a sign at the bottom of the stairs embedded into one wall that made her jump for joy: munitions, with an arrow pointing to the right, and gates, with an arrow to the left.

Namid didn't know how much time she had left, but she stomped her foot against the ground and raised as many pillars as possible to obstruct the stairs against her pursuers. She was tempted to go to the munitions and set something on fire, but she didn't think she had time for a distraction like that.

Racing down the hallway towards the gates, Namid found a large room full of archways. She'd expected them to be lined up against a wall, or in a large circle. Instead, each gate was placed in a seemingly random location in the room. This actually made sense, since the gates had to be arranged exactly right in order for the portal to go to the right place, and that didn't always line up conveniently with the architecture of a room.

She had no idea where each gate went, and she didn't care. Anywhere was better than here. She would rather be lost in the Duat than dead in Azzitha.

Looking at the gates, Namid realized she had no idea how to activate one. Glancing around for some sort of clue, she spotted a podium in one corner of the room with a black bound book on it. Grabbing the book, she flipped through it and found a set of codes and spells to open each of the gates. Apparently, liches were just as bad about remembering passwords and bank account numbers as normal people.

One of the gates was marked as "Hadesh: Institute of Theurgy. A chant in a language Namid didn't understand was written alongside it. Hopefully, pronouncing it would be enough.

Grabbing the pillars of the marked runegate, Namid whispered the chant in the book, praying something would work. To her relief, the gate sparked and sprung to life, revealing an image of what looked like the inside of a broom closet.

"Stop right there."

Namid followed Amenhotep's voice and looked back at the lich.

"You have something that belongs to me." He held out his hand. "Give it here, or I can come after you and collect it later."

Digging through her pocket, Namid produced the ring she stole and showed it to the Tomb Lord, before chucking it through the portal in defiance.

"Very well," the lich chuckled as Namid climbed through the gate. "I'll see you soon."

70

Setting the Trap

AMENHOTEP

As the runegate closed behind Namid, Arkeon and Djedefre joined Amenhotep in the portal network room.

"Well, that went about as well as could be expected." Amenhotep clasped his hands jovially. It had been a fun day for him.

"My godking," Arkeon stuttered. "She escaped! With the Ring of Solomon!"

"Of course!" Amenhotep turned to the sorcerer. "Did you forget the plan? I was just pondering this morning how we were going to get the ring into the empire in a place conspicuous enough to lure in the dragon. And then the girl showed up in the conference room, and the perfect opportunity presented itself to me."

"But..." Arkeon looked confused. "You ordered her to be brought to you! You put out a bounty on her head!"

"Yes, convincing, wasn't it?" Amenhotep chuckled. "She seemed to believe it, hook, line, and sinker. And you should have seen her face when she opened that door in the service tunnel and saw me." Amenhotep couldn't hold in his laughter anymore.

"The people of the city knew that you wanted her captured..." Arkeon still seemed to be having trouble connecting the dots.

"Ah, yes." Amenhotep nodded. "The people completely failed to apprehend the girl. Really, so disappointing. But what more can we expect from mere peasants?"

Wheels turned in Arkeon's mind, and he finally realized that Amenhotep had orchestrated the girl's escape in a way in which all the blame could be pinned on the people of Azzitha. "What if one of the peasants actually succeeded in catching her?"

The High Tomb Lord shrugged. "Then the girl is brought to me, with the ring, I figure out a new plan, and I'd have lost nothing." Amenhotep grabbed the columns of the runegate and spoke a new chant, different from the one Namid had used to open the portal. This time, the gate columns shattered and crumbled to dust, making it impossible for someone on the other side to prove there was a portal between Azzitha and the Institute of Theurgy. "The best part is that the girl believes the ring is powerful, and that it's important enough to either turn in to one of the mage academies, or to their emperor himself. She'll pass it off to someone important enough that it will be announced, at least loud enough for the dragon to catch word of it."

"Why are we trying to get the dragon to attack the Borealans again?" Djedefre growled, examining the shattered runegate. "How are we supposed to lure him into a trap—"

"The trap is in the Borealan Empire," Amenhotep replied.

"You built a trap in the empire?" Djedefre cocked his head.

"The empire *is* the trap," Amenhotep replied. "Let them fight each other. I want the Borealans to think that the dragon isn't a problem for those under my rule. Let them think that the dragon is too afraid to enter Kemet. And let the dragon tear their infrastructure to shreds looking for a single ring."

"And if the dragon finds a way to use the ring?" Arkeon asked.

Amenhotep laughed. "He won't."

71

Sibling Reunion

AMRI

The autobus was packed with people heading for the Academic District. Amri felt a number of eyes from standing passengers glaring at him as he sat in a seat, with the girls holding the fiercest expressions.

Makes sense, Amri thought. *Men stand for ladies.* But he also thought of the bandages that had been replaced on his injuries, and how Marduk had berated him for risking the loss of his legs the night before. He smiled and waved to a few girls, who frowned at him as the next stop filled up with even more people. If Amri could have moved, he would have lifted enough of his pant leg to show the bandages on his calves, but there wasn't enough room in this tiny little vehicle.

Amri could tell that most of these people were heading to get new textbooks, like him. The new school year started tomorrow, and the bookstore was only open on the weekend. Of course, if he'd been well enough before, Amri would have taken care of this sooner than the last day before class. He hated dealing with things at the last minute.

Finally, the autobus came to the Academia stop, near the Institute of Theurgy. Amri grabbed the walking stick that the monks had loaned to him and made his way towards the door as soon as the rest of the crowd had filtered out.

Once he'd gotten off the autobus, Amri started heading for the Academy of Sorcerers when he heard a commotion behind him. Someone was causing trouble over at the bookstore line for the theurgists.

"Let me out!" A familiar voice cried. "They could be chasing me right now!"

"Namid?" Amri hobbled over towards the theurgists.

"Get off me, you idiots!" Namid struggled against a pair of creatures trying to restrain her by grabbing her arms. These creatures looked mostly like piles of clothing bundled up with glowing blue eyes underneath their headwraps. *Windbags*, Amri remembered. That's what they were called. Air elementals that served as groundskeepers for the Institute of Theurgy.

"What were you doing in our school?" A professor scowled at Namid. Amri noted that this professor had the face and body to become anything from an advertising model to a starlet in an opera house were it not for her facial expression, which seemed to say things like "why are people like you allowed to exist?" and "what is the quickest way to for you to get out of my sight?"

"I told you!" Namid snarled. "I fell out of a runegate and landed in your broom closet!"

"We don't have runegates in our broom closets," the professor replied. "You're lying."

"Sis!" Amri tried to push his way through the crowd gathered around Namid and the professor. "Let me through!"

When he reached his sister, Amri was taken aback by how bedraggled she was. Namid was wearing ill-fitting, dirty clothing, smelled like she hadn't had a decent shower in a while, looked like she'd missed more than a few meals, and had an unwashed trail of blood from her nose. She looked like a wreck, but it was definitely her.

"Why are you trying to restrain her?" Amri asked the professor.

"Because she was snooping around in our campus, and she isn't one of our students," the professor hissed. "She said so herself."

"She said she fell through a runegate," Amri started piecing together possible explanations for where Namid had been all of this time. If she'd been lost in the Spirit Plane, that would explain a lot, even why Marduk couldn't find her. It would also explain how she'd managed to disappear without a trace in the first place.

"She's lying," the professor snarled. "We don't have a runegate in any of

SIBLING REUNION

our broom closets."

"Then let her show you the gate," Amri replied. "We could settle this quickly if she—"

"NO!" The professor growled.

"Why?" Amri asked. He tried to read her face, but there was nothing there except for disgust and refusal. He knew that in negotiations, you needed to figure out what the other person wanted and try to find a way to make a deal. But this woman seemed to be refusing to compromise just because she could. Either because going to the broom closet would be too inconvenient for her, or because she might lose face if it turned out there actually *was* an old gate in a corner of the school that no one had used in a long time, but Amri didn't think that was it.

It felt like the professor was refusing to let Namid confirm her story purely because she could.

She's an adult bully, a voice in his head thought. *Treat her like any other bully.*

"Okay," Amri thought for a moment. "So, you're restraining my sister with your gasbags; air elementals you've sicked on her for... 'intruding,' I'm guessing? So, shall we let the police settle this?"

The professor paused and let the weight of the sorcery student's words go through her head. Her face was a mix of anger and confusion.

Relying on authorities again? The voice whispered. *Not a bad opener, but what will you do if that doesn't work? Are you ready to tear those gasbags apart to protect your sister?*

"Of course, the police will want more information," Amri added, trying to ignore his own thoughts. "They'll require a search of the school, and will have to get a search warrant to check and see if you actually have a runegate in one of your closets."

Through gritted teeth, the professor pulled herself to her full height, which was significantly taller than Amri. "No! No police, no searching our school!"

"Okay." Amri shrugged. "Then just let my sister go. Because if you don't want the law to get involved or prove she's right, then you can't press charges. And if you try to hold her against her will without reason, then *we'll* press charges."

The professor's jaw dropped slightly, her eyes piercing into him, as if she were willing needles to shoot out and puncture the boy in front of her. But she finally closed her mouth and snapped her fingers. The gasbags released Namid. "Take her and go."

Amri breathed a sigh of relief as he grabbed his smelly sister in one hand and limped away with his cane in the other. Once they'd gotten away from the crowd, Amri pulled his sister aside. "Where in Peppi's unhinged jaws have you been?"

"That's not a bad guess," Namid replied. "It certainly seemed like hell."

"Do you have any idea how worried everyone was back home?" Amri glared at her, but he kept his voice low. "Uncle Mido's been putting up missing person posters, the police were called...what did you think would happen if you disappeared again?"

"Do you really think I ran off on purpose?" Namid gestured to the raggedy clothes she was wearing. "Do I look, sound, or smell like I've been having fun times in some fancy spa?"

"Then how...where..." Amri's tongue stumbled for words; he was too angry to form a coherent thought.

"I was dragged through a runegate, went through a living hell, and had to find another gate to come home," Namid explained. "None of this was by choice."

Amri paused. It *was* possible that Namid had simply slipped through a runegate, got lost for a while, had to make do with whatever she could while lost in the Spirit Plane, and only now found a way back through a gate no one had used in a while. It was also possible that the gate was in a broom closet, where it had been forgotten about because it hadn't been used in ages.

But it was also possible that Namid was lying through her teeth. And the thought that she might be lying drove away the relief of seeing her alive and well and replaced it with more anger.

"Where did those clothes come from?" Amri gestured to the rags his sister was wearing.

Namid's face fell. It wasn't the look of a lie exposed; it was something else. Was it...shame?

SIBLING REUNION

"I...needed a disguise. To hide." Namid's eyes didn't meet Amri's for a moment. "So...I stole these."

"That just raises more questions," Amri replied. "Who were you hiding from?"

Looking around to make sure they weren't being watched, Namid produced a ring from the pockets of her ragged clothing. "Listen, I wasn't lost in the Spirit Plane. And I didn't fall into a runegate. I was abducted by the Tomb Lords."

"Okay." Amri threw up his hands. "I can't make you tell me, but I'm not going to sit here and listen to you lying about where you've been."

"Look at this ring!" Namid held up the trinket. "I stole it from the Tomb Lords themselves!"

"You've always been a good liar, but that one's just not believable." Amri's face fell. He had run a number of scenes through his head, imagining how his confrontation with his sister would eventually go when she showed her face again, but he hadn't prepared for this. "You expect me to believe that you stole a ring from the liches that rule Kemet and escaped with your life?"

"This is supposed to be the Ring of Solomon!" Namid pointed at the golden band. Amri hated to admit it, but the ring looked fancy enough to at least be valuable, if not supernatural. There was something about the six-pointed star insignia and the writing embedded within it that suggested it was more than just an expensive piece of jewelry.

"The liches said it can control demons!"

Amri tapped the ring with his finger. "I don't feel any power in it," he replied. "Maybe it is magic, but I can't sense any."

"Then I'll take it to someone who can." Namid gritted her teeth as she pocketed the ring. "After I get a decent shower and a change of clothes."

"Well, that's going to wait." Amri crossed his arms. "This is the last day before classes, and that means we have to get our books today. I'm not fighting through the autobus with these legs again until we have those books."

"Seriously?" Namid frowned, but then realization lit up her face. "Fine. Do what you need to do. Can you get mine too while I go home and shower? I'll pay you back—"

Anger welled up in Amri like a shaken bottle of beer. "You'll do nothing of the sort! You either ran off or fell through a portal – fine. But you're not going home by yourself just to disappear again. You'll stay put until I'm back with our books."

Namid froze, clearly not used to her brother acting like this. "What the hell got into you?"

"Some floor tiles, and a number of other things," Amri calmed down. "Seriously, just wait here until I'm back. Get some water, or something."

An hour-long wade through the lineup at the book sale later, Amri returned with a stack of books crammed into his bookbag and a second stack in his arms.

"Alright, let's head home." Amri handed Namid her stack. "But you're holding these. I can only go so far with these legs and carry so much."

"What happened to your legs, anyway?" Namid eyed the cane he was using for support.

"Bad fight with an alchemist," Amri replied. "You should see the other person. At least I still have my arms."

"What the actual hell?" Namid's eyes shifted from her brother to the bus stop, which was crowded with people. "Could you handle walking home from here? I've got no money for the autobus, and I don't know if I want to be in a can full of people right now."

Amri sighed as he shifted his weight onto his cane. "Alright, but we go at my pace. That might mean I stop and rest from time to time."

As they walked, Amri told his sister about Dr. Malbim and Izaac, and how he'd gotten involved with the abbey. In turn, she told him about what she'd been up to before she disappeared.

"You were in a winery?" Amri eyed his sister. "And they had a runegate in there?"

"Yeah," Namid nodded. "I'm not going to explain it further if you aren't going to believe it."

"Hmph," Amri struggled with his cane and the weight of the books in his bag. "I think you should just stick to the details our uncle will believe when you see him later. Tell him you fell through an old runegate in a shop no one knew was there, that you fought tooth and nail to find a way back, and you reemerged somewhere in the Institute of Theurgy. He'll believe that."

"Okay," Namid shifted the weight of the books she was carrying and produced the ring again. "So, what do I do with this?"

"You're asking me?" Amri shrugged. "You're the one who knows where to get stuff appraised. Go find out what it's worth and sell it. That should be easy for you."

Namid didn't reply, but her mouth made a noise like she wasn't satisfied with this answer. Amri had never seen her upset at the thought of selling valuable (and possibly stolen) jewelry for money before. Was any part of her crazy story actually true?

72

How to Design a Spirit

EPHORAH

Several days had passed since meeting the translator. Since then, Ephorah had been fretting over the possibility that giving a woman she'd never met before an illegal book of Empyrian writing had been a bad idea. She wondered if one day the police would come barging into her house, or if she'd go to class at the institute and get called in to see the headmistress, where some imperial agents would be waiting for her.

But so far, nothing had happened. During their lunch meeting, the headmistress had seemed polite enough that perhaps she wasn't going to have her arrested, but Ephorah didn't like the other professors. Professor Sayegh came off as the kind of person who would have someone arrested just so she didn't have to pay them for painting her living room, and Professor Meir seemed like the sort who would have you thrown in jail just because she felt like it that day.

And now, Ephorah was on an autobus, headed for her first day of classes for the new school year. Instead of several classes scattered throughout the day, her new classes would take more time, usually one long course in the morning and a different one in the afternoon. For the morning, she would start with Professor Maroun, who taught Spirit Sculpting.

"Form defines function," Maroun explained. "And for spirits, form defines personality. I want you to look at the following picture."

The professor unrolled a large canvas of what looked like a beach, or at least a shore, in front of the classroom. Several types of rocks were visible in the painting. Some were large and jagged, some were smooth, a cliff face in the background stood over the water, with a single large rock sitting on top of it. Then there were pebbles, rough rocks with less-jagged edges, and some round stones that were aimed towards the footprints of people who had recently strolled along the beach.

Professor Maroun took several sticking notes and pressed them against the canvas, labeling different rocks along the beach with different letters. "I want you to tell me what personality traits come to mind with each of the rocks you see in this picture. Use the labels to tell them apart, and don't bother telling me what they look like or what they might be used for; describe the characters of each inanimate object. I want to know what comes to your mind when you see these things."

Ephorah looked at the rock labeled "A," which was a large, jagged, scary-looking outcropping. She wrote "fierce and menacing," before moving on to the next, which was a tiny pebble next to the sea. "Small, feels insignificant."

The class set out to identify the personalities of each rock formation in the picture. A year ago, this project would have seemed silly, but Ephorah now knew that spirits were born from people imagining inanimate objects having their own goals, desires, and even lives. Humanize an object, and a spirit forms in the Duat to match it.

After a few minutes, the students finished assigning character traits to rocks, and the professor looked at some of their answers.

"Ah, I see you all wrote that the jagged rock was 'menacing,'" the professor smiled. "And the smooth piece of sandstone near the footprints liked to watch people stroll along the beach. Oh, and this is nice. One of you wrote 'the rough, smaller stone without any jagged edges looks like he wants these dang teenagers to be quiet and let him sleep!'" She put down the students' responses. "You all wrote very similar characteristics to these rocks, all based on their physical appearances. This is the primary force behind spirit sculpture; once you understand how people will react to the shape of an object, you can predict how they will characterize it. The truth is, this is a painting of a real beach filled with rocks that theurgists arranged in just the right way to ensure people would have these reactions. Over the course of this semester, you're going to learn how to form physical objects like this into spirits ideal for your own use."

The rest of the class period was dedicated to ways objects of other elements could draw their personalities from their forms, such as how air spirits could be formed from people seeing shapes in the clouds, the purpose of a fire could determine what kind of elemental would be formed by it, and which types of puddles would become herba elementals in the spring, and which would become bestia elementals based on the croaks from real frogs that lived in them.

At the end of the morning lesson Ephorah left for the Academia Food Court, where she could grab some lunch before her next class. Once she'd bought a sandwich and found a seat at a table, Namid slipped in and sat down across from her.

"Oh," Ephorah frowned. "So, you're not missing anymore?"

"Yeah, I got back yesterday," Namid looked around, as if she was afraid of being watched. "Listen, I need your help to identify something." She reached into her pocket and produced a strange golden ring. It had a six-pointed star in the middle, along with a number of sigils that Ephorah had never seen before.

"What is that?" Ephorah asked.

"It's what I need your help identifying," Namid leaned closer. "I stole it from Kemet. It's supposed to be able to control demons," she whispered.

"Right..." Ephorah leaned away from Namid and took a bit of her sandwich. "Whatever you're scheming, I want no part in it."

Namid flinched. "Do you at least believe me?"

"Nope," Ephorah took another bite. "But I don't really care, either. I've gotten enough trouble with controlling spirits as it is." Ephorah wouldn't admit it to Namid, but she still wasn't happy about the school's decision to start using the *Incontio* spell to make more artifacts from lobotomized spirits.

"That's why I'm turning to you," Namid whispered. "If anyone knows how to identify this thing, figure out how it works, you know – it's got to be the theurgists. You guys have a whole department around enchanting artifacts."

Ephorah paused. "Don't you have anyone at the sorcerer's academy who can help you?"

With an expression somewhere between anger and bewilderment, Namid sighed. "No. Our professor who teaches magical safety is Professor Malouf, and he's the resident expert on wards and thaumaturgical devices. If this ring was one of those things, he'd be the one to talk to, but he burned himself while filling the school pool with gravy yesterday, and he's not seeing students until he gets out of the infirmary."

"What the actual hell?" Ephorah shook her head.

"Don't ask," Namid replied. "When it comes to Malouf, it's better that way."

"Okay," Ephorah rubbed her temples. "I believe you when you say one of your professors is insane. That's...kind of relatable, actually. But if that ring isn't an artifact, then it has no connection to theurgy. Why not just ask around and see if any of the other professors know what to do with it?"

"Are you nuts?" Namid hissed. "I stole this from the Tomb Lords themselves! And if it can do what they say it can, then I can't just go waving it around and letting every wizard in the area know about it!"

Ephorah blinked. On one hand, she most certainly did not believe that the ring belonged to the Tomb Lords, or that it came from Kemet, for that matter. But at the same time, she could completely relate to not wanting to share a ring that potentially commanded demons with the faculty at a wizard school. There was no telling what the professors would do with it.

"Alright," Ephorah sighed. "There's one guy: Professor Massouh. If anyone can identify what that ring is, it'd be him."

"Thanks," Namid slipped away from the table, leaving Ephorah to finish her lunch.

Once she was done, Ephorah headed for her second class of the day: Advanced Control of Spirits, with Professor Sayegh.

"Control comes from inconsistency," the portly professor explained. This class wasn't in a stuffy room in the school, but out on the school grounds, where they'd be able to conjure up spirits to use for demonstrations. "To keep a spirit under your complete control, especially when they start to question you, you must keep them confused. Now, pay close attention."

Sayegh called up an air elemental from the Spirit Plane. A living cloud in the rough shape of a man emerged from the ether, its legs were miniature tornados, its arms were rolls of mist. And its eyes were a pair of bright blue orbs, like precious gems.

"Stratos, we need to talk." The professor clasped her hands in front of the spirit, as if trying to be diplomatic. "I don't think you fully understand our current relationship. When I ask you to do something, I don't feel confident that you're going to get it done."

"What tasks have I left undone?" The spirit's voice was like a fierce gust of wind. Ephorah could feel the air scrape against her skin as it spoke.

Rather than answer, Proressor Sayegh shifted the subject. "There've been plenty of occasions. You just don't know of any right now because you don't listen!"

"Listen?" Stratos shifted, and as it did the winds blew all of the girls' hair every which way. This was no weak spirit. "I'm listening now."

"But you always make excuses!" The professor threw up her hands. "There's no way I can ever get any progress with you if you always have an excuse!"

The elemental shifted its gaze in confusion. "What excuses?"

"This is what I'm talking about," the professor continued. "You don't listen!"

This banter went on for a while, but Ephorah was catching the main points. It was clever, and while Ephorah understood how it worked, it would be a long time before she could do it herself.

When the professor finally dismissed the spirit, she turned back to the students. "Alright, who wants to explain what I just did to the class?"

Ephorah raised her hand. "You pinned him between two contradictory statements. You told him that he wasn't listening, and that he always had an excuse. But you can't make excuses if you're never listening."

"Very good," Sayegh smiled. "The key ingredient is that both of those statements can be perfectly reasonable on their own. This gives the spirit the impression that what you're saying *should* make sense, even though it doesn't."

One of the other girls in the class raised her hand. "Why can't you give him orders and criticism that does make sense? If the spirit figures out that he's being tricked, he'll get upset."

"The overwhelming majority of humanus elementals will not recognize the trick," Sayegh explained. "Elementals are made from people assigning living qualities to non-living things, like imaginary friends. Think back to when you were a child: when was the last time you lied to your imaginary friend? Spirits with human intelligence don't assume they're being deceived because deceit isn't something people think to give them."

"Remember that the easiest way to capture a humanus elemental, presuming it's passive or friendly, is to weaponize the spirit's own sense of morality against it." Sayegh had been Ephorah's first-year teacher for capturing spirits, and she remembered how the professor had instructed her to capture Aquaria. "Convince the elemental that they are incapable of currently following their own morals, and the spirit will submit to you in exchange for moral guidance."

"But giving a spirit reasonable instructions creates a problem," the professor continued. "Because if you give a spirit orders or complaints that make sense, it will probably find a way to fulfill them, or fix whatever you're complaining about, and then you're left with a spirit that isn't confused. Then it will think it has learned something about morality, and start to reassert its independence. But an elemental can't see the logic behind complaints that don't have any, and it's the confusion of not knowing what it will take to satisfy his master that keeps the elemental under control. As long as they're always on edge, always thinking about how they can comply with their master's orders, and always afraid that they will do something to upset their master, they won't ask whether they should be following those orders in the first place."

The professor assigned them homework of trying to come up with verbal commands that would be in direct conflict with each other, but would appear to be reasonable as long as the spirit didn't question them. They could get extra credit if they made certain that the commands were accusatory in nature.

When the class ended, Ephorah headed for the lobby. She'd seen a flyer for fencing lessons and wanted to sign up. If she was going to keep a bloodthirsty magic sword under her bed, she might as well learn how to use it.

As she looked to find the flyer in the building lobby, she felt something approaching behind her. Snapping around, she glared at the dark-haired goddess without a name.

"Oh, hello!" The goddess smiled. "Looking for extracurriculars, are you?"

"Get out!" Ephorah brandished a textbook at her.

The goddess rolled her eyes. "Really? A book?" Her right hand sprouted long, sharp talons like those of a hawk, while her left hand grew the claws of a lion.

Ephorah held her ground. "I'm not afraid of you. You don't have enough power to take on a physical form. So shapeshift into whatever monster you want; you can't actually hurt me."

"Oh, done your homework, have you?" The goddess retracted her claws and clasped her hands behind her back. "Well, it's no matter. I wasn't here to harm you, anyway."

"Then what do you want?" Ephorah kept her guard up.

"No, no. You've got it all wrong." The goddess chuckled. "What do you want? What can I do for—"

"Get lost!" Ephorah waved the book through the goddess's image, dissipating her like fog.

"You can't get rid of me!" The goddess cackled as she reformed leaning against a wall. "I feed on your darkest desires, your unspeakable wishes. As long as there is entitlement in your heart, I will have a direct link to your soul!"

Ephorah paused. Something clicked that she hadn't thought of before. "Entitlement? All you need is for people to believe we deserve what we want... You're the goddess of entitlement!"

"Not quite," she smirked. "When my nephew took the crown and handed out jobs to the gods, I never accepted one. I have no title, no official domain."

"But you feed on entitlement..." Ephorah tried to remember what she'd learned about the Babylonian myths. "And your nephew took the crown... Marduk? Your nephew is Marduk!"

At this, the goddess scowled. "As if mentioning him will get you any help. Let me tell you a secret: the god of civilization would keep you away from everything you desire. You want to see your people ascendant? Marduk won't lift a finger to do that. You want the Borealans to pay for conquering your ancestors' lands? Marduk would use his full powers to stop you. And your plans for special access to education for the Empyrians? Your school's desire for the government to make more theurgy jobs in the empire? Take a guess how the god of 'fairness' will react to that. The only way you can achieve any of these things is by embracing different ideas, a different set of values."

Ephorah didn't want to say it, but everything this evil goddess said was something Ephorah already knew. Marduk was the god of fairness, and if he was going to step in and make things more fair for the Empyrians in these last few generations, he would have done so already. And yet, there was no way that it was just or fair for her people to be second-class citizens on land that was once their own.

"You know, I hear mortals whisper all the time that money only has value because humans believe it does," the goddess giggled sadistically. "What they never realize is, even when they know how the trick works, they still believe that their coins are worth something. That's where the real magic lies; even when you know it's all in your head, you just can't stop believing."

"I. Don't. Want. What. You're. Selling!" Ephorah swung the book wildly, trying to smash the apparition of the goddess until she'd go away. The deity just snickered.

"No one says 'no' to me," she giggled as Ephorah dispersed her image. "Not forever, anyway."

Ephorah kept swinging the book until she realized she wasn't alone; a number of other girls were watching her randomly striking the air with a textbook, and the goddess was nowhere to be seen.

"Damn," Ephorah calmed down, grabbed the flyer she'd been looking for and hurried out of the lobby before any of the confused and worried-looking girls started asking questions.

73

Unforeseeable Consequences

NAMID

"And...where did you say you found this?" Professor Massouh examined the ring.

"From a set of ruins adrift in the Duat," Namid lied. There was no way she could explain to this man where the ring actually came from. "Found it while I was lost between runegates."

"Uh-huh." Massouh turned the ring over in his hands. "Bit of a weird story, that." He handed back the ring. "Look, this isn't enchanted. There is no magical power contained within it. The symbols etched into it are too old, too unknown for me to decipher, but if they're some kind of ancient ward, I can't identify it."

Namid sighed. "It doesn't look like anybody can. According to...some writing in the ruins I found...the ring can command demons, but I have no idea how or even if it's true."

"Well, have you tried talking to a priest?" The professor offered. "If the ring can't be identified by a wizard, then maybe you need to get the clergy involved. If nothing else, the gods could seal this away and keep it from causing trouble if it actually has any sort of powers."

Taking back the ring, Namid placed it in the pocket of her skirt. "Great. Well, better head over there before the temples are closed for the day."

Although she wasn't happy that she still had no answers, she was glad to leave the Institute of Theurgy. From Massouh staring at her back as she left, to the fact that somewhere on these grounds was that professor who had captured her with the windbags earlier, she had enough reason to give this place a wide berth. But there was something else; a general malignant presence seemed to hover in the very air around the building. It wasn't like the hopelessness of Azzitha, or the near lawlessness of the Kemet countryside; this was something...else.

Upon returning home yesterday for her first shower, warm meal, and good night's sleep in what had felt like a lifetime, Namid had received what could best be described as "a very stern talking-to" from her aunt and uncle. First, there had been a moment of sheer relief and smothering from the two after seeing Namid come home. And then, somewhere, between a face red enough to make a baboon ashamed of his under-colored backside and enough spit to make a rainstorm, Uncle Mido had managed to give Namid a list of new rules and demands that had to be followed if she did not want to be disowned. One of them was that she was to come home with Amri from school, and could not go out in public without him.

This meant she had to convince Amri to go with her to the temple district.

"Why are we running around taking a ring that you stole to the priests?" Amri eyed his sister. "I told you. That ring doesn't appear to have any significant magical powers, and if the theurgy guy said that it wasn't enchanted–"

"Can't you help me be thorough?" Namid whined. "Look, we take the ring to the temple district. We bring it to the priests of...I don't know, Horus or something. We tell them everything we know, and if we're wrong and the ring isn't some lich's secret super weapon, we tell the priests they can keep it as a donation. Then we'll be done with it once and for all."

Amri paused for a moment. "If this gets you to leave this thing alone and stop worrying about it, then alright. We'll take it to a temple. But why bring it to the Temple District when The Abbey of Truth is just a short walk away? They could deal with a cursed ring just as easily as the priests of Horus."

"But they're close by to our house," Namid frowned. "And I want this thing further away from our house in case the Tomb Lords come looking for it."

Her brother just rolled his eyes as they grabbed the first autobus for the

Temple District.

Once they were on the bus, Namid eyed her brother. It was subtle, so much so that she wouldn't have noticed if she hadn't been gone for so long, but were those...muscles, on his arms?

"What exactly have you been up to at this abbey you hang out at?" Namid furrowed her brow. She didn't mind her brother learning some new skills and building up some upper arm strength, but she wasn't sure what to do if he started dedicating himself to a new religious cult. She tried not to shudder as she remembered the necrophyte who had proclaimed Amenhotep to actually be some sort of a god.

"Learning, exercising, healing." Amri tapped his bandaged calves. "They're the hospital I was taken to when I had my fight with the alchemist."

"Learning?" Namid raised an eyebrow. "Could you have at least learned something that might have helped your odds of getting a job?'

"Already did that earlier in the off-season." Amri grinned. "Turns out, I can make a living inventing things and selling the patents."

"You can do what now?" Namid blinked.

"That gas cannister thing I was working on over at the industrial park? That paid off. Got my name on a few patents and made off with almost a thousand Ioseps after fees and taxes."

Namid's jaw dropped. "A thousand..."

"Diamond Energy bought the rights to the patents, even before they received any grant from the Imperial Palace. They didn't want to risk us selling to someone else. But the best part? I enjoyed doing it. It was fun."

"Okay..." Namid rubbed her forehead as she took this all in. "You've been busy." Did he actually start to outpace her? Was she really set back that much from her time in Kemet?

Namid would never admit this to her brother, but part of her had always been glad to believe she was a better wizard than him. During the Grand Wizard Tournament, they'd both had their power levels tested, and Namid had secretly enjoyed learning that she could turn more magical energy into work than her brother. But power levels aren't fixed, and she was only a little ahead of him back then. If they had their power levels tested now, he might score higher than her.

On the one hand, Namid had partly resented the fact that her brother was too useless to defend her if she were attacked. But this new Amri was different. In some ways, it made her feel worse.

When they reached the bus stop, Namid dragged her brother to the temple of Horus. A protective deity like him would probably be their safest bet.

Making her way passed a number of worshippers, a guy selling doves to offer as sacrifices, and a sickly old man with jerky movements huddled outside the shrine begging for alms, Namid marched up to the closest priestess and whipped out the ring.

"I found this in a place not far from hell. The dead there whispered that it could command demons." It was mostly the truth.

"Um." The priestess looked at the ring. "That's...not something we usually deal with."

"If you can keep it somewhere safe and invoke Horus or any other gods you need to figure out if this ring is actually dangerous, you can keep it. Call it a donation, or a contribution, or just a safekeeping fee." Namid pressed the ring into the priestess's palm. "Have you got that?"

"Uh...I think so." She held up the ring and seemed to be admiring the artwork. "It looks rather nice. Thank you for your contribution."

"And you're going to pray for a revelation, or something?" Namid asked.

"Oh, yes. We have a cleansing ceremony for these sorts of things. No demonic magic can stand up to Horus."

"Right." Namid backed away from the priestess. She still wasn't satisfied. Something had been gnawing at her ever since she'd woken up that morning, as if her first good night's sleep had made her aware of some wound she couldn't quite find on her body.

As the pair left the temple, Amri prodded her with his elbow.

"What's wrong with you?" He asked. "I mean, really?"

Namid shook her head. "You wouldn't understand." And he wouldn't. He didn't believe she had actually been in Kemet, or that the liches were planning to conquer their homeland, or that there was any real danger on the horizon. Namid was the only person who knew what was coming, and trying to warn people just made them think she was lying, especially people like Amri, Ephorah, and anyone else who'd known her for years.

Damn, Namid thought. *Who knew years of lying, manipulating, and scheming would come back to haunt me? What's really unfair is that it's going to haunt everyone else, too.*

On the autobus home, Amri nudged his sister out of her thoughts.

"By the way, Aunt Panya says you had a number of deliveries while you were gone. Something like clothes you ordered, but they were all too big for you."

Namid sighed. "Oh, Ephorah's birthday gifts. I completely forgot about that."

"You went out of your way to spend money on nice new clothes for Ephorah?" Amri raised an eyebrow. "Did you two have some sort of falling out and feel the need to get back into her good graces, or something?"

Yeah, pretty much, Namid thought. Except, something odd came to mind. Namid didn't care. She didn't care that Ephorah had acted earlier like she was still upset with her, or that her plan to win back Ephorah's good graces was dead in the water, or that her brother had read the situation like a comic book. None of that mattered now.

Even if she succeeded in getting Ephorah to get over their spat from before, it wouldn't change the facts regarding the Tomb Lords and their plans for her home.

Now more than ever, Namid was alone.

74

A Guilty Conscience or Two

CYRUS

"This will be your room while you're on campus," the housing director gestured. "Small, but you have the place to yourself. There's a kitchen in the basement, along with an icebox. Make sure your stuff is labeled."

"Thank you." Cyrus pulled his luggage into the room and stuffed his bags under the bed that was in one corner. It wasn't exactly luxurious, but better than going back to his parents' house.

Once he'd unpacked his things and had gotten setup, he went down to the Academia Food Court, where students of all the universities in Hadesh would often come for meals.

"So, you're the guy who applied for the bakery job?" The head cook looked Cyrus over. "You ever work in a bakery before?"

"Yes. Quite a bit, in fact." Cyrus wished the cook could just read the résumé he'd printed out. He had all of the answers to her questions right there.

"Uh-huh." She looked back at the paper. "Oh, I see you've done a few years at this. Well then, what made you want to work for the campus bakery?"

Because I need a job that covers the cost of room and board, Cyrus thought. *What a stupid question.* "Because chemistry started in the kitchen, and it's good for alchemists to return to our roots."

The cook nodded. "Alright. We'll have you in the kitchen making rolls, baking bread. Can you do pie crusts?"

"Yes," Cyrus replied.

"Good. We'll have you doing some of our pastries as well." She handed him a contract. "Just sign here."

Afterwards, Cyrus spent his first shift preparing the sandwich bread for the next day. Simple, monotonous work. Too much would drive him insane, but the right amount was a nice break from studying chemical equations.

The others working in the campus store were Rosa, a rather chubby girl who was a bit of an airhead but took care of most of the rest of the baked goods, Inna, a good-looking girl whose job involved staying close to a display case for customers and seemed to have "attract nerds to the campus store" in her job description, and Caleb, who ran the cash register up front. Cyrus, for the most part, didn't even need to come out from the back room where the oven was located. That was just fine for him.

There was something about watching the heat turn raw dough into a crispy, flaky crust that Cyrus had always enjoyed. Heating matter without burning it was a physical change, not a chemical one. And yet, the bread came out was like a different substance altogether.

While he kneaded new loaves and popped them in the oven, he thought about how ancient societies figured out how to smelt the first metals. For most of the metals of antiquity, like copper, tin, and gold, they just needed to build a stone furnace and light up a fire hot enough to melt the ores. But iron has a higher melting point than most rocks. To smelt the ore without melting the oven, they had to throw sand into the ore and exploit the flux effect; making the ore melt at a lower temperature than normal.

"Next set of loaves are ready!" He called as he emptied the oven.

"We need two more pie crusts and a half dozen tarts!" Rosa called back.

"On it!" Cyrus replied.

Several hours later, he was finished with his shift. The Academia Food Court closed at seven; he had plenty of time left to finish up his first assignments for classes. Tomorrow was the first day of his third year at the College of Alchemy. He was half done.

"Oh, no."

Cyrus looked over at Caleb, who was holding a letter in his hands. "Something wrong?"

"It's my cousin." He nodded. "He's got something inside of him that looks like a tumor."

"A...tumor?" Cyrus's eyes widened.

"Yeah," Caleb nodded. "It doesn't appear to be cancerous, at least not yet. But it's located in a spot that'll cause him problems if it isn't removed."

"...Right." Cyrus breathed a short sigh of relief. "Can they remove it?"

"I don't know." Caleb shook his head. "It's located on his esophagus. That's not an easy surgery, but it's making it hard for him to swallow food. It'd be terrible to live with it, but he's not guaranteed to survive the surgery."

"How old is he?" Cyrus asked.

"A few years older than me," Caleb said. "So, still young."

Cyrus nodded. "If he's in his twenties, his chances of surviving the operation are pretty high."

"You some kind of medical student?" Caleb asked.

"Medical alchemist," Cyrus replied.

"I hope you're right, but he lives in Madanaj. That city's been having a major shortage on pain killers, and it's not a surgery you can do without those. It'll be a while before they can treat him. At any rate, it could have been a lot worse. It could have been cancerous."

"...Yeah," Cyrus gritted his teeth. "That could have happened."

Cyrus didn't say anything else, but thoughts tore through his mind as he walked away from the bakery. If Caleb's cousin had antibodies that could fight cancer, his immune system would take care of that tumor without any need for invasive surgery.

But all of that was beside the point; for every young person out there with a tumor that turned out to be benign, there was someone else whose results came back positive. Sure, this particular person that Cyrus sort of knew had a cousin who probably won't die, and most people would relax as long as the only people suffering were distant strangers.

Up until now, Cyrus had tried to calm himself with the knowledge that most people with cancer were old and had lived full lives. Any treatment that revolved around sacrificing people to keep the elderly alive wasn't worth it, but a man in his twenties? He had a lot more to lose.

"Will this haunt me forever?" Cyrus looked up at the sky, where the sun was starting to go down. At the end of the off-season, night would descend faster, and the moon would be visible a lot sooner. The very same moon that ancient Egyptians once associated with Thoth.

What the hell have I done? Cyrus imagined how Thoth would react if he were there. What would the god of knowledge say about Cyrus destroying an entire laboratory and all of its research? Who was Cyrus to decide that Monroe's experiments needed to be stopped? Thoth hadn't just been killed in front of him by Amenhotep; he'd died keeping Cyrus and several other students alive. How did Cyrus repay him? By destroying life-saving research?

Try as he might, Cyrus couldn't sleep. He merely shut his eyes and rested in bed, thoughts swirling in his head until morning.

A cold shower and cup of coffee later, Cyrus was in his first class of the day: Neuroscience. The discussion was focused on neurotransmitters, and the chemicals the body uses to communicate between cells and organs.

While he got the gist of his classes, he couldn't really focus. Even in his job at the bakery, he found his mind wandering. Not enough to put him at risk with the oven, but no matter how much he tried, he couldn't rest.

The next morning, he had an early shift at the bakery. Students who ate breakfast at their respective schools would come to the food court, and most would grab a bagel or some toast in the morning. Simple enough, and Cyrus could use the hours and the distraction.

Most of the others who worked at the bakery weren't morning people, so Cyrus was working the bakery with Rosa. Rosa was good with a lot of things behind the counter, but the cash register wasn't one of them; she wasn't a math person.

"Alright," Cyrus looked at the order he'd written down for the guy in front of him. "One Iosep for the tart, two more for the bagel, and six Jaydons for the sales tax."

The boy handed Cyrus some money and took his breakfast. So far, simple enough.

The only thing that caused a problem was change; neither the bakery, nor the food court, nor the emperor himself could expect him to get exact change for the copper Jaydons and silver Ioseps. Since the coins got their value from their content of precious metals, and the value of precious metals changed from time to time, they weren't going to be exact. As long as Cyrus treated every Iosep as being equal to twelve Jaydons, he'd be fine, but that kind of math was the reason why Rosa didn't like working the cash register.

Whenever he could catch a break from taking orders, Cyrus would duck behind into the kitchen and make more bread. Some bakeries with more money to spend might use machines that could make this job easier, but Cyrus needed to mix, pound, and knead the dough mostly by hand. That was more than Rosa could handle, but it was fine by Cyrus. One more thing to distract him.

But the real distraction came from the next girl to order breakfast.

"I just want toast and some jam," Namid said.

"Uh, sure." Cyrus rang her up. "Aren't you the one who introduced me to Rostam?"

The girl blinked, as if just now recognizing Cyrus. "Oh, wow. Small world. How'd that go?"

"Eh, well enough. I fixed their ship, repaired some of their equipment, cooked them some meals. Things changed for the worse when the researchers who were supposed to pay Rostam and his crew were all dead, and we almost got eaten by a demon."

"...A demon?" Namid frowned. "You're screwing with me."

"Nope." Cyrus shook his head. "He ate the whole research team, and at least one of their dogs, and he was going to do the same to us. Although, I can't quite say if the demon was better or worse than the guy being possessed at the time."

"Wow, okay." Namid's face furrowed in confusion. "First I've heard of any of this. Uh..." She looked around, like there was something she wanted to ask, but wasn't sure if she should. "Listen, if you really have encountered a demon before and come back alive, there's something I need your advice about. What time do you get off from this?"

"Ten, but I have class immediately after," Cyrus replied. "I finish up for the day at three thirty."

"Ok," Namid nodded. "That's when my last class ends, too. I'll have about a half hour before my brother gets done with his class after that. Let's meet here then."

Shrugging, Cyrus agreed. He still owed her for helping before, and while he didn't know her very well, he might as well give her a hand.

At three thirty, the food court was mostly empty. No surprise; people went home around this time, and the only people left were students who lived on campus, grabbing light snacks before heading back to their study rooms to cram.

Namid was waiting at a small round table in the middle of the food court, and gestured for Cyrus to sit down.

"Alright," Cyrus took a seat across from her. "What did you want to talk about?"

"I need medical advice," Namid admitted. "Of the supernatural variety."

"How so?" Cyrus asked.

"Well, this last week and a half, I was...missing." Namid paused. She was clearly trying to decide how much to share with him.

"Missing...where?" Cyrus frowned. "If you don't tell me everything, there's not a whole lot I can do."

"Maybe this was a bad idea..." Namid whispered.

Cyrus cocked his head. "Something wrong?"

"Look," Namid glanced over her shoulders. "I need to know if demons can inflict any kind of lingering wounds that don't leave physical evidence."

"...You mean like a curse?" Cyrus asked.

She nodded.

"It's possible," Cyrus admitted. "But I'd need details. When did you start noticing it?"

"When I got back home, and I wasn't in danger anymore."

"Okay, and can you describe the effects?"

"Well, I've been restless for these last few nights, even though I'm back in my own bed at home, with my family. My brother...helps me a lot. ...yeah, and my mind keeps latching onto thoughts of Rana."

A GUILTY CONSCIENCE OR TWO

"Who is Rana?" Cyrus asked.

"She's a girl I met while I was lost," Namid admitted. "She and I were trying to escape in the desert, and when...monsters had us cornered, she ran out and drew them away so I could flee. None of them landed a scratch on me, but I still feel like something's wrong."

"Wait," Cyrus tilted his head in suspicion. "What happened to Rana? Did she get out of there okay?"

"No," Namid admitted. "I'm pretty sure she was killed by zombies."

Cyrus furrowed his brow and rubbed his eyes, trying to make sense of the girl in front of him.

"What?" Namid asked. "What do you think is wrong?"

"That's called 'guilt,' you sociopath!" Cyrus finally said. "You're upset because your friend is dead!"

"What...really?" Namid scratched the back of her head. "That doesn't sound right."

"Oh, trust me. It's right!" Cyrus shook his head in bewilderment. "What the hell is wrong with you?"

"That's what I wanted to ask you about," Namid replied. "You're sure it's not a curse?"

"No! It's not a curse! That's normal!" Cyrus rubbed his eyes. "How is this the first time in your life you've had this?"

Namid leaned back thoughtfully. "Well, if I had to guess, I'd say it's because I'm not sure why she sacrificed her life for me. It might have been so she wouldn't end up as another dog in a dog-eat-dog world, or it might have been to save me, specifically. Pretty weird, either way."

Cyrus pinched the bridge of his nose and squinted. "Okay, that just raises more questions. Where were you that you were getting attacked by zombies, anyway?"

Shifting her gaze away, Namid took a while to respond. "Would you believe me if I told you I was in Kemet?"

"Kemet..." Cyrus took a moment to grasp what she was saying. "You mean, you were in the south? Were the Tomb Lords involved?"

"Kind of," Namid admitted. "We were being chased by necrophytes. They were the ones who sent the zombies. Except, from what I've gathered, necrophytes just control the zombies raised by a proper necromancer, like one of the liches. So... you know."

"How did you end up in Kemet?" Cyrus asked.

Namid leaned closer and looked over both shoulders. "There was a winery. I went there to order drinks for a party. Then I get there, and the staff are dead, and the woman at the counter turns out to be a zombie. Then the liches pop out from below the main floor and drag me through a runegate. There was another gate; I had to escape through that to get home."

"Tomb Lords..." Cyrus's eyes widened. "Killing Thoth wasn't enough for them."

"What?" Now it was Namid's turn to act surprised. "Killing Thoth?"

"The liches." Cyrus's tongue turned dry as the desert. "They were the ones who killed Thoth after the tournament. Not the dragon."

"By the gods." Namid perked up. "You believe me!"

Cyrus nodded, eyes unblinking. "Yup. That's totally something they'd do. Do you know what they had planned for Hadesh?"

"I don't know why they were in a winery," Namid admitted. "Something about agents and a listening post. But before I escaped, they had a ring. It was supposed to be able to control demons. They were planning to use it in a war they want to wage against Hadesh."

"A war," Cyrus sighed. "What the hell do we do?"

"Contact a mercenary guild?" Namid suggested.

"Have you got the money to hire a mercenary company to fight off an undead army lead by a bunch of liches?" Cyrus asked.

"No," Namid admitted. "But we could tell the emperor."

"And what would he do?" Cyrus asked. "Spend a fortune on a war against an enemy that has played at being our peaceful neighbors for over a century? Do you understand that the Tomb Lords have avoided fighting us directly since before the Empyrian War?"

Namid paused. "Why is that? If they wanted to conquer this land, why not take your people out before you were an empire?"

"They tried," Cyrus replied. "Two hundred years ago. And we fought them off. And a century before that, we fought them off again. The terrain, the fact that we rely on mercenary companies instead of standing armies, the way our militias were setup…our society has never really been good at mobilizing to invade another nation, but we've always been quick to react to invaders — every home its own fort, every man a skilled rifleman. Throw in the dangers we already face in the area that we've learned to fight and an invading army like the Tomb Lords hasn't, like the Greymarch, or the dragons that used to live in the surrounding regions, and the liches had no chance."

"What are their odds of success this time?" Namid asked.

"…I don't know," Cyrus admitted. "On paper, we have more land, more resources, more advanced weapons and guns, but…" he looked up from the table towards the east horizon. "I've seen what the old Empyrian lands are like. Maybe not much, but enough to know that we're not going to be a unified force like the last few times. And it sounds like the liches are planning something sneakier than before." He looked back at Namid. "Tell me everything you saw. Everything."

75

Fiery Introductions

ROSTAM

"You know what's weird?" Cindrocles puffed a smoke ring into the air above the stern of *the Endurance*. "I barely have a concept of time, but somehow, I hate Mondays."

Rostam glanced over at the fireball from the railing of the ship. "Why on Earth would you hate Mondays? We work everyday on the ship, and you don't even know what a weekend is."

"I don't know," Cindrocles replied. "I just remember hating Mondays when the people would go to work and everyone was grumpy about having to start a new week."

Before Rostam could ask more, Nadia came out of the captain's quarters and turned to the crew. "We're going to be here longer than I expected," she said with a pause. "Around this time, we usually have contracts to supply the universities with materials they didn't think they'd need, but we made it back right as the schools are starting up again. I'm going to be keeping an eye out for more cargo jobs, but I don't know how long it's going to take."

"Need us to help you sniff out more work?" Rostam asked.

"Thanks, but no," Nadia replied. "It's best if only one person is out there hitting the streets and possibly getting us committed to a particular job. Take a few days of shore leave, just make sure you come back each evening. You all have bunks."

The crew all nodded. Of course, they could get comfier beds at an inn around town, but if you fell asleep in a bed like that, you might wake up without a ship to work for in the morning.

"Time to visit people," Rostam stretched out his arms before turning to Cindrocles. "Want to come with?"

"Are any of the people you're visiting theurgists?" Cindrocles asked.

"It's possible," Rostam admitted. "But lately, she's been more of an... acquaintance than a friend. Let's just say that if you two were to fight, I'd break it up and make sure she didn't harm you."

Cindrocles held in the air and burned slowly for a moment, and Rostam realized this was the fireball's thinking face.

"Alright," he eventually said. "I can't stay away from people forever."

The two made their way off the ship through Silverstack Docks, down the elevator to the ground level, and strolled through the Market District. Rostam had noticed the way people looked at a loose fireball floating through a town before, but the last time, it had mostly been between merchants. A lot of people crossed the streets and kept as much distance between themselves and Cindrocles as possible.

The Garden District was on the opposite side of town. Rather than try to get Cindrocles on an autobus, Rostam decided walking was better, and with the way people often reacted to a fire spirit with no theurgist master, traveling near the Imperial Palace didn't seem like a good plan.

Instead, Rostam led Cindrocles through the Industrial Zone and then through the Empyrian Quarter. This seemed like a better idea than taking the elemental through the Academic District, where the Institute of Theurgy would be right on their path.

In Hadesh, there is no part of town that is especially dangerous at night. The city wasn't entirely crime-free, but it was low-crime, or at least crime-light, depending on how the subject was pasteurized. But if one were to comb through Hadesh and go looking for crime, the place to check would be the Empyrian Quarter.

When you walk about with a living ball of flame as a traveling companion, you don't usually have too much trouble with crooks. Thugs armed with knives or even guns will jump out at you from alleyways and then immediately scurry back into them. But Hadesh was different, because sometimes, those thugs might have a degree.

"What do we have here?" A woman only a few years older than Rostam came out of a house and leaned against a balcony railing to eye Cindrocles. "Whose fire elemental is that?"

Rostam wasn't sure how to respond. Part of him wanted to say, "he's mine," or "he's my Captain's," or "he's my ship's," but none of those quite seemed right. Instead, he just answered: "what's it to you?"

This answer was about as effective at driving the woman off as if Rostam had said "he's his own elemental." Which is to say, it just made the woman more interested.

"That looks like a humanus fire elemental," she said as she took a step closer. "Yes?"

Cindrocles looked visibly uncomfortable and started floating behind Rostam.

"He might be," the shipmate replied. "Again, what's it to you?"

"Do you have any idea how valuable those are right now?" The woman replied. "I'm between jobs at the moment, but the Institute of Theurgy has put out a bounty on humanus spirits. Especially fire elementals. I'd split the reward money with you."

"He works on my boss's ship," Rostam felt himself putting up his arm between Cindrocles and the theurgist. "I'm getting him some air, but then he needs to be back in the boiler for us to take off again."

Frowning, the woman cocked her head to look at the fire elemental behind Rostam's back. "You know, the institute is looking for spirits to test out a new boiler experiment. If it works, you'd have a spirit permanently bound to the boiler as an artifact with no worries. You'd never need to take him out for fresh air again, or keep him satiated with expensive coal."

"Experiment on someone else," Rostam replied.

The woman opened her mouth as if confused by his words. Either, in her opinion, he had just implied that she intended to experiment on him, a human who could not be used to power a boiler, or he had just referred to Cindrocles as a "someone," which was unheard of to theurgists. Rostam took her moment of bewilderment as an opening to rush Cindrocles away from the area.

"On our way back, we're taking the long way outside the city wall," he whispered to the fireball, who nodded in agreement.

When they finally reached the Garden District, Rostam told Cindrocles to stay back a ways as he knocked on Amri and Namid's front door.

Panya Seluk opened the front door and looked over at the fireball hovering above her garden. "What is that thing doing so close to my irises?"

"He's a friend," Rostam replied. "I came to see Amri, and check on Namid, but I don't think it's safe to bring him into the house. Can I take him around to the back porch?"

Panya looked at Cindrocles again, who was fidgeting to avoid a moth drawn to his light. When the insect got too close and burst into flames, the fireball instinctively flinched back as the burning bug landed on a flower.

A slack-jawed Panya pointed at the elemental as Rostam went over and stamped out the fire spreading in her flowerbed.

"There, all better!" Rostam gestured to the trampled burnt flowers. "I'm going to take Cindrocles to the back patio where there aren't any flowers now."

Panya, frozen in shock, didn't respond as Rostam quickly guided Cindrocles around to the back of the house. To his surprise, he found Namid and Cyrus on the back patio, sitting around a table with a fancy-looking incense burner in the middle.

"What— Namid?" Rostam looked at the two. "And Cyrus?"

"Oh, hi again!" Cyrus smiled at Rostam. "Namid was telling me..." he glanced at Namid, who locked eyes with him but said nothing. "Telling me... about the things she saw while she was missing."

Namid nodded, as if this was an acceptable cover. Rostam wasn't buying it but knew better than to press the issue right now.

"So..." Rostam turned to Namid. "You're back. Last time I was here, there was a big commotion over you being missing."

"Made my way home," Namid replied. "Wasn't easy, but I found a runegate that dropped me off in the Institute of Theurgy. 'Nuff said."

"Uh-huh," Rostam frowned. "So, where were you?"

"...Lost. In a really bad place," Namid replied. "The kind I needed a runegate to get back from."

"And her aunt and uncle have put her under a sort of house-arrest," Cyrus added. "They're making her bring her brother with her whenever she leaves the house, so it was just easier for me to come here than to explain to her family why she was staying late at the college."

"Right, but why are you here?" Rostam asked. "I didn't get the sense that you knew each other that well."

"Don't question it," Panya came out onto the back patio with a plate of snacks. "This is the first time Namid's brought a boy home."

Cyrus nodded. "Sure, let's go with that reason."

Rostam pondered the two for a moment. He was glad to see Namid was back safe and sound, but she and Cyrus were acting incredibly suspicious, and not even like a teenage couple sneaking around.

"Guys..." Rostam eyed the two and didn't even hide his suspicion. "What's really going on?"

Cyrus looked at Namid with an expression that read "should we tell him?"

"I wasn't just lost in the Spirit Plane," Namid sighed. "I was dragged through a runegate by several Tomb Lords into Kemet, and I had to find my way back through another runegate."

"...Right..." Rostam looked at Cyrus for clues.

"I think she's telling the truth," Cyrus said. "It lines up with what I saw at the Grand Wizard Tournament."

"What?" Rostam blinked. "What happened at the Tournament?"

"The Tomb Lords murdered Thoth." Cyrus gritted his teeth. "And they had a complex plan for it, too. They used mechanical warriors, undead monsters, and some sort of metal made from people's jealousy. Poison to the god of reason."

"Okay, both of you." Rostam pulled up a seat next to the table. "Start from the beginning."

"Oh, hey," Cindrocles floated closer to the table's incense burner. "Incense! Mind if I try some?"

The others dismissed the elemental as he popped a stick of incense into the hole that served as his mouth while Cyrus explained his story.

"Why didn't you bring this up before?" Rostam asked. "You could have said something while we were waiting for the captain to heal at the research station."

"Would you have believed me?" Cyrus asked. "And even if you did, what then? Would you go on some adventure to fight an ancient tyrant before he brings his armies to the empire? That's a pretty big ask from someone who was bumming room and board from your crew for a week."

Rostam sighed as he realized he wouldn't have been able to do anything. "Okay, so what else is going on?"

"The Tomb Lords had some sort of demon-commanding ring," Namid replied. "I don't know what they had planned for it. Everyone I showed it too insists that it had no magical powers, but..." Namid's gaze shifted. "I swear, Amenhotep himself made it sound like he had some big plans involving that ring. So I stole it, brought it back here, and gave it to the temple of Horus."

"Did you catch any of their other plans?" Rostam asked.

Namid shook her head. "I saw some of their weapons. The Tomb Lord who's obsessed with technology – I think he was making mechanical soldiers. That's all I know."

Something else clung to Rostam's mind. It might not have been related, but...

"I saw a man blow himself up in a market," Rostam said. "Back in Taisha."

"You told about this," Namid replied. "When you came back from your trip."

"Yeah, but I didn't tell you the guy looked like he hadn't had a decent meal in his entire life," Rostam added. "And...I think he might have been Coptic."

The others paused and looked at each other. Rostam realized he'd just said that to one of his Coptic friends, as a guest in their house.

"Sorry," he backtracked. "I wasn't trying to imply...it's just, where does a guy who can't afford food get his hands on explosives?"

"It's alright." Namid's face turned grim. They all knew where this could lead. "It isn't exactly proof, but it makes sense."

"Why have him blow up a marketplace, though?" Cyrus asked. "Did this bomber have any plans, make a speech first, have an agenda?"

Rostam shook his head. "No. There was no warning. One minute, everything was fine, the next...people were dead."

"That...might be their actual goal," Namid paused. "To make people afraid of going out in public, or just living their regular lives. Amenhotep's minions genuinely believe he's some kind of godking who will bring prosperity as soon as everyone who opposes his order is destroyed. Maybe this is part of how he does it. Get people as scared as possible and then offer protection. Even better if people don't know he's the one who caused the problem in the first place."

"Woah," Cindrocles interjected. "Did you guys know...I don't have hands?"

Rostam looked over at the elemental. "What?"

"Yeah, and they've got like...no fingers, either."

"Cindrocles, how much of that incense have you had?" Rostam asked.

"Hmmmmmmmmmmmmm" the fireball dragged on. "I don't...know."

"Okay...maybe that's enough for you." Rostam blew out the fire in the incense burner and covered it up. "Note to self, the fireball gets high on incense."

"What are we supposed to do?" Cyrus asked.

"Eh, just give him a bit," Rostam replied. "He'll sober up eventually."

"I meant about the Tomb Lords," Cyrus rolled his eyes. "How do we stop the liches?"

"We can't," Namid looked down at her hands for a moment. "We can try to make more people aware, but that's not much. Maybe...maybe the reason they're still sneaking around to get things done is because their plans would be ruined if people knew what they were up to."

"Then we should be spreading the word," Cyrus drummed his fingers on the table. "Except...Namid's already having trouble getting people to believe her story...and while I haven't been running around telling people about who really killed Thoth, I have a feeling it's because no one would believe it. And...to be honest, maybe we shouldn't just randomly start telling people about the stuff we've seen."

Namid and Rostam looked at each other. "Why not?"

"Because you saw a Coptic man blow himself up in a marketplace," Cyrus pointed at Rostam. "And right now, maybe the last thing we want is for everyone in the empire to start suspecting Coptics of working for the liches." Cyrus tilted his head at Rostam and raised an eyebrow inquisitively. "You know it was already on your mind. You might've been trying to be polite, but lots of people are going to start suspecting any Coptics they see if we aren't careful who we share stuff with."

Rostam knew he was right. "Can we let Amri in on this?"

Namid sucked her teeth. "He didn't exactly believe me when I told him where I was. And he doesn't even know you." She pointed to Cyrus. "He's got no reason to trust you. And Rostam's story is the weakest one we've got."

"What about Ephorah?" Rostam asked.

"Do you really want to introduce her to him?" Namid whispered to Rostam, though not quietly enough so that Cyrus couldn't hear. Even so, the Borealan alchemist rolled his eyes and got the message.

"Alright," Rostam sighed. "But I think we should at least tell Ephorah and Amri what I saw in Taisha. And we should try to bring them in on this, even if it is slow."

"Slow," Cyrus paused. "I wonder how much time we've actually got."

76

The Game of the Pharaohs

DAURGO

The dracolich could feel another group of zombies turn to ash. Medjed was loose on the centipede again.

"Okay, I've had enough of this frickin-bedsheet-laser-ghost!" Daurgo directed a group of cauldron-borne ogres to grab mirror shields he'd crafted for this purpose.

"Mirrors?" Aquila asked. "What are mirrors going to do?"

"Have I told you how a laser works?" The lich asked.

The thief shook her head.

"Well, those things Medjed shoots from the eye? They're a bunch of photons with identical energy levels–"

"Never mind!' Aquila turned away and threw up her hands. "Magic, science things. Whatever!"

"They're reflective," the lich hissed. "Just...stay out of sight and try to keep a mirror between you and the weirdo in the sheet."

As if on cue, a shadowy bedsheet emerged from the floor of the centipede's control room. The lights of Medjed's eyes glowed as he or she was about to attack, but each of the cauldron borne ogres in the room raised reflective shields, all curved to aim Medjed's own gaze back at the smiter.

Unsure how to react, the god hesitated. Long enough for a murder of undead crows to tackle the deity's head and peck at their eyes. While some were reduced to ash, the god's eyes were ripped out as it stumbled around the room.

Several cauldron borne seized the opportunity to grab the smiter and rip it apart piece by piece, gobbling up each severed limb or rib until there was nothing left.

When the dust settled, there was nothing left but an empty bedsheet with eyeholes where the god of the unseen had stood. A few skeletons came to sweep up the piles of ash that had been crows, and Daurgo returned to his work.

"That weirdo is getting better at this," the lich muttered. "I need a more permanent solution."

"More permanent than sending the gods taunting letters?" Aquila asked.

"Ah, that!" Daurgo chuckled. "I think that joke has run long enough. Now I need to do something more...brutal, to get my point across."

Aquila rolled her eyes. "Exactly how do insulting letters and acts of violence get the gods to leave you alone?"

"There are two ways to get the law off your case," the lich replied. "Doesn't matter what country, or culture, or whether it's mortal laws or gods. The first is to prove you're not the one they're looking for. Which, I'm not, but they don't believe me, and I have no evidence to show them. The other way is by showing them so much force they have no choice but to leave you alone. A cop is just a thug with a badge, a divine law enforcer is just the same thing, scaled up. Never forget this."

"So...you're going to intimidate the gods into backing off?" Aquila's eyes widened. *The rook was right. He is insane!*

"Something like that," Daurgo admitted. "Not just with force, though. Control what something eats, and you've got 'em by the throat. Hold on... what's this?"

Daurgo turned his attention to the eyes of one of his zombie puppets located in Hadesh. This one was an elderly man who had died of old age and smelled bad when he was alive, so no one thought much of his condition now. The old man's corpse sat on a beggar's mat outside the temple of Horus, where Daurgo could monitor the Egyptian god's house on the mortal plane. And from this old beggar's milky white eyes, he had spotted a strange gold ring with an unusual symbol.

"No. It can't be." Daurgo focused his attention through the old man's eyes. He couldn't get closer; if the corpse set one foot inside the temple, Horus would immediately notice an undead creature in his house. But even from here, the symbol on the ring was unmistakable.

"The Ring of Solomon." The skeleton shambled to the nearest bookshelf and started digging through old tomes until he found what he was looking for.

"The ring of solid one?" Aquila cocked her head. "Never heard of it."

"Legend has it that Solomon was a mighty king with a ring that had amazing powers," Daurgo explained. "It could tell him anything he wished to know, and it was said that he used it to command demons to build a temple to the deity he worshipped."

Aquila shrugged. "It's probably fake. There's no way—"

"Impossible," Daurgo replied. "There's no one alive today who would even know how to replicate the symbols on that ring. No one could fake that..." If the lich still had lungs, he would have sighed. "Arrrgh, there's no one alive who even knows about the ring. So...the Tomb Lords...That ring's a trap. I'm certain of it."

"How could that be?" Aquila asked. "That girl who brought it in—"

"There can be no other explanation." Daurgo marked the page in his book detailing the ring and its markings. "No living person could make a fake, in part because no one alive would remember it. It's a relic of a religion no one practices anymore. A kind of...supernatural debris. Whether it's real or fake, the only way that ring could be here is if the Tomb Lords planted it. And they must have realized...I'm the only one in the area who would recognize it."

"Aren't you jumping to conclusions a bit?" Aquila asked. "Not everything is about you."

"I don't like working the same city twice," Daurgo muttered, ignoring the thief. "Not within the same century. I can't just send you to steal from a temple; you can hide from mortal eyes, but nothing in the house of a god slips by their notice." The lich paused for a moment. "That must be their plan. Pit the dragon that's caused them trouble against the gods of their enemies. Soften up the empire for...whatever they have planned, weaken their gods if possible, and get me knocked out of the picture."

"Okay, now I know you're jumping to conclusions," Aquila said.

"Oh, I can just see Amenhotep's self-assured face, thinking he's got everything under control." A thought occurred to Daurgo, and an uncontrollable laughter overtook him. "Oh-ho-ho! I can just see his face! Thinking he's got everything under control!"

A worried expression crept along Aquila's face. "What are you doing?"

"A trap that I know about is one I can work to my advantage..." the lich grabbed several sheets of paper and started scribbling plans. "Let's see...I'll need ambiance — I've got to check my vinyl records and see what I can spare. Then I'll need herring. Lots of herring! I'll have to check the train schedules in Hadesh to send them where they need to go. And then the golden frying pan...do I have enough confetti and balloons?"

"Do you want to fill me in on your plans?" Aquila asked. "Or at least, whatever you have going on in your skull that you think is a plan?"

"...There is no way that arrogant jerk will be able to resist..." Daurgo tapped a bony finger against his table as his plans began to take shape, before finally turning to Aquila. "I will need something from you."

"Okay," Aquila gritted her teeth. "What do I need to steal?"

"Nothing," Daurgo replied. "I need you to head back to Aestival." The lich wrote down several instructions. "Bring this to the undercity and tell the janitors that I'll pay them in gold bars."

Aquila took the list. "...anything else?"

"Yes, a delivery." Several skeletons brought out a machine the size of a typewriter and placed it on a table near Aquila. "Bring this to the Imperial Palace. Make sure it gets to the emperor himself."

The thief eyed the contraption. "What the hell is this?"

"A message," the lich replied. "In the meantime, I need to get some moonlight."

"What?" Aquila balked. "You're going to go stroll around in the night air?"

"Not exactly," Daurgo muttered. "It's a good thing I've had enough time... I'll be back soon. As soon as you've made the delivery, lie low. I'll do the rest."

"But...what about the ring?" Aquila asked. "Don't you want me to steal it?"

"This won't be like last time," the skeleton shook its head. "Last time was about stealthily taking things out from under the gods' beaks and noses, and keeping a low profile until the last possible moment. This will be very different. We're stealing from a temple."

In the Spirit Plane, a corpse dressed in black robes and a bronze mask approached a pale white house that gleamed in an endless sea of night. This was the house of the moon. Stepping through the front gate into the main hall, Daurgo confronted Konshu.

The Egyptian god of the moon sat across a large table and dressed in a silvery business suit, a pair of dark-tinted glasses, and a false beard. His head was cleanly shaved, and in the limited illumination of his house, his scalp gleamed with the light of a cloudless night.

"I take it you know why I'm here," the skeleton approached the table.

"Yes, yes." The god smiled. "There's only one reason anyone comes here anymore."

"Then let us begin." Daurgo reached into his robes and pulled out a deck of cards. "I've done my research, and I've built my decks. This is the game you do your dealings with these days, even if it is stupid."

"Stupid is as stupid does," Konshu chuckled as he pulled out a deck of his own. "Here are the terms. Each round you win, you gain an hour of moonlight to be used at a time of your choosing. Same deal I made with Nut when she needed to add time to the year to give birth[AC1] . Each round I win, I will devour the memories of one of your kind. Their name, their relationships to you and to others, everything. Even if you find some way to raise up their soul from the afterlife, you won't even remember to call them. They will be forever lost."

"Very well," Daurgo placed his first deck on the table. "If you're making the rules, then I get the first turn on the first hand."

Konshu gave a toothy smile. "Draw up to five cards each turn. Chamber Pot of Greed and Shapeshifting Jar are prohibited."

"Yes, yes…" Daurgo drew his first hand of cards. "For the record, this game is stupid."

THE GAME OF THE PHARAOHS

Looking at his hand, Daurgo laid down his first monster card. "Zombie Clown Car. With this in play, I can summon an Undead Clown every turn. I also play a card facedown. I cast Fertile Graveyard. All of my undead minions have double health. I place a second card facedown, which requires me to discard my one remaining card from my hand. Your turn."

"Very well," Konshu drew his first hand. "I summon a Moon Maiden. I also play Extra Summon which allows me to also play Dark Magician Cow, which I equip with Massive Udders to give her a total of eight thousand and eight attack power. Both of my monsters attack your Clown Car."

"And that activates my trap card." Daurgo flipped one of the cards he'd placed facedown. "Hand of Death. Dark Magician Cow gets dragged to the graveyard, and your Moon Maiden doesn't have enough attack power to destroy my Clown Car with the Fertile Graveyard in effect."

Konshu played another card. "Grace of the Moon. Dark Magician Cow returns to my hand."

"Second trap activated." Daurgo flipped his other facedown card. "Gravedigger's Trick. Your Cow goes back to the graveyard, and you lose two thousand health. I did tell you this game was stupid, right?"

The moon god looked at his cards again, folded them and frowned. "Very well, your turn."

Daurgo drew five new cards and placed an Undead Clown in front of his Clown Car. "I give my Undead Clown a Sword of Unholy Power, which triples the strength of its wielder if they're undead. When the Undead Clown is the only monster on my side, he has the effect of dealing an extra seven hundred attack to his initial eight hundred, meaning that he does forty-five hundred damage when he attacks."

"Which will all be absorbed by my Moon Maiden," Konshu smiled. "She only has five hundred life, but you can't strike me without killing all of my monsters on the field first."

"Which is why I play the spell Disturbing Mental Image." Daurgo laid the card with an image of a censor block down on the table. Your Moon Maiden is too nauseated by a horrific mental image to defend, allowing my Undead Clown to sneak passed and strike you for forty-five hundred damage."

Konshu frowned at his hand. "Hmph. Alright. Anything else?"

"One card played facedown, the rest I'll hold," Daurgo replied.

The match continued for another turn until Daurgo struck again with his Undead Clown, finishing off the last of Konshu's life points.

"Alright," Daurgo reshuffled his deck. "That's one."

77

Memories of Eternity

MARDUK

"So, your sister's returned?" Marduk sat at his desk translating the works of the Roman poet Juvenal. "Hm. That's good, but...her story bothers me."

"Well, she has something of a reputation for saying whatever gets her out of trouble." Amri winced. Admitting this about his own sister must have been unpleasant for him.

"Yes," Marduk sampled the thoughts currently flickering through Amri's mind. They were memories of times when his sister had overtly lied about things, omitted key details when her parents had been upset, and even threatened to spread false rumors about people to get what she wanted from them. Marduk also caught a glimpse of one time she didn't lie about a vase she broke and how her parents had reacted.

"But I have to ask...what does she gain from this story about getting lost in Kemet?" Marduk looked up from his desk. "Apart from some people accusing her of lying and asking uncomfortable questions, what benefit is it to her to lie right now?"

Amri didn't have an answer to this. Marduk could sense that a part of the boy had been worrying about it.

"Do you think her story might be true?" Amri asked.

"Possibly," the god replied. "Amenhotep forbids the worship of gods in Kemet, so it's outside the reach of my sight. That would explain how I wasn't able to find her anywhere while she was gone. There aren't that many other ways she could avoid my sight for so long. And it's not as if anything she's describing is out of character for the Tomb Lords."

"Then...you think she's telling the truth?"

"I can't say. A god's knowledge over things only one person knows about is...limited," Marduk admitted. "I know what the collective consciousness of mankind knows. Unfortunately, one person in a sea of minds isn't very loud. If she were here in front of me, I could pick through her thoughts and determine whether she believes her own story, but otherwise, I can't be certain."

"...Should I...bring her here?" Amri asked.

Marduk shook his head. "Not against her will. And don't give her an ultimatum, either. If you offer to bring her to a god who can confirm if she's telling the truth, and she accepts, that's fine. But if you tell her 'do this or I won't believe you,' you'll just make more friction between you two."

Amri wanted to ask Marduk whether he had any suggestions, but wouldn't outright ask. Marduk rolled his eyes.

"Kings do not sit and wait for someone to read their mind," he pointed a pen at the boy. "You have questions, ask! If you don't have the knowledge you need, seek it out!"

"What should I be doing?" Amri finally asked. "About my sister. How do I figure out if she's telling the truth or not?"

Putting down his pen, Marduk stretched out his arms and cracked his knuckles. "You study how to observe with your third eye."

"Third eye?" Amri blinked and rubbed his eyes, as if checking to see if he had an extra he never knew about.

"It's metaphorical, but many religions bring them up for a reason," Marduk explained. "Just as two eyes allow you to see things one cannot, your third eye allows you to see things people try to hide. People are the only creatures on this planet that will lie, and piercing their deceptions requires a sight beyond your base vision."

"Okay," Amri's mind was filled with confusion, but he was interested in learning. "How do you start?"

"Your third eye is composed of your other senses combined. It is, in essence, the center point of your eyes, ears, and your mind. First, you must start by listening carefully to what people say, but also observing what they do. Actions speak to priorities, but speech can tell you when a person's words are aligned as well. A man who never exercises clearly does not consider getting into shape a priority, but if he says he wants to get stronger on top of failing to exercise, what does that mean?"

"He's...lying?" Amri offered.

"To whom?" Marduk replied.

"To..." Amri paused. "To himself. There's...no one to fool. If he doesn't exercise, people who look at him and see his lack of muscles aren't going to be tricked by his words. So the only person he can deceive is himself."

"Exactly," Marduk allowed himself a little smile. "The third eye comes from enlightenment. Learning how to see through illusions is all about..."

The god trailed off as he sensed an owl outside the library window. A single tree stood across from the library in the abbey's yard, and the night bird sat on a branch in broad daylight glaring at Marduk through the window.

"Creatures of the night." He stood up from his desk. "Out in the sun."

"Uh, sorry?" Amri asked.

"I have to go." Marduk turned to the boy one last time. "Use your best judgment to figure out what's going on with your sister. She's a liar; that won't make it easy. But that doesn't mean she lies all the time."

Amri frowned. His mind had picked up that Marduk was on edge over something. "Is there something wrong?"

"Yes," Marduk admitted. "And since I did tell you to seek the information you need, I'll be sure to fill you in later."

Marduk slipped out of phase with the material plane and made his way invisibly to the Institute of Theurgy. Sure enough, the closer he got to the institute, the more creatures of the night he could see active in broad daylight, with owls perched above, as if ruling or commanding the other beasts. She was here.

"You can cower in the shadows," Marduk growled as he patrolled the university grounds, still out of phase for mortal eyes. "Or you can come out and face me. Makes no difference to me."

Sounds of laughter were followed by a dark-haired girl materializing out of the ether nearby. "Doesn't really matter to me either, nephew."

Marduk's weapons materialized in his hands. "You have no place in civilization."

"Yes, I do," the girl cackled. "I'm it's shadow."

The god of civilization sighed and sheathed his weapons. No amount of force could stop his ancient enemy.

"You knew I'd come here," the goddess smiled as she looked around the campus. "That's why you stuck around, long after they turned away from your teachings. Even when they started to besmirch your name by torturing spirits while you were still their figurehead. You knew I'd come fill the void in your absence."

Marduk could remember what she could not. This goddess couldn't be reasoned into backing off or bargained with. He knew from experience now that it was pointless to try.

"Heheh," she strolled up to him, still wearing the form of a schoolgirl. "Tell me, how do you like this culture? What's new about it? There has to be something you haven't seen before."

"The slaves," Marduk sighed. "This empire doesn't force people into slavery. The Persians, the Parthians, the Babylonians, the Sassinids, they all went to war to take captives for slave labor, but not the Borealans."

"Good, good!" She smiled. "And...that's why they have all these machines, isn't it? The Empyrians didn't have these...factories, or billowing smokestacks. Neither did the raiders that used to live in the wastes to the north. And all those ancient peoples, they had steam engines too, didn't they? But they didn't have this...industrialization. The rich would just buy more slave labor. Here, rich people couldn't do that, so they invest in automated labor instead. Isn't that right?"

Marduk closed his eyes and nodded.

"And you were hoping that would be this nation's saving grace?" The goddess laughed. "Their ace in the hole, right? No slaves, no slave rebellions? And the women, the upper-class women can't repeat history if they can't buy slaves, right? Did you not notice what was happening here?"

The god of civilization knew why she was enjoying this so much; he had hoped that this time around, things would be different. And crushing that hope was her favorite thing in the world.

"Of course, I knew they were enslaving the elementals," Marduk replied. "I tried talking them out of it, but they do not recognize these spirits as people. They do not age or procreate the way mortals do; they don't have the same bodily needs, and so humans think the rules against forcing someone into slavery don't apply."

"Oh, don't give them that much credit!" The goddess sneered. Her form was starting to grow, giving way to the lie that she was a harmless young girl. "They know full well what they're doing is wrong! I can hear them, you know? Even now – even before I started manifesting in front of them. There was a girl last year who pointed out in front of her class that if they treated humans the way they treated spirits, they'd be thrown in prison. And the headmistress responded by beating her until she shut up! It isn't ignorance that allows them to exploit the elementals like this. It's good old-fashioned selfishness."

Licking her lips, the goddess' form stretched out, almost serpentine, as she began to tower over Marduk. "Selfishness, and laziness, and entitlement, and...and...vanity! The vanity!" She cheered. "This entire campus has become my buffet!"

"So..." Marduk sighed. "Do you want to gloat about how you infected this place?"

"Infected?" She smirked. "No, no. I didn't need to. Theymanaged to do that for me. I just had to move in."

"Then what do you have to brag about?" Marduk asked.

"Pick an elemental," she replied. "Any elemental you want, as long as it's sapient. Summon it, and let me show you what I'm up to."

Marduk conjured a water elemental. This one had the form of a serpent, but winged plumage around its head and beak. With its watery feathers, it was able to take notes in clay stone.

"Yes, there we go." The goddess stepped closer, and Marduk was ready to smite her with lightning if she tried to harm the spirit, but she only traced her finger under the confused elemental's chin. "They say that water has memory. Strange, but apparently, it does. And here you have a living river that makes records for you. Now...what do you remember about the rivers in Ancient Rome? What did they use to dispose of in the Tiber?"

"Why are you bringing up Rome?" Marduk growled.

"Oh, I'm sure you remember," she giggled. "If I can, so can you. All those little babies?"

Marduk dismissed the spirit back into the Aether. "That has nothing to do with me!"

"Oh, but it does!" The goddess whispered. "It has everything to do with civilization. In Rome, they were drowned. In the East, I think they were...buried alive? And then there's Baal—"

"No!" Marduk lashed out at the goddess with his mace, but she merely slithered out of his reach.

"Haha! Don't you see?" She smiled, her teeth now with the fangs of a lioness. "You're no longer necessary for these people, and now they'll turn to other gods. Gods that don't require them to have self-control. Gods that don't make them take personal responsibility. Why be diligent and clean your home, when you can just live in your own filth? Why be reasonable when logic doesn't entitle you to the things you want? Don't want to be chaste? Sleep around and have an unwanted baby? Just dump it in the river! After all, each one is a sacrifice in my name!"

At this point, she had grown to twice her original size. Hair extended from every visible part of her body, her feet had become talons, and her hands claws. A pair of feathered wings like an owl's extended from her back.

"You asked me what I have to brag about?" She roared. "It's the fact that there is nothing you can build that I can't take from you! You want peace, then I will bring war! You want to bring the best out of people? I will make them monsters! For I am Lamashtu – I am evil itself! This oasis you've made, this sanctuary from the barbarism of nature? It will become hell! And the worst perdition will fall upon those who try to push back; those that cling to virtue will be the most tormented. But..." she chuckled. "Why am I explaining this to you? You know better than I! How many times have we already had this conversation? I can't remember, but you can."

Marduk didn't answer, but Lamashtu could read his expression.

"Ahahahah!" The monster roared. "You're not even going to argue, or swing your little club at me, are you? Let me guess, you've tried all that before, and none of it ever worked? Then I'm right when I say I don't need to teach you about hell. You're already there, aren't you?"

That laughter. Marduk had heard his aunt's laughter more times than he could count. And, for the first time in centuries, he wished he could return to the void of unconsciousness, where gods go when they are forgotten by mortals.

78

Is This Thing On?

DAURGO

"I equip the Moon Princess with Skimpy Warrior Women's Bikini Armor." Konshu placed his equipment card on top of his Moon Princess monster. "She gets five hundred extra life and two thousand additional attack."

"You've just activated my trap card." Daurgo revealed the spell card he'd placed facedown. "Confetti Confusion. Your Moon Princess's armor explodes into confetti. Lose the equipment, and your monster is too confused to act this round."

Frustrated, Konshu removed the Skimpy Warrior Women's Bikini Armor from play and turned the Moon Princess sideways. "My Blue-Eyed Moon Dragon..." he looked at his options for a moment.

"He can attack and destroy my Undead Clown," Daurgo admitted. "But he won't have enough attack left to destroy the Clown Car this turn, even with his special ability to split his attack to hit three separate monsters. You won't have the attack power left to kill the car and the Undead Clown. And you can't attack me without getting passed my monsters."

Konshu fiddled with his hand for a moment. "My Blue-Eyed Moon Dragon kills the clown anyway. I've got nothing else this turn."

Daurgo drew his next hand and placed a new Undead Clown in front of his Zombie Clown Car. "I play Exploding Zombie." Daurgo placed a monster card depicting a zombie with dynamite sticks poking out of its flesh next to his

Undead Clown. "This card can be used as a spell instead of a monster. Instead of fighting, he charges at one of your monsters and explodes, killing it and a monster with up to three times its life value." The lich pointed at Konshu's field. "Which means, your Moon Princess."

The moon god sighed and placed his monster in the graveyard as Daurgo placed the Exploding Zombie into his own.

"And then I play Call of the Grave." Daurgo put down his final spell card. "For every monster in your graveyard, I summon a Skeletal Puppet at the cost of two hundred of my own life per monster."

Konshu went through his graveyard and counted the number of defeated monster cards. "Nine monsters."

"Nine Skeletal Puppets," Daurgo placed several dummy cards out in front of his field. "At the cost of eighteen hundred life. Now, with the aid of my zombie clown, we kill your Blue-Eyed Moon Dragon and deal five hundred life damage to you."

Grumbling, Konshu looked at his hand for options, but he only had two cards. Apparently, neither of them could stop the undead horde. "Are you done?" He finally asked.

"Yes," Daurgo replied.

"Good," Konshu laid one of his cards down. "I can play this before drawing – Strength of the Moon. I recover one hundred life for each monster in my graveyard. I then play Arcane Explosion. At the beginning of my next turn, you take one hundred damage for every spell card in your discard."

"Carnival Hall of Magic Mirrors," Daurgo flipped over one of his trap cards. "The effect of your spell hits you, not me."

"Do you have some kind of control card for everything I cast?" Konshu growled.

"Can't spell 'control' without 'troll,'" Daurgo replied. "Well, kind of. And really, don't blame me just because you're not good at this card game for children. I would have been happy gambling over Senet, or Nine Men's Morris."

"But how do you always seem to have exactly what you need to counter my deck—"

"I don't." The skeleton shook its head. "I'm not playing against your deck. I'm playing against you, the god of the moon. The god who looks down on all the world and thinks himself above it all, and never expects mere mortals to reach him. Your entire deck is built around a handful of really powerful monsters and some supporting minions, with no flexibility for when the big monsters are unavailable. You have no idea what to do if someone actually manages to reach you and plant their flag on your face."

Pointing to the cards on the table, Daurgo placed a new card facedown. "Unholy Enervation. My undead minions gain one hundred extra attack this turn. Now they swing and attack your health. You're down to fifteen hundred life, and at the start of your turn, your spell goes off and kills you."

Konshu looked at his cards again in bewilderment. "No...that's..."

"That's game." Daurgo folded his hand. "And that's three wins, zero losses. You owe me three hours."

Sighing, the moon god folded his hand and took out a small, empty hourglass. Touching it with his finger, he filled the bottom half with sand. "Very well. Three hours of moonlight, to be used at a time of your choosing. And you understand that this is just the idea of the moon?"

"Yes, yes, you can skip the formalities." Daurgo tucked his card deck back into his robes. "No meteorological effects, etcetera."

"Then our business is concluded." Konshu handed the skeleton the hourglass. "Now, get out."

Returning the skeleton back to the material plane, Daurgo looked over the hourglass.

"Alright, what's left?" He looked over the plans he'd drawn earlier. "I need to get those crates delivered throughout the empire, and soon Aquila will have delivered my device. Then we can get started."

A few days later, Aquila returned. "Alright, I'm back. Dare I ask what that contraption was you had me deliver?"

"The latest in communication technology," Daurgo chuckled. "Except, it's more of a reinvention than a new invention."

"Wait, seriously?" Aquila asked. "You sent me to deliver a machine that will help you send more messages to the emperor? What for?"

"Oh, no. Just one message. But it'll be a verbal one, not handwritten." The lich pulled out another machine exactly like the one he'd sent with Aquila. "Let's see if they're listening."

Daurgo turned a crank and adjusted dials until he could to get some sort of static noise from his makeshift radio. The one he'd given to Aquila was fixed with only one channel, so they were tuned in to his machine even if they didn't know it.

"...and that's why we believe at the Institute of Theurgy that this proposal is just," a elderly woman's voice came through the radio speaker. "For the betterment of the empire, its socio-economic relations, and to calm racial tensions, this grant for Empyrian and impoverished students should receive imperial funding."

"Excuse me," a man's voice chimed in. "But what power are we to use to justify this expense? Where in our nation's constitution does it say we have the authority to spend taxpayer money like this?"

"We believe that the nation's constitution should not be your primary concern," the woman's voice sounded more irritated. She was clearly older than the man who had questioned her. "The purpose of a document like that should be to protect and provide for the citizens of the empire, not to keep them from education."

A few murmurs in the background rose and Daurgo could make out at least one person saying "the constitution doesn't say anything about providing for citizens."

"Why give money specifically to Empyrians?" Another voice asked. "Why not make it a grant to people who are too poor to pay for school? It doesn't make sense to fund a wealthy Empyrian student when there are impoverished Borealans and Coptics seeking an education."

"What treasury is this supposed to come out of?" A third voice added. "If it isn't benefiting people based on the amount they pay in property tax, it can't be the property treasury. If it doesn't help people based on the income tax they pay, it can't come the income treasury. Can we really justify it under the sales treasury?"

"This is a bill meant to help people!" The older woman sounded furious now. If Daurgo had a stomach, he'd be eating popcorn to this. "If we don't pass this grant proposal, how will the stupid monkey people be able to afford tuition?"

"...what did you just say?" One of the other voices asked.

"How will the super unlucky people be able to afford tuition?" The woman replied.

"This has been extremely entertaining to listen to," Daurgo said into a microphone. "But I'm afraid I'm on a bit of a schedule."

"Who said that?" People on the other side muttered in confusion. "Where is that coming from?"

"Over here, from the machine that was delivered to the palace," Daurgo replied. "This thing is called a radio."

Daurgo could hear someone picking up the radio on the other end of the call and bringing it towards the others in the room, their mutterings growing louder as it got closer.

"Ah, that's better," Daurgo mused. "You can all hear me now, I presume?"

"Who are you?" This was a new voice, much more authoritative than any of the others.

"I am Daurgo, the dracolich that attacked your city a few months ago. Do I have the honor of addressing Emperor Andreas Charvette?"

"Very funny," the authoritative voice replied. "And tell me, how do we know that you are, in fact, the same dracolich that attacked during the Grand Wizard Tournament and not some prankster?"

"Can't I be both?" The lich retorted.

"It's probably him," one of the other voices muttered. "No one else is that cocky." Several others murmured in agreement.

"Then why have you sent us this...contraption? As the emperor, I should have every one of your machinations destroyed on sight."

"Where would the fun in that be?" Daurgo chuckled. "I've sent you this device so I could inform you that I have something very special planned for your capital city. I don't usually operate in the same city twice in such a short period of time, but...what can I say, I like the view!"

"What!" The emperor and several others gasped. "Another undead invasion?"

"I never said that," Daurgo replied.

"We need every gun in the city aimed at the sky!" One of the other voices cried. "We've got to be ready shoot his cans of corpses down before they land!"

"Our cemeteries are all outside the wall," another added. "We could reinforce every ward we have to keep him from animating our dead!"

"The amount of revenue the city– no, the nation lost from his last terrorist attack – we can't afford another!"

"Okay, you're really twisting my arm here," Daurgo tapped his microphone with a bony finger. "I suppose I *might* be able to release an army of flesh-hungry zombies in your city to eat all of your brains. No promises, though. And you have to be on your best behavior," he added in a sing-songy voice.

"We need to evacuate the city!" One of the men shouted.

"Are you mad? We'd cause a panic!"

"But if we don't–"

"Okay, you bean-counters are really killing all the fun here, you know that?" Daurgo growled. "Look, in the near future, at a time of my choosing, I'm going to throw a party in your city."

"A party?" An older voice with traces of senility asked. "What kind?"

"Let's just say it'll be to die for," Daurgo continued. "But if you're so concerned, perhaps you should pray to whichever gods you worship to intervene on your behalf. Goodness knows they did so well facing me at your little magic sports festival. If you're lucky, it'll just be your capital city."

Daurgo laughed as he heard the terrified bureaucrats running around like disorganized chickens before turning off his radio.

"Why are you warning them that you're going to attack?" Aquila asked. "Wasn't the element of surprise a big part of your plan last time?"

"Of course it was," Daurgo chuckled. "That's why it's so important that I do without it now. I need to show the gods of this city that I can grind them into paste even when they know I'm coming."

Taking out a sheet of paper on which he'd drawn his plans, he went through and checked that everything was all set.

"Do we have the fish loaded and ready?" The lich asked his assistant.

"Yes," Aquila sighed. "They're on trains to be delivered to all the cities you requested. In ice cars warded to keep them cold and fresh. Why did you need me to organize that?"

"To keep them fooled," the lich replied. "Just because I want them to know that I'm coming doesn't mean I want them to know everything I have planned. I'll show them that I'm one step ahead of everyone else."

"Got the golden frying pan, the confetti, music, moonlight, and even the hallucinogenics." Daurgo laughed as he checked off the last items on his list. "Now I just need to give them time to prepare their best defenses."

79

Secret Wrestling

EPHORAH

Holding the blade in her hand, Ephorah's arm screamed at her to let it drop. But the assignment for fencing practice was to hold her sword up and extended from her body as long as possible to strengthen her muscles and stamina.

"It has been two minutes," her instructor called out. "Keep those swords up!"

Around her, several students had already dropped their arms. Ephorah's elbow buckled and she struggled to keep it up, but her arm wouldn't listen to her as she tried to straighten it out.

Professor Rashaa Kabir was a woman who taught some of the elective classes at the Institute of Theurgy, which mostly meant she couldn't find a job with her degree. She was also tall, and had the kind of muscles one would expect from a sword training instructor. Ephorah wondered if that had kept her from finding an MRS degree as a backup plan.

Finally, Ephorah's arm completely gave out and she dropped her arm, her training sword clanging against the floor.

"Pretty pathetic," Kabir looked over the rest of the class. It was entirely made up of girls from the Institute of Theurgy. Technically, students from any university were allowed to join. Even students from the Hadesh School of Architecture and the Engineering Academy could apply, but their schools had to pay a fee for each student who attended the class, so they didn't tend to advertise it much.

The professor sighed. "How many of you are only here because you want to learn how to use an enchanted sword?"

Every student raised their hand.

"And how many of you already made some magical sword that you don't know how to use?"

Ephorah kept her hand raised. She glanced around and saw she was the only one.

"I see." The professor eyed Ephorah. "This class is meant to teach you how to use a sword in general. It won't be tailored to your specific enchantment. Perhaps you should see me after class."

The rest of the course was focused on how to properly hold a sword. The instructor noted that different swords needed to be held in different ways, and that you wouldn't try to wield a falchion the same way you'd hold a gladius. But the training rapiers seemed similar enough to the officer sword that Ephorah had enchanted that she wasn't too worried about it.

Once the class had ended, Ephorah went up to Professor Kabir's desk. There was something about Kabir that made Ephorah instinctively put on her strength gloves. It was probably the fact that Kabir was two heads taller than Ephorah tall and had arm muscles that could bench press a crocodile.

"Ah, the girl who makes swords without training," Kabir folded her arms, but her expression wasn't threatening. "Hang on, haven't I heard of you before?"

Ephorah shook her head. "Don't think so."

"Hold up," the professor looked down at her student attendance book. "Ephorah el-Sabet. You're the one that the others in the faculty were going on about. The one who discovered a new sigil."

"Oh, yeah," Ephorah admitted. "You meant that."

"Impressive work. And the sword you made...is that one that includes the new sigil?"

Ephorah nodded.

"You should bring it here next class period. If you're worried about knowing how to use a powerful weapon, let me see the kind of sword you used as the base. Then we'll–"

"Kabir!" Professor Massouh barged into the room.

"So help me," the fencing instructor growled. "I am not going to sit on–"

"The headmistress is calling all staff to the faculty room," he panted. "There's some sort of emergency."

"What kind of emergency?" Kabir asked.

Massouh eyed Ephorah. "The kind we can't talk about in front of a student."

"Ugh." Kabir rubbed her eyes with her exceptionally large palms before looking back at Ephorah. "Listen, I'm always happy to talk to girls who aren't just in my class hoping to find an MRS degree. Come back during my office hours and I'll give you some one-on-one training for that sword you made."

The professors hurriedly left Ephorah alone in the training room.

"Oh, like I'm going to just let that go," Ephorah thought aloud as she snuck after the professors.

Careful not to be heard, Ephorah followed the two professors to their faculty room. She had a rough idea of where the faculty room was, but she'd never felt the need to seek it out before.

Ephorah was aware that in a school of wizards, there could be alarms or other systems meant to keep students from eavesdropping on the staff. Was it really worth the risk to figure out whatever they were worried about? She hung at the end of the hallway away from the room for a moment.

"Some sort of remote talking machine?" Ephorah overheard a voice coming from the faculty room.

"Yes, like a speaking tube, but it wasn't connected to anything!" That was the headmistress's voice.

"That's...I've never heard of magic that can do that," Professor Massouh added.

These voices were loud enough for Ephorah to hear from the hallway, but she needed to get closer if she wanted all the details. She'd learned from Namid that if you want to eavesdrop on someone, you do not block their only exit by sticking your ear against the door. Ephorah only knew of one door to the faculty room, so she'd need to find another eavesdropping point.

The faculty room was on the first floor, so all she had to do was go around to the courtyard and listen from the outside window. Huddling against the wall below the window, she kept her body low enough that anyone who glanced outside wouldn't be able to see her.

"The dragon had technology that seemed advanced," a professor's voice added. "I think he even did something from the arena that called in those big metal containers full of corpses. I could see him having some sort of remote-communication device."

"It was Daurgo's voice!" The headmistress announced. "Garbled, but it sounded exactly like him! And he declared that he was going to attack the city again!"

"Dear gods..."

Out in the courtyard, Ephorah noticed a windbag that was out cleaning the grounds. It had removed the glove from its right hand and was now sucking up autumn leaves that had fallen from trees. Ephorah crawled along the edge of the wall behind a bush where the elemental wouldn't see her.

"Why would he just...announce that he's coming like that?" One professor asked. Ephorah was no longer focused on which instructors were talking.

"I have no idea," the headmistress replied.

"Because he's nuts!" Another said. "Why else would he do half the things he does?"

Out in the courtyard, the windbag had finished sucking up all of the leaves, and was now in the process of trimming bushes. Ephorah scooted away from her current bush and realized it might be time for her to leave.

"He even told us to pray to whichever gods we worship to try and stop him," the headmistress said.

"You see what I mean!" This voice was unmistakably Professor Meir. "We cannot afford to be godless anymore. If that dracolich attacks again, we will have no divine protection for our school. Do you think we can handle the rebuilding costs?"

As Ephorah tried to inch her way to the nearest exit, the windbag suddenly glanced up at the suspicious-looking student who was right next to the wall of the faculty room. The elemental had no visible mouth, but it pointed at her with bright, glowing opals for eyes and waved at the professors inside the faculty room to get their attention.

As the spirit tried to alert the faculty, Ephorah tackled the elemental, trying to squeeze it with all her might. She tried to focus all the pressure into her arms, which were enhanced by her gloves and came up to just below her shoulders, but it was like trying to wrestle a miniature tornado in a burlap sack. The spirit writhed and bucked, trying to throw Ephorah off as she squeezed its arms together.

"We don't need to worry about property destruction," the headmistress argued. "We have insurance."

"Have you *paid* the insurance?" Meir hissed.

Ephorah didn't hear a response from the headmistress, but that might have been because she was hanging onto the windbag for dear life. The thing tried to gain some height by floating off the ground, but Ephorah headbutted the sackcloth hood that covered its head, disorienting it enough to fall back to earth.

As Ephorah wrestled on the ground with the elemental, the professors continued bickering, like they didn't notice the struggle outside.

"This is why we need to accept that goddess's offer!" Meir shouted. "We're better off having her, then having none look after us!"

"Eh, she might be right about this one," another professor offered. It might have been Maroun. "It's not like we have to go completely public about our new patron."

Ephorah squeezed the windbag harder, desperately trying to think of a way out of this situation. As she did, the sackcloth ripped, and the air elemental burst out of its work outfit like a tube of toothpaste, leaves exploding everywhere. Confused, Ephorah looked around for the air elemental that was now a whirling vortex of leaves and dust in the rough shape of a human upper torso. It floated above Ephorah and tried to wave to get the staff's attention again.

"Oh, no you don't!" Ephorah clapped her hands together above her head at full force, right in front of the elemental. With the strength of ten men, the resulting sonic boom was enough to sunder the windbag, who floated helplessly to the ground.

Unfortunately, it was also enough to snap the faculty out of their argument and look at the girl fighting an air elemental in the courtyard. Ephorah could hear some of them shout "stay right there!" before leaving the room to come and deal with her. She only had a few seconds to come up with an explanation.

"Sorry about this," Ephorah said as soon as two faculty members entered the room. She wasn't familiar with either teacher. "Wind blew some leaves off a tree into my face, and the windbag was in the middle of sucking up leaves. Thing went haywire, and started attacking me." Ephorah gestured to the leaves that had fallen all over her when the windbag's outfit had burst.

The two professors gave each other quizzical looks. There was a chance Ephorah was telling the truth. An elemental can act oddly if it's following orders that get into conflict with one another, like "collect leaves from the courtyard" and "don't bother the students." Sometimes the elemental doesn't know which command to follow and which to ignore.

"So, why did you knock the elemental out?" One professor pointed to the air elemental collapsed on the ground.

"Well, it wouldn't leave me alone," Ephorah replied. "And have you ever tried to fight a living bag of air? Not a lot works on them."

The professors looked at each other again and winced. It was better to let the student go than risk a lawsuit.

"Are you alright then?" The other professor asked.

Ephorah nodded. "I've got to get going, though. I'll miss my bus."

"Of course, of course," the professors waved her away. "Run along."

And with that, Ephorah left the campus, processing what she'd overheard.

80

Final Preparations

ROSTAM

"So, you're here for three more days?" Namid asked Rostam across the card table. "Long shore leave."

"Yeah," Rostam admitted as he looked at his hand. "We had some trouble with our last job. My captain is trying to get the College of Alchemy to cough up hazard pay. I don't know if she'll succeed, but I'm keeping an eye out for job prospects for now."

"Shame you didn't bring Cindrocles again," Amri played a card. "He was fun."

Rostam chuckled. "Yeah, but he set a lot of your aunt's flowers on fire, so…"

A pounding at the door interrupted their game. Amri set his cards down on the table to go check on it while Rostam thought he saw Namid slip a card into her hand from her sleeve.

As soon as Amri opened the door, Rostam and Namid could hear frantic yelling that sounded like Ephorah's voice.

"Probably should go check on that." Rostam slid his chair back and got up, while Namid leaned back in her seat holding a glass of water and made a face that read "do I really have to?"

At the front door to Amri and Namid's house, Ephorah was in an exhausted panic, yelling so fast that nobody could understand her. Amri was clearly in over his head, trying to calm her down.

"Ephorah, slow down!" Amri looked to the others for help.

"Hang on, let me try something." Namid walked up to Ephorah and threw the water from her glass into the panicked girl's face.

Freezing with a look of confusion, Ephorah stopped raving long enough to glare at Namid while the boys pulled her into the foyer of the house.

"Okay," Namid crossed her arms in satisfaction. "Now, start from the beginning."

"I'm gonna kill you," Ephorah wiped the water from her face before starting up again. "The dracolich is going to attack the city again!"

Namid shook her head. "That doesn't sound like the beginning."

"Look, I was at the theurgy school," Ephorah explained. "They had some kind of emergency faculty meaning. So, I went over to eavesdrop."

"Nice," Namid nodded. "I've taught you well."

"Then the headmistress came in and said that after going to the imperial palace to convince the government to do a grant fund for Empyrian students, the dracolich that attacked during the Grand Wizard Tournament announced he would attack the city again! And then there was some political junk about not paying the insurance and wanting to worship a new patron god now that Marduk left."

"Okay..." Rostam tried to filter the important parts out of that speech. "So the dracolich...announced he was coming? Wasn't the last time a surprise attack or something?"

"He's doing something different this time," Ephorah replied. "Something that might involve armies of zombies eating people in the streets. We have to do something."

"Why hasn't there been any formal word from the government about this?" Amri asked.

"Isn't it obvious? To prevent people from panicking." Namid scratched her head. "Okay, so do we know when the lich will strike, or what part of the city? Because I know a guy who can get us some carts if we want to get in on looting the Market District once the zombies attack."

Rostam glared at Namid. "Not helping. But...it would be good to know when and where he'll attack."

Ephorah shook her head. "We don't know. The lich didn't announce where he'd attack, only that he would. He's deliberately making the city raise their guard before he strikes. Maybe he wants us to panic, or something. I don't know."

"Looters could probably use some wizards to keep zombies off their backs." Namid shrugged. "Just saying."

"So...we should be warning as many people as possible?" Amri asked.

"I don't think so," Rostam rubbed his chin. "If we did, there'd be riots. And that's if people believed us. All we have to go on is what Ephorah heard from a meeting she wasn't supposed to be listening to, and that meeting probably wasn't even supposed to happen in the first place. I'm pretty sure the headmistress would never have found out about all of this if she hadn't been in the palace with all of those bureaucrats when the dragon...wait, what did you say she was doing again?"

"Trying to get the government to fund a grant for Empyrian students," Ephorah replied. "Specifically, students who can't afford tuition."

"Wait, what?" Namid closed one eye and made a "thinking face." "Why only Empyrian students? And why just the theurgy institute?"

"It's a reward for potentially saving the school." Ephorah tilted her head in a sort of submission. "I'm not exactly happy with what they're using it for, but the school discovered a new way of controlling elementals that might be a huge shift in artifact enchantments and other stuff thanks to me. So, as a way of saying 'thank you,' they're going to try and get the government to fund tuition for Empyrians who can't afford it."

"Um...isn't that..." Amri blinked a few times. "I think that's against the law. Or the imperial constitution. Or something. I don't think the government is allowed to do race-based laws."

"Well, originally we agreed to focus the grant on poor people in general," Ephorah admitted. "But I did specify that I wanted the money to help Empyrians, specifically. It sounds like the headmistress decided to push for the grant to be aimed at Empyrians."

"Yeah, but there's a lot of other people who are equally poor who are going to be short-shafted," Amri countered.

"Oh, don't complain." Ephorah scowled. "You're living with your rich aunt and uncle. You'll be fine for tuition! You probably didn't even need a student loan!"

"Yeah, I'm not jealous, I just don't know if I like the principle," Amri shook his head. "It doesn't affect me, but I don't like the idea of the government making a law based on race. They won't stop at one."

"Do you know if it'll pass?" Namid asked.

"No," Ephorah admitted. "I think they rescheduled the discussion because of the dragon's threat."

"All right," Namid shrugged. "But if it doesn't, and you're already set on taking other people's money to pay for tuition, I could save you a spot on the looting cart."

Ephorah clenched her fists. "That is not the same!"

"Eh, it kind of is," Rostam added.

"No, it isn't," Ephorah huffed. "First, I am not the only person who would be getting government money. All Empyrians would."

"I won't," Rostam replied. "I'm not studying theurgy. And I pay taxes."

"Well, that was your choice," Ephorah hissed. "And second, the bureaucrats are mostly elector counts, who people voted into office. The emperor gets the final say on the project, but he only gets to stay in office if the elector counts don't vote to have him removed. So every step in this process has people voting for it. If the counts pass the grant, it's only because people voted to give them that power in the first place."

Rostam shook his head. "That isn't the same."

"Why are you so opposed to something that's meant to help poor people?" Ephorah asked. "Do you just hate helping poor people?"

Amri raised an eyebrow. "Is this thing supposed to help poor people or Empyrians? Not all Empyrians are poor. You were able to get money for tuition without help."

"I have a student loan," Ephorah snapped. "That's different. And anyways, this is meant to help make the empire give our people the respect they deserve. If the empire respects wizards and people with degrees, then this is for the best."

Rostam wanted to argue further, but there was no point. Wizards with degrees.

"So..." Amri changed the subject. "What do we do now?"

"We stay alert," Rostam replied. "We make sure we're ready at a moment's notice."

Namid frowned. "We can't be on guard all the time."

"No, and if we are, people will notice." Amri rubbed his eyes. "Guys, we can't handle this alone. We have to tell someone."

"Agreed, but who?" Rostam asked. "You going to run to one of the mercenary companies and tell them?"

"No, he's going to run to his friends at the abbey." Namid rolled her eyes. "Like they're going to be able to do anything."

Amri gave his sister a scowl, and Rostam realized he'd never seen him look at anyone like that before.

"Amri's new friends aside, who else can we talk to?" Rostam looked around. "I can tell my captain and the crew; they've seen weirder things already."

"I'm telling Cyrus," Namid added. Then her eyes widened and drifted towards Ephorah, who looked at her in confusion.

"Who's Cyrus?" Ephorah asked.

"Um..." Namid looked away and rubbed the back of her head nervously. "A friend. From the College of Alchemy."

"He boarded passage on *the Endurance*," Rostam added before Ephorah could ask more questions. "He ended up helping me fight off a ghoul on our last trip, and he studies medical alchemy, so we might need him."

"...Okay..." Ephorah looked like she was suspicious of something, but not certain what was going on. Rostam thanked any gods responsible that Cyrus didn't have a more traditionally Borealan-sounding name. When did they all have to start walking on eggshells around Ephorah?

"So, we have a plan, then?" Amri looked around. "Ephorah, why don't you go on and warn your family? They'll listen to you, right?"

Ephorah nodded. "Yeah. They probably will."

A shadow suddenly loomed overhead. All four friends looked up at a battleship floating above the city. This was a vessel so massive, held aloft not only with hot air balloons, but tanks of helium refilled by air elementals, and with enough weight to the vessel itself that it could carry heavy cannons along the prow. If any smaller airship tried to fire guns like that, the recoil would shake the ship so much it might tip over in the sky.

"That...is a big warship." A strong wave of awe hit Rostam at the sight of such a vessel; it was larger than anything he'd likely ever board, and even if he did...does the captain think he's in control of such a beast? Or is he just another cog in the wheels that keep the thing airborne?

"They're mobilizing the military," Namid whispered. "They might try to pass it off as some kind of parade, or a show of the empire's might...but we know different, don't we?"

Rostam nodded. "We don't have a lot of time."

81

Alchemical Healing

CYRUS

In a large, open laboratory room, Professor Kagan took a mouse from a small terrarium and secured it against a set of leather restraints. Once it was stuck and unable to move, Kagan cut off the mouse's tail with a pair of scissors. Cyrus and the rest of the class looked closely, a few students wincing as the mouse squeaked in pain.

"Now, the mouse's tail will die in a few seconds." Professor Kagan checked his watch. The mouse tail twitched for a moment longer, but it finally stopped moving.

"There we go," Kagan placed the tail next to the secured mouse, clapped his hands, and reattached the tail. The tissue of the mouse tail reconnected to the stump, but it didn't move. The mouse continued to squeak in pain, but nothing happened. The tail was still dead.

"As you can see, reconnecting dead tissue to a live organism doesn't bring the dead parts back to life," the professor explained. "No alchemist, no matter how skilled, can bring life to dead or inert matter. When a piece of an animal or person has been removed from the rest of the body, there's a very short window of opportunity to reconnect it before it dies. Once that happens, there's no fixing it."

"Now, there are ways of slowing down the process of death for the severed parts," the professor continued as another wizard carrying a large wooden box walked into the laboratory. This new wizard had odd, frizzy hair, stormed into the room with a sense of importance and purpose, and appeared to be in the process of regrowing his eyebrows.

"I have done it!" The new professor slammed the wooden box down on the table. Mysterious honking could be heard inside. "The latest great breakthrough in chimera research!"

"You!" Professor Kagan's face turned red with rage. "Professor Malouf, you are in violation of your restraining order! You are not allowed within ten meters of this campus!"

The other professor, whom Cyrus assumed must have been Malouf, looked around the room for a moment. "This isn't the Hadesh School of Architecture. I'm certain the restraining order said I was not allowed near the architects' university."

"That was a different restraining order!" Kagan fumed. "You tried your hand at chimerafication, and your flying pigs full of hydrogen gas set the building on fire! Repeatedly! Every time they broke wind!"

"Indeed!" Professor Malouf gave Kagan a very proud smile, seemingly ignoring the class of confused students. "And what about the cows I fused with cocoa beans? Brown cows that can produce chocolate milk!"

"It tasted terrible," Kagan hissed. "You don't add the chocolate before you pasteurize the milk! Your chimeras are a disgrace, you belong in an asylum, and if you don't get off this campus immediately, I'm calling for security to drag you off to jail!"

Professor Malouf looked around at the students, finally realizing they were there. For a moment, it looked like he was genuinely upset and having a brief moment of clarity.

"I'm interrupting a class, aren't I?" Dejected, Malouf made his way towards the door. "I'm sorry. Just...keep the chimera. Consider it a gift to the sciences. I'll see myself out."

As he left, Professor Kagan kept a close eye on him, even going up to the door and watching the professor in the hallway to make sure he was leaving. "I'm sorry about that," Kagan closed the door behind him.

"Who was that guy?" A student asked.

"A dangerous maniac with a long history of disastrous experiments," Kagan came up to the box that Malouf had left behind. Opening a latch on the top, he looked down at the chimera inside. Carefully, he picked up what appeared to be a five-headed goose, each confused head honking in different directions.

"What the hell are we supposed to do with this?" Professor Kagan held the creature up for a moment before putting it back in the box.

"So, was he like...an alchemist?" Another student asked.

"Not exactly," Kagan sighed. "Professor Malouf is the teacher of Magical Safety at the Academy of Sorcerers. Although he's primarily a sorcerer, he's the sort to try and combine alchemy with his line of wizardry, which would be fine if he wasn't a deranged lunatic."

Cyrus thought about that for a moment before raising his own hand to ask a question. "Is that normal? To combine sorcery and alchemy? I haven't heard of many wizards who do that."

"It isn't normal," Kagan admitted. "Alchemy as a field of magic is heavily focused around hard sciences and logic. For example, if I add a specific amount of ammonia to an amount of nitrogen, I can expect a specific amount of ammonium nitrate as a result. This is why our patron god has always been Thoth, the god of logic and reason."

"But sorcery involves a lot of places where logic fails," Kagan continued. "The field tends to split into wizards who can understand the scientific principles of their craft, but struggle to actually cast any spells, and wizards who are good at putting those principles into practice, but have difficulty discovering their own. 'Thinkers' and 'doers,' if you will. For a sorcerer to be able to cast their own spells and understand alchemy, they need to be both a thinker *and* a doer. Those people are rather rare, and they usually have a screw loose. And now..." the professor looked back at the goose chimera. "I'm going to end class early so I can make sure he's left the campus. And to go figure out what to do with a five-headed goose."

Places where logic fails, Cyrus thought to himself. Ever since he'd joined the College of Alchemy – no, ever since he'd first met Thoth, he had assumed logic and reason had the answer to every problem. Where were the places logic didn't work? No...he knew plenty of places where reason didn't solve things. Reason couldn't convince people that a tournament was fair if the "wrong person" won the final match. Reason couldn't get you out of jail if there were political reasons to keep you in prison, regardless of whether you'd done anything wrong. And reason couldn't solve the problem of whether it was okay to torture one person to save five more.

Making his way to the cafeteria for his job shift, Cyrus continued to ponder this in the back of the bakery until Inna called him from the front.

"There's someone asking for you," she smiled. "A cute girl, by the way."

Cyrus took off his oven mitts and apron and went around to the counter, where Namid was waiting.

"We need to talk," she said.

"Can it wait until my shift is over?" Cyrus asked.

"Yeah, yeah," Namid rolled her eyes. "There's just...a problem. I...can't invite you to our house tonight to discuss it."

"Why not?" Cyrus raised an eyebrow.

"Look, my brother, Rostam and I...have a friend, who has told us about something big that's happening. Soon. But if she sees you, I don't think we'll get anything done."

"Uh-huh." Cyrus had a fairly good idea of what was going on. "And what do you suggest?"

"Do you work tomorrow at lunch?"

Cyrus shook his head.

"Then meet me for lunch tomorrow. I'll fill you in on the details."

With that, Namid walked away. Cyrus turned back to his work, ignoring the confused Inna behind the counter.

"Was that supposed to be flirting?" Inna asked. "It didn't look like—"

"Inna," Cyrus turned his head towards her. "Just let me get back to work."

After he'd finished his shift, Cyrus had his second class of the day: Introduction to Genetics.

"Whether it's chimerafication you intend to study, or simply medical alchemy, genetics are an essential component of a bio-alchemist's work." Professor Basara explained how an alchemist could use the DNA structure of an organism to knit matter back into place and close wounds, something Cyrus had already learned and even put into practice from Doctor Monroe.

When the class was over, Cyrus dropped off his books in his dorm. He had a lot of homework to do, and his shifts at the bakery meant he couldn't do any of it during the break between classes. But even still, he had something else he needed to do first.

The College of Alchemy maintained a shrine dedicated to their patron god. It wasn't seeing much use lately, due to the fact that everyone in the city now knew Thoth had been killed during the dragon attack, but it was still open for students to use.

Cyrus had never been here before; he'd never needed to. Before the Grand Wizard Tournament, Thoth had regularly come to him. Cyrus sort of understood that, as an idea, he could be in multiple places at once, and so after a while, he stopped feeling like he was taking up the god's time. Once, he'd asked Thoth if he had nothing better to do than to train some stupid kid, and Thoth had replied that there was nothing more important than guiding people who wanted to improve. Now that the shrine was empty of students, and, Cyrus felt, empty of its dead god, feelings of guilt at having gotten to train under Thoth oozed back up inside the boy like mud overflowing from a bog.

The shrine itself was a small room with simple wooden pews, candles that hadn't been lit much as of late, and a stone statue of Thoth in his ibis-headed form at the center. The shrine had no offering plate; it wasn't for making sacrifices. This wasn't a temple with clergy to staff it.

Crossing his legs as he sat on the floor across from the statue, Cyrus closed his eyes and tried to meditate on Thoth. He had no real idea what he was doing; he hadn't tried to contact the god this way before, and he didn't actually expect him to answer. But that wasn't the point.

Is this prayer? Cyrus mused. *To a god I know can't hear me? Maybe it's just meditation. Not the point. I keep trying to convince myself logically that what I did in Doctor Monroe's lab was the right thing to do, but it's like I'm spinning wheels in the sand without any traction. I don't even think I'm trying to figure out what the right thing to do was. I'm just trying to reason myself into a clear conscience.*

Maybe that's why I can't get anywhere with it.

Opening his eyes, Cyrus looked up at the statue of Thoth. He'd heard alchemists describe the Philosopher's Stone, and how it could only be found if lost or made by a scientist who wanted to have it but had no desire to use it. Now, Cyrus felt that the moral roadblock he was stuck in worked the same way; he couldn't find the answer as long as he was trying to justify his own actions.

82

Dispatch of the Gods

HORUS

Gods play politics, just like humans. As above, so below.

When human politics get complicated, divine politics follow suit. If human kings and clergy start backstabbing and usurping one another, the gods do the same.

But every now and then, human politics become curiously simple. And divine politics, in turn, become simple. Sometimes, so simple that they bring in allies from a neighboring pantheon.

"The dragon...*announced* he would attack again?" Nergal, the Babylonian god of war and plagues, sat in council with the Egyptian war host, along with Marduk, Enlil, Enki, Adad, and Ereshkigal. They sat across from Horus, Sobek, Isis, Sekhmet, Bast, and Ptah around a large table with a layout of the city of Hadesh.

"Indeed." Horus placed several letters that Daurgo had snuck into offering plates on the table and presented them to the other gods. "The dracolich has been sending us taunts ever since we failed to apprehend him in the Blasted Wastes. Now he's moved on to threatening mortals as well."

"This is a challenge," Marduk said as Enki looked over some of the letters. "The dragon knows that alerting the mortals will alert us as well. This is his way of throwing down the gauntlet."

"Agreed," Horus nodded. "It cannot go unanswered. If the mortals expect their gods to protect them at all, it has to be now. No god with any significant following in Hadesh can ignore this without the mortals losing faith."

Isis sat next to Horus on the war council. "This is obviously a trap."

"Does it matter?" Horus asked.

"Hrm..." Sobek gave a low growl. "The lich knows that force is the base of all authority. His chances of succeeding in this fight are low, but if he shows more courage than us...it would be better to walk into a trap than stay away out of fear."

"You would deliberately spring a trap on yourself?" Isis scowled.

"Imagine how the mortals will react if we do nothing while the dragon terrorizes their cities," Sobek replied. "Failing to show courage here is worse than failing to show strength."

Isis folded her arms and didn't reply. Sekhmet, on the other hand, drummed her fingers impatiently on the table.

"I agree that this is not a fight we can back away from," the lion-headed war goddess added. "But that doesn't mean we face this monster without a strategy. Do the mortals have guns that can fire at the sky?"

"Some," Horus admitted. "They're mostly for the case where an invader were to attack with airships, though."

"The guns along the walls of Hadesh are mostly cannons and mortars," Marduk added. "They were mostly designed for fighting enemies on the ground, especially the Greymarch. But they also have stationary gatling guns that can be aimed at the sky. They won't be much more than a nuisance to the dracolich, though."

"I am mostly worried about the dragon bringing in cans of zombies again," Sekhmet replied. "The last time he attacked, he called in several metal cans of corpses and raised them as an undead army on the spot. Our first priority should be to make sure he can't do that again."

"He raised those zombies in broad daylight." Isis looked over at Enki, the patron god of sorcerers. "The sun should have stopped him from doing that."

"The sun can cause problems for necromancy," Enki said as he continued looking through the lich's letters. "But if he charged those corpses with power before he dropped them into the city, it's possible he just gave them the last spark of unlife after the cannisters landed. That's a lot easier for a necromancer to do in broad daylight than trying to animate fresh corpses."

"So, if we could get the city's cannons focused on the sky, how well could we prevent him from playing that trick again?" Sekhmet asked.

"Those containers maintained their shape pretty well even after crashing into the ground." Marduk replied. "It's unlikely that the human cannons will be able to shoot them down, however... a direct hit should knock them off course."

"The gatling guns might be able to fill them with enough holes to break the cannisters apart," Ptah smiled. "That might be even better. But beyond static defenses, the city has several military airships that are large enough to mount several cannons, including puckle guns that are like a cross between a cannon and a revolver. Those should be able to intercept any reinforcements he tries to drop into the city from above."

"And the lich won't be able to raise the dead within the city itself?" Ereshkigal asked.

"There won't be any to raise," Horus replied. "The Borealan Empire has long maintained a policy of burying their dead in graveyards outside the city walls, specifically to prevent necromancers from raising an army. Burial rites include pouring salt on the bodies for consecration and whenever possible, pouring concrete over the casket to ensure the dead can't crawl out. Smaller towns don't usually resort to such measures, but the capital city and all of the major ports do the same."

"What if he starts slaughtering people in the city and reanimating them?" Enlil asked.

"That's our greatest concern," Horus answered. "The sun will prevent him from doing that during the day; a necromancer can't raise the freshly dead in direct sunlight without having a dark area to fill them with unholy energy first. If he strikes in broad daylight, he can't do that."

"So," Enlil stroked his beard. "We need to worry about him attacking at night."

"The airships can't stay in the sky all the time," Ptah admitted. "We could tell the mortals to keep them grounded during the day and stay on patrol at night."

"What about underground?" Adad pointed to the lower layers of the city schematics. "The dragon has made plenty of use of undead animals before, especially rats. He could raise an army from the sewers, even if it isn't human."

"I have personally seen to the purging of all vermin that might be hiding out of the sun's reach," Bast replied. "By influencing the cats in the city, I will ensure there are no rats, mice, or other pests he can animate."

"Some of these letters don't make any sense." Enki squinted at one of the lich's messages, as if trying to piece together some hidden clue. "What's this about how he's never going to give Horus up, or let him down, or run around and desert him?"

"All of the major ports..." Marduk ignored his father. He clearly had other things weighing on his mind, but he was at least partly focused on the present matter. "The lich mentioned in his threat that he might attack other cities. What do we know of this?"

"Ah!" Ptah beamed. "I'm already onto that! We've identified trains with suspicious packages to each major city on the west coast of the empire, and even a few along the southern border. Someone appears to have commissioned additional packages in refrigerated freight cars on each of these trains, using the aliases Baram Duchen, Nebum Chadam, Maruch Daben – all anagrams. We couldn't trace the fake names any further, or identify what was in them–"

"But the fact that the paper trail was falsified was enough to grab your attention." Marduk sighed. "And that means we need to spread out our forces if we want to stop him."

"Well, yes," Ptah admitted.

"Refrigerated cars?" Isis frowned. "He could be smuggling anything from bombs to more zombies in cold storage."

"We have the demon hunting gods Bes and Tawaret stationed in Dumiabet and Zarash." Horus turned to Enlil. "We can't take any chances, so they've manifested in their physical forms. Taisha has already been attacked recently by someone else, a bomber not connected to Daurgo. Aside from Hadesh, that city needs to be kept safe to prevent civil unrest. Can you handle it?"

"I can manifest there, and guide the local authorities to the train when it arrives." Enlil looked back at Ptah. "Speaking of, how long do we have until the trains reach their cities?"

"The first will arrive in Tiberias in one hour," Ptah replied. "The last reaches Baltithar in ten."

"Which means Daurgo will likely make his move soon after," Marduk rubbed his eyes with his index finger and thumb, as if he knew there was something else, but couldn't put his finger on it.

"Wait, that means..." Isis' eyes widened. "The sun sets in an hour. He'll be able to attack at any moment!"

"You and I have to be on Ra's sun barge as soon as we're done here." Horus nodded at Isis before turning back to the Babylonian gods. "That's why we need your help. We cannot pull every god from every one of their duties to focus on rooting out one dracolich; that one case in the desert required us to turn our eyes away from the rest of the empire, and that was during the day, when the Red Serpent and his minions lay dormant."

"Then we mobilize the mortals to reinforce their defenses during the night," Sekhmet examined the defenses along the cross-section of the city walls. "The human guards can take shifts, but I don't think they have enough airships capable of air defense to cover every city day and night."

"Then we will have to fill the gap where possible," Sobek growled.

"Throwing down the gauntlet..." Isis paused. "No, we're missing something. That dragon attacked the city before, and the Philosopher's Stone went missing. He definitely stole it in the confusion. If he really is going to attack the same empire again, with such short notice, there'd have to be a bigger reason than just to blow up trains or release more zombies. Even last time, the undead he let loose in the city were another distraction. So, what is he really after this time?"

"Crippling us," Nergal hissed. "We've openly attacked him for killing Thoth. He knows we aren't going to stop trying to bring him to justice. So now he's trying to disrupt us, like taking out the police headquarters so they'll leave him alone."

"Hm," Sobek murmured. "The weapons that killed Thoth were tailor-made for him, specifically. They would have taken a long time to craft. He likely doesn't have a weapon like that designed to kill the rest of us. Even in both of his fights with you, Marduk; he only had mortal weapons. Albeit, technologically advanced ones."

Marduk clasped his hands in front of his face, concealing his mouth and thoughts. "Yes, I believe that's correct."

"So, bombs on trains, or a horde of the undead released from the stations all at once." Horus clenched his fists. "He intends to make the mortals believe we can't protect them, weakening their faith in us. We have to split up to cover more ground."

"We go in pairs," Marduk murmured. "We need to limit the odds that anyone faces the dragon alone."

"I will guard the capital as soon as the daybreaks," Horus declared. "Sekhmet will watch over the city in my stead, and we can call up Nephthys to support her until the morning."

"I should cover the port in Tiberias," Enki replied. "I think it best if Ptah join me."

The Egyptian god of creation nodded, while the others exchanged looks. Having gods from different pantheons working together could be a good idea. Or a terrible one.

Isis stood up. "I should go to Dumiabet before the sun sets. That city is too close to the border of Kemet; someone apt with magic should ward the place there in case he tries to tap into the necromantic power there."

Adad looked at the other Babylonian gods. "Should one of us—"

"I will meet up with Bes," Isis replied. "He's already stationed there on search for demons."

"And Tawaret is in Zarash," Sobek added. "I should be the one to join her."

"Fine," Ereshkigal got up to leave. "I can't return to the land of the living, anyway."

"That leaves Baltithar and Petryan," Marduk rubbed his eyes again, as if still hung up on some missing clue. "I shall go to Petryan."

Nergal raised an eyebrow. "That's the smallest city on the list. After the Egyptian king steps up to protect the capital, you want to go to the least-populated area?"

"Call it a hunch," Marduk replied. "And I can defend a city of that size alone."

"Very well," the plague god raised his hands. "Then I shall go to Baltithar. A city of that size needs protection.

"I will join you." Bast smiled. "It's been a while since I've been there."

"Then it's decided," Horus announced. "To your stations! We'll not let the dracolich surprise us again!"

83

Lessons Recapped

AMRI

"Something's coming."

Marduk stood on the rock that floated in the void of Amri's dreams. The god's face was a mix of worry and confusion.

"More than one thing," he added, talking less to Amri and more to himself. "The dracolich is up to something again, and I don't fully know what. And at the same time, something wicked stirs in the Institute of Theurgy. And I still don't know who sent a suicide bomber to Taisha."

"Excuse me," Amri raised a hand. "Are you trying to get me to do something?"

The god paused and looked at the boy, as if just noticing the person whose dream he had entered. "Yes, actually. I need you to be on guard. The dracolich has challenged the emperor of your nation, and–"

"I already knew that" Amri interrupted. "Ephorah heard it from her teachers holding a secret meeting, and she told me, Namid, and Rostam."

"...Great," Marduk clenched his teeth. "The entire city is going to be panicking. Soon."

"Wait," Amri squinted. "How did I learn about this before you knew that I knew?"

"If it originated from the faculty Institute of Theurgy, then it's because the professors who work there no longer believe in me." Marduk grimaced, and

Amri was grateful the god's anger wasn't aimed at him. "Now they've started worshipping something else."

Amri wanted to ask what they were now worshipping, but Marduk's angry expression told him it wasn't a good idea.

"So, what should you or I be doing?" Amri asked. "About the dragon, that is."

"I keep watch, and be prepared for when he strikes," Marduk replied. "You keep your head down, and once he does make a visible move, get as many people as you can to safety."

"Shouldn't we be trying to prevent the dragon from killing people?" Amri asked.

"Can't be done." Marduk shook his head slightly. "There's no way for me to predict where he will strike; we can only react swiftly when he does."

"But that means..." Amri tried to search the void of his dreamscape for an idea, but nothing appeared. "That means lots of people are going to die!"

"Yes," Marduk nodded. "It probably does. Even though the lich spent most of his attention on me the last time he appeared, the damage he did to the city still killed and injured a lot of people. Even more died in the panic and looting that occurred afterwards. There is no reason to think this will be different."

"And..." Amri stammered. "There's...there's no way to—"

"Prevent it?" Marduk sighed. "No. There isn't. Some terrible things can be stopped before they happen; others can only be mitigated. What we can do is fortify our defenses."

Amri could feel the god peering into his thoughts, as if searching for something specific.

"Tell me," Marduk asked. "What did you learn from your encounter with Doctor Malbim?"

"I...well..." Amri paused. What had he learned? That there are people who don't care about the laws of society? Or that an alchemist can turn a person into red paste in a second?

"I learned that...there are some problems that can't be solved with reason," Amri finally said. "And that you can't always expect the law or justice to work, or for the police to do their jobs."

"Hm," Marduk sighed. "These are...terrible lessons, but they're all true. It is good that you looked for non-violent solutions to the problem of the doctor and her son, and that you tried going to the authorities first. But the part where you made your biggest mistake was thinking that a woman like Malbim was going to listen to something like a law against practicing medicine on family members. Anyone as evil as her wouldn't care about a technicality like that." Marduk looked Amri dead in the eyes. "Some problems cannot be solved with violence. And some problems can *only* be solved with violence. Do you understand?"

Closing his eyes, Amri nodded. "When the dracolich shows up, there's no talking him down. The only way to stop him is with force."

"Exactly." Marduk gave the smile of a teacher whose pupil was finally understanding the course material. "At the end of the day, all law, order, and authority come from force. It is why the Babylonians imagined the god of civilization as a person with nearly limitless power. Every rule of society either has a threat of force if people don't follow it, or it isn't a real rule. And if the level of force a society can muster isn't enough, then the rule doesn't matter. If I and the other gods want that dragon to leave this empire alone, we must answer his challenge and crush him."

Amri nodded. He didn't want to think about what would happen if Marduk failed.

"I'm...not going to lie," Marduk's glasses hid his eyes, but Amri could tell he was avoiding the mortal's gaze. "There's a good chance the dragon has tricks up his sleeve we aren't prepared for. If he strikes your city, and I'm not there right away, I do not expect a mortal to drive him off."

"Have you told the abbey yet?" Amri asked.

"Not all of them," Marduk frowned. "Not all of them talk to me. But I have told Esfan."

"Right," Amri nodded.

"Hold firm, and stay vigilant," Marduk looked Amri over one more time. "You...will not die in the days to come. For better or worse."

With that, the god flung Amri out into the void of his subconscious, disappearing from his mind.

84

Unmasked

NAMID

Fluid Dynamics was not a class Namid particularly liked. Even on a good day, aquamancy was her weakest subject, and every lab experiment had her gritting her teeth. But today she was more on edge than normal. The battleship flying overhead outside the class window didn't help. The dragon was plotting an attack any day, or maybe any hour, and the Tomb Lords had plans to conquer the empire in the not-too-distant future. Admittedly, to a bunch of immortals, the not-too-distant future could be after Namid was dead from old age, but it could just as easily be next semester.

But there was something else bothering her today. Namid had taken it upon herself to bring Cyrus into the fold, and now she was starting to think that was a really terrible idea. Of course, Rostam couldn't do it. He wasn't a student, and it would be weird for him to be walking around the Academia Food Court by himself. Amri hadn't offered, and now Namid wished he had. Just this once, she didn't want to play the diplomat.

Cyrus was waiting at a table by the bakery. Rather than sit at the table, he was standing next to one, looking somewhat nonchalant, but also alert. Namid wondered if he already knew something was up.

With a deep breath, Namid forced herself to approach the young alchemist. "You're here. Good." *Let's get this over with.*

"Yeah, I'm here." Cyrus looked around and glanced up at the battleship circling the city. "That's rather ominous. Did they say anything about a parade?"

"I think that's going to be the official reason for it," Namid gestured to the table. "Have a seat."

Cyrus sat down across from Namid, who drummed her fingers against the table for a moment.

"Ephorah overheard her teachers in a private meeting," Namid started. "Their headmistress was in the imperial palace when the dracolich gave a message to the emperor himself. He's planning to attack the city again. Soon."

"Okay..." Cyrus made a confused face. "First, who's Ephorah?"

"Oh, that's right," Namid gritted her teeth. How much should she share with him about Ephorah? "She's an old school friend of me, my brother, and Rostam. She's...Empyrian, like Rostam."

"Okay...and I'm taking it you're being dodgy about the subject because she doesn't like people like me?" Cyrus raised an eyebrow.

"Wow," Namid whistled. "That was quick."

"It wasn't hard to put it together," Cyrus frowned. "There's only so many reasons you'd be so sensitive about something like this."

"Right," Namid gritted her teeth. He had somehow made this discussion easier and harder at the same time. "So...main point is, the dragon. He's going to attack again."

"And...I take it we don't know when or exactly where?"

"We think he'll attack Hadesh again, since it's the capital. We don't know much else," Namid admitted. "We do know that the government doesn't know much else, either. That's the real reason they've got battleships circling the city."

"Of course it is," Cyrus rolled his eyes. "They want the military's guard up, but they don't want to start a panic. I wouldn't be surprised if the gods themselves are on watch for him; he made a mockery of both of the local pantheons at the tournament. So...what are you all planning to do?"

"Not much," Namid shrugged. "Mostly just stay on our guard. Although, I was asking the others if they wanted to get involved in some looting once the chaos starts." As soon as Namid said this, she immediately regretted it. Cyrus didn't really know her like the others; she shouldn't be trusting him with stuff like that. She didn't even have any dirt on him to blackmail him with.

"Uh..." Cyrus blinked. "Your plan for when the dragon attacks is to commit crime, and you're announcing you plan to commit that crime ahead of time? Is this a bad attempt at a joke, or some kind of cry for help?"

"Well..." Before Namid could answer that, she spotted an odd-looking figure who stole her attention. A man (maybe?) was walking around in broad daylight wearing fully-concealing black hooded robes, despite the afternoon heat, along with a bronze mask that completely concealed his face. The mask didn't even have much for features; it was mostly blank with eyeholes. The man himself walked more like a puppet than an actual person; like someone maladjusted to their own body proportions, or even human anatomy, for that matter.

"Who on Earth dresses like that?" Namid thought aloud, and apparently her distraction got enough of Cyrus's attention to turn and look too.

The figure went up to a couple of students who were in the middle of making out. They were poorly hiding this behind a textbook that was deliberately low, so everyone around could still see them kissing in public, and the couple could just barely look like they weren't deliberately making everyone around them uncomfortable.

Leaning over the textbook and invading the couple's personal space, the masked figure seemed to be examining the girl closely for a second. "Ew, you are one ugly female!" He turned to the boy. "My condolences, young man."

"What the hell is wrong with you?" The boy asked while his offended girlfriend slapped his mask so hard it fell off of his face. The couple then screamed as the figure started laughing.

"Boo!" He lifted his hood, revealing a rotten, half-decayed head of a zombie. "Time to start the party."

"Looks like we know when and where he's attacking." Cyrus clapped his hands and touched the table, splitting a large piece of wood off with magic to use as a club.

85

Son of a Fish

ENKI

Tiberias' railroad stations were always packed with people. This was one of the biggest port cities in the empire, and the one that received the most traffic from Taride, and usually the last stopping point for ships coming from or leaving for Meditia. This made it a hassle to try and find the dragon's secret cargo shipments.

Since no one actually observed the lich's cargo, and most people didn't bother memorizing the trains' itineraries, there was no way for Enki or Ptah to locate the cargo through the collective consciousness of mankind. Even if someone did know, their thoughts would be drowned out by the sea of merchants worried about their profits, the travelers returning from vacations, and the angry passengers upset about lost luggage.

Fortunately, most people knew to clear a path when two gods of different pantheons were trying to search a station and its cargo trains. Even if the gods in question were well-known for being friendlier than most, mortals still did not get in the way of a physical god on business. Deities did not normally bother to physically manifest in train station at all; any crime or trouble was left up to mortals. If gods felt the need to get directly involved, it meant mortals usually wanted to move in the opposite direction of wherever they were going, since the problems they were dealing with were probably not mortal, either.

With a small contingent of the station's security around for support, Ptah

SON OF A FISH

and Enki sent them out to search all refrigerated cars that had arrived recently. They had not, unfortunately, all come from the same cities, and this was why the gods employed mortal assistance; they needed extra eyes and extra minds focusing on the task if they wanted to find all of the trains the dragon had arrive in this city in time.

After several hours, one of the security guards pointed to a train car and held up a checklist. This one was refrigerated, held cargo that had come from Hadesh, and had arrived at the right time to be on one of the lich's trains. Of course, neither Ptah nor Enki would allow the mortals to actually enter the car by themselves; there was too much risk.

Opening the door, Enki was greeted by a large, wooden crate with big red letters on one side that said, "Looking for this?"

"I guess we shouldn't be surprised." Enki looked at Ptah. "You know we can't just walk over there and open it, right?"

Ptah nodded. "There could be anything in there. One moment. *Extra long crowbar.*"

As the god of creation spoke, his words became matter and a crowbar with an exceptionally long handle appeared from his mouth and into his hand. Standing back from the crate, Ptah wrenched open the top of the box from a safe distance, as Enki prepared himself to fight whatever came out of it.

A few seconds passed, and nothing happened. Ptah poked the box with the crowbar, and still nothing happened. Finally, the confused gods approached the crate and looked inside.

"Salmon?" Ptah peered inside the box. "He shipped a crate full of salmon?"

"No," Enki picked up one of the fish. "These are herring."

"But they're all red. *Lantern.*[4]" Ptah produced a lantern and held it up to see the fish more clearly. "Yes, they're just the red ones. I know red herrings exist, but it's like he collected only the red ones—"

"Son of a fish.[5]" Enki clenched his teeth. "We've been had. We have to go—"

The two gods were interrupted by the sounds of laughter mixed with screams

---

[4] As the god of creation, Ptah's words could speak things into existence.

[5] This was an actual insult used in the Epic of Gilgamesh.

of terror and weeping from outside. Enki tried to tap into the collective consciousness of mankind to find out what was happening before leaving the train car. Instead of reading the thoughts of the mortal security guards, or any others, he was bombarded by images of dancing goats, purple mists, a baby's face where the sun should be, and a host of other maddening hallucinations. The more he tried to focus on a particular person to get a clearer read on their thoughts, the more confusing and horrifying the images became.

Stepping out of the refrigerated car, Enki saw the security guards falling over, laughing maniacally, scratching at their own skin, and waving their weapons about at imaginary enemies.

"What is this?" The sorcery god asked.

"Some kind of hallucinogenic," Ptah touched a powder on one of the guard's gloves. The creation god could understand matter and it's function by merely handling it. He then felt around in the web of human consciousness for more answers. "It's not just these people. The stuff was laced into the food on the train's dining car. It activates slowly, needing to be exposed to the air for a while before it can start taking effect, but once it's active, it can drive a person mad immediately. That's how it was able to go off at exactly the time the lich planned."

Enki tried to read the thoughts of mortals in the other cities. Zarash, Dumiabet, Baltithar; it was all the same. Each city was now overrun with people driven insane by the hallucinogenic. The only city that didn't seem to have a sudden epidemic of raw madness was Hadesh. "This is a distraction. We have to get back—"

A rumbling sound from outside the station drew the gods' attention. Having no way to chcek the minds of mortals to know what was going on, the gods ran outside of the station into the streets of Tiberias, where a swarm of cauldron-borne ogres ran through the city, slaughtering citizens who were too intoxicated to even realize they were in danger. The only ones who could stop it were Ptah and Enki.

"Curse that dragon! *Revolver!*" A high-caliber pistol appeared from Ptah's mouth and the god of creation shot the first ogre zombie he could in the head. "First he jams our omniscience with madness, now this? How'd they get through the city walls?"

"We can't just leave the mortals like this." Enki summoned a strong gust of wind to shred another ogre nearby. "We have to hope the forces at Hadesh can—"

In the corner of his eye, Enki spotted an unusually bloated ogre. To his horror, the corpse had been stuffed with explosives, poking through bits of ragged flesh, and was charging into the middle of a crowd of people rolling around in various states of stupor.

There was no spell Enki could cast to strike the cauldron-borne ogre without setting off the bombs. Instead, Enki focused his magic on the waterworks beneath the streets and forcing the pressure to burst through the ground. He then directed the water to envelop the zombie, trying to contain the blast.

The explosion splattered water and wind everywhere, but it looked like most of the intoxicated mortals were okay. Then Enki noticed a single man who was writhing on the ground with a giddy smile on his face, his ribs impaled by a single piece of shrapnel.

More ogres swarmed the city. Ptah tossed his empty gun away and created a new one.

86

Fireworks

DAURGO

Human students scattered from the zombie puppet as Daurgo scanned the skies. A heavy object struck the zombie in the head, snapping the corpse's neck and leaving it hanging by a few layers of sinew.

"Now, that wasn't very nice." Daurgo ripped the head off of the body's shoulders and held it aloft as the boy with the club tried to strike him again. "A wizard student, and your first instinct is to hit a zombie with a club?"

As he said this, a girl behind him snapped her fingers and the edges of Daurgo's robes caught on fire.

"Ah, that's more like it," the lich chuckled as the pair tore his puppet apart. "But these are just bystanders. Where are my real opponents?"

While the students destroyed the zombie in the Academia Food Court, Daurgo's consciousness shifted to a corpse waiting by a set of fireworks in a clearing right outside the Temple District. As the battleship overhead, Daurgo's zombie lit the small set of party rockets he'd setup. They were not meant to do enough damage to actually wreck the ship; that wasn't the point.

As several firecrackers bombarded the underbelly of the battleship, the vessel slowed down, as the confused crew tried to figure out what attacked them. This brought the ship in just the right spot for the cannon on Daurgo's centipede.

A massive artillery cannon launched a shell aimed for the stationary battleship. The explosion ripped the vessel in two, leaving the ship's engines and stern in one half, the bow and remainder of the hull in the other. The ship's balloon was still attached to both ends, which tipped downward and dumped the screaming crew out above the city.

"Alright, that's enough appetizers. Where's the main course?" Daurgo looked at the shipmates as they fell to their deaths. His surroundings told him this was in the Southern Residential District. "Well, what's a party without favors?"

Shifting his consciousness to another corpse in the Industrial Zone, Daurgo set off a much larger array of fireworks. These weren't meant to strike anything; they were meant to send a message.

Bright, burning fireworks filled with alchemically altered powders lit up the sky with the words: "Come and get me, gods of the city!"

When several seconds passed with no signs of any gods showing up, Daurgo set off the second array of fireworks, which spelled out the additional message: "Unless you're a bunch of chickens!"

At last, a furious armored god with the head of a falcon landed on a rooftop overlooking the corpse that had lit the firecrackers.

"Finally!" Daurgo huffed. "Took you long enough. I've only got so many of these things. Do you have any idea how much they charge in this city for quality fireworks?"

"You!" Horus bellowed. "How dare you!"

Daurgo wasn't intimidated. "Are you the only one that came to my party? I gave you all clear invitations! I even threw up big flaming letters to let you know where I was!"

"Wow," Horus clicked his beak menacingly. "You made your move in broad daylight? Now I just have to destroy you and any other corpses you've sent here, and then I can find that cannon."

"Oh, please." The skeleton didn't have eyes to roll, but his skull managed to mimic the expression. "Do you really think it takes me more than three months to regenerate my body?"

Horus had just enough time to jump off the rooftop as the dracolich burst out of the building beneath him. Unfortunately, he was not fast enough to escape the lich's jaws, which bit him in half at the waist.

The god screamed as he felt his lower half slip down the dragon's new armor. Unlike last time, where he had simply spat out enemies that he could bite but couldn't swallow, Daurgo had outfitted his armor with a new machine in the neck. Throwing a lever labeled "puree," the dragon turned Horus's severed half into a thick paste. The machine in Daurgo's neck released a cannister beneath his throat, holding the god's blended body like a macabre beverage.

"I was hoping I'd get your entire body," Daurgo admitted. "But I guess half a surprise is better than no surprise."

Crawling away with his arms, Horus's body was starting to regenerate, but it wouldn't be easy. With half his body mass kept in a separate container, he would either have to rebuild himself from scratch, or find some way of getting to the rest of himself back. This was one of the drawbacks gods took on when they adopted a physical form.

Daurgo examined the falcon-headed god for a moment. He could, in theory, use his plan on Horus and kill the king of the Egyptian gods. But as the old saying goes, "as above, so below." If Horus died, the consequences of killing him might be so severe that even the dracolich would have to deal with them later on. He needed a better victim.

"I suppose this is the part where I'm supposed to bat you back and forth like a mouse?" Daurgo slapped the dismembered god with his tail, sending him straight into a wall.

Where were the other gods? He'd expected there'd be more than one in Hadesh; that was why he set up his trap to take one of them out as quickly as possible. He had gone to all this trouble with the herring, and the fireworks, and the train fare, and now the gods weren't even going to show up?

"Maybe my plan worked better than I intended," the dragon thought aloud.

The dragon got his answer when the sun bore down upon him with an intensified fury. Feeling the focused rays of light, he peered up and felt the full anger of the sun coming down on his undead form. This wasn't just the normal, annoying effect of sunlight on a lich; Ra must have been warned by the other gods to focus his divine power on weakening the dragon. Even his armor wasn't enough to protect him from the holy rays.

FIREWORKS

"Looks like they're trying to soften me up for an attack," he muttered to himself. "I'd better play along, or they won't be brave enough to engage."

Daurgo could feel the sun whittling away at the necromantic powers holding his body together. With a quick spell and a gust of wind, he blew up enough dust to cloud the sky above himself, giving him a brief reprieve. Then the winds angrily blew away the dust, leaving him exposed again to the sun's might.

"Ha!" A goddess with the head of a lioness appeared behind Daurgo and slashed at his armor. Although it barely pierced the plating, the dragon let out a roar as if he were in genuine pain.

"And you might be?" The dragon snapped as he turned to face the goddess. "No, wait. Don't tell me. Sekhmet? I could tell from the stench of hairballs!"

"Tch," Sekhmet spat. "You're partly right. You're one cocky bastard, you know that? First you attack in broad daylight, you don't even try to sneak in an undead army, and you think those toys in your armor are going to save you? Maybe I should let the sun bleach your bones a bit before tearing your skull off. That's the only part we need to capture you, isn't it?"

"Maybe so," Daurgo chuckled. "But arrogant as you are, I accept your surrender."

"HA!" Sekhmet sneered. "Defiant to the end? I can respect that."

Daurgo took out Konshu's hourglass and tipped it over, letting the sand start to fall. "Now."

At one moment, the sun continued to rain holy light on the undead monster, weakening his necromancy and draining away his magic. Then, a circle of darkness crossed the sky and slid in front of the blazing star. A total eclipse.

"The...the moon?" Sekhmet gasped. "Did Konshu lose at his stupid child's card game again?"

"And that, ladies and gentlemen, is the sound of three hours of unrestricted, unholy power!" Daurgo rose up, his necromancy fully restored, and slammed the ground with his foot, channeling energy into the soil that sought out corpses. "Would everyone who died gruesomely in the past twenty minutes please raise your hand?"

Among the wreckage of the fallen battleship, the corpses from the crew of the vessel each lifted their mangled arms in response to the lich's question. "Excellent!" He turned back to Sekhmet. "Now, about that surrender…"

87

One Bad Idea After Another

AMRI

Trying to run with legs that hadn't fully healed, Amri scampered for the Academia Food Court, where his friends had agreed to meet if the dragon attacked while they were in class. Amri swore that as soon as he was able, he'd get back in the gym and practice running until he could sprint for a kilometer without stopping.

Hobbling from the Academy of Sorcerers to the food court, Amri looked around and saw Cyrus turning what was left of a skeleton into chalk with his alchemy. Namid was standing around looking for other undead, ready to fire spells if she saw any.

"Where's Ephorah?" Amri asked.

"I'm coming, I'm coming!" Ephorah grumbled. "I didn't think the dragon would attack during daylight hours."

"Why did no one know there was an eclipse today?" Namid asked. "Those don't usually happen out of nowhere."

"I don't think that's a real eclipse," Amri shielded his eyes and glanced up at the sun. Unlike a normal solar eclipse, where a sliver of light is still visible behind the moon, the sun was completely dark, and the sky was a dim red. "That's something else, like...just the idea of the moon, not the actual moon."

"So, what?" Namid asked. "The dragon managed to block out the sun? What for?"

"Because sunlight messes with necromancy," Amri replied. "Remember the library in Grand Spire? They had a whole area on the subject, and sunlight causes all sorts of problems for the undead. I'd bet that if the gods knew the lich was coming in advance, they probably tried to get Ra to focus the sun on him directly."

"And now, they can't do that," Cyrus gritted his teeth. "Anyone see where that battleship went down?"

"It was right above the Temple District," Namid pointed. "Right along the edge of the Industrial Zone."

"Oh, gods!" Ephorah's eyes widened. "My family's home is over there!"

"And probably a number of freshly raised corpses," Cyrus added. "We should—"

"Excuse me, who in Peppi's unhinged jaws invited you?" Ephorah scowled at Cyrus.

"Oh, yeah." Namid tried to smile, but it came out as more of a grimace. "You haven't met yet—"

"Yes we have!" Ephorah snapped. "He's the bori trash who jumped on my back and nearly broke my ribs during the tournament!"

Cyrus scratched his head. "Oh, yeah. We have met. Didn't you get slapped by my platypus one time?"

Namid shot Cyrus a look that said "stop digging yourself deeper."

"Why on Earth did you bring this scum here?" Ephorah hissed.

Amri nudged her arm. "Zombies close to your family home, remember?"

"Oh, damn it!" Ephorah threw up her hands and started running towards the Temple District. "When this is over, you all have some explaining to do!"

"Wait!" Amri clutched his calves. The pain in his legs told him he needed to stop running. He didn't want a repeat of last time. "I'm sorry, I can't run anymore. I can walk, but not run."

While Namid rolled her eyes in frustration, Cyrus looked at her and Amri for a moment.

"Can you go on ahead?" He asked Namid. "We'll catch up to you—"

"You want me to run headfirst into danger by myself?" Namid scowled. "What is wrong with you two?"

ONE BAD IDEA AFTER ANOTHER

"Where's Rostam?" Cyrus countered. "Can you go find him and get his fireball friend?"

Namid paused. "He'll be at Silverstack Docks, since he sleeps on that airship. Yes, I could go get him. And Cindrocles."

"Then we'll meet you at the Temple District." Cyrus gestured to Amri. "I'll walk with him."

Namid ran off for the Market District while the two boys walked together.

"So, you guys didn't tell that Empyrian girl about me, did you?" Cyrus smiled sheepishly.

Amri nodded. "Her name's Ephorah, and, well…you know."

"Yeah, this is why I didn't ask Namid to walk with you so I could run off to join her," Cyrus admitted. "She's probably headed for the Empyrian Quarter, which I don't know very well, but I do know I'm not welcome."

"Yeah." Amri continued walking. "I'm sorry for this, not being able to run."

"I heard you got stabbed in both legs," Cyrus replied. "You're young, so you'll probably make a full recovery, but not if you don't let them heal. I might have tried my hand fixing them with alchemy if I'd been there, but now that the wounds have closed themselves, it's best to just let them heal naturally."

"Thanks," Amri pointed to a bench along the road they were walking. "Because I need to stop for a moment."

Amri sat down while Cyrus looked over in the direction of the Temple District.

"Once we get there, what are you going to do?" Cyrus asked. "You can't run, and I doubt any spells you perform can rely on footwork."

Amri lowered his head for a moment. He truly was useless. "I don't know. Maybe I should start carrying a gun. But if I don't try to help, I know I'll regret it."

Cyrus tapped his fingers on the bench for a moment, as if trying to decide what to do. "Yeah, and I'm probably going to regret this."

In a flash, Cyrus picked up Amri and hoisted him onto his back, supporting Amri's legs with his arms.

"What are you doing?" Amri grabbed Cyrus's shoulders for balance.

"Using up the stamina I need for alchemy before I even get to the danger," Cyrus took off towards the Temple District. "I did say this was probably a bad idea. Just hang on."

88

Street Fighter of the Dead

EPHORAH

Sprinting through the streets to get to her parent's home, Ephorah took a detour around the Temple District opposite the Industrial Zone. Sure enough, most of the fighting was above the area between the two districts. She didn't have to worry about zombies yet.

But she did have to worry about terrified mobs sweeping through the streets away from the temples. Ephorah had kept her strength gloves literally on hand in case the dragon attacked, but she knew she couldn't just pummel her way through people fleeing in terror.

Instead, she raised her arms like a shield and forced her way through the crowd, her arms taking the brunt of people in front of her as she slowly advanced. She had barely learned anything in her fencing class, but the first lesson on footwork taught her how to make herself immovable from attacks to the front by straightening her back leg. With arms up for defense and a lowered center of gravity, Ephorah managed to take one step at a time through the mob.

After a while, the crowd thinned out. There were only so many people praying at any given time, and now it looked like the temples were evacuated. But when Ephorah reached the Empyrian Quarter, people were still frantic.

Some were in the process of boarding up their windows and bracing their doors. Others were evacuating their homes, running for the southern wall or to another district.

"Why here?" Ephorah muttered to herself. "Last time the dragon attacked, we got the worst of it. Now he attacks again, and he aims for the temples nearby?"

Ephorah was aware that the government did not know when or where the lich would strike. She was also aware that keeping the dragon's announcement a secret was meant to prevent mass panic. But she was also aware that not warning the city had left them unguarded, and the idea that it just so happened to result in zombies swarming the area surrounding the Empyrian Quarter wasn't something she could just ignore.

As soon as she reached her house, Ephorah scrambled for the front door. It was locked. Fiddling with her house key, she heard her mother's voice from inside.

"Ephorah? Is that you?" She called. "We've already blocked the front door. Go around to the back. We haven't barricaded it yet."

Sighing, Ephorah ran around the other side of the house, where her father opened the back door to let her in. Panting, Ephorah realized just how worn out she was. She had run all the way from the Academia Food Court to her house in the Empyrian Quarter. Now she was completely exhausted.

"Thank the gods," her father said. "You made it before we sealed this off."

"What are we going to do?" Ephorah doubled over panting.

"We're going to barricade this door," he replied. "And stay safe until the zombies leave."

"No, I mean..." Ephorah leaned up. "What are we going to do? About the zombies, the dragon, our neighbors..."

"We do nothing." Her father braced one of the kitchen chairs against the door. "We're going to stay put, keep safe, and let this thing blow over."

Ephorah thought for a moment as she caught her breath. She and her family could probably stay safe inside the house without too much trouble. If zombies take the path of least resistance to get to food, then it made sense that they'd ignore a boarded-up house and look elsewhere. But elsewhere might mean terrorizing the rest of the Empyrian Quarter, along with the neighboring districts, and they had just rebuilt from the last necromancer attack. She could stay safe in her family's house and allow the undead to ravage her city again.

Or she could do something else.

Having caught most of her breath, Ephorah made her way to her room and took off her sweaty school outfit, changing into her gym clothes. Then she pulled the box out from under her bed where she'd hidden her sword.

The blade was a sickly, corroded color. Ephorah realized the sword never rusted because rust was what gave blood its red color; this thing had no rust to spare. Carefully picking it up by the hilt, the blade twitched on its own. It couldn't die of hunger, but it was starving. It smelled her blood, and the blade tried to pull against Ephorah to reach her flesh, but she kept arm firm.

"Behave," Ephorah whispered. "And I'll feed you."

The weapon gave off an aura that it wasn't convinced Ephorah was telling the truth, but it stopped struggling against her for the moment. She thought about trying to go through the house to the back door, but pushed that thought out immediately. There was no way her family would let her out, and the blade might try to lash out at them if they tried to stop her.

Almost a year ago, she had snuck out of her house through her bedroom window with Namid. Sliding the window open, she glanced over her shoulder one last time, hoped she wasn't making a terrible mistake, and jumped out onto the lawn below.

The howl of zombies nearby told her they were close. She had recovered enough stamina to swing her sword for a bit, but if she didn't feed it blood soon, she wouldn't be able to fight for very long. She still barely knew how to hold a sword; she was banking everything on a hunch.

Across the street, a swarm of zombies in military uniforms scampered through the neighborhood, looking something to kill. A battleship like the one that had crashed earlier had at least a hundred crewmen at any given notice. Figures she wouldn't be lucky enough to fight the undead shipmates one at a time.

Picking up a nearby pebble from her neighbor's garden, Ephorah whipped the stone at the closest zombie, hoping to get the attention of just one.

Instead, the pebble missed the zombie and crashed into a flowerpot sitting on a retaining wall near a house. All seven zombies turned their heads towards the girl who'd thrown the rock.

"Crap!" Ephorah raised her sword in a low guard stance as the undead raced for her. Timing her thrust, she jabbed at the first zombie with the blade and jumped back once it had pierced the corpse's shoulder.

As she'd hoped, these zombies were freshly dead. Sure, zombies don't need their blood, but that doesn't mean they don't have any. The corroded sword tasted the first few drops of blood from the corpse and vibrated with new life, rejuvenating Ephorah's stamina. In the split second it took the sword to feed her the zombie's strength, another zombie raced past the first and tried to tackle Ephorah. She had just enough time to turn her sword so that the zombie skewered himself on the blade.

The sword gorged itself on the zombie's blood. Even while the zombie was still moving, the blade made a noise like a hungry wolf and greedily siphoned the crimson fluid. The corpse twitched for a second, and it almost looked like whatever magic animated the thing had been drained away as well. Then it lurched forwards, trying to lunge at Ephorah while impaled on her sword. The other zombies swarmed around the two that Ephorah had wounded and were almost upon her.

With strength fed to her through the sword's bloodthirst, Ephorah wrenched her weapon through the stuck zombie's ribcage and sliced three more of the attacking corpses in half, but this left her right side open for three more zombies to tackle her.

Ephorah yelped in pain as a pair of jaws bit down on her right arm, tearing out chunks of flesh. Remembering what Namid had told her once about muscle groups, she realized her right arm would be useless if the zombies had severed her tendons. Two more jaws bit down on her arm, and between flashes of pain Ephorah started to lose feeling in her hand.

Instead of trying to pry her arm out of the zombie's mouth, she let go of her sword with her right hand and snatched it up with her left, stabbing each corpse in the skull. A red weave of blood flowed around the blade. The sword, no longer corroded but a gleaming black polished metal, drank up the blood with such force that it no longer needed direct contact with the corpses, sucking it out of the open wounds through the air.

With three quick strikes, Ephorah skewered the heads of each zombie that had bitten her arm. As the blood was drained from their corpses, the skin grew paler, fragile as paper. Ephorah did not understand exactly how necromancy worked, but there was a general understanding that the magic holding a walking corpse together had limits, and if you do enough damage to an undead creature, the magic will run out. The zombies might not have needed blood to "live," but they did need it to keep their fleshy bodies strong and, for lack of a better word, "healthy."

Ephorah slashed one of the drained corpses with her sword, chopping his head and shoulders off the rest of the body. The dried out skin and muscle tore like tissue paper, and with a few more successive strikes, Ephorah found herself standing among seven borken, no-longer-animated corpses.

Checking her right arm, Ephorah was surprised to see the bites were already knitting themselves closed. What had been a series of deep flesh wounds had stopped bleeding, and scabs that would have taken days to form were already turning to scar tissue.

Looking down at the sword, Ephorah could feel the weapon continuing to pump her full of vitality. She knew this thing could refresh her stamina when she was drained from a fight; she had no idea it could heal her wounds.

Walking out into the street refreshed and ready for more, Ephorah kept an eye on her sword. For now, it was satisfied. She knew that wouldn't last.

Two boys, one running with the other on his back, made their way down her street. They were both looking around the street in case more undead were still about. As they got closer, Ephorah realized the one running was the Borealan from the food court, and Amri was riding on his back.

"We...um..." Cyrus looked around like he was almost disappointed. "Thought there'd be more zombies."

"I got the ones on this street," Ephorah gestured to the severed corpses in tattered military uniforms. "Didn't need your help," she eyed Cyrus.

"That battleship needed a crew of over five hundred people to fly," Amri sat up on Cyrus's back and scanned the area. "There are going to be a lot more than seven zombies."

"Why are you riding his back?" Ephorah asked.

"Because my legs are still healing," Amri replied. "I can walk, but not run."

"And alchemy boy here can't fix them?" Ephorah raised an eyebrow at Cyrus, who was still standing with Amri's legs tucked under the alchemist's arms.

"Alchemy is like surgery," Cyrus replied. "Do not use surgery to fix something unless it's truly necessary. Besides, he's not that heavy."

"Uh, actually," Amri mumbled sheepishly. "Could you put me down now?"

Cyrus dropped Amri down next to him, who visibly didn't like how easily the alchemist was able to do that. Cyrus was visibly strong, even for an alchemist, but not so much that he should be able to pick up another boy close to his age and haul him around like a large pillow. *That can't be good for Amri's ego*, Ephorah snickered to herself.

"Here, hold this a second." Ephorah handed Amri her sword.

"Okay…" Amri looked at the blade for a moment and then jolted when he realized the weapon was alive. "What the?"

Ephorah looked through the pile of zombie corpses and found a body that had stopped moving after she had cut it in half through the ribcage. The upper half was so drained that it looked like a natural mummy. The lower half, on the other hand, was still bleeding out onto the ground of the lawn of the poor person who was going to have to clean up this mess tomorrow.

"Here, stab this with the sword," Ephorah instructed.

"What? No! Why?" Amri asked.

"Because it'll heal your legs faster," she growled. "Just trust me. It's a magic sword."

Reluctantly, Amri did as she said, and thrust the blade into the zombie's buttocks. Ephorah had never gotten to watch someone else using the sword before, and now she could watch it hungrily devour blood from a new angle.

The corpse shriveled and wrinkled as it was drained, and Amri's expression told Ephorah he could feel it working. When it had finished, Amri flexed his legs with a few squats before handing the sword back to Ephorah.

"That's amazing," Amri rubbed the backs of his legs. "Where did you get a sword like that?"

"Made it," Ephorah sheathed the weapon. "Now, who wants to try and round up the other five hundred zombies?"

89

Divine Food Fight

DAURGO

Sekhmet slashed at the dracolich with weapons and claws, but Daurgo simply slipped through space away from her and left her scratching at empty air.

"Too slow," Daurgo tossed a smoke bomb at the goddess, which exploded in a blast that covered the confused cat's face in soot.

Sekhmet responded by summoning a bow to her hands and firing arrows at the dragon faster than any human eye could perceive. Daurgo simply folded the space in front of himself so the arrows struck Sekhmet in the back.

As the goddess howled, partly from pain, but mostly in rage, Daurgo snapped his consciousness to another skeletal puppet, ready to start the record player he'd set up.

"This is getting boring," the lich sneered. "Let's liven it up with some music!"

Daurgo's skeleton placed a vinyl record on the player and started the first song. All throughout the Temple District, the nearby Industrial Zone, and even the Imperial Circle, music started to blare from a system of speakers Daurgo had secretly hooked up before the fight.

"It's time to party, let's party
  Hang out with yourself and have a crazy party
  Hey you, let's party

DIVINE FOOD FIGHT

Have a killer party and party!"

"What?" The goddess looked around in confusion. "Where is that coming from?"

"Wherever I feel like it," Daurgo chuckled. "Hey, want to see a trick I learned from Medjed?"

Daurgo pointed his right claw towards Sekhmet and made a laser of energized photons. This did nothing more than make a red dot that danced along the ground before landing on Sekhmet. The confused cat goddess poked at the red dot, unsure of what it was supposed to do.

Then the lich sent a bolt of electricity from his claw, arcing across the laser and slamming Sekhmet with enough heat to burn through her armor, flesh, and come out the back, starting a small fire on the ground behind her.

The goddess flailed around until she fell forward, clutching her stomach as her body started to regenerate.

"The best part? It aims itself!" The dragon laughed as Sekhmet got back to her feet.

"Let me guess," Sekhmet spat out a wad of golden ichor. "You don't have very good eye-hand coordination? So you need that cheap light trick to help you aim? I think I can take advantage of that."

Sekhmet fired three more arrows at Daurgo. This time, she aimed above, below, and around the dragon, who tried to create his previous folds in space again, but this time the pockets of space he tried to fold were completely off. As an arrow whizzed past his head, he turned his attention on the projectile just long enough for Sekhmet to fire another arrow.

This one punched a hole through the lich's armor and embedded itself in between Daurgo's ribs. Daurgo looked down for a moment and scoffed.

"Oh no, a piece of metal on a stick. My one weakness." The lich casually pulled the arrow out of his ribcage, only to realize the shaft was tied with a red linen ribbon.

The ribbon burst into a blaze of holy red light, burning the lich even through his armor, and forcing him to drop the arrow and instinctively fly higher above Sekhmet.

"Ha! Easy target!" Sekhmet fired several more arrows at the lich, lodging each one inside dragon's skeleton. This time, the holy ribbons burned him from within, paralyzing his wings and causing him to fall like a stone onto the rooftop.

Writhing in pain, Daurgo slipped himself out of sync with the normal flow of time, offering him a brief respite from these holy arrows. "Enough!" The dragon gritted his teeth. "Time to get comical."

Once he'd recovered, he slipped back in sync with time, where Sekhmet was waiting to fire another arrow at him. Snapping his claws, he stopped the flow of time just as she let the arrow loose, sidestepping the projectile. Sekhmet knocked another arrow; even if she couldn't fire it with time still stopped, she'd be ready to let it fly once it did.

"I think that's enough of those," Daurgo snapped as he swept his tail around to smack the bow out of the goddess's hands. She jumped up with cat reflexes to avoid the strike, but wasn't able to dodge the dragon's follow up as he clamped down on her bow with his teeth, snapping it in half between his jaws.

"Ah, much better," Daurgo spat out the remains of the bow as time was allowed to flow again. "Now then..."

Daurgo had practiced this over and over in the Blasted Wastes before trying it in a real fight. Try as he might, he only had about a ten percent success rate of teleporting items without direct line of sight. Fortunately, he'd prepared a lot of pies.

With great focus, a single pastry appeared in the air above Sekhmet, spinning as it fell and smacking the goddess in the face.

"Yes!" Daurgo squeaked before hiding how surprised he was that he had gotten that to work.

Sekhmet wiped whip cream off her face and tasted a bit. "Seriously? A pie?"

Daurgo nodded. "Consider it your just desserts."

The lich opened more portals, dropping in dozens of pies. Sekhmet didn't need to know he was firing them at her by the hundreds.

The goddess managed to dodge the first few pastries before one hit her in the face. Once she was blinded, more pies struck her from all sides until she was completely buried under a mountain of whip cream and flaky crusts.

Elsewhere, tons of pies that were way off target splattered all over other parts of the city.

Struggling under the strain, Daurgo finally relaxed. Trying to get a single pie to fall through the currents of the Spirit Plane where he wanted it to was hard enough, and he couldn't use the logic engines on his centipede to help him from this distance. Still, it was worth it to make a mockery of the goddess.

"Oh, that's just disgusting," Daurgo scowled. "I hate finding cat hair in my food. Things covered in cat hair are just gross."

Sekhmet wriggled her way out of the pile of pastries and wiped whip cream off her face. Even as she did, she still had pie filling stuck to her fur and whiskers.

"First, you challenge the gods themselves to a fight, then you pelt me with pies?" The goddess bent over like a real cat and tried to shake more of the pastries off her fur. "Why aren't you taking this seriously?"

"Because that's no fun." Daurgo aimed another red laser at Sekhmet and fried her with as much electricity as he could muster. The lightning flooded her body with so much heat her fur caught on fire and most of it burned away, leaving nothing but her twitching, cooked flesh.

Heaving, it took Sekhmet a few minutes to regenerate her skin and fur.

"See? That wasn't funny at all." Daurgo pointed another laser at Sekhmet, but this time blasted her with only a small amount of electricity. Instead of burning her, this time the shock left sparks jumping between her fur, which stood up on end and turned the war goddess into a confused puffball of fluff.

"Now that was fun!" The lich chuckled. "If only I had a mirror to show you. You look ridiculous!"

The fluffed-up Sekhmet roared and leapt off the rooftop into the air, drawing a pair of daggers and trying to slash at the dracolich. Daurgo slipped out of phase with time, letting Sekhmet slash at the air where he'd been before falling back to the roof. Once she landed, Daurgo realigned with the flow of time, and she leapt into the air to try and strike him again.

Daurgo shifted through space again, slipping behind her. Sekhmet managed to somersault in midair to redirect towards the dracolich, only to collide face-first with a golden frying pan. The goddess hit the pan with so much force that she bent the metal, almost leaving the impression of a bewildered lioness' face in the middle of the pan.

Sekhmet fell, crashing into the rooftop on her back and dropping her weapons, the frying pan still stuck to her face.

"What's the matter, kitty?" Daurgo chuckled. "Dragon got your tongue?"

Stunned, Sekhmet fumbled with the pan until she could pry it off her face, the soft metal tearing like foil as she wrenched it off her jowls.

"Did..." the goddess wheezed. "Did you make a solid gold frying pan...for a single joke?"

"Maybe." Daurgo smirked. "Worth it."

Still dazed, Sekhmet looked around at their rooftop battlefield. Pies had been thrown everywhere, an extremely expensive frying pan now lay at her feet, and somewhere, some strange contraption was still blaring loud, fast-paced music.

"Why...I don't understand," she finally said.

"Of course you don't," Daurgo chided. "You're an idea. And a war goddess at that. You have no idea what I'm doing to you, do you?"

90

Face the Music

ROSTAM

Ever since they'd fought a ghoul in the underground lab, Rostam had held onto the silver-plated axe Cyrus had made. As it turned out, silver worked well against the undead, too.

Namid had run to Silverstack Docks and told him about the undead that attacked the wizard students. Much to Namid's disappointment, Captain Nadia insisted on keeping Cindrocles on board *the Endurance*. She wasn't going to risk him being snuffed out or extinguished like he nearly was in Taisha.

"We could really use a living ball of fire right about now!" Namid grumbled.

"It's alright." Rostam brandished the silver-coated axe that Cyrus had made. "Let them hold down the fort here." He turned to Nadia. "That is, if the undead do make their way here, can you defend yourselves?"

The captain shrugged. "We can always take off if the zombies get too close."

"The lich already blew an airship out of the sky," Rostam replied. "I don't think the skies are safe. Do you want me to stay here?"

Nadia scanned the ship for a moment. "No. Go help your friends. We'll be alright."

Rostam followed Namid through the city. They took a longer way around the inside of the city walls to reach the Empyrian Quarter, hoping to meet up with the others. Even along the edges of the city, people were starting to panic, trying to fortify their homes or head for the city gates. An old man who was probably too senile to notice what was going on tried to sweep garbage from a sidewalk and was nearly run over by a panicked crowd. Some huddled inside their businesses and tried to protect their livelihoods from potential looters. Rostam couldn't help but notice that Namid didn't even mention the wealthier shops tightening their security.

Somehow, they reached Ephorah's street, where she was standing holding a black sword next to Amri and Cyrus. A pile of mangled zombies told Rostam that they'd been busy.

"Hey!" Cyrus smiled. "Reinforcements are here!"

"Not a moment too soon!" Amri pointed off at a cluster of corpses running towards them.

During her time in Kemet, Namid had apparently learned a thing or two about fighting the undead, because she was able to blow them up with small, well-time air explosions. Cyrus, Ephorah, and Rostam could deal with them in close quarters, but Namid could take them out from a distance.

Amri wasn't doing as well. He could set a zombie's clothes on fire with the snap of his fingers, but it turned out zombies didn't die when you set them on fire. They just got angrier and would set other things on fire while running around.

"Amri, can you try something else?" Cyrus dodged a flaming zombie's arm and touched his forehead. A blast of gunpowder exploded out the back of the corpse's skull. "Like, anything else?"

"Uh...well..." Amri looked around for a moment. "If fire's not working... logically..."

Rostam swung his axe at a zombie in a military uniform. The silver seemed to burn through the undead flesh like a hot knife through humus. As he did, another cadaver charged at Rostam with a bayonet.

As the corpse ran, ice crackled up the zombie's shins, and the zombie's legs snapped below the knee. It tumbled onto its belly, sprawled out in front of Rostam, who split its skull with his silver axe, and the corpse stopped moving.

"Ice is better, thanks!" Rostam called out to Amri as the next zombie tried to tackle him.

Pretty soon, the five of them had managed to defeat enough zombies that they had some breathing room. They could still see some running off through the city, but they seemed to be looking elsewhere for targets. Either they didn't know Rostam and the others were still alive, or they weren't interested in attacking a group that had just destroyed twenty or so zombies.

"That music," Amri looked up at the rooftops. They were near the Industrial Zone, where all the rooftops were flat slabs of concrete. "Where is that music coming from?"

With no more zombies attacking at the moment, Rostam paused and realized that somewhere, someone was playing some sort of fast-paced music:

"Cause we will never listen to your rules (NO)
 We will never do as others do (NO)
 Know what we want and we get it from you
 Do what we like and we like what we do!"

"What the hell is that?" Namid asked. "It sounds...mechanical."

"It's a recording," Rostam replied. "Like on a vinyl record."

"I have never heard a recording of a song like that." Cyrus scanned the streets to see if any new zombies were coming to attack.

"That lich has stuff from the Ancients," Amri replied. "It wouldn't surprise me if he had music recordings from that time. And I think I know what he's doing."

"Music has its own magic." Rostam's eyes widened. "Someone – Irene, a girl we transported – she told me that music was magical."

"It's psychological warfare," Amri added.

"Okay...so just try to ignore it, and it won't bother us, right?" Namid shrugged. "Psychological warfare can't hurt you if you don't let it get to you."

"The gods are made of psychology!" Armi gritted his teeth. "It's not for fighting us. There!" He pointed over at the rooftops where a goddess and Daurgo were fighting. Daurgo opened portals and pies came raining down on top of Sekhmet.

Splat!

"Ack!" Namid cried.

Rostam and the others looked at her, now covered in whip cream and pie filling. Around them, more pies fell from the sky, landing on buildings, lampposts, and in the streets. Ephorah wiped a finger on Namid's shoulder and gave it a taste.

"Cherries?"

"An evil dracolich pulls pies in from who-knows-where as a weapon against the gods, and your first thought is to lick some off somebody's shoulder?" Cyrus asked.

"No, wait a minute." Amri tried a finger of pie filling off his sister's sleeve.

"Has my shirt become a desert sampler?" Namid growled.

Amri ignored her. "She's right. It's just ordinary cherry pie. Which means... the act of hitting a goddess in the face with a pie..."

"I think you're reading too much into this," Ephorah pointed back at the goddess and the dragon. "See? He just hit her in the face with a frying pan. He's not some 'master planning' schemer. He's a buffoon who likes to make jokes."

"A god is an idea that people worship until it gains a personality of its own." Amri looked down at the ground, his eyes deep in thought. "If you throw a pie in a god's face, does he still look like a god to you?"

"Well...no," Ephorah admitted.

"And now he just hit her in the face with a frying pan." Amri squinted in the direction of the duel. "Forget the zombies. We need to stop that music!"

Rostam cupped his hand to one ear and listened for where the music was loudest. "I think there's a source over in that building!"

As the group started running for what sounded like a source of the music, Rostam couldn't help but glance back at Daurgo and Sekhmet. The lich had impaled the goddess on the blades on his tail, and now had her held close enough to give her a noogie, much to the cat-goddess's frustration. Try as he might, Rostam couldn't help but laugh at the flustered goddess trying to escape her captor. As he did, he thought he saw the goddess shrink slightly.

Crap, Rostam thought. *That's exactly what the lich is trying to do.*

FACE THE MUSIC

The building where the music seemed to be coming from was a warehouse with a fat lock on a thick steel door. Cyrus clapped his hands and touched the lock, but nothing happened.

"Hrm," Cyrus lifted the padlock and examined it. "Warded against corrosion. Oh well." The alchemist turned and touched the steel door, quickly turning the metal around the lock into rust, which crumpled as he kicked in the door, the lock clattering to the ground still intact and unopened. "Probably should've warded the door, too."

Ephorah scoffed. "I could have just smashed it open."

"We don't care!" Namid slipped into the warehouse and looked around. "There!" She pointed up at the ceiling, where a box-like contraption with a brass round horn had been installed. Inside the warehouse, the music was louder than ever.

"Strange," Amri squinted in the dim light of the building. "I don't see a record, or anything else to play the music."

"But it's definitely coming from that thing." Namid raised her arms to cast a spell. "I can take it out with an air explosion."

"Wait!" Amri called. "I need to get up there. I might be able to track the rest of the machines if I get up there before we break it."

Cyrus grabbed one of Namid's arms and lowered it. "It's worth giving him a shot."

"Okay..." Namid took her arm back. "But how do we get up there?"

"Look!" Rostam pointed to a ladder on one wall that lead up to a catwalk. Along the walkway, a door lead to the outside.

Ephorah followed the catwalk with her pointed finger. "That doesn't lead under the sound machine."

"Doesn't need to," Rostam replied. "It leads to the second floor. We can get to the ceiling from the outside, then reach the machine from there."

The five of them climbed up the ladder, with Rostam taking the lead, Amri and Cyrus behind him, and the girls covering the rear. Ephorah kept an eye on the floor as the others reached the catwalk, only climbing up herself once everyone else had made it.

Rostam opened the door along the catwalk to reveal a metal balcony along the side of the building. It must have been some sort of service access. Unfortunately, the roof was about three meters above them, and there didn't appear to be a ladder. Worse, the music was blaringly loud now, and Rostam could barely think.

"Anyone got any ideas?" The shipmate called over the noise.

"Give me a boost," Amri hollered back.

Rostam looked at the edge of the concrete roof and tried to imagine someone as weak as Amri pulling himself up. "Yeah, no offense, but you're not—"

"On it." Cyrus held his hands low enough for Amri to step up. He then lifted Amri onto his shoulders, getting him high enough for Amri to grab the edge of the roof with his arms outstretched.

Rostam shook his head. "How are you going to pull yourself up?"

Grunting, Amri pulled his chin above the edge of the roof, his legs flailed around for a moment, before he lifted one foot high enough to catch ahold of the ledge and pull himself up.

"Okay...I didn't actually think you were strong enough to do that," Rostam admitted.

Amri scanned the top of the warehouse. "What's this?"

"We can't see from down here!" Cyrus yelled. "So why are you asking us?"

"This thing is communicating with another machine!" Amri called back. "I can't see it, but I can feel some sort of energy moving between this machine and another device somewhere else!"

"Can you track the source?" Rostam asked.

"No," Amri hollered. "Wait, maybe...If I can use a magical energy reading spell... the source is another building several blocks away!"

"Can you disable it?" Cyrus asked.

"Hang on..." Amri placed his hands on the dragon's device. "There's no wires. It's using some kind of radio wave to send signals. If I can use that wave to send a pulse..."

All at once, the music stopped playing. Instead of whatever music Daurgo had setup, the machine only made scratchy, fuzzy sounds, like rain on an old carpet.

"What did you just do?" Namid asked.

"I sent a jolt of electricity back to where the signal was coming from." Amri came back to the edge of the roof and looked down at the others. "I think it fried the source, wherever it is."

91

No Witnesses

DAURGO

Holding Sekhmet over a beam he'd ripped out of one of the nearby buildings, Daurgo kept one foot on the goddess's body to pin her down while he repeatedly bonked her on the head with a balloon shaped like a sledgehammer, making a squeaking noise with each whack. All of a sudden, Daurgo's music stopped all throughout the city.

"What?" The lich looked around at the buildings where he'd rigged his music devices, eventually spotting a warehouse with several young humans, one of which was on the ceiling, and smoke coming out of the building where he'd hidden the record player.

"Do those meatbags have any idea how hard it is to find pre-Calamity music records?" The dragon squeezed Sekhmet like a furry stress ball. "Still in working condition, no less?"

"Ha!" Sekhmet wheezed. "Your plan has failed! Foiled by mortals!"

"Mortals were part of my plan," Daurgo replied. "Oh, sure, a handful have figured out what I'm doing: make a mockery of you until you no longer look like a goddess to them. Doesn't matter; the mortals who can see us have done more than enough to fill their end of the equation."

Confusion filled Sekhmet's face. "Their end?"

"That's right, other people's beliefs about you are only half the formula," Daurgo grinned. "The other half is what people believe about me. It turns out that if you act like an unstoppable cheeky bastard, people start to believe you *are* one. But the coup de grâce, the final ingredient, is what *I* believe about myself. If I believe you are nothing more than a joke and act as if that were true, then you *are* a joke to ME!"

With that, Daurgo bit Sekhmet's head clean off of her shoulders. Instead of golden ichor dripping out, red blood, as mortal as a human's, flowed from her neck. The dracolich spat out the head, tossed the rest of her body on top of it, and aimed another one of his electrified lasers at the corpse, incinerating it with the intense heat.

As he finished off what had been a goddess, Daurgo felt a ripple between the material world and the Spirit Plane. The universe itself recognized that Sekhmet was dead.

"As above, so below," the lich muttered. "Now then, time to tie up some loose ends."

The dragon shifted space around himself, appearing just above the building where the humans had destroyed one of his music machines. Those hooligans knew too much.

One of the humans on the rooftop scrambled for the railing he'd used to get up there as Daurgo flew up to the building. The lich couldn't aim one of his electrolasers at the boy quickly enough to stop him. Instead, he fired a sweeping arc of lightning along the side of the building, cutting through the walls and masonry with intense heat.

The human, a smaller-than-usual boy, stopped himself just short of running through the superheated brickwork and looked up in panic at the dracolich hovering above him.

Yes, hold still for me. Daurgo focused a laser of magic. A red dot fluttered on the rooftop towards the boy as the dragon aimed at his target.

And then, just as Daurgo pulsed a bolt of electricity along the laser's path, the boy dive-rolled out of the way. Surprised, Daurgo's gaze shifted from the scorched, molten spot on the ceiling to the boy who'd dodged his blast.

"You use that red light to aim the lightning, don't you?" The human asked. "A bolt of lightning like that should have made a clap of thunder. Which means...you're using that light as a medium for the electricity. The same way

I used the radio wave to fry your device."

"Interesting theory." Daurgo descended onto the rooftop. "Too bad it won't save you."

The lich swept another electrolaser across the top of the roof, slicing through the space where the boy was. Except, the human stomped his foot into the ground and pulled up a pillar of bricks, mortar, and plaster dust in between himself and the dragon. The laser hit the dust and refracted all throughout the cloud of particles, scattering the electricity into a ball of lighting that forced Daurgo to recoil.

"You have terrible aim," the boy said matter-of-factly. "That's why you can't just point that red-lightning thing at me. You have bad eye-hand coordination. Probably because you have six limbs and a prehensile tail."

Daurgo frowned. "You wreck my machines, you know too much, and now, you're getting on my nerves. Just how dead do you want to be, meatbag?"

"Wait a minute..." the boy seemed to be ignoring Daurgo and was merely thinking aloud now. "When you attacked the tournament, you teleported in and made a big explosion of air. Probably displaced by your sudden appearance. But just now, you showed up above me without so much as a breeze. You use different methods to teleport, don't you?"

"Seriously?" Daurgo lashed out at the boy with his tail, but the kid threw himself to the ground and slipped under the blow. "You just don't stop, do you?"

The kid jumped up and ran for Daurgo's legs. The dragon tried to kick him, but he was too small and fast for the lich to stop him. In seconds, the boy was between the dragon's legs and tail, a spot dragons are sensitive about, as it's difficult for them to defend and often lead to many undignified dragon deaths.

"Enough!" Daurgo looked up and teleported above the building again, turning himself around in mid transit to look down on the building. Noting the four other humans on a metal walkway trying to get up to the rooftop, Daurgo aimed his red light at the walkway, only for his laser to disappear before he could electrify the humans and cut the boy on the roof off from his only escape.

"What?" Daurgo looked at the walkway in confusion. "Where did my laser..." then he realized what was wrong and looked down. "No...my arm is gone."

NO WITNESSES

One of the humans, a girl this time, had her hands up to perform some kind of spell. Before Daurgo could figure out what it was, a small vacuum of air under his left shoulder burst and snapped his left arm off, armor and all, landing on the ground next to his severed right arm.

Reappearing on the ground next to the building, Daurgo reached out with his mouth and lunged for the walkway. The humans scattered out of his way, letting him chomp down on the metal floor, ripping it out from the side of the building.

One of the humans had managed to scamper back inside before the lich ripped the floor out from beneath them. Another hung onto the remaining floor near the doorway. A male human clung to a metal pole stuck to the side of the warehouse, and the girl with the air explosions was hanging onto one of the pole-clinging boy's legs.

In their confusion, Daurgo was able to restore his arms with necromancy and used another electrolaser to set fire to the ground below the dangling humans. The boy on the roof took the bait and ran up to the edge waving his hands, raising a cloud of dust along the ground that extinguished the flames.

"Got you!" Daurgo lashed out with his claw and caught the scrawny human boy. "Bad aim? Maybe. But not for catching prey." He held the boy up to his head and smirked. "Oh, and just for the record? I slip in and out of the Spirit Plane to teleport, and fold space to go places I can see."

Daurgo felt a thud as something landed on the side of his helmet. One of the other humans, the one that had been standing on what was left of the walkway, had leapt off the building and jumped onto him, hacking away at his skull armor with an axe. At first, this was nothing more than a nuisance. But as soon as the lich tried to bite the boy from the roof in half, the new boy's axe struck his jaw, and Daurgo felt the silver blade burn through his necrotic body.

The dragon roared in pain and confusion, and as he did, he felt spikes of stone pierce his feet and root him to the spot. Then he felt something smash his left leg, shattering parts of his ankle bone and denting his armor. As he turned to see what was attacking his left leg, something else corroded the armor around his left leg and wove the rusted metal into the gaps of his leg bones. Losing all balance, Daurgo fell forward, his feet still pinned to the ground, but smacked the bottom of his skull on the pavement below.

As if that weren't enough, his vision began to blur. Frost spread across the lenses of his helmet and clouded his sight. Sure, he could see in the dark, but not through ice. He could even smell the magic coming out of the boy in his hand making his helmet freeze.

Trying to think of options, Daurgo activated the tesla coils on his back. He could hear the energy arc to the remains of the metal railing, likely avoiding the humans altogether. No good. His tail wasn't flexible to strike the humans at his feet. He silently cursed himself for letting humans get between his legs. If he could still breathe fire, he'd burn the one freezing his helmet and...

Wait, the lich thought. *It doesn't have to be fire, exactly.*

Daurgo let go of the boy in his claw and pressed a release valve that opened two flaps along his neck. Steam from inside his chestplate engulfed the boy in scalding hot water, melting the ice off of his helmet at the same time.

The teenage sorcerer screamed as his skin became covered in burns, and one of the other humans ran away from the lich's legs towards the burned one. Clapping his hands, this other boy tried to heal the sorcerer.

"Got you!" Daurgo lunged forward to bite down on the two boys, fangs bared to tear them to shreds.

Then he bit down on something metal, something that was wedged into his mouth. The other boy, the one with the axe, had shoved his weapon in between his jaws. Worse, the head of the axe was silver, and as Daurgo bit down, the pure metal ground against his undead fangs. Genuine pain, not just the fake pain liches allow themselves to feel to know when they've been hurt, flooded his skull. Daurgo furiously bellowed every swear word in every language he knew as the silver burned his unholy body.

Swinging his head around, trying to get the painful metal out of his mouth, he barely paid any attention to the two human girls. One of them had been pounding away at his legs with inhuman strength, while the other attacked him with more explosions of compressed air. If he hadn't been thrashing around, she might have succeeded in blowing his arms off again.

Somehow, in all of this confusion, Daurgo felt something snap. The girl with super strength had broken his right leg completely, leaving his foot behind.

NO WITNESSES

And now, everything from the ankle up was free to move again.

An idea occurred. He could repair any damage to his feet with necromancy later. If he sacrificed his remaining foot for now...

Daurgo ignored the pain in his mouth and rolled over to his left with all the strength he had left. The twisted, corroded metal that had been melted into the bones of his ankle cracked and broke, wrenching his angle off his left foot, allowing the dragon to roll freely on his side. He kept rolling until he was back on his belly, far enough away from the humans to spread his wings. He might not be able to walk with broken feet, but he could still fly.

Once he was airborne the dragon shook his head against a nearby wall and knocked the silver axe out of his mouth. Finally relieved and able to assess the situation, he looked down on the humans and smiled.

"What does your kind call this again?" He asked. "Oh, right! Death from above."

92

Cooking with Gas

NAMID

The dragon hovered above the roof of the warehouse. Ephorah had pummeled his legs so badly that they were practically useless, but that didn't matter while the lich was in the air. Namid had tried to blast his limbs off again with compressed air, but the dragon had started moving about so much that her trick wouldn't work again.

Amri had been burned by a blast of steam, and Namid couldn't help but wince at the sight of him. She'd been hit by a similar blast during the Grand Wizard Tournament and ended up unconscious for a while. For some reason, she'd woken up without any burns. Must have been because of the medical team on duty at the time.

Cyrus had started healing Amri with alchemy. Rostam had lost his axe and was now looking around for something to fight with. And Ephorah had no way to fight the dragon in the sky.

Daurgo descended until he was only a few meters above the boys and pointed one of his claws at Amri and Cyrus. A green gas sprayed from a tube on the lich's wrist. Namid didn't know what that cloud was meant to do, but she didn't want either of them to find out.

Namid summoned a gust of wind and blew whatever gas the lich had sprayed away from the boys.

As the gas was blown away, the dragon turned his gaze on Namid. "Oh, that's right. You're the one who plays tricks with the wind."

Daurgo created a vacuum of air in the palm of his left claw, then made a high-pressure bubble around his green gas. The chemical weapon flowed up into his left claw, and he glared at Namid.

"That's an interesting trick with the air pressure," the lich chuckled. "Figured I'd give it a try."

The dragon funneled all the gas towards Namid. She tried to blow it away, but the lich's magic overpowered hers. Namid was enveloped by the green gas within seconds.

"Hold your breath!" Cyrus called.

Namid had just enough time to plug her nose as the gas surrounded her. The gas burned her eyes, and she shut them tight to keep out the pain.

"Smart move," Daurgo flexed his magic and encircled the poisonous gas around her. "But how long can you—"

The lich was interrupted by a gunshot. Rostam was holding a smoking pistol. He must have grabbed it off one of the zombified soldiers from earlier.

"A gun?" The dragon turned his gaze to Rostam. "Not even a big gun, but some tiny caliber like that? You must be really desperate."

Rostam took another shot, which glanced off the dragon's armor. Although it bounced off harmlessly, the *ping* of a bullet on metal plating was annoying enough to keep Daurgo distracted. With the dragon's attention on Rostam, Namid managed to blow the gas away from herself and took in a deep breath.

Cyrus scooped up some sand off the ground and started alchemically shaping it into some sort of flask. "Can you get the gas in here?" He called.

"Why?" Namid asked, but she began channeling the wind around her to direct the poison gas into his container anyway. "What are you going to do?"

Once the gas was safely compressed into his make-shift container, the alchemist clapped his hands and poked one finger into the hole. The green cloud inside quivered and turned clear.

"Hydrochloric acid," Cyrus formed more glass to close up the flask. "If we can hit the dragon with this, it should screw up the gadgets on his armor."

Namid made a mental note to question how Cyrus knew what kind of poisonous gas the lich had used, but put it aside for now. Rostam couldn't keep the dragon distracted forever.

"Who here has the best throwing arm?" Cyrus asked. "Can Ephorah—"

"My arms are enhanced," Ephorah admitted. "Not my back or other muscles. These gloves don't do much except punch."

"But it's a gas, right?" Namid asked.

Cyrus nodded. "In this form, it'll corrode everything from machinery to bones."

Rostam had ducked inside the warehouse and was shooting at Daurgo from the door frame. The dragon still couldn't land; his legs were completely busted. He tried spraying more gas at Rostam, but the boy ducked inside the building while the lich zeroed in on the upper floor door, being the only other exit Rostam could use. Instead, Rostam smashed a window on the upper floor and took another shot at the dragon from there.

Out of frustration, Daurgo focused a beam of red light on the furthest window and blasted it with electricity, which he then swept across the entire wall of the upper floor, shattering every window in his path. Namid wasn't sure Rostam was okay until a gun popped out from behind a window frame and fired again.

"Now's our best chance," Namid looked at Cyrus. "Throw that flask as close to the dragon as you can. I'll take it from there."

Cyrus nodded and hurled the makeshift flask at the ground beneath the dragon. It shattered on the pavement below, releasing the gas, which settled on the ground and started to flow outward.

Namid willed the air around the gas to rise in pressure, with a single shaft of low pressure between the gas on the ground and the dracolich. The acidic gas funneled up into the lich's armor from the bottom up.

"Hold it there!" Cyrus called. He had grabbed a piece of metal off the railing and turned it into powder with alchemy.

Daurgo must have realized he'd been encased in some kind of gas, and turned away from Rostam in the warehouse and zeroed in on Namid. She could feel the dragon realizing she was a bigger threat now than the small-caliber gunfire as he swooped down until he was right above the ground. The dragon flew at the girl, who did her best to keep the bubble of acid gas around him.

As soon as he came near Cyrus, the alchemist threw a handful of powder at the lich. The dragon looked surprised just long enough for Namid to dive out of his way, releasing her spell on the gas.

The acid started to react with whatever Cyrus had thrown, fizzling all over the lich's armor. Patches of yellow started to appear all over the armor, caking onto him like flies on honey. Something inside of him creaked and strained, and steam burst out of a tube inside his armor.

Confused, Daurgo stopped in midflight and felt around his torso. Steam burst a hole in his chest plate, and cracks started to appear all over his armor. Piece after piece flaked off, and Namid could see some of the machinery inside. The lich had actually designed his armor so that parts of the machinery took up space inside his hollow ribcage. One of his ribs even snapped off, despite being thicker than a man's arm, and Namid remembered what Cyrus had said about the acid weakening bones.

"Ah, I see." The lich looked at Namid and Cyrus. "Hydrochloric acid, and some iron dust as a catalyst. I've been fighting too many gods; they're never this creative. They can't be. Only mortals can come up with novelties like this. And that's exactly what I love to see."

The dragon smirked and pointed his claw at a nearby office building. He fired another electric blast from one of his red lights, sweeping it around wherever he could and starting fires on every floor.

"Now then," the dragon chuckled. "How many people are in that building, I wonder? And how many of them barricaded their doors to keep my zombies out?"

"Who cares?" Namid asked. "You think we're going to–"

"Ah, dammit!" Cyrus ran towards the burning building.

"Hey!" Namid called. "Get back here!" But he was already out of earshot. And before she could say anything, Rostam had run after him.

Daurgo raised a bony arm and green energy swirled around his claws. The bones from his shattered feet flew up from where he'd left them and reattached themselves to his legs. Then the lich landed right next to Amri, who was finally starting to get up from his previously being burned and reconstructed by Cyrus.

"This is the only human who was able to figure out my spells so quickly;" he chuckled. "So he's the only one who's a real threat for now."

The dragon opened his jaw to bite Amri in half. Then the lich paused, his skull twitched like he was sniffing Amri for a moment as a short panic washed over him.

"No," he whispered. Then the lich heaved, as if he were trying to vomit. "You've got to be kidding me! That smell...That's absolutely foul!"

A bolt of lightning from the skies came down and struck the dragon's head. Dazed, the dragon held up one claw and froze time. Then he looked up and, sure enough, another bolt of lightning was overhead, slowly coming down to strike him again in the exact same place.

Time must not actually be stopped, Namid thought. *Or that bolt wouldn't be moving. It must just be really slow.*

"Hm," the dragon looked at Amri again. "Another time, I'll have to plot out your demise later. For now, I've got bigger fish to fry."

Daurgo spread his wings and took off into the sky, letting time return to normal after he was far away from where the lightning bolt struck, leaving Namid next to her brother.

93

New Solutions, New Problems

DAURGO

"I know this is rich coming from me, but your powers are bull crap," the lich snarled as he landed near Marduk, who was standing on a balcony of the Imperial Palace. He knew comedy wouldn't weaken Marduk like it did other deities. When mortals defined a deity or similar immortal as being a particularly powerful fighter, it was almost impossible to break that belief with jokes.

"I just got back from Petryan," Marduk frowned. "Red herrings, psychotic drugs, ogre zombies...but there was one thing about your scheme that never made sense. Why use anagrams for all of your train deliveries...unless you wanted us to find them?"

"Yes, yes. Very impressive," Daurgo nodded mockingly. "You figured out I had laid a trap and then you walked right into it anyway. I know you're probably expecting us to have some final match, but the fact is that you're too late to stop me. I killed the cat goddess, Horus is still pulling himself together, and my other plans are all tied up with a nice little bow."

"If you think I'm going to let you leave this city," Marduk gritted his teeth. "After all you've done—"

"I don't need you to *let* me do anything," Daurgo drew a grenade from his armor, pulled the pin, and tossed it underhanded at Marduk. "Here, hold this a second."

Marduk caught the pin-less grenade with wide eyes and threw it across the balcony, where it rolled along the floor harmlessly. Confused, he pointed his finger at the grenade and launched a beam of fire at it, blasting off the metal casing and revealing a small block wrapped in brown, shiny paper.

"Another one of your pranks?" Marduk glared at the dragon.

"Kind of." Daurgo pressed a trigger in his armor, detonating the brick of C4.

The explosion shattered the balcony floor, unmooring it from the palace and sending Marduk tumbling to the ground below. He was able to fall somewhat gracefully, but he couldn't stop Daurgo from activating his logic engine. Before the god could react, the dracolich was safe inside the Spirit Plane, on his way back to his centipede fortress.

Inside the centipede's control center, Daurgo turned to Aquila, who had been monitoring things from a swivel chair.

"So..." the thief tilted her head. "How did it go?"

"Killed a goddess, did lots of damage, minimal harm to my own plans..." Daurgo didn't hide his frustration. "But one of the humans figured out more than he should have about my powers. And I couldn't kill him."

"You can kill gods but not a mortal?" Aquila asked.

"Not just any mortal. He had the scent of a god's manipulations on him," Daurgo hissed. "Someone is playing games with that boy's fate."

"What?" Aquila leaned back in her chair. "How do you mean?"

"Gods can play with the fates of mortals," Daurgo explained. "They can manipulate the winds of destiny, bend the rules of biology, even the laws of probability to keep mortals alive for their own purposes."

"So...the guy's functionally immortal?" Aquila's brow furrowed.

"Not really," Daurgo admitted. "He can still die of old age, obviously. And as soon as his usefulness to whichever god favors him is complete, he'll be fair game. But until then, he might survive literally anything. You stab him, and you'll somehow miss his vital organs. You shoot him, and he'll wind up having some pocket watch that stops the bullet. And worse, the bullet might bounce back and hit you in the face; funny things can happen to people who try to play with fate."

"Oh," Aquila nodded with wide eyes of understanding. "So, he's got plot

NEW SOLUTIONS, NEW PROBLEMS

armor."

"What?" Daurgo shot Aquila a look. "No, he's just got someone pulling fate's strings to keep him alive, even when it defies probability or logic."

"Right," Aquila nodded again. "Plot armor."

"Oh, for crying out loud!" Daurgo rolled the green lights in his eye sockets. "The point is, unpredictable supernatural shenanigans can occur if I try to kill him. And that's a problem, because he knows too much, and someone is protecting him."

"Hang on," Aquila paused. "From what I remember...when Zeus wanted to save Sarpedon from dying to Patroclus in *the Illiad*, all of the other gods demanded that they get to save their favorite mortals too, and Hera told Zeus the others wouldn't approve of him meddling in fates if he didn't allow it. And the price ended up being so steep Zeus backed out of preventing Sarpedon from his brutal death."

"Okay, seriously," Daurgo growled. "How do you know that?"

"So, assuming the rules are something like that," Aquila ignored her boss. "Shouldn't there be some heavy cost to some god playing with that guy's fate? Like, opening the door for other gods to do the same, or something like that?"

"Yes..." Daurgo wasn't about to overlook his minion's knowledge of old literature, but she'd raised a good point. "Every action has a reaction. If a god is playing games with fate, it will have consequences. And fate has a sense of humor; I can exploit that. I'll need to pull back and observe the situation to figure out my next move. Speaking of which, what did our friends over at the Super-Secret Society of Elderly Janitors have to say about their little assignment?"

"I offered the society enough gold to post their janitors all over the capital city," Aquila smirked. "Of course, I didn't tell them who I was working for, but I did give them your instructions. Just as you suspected, the Tomb Lords couldn't resist watching your...performance. They had undead rats and ravens pouring out of specific spots, where runegates are guaranteed to be hidden. It'll take time to get all of the reports in, but you should have details of their entire portal network in Hadesh in a day or two. Wasn't able to get them positioned in other cities, though."

"My undead ogres and rats covered that for me," Daurgo directed a skeleton to pull out a map and lay it out on a table in the bridge. This map showed some of the details of Janaan's topography, but it primarily featured known points of connection between the material plane and the Duat. Places where one person could open a permanent gate between two distant locations were marked throughout the region, with leylines – fissures between the worlds were magic could pour easily into the physical world – drawn in shades of purple.

"It must have taken them centuries to map all those routes," Daurgo chuckled. "Even without the Calamity, millennia of changes in the landscape would shift the navigable paths through the Spirit Plane. And now, I will be able to mark every place they know and keep a record stored in my logic engines; no more slow calculations before teleporting. I can also keep a close eye on the Tomb Lords' activities if they cause any more trouble, and I was able to humiliate the Egyptian gods in the process. Not a bad day."

"You're not worried about playing right into the Tomb Lords' hands?" Aquila winced and looked up at the dracolich.

"You must have known that they wanted you to do this."

"So?" Daurgo shrugged. "What do I care for their plans? Let them have their schemes. I'm playing a much bigger game with more important players."

"And there aren't going to be any major consequences to killing a god?" Aquila asked. "Sekhmet's still a goddess. Killing her has got to have some kind of effects, right?"

"Probably not," Daurgo shrugged. "She's a war goddess. The Borealans haven't been to war in two generations. All she did for them is consecrate weapons to fight things like me. How important could she be?"

"I guess." Aquila pointed to the Ring of Solomon. "It was easy for one of your zombies to steal this and hand it off to me. They didn't even bother trying to secure it, and with everyone panicking, there wasn't much trouble."

"Oh, yeah." Daurgo looked at the ring. "Almost forgot about this." He picked up the ring and looked it over. It was a beautifully ornate piece of jewelry, but it had no signs or traces of any magical power. The strange symbols engraved into the ring's head could not be ward lines, and there

NEW SOLUTIONS, NEW PROBLEMS

were no signs of spirits or other entities bound within it like an artifact.

Examining the ring further, a thought dawned on the dracolich. "Wait a minute...a ring that could tell the king anything he wished to know...and the king was known for being wise and specifically being humble enough to ask for wisdom..."

Daurgo sent one of his undead rats to rummage through the artifacts of power he had in storage and retrieved the Philosopher's Stone. The rodent scampered with the stone in tow and presented it to its draconic master. Daurgo took the stone, a piece of plain-looking sandstone, and placed it against the Ring of Solomon.

As soon as the objects touched, the stone shrank until it could socket itself within the ring's head, a perfect fit.

"Figures," Daurgo muttered.

What you are trying to do is impossible, the stone whispered back through the ring. Its voice was Daurgo's own, echoing through the lich's skull. *You cannot bring back the dead. Nothing will change that.*

Daurgo chuckled and placed the ring on one of his bony claws. The ring expanded until it could fit his draconic appendages exactly. "Are you the type to take out insurance on your universe?" He asked the stone. "You might want to start, because I'm about to wreck it."

94

One Step Closer

AMENHOTEP

Sitting on his throne, the High Tomb Lord waited for his fellow liches to be brought into his council chamber on their thrones. Mereshank and Djedefre were carried by slaves and set down on Amenhotep's right; Arkeon and Sekhet were brought over to their godking's left. Then Pausiris' scarab throne entered last, crawling on mechanical legs and depositing him next to Sekhet.

"So," Arkeon began. "The dragon took the bait."

"You sound surprised," Amenhotep tilted his head at the sorcerer.

"I had my doubts," Arkeon admitted. "Forgive me, my godking."

"Such a pity, but I will forgive you. This time." Amenhotep made it sound like he was disappointed in the sorcerer, but in reality, it was good to keep his underlings surprised once in a while.

"I am not convinced the dragon was completely fooled;" Pausiris added. "He killed Sekhmet. He could have simply beaten her into submission, stolen the ring, and left her alive. Instead, he went through the proper planning to fully murder a goddess. I think that was his real goal."

"It doesn't matter." Amenhotep smirked. "The death of the war goddess will make things even easier for us going forward."

"What is our next step, my godking?" Pausiris asked.

Amenhotep looked at Sekhet, who bowed her head before answering the scientist's question.

"Subterfuge," the sage explained. "I have agents spread throughout the empire now. Some of them have managed to climb into high positions, others have simply bribed imperial citizens to move things in the right direction."

"And that direction is?" Pausiris' voice was trying to hide some form of impatience, but he wasn't doing it very well.

"For the empire to tear itself apart before we even invade," Sekhet replied. "In the ancient times, older empires could never really do this; their leaders could be excessively decadent and drive their civilizations into ruin, but the destruction couldn't really come from the commoners; they had no power. But things are different for the Borealan Empire. Their commoners have lots of power. We just need them to aim it at each other."

Djedefre, who had been looking bored until now, stirred his head to look at Sekhet. "What kind of power? Is it the guns?"

"No, you imbe– well, maybe." Sekhet paused. "Almost everyone in the empire does own a gun. That might actually happen when the riots start."

"And how does that happen?" Arkeon asked. "The riots starting?"

"Ah, I'm glad you asked." Amenhotep stood from his throne. "I would like all of you to follow me. I have something to show you all."

The other Tomb Lords looked at each other. It was highly unusual for them to leave their thrones during one of these meetings. And yet, the High Tomb Lord had simply gotten up from his seat and walked to a door too small to fit a throne carried by slaves. What was he planning?

Arkeon was the first to get up, followed by Pausiris, Sekhet, Djedefre, and finally Mereshank. All of the liches followed their master through a side door into a smaller room where a young boy who couldn't have been older than five sat in one corner with his legs folded under his chin. He was the same boy Sekhet had brought in from her laboratory; one of the ones who had chosen to starve instead of follow her commands for her experiments. Now, instead of the starving, emaciated child from before, he had been fed back up to a healthy weight.

"Good afternoon, Ali," Amenhotep clasped his hands politely. "I've heard you requested an...opportunity."

The boy, who must have been named Ali, bowed his head politely before the

High Tomb Lord. "Yes, my lord. I wish to serve you. Properly."

"Well, I must say," Amenhotep gave a knowing look to the other liches. "That is wonderful news. Do you think you'd be up to a task right now?"

"Yes," the boy said emphatically.

"Excellent." Amenhotep signaled for two guards. "Bring him in."

The guards dragged a man bound and gagged from outside the room. His head had been covered by a sack cloth bag, and when it was removed the man's face had been so visibly bruised that he could barely open one eye.

"This man operated an inn that harbored two girls recently," Amenhotep tilted his head as he inspected the innkeeper. "One of them was the girl who escaped from the city with property stolen from my administration building. He has aided and abetted a spy."

The innkeeper's throat had been cut, not so as to kill him, but to sever his vocal cords. But even if he could speak, he was too badly beaten to respond.

Amenhotep received a sword from one of the guards and handed it to Ali. "Bring me the traitor's head."

Ali paused, took the sword, and then looked at the innkeeper. He hesitated one last time before swinging the blade at the man's neck. Of course, a five-year-old wasn't going to cut through a man's neck in one blow. Ali spent several minutes trying to cut off the head before it finally came off. He then picked up the head and presented it to the lich.

"Thank you," Amenhotep nodded. "You will go far one day." He turned to the guards. "Take him to training."

"Okay..." Sekhet waited until the guards and Ali had left before asking questions. "How did you do that?"

"Hm," Amenhotep chuckled. "This one is harder to show, easier to tell. What you saw was a boy broken by isolation. For the last week, the girls who I showed you earlier have turned against this boy. They have teased him, berated him, and finally ostracized him. You see, the girls are convinced that service to me is good, and so a boy who refuses to serve must be evil. He has no other peers, no other family. This isn't like your pit where you dumped all of the disobedient youths together, and they all still had each other." The High Tomb Lord gave Sekhet a dismissive glance. "This was different. And so, he could either accept the...narrative of his peers, or he could sit forever in isolation. An older boy would have taken more time. That's why it's best to get them when they're young."

Amenhotep finally took one last look at his fellow Tomb Lords. A handful of people he'd personally picked to build his empire. Two nobles too incompetent to do anything with the high status to which they'd been born; a sorcerer who wanted to practice the blackest magics with impunity, a scientist who wanted to explore the world...and a former priestess, who sought to climb the ranks of society at any cost. Two idiots. Three geniuses. None the wiser.

Soon, Amenhotep thought to himself. *This world will be mine. And after that, so will the stars.*

95

An Incorporeal Warning

AMRI

"So, you were able to identify some of the dragon's magics?" Marduk stood in the street where his winds had dropped the boy off safely and examined Amri as if he were a piece in a puzzle, trying to decide where to put him. "That's certainly progress."

"Thank you, for saving us." Amri bowed his head before the god. "I know it was you who stopped the dragon from finishing us off."

"Don't worry about that. Your friends were the ones who put out the fires he started." Marduk held up a large leather bag that he seemed to materialize from thin air and produced a red fish from inside of it. "Now we know why he's so powerful; why he can throw gods around like we're a joke."

"Is that...a herring?" Amri asked.

"It's because he genuinely believes we are a joke, and he acts as if that belief were true." Marduk gritted his teeth. "In short, he has an unshakeable faith in his own abilities."

"Does...does it actually work like that?" Amri gazed at the fish for a moment. "I mean, I had my suspicions he was using comedy to make other people stop believing in gods, but does believing in yourself really make you unstoppable?"

"Sometimes," Marduk admitted. "There are limits, like with all beliefs. But you can't even imagine the reality-bending things mortals have pulled off just by sheer force of will, and technically, Daurgo is still mortal. At least, his soul is, wherever he's hidden it."

"You'd also be surprised at how much of your current world is built on such beliefs."

This was a new voice. A girl Amri didn't recognize. Amri turned to see a young girl, about Namid's age, sitting on top of a garbage can with her legs folded and a sinister smirk on her face. She had dark hair, and was dressed like a schoolgirl, but Amri had started to get a sense for when the person in front of him wasn't human.

"You!" Marduk summoned a bow to his hand and drew a bolt of lightning as if it were an arrow.

"Oh, please," the girl rolled her eyes. "You know damn well I'm not corporeal. What is a bold of lightning going to–"

Marduk released the shaft of electricity, which passed through the girl's legs and struck the garbage can. The bin exploded, sending trash everywhere. The entire top half of the trash can was vaporized.

The girl floated in midair above where the bin had been for a moment. And then, as if gravity finally realized that she should be falling, tumbled into the garbage below. Amri didn't understand why an imaginary girl would be covered in filth after falling into real garbage, but then, his brain was probably filling in the gaps, and a normal girl would be covered in hot trash if that had happened to her.

"Okay..." The girl made a disgruntled face as she stood up from the trash. "Rather immature for you, nephew."

"Who is this?" Amri pointed his thumb at the girl as he looked at Marduk.

"She is Lamashtu," Marduk snarled. "Evil goddess of the Sumerians. And my eternal enemy."

"But she's not physical..." Amri observed. "At least, not right now."

"She can't fully enter the physical world," Marduk maintained his guard. "Not inside of civilization."

"Well, well," Lamashtu didn't even bother dusting the filth off of herself as she examined Amri. "So this is the new mortal you've taken a liking to? He's perfect!" She laughed.

"Leave," Marduk ordered. "Right. Now."

Lamashtu shuddered, as if Marduk's order held some mystical power over her. Scowling, she flung herself to her hands and knees and shook, her body morphing from that of a girl to a grotesque, monstrous beast larger than an ox. Her head became that of a lioness, her feet talons, her hands clawed. Her body became matted with fur, and a pair of feathery wings burst from her back.

"I will give you this warning, mortal!" Lamashtu's wings began to flap, as if against her will, and lifted her off the ground. "If you think this god is your friend, your role model, or anyone else you respect, you will live a long, wretched life, until you die broken and alone! YOU CANNOT ESCAPE YOUR FATE!"

As her wings beat, a cloud of dust enveloped Lamashtu. When the sky finally cleared, the goddess was gone.

Amri turned to Marduk for answers, but the god just gritted his teeth.

"I have work to do," Marduk looked to Amri. "The fact that she's able to start manifesting even as a shade is a sign of things to come. We used to have Pazuzu to keep her away, but...myths change. I must reinforce the barriers keeping her out of your world. Go. Join your friends. We will speak again soon."

96

No Going Back

EPHORAH

After the dragon had left the city, things never really returned to normal. No one in Hadesh truly believed they were safe anymore. While the dragon hadn't caused anywhere near as much damage to the city this time, the initial panic, followed by more looting than the last time, had done enough.

As before, the Empyrian Quarter faced the worst of it. First, because the zombies had initially ravaged that part of the city, and then when the zombies had been dealt with, some people took full advantage of the situation and robbed the homes of their own neighbors.

Ephorah couldn't shake the thought that if she, Rostam, Amri, Namid, and the other guy hadn't gotten involved, the zombies might have kept robbers from looting the Empyrian Quarter.

After the winds themselves had saved them from falling to their deaths, the five had agreed to return to their respective homes and try to protect their families. Except the alchemist; he apparently went back to the College of Alchemy. *Family must not mean much to bories,* Ephorah had thought.

The group had agreed to meet the next day at the Academic's Food Court. Ephorah approached a table where Amri, Namid, and the bori were already seated.

"We knew it was coming," Namid sighed. "And we still missed all the looting."

"Oh, shut up," Ephorah sat down. "Is Rostam coming?"

"I'm here," Rostam pulled up a chair next to her. "Sorry, I always feel weird on this campus. I'm not a student, remember?"

"Right..." Ephorah looked at the others. "What the hell do we do?"

"Do we need to do anything?" Namid asked. "We're a bunch of students." She glanced at Rostam. "Well, mostly. Why is it our responsibility to do anything?"

"Because we can," Cyrus had his eyes downcast at his hands. "Because this city is our home, and if we do nothing, we might lose it."

"We learned a lot," Amri added. Ephorah noticed his expression was more haunted than normal. "I saw a lot of what the dragon used for his spells. And I got a good enough look at his music device to know he has tech we don't. That music machine ran on electricity, but there was no magic coming in or out of it. It had no wires, no cables to any kind of power source, but it ran on electricity. And somehow, he was able to send music from another machine...just using radio waves. I went up there again afterwards to see if I could study it, but it had been blown to bits by the time I could check."

"Wouldn't surprise me if the dragon did that himself," Cyrus muttered. "Doesn't want people studying his stuff."

"That's all well and good," Ephorah eyed the Borealan. "But what about the dragon himself? What does he want? Why has he attacked our city twice? He's clearly not from around here, and we have no way of learning anything about him."

"Actually, that might not be true." Rostam set a large book down on the food court table. "I bought this a while back from some traveling dragon experts."

Namid eyed the book. "What kind of experts?"

"The kind who sell live dragons as pets," Rostam replied.

Namid scowled. "You don't actually believe anything in a book about pets is going to–"

"Wait, this might work," Amri looked at his sister as he interrupted before pointing to the book. "Namid and I saw a whole exhibit on dragons in Grand Spire. If we pool the stuff we learned with what's in that book, we might be able to get at least a good idea of what kind of dragon we're dealing with. From there, we could probably figure out what he wants."

"And then we could prepare for his next move," Cyrus had his chin resting on his palm, his mind visibly on other things. "Anyone else see what the dragon did when Rostam started shooting at him? Even when the bullets bounced off his armor?"

"He ignored the rest of us on the ground," Namid paused. "He turned all of his attention to the one person with a ranged weapon and practically let us put together a counterattack."

"I'd wager one of his instincts is to focus his attention on anything that can attack him when he's airborne," Amri added. "Even if the bullets don't do much damage. Of course, it could be he was worried one of them would actually hit something important."

"That's all well and good, but what do we do about our other undead problem?" Cyrus asked. "The one Namid discovered?"

"Could we get mercenaries to start arming themselves with holy weapons?" Namid offered. "Cyrus, didn't you once say your ancestors fought off undead armies with something like that?"

Cyrus didn't pick his head up from his hand. "I said they used weapons tied with a red linen ribbon, blessed by Sekhmet to fight evil."

"Okay, so we get some red linen..."

Cyrus shook his head, still not lifting it from his palm. "Namid, 'blessed by Sekhmet.'"

"Oh...oh." Namid's eyes widened. "You mean...they won't work now...You don't think..."

"What, that the dragon and the Tomb Lords are working together?" Cyrus finally sat upright; his face still stuck in a frown. "It's possible. But it's also possible Daurgo just targeted a goddess he really wanted to get rid of for his own sake."

"I'd be shocked if there weren't other gods who can deal with the undead," Rostam looked at Amri. "Haven't you been hanging around a temple of some sort lately?"

"The priests there don't fight," Amri frowned. "And I don't think they have any powers. Marduk might be able to help, because he's a protector deity, but...if he had the ability to empower mortal weapons to fight evil, he probably would have done it already."

"Thoth could destroy the undead with a touch," Cyrus murmured. "I've seen him do it."

"Then there are probably other gods who can do the same. And we have this." Rostam placed his axe on the table, to the surprise of everyone else. Something about the weapon, or the fact that Rostam had brought it to a food court, had shocked everyone else out of their slump. "Silver weapons will work, with or without a god's interference."

"Yeah...good luck getting enough silver to make a real difference," Cyrus examined the axe. "Normal weapons...you'll have to wear down an undead creature until the energy that keeps them together wears out. That's what we were always taught in school, anyway."

"...There's really no going back to the way things were, is there?" Amri asked. "Peace with Kemet for generations, almost no wars in living memory...I never thought I might actually be drafted as a military wizard."

"I'm going to need more elementals," Ephorah folded her arms. "Could use an army, in fact."

"Miss," a voice came from behind Ephorah.

Turning around, Ephorah was greeted by the sight of a girl her own age who must have been thirty centimeters shorter, wearing some kind of scarf that covered the bottom half of her face, and holding a book and a packet of papers.

"Are you Ephorah el-Sabet?" The girl asked.

"I am," Ephorah replied. "What's this about?"

"I have a delivery from the office of Daniela Sachar." The girl handed Ephorah the book and papers. Ephorah recognized the book as the old Empyrian heirloom she had asked Sachar to translate.

"She says this is yours. The papers are the translated copy." The girl looked up at Ephorah. "Her fee is included. Please deliver payment within one week."

Ephorah cradled the book and the stack of papers. She looked at the fee slip. Five Ioseps per page, totaling two hundred and fifty Ioseps. A small price to pay.

"I'll deliver it tomorrow," Ephorah offered her hand to the girl, who shook it.

"Very well." The girl turned and left.

Placing the book and papers down on the food court table, Ephorah was about to read the first page of the new translation when Cyrus spoke up.

"Might I ask what's got you so excited?" The Borealan asked.

Ephorah glared at Cyrus, then packed the book and papers into her bookbag. "No, you may not." She turned to the others. "I'm going to look for ways to get more elementals. Might as well fight the dead with spirits. But for now, I'm going home."

The others exchanged glances as Ephorah left the food court. It didn't matter. As much as she wanted to read the translation immediately, it was dangerous to read it around Borealans. So, Ephorah took the first autobus home. Her father and brother were still at work, and her mother was busy mending clothes in the living room. Ephorah greeted her mother as she came into the house but let her work as she went to the kitchen to read.

"Alright, here we go." Ephorah took out the translation and held it next to the original book. Then she read the title aloud.

"*The Gentleman's Guide to Beating His Wives and Children with Sticks.*"

Ephorah blinked as she read the title again. "What?"

Glossary

Egyptian Gods

Mythology is a lot like superhero comics. The gods' characters depend on the writer, canon is constantly changing, and continuity is messy. There are a number of different versions of each myth, and the gods in Janaan follow only the versions detailed below. Any name without a guide is pronounced phonetically.

ATUM - Name means "the completed one" or "the finished one." Egyptian creator god who made the universe.

RA - The sun god, whose name was also the Egyptian word for the sun itself.

APEP (ā'pep) - A massive snake that wanted to devour the sun and destroy all of creation. Technically the god of chaos, if he's even a god at all.

KHONSU (kan'shü) - God of the moon. Name means "traveler".

MA'AT - Goddess of order, morality, and truth, whose name literally meant "truth" or "order." Sometimes interpreted not as an actual person but as the abstract concept of truth.

THOTH (thōth) - God of science, wisdom, medicine, reason, and logic. Also associated with the moon, and portrayed with an ibis head.

PTAH (p'ta) - God of craftsmen and architects, whose name means "the forger."

SOBEK (sō'bek) - Crocodile-headed god of the Nile, fresh water, fertility, and often the patron god of the army.

SHU (shü) - God of the air and winds, whose name means "emptiness" and "he who rises up."

TEFNUT (tef'nüt) - Goddess of moisture, whose name means "to spit."

GEB - God of the earth, whose name is a translation for "earth."

GLOSSARY

NUT (nüt) - Goddess of the sky, whose name is a translation for "sky."

BAST - Cat-headed goddess who destroyed vermin, kept farms and houses safe from rats and other pests, and protector of children from disease. Her name meant "she of the ointment jar."

OSIRIS (ō'sI'ris) - Egyptian god of the underworld. Formally the king of the gods, but retired to the underworld after being tricked by Set.

ISIS (Is'is) - Also called Aset. Goddess of magic, healing, and motherhood. The only deity who could match Thoth in a contest of magic to a draw.

HORUS (hô'rus) - God of the sky, and later king of the gods. His name meant "falcon."

SET - Originally a protective deity associated with storms, and Ramses claimed to be descended from Set. He would later become god of the desert and foreigners. He would later be associated with anarchy and evil after foreigners invaded Egypt.

NEPHTHYS (nef'tēs) - Wife of Set, associated with rivers.

HATHOR (ha'thôr) - Goddess of beauty, love, fertility, drunkenness, and music. Wife of Horus, whose name means "Horus's sanctum."

ANUBIS - God of the dead, who collected the souls of the dead like the Grim Reaper, and protected them on their way to meet Osiris.

MEDJED - God of the unseen, also called the Smiter, who "shoots from the eye." Very little is known about him, other than that he's depicted wearing what looks like a Halloween ghost costume without armholes, and he appears to be able to fire laser beams from his eyes. Also, we don't actually know if Medjed is a "he," either.

Babylonian Gods

Many of the gods worshiped in Babylon were derived from older Sumerian gods, but like the Egyptians, myths would change with rise and fall of empires and the gods in Janaan follow only the versions detailed below. Their gods tended to be like nesting dolls, where one god would be in charge of the entire heaven, another would rule the sky, and a third would just govern the winds. Also, some of the goddesses may sound like they were copied from each other. This is because the Mesopotamian cultures had a lot of goddesses whose only roles were to be wives and mothers of more important gods. Any name without a guide is pronounced phonetically.

APSU (ap'sü) – God of fresh water, and in a sense the god of order. The first king of the gods.

TIAMAT (tē'a'mat) – Goddess of the primal waters, and often associated with salt water, and later the goddess of chaos.

LAHMU (La'mü) **and LAHAMU** (la'ha'mü) – The first and most powerful children of Apsu and Tiamat, who were both gods of stars and associated with constellations. Some depictions show them as dragons.

MUMMU (mü'mü) – God of practical knowledge and technical skill, or skilled trades. His name meant "knowledge."

ANSHAR (An'shär) – God of the heavens, whose name meant "whole heaven."

KISHAR (Kē'shär) – Goddess of the earth and wife of Anshar, whose name meant "whole earth."

ANU (A'nü) – God of the sky, whose name meant "sky."

KI (Kē) – Another earth goddess, married to Anu.

ENLIL – God of the winds, air, and initially, storms. Also the god of patriarchs and initially granted mortal kings their divine right to rule. King of the gods in Sumeria, and largely inspired the Assyrian god Ashur, who was king of that pantheon. His name meant "lord of the wind."

NINLIL – Husband of Enlil, goddess of air, fertility, and sailors. Her name means "lady of wind."

ENKI (en'kē) – Also called Ea (pronounced ē'a). God of water (especially rain), craftsmen, fertility, intelligence, magic, mischief, and civilization.

NINHURSAG – Wife of Enki. Goddess of fertility, mountains, and rulers. Name means "lady of the sacred mountain."

NANNA – God of the moon. Later replaced by Sin.

NINGAL – Goddess of reeds. Wife of Nanna, whose name meant "great lady."

NERGAL – God of war, plague, death, and disease. His name is often interpreted as "scorched earth."

GLOSSARY

ERESHKIGAL (ē'resh'ki'gal) – Queen of the Sumerian underworld. Name meant "Queen of the Great Earth."

GUGALANA (Gü'ga'la'na) – The Bull of Heaven. First husband of Ereshkigal, whose name meant "Great Bull of Heaven."

-REDACTED- By order of Marduk, this entry has been removed.

DUMUZI (dü'mü'zē) – God of shepherds. First husband of -REDACTED-.

ADAD (a'dad, or ad'ad) – God of storms, rains and floods, and weather. Name meant "thunderer".

UTU (ü'tü) – God of the sun, and god of justice, truth, and morality. Would later be combined with Marduk and called Shamash.

KINGU/QINGU (king'ü) – Tiamat's escort after Apsu's death and brother of Mummu, usually depicted as a dragon. His name means "unskilled laborer."

MARDUK (mär'duk) – The patron god of Babylon, he was the god of magic, justice, healing, compassion, truth, and became the king of the gods in the Babylonian pantheon. Name means "calf of the sun," or "child of the sun." Married to -REDACTED- at first, later Sarpanitu.

LAMASHTU (la'mäsh'tü) – An evil goddess born from Anu and Kishar after the death of Apsu. Not really the goddess of anything, but always referred to as a goddess, not simply a demon.

Made in the USA
Monee, IL
22 October 2024